TESTING OF THE POTTER

APOCALYPSE: THE LIFTING

OF THE VEIL

A. C. DeLozier

ISBN: 0985706724
ISBN 13: 978-0985706722
Library of Congress Control Number: 2014905244
A.C. DeLozier, Maryville, TN

To my family, without whose support this work would not be possible. They have been dependable sources of inspiration, encouragement, editing, and computer expertise.

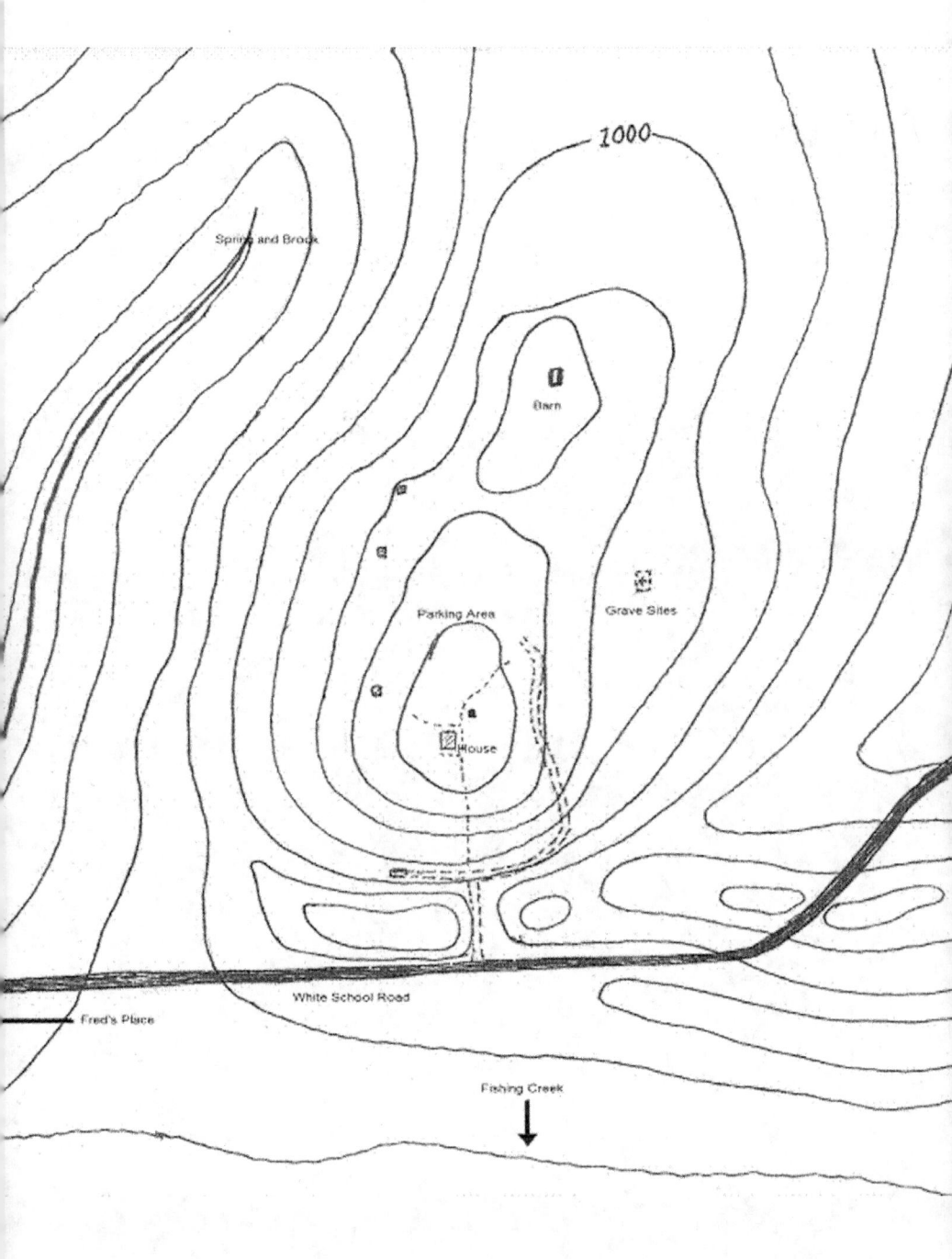

PROLOGUE

"In the beginning God created the heaven and the earth. And the earth was without form, and void; and darkness was upon the face of the deep. And the Spirit of God moved upon the face of the waters" (Genesis 1:1–2, King James Version).

Now there was a day when the sons of God came to present themselves before the Lord, and Satan came also among them. And the Lord said unto Satan, "Whence comest thou?"

Then Satan answered the Lord and said, "From going to and fro in the earth, and from walking up and down in it."

And the Lord said unto Satan, "Hast thou considered my servant Job, that there is none like him in the earth, a perfect and an upright man, one that feareth God, and escheweth evil?"

Then Satan answered the Lord, and said, "Doth Job fear God for nought? Hast not thou made an hedge about him, and about his house, and about all that he hath on every side? Thou hast blessed the work of his hands, and his substance is increased in the land. But put forth thine hand now, and touch all that he hath, and he will curse thee to thy face."

And the Lord said unto Satan, "Behold, all that he hath is in thy power; only upon himself put not forth thine hand." So Satan went forth from the presence of the Lord. (Job 1:6–12).

Satan returned, saying, "It is done, God, and done. My thoughts were but foolishness. Your created being cursed not thee while all lies about in waste and ruin. His seed is no more."

God replied, "Behold! My work is yet an eternity. My will doth reign and endureth forever and ever. My time is infinite; I and the seed are one and...I AM."

THE BELL

Maymum Abbas focused on the tiny, round pebble on the blade of his short-handled spade. It was somehow different from the other small stones he had sifted from the dirt of the spoil pile.

Hunkered in the excavation trench, his knees tight to his chest, he flicked away the surrounding crumbs of dried dirt and picked up the tiny object. *Heavy...and hard,* he thought as he applied light pressure to it between his thumb and forefinger. Holding it close to his aging eyes, he scratched at it with his thick thumbnail until a dull glint showed through. "Gold!" he breathed to himself.

Standing at the top of the ditch, about five meters away, Dr. Cohen saw Abbas abruptly drop his shovel and straighten. From having spent years working beside the ancient Palestinian—or to be more correct and as Abbas would say, Palestinian *Christian*—Cohen knew what that gesture meant: *He's found something—something significant!*

Abbas was born in East Jerusalem and had been orphaned at age two, his parents having had the bad luck one day to choose the bus seat immediately behind an Islamic suicide bomber whose nervous thumb was to prematurely ignite the shopping bag on the floor between his knees. With no close relatives, the boy eventually had been placed in a Catholic-supported orphanage in Hebron, where he stayed until he had completed his studies at a West Bank Arab high school. Then, having developed adequate multilingual skills—Hebrew, English, and the Palestinian dialect of Arabic—and seemingly unburdened with any extreme political convictions, Abbas had attached himself to an ongoing archeological dig in the Old City to learn his eventual trade.

It had been a good career choice for him. He possessed a quick, inquiring mind and a jovial personality that usually had made him an early pick for any of the excavation projects of the Israeli archeologists and the visiting professors. There had been few breaks in his employment, particularly with those digs that centered on the Old City, and as he had amassed experience, his positions gradually had become less "laborer" and more "consultant."

That is how he and Dr. Eli Cohen had come to meet. Cohen was working on his dissertation involving the study of the Gihon Spring outside the City of David, and the older Abbas had been recommended by his archeology sponsor to assist the aspiring candidate. The relationship had proved to be of mutual advantage: Cohen had breezed his way to his PhD, and Abbas had rounded out his reputation as somewhat of the local expert on the geography of the Old City. And that is how they had come to be working together today: Cohen had secured the funding and the permission of the Israel Antiquities Authority (IAA) to excavate an ancient sewer line in Jerusalem's Old City, and had hired Abbas, already possessing much practical knowledge of the Roman-era sewer system, as his consultant and on-site supervisor.

As to his self-identification as a Christian Palestinian, Abbas was one of the very few non-Muslims to come from the West Bank. He supposed he had learned of the life of Jesus Christ from the teachers at the orphanage, even though the authorities expressly had forbidden its Christian benefactors from formally teaching their theology to the orphans. At any rate, as he grew to adulthood, he became as firm in his faith as any of his Muslim or Jewish associates were firm in theirs—and twice as discrete in his worship. He neither wore his cross outside of his shirt nor sprinkled his language with Christian phrases. And while he kept his Bible handy in case someone came to him for sincere inquiry and discussion, he did not proselytize or overtly advertise his faith to anyone, with the exception of Dr. Cohen. Abbas figured his nonpracticing Jewish friend was fair game, and for some reason, he carried a great concern for the soul of Dr. Eli Cohen.

"Mr. Abbas?" Dr. Cohen called. "Find something?"

Abbas looked up and raised a cautionary forefinger to his lips. Then he waved Cohen away, pointing him toward the ladder that leaned against the side of the ditch a discreet distance from the other workers.

Minutes later Abbas joined him there, grunting to the top of the ladder from the trench and, with Cohen following, ambled on to the relative privacy of the water tent. There, in its shade, he spat the found object onto his palm, briefly rolled it between his finger and thumb, then held it out, his saliva having loosened the remaining dirt. A tiny, golden bell glistened there, damp and exquisite yet unknowably foul.

Dr. Cohen daintily picked the bell from his site supervisor's hand. After a cursory examination, the archeologist asked, "What are you thinking you've found, Mr. Abbas?"

Abbas started to reply but stopped, holding up his hands. "Just please, a minute. I have come to realize I should to rinse the dirt from out of my mouth." Taking a cup from the stack on the nearby table and drawing water from the tall Igloo cooler, he gargled and spat, gargled and spat. The cool water hurt his failing teeth. "Dirt tastes like to very bad, very bad. I forget we were to excavate that which was once a sewer."

Cohen laughed. "It was a long, long time ago, Mr. Abbas, when this was really a sewer here. I think you were just afraid of keeping this in your pocket while climbing the ladder, fearing it might fall out. But I believe you'll be all right. So now what are you thinking?"

"I am to think it is a golden bell—perhaps from hem of a Temple priest—maybe lost while to walk along the street. Here, wait but a moment." He stooped to retrieve a canvas bag from under the table that held the cooler and stacked boxes of paper cups. Abbas and the other workers, Cohen knew, used these canvas bags to bring their lunches and any noontime reading materials: a Bible for Abbas and mostly Qur'ans for the others. Abbas rummaged through his bag and located his book, immediately thumbing to its beginning chapters. "I to have find it," he announced, obviously pleased with himself. After another quick survey around, confirming their privacy, he softly read, "Exodus, chapter twenty-eight, verses thirty-three and thirty-four: 'Make pomegranates of blue, purple, and scarlet yarn around the hem of the robe, with gold bells between them. The gold bells and the pomegranates are to alternate around the hem of the robe.' A golden bell—a priestly bell—that is what I believe it to be."

Cohen gently shook the bell which gave off a faint, metallic click. "I think you're correct, Mr. Abbas. Yes, I believe you are correct! A priest once walked along the drainage channel…beside this very road…and lost one of his golden bells, Mr. Abbas…lost a bell from his robe." He stroked his chin, his eyes distant with the imagery. "It must be at least two thousand—no!—three thousand years old!" he finished in a rush. "Perhaps the archeological find of the decade!"

A couple of the workmen sifting soil on the far side of the ditch paused to glance in their direction. Abbas turned his back to them and gently closed Dr. Cohen's hand on the bell. In a low voice, he suggested, "Suppose you are to find a safe place to put. I shall go to see if there should be more such pebbles in the waste piles. And then to allow you to again examine the sites where we to have removed the dirt. OK?"

Dr. Cohen could only nod in agreement as the enormity of the find began to sink in.

✳✳✳

By late afternoon Abbas's eyes burned, and his head and neck ached; he was beginning to feel a great weariness. He supposed his fatigue and headache were brought on by his having skipped lunch and by the searing heat of the day. He simply had been too excited to waste time either eating or napping; he envisaged that this bell would be among the greatest finds in Israel in recent years. *Maybe of the century!* he thought. *My life is sure to change forever.*

He and Cohen had used the remainder of the day to repeatedly walk the entire length of the excavated sewer line, picking at uneven dirt protuberances in the channel's walls and spreading the collected soil, but had found no more strange-looking pebbles. And now the shadows were deepening in the digs.

Dr. Cohen called his name, again from the top of the ladder. "Mr. Abbas, are you ready to end the workday and dismiss the men?"

"Yes," Abbas answered. "Already I have distributed the weekly pay sums and dismissed many of the mens for the weekend. I shall to leave my trowel here, at the wall, to mark my place to again, yes? To begin...tomorrow?" He glanced over to the piles of waste dirt he intended to resift over the weekend—without the presence of any curious assistants.

"Well, I understand then and am sure it will be right there, waiting for you...tomorrow," Cohen replied, leaning over to give Abbas a smile—a tight, confidential grin. "Bright and early tomorrow, you will be back doing what we both love, but I will be on my way to Tel-Aviv to the annual archeology weekend...with our new find." He whispered the last four words. "Our timing could not have been better. I'd quite forgotten in the excitement that I'm a speaker this year, yes? I shall see colleagues from Paris and London! And New York! Dorfman will come from New York. Imagine when he sees our..." Cohen had to pause to settle himself, as he had done several times that afternoon. He was getting carried away in his imaginings: Dorfman's jealous eyes, Spiegel's pinched mouth—*Oh, this will be good!* "...our find. And I shall be sure to remember to give them your regards," he added brightly.

From the ditch Abbas nodded, coughed repeatedly, and managed a weak smile. "May God keep you, Doctor."

***

Abbas awoke at 2:15 a.m. His headache had gotten worse and his coughing spells more violent and prolonged; sleep was impossible. He decided to go to work early and perhaps stop by the hospital's walk-in clinic on his way to the Old City. *Maybe it's the flu*, he thought, his joints aching as he felt around in the dark for his bedside lamp's chain switch. Then, in the resultant flood of light, he recoiled, shocked to see that his pillow was red stained and damp, maybe with blood that had come from his nose—or from his harsh coughing. Fighting back panic he quickly pulled on yesterday's work jeans and shirt and headed for the door. *Do not forget the jacket*, he cautioned himself. *Now, to my soul, I am feeling chilled from the flu.*

At his front stoop, he sneezed and coughed again into his handkerchief; it was speckled with blood droplets. He folded the cloth and tucked it away, pulled tight his door, and turned to his car parked at the curb.

He made it to the first security checkpoint before he knew he could go no farther.

Several Israeli soldiers warily approached the ancient vehicle that had coasted up to the lane barrier and stopped; the car's driver had not yet lowered his window to present his identification papers. Slowly they advanced, now with their weapons held high and their powerful flashlight beams trained on the car's windows. Through the driver's side of the windshield, they saw a man; he was leaning forward, his head resting on the steering wheel. Raising a bullhorn, one trooper gave several amplified challenges to the car without receiving a response. Finally they withdrew, summoning the bomb squad.

***

"Mr. Abbas?" a nurse softly called.

Maymum Abbas slightly cracked his eyelids. He felt miserable. His eyes burned; his arms and legs ached; and he could hardly swallow. And he had no idea where he was, so he asked the woman who was leaning over him. "Where please am I to be?" he croaked.

"You've taken sick," she replied. "You passed out in your car and were brought to the hospital by ambulance. I hope you don't mind, but we retrieved your identification papers from your wallet and—"

"Nurse," a doctor interrupted, striding in from the hallway, "let me have some time to talk with our patient, please." He had overheard Abbas and the nurse talking.

"Of course, Doctor." She hurriedly retreated to the far side of the bed, awaiting further instructions.

Abbas watched as the doctor dragged the metal chair from its place against the wall and heavily seated himself beside the bed, pulling at his lab coat until he was comfortable. The man was obviously preparing to spend a considerable amount of his valuable time here. *Strange*, thought Abbas, his mental processes clearing. He seldom had received anything other than the most cursory of attention from the state's harried physicians, Palestinian or Israeli. *This is to be serious.*

"Um…Mr. Abbas, I am Dr. Eliphaz." The doctor introduced himself as in afterthought; he was engrossed in reading the forms he carried. After studying the first five or six pages of the sheaf of paper clipped to his board and pulling the ballpoint from its Velcro rest, the doctor was now ready with his questions. "Mr. Abbas, you were brought unconscious to us this morning—very early this morning, about six or seven hours ago. We have performed certain vital examinations and have taken blood samples for further analysis. Now, if you're able, I must make certain inquiries then proceed with further treatment." He folded back the first page.

"Proceed with further treatment" sounded minutely comforting to Abbas, while "must make certain inquiries" slightly alarmed him. After all, he *was* Palestinian, and this *was* Israel. Regardless he nodded his acquiescence; he felt too miserable to do much else.

"Mr. Abbas, are you sexually active?" the doctor asked.

Abbas blinked at the question. Apart from the bluntness of the inquiry and his obvious advanced age, he believed that had he felt the least bit well, he would have managed a better answer—a humorous answer—for the doctor…but not now. "No," he simply replied.

The doctor continued with his questions, and Abbas continued to softly respond in the negative: "Have you traveled outside the country? Have you recently eaten shellfish? Have you recently had contact with an ill person? Have you had anything to drink from any nonmunicipal water sources? Do you have a dog or cat?…"

Halfway through the second page, Abbas choked and hacked out a long, ragged cough, interrupting the doctor's stream of questions. When the spasm subsided, and he was again able to open his eyes, he saw he had sprinkled the physician and his white lab coat with his bloody flecks. He had tried to cover his mouth, but the simple act of raising his hands had brought new waves of searing, burning anguish to his chest and armpits. "Doctor, I am sorry, so very sorry," he whispered in apology. Feebly indicating the sites of his torment, he attempted to explain, "I can no to lift my arms. Here I am to hurt."

Dr. Eliphaz nodded to acknowledge Abbas's apology and removed his eyeglasses from his forehead, where he customarily carried them. He leaned over the bed to give them to the nurse to clean away the blood droplets. "I suppose I should have been wearing them," he said, now standing and pushing his chair back from the head of the bed, its legs making alarming, rasping noises against the tile floor.

Taking the glasses from him, the nurse handed the doctor a sanitary wipe in return, one of several she had pulled from a box beneath the side table. "Quite all right," she cheerfully replied. "I'll have them sparkling in a sec. Considering that cough, I suppose we both should be wearing masks."

"A tad late, I'd say, Nurse. Next time," he suggested, waving off her feint toward the supply cart.

After having thoroughly wiped his face and hands with the cloth, Dr. Eliphaz again turned his attention to Abbas. He helped the old man slowly lift his arms to the pillow underneath his head and pulled low the top sheet.

"My God!" With the unveiling of the dark swellings, the whispered words inadvertently escaped the doctor's lips. He glanced up to the nurse. "His armpits—how long has this man…ah… Never mind." *This is Israel and the patient is a Palestinian.* He realized Abbas's identity verification alone would have consumed several hours. *Probably doesn't have his insurance card either. Oh, well.*

"Now hold your arms there, Mr. Abbas, while I feel around here." The doctor ran his gloved hands along Abbas's bare body, pausing when he reached the grotesque lumps at his armpits and on his neck. "Does that hurt?" he asked, as he applied light, intermittent pressure to the swellings.

Abbas almost screamed. His clenched teeth and squinted eyes were answer enough for the physician. Dr. Eliphaz lifted the sheet aside to similarly examine Abbas's groin area, where he immediately found more enlarged lymph nodes.

Replacing the covers and sitting back down, the doctor furiously scribbled on his clipped pages for several minutes. The nurse—Cynthia Silverman, RN, according to her name badge—came around the bed to return the freshly cleaned spectacles. The doctor murmured his thanks and slipped them back onto his forehead, then turned again to his patient, pushing his chair farther from the bedside as if to better view the old man. "Mr. Abbas, I initially had suspected you had contracted either typhoid fever or...perhaps syphilis. But these enlarged lymph nodes, these tender swellings..." He softly touched around Abbas's groin area. "...lead me to believe you...have something else here. See, these inflamed areas are called 'buboes,' which usually are associated with bacterial infections. Years ago, while working in India, I had occasion to see similar buboes, but that was from...something we seldom see around here. But...ah...we are awaiting lab tests—no need to jump to conclusions. We should know more—maybe have a better prognosis—tomorrow morning."

Tomorrow morning? Abbas first thought to tell the doctor that he couldn't stay, that he had much important work to do, but somehow that work no longer seemed so important. *Anyway, Dr. Cohen will not be returning from...I cannot remember where he is going. I hurt so.*

As he again slipped into unconsciousness, he heard Dr. Eliphaz's fading words to the nurse to set up a drip with streptomycin...and then the doctor stifled a sneeze.

***

It was dark outside when Abbas awoke—the wee, dark hours in a hospital—a very lonely time for all patients.

But he was well past the point of actually feeling single miseries. His eyes hurt, even in the muted light; his head hurt; his stomach hurt; and he dared not move lest he aggravate the flaming agony of the buboes and his bowels. In fact he hurt so much that he found he could not even pray coherently to God, the savior.

And he knew with all certainty he was going to die. The doctors and nurses would be unable to cure him; drugs would not heal him; he would die. Abbas wanted to pray, to thank God for this insight and perhaps to find comfort in the knowledge of God's purpose, but he was unable to even fashion the question and then to connect with God. The pain was too great; he could not concentrate; he could not separate. He again lapsed into unconsciousness.

At the doorway Nurse Silverman and an aide watched Abbas as he grimaced and struggled then collapsed. "Do I need to change the sheets again?" the aide asked.

"No," the nurse brusquely replied, looking at the chart in her hands. "We changed them just three hours ago, and frankly, I don't think this old fart is going to make it to morning."

The aide glanced sharply at Nurse Silverman, then, just as quickly, looked away. She knew they were shorthanded, and the nurse was working a double shift; she was probably justified in her moodiness. She would say nothing about the RN's breach of professional proto-col—her loud voicing of her opinions well within the patient's hear-ing distance, whether he was conscious or not. *I'll talk to her tomorrow,* she thought. *Or not. Cynthia doesn't take any criticism well.* Aloud she volunteered, "Then I'll just go over here and wash his face with a little cool water and…"

Abbas stirred again, sat bolt upright in bed, murmured a few words, and slowly fell back. He was now totally still, his unblinking eyes fixed on the ceiling.

"What'd he say?" Nurse Silverman asked.

The aide did not answer right away; she sucked on her bottom lip and lowered her gaze, considering what she thought she had heard. "You know, it sounded like he said, 'My father, God, I now understand'...or something like that. He said it in Hebrew, and my Hebrew isn't that good. Is he a religious person?"

The nurse eased the door fully open and walked to the side of the bed. She lifted Abbas's wrist and felt for a pulse: "Who the hell knows, these old guys...Yeah, I think he is—*was*. For all the good it's done him; he's going to be dead soon. It doesn't appear his gods are particularly anxious to save him."

"Well, he looks like he's at ease now," the aide replied, having followed the nurse into the room. "Actually I think he's...smiling."

"Like an idiot if you ask me," the nurse scoffed. "With the agony he's going through, I certainly don't know why." Yet she continued to study Abbas, absently making faint ticking noises with her tongue as she watched. Minutes passed, and she turned to the aide. "I'm feeling like crap myself, so I'm going home. Tell them at the office, would you? Tell them to call me at my house if they don't like it. Tell them...Never mind." *Tell them to call me when they find out what this old fart has.*

***

The hospital's personnel director called Nurse Silverman's home at nine the following morning; he got her answering machine and left a message. He said the lab samples had come back, and well, they suspected they might have a problem on their hands. The ministry of health had been contacted; would she mind returning to the hospital as soon as possible? "Oh, better yet," he said, other muted voices murmuring in the background, "we'll be sending someone directly to pick you up, Nurse Silverman. Say at eleven? Eleven-thirty at the latest?"

At ten that morning, Cynthia Silverman backed her car out of her parking space to journey to the airport. She would take her vacation—and chances—in New York City.

***

From just inside the now barred door, two hazard-suited physicians studied the dying Mr. Abbas.

One asked the other, "Have you heard anything more from Dr. Eliphaz?"

"Yes. He's admitted himself to the hospital. The day nurse also may have been infected, but we haven't yet located her. Me? I believe she panicked and ran. The police have been notified."

They again considered Mr. Abbas in the bloody, vomit-and-diarrhea-soaked bed.

"I wouldn't blame her," the first physician added.

2

ORDINARY DAY ON THE FARM

Homer Clark lifted the window shade and looked to the north, up past the barn's roof line, to the early-morning skies above the black hump of the distant mountain. *Gonna be a real nice day,* he silently judged. *Clear as a bell.* From the multitude of stars, blinking clear and cold in the inky heavens, he easily picked out the Big Dipper, now low to the north, its leading edge pointing out the North Star, Polaris. *No clouds to speak of,* he thought.

He bent across the bed and shook the mattress. "Jimmy," he whispered.

The boy slowly came to consciousness, his first thoughts for the new day: *So I'm not in Florida in the middle of an earthquake. But it's still dark as...night? Where the heck am I?*

Homer whispered again. "Hey, sleepyhead. It's time we head to the barn."

Oh, yeah, Jimmy remembered. *I got kicked out of bed last night when Zula rented out my bed, and I had to sleep with Homer. But gosh, wasn't that, like, only about ten minutes ago? Crap!*

Jimmy flipped the covers back and pushed sideways to balance upright on the edge of the bed, his socked feet dangling six inches from off the floor. Homer's bed *was* rather ancient, Jimmy guessed, with its heavy, wooden headboard and enormous old-timey mattress, stuffed tight with the feathers of generations of chickens and ducks. *But it's comfortable...and it sure helped to drown out Homer's snores. But gosh, it's hot!*

"Homer, you snore like a freight train, and you hogged all the air from the fan," he complained.

"And you need to turn around and sleep right side up, boy," Homer replied, trying to find his crusty voice. "When did you decide to start sleeping upside down anyway?"

"When I found myself trading breaths with you. And besides you leaving little oxygen, you don't leave much space in the bed neither."

"So now I get to smell your stinky feet all night? Why don't you just stop growing, son? That's the problem—you're gettin' too big," he concluded. "And keep your voice down," he warned. "The old woman's got about a dozen tourists in the house." When Zula wasn't around, like now, Homer referred to his wife as "the old woman."

As to the tourists, Zula had negotiated an ongoing arrangement with a motel out on Chapman Highway for the referral of their over-flow guests to her "tourist home" during the summer months. Last night, Jimmy figured, the number of visitors to the Great Smoky Mountains must have *really* exceeded the motel's capacity; he remembered the phone ringing long after Zula had roused him from his bed to double up with Homer.

Jimmy slid to the floor to feel around with his feet for the bundle of clothes Zula firmly had pushed into his arms last night when he had stumbled past her on his way to Homer's bedroom. Obviously she wasn't about to chance a repeat performance from last week when he had forgotten to grab his jeans and had instead worn a pair of Homer's old overalls to the barn. According to her, he had made quite an impression with the tourists when he had later "traipsed past the breakfast table—shirtless, shoeless, and sporting old, worn overalls rolled to your rear end and tied with rope—looking like one of those idiots in Gatlinburg trying to look like…a hillbilly! We got enough real hillbillies around here who look like that anyway," she had added. "Next thing you know, our guests will be expecting to see a moonshine still out behind the smokehouse." Homer had then opined that he could take care of that and go ahead and move it right alongside the outhouse. *Homer always kids around like that,*

Jimmy thought. *He* wasn't quite sure what a real moonshine distillery looked like, but he knew they didn't have an outhouse anymore.

Still rubbing the sleep from his eyes, the boy heard Homer ease open the bedroom door and step out, feeling his way down the back staircase as the treads creaked in protest, announcing each movement as he carefully shifted his weight from step to step. *And he's worried about me waking up the tourists?* Pulling his T-shirt over his head as he walked, Jimmy joined Homer on the stairs, taking care to edge his feet to the extreme ends of the treads so the stairs wouldn't announce his descent with more creaks and squeals. On the bottom step, he caught up to Homer. Then, touching and taking a firm grip on the old man's overall straps at the back, he sock skied the linoleum in the dark, as Homer dragged him across the enclosed porch clear over to the screen door.

"Boy, I think you've put on five pounds since yesterday," Homer puffed.

"Do you really think so?" Jimmy liked it when Homer kidded him about growing and getting bigger. In actuality he was a rather slow-developing kid physically and, over the years, consistently had been among the smallest of his classmates.

"Yeah. You'll soon be looking down on us all, fatso." Homer located the flashlight on the tiny shelf beside the door. He clicked it on and focused the beam on the grimy pair of tennis shoes aligned next to his rubber boots. "Jimmy, why don't you let me get you a pair of boots, like mine?"

"Homer, my shoes are fine for the few weeks I'm up here. As long as I don't forget and come in the house with them on, Zula ain't apt to kill me neither. I'll just wash them off real good when we get back."

The truth was both Homer and Zula were getting on in years, and well, farming wasn't very profitable anymore and hadn't been for a long time, according to Jimmy's father. His dad had taken him aside after Jimmy's visit last fall and had pointed out the relative value of the bills and coins Homer and Zula had slipped into the boy's pockets as he was leaving. Consequently, as Jimmy was departing to go home after his next stay, this last spring, he loudly had objected to Homer and Zula's paying anything for his "labor," saying that they were his cousins and that he was just helping out… and that the work was a lot of fun. And in truth, a lot of it *was* fun. So the money he had refused in the spring he found awaiting him in an envelope on the bedside table when he had returned this summer.

Holding the light steady so Jimmy could see his laces, Homer teased, "Yeah, like you could possibly do anything wrong in the eyes of the old woman. And just look at those shoestrings. They've got enough cow shit on them to fertilize a couple hills of potatoes."

"Ooh, you said 's-h-i-t.'"

"Yeah, but how are you going to turn me in without sayin' the same thing?"

"I'll write it down for Zula."

"Smartass."

"Ooh, you said…"

They kept it up that way, all the way to the barnyard gate.

Relatching the wooden gate behind them, Homer clicked off his flashlight, and the heavens *exploded* with stars. "Dang!" Jimmy exclaimed. He reckoned aloud that he never had seen so many stars in his life.

"And can you imagine that this is only *our* galaxy?" Homer marveled. "That beyond, in the universe, there are endless more galaxies? More solar systems and planets? Can you even begin to imagine that?"

Jimmy couldn't. Standing in wonder and appreciation, he slowly circled in place to take in the whole of the magnificent skies, horizon to horizon. For several more minutes, they were silent.

Then, in a low voice, Homer recited from memory, his hands slightly raised, his palms up, "'Because that which may be known of God is manifest in them; for God hath shewed it unto them. For the invisible things of Him from the creation of the world are clearly seen, being understood by the things that are made, even His eternal power and Godhead; so that they are without excuse.'

Romans chapter one, verses nineteen and twenty...I think. That's what Grandma Clark used to quote all the time."

"Your mother?"

"Grandmother. She passed on long ago, but when she was at home and we were just little kids—like you used to be—we had to memorize Bible verses to say aloud before eating supper. That happened to be one of my favorites, and one of Grandmother's favorites. She let me reuse it several times."

"Pretty heavy memorizing for a little kid," Jimmy determined.

"Know what it means?"

"Homer! I'm almost fifteen!"

"Oh, right. So what's it mean?"

"It means that even nature is a witness to God. We studied that in Sunday school. Your grandma must've read the Bible a lot."

"Well, yeah. But she was Primitive Baptist—didn't hold with missions and missionaries—figured God gave enough hints about himself already. I think that was her Scripture to have ready for when the Southern Baptists came calling."

"Yes, but—"

Moooooooo! A cow had moved in close in the darkness and loudly introduced herself.

They both jumped then laughed in relief when they realized what had happened.

"Whew!" Homer snorted, still catching his breath. "You know, I never realized what a good dancer you are, boy. That was a tidy little jig you were doing right there—a real feet beater."

"So do you want me to help you find that flashlight now or not?" Jimmy countered. He had heard it hit the ground when the alarmed Homer had flung it down while performing his own jig.

"OK, OK." The old man chuckled. "I guess I might be needing to change my own drawers, too, eh?"

The boy quickly located the flashlight and switched on its beam. "I don't think the cows will care one way or another. Besides, ol' Elsie there's just waiting to be milked...or maybe she was doing some witnessing herself." He shone the light her way.

"Yeah, doesn't look very impressed with our theological musings, does she?" Homer observed. They laughed again. "Yeah, no excuses," he added, summarizing and closing their discussion.

"So anyway, boy, how 'bout you getting the feed, and I'll turn on the overhead lights and open the stalls?" Creatures of habit, the cows were lined up in front of the stall doors where they usually were milked. That's why the doors were kept closed—to limit the number of cows in a stall at one time.

While the overhead bulbs buzzed and sizzled to full brightness, Jimmy climbed into the storeroom and cautiously lifted the cover from the big feed drum, vigorously kicking its steel sides as he tipped back its lid. He then leaned well into the drum to fill two gallon-size cans with the sweetened feed mixture. He liked this part of farming—feeding animals and smelling the molasses in the oats and corn in the barrel—unless the last person feeding the cows hadn't securely replaced the heavy metal lid. Rats had a special taste for the sweet mixture too, and meeting one, or several, face-to-face in the confined space wasn't usually a pleasurable experience.

Homer was waiting for Jimmy when he climbed back down from the elevated doorway at the front of the barn and had ready two stainless-steel pails partially filled with the diluted disinfectant used for cleaning the cows' udders before milking. Not needing verbal direction, Jimmy traded one of his buckets for one of Homer's and tromped on to his assigned stall. Like the cows, the humans were well familiar with the daily routine.

In the first two stalls, Jimmy's cows awaited his attention—the Jersey, Elsie, in the second stall and the Guernsey, the one with the reddish-brown coat and white highlights, in the front stall. Because of teat size and bovine temperament, Homer had told Jimmy it would be better if he, Homer, kept milking the other cows, the three Holsteins and the wild Ayrshire, for a while more. He had allowed to Zula that Jimmy had "perhaps a few more months of growing to do, in both intrepidity and hand width, before we should be doing any changing of charges." Inwardly relieved to not be tasked with milking the Ayrshire, Jimmy still meant to look up "intrepidity" before he voiced any protests. *Homer might have been saying something good...like "big, hairy forearms" or something.*

Jimmy dumped his feed into Elsie's box and positioned his three-legged stool to her left side, her accustomed milking side. With the top of his head pressed tight against her gray flank, he first thoroughly washed her bag then grabbed her farthest teats to begin the milking process, holding his clean, empty bucket between his knees and off the ground. He had learned from harsh experience that cows often shift their stance during milking, usually kicking over any nonheld buckets. *And then there's the Ayrshire, who goes out of her way to kick at you,* he thought.

After seemingly an eternity of squeezing and pulling, Jimmy sensed Elsie was again comfortable, having eaten her feed and dropping all the milk she was willing to give this morning. *One more time around to strip her,* he determined. While he was making this final circuit of her teats, Elsie decided the time was also right to flip her tail at a fly on her side, slightly above and to the left of Jimmy's head.

"Damn it, Elsie!" he swore, raising himself from his stool. Her manure-laden tail had left a warm ring around his head and across his forehead.

From the far end of the barn, Jimmy heard Homer slowly spelling, "D...a...m..."

***

Homer was releasing the last Holstein from the stall across the way as Jimmy finished up with his Guernsey. The boy liked this old cow because she reminded him of a friend at school, a guy named Gary. Both had reddish hair and rather passive, gentle faces. *Kind of vacant-looking,* he thought. But of all the cows, he preferred the little Jersey, even after the tail swipe this morning, because she had these large, dark eyes—*pretty eyes,* he thought—a short nose, and small, perfectly curling horns. *No wonder PET milk shows Jerseys on their can labels.* Seeing Homer still standing at the stall door, he yelled, "Do you know why PET milk chose Jerseys for their labels?"

"Because Jerseys have pretty eyes and remind you of a girl named Susie you once loved in the third grade?"

"Homer!"

"Oh...maybe that wasn't you. How 'bout that their milk has an outstanding cream composition, and the company wants you to think their milk has lots of cream?"

"Yeah, that one. That's why," Jimmy agreed, following the Guernsey from the stall.

Homer laughed and took the boy's partially filled pail from him and poured its contents into the tall, steel milk can topped with a paper filter. He then added his three full, froth-covered buckets and tapped home the can's stainless-steel lid. "Well, that should about do it," he declared, clapping imaginary dust from his hands and reaching above for the wall switch to turn off the barn's lights. The stars were long gone now, and the sun was beginning to peek over the eastern horizon; low ground fog still hugged the bare dirt of the barnyard. "So my boy, how 'bout you taking the cows to pasture while I tote this milk down to the hard road? I expect that ol' milk truck should be getting here pretty soon." The big dairy companies sent their trucks around to the small dairy farms throughout the county, picking up the filled cans along the roads and leaving empties for the next day's production.

"You bet!" Jimmy agreed.

He liked that job—herding the cows down the sloping trails cut in the hillside and through the creek bottom to the paved road then along the asphalt for a short distance to the fenced fields on the other side. Occasionally an automobile would pass and slow to allow the small herd to clear the road. Then Jimmy would imagine himself as looking lean and rugged to the car's occupants—hopefully female occupants—as he courageously guided his bovine charges to the ditch and safety, his sturdy tobacco stake in hand and his obedient dog to his side. However, this summer all he had was the stick at his side. The stray mongrel he'd named Lassie, which had been allowed to stay on the farm for most of the prior year, had taken to slipping into Zula's chicken pen and sucking egg yolks from their shells. So, as Homer had told him, they'd had to put down Lassie before more damage could be done. Of course the news had saddened Jimmy for a day or so when he had first arrived this time, but Homer had spent much additional time with him, taking him along on trips into Sevierville for nails and supplies, including a couple of side trips to Cline's Drugstore for chocolate sodas. That had greatly helped the boy through his period of mourning.

"Well, OK then!" Homer brightly replied. "I'll even run ahead and catch that gate for you." He heaved the heavy milk onto the handcart then walked on outside, crossing the barnyard to the side fencing to loosen the barbed-wire span there from its wire loops and to hold it aside for the boy and the cows to pass. When they had filed through, he refitted the end post into the loops to stretch the barbed-wire back across the barnyard's access to and from the steep hillside. Jimmy was still too short to easily open and close the gate by himself but had impressed Homer in developing his own methods years ago, which involved first securing the top of the gatepost before fitting the bottom loop, the lower portion being much easier to reach and to either pull into place or lever into place, using the tobacco stake as a fulcrum. "I see you're using a little physics theory," Homer once had remarked after watching him close the pasture gate.

Now clear of the gate, Jimmy waved his thanks and followed the cows, whistling and talking to them, disappearing over the hill's edge and down the well-worn paths that crosshatched the brushy slope. This type of hilly East Tennessee terrain, called "knobs" by the locals, was often grazed by cattle but wasn't usually designated as primary pasturage. The grass was sparse and the grazing so exerting that most farmers, like Homer, used the knobs for their houses and barns and the flatlands for their gardens and pastures...and jokes. Homer seldom tired of spinning tales for the tourists about his knob cattle— specially bred cows with shorter legs on one side to keep them from falling off the hills while grazing.

At the base of the ridge, the paths converged and continued across a small brook, still misty in the early morn, and ran parallel to the fenced pasture to the west of the house. Homer used this pasture to hold Red, his big Hereford bull, separating him from the herd until his services were needed.

Today, as with every day this week and last, Big Red obviously felt his services were soon to be sought as he walked along his side of the fence, escorting the herd on its way down the valley. His pleading bawls, while mostly ignored by the passing ladies, grew louder and more desperate as they neared the pasture's end. And as on prior mornings when they had finally reached the fence that ran alongside the road, in his last-ditch effort at joining with the cows, Red lowered his mighty horned head to administer several test butts to the corner fence post.

Today, however, unlike prior mornings, he charged the post repeatedly—once, twice, three more times—bawling, snorting, and kicking dirt clods and dust over his dew-wet, muscular flanks—before surrendering…for the morning.

Whew! Today the post had held; Jimmy could feel safe for another day. He could breathe again. But his concern had reached a new high this morning because the brute was making headway; each day the post had appeared to be a bit looser in its hole, and this morning, the wire staples looked to be drawing back from the wood of the post itself. When the big bull had charged these additional times, the boy actually had found himself gauging the distance to the road beyond the fence gate—in the event he had to outrun Big Red. He remembered also noticing that one of the Holsteins was beginning to dawdle and take a tad more interest in the raging bull—and that was real bad. This last spring, when he had been walking through the valley to go fishing, he witnessed the neighbor's heifer going *through* three strands of barbed wire in two fences to get to Red. It wasn't the bull exerting all the effort; it was the heifer, and it was her time! And that effort had been impressive. *There's no way that fence is gonna stand up to Red and that big ol' Holstein,* Jimmy determined. He already had told Homer about the progressive weakening of the fence, but Homer had a lot of other duties to first attend. "I'll get to it tomorrow," he had said—and that was last week. Now Jimmy needed to tell him of the Holstein's increased attention.

From ten feet away, the snorting bull fixed Jimmy with a malevo-lent stare as the boy held open the gate and the cows clomped past and away, onto the hard road. "You think this is my fault, don't you, old feller?" he addressed the fiery, evil eyes. "You think it's me that's keeping you in, don't you? Well, it's not!" The bull continued to glare, still breathing hard and tossing his head, blowing strings of snot onto the grass. The boy suspected the bull didn't really care anyway, even he was understanding his words. *Red's going mad,* he thought. The big Hereford, not having had his horn buds removed as a calf, had grown one sharp-tipped appendage that formed a respectful arc to the front, while the other horn curved downward and into the bull's temple. Jimmy imagined how the continued growth of that lower horn was affecting the animal's sanity—and disposition—and that image made him super wary around the bull. *Won't turn my back on you for long, big guy. Ever.*

Even those times when he was assigned laundry duty on the long set of clotheslines just inside the pasture at the top of the hill, Jimmy took care to locate Red well before he muscled the clothes basket over the fence and into the unprotected territory—even when there were no enticing cows close by to inflame the bull. As a result he'd noticed that ol' Red had taken to frequenting the high weeds beyond the clothesline poles on wash days. "Hiding in ambush," he had told Homer. And on more than a few occasions, he was certain the loitering bull was closer to him than when he first had turned away. "Dang thing is plotting to get a better angle on me—to beat me to the fence," Jimmy had declared with all certainty. "He's grazing sideways now!"

The old man had just laughed. "Ain't no cow that smart," he had said. However, as the boy also had noticed, ol' Homer himself seemed to be paying more attention to the bull's whereabouts when *he* entered the pasture.

Using his special technique and the tobacco stake, Jimmy hur-riedly refastened the gatepost then trotted to catch up to the herd, now hungry for the tender grass in the big fields. But he knew he wouldn't have to run to get to the gate first because he purposely had left the pasture's entranceway pulled back and open when he had gathered the cows the previous evening. And as he expected, at the break in the wire, they properly turned in on their own and commenced eating their way across the grassy bottomland.

After the last cow was through, Jimmy secured the fence. Deciding that he wanted to watch the cows for a while, he scrambled atop the adjacent V gate stile. The wooden posts of this ancient gate were set close together so the cows couldn't bend their bodies to get through the opening while allowing skinny kids—*Like me,* Jimmy thought—and sometimes exploring tourists to slip through without having to latch and unlatch the wide gate. *Or according to Homer, to forget to latch the gate.*

At the far reaches of the pasture, the boy clearly saw the forested knobs, now lit by the rising sun, and the dark shadow line along the base of the hills, where he knew the creek ran deep and slow. He would steal away early this afternoon, he planned, to get in a bit of fishing before he had to gather the cows for the evening's milking—that is, if he could finish picking up the ground leaves in the tobacco patch beyond the barn; or finish hoeing the long rows of corn, beans, and tomatoes in the garden patch to the east of the house; or finish with the...*Crap! I think I'm supposed to help haul hay today.* Yesterday, he remembered, he had seen the neighbor, Fred Rogers, pulling his big baling machine behind his Ford tractor and heading down the paved road in the opposite direction toward the hayfields. He knew Homer already had raked the dry, mowed grass into long rows, so they were now ready for Fred's attention. *Well, maybe tomorrow I'll go fishing. Maybe.* Jimmy dropped from his perch and trotted back down the road, past Red's pasture and on, to the driveway that led up the hill to the house.

Across the road from the driveway entrance, Homer was waiting for him beside the mailbox, having carried the heavy milk can on the handcart down the rock drive to deposit it there to await the milk-collection truck. He nodded to acknowledge the approaching boy. "Have any trouble with them?" he called.

"No...but ol' Red's about to bust outta his pen down next to the road. And I think one of the big ol' Holsteins is about ready to come into season."

Nodding again, Homer squatted to pull a tall weed from alongside the road. He clouded over in thought for a minute as he chewed on the long stem and vacantly stroked his wispy chin whiskers. "I think I know which one you're talking about. She was a bit off her feed this morning and gave me a little trouble about letting her milk down." He chewed some more. "I'll take a look at that fence after I get done with the hay. Say? Did I mention I could sure use your help today? Fred's gonna bale my hay down in the east pasture, and the Parton boy and the Davis boy are coming down to help me get it in the barn. What do you say?"

Jimmy had pulled his own weed to chew. "Sure," he replied. *I really don't have a choice, but it's nice that Homer asks anyway.* "Sure. Will Zula be feeding us all? Like last time?"

"You betcha. The tourists will be all gone and...Say, I bet she'll make a nice dessert too. Whatcha want? Banana pudding or blackberry cobbler?"

Homer sure has a way with words to a guy who hasn't had breakfast. "Oh, banana pudding of course. You like it best too." But he had more on his mind. "Couldn't...couldn't just me and you and Fred and Tom Parton do the haulin'? We don't really need Daniel, do we?"

Homer looked up to Jimmy from his squatting position. "Don't much care for Daniel Davis, do you?"

"Oh, he's all right, I guess. He just...likes to tease around a lot and...it's not the good type of teasing." Jimmy rearranged the gravel on the side of the road with the toe of his sneaker. "He's kinda mean to the mules too."

Homer puffed a tiny laugh through his nose. "I understand, and if it makes you feel any better, I don't exactly care for his old man neither. Young Daniel is a lot like the Reverend Dilbert was when he was growing up—a bit of a bully, God's gift to womankind, and so on. I was a bit surprised when he got his call from the Lord to preach…but that's not for me to speculate on. Tell you what…" Homer reached up to grasp Jimmy's forearm, to help him get back to his feet. "I'll keep a special eye on the boy today and team him with the Parton boy. Tom and the mules are big enough and nasty enough to take care of themselves."

"Homer…thanks."

"No thanks needed, but my thanks to you. Now do you think you can outwalk an old man back to the house for some breakfast?"

3

BRINGING THE BELL
TO THE WORLD

Holding his seemingly empty wineglass aloft and tapping his plate, Dr. Eli Cohen loudly called for the attention of his fellow diners, especially that of the bald, bespectacled man sitting across the table from him.

"Dr. Biran," he began, "I feel compelled to take this moment of your time to conduct important business with the IAA." The table quieted further. He then, rather formally and perhaps somewhat pompously, acknowledged his other tablemates—Dr. Dorfman on his left side and Dr. Spiegel seated to his right—bestowing his tight smile on each man along with his nods. He had awaited this moment for a long, long time.

Dr. Biran, however, wasn't in a mood to stand on ceremony. He had endured the first day of the annual archeology conference and frankly was a bit tired—tired of refereeing the squabbles among his learned colleagues, tired of defending his employer's official positions taken during the year (*All day long, that legal action involving inscriptions and ossuaries—bone boxes, for God's sake!*), and tired of listening to self-important, aged archeologists extolling their particular "discovery of the century."

"Cohen," he replied, "you invited us to dinner...to do business? You think we don't have office hours maybe? Or you think perhaps I and the IAA are obliged...to refill your wineglass for you?" Avi Biran could be a tad feistier than his diminutive appearance would have one expect. "Besides, you've had enough wine already," he sniffed dismissively, removing his eyeglasses and holding them aloft, inspecting the lenses for potential smudges.

"Avi, I'm wounded," Dr. Cohen protested with feigned aggrievement. "No, I...I actually want to report my finding to the Israel Antiquities Authority...right and proper...at this time." *And in this company.*

"What do you mean? See here, Cohen," Professor Dorfman blustered. "It's getting late, and Spiegel and I have flights out tonight. You've been acting like—"

"Observe..." Cohen lowered his wineglass to present the tiny golden object within. "...and see the beauty of the Israelites from two thousand or even three thousand years ago. See the golden bell that once adorned the hem of a holy priest of our great nation, once lost in the sewers of old Jerusalem, found by me just this week in my excavations." His well-practiced speech was slightly more slurred than he would have preferred. "Maybe once adorning the robe of Joshua, Annas, or even Caiaphas."

"Eli, we are to be notified of such a find while the object is in situ!" Biran sharply interrupted, returning his spectacles to his nose. "You are required to notify the IAA immediately! And not to sport around a sacred object...in a wineglass!"

"An unprovenanced object, for the record," Dorfman gleefully noted.

"Yeah," Spiegel added.

This was not going the way Dr. Cohen had expected—even though the eyes of the other three men had not left the wineglass. "But...but," he declared, "it was not originally found in situ...by my workman. It was sifted from waste material, from the waste material from Fulbright, who started the excavation—from Dr. Fulbright— found just yesterday morning! Avi, I *am* notifying the IAA almost as soon as it was found! This is it!" Cohen knew then he should have made his announcement about three glasses of wine earlier.

"Calm down, Cohen. I'm just having a bit of sport with you." Dr. Biran's eyes sparkled. "I thought you had something going on today—smugly smiling at everyone—buying us dinner tonight. You've never bought me dinner before in your life! And the wine…" He raised his hands and eyes heavenward.

Dorfman and Spiegel were now confused; their expressions appealed for clarification from Dr. Biran. They, too, obviously had thought the IAA man was serious and angry—a state they much preferred at the moment.

"So let's see what you've got," Biran cheerfully concluded, as he deftly scooped the golden bell from Cohen's glass. He then pulled his key ring from his vest pocket and thumbed around his few keys and nail clipper to the tiny jewelry loupe attached. "Some people carry a pocketknife." He shrugged, unfolding and raising the magnifier to his eye. "And I suppose your foreman, Maymum Abbas, did the actual finding, eh?"

Cohen felt a momentary urge to reclaim the credit, but that impulse quickly passed when he noticed Dr. Biran appraising him from above the loupe. "So you also know old Abbas then?" Cohen said with a sigh. "So yes, Avi, Mr. Abbas brought the golden bell to me from the excavation of the sewer. And yes, Mr. Abbas recognized the bell immediately for what it was…and is." He felt the color rise in his face.

Biran smiled slightly and returned his eye to his examination. "I would imagine old Abbas also gave you a figurative eyewitness account of the priests' procession to the Temple, replete with descriptions of the gold-threaded robes, the stately banners flowing overhead, and the sounding of the cymbals," he absently observed.

"Ah, yes," Cohen snorted. "All the glory of a fictional time, a period of myths and stories, told to fearful, oppressed minions to keep them in line."

Dr. Biran lowered his loupe and appeared to be silently contemplating Dr. Cohen's comment as he unwound the magnifier from his key ring. Then he passed the loupe and bell over to Professor Dorfman.

"Eli Cohen, you do not believe in the God of our fathers?" Dr. Biran softly asked, leaning back in his chair as to await Cohen's reply.

The question had surprised him. He slightly shook his head to clear his thoughts. *Is this midget just having me on again?* He found he could not reply. He had spent his life studying a civilization that was held together by its belief and reliance upon the concept of God, but inside, in the depths of his being, he wasn't sure what he believed. *No, I am sure; Yahweh of the Hebrews is no more to me than Marduk of the Babylonians, Ba'al of the Phoenicians, or Seth of the Egyptians. Just…myths.* Yet he found himself getting angry with Biran. "Now see here, Avi!" He used the bureaucrat's first name because he didn't want him getting mad at him in return. "That's a very personal question, not a professional topic for discussion."

"I don't know, Eli," replied Dr. Biran. "The God of that man who once wore that bell"—he gestured to the bell and magnifier Dorfman was now passing to Spiegel—"was as *personal* to him, that priest, as anything could have been to him—personally. A concept? An understanding? A relationship to die for…even willingly daring to risk being in *God's* presence in the Holy of Holies or to venture forth in battle at *God's* urging? Would any of us be willing to die for such an intangible concept today? Can we even begin to understand the kingdom of God, the workings of the Yahweh of our forefathers, God's reality to them? I'm thinking perhaps God is more real to Mr. Abbas than he is to any of us. And I'm afraid that's our loss."

The other two men were closely watching Avi Biran, wondering where he was going with his dreamy discourse—and secretly glad it was Cohen rather than themselves who was in the hot seat.

Biran leaned over and picked the golden bell from Spiegel's palm. People at neighboring tables were now casting glances their way, obviously interested in their animated conversation and in the tiny, bright object held high by the tiny bald man.

"Suppose, gentlemen, Yahweh is addressing us all through this piece of our history, when we knew God well, when we feared him and sought his protection from the evil one and our enemies. Will our *personal* positions now mean anything to him—or us—should the priests of God in our world today be correct in their warnings of the unseen eternity awaiting us? Will we still be able to communicate, to be drawn to God at some level? What if..." Biran's words trailed off as he looked up.

A well-to-do matron and a pretty little girl were standing beside Dr. Spiegel. "We couldn't help overhear. Would you mind if my granddaughter held the artifact for a moment?"

***

"Say, have you heard anything about where the old guy worked? Where he's been? Where he might have picked up that infection?" one physician asked the other, still in their hazard suits, both just leaving Abbas's hospital room.

"Not much. He hasn't regained consciousness, even though we've trimmed the pain medication. Best I understand, he apparently has been working with a group of archeologists nearby in the Old City. Remember reading about the excavations of the ancient sewer lines there? Roman-era systems, I believe? No? Well, anyway... hey! Did you hear the latest about Eliphaz?"

"No, what?"

"Aside from obviously being in great pain, he's conscious and talking. He seems to believe the infection is a variant infection and much like...bubonic plague." He turned his face to his associate when he said the last part and lowered his voice.

At the very mention of the words, the other physician shivered, visible even beneath the layers of his suit's protective fabric. "No shit?" he managed to croak in reply.

"Yeah, Dr. Eliphaz told Bildad the infection's symptoms are much like he saw years ago in India. Or maybe it was Peru. At any rate he says the communication medium, the transmission means, has morphed somehow. He's certain he wasn't bitten by a flea and didn't contract it from any other more common means to transfer bacilli. He thinks he got it from a simple cough from Mr. Abbas. Now *that's* frightening!"

"Any lab reports yet?"

"Yeah, but *Yersinia pestis* wasn't evident. Didn't matter. Dr. Eliphaz requested we immediately contact the CDC in Atlanta, but we'll probably wait for all the lab results before we do that. Dr. Bildad doesn't want us alarming the world before we know what we've got. Eliphaz also has asked for antibiotics, tetracycline and such—IV fluids. Bildad agreed, and that's all in place."

"Wow!"

"Oh, yeah, and Eliphaz has asked for a priest too."

"A priest? I thought he was Jewish—go figure. Well, he must *really* believe he has no chance." He leaned his head toward the windowed isolation room. "I bet he's really pissed at Abbas for coughing on him."

"No, actually he's not. They say he's rather philosophical about the whole thing. And he's asked about Mr. Abbas's condition several times. Says he's recognized a kindred spirit or traveler or something like that, in the old man."

"Well, I'd certainly be pissed. Anything else?"

"Yeah, believe it or not, Dr. Eliphaz is even concerned about us. Imagine that—in his pain and all—he recommended prophylactic antibiotics for us and for Nurse Silverman. He doesn't know she's split."

"Hah!" The first physician laughed bitterly. "Prophylactic antibiotics? There couldn't be any better protection than all this gear we have on. And when the CDC is contacted, they will, of course, want to take over everything. And we will, of course, step back and let them risk *their* respective arses."

They sagely nodded in agreement.

Little did the cloaked doctors suspect that they were already infected...and were carriers themselves. Dr. Eliphaz had stopped by the cafeteria early that morning, as was his custom, and had poured himself a large cup of coffee from the urn. Feeling a coughing fit coming on, he had grabbed several paper napkins to stifle his expulsion then had left the room. He had deposited his used napkin in the lidded receptacle at the entrance to the men's room and grabbed replacement tissues from the box above the sink as he had exited, those having been quickly put to use during his elevator ride up to his office. Then, after he had violently coughed several times in the elevator, amid the other passengers—a night guard, a couple of visitors, and several frowning nurses—he had gotten off at his floor, noticing then the bloody flecks on his tissues. At that moment he had decided to admit himself in the hospital.

Meanwhile, a housekeeping attendant had emptied by hand the adjoining bathrooms' receptacles into his own larger waste bag because he had forgotten to bring replacement bags, and then he had restocked the bagels on his way back to the kitchen as a special favor to the cafeteria attendant—his girlfriend.

The doctors had both eaten untoasted blueberry bagels with cream cheese that morning; it was staff appreciation day at the hospital and breakfast had been free.

"Say, have you heard anything more about Silverman...more than you think she's split?" the first physician asked.

"Just that no one's been in contact from her since yesterday," the other shrugged in reply. "I don't know if she was scheduled to come in but the hospital administrator sent a guard to her apartment to check on her anyway. Then they called the police when they couldn't raise anyone inside.

"So I guess I don't know anything about what's going on with her now."

***

Cynthia Silverman already had cleared customs and was taking a cab to downtown Newark. The sun was still high in the sky, so she knew her sister would be at work; she would just wait for her in the little bar at street level in the same building. *Make it easier for Sis to find me.*

Cynthia's panic had subsided somewhat since she'd left the hospital. *Was that only yesterday?* The direct flight she had managed to catch this morning in Israel was divine intervention, she had told her seatmate. "Not that I'm particularly religious," she quickly had added. Since the flight time was exceptionally long, about twelve hours, she normally would have gone on to talk more about her nursing life and her experiences, and maybe about Mr. Abbas, but for some reason, she had wanted to keep those thoughts far from her mind. Yes, the very reasons for this trip were these recent events and her desire to flee to the only one who unconditionally would love and reassure her—Sophie, her older sister and sole remaining family member—but now she wanted to forget all that. She had not even thought to place a call to Sophie prior to her departure. *But I'm OK…I'm feeling OK,* she comforted herself. *Just too much work. This will just be a nice time with Sis.*

The cab pulled to a stop in the middle of the block, in front of Woodrow's Tavern. Cynthia paid the driver and rolled her suitcase through the door and into the dim bar. She would find a phone and call her sister to let her know she was going to have company—company that would be found waiting and seated in the bar downstairs. *But first a stiff one. It's nighttime for me.*

She walked and rolled over to the nearest barstool at the corner of the long bar, her back to the door. The bright light seemed to bother her eyes now. She also had noticed a rather nice-looking gentleman seated two stools down.

"Randall Sells," he introduced himself. He softly took her offered hand and signaled the bartender with his eyes to give her whatever she wanted.

"Sells in sales," he responded to Cynthia's inquiry. "Computer executive. Based out of Atlanta. Traveling the nation," he offered, then added, "Here to look into problems and ride herd on the local sales guys." He wanted to let her know he was also a person of worth, a boss, a leader, an independent stud, and secure in himself.

In her peripheral vision, Cynthia watched Randall fumble with the removal of his wedding ring beneath the bar's elbow cushion. He didn't know she already had spotted his ring and had absolutely no concern about his marital status. If they were going to hook up, they were going to hook up; she was a liberated lady.

They talked on, and Cynthia decided she liked Randall very much. He now had his hand on her thigh and hotly suggested,

"Maybe we could have dinner…later?" His left eyebrow mischievously bobbed up and down with the real question. Cynthia had no trouble at all interpreting his message. Soon she and Randall were rolling her suitcase down the sidewalk, back to the nearby Marriott he had checked out of not two hours before.

Upon entering the hotel room, Cynthia excused herself, closing the bathroom door.

Attending to female things, thought Randall. He complimented himself on his extraordinary luck as he toed off his shoes, one foot against the other, as he sat on the edge of the king-size bed. He actually had been on his way to the airport when he had decided to have one more little drinky poo before he headed home to the old lady and the brats. Besides, the trip had been crap, and he needed a bit of a break. *This lady's not a knockout, but she seems pretty well put together under her clothes. Just that she tasted like liver or something when she gave me the tongue in the elevator.* But Randall was hardy; he could get by that. *I've got a rubber, and I've got the time…just as long as she doesn't have another one of those coughing fits.*

In the bathroom Cynthia looked at the dark sprinkles in her hands. She hadn't felt that well after all. Then Abbas's gray face and crimson-streaked bedcovers flashed vividly across her mind. *I've caught the stuff he's got! I'm too young to die!* She sat heavily on the toilet seat and buried her face in her hands, willing herself to smooth the gasps in her breathing. But she had already known that…hadn't she? Wasn't she just lying to herself since she had run from the hospital yesterday? She knew already she had caught Abbas's disease. "Damn you, God!" she cursed. "Damn you. Damn you all to hell!" But she wasn't going to go alone! She no longer felt like having sex with this guy but…*Couldn't call it love anyway,* she thought. *And I'm not going alone! Damn them all to hell!* She started to unbutton her blouse.

Randall was in the bed and naked when Cynthia opened the door. "Baby, I missed you," he crooned. *Sure took your time, bitch,* he thought. "You look fabulous. Were you talking to me in the bathroom just now? Here, crawl in here beside me." He held the sheet back so she could see his ready manliness.

Cynthia closed the window curtains and turned off all the lights. *In case I cough,* she purposely thought.

Three hours later, Randall Sells was on an airplane, winging his way back to Atlanta. In the days ahead, he and Cynthia Silverman would go on to infect dozens of other people before they would both lie in their respective blood-and-diarrhea-soaked deathbeds.

***

"Did the police go to Mr. Abbas's house?" the first physician asked, gesturing with his gloved hand, pointing to the dying man on the other side of the thick, protective glass.

"Yeah, I think that's where they got the tie-in with the archeologists in the Old City. My brother-in-law, a cop, says the chief archeologist, a Dr. Eli Cohen—you've probably heard of him. Been around here forever, I think; I remember seeing him on TV. Anyway, Dr. Cohen is in Tel-Aviv at some kind of conference. They're trying to contact him there about Mr. Abbas. I imagine if Cohen has been in Tel-Aviv all week, he probably doesn't know anything about what Abbas has come down with or what. Oh, another thing—Abbas handed out paychecks the day before he was carted in here. Another old guy, a Palestinian—someone who works with Abbas at his archeology dig—was admitted at that Palestinian West Bank hospital in Ramallah. He was coughing blood and all, had swollen lymph nodes—just like Abbas—and the authority contacted the police here. The Palestinian tried to cash his paycheck at the hospital to pay for his admission, and he told the police he had received his check from Abbas just before leaving for the long weekend."

"Wow!" exclaimed the first doctor. "Maybe Eliphaz..." His voice trailed off. He had talked about the bubonic plague, but only now was it becoming real to the man, in his heart of hearts.

***

That turned out well after all, Dr. Cohen told himself. He had paid the bill, leaving a generous tip for the headwaiter, who somehow had become his publicity agent for the evening. And he believed he must have told every table in the place about his magnificent discovery: people from Spain, Portugal, Los Angeles, Hong Kong. *Everywhere! And they all just wanted to see, to hold the tiny, golden bell and to shake my hand. Maybe there is something to this God-blessing thing after all!*

Dr. Spiegel and Dr. Dorfman had departed for their evening flights—Spiegel to Paris and Dorfman to New York, where he ostensibly had a morning lecture to prepare for his freshman class at the university. *Hah! That SOB just couldn't wait to be away from this attention—my glory. So jealous—I hope.*

Dr. Biran was waiting patiently at the restaurant's exit. He had ordered a cab to take them both back to the hotel and had secured the golden bell in his handkerchief for an early-morning visit to the IAA offices. "Shouldn't be too much longer," Biran confided to the maître d'. "Dr. Cohen is having his moment in the sun and appears to be rapidly losing steam. I think that's the second or third coughing fit he's had tonight."

When they reached the hotel, Biran had to help Cohen from the cab and through the revolving doors. The health ministry's man, waiting in the lobby with his message from Jerusalem, met them there and took over for Dr. Biran. He asked if he could have a private moment with Dr. Cohen, and Biran was only too happy to oblige. He was very tired and had to get up early.

"So Cohen," he said, "I'll see you in the morning. You and this fellow have your discussion without me, and I'll take that lift over there. Good night all." The elevator doors snicked closed behind him as the stranger leaned in to deliver his short message.

Cohen didn't receive the summons well. "You say I'm to return tonight to Jerusalem, to admit myself to the hospital—for testing?" He snorted his displeasure. "Don't be daft, man. I have a presentation tomorrow. I just need a good night's sleep because I think I'm coming down with a bit of a cold. Just tell them that, and say

I'll be along presently…after I've made my presentation tomorrow. Terribly important, you know."

The ministry man persisted and was relating the events concerning Mr. Abbas when Dr. Cohen coughed violently and staggered backward, then slid slowly down the wall beside the elevator's doors, lighting the buttons before reaching the floor.

High above, as the elevator door opened to his room level, Dr. Biran patted his breast pocket, where the golden bell was now secure in the folds in his handkerchief. *I'll return this to old Cohen tomorrow— after my chaps have had ample microscope time with it.* Israel was awash in counterfeit artifacts, and he believed it was his primary job to ferret out such fakes. *We'll just see what the patina experts have to say about this priestly bell.*

4

NEWS COMES TO THE FARM

The driver in the Mayfield truck waved through his open door as he pulled away. "Thanks, boys!" he yelled. "See ya tomorrow!" Gus had arrived just as Homer and Jimmy had started up the driveway, so they dutifully had turned and walked back down to the hard road to help old Gus lift their milk-filled can into one side of the gleaming-yellow, refrigerated truck and lower an empty can down from the other.

On their way again, returning to the house and breakfast, Jimmy sprinted ahead up the rise, leaving Homer and his handcart well behind and out of sight, hidden by the elevation of the broad, covered porch that spanned the house's front and eastern sides. Seeing his chance, the boy slipped in behind the row of bordering boxwood shrubs to hide in Zula's prized flower bed, waiting to ambush the puffing old man when he rounded the hedge. Jimmy was betting Homer would choose to go in the house by the back door at the TV room, and he would follow around on the broken-marble sidewalk branching off from the front walk. *But I'll be careful in jumping out to scare him,* Jimmy told himself. Homer wasn't a spring chicken anymore, as he often reminded the boy, and the flower bed *was* elevated a bit above the walkway. *I'll be careful.*

Long minutes passed, and Jimmy realized he could no longer hear Homer's wheezing progress up the walkway; he'd take a quick peek to see what had delayed his victim. *Slowly. Slowly.*

Pit-too-ee! A stream of ambeer shot by, about six inches in front of his nose.

"Homer! You almost spit tobacco juice on me!" cried the boy.

"Well, what are you doing up there amongst Zula's flowers anyway? That's where I dump my chaw in the mornings—to fertilize the ol' woman's zinnias."

"You saw me getting ready to ambush you, didn't you?"

"Boy, there's not a jury in the land that'd convict me. By the way," Homer snorted, "if you'd stepped back on that marigold there behind you, I'd have to go out and find a new favorite relative. But I'd be sure to tell your hide hello every morning as I passed the pump house door…where Zula nailed it."

Jimmy looked around his feet and carefully stepped out again to the sidewalk. "So did you see me?"

Homer was scraping his shoe bottoms off on the metal blade set in the concrete at the edge of the sidewalk, right before the single step up to the back walkway. "Naw, I didn't see you. I just figured you'd be doing something I'd be doing if I were your age. And you know what I'd be doing next if I were your age?"

"What?"

"Taking my shoes off before going in the house for breakfast. You've got manure on your laces, and I'm expecting that the bottoms of those tennis shoes are loaded up too. And you know what else?"

"What?"

"You got cow manure splattered all up the front of your britches! Did one of those cows explode on you or something? Maybe you got too close behind one of those long-legged Holsteins on that hard road, and it splattered?"

Aw, man! "Where, Homer? I don't see it." Jimmy, having slipped off his shoes, was standing in his socks on the edge of the step, leaning well over and pulling outward on the legs of his jeans.

"Right there, boy. And there. Maybe you have to have the light positioned just right to see those spots? Regardless, you smell pretty bad too. You'd better hustle around to the other door and go through the laundry room. And you'd better hope the ol' woman has done the wash and you've got a dry pair of pants back there. You can't go to the breakfast table and sit down next to some tourist lady a'smellin' like some ol' cow with terrible hygiene."

That made sense to Jimmy. "You won't eat all the ham, will you? You'll save me a piece?"

"Yeah, yeah, I'll save you a piece. And a biscuit too."

Zula cooked a breakfast buffet when they had tourist guests, charging one dollar per adult head (children were free) for the privilege of pulling up a chair to the long table and spooning off any appealing victuals from the big serving dishes as they were handed down the table. She would start early in the morning by cutting thick slices from the country hams hanging in the smoke-house then soaking these slices for an hour or so to cut their saltiness before pan-frying them. Then she would bake, fry, simmer, or boil the remainder of the fare: eggs (any way you wanted them), bacon, home-seasoned sausage, sausage gravy, redeye gravy, buttermilk bis-cuits, toast, hash browns, and sometimes either grits or mush. The finely ground corn mush was usually prepared toward autumn then usually only on request by those Cream of Wheat–desiring tourists. Since East Tennessee was above the grit line, the preparation of grits also was seldom done without tourists being in the home; it was just something the Northerners seemed to expect throughout the South. And then there were the assorted offerings of homemade jams and jellies—something Jimmy hated seeing consumed in copi-ous quantities because, as the youngest, it was still his job to wash the innumerable jars during the annual jelly-making season. He equated consumption with demand—and the more jars he'd have to wash, come next summer.

Jimmy could smell the frying sausage as he padded across the enclosed porch on his way to the laundry room. He'd hurry because he knew Zula took great pride in timing her meals so that each dish was on the table at its optimum temperature—and she wanted her sausage to be hot when it left the kitchen.

But he couldn't quickly locate his other pair of jeans today. He searched garment by garment along the shelves of clean clothes and even checked the washer to see whether anything had been skipped in the hanging. *Nothing*. So he didn't really have a choice; he'd give his pant legs a good brushing and shaking, and then he'd see if they'd pass Zula's muster. He slipped off his jeans and returned to the porch to spread them on the big chest freezer there, all the while hoping some female tourist didn't decide just then to come down the back steps from an upstairs bedroom.

Squinting his eyes and turning his pants at all angles, he still couldn't see the spots Homer had seen, even with the light of the overhead bulb. And he certainly couldn't detect any manure aromas emanating from his cuffs or from his seat, supposing he might have sat on a cow chip or two at the barn. *Still nothing*. Shaking his head, he pulled on his jeans again and, after a final hearty brushing, headed for the kitchen, hoping to find Zula there and not already in the dining room.

That wasn't to be. From the kitchen, Jimmy saw Zula sitting in her usual chair, her back to him and the kitchen door, and Homer sitting at the far end of the long table, now lined with tourist strangers. *Oh, boy, I'll just wait for a while and grab a biscuit later*, he told himself. But Homer must have been waiting for him because he immediately noticed him and waved him in. "Oh, well," the boy said with a sigh. He checked his fly once more and sauntered in.

Strange. He wasn't hearing the normal clanking of silverware or the hum of conversation. *They must still be saying the blessing because no one is eating!* He almost skidded to a stop, bowing his head and closing his eyes.

Then: "Happy birthday to you. Happy birthday to you…" They all robustly sang to him, even the tourist-guests. *Today's my birthday? And Homer musta wanted me to come in late—after everyone was at the table—so they all could sing to me. That's why I couldn't see the cow shit on my pants—there wasn't any! Homer!* But Jimmy didn't say anything right then. To him it…just felt too…*Darn it, Homer! It's not my birthday! You just told them that!*

The furiously blushing boy slipped onto the nearest vacant chair.

"Got your seat, Jimmy? You know I saved you a biscuit here," Homer boomed, grinning and holding aloft the bread. He then confided to the table: "It's almost like a hillbilly bar mitzvah—'cept maybe a tad early. Right?" He winked at Zula.

Zula stared back from her end, obviously not amused with her witty husband. *What's he pulling now?* She knew it wasn't Jimmy's birthday and...*Hillbilly bar mitzvah!? Sometimes that man can be so embarrassing!*

But Jimmy couldn't stop smiling anyway. *No matter; that was pretty good.* He thought he probably could have even managed a tear or two—if the tourist lady seated next to him hadn't seemed inclined to hug on him some more. So he and Homer just exchanged meaningful glances over the tops of their coffee cups. *There will be vengeance taken, Homer,* Jimmy promised. *Terrible vengeance.* But he knew it would take a while to think up something to top this one. *So embarrassing.*

After breakfast the guests lingered over their coffee and conversation and helped themselves to more of the flower-shaped butter mounds (churned and pressed by Zula of course) and jelly. *Darn!* Jimmy counted a half dozen empty jars on the table.

Then Zula caught his eye and gave him a nod and the thumbs-up signal; if he and Homer didn't want to do dishes, they had better get on with the day's work. *Time for us to go to the barn.* Homer and Jimmy pushed back from the table and politely waited for the man from New York to finish his conversation with the man from Philadelphia before they stood and excused themselves.

But as they listened to the men, they realized the conversation had turned sober; both men were returning home today with their families, cutting short their Smoky Mountains vacations because their elderly parents suddenly had taken ill. Then the woman seated beside Jimmy spoke up. "I'm from Jacksonville, but I wasn't on vacation here in the mountains. I got a call yesterday that my older sister in Milwaukee is very sick with some kind of flu or something that apparently is going around. I was planning on driving through the night when I got tired outside of Knoxville. That's when I discovered all the motels along the interstate were filled to capacity. Apparently a lot of people are traveling right now."

"Yeah," said a man seated farther down the table, an engineer from Little Rock who was working in South Carolina. "I got a call from my dad in Arkansas to come home. He's taken the flu and was admitted to the hospital. Yeah, the roads between here and Charleston were packed yesterday."

"Do tell." With his eyes lowered in thought, Homer scratched his scraggly beard and absently observed, "Lots of people traveling and lots of sickness at the same time—that's all very unusual...but it reminds me of another time." He proceeded to recollect aloud about the flu epidemic of 1918 that had taken a cousin of his who had lived in Kansas. "It started out the same way—notices of illness coming in all at once. And then later the government told us we had an epidemic on our hands—the Spanish flu, they called it. Told people to stay home and not to travel. But the warnings came too late; it spread like all get out and continued spreadin' on up through nineteen twenty. All around the world. You know, I bet ten million—no, twenty million—people were killed by the stuff before it was through. And then it just stopped. But you know what was really strange? The Spanish flu seemed to hit the young and the healthy the hardest. More of them died then—oh, damn!... But that doesn't sound like it's what we have here today!" he hurriedly added, concluding his pondering. He had glanced up to see pained expressions replacing thoughtful ones. *Too late.* He knew then that any further attempts at providing comforting qualifications would only be drowned out by the ensuing screeches and rumbles—sounds of chairs being pushed back and of diners standing to hasten upstairs to finish their packing of clothes and their zipping of suitcases.

Zula glared, and Homer grabbed Jimmy's shoulder, rushing the boy and himself out of the house and away from his wife's sharp tongue. "I think I might have done it this time," he quietly observed as the door slammed shut behind them.

"You betcha," Jimmy seconded the observation.

They strode on, taking the long way to the barnyard this time, walking but not talking, as Jimmy sensed Homer's present need to do some cogitating, as he would say. They tromped through the weeds behind the smokehouse then past the partially completed cinder-block building that was someday to be Homer's milk house. Jimmy had two uncles in the dairy business so he knew what Homer was aiming for: elevated stalls and automatic feeders; electric milking machines feeding into clear, overhead tubing; cow head locks; and concrete floors. *Especially concrete floors,* he concluded. *And maybe this would be the time to hear all about that again. Homer could use some cheering up right about now, I think, and talking about the ol' milk house usually brightens him up considerably.*

And it did—sort of; Homer detoured into the gloom of the half-built structure, his hand on Jimmy's shoulder, to point out where fixtures someday would be installed and electrical cables eventually run. But the information was basic; the old man remained reserved and quiet like; he was still cogitating. "And this will be where the cows come in. 'Course we'll have a lot more cows too, and…"

"Homer!" A shout from the other side of the wall interrupted them. It was Fred Rogers from the next farm over. "Homer Clark!"

"In here, Fred!" Homer yelled back.

"In here, Fred!" Jimmy helped.

The old farmer shuffled in to lean against the doorless jamb, his thumbs hooked in the straps of his overall's bib. "You a'tellin' the boy again how great and wonderful things are a'gonna be?" Fred grinned. "Why, I expect that the boy should be able to do his own tour by now. How old are you now anyway, Jimmy?" he asked.

Jimmy was about to tell Fred of his newly discovered birth date when he caught Homer's subtle headshake. *Probably knows ol' Fred will head off to the kitchen to tease Zula so…I'd better not. That might result in something a bit harsher than just vengeance. Maybe later.* "Fourteen," he answered. "Almost fifteen."

"Well, Homer, I expect that the boy here has heard about your milk house at least fourteen times now. Jimmy, did you know that this here roofed pile of cinder blocks is about three years older than you?"

"Naw," Homer halfheartedly disputed. "Couldn't be that old."

But he didn't laugh along with Fred—and Fred felt it: *Homer's burdened*. So he waited, inclined there in the doorway and chewing his tobacco. His friend had thoughts he needed to share.

After a prolonged silence, Homer obliged and slowly recounted the breakfast events and conversations...and his developing fears as best he could in the boy's presence. Fred listened but said nothing, even when Homer obviously had finished. He just looked at the ground, nodded a few times more to show he understood, and sucked in his top lip to indicate the gravity of his thoughts. Then, like most old farmers do when their opinions are not specifically sought—or there is no solution to be had, Fred changed the subject, reaching over to ruffle Jimmy's sandy hair. "See, boy, every man's gotta have a dream, a goal in his life, to make it meaningful." He'd picked up where he had left off. "Ol' Homer's dream centers around this here milk house, and I don't doubt he'll properly finish it... probably when the milk prices get a bit better."

"Yeah, and when pigs fly," Homer added.

This time they all softly laughed.

"Actually, Homer, I walked over here for a purpose—to see if you're gonna get around to hauling in the hay today as I bale it. I hear it's gonna rain and all, the rest of the week." He paused to lean far back to spit his chaw juice outside the doorway. Wiping his mouth with the back of his hand, he winked and explained to Jimmy, "Can't be a'spittin' inside the milk house, now can I?"

Homer snorted. "Fred, you've always had some real class about you—worried about spitting outside whilst you dribble down your chin."

Fred just returned the sideways grin, chewing and nodding, while obviously trying to think up his own snappy rebuttal.

Homer continued on. "Now, old man, me and the boy were just going to the barn to hitch up ol' Blackie and Whitey to the wagon to haul in that hay." Blackie and Whitey were two elderly mules Homer had owned for many years and still used for close-in plowing and wagon hauling. He preferred them to horses because, according to him, they could plow a straighter line and were more intelligent;

they pulled the wagon around the hayfield and tobacco patch at a constant speed, needing only occasional course corrections from him. That freed him to help with the transferring of hay bales or tobacco-filled stakes from the field to the wagon's bed—one less hand to have to pay.

"You penned them up already?" Fred asked, his head lifted. He knew the mules tended to stay far away from the barn when Homer hung their harnesses on the nails at the barn's entrance, ready for the next day's labors.

"Yeah, yeah. I shut them up last night in the pen at the back so we won't have to spend the time a'runnin' them down. Took me about a gallon of shelled corn apiece to coax them into the fence yesterday, smart ol' critters."

"Them ol' mules still chasing you around the barn, Jimmy?"

"Just Whitey, for the most part, Fred," he softly answered. For some reason the mules intensely disliked children. *And not just me,* Jimmy thought. For as far back as he could remember, he had been warned to watch out for the mules—and Red, the bull, but mainly the mules. They *were* smarter than the average farm animal and *were* entirely capable of inflicting significant, permanent damage on any nonvigilant barnyard visitors but especially kids. *And not just kids.* Jimmy recalled the time Blackie had waited for Lassie to round the barn door and had caught him with a kick that almost had knocked him cold. The mule would have finished off the dog if the animal hadn't been lifted to the far side of the fence wire with the kick. On another occasion Whitey, the other mule, had kicked back at Homer when he had gotten too close to the front of the wagon. She had reached over the top of her traces, just barely clipping the top of the old man's nose with the tip of her sharp, unshod hoof. Since the mules rarely walked on paved roads, Homer never had felt the need to have them shoed. *It split his nose so that the doctor had to push it back up and hold it in place with a pencil to tape it,* Jimmy remembered. *Homer's got a scar there now between his eyes and on top of his nose…but it coulda killed him if he'd been three inches closer.* That also had been the day Jimmy discovered his sensitivity to the sight of blood in his earlier years; after witnessing the kick, he immediately passed out in a row of cabbages while Homer staggered about, his blood squirting from between his fingers and running down his forearms.

"You know, sometimes I think those ol' mules can actually talk to each other," Jimmy continued. "There've been so many times when I've started out across the barnyard, first seeing one mule standing with its back to me like it was ignoring me and, then a few seconds later, hearing the other one come thundering through the barn from where it was hiding. See, it was just waiting for the signal from the other mule that I'd come through the gate." Fred was still looking at him. "Just Whitey, for the most part," Jimmy repeated, a little louder this time. *Maybe Fred's not wearing his hearing aid.*

Fred nodded and grunted in agreement. "Ah, boy, you gotta stay on your toes around here, don't you? And near those ladders to the loft? Hah! Between those ornery ol' mules and ol' Red, you can't be in your unawares anywhere, can you, boy? Hah!" Fred leaned and spat again. "Say, what do you do around that big ol' white leghorn rooster of Zula's when you go to gather eggs? That ol' boy's got to have spurs that are at least three inches long. You'd have to be watching out for him too."

Jimmy looked confused. Now that Fred had mentioned it, he remembered having seen—and avoided—the rooster when he had come to stay in the spring, but now he realized he hadn't seen the bird on this stay, nor had he noticed its absence. He looked to Homer with the question.

"Remember the fried chicken dinner we had when your folks first brought you up?" Homer waited for Jimmy's nod. "Well, that was Hercules."

Jimmy's face screwed up, first in delight and then in thought. "Don't you need a rooster for, eh, you know, eggs?"

Homer laughed brightly. "Chickens don't need a rooster around for much of anything. Go ask Zula; she'll let you know right quick the worth of anything male on a farm."

They all laughed again. *It's good to see ol' Homer almost back to normal,* Jimmy thought.

"We've wasted enough time. Come on, boy," Fred said, pulling Jimmy close. "You can ride down with me whilst Homer hitches up the hay wagon. He ain't gonna need you there any more'n I'm gonna need you now. The tractor's out yonder in front of the barn." He pointed the way. "I left the Parton boy and the preacher's kid down at the gate to the bottom, waiting for us to start in."

Now it was Jimmy's time to become thoughtful; he had forgotten he would be seeing Daniel Davis today.

And Homer noticed that. "Jimmy," he said, "I believe I'd rather have you mostly stay on the bed of the wagon and up top in the loft today, if you don't mind. You can stack the bales as we toss them up. OK?"

Jimmy nodded and smiled his appreciation to Homer. He even thought to yell his thanks a second time over his shoulder as he ran past Fred through the doorway and on out to the barn to wait for Fred atop his Ford tractor. He knew that the wagon was Homer's usual job position and that he was just giving him some separation from Daniel. *Gonna be a good day after all. But I'd better get on before Homer changes his mind.*

When the boy's footsteps had faded, Fred turned to Homer. "For what it's worth," he said, "I don't think I like that Davis kid hardly any better than Jimmy appears to. That's one kid who can brighten any room...just by leaving."

"Well, it's more than that, Fred. He's sour, yeah, but he's a lot bigger kid than most—and a mean one—and he doesn't like Jimmy one whit. Jimmy's small, and Daniel's a born bully. Always has been, even when he was younger. He likes to pick on the smaller kids, especially on Jimmy 'cause Jimmy's got a mouth on him; he'll say what he thinks, even if it means a pounding. And Daniel is only too happy to oblige. Fact is, I think that boy gets way too much enjoyment out of hurting people...and things," Homer concluded.

"Do you think he's the one that hung your dog—what'd you call him?—Lassie?"

"Fred, I told Jimmy I had to put Lassie down and let him think it was because the dog had started getting into Zula's chickens and eggs. He don't know I found the dog burned and hanging from a tree down by the creek. So be careful when you talk about Lassie; Jimmy don't know any different, and he was right fond of that animal."

"Well, Homer, ain't you concerned then about Jimmy being down at the creek by himself and playing there all alone? I mean, whoever killed your dog is one sick bastard. I saw that dog—all splayed out and nailed on that tree like Jesus, only gutted and burned too. One sick bastard..."

"Yeah, yeah, I'm concerned, but I can't watch the boy and do the farming too. Besides, Jimmy's starting to really grow and fill out, and I'm betting he'll be able to take that kid himself one of these days. And when that happens, Daniel will leave him alone—cowards are like that."

"But splayed out and crucified..."

"Fred, I've kept my eye on that pasture and around here in general. I haven't seen Daniel 'round about here since that time, so I can't rightly accuse him of anything. Hell, he might be totally innocent, and here I could be wrongfully accusing him of...some terrible act."

"I've noticed I haven't seen you much down at the church house for the last two, three months either, Homer. So as far as learning forgiveness or giving someone the benefit of the doubt..."

"Yeah, well, I guess the Lord still has some sanctifying to do in me, Fred. Meantime I expect, since that pasture and the creek lies directly across the road from your place, you'll keep your eyes open too, huh?"

"Well, you betcha!"

"And thanks for the cheering up. I think I put my foot in it with Zula and the tourists this morning—but I don't like the sounds of this one bit. Did I ever tell you about the cousin I had out in Kansas who died in nineteen eighteen of the flu that—"

"Only about a dozen times, Homer."

Homer and Fred were very good friends.

✳✳✳

"Heads up!" Homer yelled as he launched his fifty-pound load up to Jimmy to complete the fourth row of bales piled neatly atop the old, lumbering wagon. The vehicle was an ancient one Homer had inherited from his father, who in turn had inherited from *his* father, and so on. "Antebellum," he had told Jimmy. "That ol' wagon was in use way before the Civil War and probably come over the Cumberland Gap with ol' D. Boone himself. Why, just look right there," he would point out for the boy. "What's that say right there?"

"Well, it looks like it says 'Dan'l Boone,' but unless ol' Dan'l favored writing with a ballpoint pen…"

"Of course he did, boy," Homer would reply, and then off he would go, spinning some yarn about the wagon's role in the birth of the nation.

Today that old wagon looked and sounded every bit its age as it creaked and moaned beneath its heavy load and the hot sun, behind the pair of straining, sweat-soaked mules. "Homer," Jimmy shouted from his perch, "how many more bales are you planning on hauling on this trip? Think the wagon sounds OK?"

Homer squatted down to inspect the wagon's wooden-spoked wheels. "The axles are a mite dry, I'd say, but they're OK for now. I'll grease them when we get back—ouch!" He had trapped a sweat bee in his armpit and was swatting himself to finish off the stinging insect. "Damn bee," he swore as he rubbed at the spot for a while more. "Dang things can sting the pee outta you, can't they?"

Jimmy nodded his agreement from above. "So take your long-sleeve shirt off."

"Naw, too hot for that; I'll choose the sweat bees. Now what was I saying? Oh, yeah, the wagon will be OK for the day," he continued. "Besides, we can only make one more haul today anyway since the ol' bailer broke down." He glanced over to the shade beneath the trees alongside the field, where Fred was only partially visible, his upper body totally buried in the partially disassembled machine. "We'll come back out once more for the rest of the bales on the ground then call it a day—then go to dinner." In the South "dinner" referred to the large, noontime meal, while supper was the lighter evening fare. "I'm about pooped out anyway. What'd you say to that?"

"OK by me," Jimmy answered.

"Well, it's not OK by me," Daniel Davis yelled from the other side of the wagon. "'For the Scripture says, Ye shall not muzzle the ox that treads out the grain. And the laborer is worthy of his reward,'" he quoted.

"Daniel," Homer explained, "you're going to get fed—just a little later—at, say, one o'clock or thereabouts. Then we'll be done for the day, and Fred can fix his machine and go to town if he needs parts."

"Well, I dunno. I'm hungry now. Will we be paid for the full day? 'For the kingdom of heaven is like a master of a house who went out early in the morning to hire laborers for his vineyard—'"

"Daniel, I know the parable!" Homer interrupted. He sounded a tad exasperated to Jimmy, seated high above. "You'll get paid as much for half a day as a full day. OK?"

"Why, Mr. Clark, that is perfectly acceptable." Daniel smiled, allowing the wagon to clear and dropping his bale then straightening to wipe his face with the enormous, red-checked handkerchief he pulled from his back pocket. "Totally acceptable."

"How about you, Tom Parton, seeing as how you've done most of today's work anyway?" Homer shot a dark look Daniel's way.

"Oh, that's fine by me, Mr. Clark," Tom replied, appearing from around the front of the mules and carrying a couple of hay bales with him, his leather-gloved hands gripping the twine of each. "But you don't gotta pay me for 'nother half day tomorrow, 'cause that's all hit's gonna take. 'Sides, I'm a'needing to spend some time down here in Miss Buelow's tabacky patch a'picking worms and ground leaves. You be doin' me a favor."

Tom Parton lived on the other side of Chapman Highway, northwest of the city limits of Sevierville. Homer knew the boy probably had walked for more than an hour just to get here this morning, around and over the many knobs and creeks between here and his home, a ramshackle old house that probably didn't yet have indoor plumbing, located as it was at the end of an anonymous, overgrown hollow far out in the county. And Homer knew the boy and his older sister were his family's sole source of income—a family that included two younger children, the youngest being a Mongoloid child; Tom's mother, who was chronically sickly, probably with TB; and his father, who had been injured a year or so ago while working his own coal seam in the ridge behind his house.

In fact Homer had known the boy's grandfather since his own childhood, both having attended Harrison Chilhowee Academy, a boarding school located to the west, toward Knox County. *In these hills,* Homer reflected, *education alternatives were few back in those days, and Parton didn't quite get enough of it.* The elder Parton had withdrawn from school when his family had fallen on hard times. *And so it has gone on. This family has known nothing but toil and hardship, and here this boy is willing to...* "Tell you what, Tom. I'm giving you the same deal I've given Mr. Davis here—the full denarius for today. Plus a full day's pay for tomorrow too—no matter if it turns out to be only a half day."

"That too is reasonable and wholly acceptable, Mr. C," Daniel decided.

"Daniel, the deal is for Tom, not you. I won't be needing you after today. I think we—Tom, Fred, Jimmy, and me—can finish up tomorrow."

"But...but Mr. Clark, that's not fair to me!" Daniel sputtered, his face reddening and his eyes narrowing to slits of hate. But Homer already had turned, and the wagon moved on, leaving Daniel behind, still standing with his bale at his feet. Only Jimmy, from his high perch, clearly saw the frightening transformation of the boy's face and witnessed the double-handed, obscene gestures he repeatedly flung at Homer's receding back.

But Daniel had noticed Jimmy too.

***

Back at the barn, Jimmy scrambled from atop the wagon and into the loft as the load passed in and through the main doors. He would now stack the bales to the left side of the loft, having already filled the right side to a six-bale height. *I can go higher, but you know, Homer's not a spring chicken anymore. Besides,* he thought, *it just might be me doing the hauling down again when the hay's needed in the stalls.*

"Hey, Tom!" Jimmy called to the figure silhouetted in the dusty sunlight streaming through the opened loft window. The bales were being thrown into the loft through the opening then heaved back to Jimmy for stacking. Since each bale weighed almost as much as Jimmy himself, he did as much dragging as he did toting. "Hey, Tom. Throw the bales off to the side there so that I got some room to grab the twine to drag 'em over back there. It's kinda dark and musty back there, so I can't go as fast as you."

"Ain't Tom, asshole," the figure growled back.

Daniel! Jimmy felt a tightness in his gut. "Ah, OK, Daniel. How 'bout throwing them off to the side to stack up? Makes it easier on me." He pointed to where he wanted the bales, turning back just in time to catch the next bale full in his face.

"Ain't interested in makin' it easier on you, asshole," Daniel replied, jerking up another bale to send it hurtling toward Jimmy, now prone and only partially visible under the first hay bale.

One...two...three...the bales were stacking up, and Jimmy, pinned beneath the rising pile, could do little to crawl out or even to cry out. His mouth was filled with dust, his tied handkerchief having been torn from over his nose and mouth by the first bale. He coughed once, twice, but he still couldn't breathe; the weight on his chest wouldn't allow him to even draw another dust-filled breath. *I'm gonna die here! Die...here.* Jimmy was fading away. *Dark.*

Then he felt himself being carried aloft on someone's shoulder then being lowered to the wood floor of the loft again, but out near the edge where there was light...and air! Jimmy sucked it in, coughed, and breathed deeply again.

"You OK?" It was Tom Parton. Jimmy saw his face close to his own. "You OK?" the boy asked again.

"Yeah," Jimmy answered, and coughed again, several times. "Yeah. Yeah, I think so. Did you—did you hear me yelling?"

"Naw. From down there, on the wagon bed with Homer, we didn't hear you t'all. I just saw that ol' boy over there a'flingin' those bales like there weren't no tomorrow. I knowed something was up for him to be a'workin' so hard, so I come up to have a look-see."

Jimmy raised himself onto one elbow to follow the tilt of Tom's head. It took a moment in the hazy, orange light, but then he could just make out a pair of upturned shoes, legs, torso, an extended arm—Daniel Davis—laid out on the loft floor beside the stacked bales and seemingly pinned by a pitchfork, its tines driven deep into the bales. And Daniel Davis looked to be dead!

Jimmy's first thought: *How in the world did this skinny guy do that to that big ol' dude?* But he just softly asked, "Didja kill him?"

"Naw, I jus' caught him a time or two in the head with the handle. Maybe once in the stomach. That ol' boy t'weren't near as hard as his talk."

"I just saw that pitchfork still quivering and—"

"Naw, I just jacked that there near 'bouts his head to give him somethin' to look at when he woke up. T'weren't no call for that ol' boy to be doing what he was a'doin' to a boy barely half his size. Figured he jus' be needin' somethin' to jus' remind him, you know, impress him with somethin' he'd understand when he come to. You know, next time?"

"This won't happen again," said an angry voice from behind. Homer had arrived, having climbed to the loft by way of the stairs at the front of the barn. He must have caught the last of Tom's words and seen the jumble of bales off to the left in the dusty gloom back near the outer wall. And he saw Daniel laid out to the other side. *Now how in the world did this skinny kid do that to that big ol' lummox?*

"No, this won't happen again," he repeated. "Me and Mr. Daniel are gonna take a drive to see the Reverend Dilbert in a little while. Gonna have a conclusion to a talk we had a few months back. That's what we are going to do. That boy..." The old man's voice trailed off. He was thinking, and now listening to an inner consultant. A full minute passed before Homer continued, his voice now calm, his anger put aside, his now unclenched hands returning to his side.

"That…boy needs help, or he's gonna come to a bad end. *Our* help. And I'm gonna see he gets it—some psychiatric help."

Homer walked over to where Daniel lay, the boy only now beginning to move his legs and head and blink his eyes. Homer tugged and slid the pitchfork from out of the hay bale, moving it to the side so he could reach Daniel's shirtfront to grip and pull him to a sitting position. "There. Now sit up there," he brusquely ordered.

Daniel was up but was still very groggy and was shaking his head, not having yet noticed the blood freely flowing from his broken nose.

Homer twisted back from his squatting position to speak over his shoulder. "Tom, Jimmy, he's…We're gonna need a few minutes here. How 'bout you boys go on to the house for dinner? We'll be there directly. Jimmy, you need to go down and get Fred to come on, and Tom, how 'bout you just going ahead and telling the ol' woman that me and Daniel are taking a trip? I'll be back directly."

"Yessir," both boys replied.

"And Tom, if Zula asks, be right careful in what you tell her. That ol' woman has got one foul temper right now." Tom nodded his understanding. "And Tom, thanks. You know what almost happened here today. We all need to let you know how much we appreciate you." Embarrassed, the boy lowered his head.

***

Homer hadn't yet returned, and Zula, her tourist guests now long departed, had collared both Tom and Fred, making them stay with her at the dining room table for further interrogation after they had eaten. She already had exiled Jimmy to the front room and well out of earshot, to watch TV while breaking her green beans. He normally wouldn't have minded; after all, that was usually the only way he got to watch TV during the day—to be doing something while he watched. But today he believed he would have liked to hear what Tom and Fred had to say.

"Don't know why I couldn't have stayed," Jimmy muttered, pouting. "Well, at least I'm not ironing clothes again. I just wish Homer and Zula got all three TV channels. And I wish it was Saturday." But it wasn't Saturday, and only CBS was coming in clear today on the tiny black-and-white screen. This afternoon Jimmy watched *The Secret Storm* followed by *As the World Turns*.

After breaking and stringing the last bean in the hamper, Jimmy stood and hoisted the two large buckets of broken beans. *Great timing; Matthew just told Lola that their child wasn't hers and that his former wife just returned from Korea—or something like that—and I'm through with the beans.* He clicked off the TV just as some special news report was coming on. *Great timing all right. I'll go see if I can go fishing in the creek this afternoon then bring the cows up for milking.* With a bucket in each hand, he padded barefoot through the now empty dining room toward the kitchen. Loitering at the doorway, he heard Zula talking in her low voice with Homer, who apparently had returned without Jimmy hearing him drive up the rocky driveway. And both Fred and Tom were gone. *Aw, dang! I didn't get to say bye.*

Seated at the breakfast table, the two adults straightened and abruptly ended their conversation when Jimmy came to the door. But the boy already knew the subject, having long mastered the subtleties of the "silent kid stalk" and having lingered out of sight at the door until he had a reasonable idea what the adults were discussing before he entered—more on Daniel Davis. Apparently the good Reverend Dilbert, having presently arrived from ministering to his flock throughout the county, had been totally supportive of his son and had refused to hear anything remotely negative concerning his progeny. He had refused to listen as Homer had tried to recount the attack on Jimmy, and to the contrary, he had threatened legal action when he caught sight of Daniel's now uneven nose. Homer had then supposed to Zula that it was a good thing he had taken the time to somewhat clean up the kid or Dilbert would have been calling the sheriff right then, had he seen the blood and all. As it was, Dilbert had snatched the boy up to haul him to the emergency room "but not before that turd, Daniel, made sure to get his day's pay, whining and skipping around there behind his pa." Homer had gone on to say that, before leaving the church house, he also had talked with the part-time custodian, old Mr. Miser, who had happened to be there this morning, sweeping out the building. "Ol' man Miser says that boy's the center of the preacher's life right now, even more than ever. The preacher's determined that Daniel is blessed with the gift of healing and is to be the center of his new healing services, to begin this very evening. Many locals seem to be afflicted with this new flu that's going around, and Daniel's touch is supposed to lessen the 'anguish of the afflicted.'"

"Well-to-do afflicted, I would imagine," Zula had added. "About the only anguish I can imagine being lessened is the strain on the ushers after having carried the offering plates out to the preacher's car." She was having a tough time keeping her voice down.

Jimmy knocked, and they both turned and smiled.

"OK if I go early down to the pasture to bring in the cows for milking?" Jimmy asked.

"Sure," Zula replied. "Just be real careful."

Homer leaned back in his chair. "So you want to go fishing in the creek and run your hands back into those holes along the bank and catch big ol' catfish and maybe a softshell turtle or two. And then find Fred's horse, ol' Hammerhead, and ride naked like an Indian over the knobs beyond the creek and…" Homer looked over from Jimmy's open-mouthed captivation to catch another one of Zula's glares. "Or maybe that's just me."

"Yeah?" Jimmy prodded.

"Sure," Homer replied. "Just be real careful."

***

They were finishing up supper early that evening. Jimmy had been unable to find ol' Hammerhead and had decided to cut short his noodling activities after three times finding water snakes rather than big ol' catfish in the holes along the creek's bank. He figured he'd be pushing his luck with a fourth hole. He also had decided he'd save the naked riding for another day, when Hammerhead was easier to locate and there were fewer mosquitoes around. Then, in returning to the house, he had found the cows already loitering around the pasture gate and ready for their evening milking. He had brought them along home with him since he was coming anyway—and the milking for the day was completed about an hour early.

Jimmy was already eating his second dessert, crumbled corn bread in buttermilk, when Thelma arrived home from work, slamming shut the screen door as she came in through the house by the back door in the TV room. "Hey, Mother, Dad, Jimmy," she wearily greeted the table as she stalked into the kitchen, plopping her purse and magazines on the counter beside the refrigerator.

Thelma was Homer and Zula's only living child. She and her husband, Billy Ray, had the bedroom at the top of the front stairs, the only room that was totally off-limits to Zula's tourist home industry because Thelma "needed her sleep" for her job as a beautician over in Knoxville.

"Did you have a good day?" Zula asked.

"Um, so-so, I guess. Kinda slow." Thelma had inherited little of either her father's personality or her mother's industriousness. For more than twenty years now, she'd worked at the same job in the same department store's beauty shop...and seemed to be still working on building her clientele. "Kinda slow," she said again, walking by the table to the stove.

"Say, did Billy Ray call yet?" she absently inquired, as she lifted the tops on the still warm pots. Her husband was an electrician and had gone off to work on the high steel buildings in New York City about three years ago, coming home now only occasionally and between jobs. But he made *very* good money—almost a hundred dollars a week—Jimmy had overheard Thelma telling someone on the phone. The boy was very impressed...and proud.

For, in addition to knowing that Billy Ray was a highly paid professional, Jimmy knew that Billy Ray was a war hero. He had seen the evidence hanging on their bedroom's walls: his German Mauser rifle, his Japanese Nambu pistol, and the assortment of decorations and medals he had brought back from World War II. The boy had sometimes managed to coax a story or two from Billy Ray about his experiences during the war: his having ridden two different bombers to the ground after having been shot down, once over Germany and once over the Philippines, *I think*. Jimmy wasn't too sure of the second location, just that it was over water somewhere. Those times—when Billy Ray was home from New York—were when Jimmy most enjoyed his stays at Homer and Zula's house.

So now, hearing his hero's name mentioned, his ears perked up. "Is Billy Ray supposed to call tonight?" Jimmy asked.

"Nosy," Homer said. "Is Billy Ray to call tonight, Thelma?"

"Yeah, he called at work and left me a message. The job he's on is to be held up for a while—this flu stuff that's going around—so he's planning on starting back down this way either tonight or tomorrow night and drive straight through. I don't know why he just don't stay around up there to see if another job doesn't open up somewhere."

"Well, I'd kinda like *seeing* the ol' boy now and again, you know," Homer replied, adding a strange twist to the tone of his words.

"Well, you don't have a payment coming up on your car neither," she scoffed. Billy Ray tended to dote on Thelma, easily giving in to her demands for late-model automobiles and new clothing to the extent that their living with her parents and his working in New York City was less a matter of choice and more a matter of necessity. Thelma really liked owning things.

"I'd like to see him too!" Jimmy seconded the motion.

Thelma fixed him with a lowered-brow stare. She hadn't wanted kids for very good reasons. "Did you polish my shoes like I asked?" she queried.

"Gosh, Thelma, not yet. See, we brought in hay today and—"

"Spare me the sob story, Jimmy. You just make sure you get them done before you go to bed tonight, hear? I've got to wear them with my new outfit tomorrow."

Homer patted Jimmy's hand on the table. "What say you and me whip them out as we watch TV tonight? I'll show you how to spit shine."

"Dad!" Thelma objected. "He's never going to learn responsibility and to do his job if you always—"

Homer stopped her midsentence with a raised hand and his no-kidding-around look. "Thelma, that's enough. I should have…Never mind. Jimmy is a hard worker already. Now would you like some supper, dear?"

"Jesus! Like I'm not a hard worker? I know what you meant. And supper? You think I want to just eat vegetables for supper? Okra, corn, tomatoes—no meat? Jesus! I gonna call Murphy, and we'll go into town to eat—at a restaurant!"

"Now, Thelma," Zula spoke up, "you know I don't like you using the Lord's name that way. And it don't look right for you to be running out to eat with a male friend who isn't your husband. It don't look seemly. Besides, Mr. Dilfer should be taking his own wife out to eat."

Thelma crossed her arms and puffed through her nose—her disgusted pose. "Mother, Murphy has been divorced for three months now and will soon be getting another promotion at the bank. He's an important man around here, and at the rate you two are going, you'll need someone in a position at the bank to get that mortgage we've been talking about."

Homer stood. "The mortgage *you've* been talking about, you mean." He tapped Jimmy's shoulder. "Take your milk, and let's go tackle those shoes, boy. Maybe there'll be a baseball game on TV this evening after the news." He left Thelma with his long, solemn gaze as Jimmy gathered his glass, dish, and silverware to deposit in the sink in passing.

Hot dog! rejoiced Jimmy. *It's my night to do dishes, but I do believe the priority has been changed.*

***

Two hours later and out on the front porch, Homer and Zula rocked in their big wicker chairs while Jimmy pushed himself to and fro, lying full length on the bench swing that hung by chains from the rafters. Night had fallen, and the moon was up.

Looking between his feet on the armrest, the boy could still make out the mailbox at the foot of the hill, where tomorrow morning they would again be leaving their milk can for ol' Gus to pick up. *A pretty good day,* Jimmy concluded. *But I'm starting to really want to go home.* He had been on the farm for three weeks already and was getting very homesick. *I bet the guys are already playing football. Besides, Mom told me she and Dad were picking me up this week—and the week's almost gone! And the TV doesn't hardly work at all now!*

They had hoped to clearly pick up at least one station—and maybe a ball game—but were out of luck tonight. Homer and Jimmy had ended up listening to the news on the radio while they shined shoes and then had moved to the porch to rock until bedtime. When Zula had finished with the kitchen, she had joined them to listen to the crickets sing and to watch the lightning bugs flashing back and forth across the front lawn. Thelma had retired to her bedroom to eat alone after Zula had conceded to broiling her a chicken breast to go with the vegetables.

"Anything on the news tonight, Homer?" Zula asked.

"Just more gloom and doom. This flu stuff is getting out of hand. The newsman said New York and the bigger cities have really been hit hard. The hospitals are filling up with folks, and a lot are dying—just like back in nineteen eighteen. Only it's the old folks this time."

They nodded together in the dark, pondering this news and listening to a lone whippoorwill calling plaintively far down in the hollow, down Big Red's way. There was no answering call.

"Did Billy Ray telephone?" Homer asked.

"Yes, and Thelma was there to pick up."

"Good thing. Did he say anything about coming home?"

Zula rose and walked to the edge of the porch to fluff off a lightning bug that had landed on her apron. Returning to her rocker, she said, "He told me he was trying to come home, but traffic was really, really bad. He left his car at a gas station out toward the interstate, but he was worried—people were stealing batteries and siphoning out gasoline and all." She paused to take a deep breath before continuing. "He...he said a lot of people were panicking and all about the flu, and there was a big exodus from New York—frightened people, you know."

"Well, I can imagine," Homer replied. "You said Thelma got on the line?"

"Yeah." Zula exhaled loudly, tired from the day—or exasperated with her daughter. "Yeah, she picked up and was short with Billy Ray. She almost hung up on him before I could get off the line. She's turned out to be a very self-centered person, Homer. You know?"

"I know Jimmy's laid out there in that swing a'listening."

"It's nothing he doesn't already know," she sniffed. "And the way she treats Billy Ray…it's a shame. Just cares about herself."

Jimmy heard the phone ringing in the front room. "Phone's ringing," he announced.

"Would you mind running and getting that, honey?" Zula asked.

Jimmy was already up and opening the screen door.

When it slammed closed and Jimmy's footsteps faded out of earshot, Zula turned back to Homer. "So what else did the newsman say about the flu?" She could always tell when there was more to Homer's stories.

"Well," said Homer, "the man said the CDC says the flu looks more like the bubonic plague like back during the old, old times. He said it seems to be hitting the oldest first, but it's now getting into some middle-aged folks. And Zula, there ain't no survivors yet. Imagine that."

"Nooo."

"Yeah. Sure hope a lot of good folks have made their peace with the Lord; may his will be done."

Jimmy returned, staying just inside the screen door. "Zula," he called, "that was the motel. They're full up at the road and pointed two carloads of tourists our way. Said they want to talk with you when you get a chance to call back."

In response he heard two long sighs released together from the darkness, followed by Homer saying to Zula, "Bet they're taking to the hills now too."

5

DAY ONE

J immy awoke slowly to Homer's gentle nudges and easy sum-mons: "Time to rise and shine, sleepyhead. Gonna be a pret-ty day." The shades were raised in the windows, and sunlight was streaming in. A light breeze momentarily puffed the gauzy curtains inward. It was already a beautiful day.

The boy pushed up to his elbows to blink in the morning light. "What time is it, Homer?" he croaked.

"Yeah, it's late, boy. I let you sleep in a bit because I don't think I allowed you much sleep during the night...with all my tossing and turning and such."

Jimmy sat up on the edge of the bed, rubbing his eyes, his feet searching for the leg holes of his jeans, which were bunched on the floor. Since the tourists had arrived before he had gone up to share Homer's bed the prior evening, his clothes lay spread out as he had taken them off for the night. "Did you already do all the milking and stuff?" he asked.

"Yeah, but it wasn't hardly any trouble. I'm letting that one ol' Holstein dry up since she'll be calving soon then breeding again. That ought to make ol' Red a little happier, won't it? So anyway, we're down a cow, and you looked right comfortable, so I thought I'd leave you to sleep in for a while."

Jimmy heard his words, but the old man seemed somehow qui-eter this morning...more reserved...sad. "You didn't already take them down, did you? To pasture?" Jimmy leaned forward, looking out the window as if he would be able to see the cows waiting outside for him to lead them to breakfast.

"No, no. I left that for you to do. You know my ol' knees don't work so good anymore going down that steep hill alongside the barn, so I left that for you to do."

Jimmy hopped to his feet and pulled up his jeans. "Then I'll go do that right now," he declared.

"Well, Jimmy, could I ask you to do that after while? See, I got some more stuff you can assist with—more important stuff maybe. See, Zula's not feeling any too well this morning, so I'm a'letting her rest a while more too and—"

"You need me to help cook for the tourist folks." Jimmy finished Homer's sentence. He knew the old man had never learned to cook and would rather take a beating than try to do it now.

"Yeah, you know, if you could just scramble some eggs and fry some bacon—that should do the trick. I believe I can still remember how to set a table and such. And make some coffee…you know how to do that, don't you? 'Sides, it looks like we're not gonna have much of a crowd anyway. I met one family leaving when I was coming in from the barn. They said they needed to get on down the road to find someplace where they could call to see what's going on in St. Louis. Said traffic was expected to be real bad, and some people were driving real crazy, so they wanted to be on their way early."

"Listen!" Jimmy commanded, patting Homer's forearm for quiet. He heard a car engine cranking to life out back, in the parking area between the house and the barn. "I think I hear another carload of tourists leaving now." A door slammed downstairs. "And that might be a third. Say, Homer, how many families spent the night here last night?"

"Three. That's all Zula wanted to take in last night, she said."

"Well, anyway, I suspect we ain't really needing my cooking skills now."

Homer flicked him on the leg. "*We?* You got a mouse in your pocket, son? I'd like to eat sometime today, and we don't only feed tourists around here, you know."

Jimmy laughed. "I could teach you how to make a boiled egg."

"I'd rather have some bacon—crispy of course—fried eggs over easy, toast...say, maybe some of those grits you make?"

"You mean with lots of butter and seasoned salt and pepper?"

"Yeah, if that's the way you do 'em."

"Heck, Homer, I think Zula has spoiled you or something. Speaking of which, is Zula hungry? I mean, how sick is she anyway?" Jimmy's tone grew serious with the last question. He remembered having dreamed about her during the night, but he couldn't recall the specifics of the dream. *She was calling me to come out front to talk, I think. She was wanting to tell me something.* But he couldn't remember if they had talked then, in his dream.

"Well, you know, she started coughing a bit last night," Homer began, his voice now low and confiding, "right about the time she called the motel folks back to tell them not to send anybody else out for the night. So she must've started feeling poorly then—you know how that ol' woman is about missing out on some tourist money. Fact is, I went to the barn first thing this morning and just looked in on her in passing. She said she wanted to sleep a tad more. I didn't hear anything then, so I didn't turn on a light—wanting her to sleep, you know. Well, her door's still closed, so I looked in and...She needs to sleep some more, Jimmy. That's why I come here; to rouse you 'cause I don't want her trying to get up and cook for everybody. I'm on my way to check on her again. I'll ask her about breakfast. OK?"

"Yeah, OK," the boy agreed, his voice muffled by the T-shirt he was pulling over his head. "Hey, Homer? Is Thelma staying home today?" *Maybe to take care of Zula?* "She might want some breakfast too."

"No, no, she was coming down the stairs when I was washing out the milk buckets. It kind of surprised me, her being up so early. But she said she had some early-morning appointments today and—what I think is the real reason for her getting out so early—she's concerned about catching the flu from one of these tourists whose folks are sick back home."

Jimmy solemnly nodded his understanding. *Thelma's taken off on him and Zula.* "Looks like she would have…" He almost had voiced his thoughts aloud.

Homer had started toward the door, but he now turned back to study Jimmy's face; he slightly nodded, having caught the wistful tone in Jimmy's voice. "Yeah, it looks like she would've stayed to help too, doesn't it? But you know, Thelma has never been able to take much pressure, and with hearing about…" *Fact is, that girl is frightened by what she's hearing. Thelma's panicking along with the rest of them.* Homer was thinking again of the stories told by the fleeing tourists and of Zula's phone conversation late in the night with her motel friends: older family members being abandoned in motel rooms, now sick and alone; policemen showing up at the intersections to direct traffic and not allowing cars to turn onto side roads, just hurrying them through town and on; looters stealing gas from the filling station across the road there on Highway 441 until it finally just closed up and turned off its pumps; and on and on. *There was too much for Zula even to relay. And that's what's making her sick, I bet—and making Thelma run off. It's not making me feel any too good neither. But no use worrying the boy. No use him worrying about his folks neither.*

"Cogitating, Homer?" Jimmy asked.

"What?" He then realized he was still staring at Jimmy, and the boy was studying him right back, waiting for him to finish what he was saying. He cleared his throat. "So Jimmy, we'll just keep on keeping on and trust the good Lord to use us and all what's happening for his purposes. And we'll remember to give your folks a call this morning too." He smiled his reassuring smile at Jimmy. "Now, need any help with any of the gates?"

"No, I can get them opened and closed all right if I take my time. I'll be back after while and teach you how to boil water. OK?" With that said, Jimmy ducked past Homer—in case he wanted to swat him one—to noisily tromp downstairs and out the door.

The racket that boy can make. Homer smiled again—his sad smile—and thought maybe he'd rest for a while before he followed Jimmy downstairs. *I'll just straighten the bed so the ol' woman…No, I'd better see to her first.*

He went out by the other door and along the narrow, upstairs hallway that led to Zula's bedroom. They'd slept apart for years now, an arrangement not all that uncommon for people of their generation. As he walked he listened at the doors of the other bedrooms then knocked before tentatively opening doors. "Helloo, one… Helloo, two…Helloo, three," he counted aloud as he went. "All gone. All empty. And they took all their family members too. I guess that's a blessing in itself."

He tapped softly at Zula's door, slowly turning its knob and easing it open so its hinges wouldn't squeak. "Zula? Honey?" he softly called to the lump on the bed in the darkened room. "Feeling any better? Want me to open the window some more or anything? Maybe get you something to drink? Baby? You feeling any better?"

The lump rolled over and extended itself the length of the bed. "'Morning, Homer. No, I'm not doing too well at all. Good for nothing, I guess. What time is it anyway?"

"About nine or so—and no need for you to get up right now!" Zula was struggling to rise. He moved quickly to sit on the side of the bed and softly guide her back to her pillow, fluffing it behind her head. "See, the tourists are all gone already. I checked. I guess they were all concerned about their families and such and wanted to get out of here and get on the road early." He tried out his reassuring smile again. "Besides, me and ol' Jimmy want to fix you breakfast in bed this morning."

Zula chuckled, her eyes closed, tired. "Breakfast in bed? Don't believe I've ever had that before. You're sweet."

They kissed, and Homer lightly ran his hands over her forehead to the sides of her head, pushing her loosened hair away from her face. "Don't think I've seen you with your hair down for years now," he said. "You still look real fine." He winked at her and made little kissy sounds.

"Yeah, you wish." She reached up to cup his face in her hands. "Darling man, I'm going to be fine. Don't worry. It's just a cold. Don't worry. So you're having Jimmy cook you some breakfast—good. Did Thelma go on to Knoxville?"

Homer nodded. "Yeah, but you know her in a crisis—something else to run away from. Now don't get upset, and let's not talk about her any more right now. OK?" He soothed Zula's furrowed brow with his warm hands and the tips of his fingers. *Danged calloused old paws.* "Honey, you just need to spend your time thinking about healing and getting better. Thelma will be back directly, hear?" He rubbed and tenderly massaged her neck and shoulders for several minutes. When he felt her ready to drift off again, he straightened and cocked his head as if to concentrate on his listening. "That's Jimmy's whistle. Hear it?" he whispered. "He's taking the cows to pasture now." He stood and looked down on Zula, his concern evident in his expression. "You rest now, darlin'. I'll take the milk can down to the road for Gus, and you try to sleep a bit more." He bent and kissed her fevered forehead. "Back soon, honey."

"You can be so sweet. You know I love you, don't you?" Zula said, looking frail and tiny on her big pillow with the covers pulled to her chin. *I don't say that often enough.*

"Know it every day. We've had a good long run of it, haven't we, ol' gal? And I believe we've been in love every day of it. So now you rest. This too shall pass."

"How 'bout 'and it came to pass'?" She corrected his quote.

"How 'bout just thinking about you getting better, huh?" Homer sniffed in mock annoyance and carefully closed the door as he left.

With the click of the latch, Zula's face pinched tight with the pain of her inner torment. She hardly knew anything about bubonic plague or any other plague; she just knew that whatever she had was going to be really, really bad. And she didn't want Homer to worry over her—not yet. "But," she whispered to herself, "we have had a good long run of it, ol' boy."

***

Jimmy dropped to the ground from the top of the big wooden gate that fronted the barnyard and trotted across the open space, angling to his left, toward the fence gate and the deep hollow beyond. Awaiting him, the cows were grouped at the barbed-wire gate because that was the way they expected to be led to pasture: down the grooved, beaten paths that crisscrossed the hillside to the valley floor where the little brook flowed, then down the valley to the hard road. They all knew the way well.

Thundering hoofbeats! Both mules! From the barn! They'd been waiting for him inside the barn's wide, open doorway and now burst from the deep shadows at full gallop. Jimmy first feinted to his right, as if he were retreating to the wooden gate, then turned to dash across the barnyard to lunge forward at the last second, throwing himself to the ground to roll in under the wire. Both mules initially took the feint, veering to head him off at the gate, then changing course to race after him across the manure-lumped, grassless barnyard. But the boy was too fast, and the extra steps were too much; they pulled up short at the fence to stomp and snort and bite at Jimmy, who now stood on the far side and safely out of their reach.

"Aha!" Jimmy celebrated his victory. "Faked you out, didn't I? Didn't I? Too fast for you suckers, weren't I? Weren't I? You guys never learn. Now go on. Go on!" He looked around his feet and farther down the fence row until he located the tobacco stakes he had leaned there the previous day. After selecting a stout one, he used it to poke at the mules until he got them to move back away from the gate. "Now go on, I say! We're through playing, and I've got work to do. Go on!" The mules grudgingly stepped back and finally turned to trot heavily back into the shade of the barn.

Jimmy watched them until they passed from his sight, and then he dropped to his knees, pushing with his stake against the gatepost to frantically lever loose the wire gate, first raising the gate pole from the bottom loop then slipping the pole down from its top loop. Yet he was cautious all the while, glancing up often, making sure the mules stayed in the barn, and again before he pulled back the gate. That done, the cows filed past, choosing one path down the hill with the others following behind. Jimmy waited until the cows were about halfway down the hill before he left the gate, now fully open, and scampered after them. He'd let the mules find their own way out to do some browsing on the grass to the back and the sides of the barn and beyond the fenced tobacco patch at the back. *They'll spend the day in the woods probably, waiting to ambush me tonight, I bet.* Homer's woods ran from behind the tobacco patch almost to Chapman Highway, to the Ogles' farm.

Dancing down the steep trail, Jimmy quickly caught up with the cows, tapping the last one, the Jersey, with his tobacco stake to reestablish his authority over the herd. "Git on now!" he yelled in his imitation of Homer's words of encouragement. "Git on now! Ya hear?" The cows plodded on, ignoring the loud human at their rear, to the bottom of the hill then south along the babbling brook.

Big Red was waiting. He walked along his side of the fence, matching the herd's progress and bawling his bovine promises every fourth or fifth step. When the cows reached the gate to the hard road, and the fence that ended Red's pasture, the bull again vented his frustration on the corner post and the sharp, prickly wire that kept him from his lovely ladies. He bawled and charged, bawled and charged, pausing only to snort and fling torn sod across his back and flanks.

All the while, Jimmy busily levered and loosened the gate there, holding it back for his cows to pass, then refitting the post into the wire loops that held the gatepost erect and its attached barbed-wire taut. *Almost...almost...there. Top and bottom.*

"Whew!" Finished, he rolled to his knees and clapped the dust off his hands...in perfect timing with the sharp cracking of the corner fence post; Big Red finally had done the deed! The wood popped several times then snapped cleanly off at the ground with a mighty crack. *Oh, dang!*

The big bull stumbled and stepped back, momentarily confused by the way the post had flipped down, its attached barbed-wire striking him on the legs with the release of tension from the adjacent poles. Then, catching sight of the last of the cows on the far side of the fence, way across the tiny stream, he instantly remembered his purpose. He bellowed again and was over the downed wire and the water in two leaps, showing amazing agility for a bull his size. Gaining the firmer footing of the creek bank, he lunged upward and twisted left toward the road, and rammed headlong into another fence. Its strands of wire rang in metallic protest, its wooden posts creaked and complained, and a staple or two twanged loose...but the fence held. And on the far side, an astonished boy scuttled away on his hands and knees, his mouth hanging open and his eyes wide with fright—but having just secured the gate.

Retreating from the sharp barbs and trembling in frustration, Big Red tossed his massive head and roared out his rage with great, heaving bellows, slinging threads of snot to the fence and his solitary audience paused just beyond.

"Whoa!" Jimmy declared, breathless in his surprise...and relief. "Whoa! If you'd made it through that fence a minute sooner, big guy, I'd be kissin' that ol' ugly horn right now." As it was, he still scrambled backward, first to his feet then up onto the hard road, in case the stomping, raging bull decided to further test this new gate. The boy wanted to make space, lots of space, between him and the wire and the bull.

From a position of relative safety on the higher road, Jimmy stood and watched the action behind, catching his breath and surveying the scene from side to side. He did a double take to the right: The barbed-wire had pulled loose at the *front* of Red's pen, farther up the hill alongside the road. *One, two, three posts beyond the gate I just closed!* He looked back to the ground-pawing, snorting bull, knowing that Red had yet to see the gap because of all the blackberry bushes growing in the fence line. *But it won't take him long to find that hole, I bet. And he'll be through it in a blink! I'll tell Homer! But right now I need to...* He searched around. The cows, obviously unconcerned with the commotion behind, had continued on down the paved road toward the open pasture gate across from Fred's place.

Maybe if I... "Hey, bull!" Jimmy yelled, hopping sideways and moving away from the gate, farther along the road beside the sound fence that extended to the west up the other side of the hollow. "Hey, bull! Hey, bull! Hey, bull!" he called, dancing and waving his arms. *Maybe if I can keep his attention.* He figured if he could get Red to follow after him, along the inside of the fence, he could get the beast away from the break in the other direction, and then, distracted by new grass and woods and maybe remembering the corncrib, the old bull would decide to go on back up the valley for the day, staying inside the fence. *Hah! Maybe he'll get to meet Blackie and Whitey at the barn. I bet they'd kick the living tar outta him too. Hah!*

The bull took the bait and quickly mounted the rise to trot after Jimmy alongside the new fence for about a quarter of a mile, arriving in time to watch the boy close yet another gate—to the pasture across the road. Standing there, behind the tight barbed-wire and an unbroken corner post, the bull could do little more than gaze down at the objects of his desire as they munched their way through the tall grass of the far pasture then out of sight. "If bulls could sigh," Jimmy later told Homer, "then that's what he done."

The excitement had now passed, and the short walk had calmed both boy and bull. Red couldn't even summon enough angry energy to give this corner post a test butt or send another spit-laden bellow the boy's way. He just stood and glared.

Leaving the simmering bull to explore his new surroundings, Jimmy turned and jogged back up the long asphalt rise toward the driveway entrance. As he trotted past that section of ruined fence and thick blackberry thorns, his attention suddenly was drawn to a shiny metal object farther ahead, glinting there in the sun beside the road. *Homer's already brought the milk down,* Jimmy noted. The steel milk can was standing there next to the mailbox awaiting Gus's yellow truck. *Bet he didn't wait 'cause he hurried back to tend to Zula.* This thought somehow touched him, bringing forward those feelings of loneliness and abandonment, feelings he had been holding in check and pushing away from consciousness. He slowed to a walk. *Mom and Dad shoulda been here yesterday to pick me up.* His lip quivered, and he sucked back a sob that rose in his chest. He loved his times with Homer and Zula, but...*Gosh, I miss home and all.* And since he was alone now, with no one around to witness his breach of Southern-boy rules, he allowed another jerky breath to escape and a few tears to fall…for just a minute. He reasoned that, with this excitement of dealing with Red and with Zula's illness—both altering the consistency of his life—he was perhaps a bit more sensitive than usual. *Quit being a baby! You're OK!* With that thought, he pushed back the flow of emotion, sniffed, and wiped his eyes on his already grimy T-shirt sleeves. *Yeah, and Homer said we'd call them on the phone this morning.* He was feeling a little better.

Jimmy had reached the mailbox and the milk can, and from far behind, he heard the roar of Gus's truck as it climbed the long hill beyond Fred's place. *Just in time. I got here just in time.* Then the engine noise faded, stopped, and started again, getting steadily louder but accompanied by the harsh sounds of gears grinding and a horn toot—like an accidental horn toot.

"Dang!" Jimmy whispered. "Ol' Gus must be having transmission trouble or something. Can't find his next gear." He waited in the gravel for Gus to arrive; he would help load their milk.

As the truck puttered into view, Gus appeared to be having problems with his steering too. He was weaving from one side of the narrow lane to the other as he came on, snatching the truck back to the middle when the tires crunched in the deep gravel to the sides. Jimmy stepped back a bit to give the guy plenty of room to maneuver as he drew near.

Pulling alongside the boy, Gus sharply applied the brakes and scraped to a stop, sending pebbles flying and his milk cans crashing in the back of the truck. *Time for new brakes too,* thought Jimmy. The old man coughed several times into his handkerchief before easing himself down from his tall truck seat to the road. When he had walked *(staggered)* around, leaning against the side of the truck, Jimmy could see Gus was in a bad way; his hat was gone, his eyes were unfocused, his shirt was wet *(Blood? Vomit?)*, and he smelled bad *(like he's pooped his pants)*.

"Gus, are you OK?" Jimmy asked, clearly alarmed.

"Yeah, yeah, OK," Gus replied. Then he looked up and gazed at the boy, his eyes shiny with rheum. "No…Jimmy, I'm really not. I'm in terrible shape, and I bet I've got that plague stuff. I've seen some real bad things this morning and…Jimmy, I don't think I can get your milk into the truck. I just want to go on home and lie down somewhere. And I want to see my wife again." Gus started to cry and coughed some more.

The boy found a dry place on the old man's shirt sleeve and patted him there. "Gus, suppose you go on back to the cab, and I'll go ahead and put this milk can in? It's not as heavy as usual, and I believe I can do it on my own. You go on now then head back to Knoxville." Jimmy believed that was where Mayfield's dairy plant was located. "You don't need to be worrying about milk and such right now. OK?"

"I'm much obliged," Gus replied. He turned, searching around to first determine his way back to his high seat then inching his way along, keeping his hand against the truck's side for support. He had ceased to bother with the handkerchief in his other hand; his chin was wet with newly coughed phlegm.

Jimmy dragged the can through the gravel to the big bumper of the truck and reached up to slowly open the rear doors, fearing that a can might come rolling out on him. He peeked inside. The milk cans were haphazardly stacked, and some were even lying outside the chain restraints that ran down both sides. *Ooh, Gus is really having a tough time of it.* Jimmy grasped his can's handles and bent to lift with his legs…and found the can to really be light. *I was just telling Gus that. Homer must've not milked all the cows. Or he must've not finished them off.* Using the bracket on the door, he swung himself up and into the truck. Then he walked his can into position, unhooking the security chain and lifting upright the cans that had fallen over. *Lucky the tops stayed on.* After more straightening and rechaining, he jumped back down to the road and slammed the doors. Trotting back around the truck, he slapped its sides as he had seen Homer do to let the driver know where he was. He saw Gus watching him in his long rearview mirror and waved to him. *I'm glad he managed to climb back into the cab.*

I'd hate to be having to push on the seat of his pants to get him up there. The old man waved backward out his door, revved his engine, and jerked forward, weaving on down the road like a drunkard.

Jimmy stood for a while, watching Gus go, until the truck turned the corner and passed from sight. *Lord, be with Gus,* he prayed. Then his stomach rumbled, and being reminded that he hadn't yet had breakfast, he decided he would next see about teaching Homer to boil eggs.

Trudging up the long drive that led to the tree-shaded parking area, Jimmy whacked at loose rocks with his stick and returned to his earlier thoughts about his home, his parents, and their preparations for his visit here this last time. His mother had made sure she remembered to bring some extra clothes for him, in the event that Zula would ask him to stay (*Like there was a doubt?*), and his father had made sure his mother had made sure (*Confusing, but Dad thinks farm work is really good for me because he was made to do it when he was a kid, I guess*). So when Zula had asked, Jimmy's mother had "just happened" to have some of his clothes out in the car. *Fortuitous, eh? That's what Matthew told Lola on* As the World Turns. Then they had eaten the rooster, Hercules, for supper—fried with vegetables and gravy—and Mr. and Mrs. Burke had said they needed to be getting back to Maryville before it got dark. *And they said they'd be back up in two weeks to pick me up.* "Or put him on a bus if he doesn't behave himself, hah hah." Jimmy was again almost to that level of self-pity he had managed earlier.

"But you're not going to cry again," he declared aloud. "You're almost fifteen!"

He often had wondered whether he would get less homesick if there were other boys around. As it was, the farms on both sides were owned by people at least as old as Homer and Zula, with their own children all grown and grandchildren visiting only sparingly. On the farms farther down White School Road, the kids were mostly all older than Jimmy and were, like the Parton boy, working—truly working—all day long. Or the kid was Daniel Davis— *mean as a snake.*

Now, if Billy Ray was in from New York, I'd be ready to stay four, five weeks on the farm, without being the least bit homesick. Besides being Jimmy's hero, Billy Ray was a hunter, a fast driver, a friendly tease, and just about anything else a kid could ask for in an idol. Billy Ray had taught Jimmy to target shoot, using the German Mauser and a few unlucky pigeons perched atop the barn. Billy Ray would take Jimmy over to Douglas Dam to fish for perch and bream. In fact Jimmy had caught his very first fish using Billy Ray's fishing pole...assuming that the fish hadn't already been hooked when he was handed the pole. Billy Ray had driven him and Thelma to Gatlinburg one late night—just for ice cream cones. *Imagine that! Just for ice cream cones. Yeah!* When Billy Ray was around, life on the farm was great for the boy.

But Billy Ray's still in New York, and Thelma's acting funny and Zula's sick. This ain't so much fun anymore, and I don't know what I'll tell Mom when I do get her on the phone. If Homer's sitting right there, I don't think I can tell her how much I want to come home and maybe hurt his feelings. And with Zula sick, I know I probably should stay 'cause I do help out some around here.

When Jimmy looked up, he was a bit surprised that he almost had reached the back door of the house. *Cogitating makes the time really pass.* He toed his shoes off without untying them and slipped inside through the back screen door, being careful to not let it slam behind. Since the house was quiet, he figured Zula was still in bed and resting.

He padded through the house. "Homer?" he half whispered up the front staircase. "Homer?"

"Yo, be there in a minute," Homer called softly back. He already was coming down the stairs and had called from the landing. Having arthritic knees, Homer took his time in descending stairs. "Whatcha got going?" he asked when he reached the bottom.

"Well, I was going to fix some boiled eggs and toast for us then see if we were going to hay some more today. And then I met up with ol' Gus down at the road—by the way, ol' Red finally took out the corner post of his pasture and is now over in the other side where I bring the cows down."

"Did he take down the fence toward the road?"

"Yeah, but he didn't notice it with the brush and all in the fence row. He's up toward Fred's place now, investigating the fresh grass."

"Well, I'll see about tacking the wire back up later today. But I need to run into town to pick up some cough syrup for Zula. Want to ride with me?"

Jimmy perked up, the rest of his news forgotten. *Maybe another soda or milk shake?* "Yeah, I'd love to go, but shouldn't I stay around in case Zula needs something?

Homer grasped the boy's shoulder and gently held him. "That's thoughtful, Jimmy. Thanks. But Thelma's come home. They closed down the department store's beauty parlor early and sent her home. She said she'd stay here while I go get some medicine…"

"And straighten up and clean Mom's room," Thelma added, yelling from the top of the stairs.

"Take inventory, you mean," Homer quietly grumbled. Jimmy barely heard him.

"Dad," she yelled again, "since you're going to the drugstore, I need some hair spray—firm—and some fingernail polish remover and a Milky Way. OK?"

"Yeah," Homer called back. He turned to Jimmy, "And a Milky Way for you too. OK?" He winked at the boy and patted his shoulder. "Let's go so we can get back."

"By the way," Homer added, when they were almost to the door, "what I said to Thelma just now? That wasn't very Christian, and I'd like you to forgive me for saying that in front of you."

"Oh, Homer, I didn't even hear what you said," Jimmy replied, pushing the screen door open for them. "Come on. Let's go!"

***

The trip into Sevierville took longer than usual. The four-lane highway was packed going both ways with very short-tempered people; horns were blaring, and drivers were trying to cut in front of one another, some riding on the road's shoulder for long ways then attempting to duck in the line. And other cars apparently weren't up to the task, having been abandoned alongside the road.

"I've never seen traffic like this before. Look at that!" Homer said, pointing ahead. The little red sports car with Virginia plates, which just minutes ago had passed them on the right, had collided with the back end of an aged Volvo on the shoulder. "That ol' boy must've not seen the Volvo and plowed right into him. He must have been watching for a gap in the traffic. Now what's he doing?" Homer asked, craning his neck for a better view.

Jimmy was already sitting high on the edge of his seat, almost with his forehead against the truck's windshield. Homer had chosen to drive the truck, his old Chevy pickup, "because it's got the most gas." But Jimmy suspected the real reason had more to do with the truck's big bumpers, oversize tires, and 4:11 rear end. Homer hated to be stuck anywhere when there was a ditch or bordering field to be driven through. And now the boy was equally pleased with the old man's selection of vehicles because the raised frame of the truck allowed him a clear view of the accident ahead.

"Well, Homer," he reported, "it looks like the sports-car guy's got his bumper in and under the old guy's bumper...make that *old lady's* bumper." They were almost even with the red sports car now. "Homer, Homer, that guy's got a gun! He's reached back in his car, and he's got a gun! He's going to the Volvo with his gun!"

Homer instinctively reached with one arm for Jimmy, to push him down in the seat and out of sight, and the car ahead suddenly stopped...and then started again. "Damn it!" He had almost just done his own rear ending. "Jimmy, now sit back..."

"Homer, the guy's trying to open the car door and...whoa! He's moving back!" Jimmy was now over against his door, almost leaning out the window. "He's..." Then he jerked back inside, sitting bolt upright in his seat and staring out the windshield with big eyes.

"What happened?" Homer asked.

"Just go on, Homer. Just go on."

They had passed the Volvo, and Homer was turning his head side to side, trying to watch in all his rearview mirrors, trying to see what was going on. The sports-car man had staggered into the road and almost was hit by the car behind Homer. He was now barfing his guts out near the dividing line. "Jimmy, what'd you see?" he demanded.

"Well, I was right the first time—the driver was a man. I thought he was a woman wearing a red scarf, but well, he's just bleeding real badly. From his nose and mouth, it looks like. And there's a lady, I think, sprawled out on the seat beside him."

"Damn, Jimmy. I wish you hadn't seen that!"

"That's called hemorrhaging, Homer. That's what ol' Bullet done when he got hit by the car in front of our house. Mom said he was hemorrhaging. And the pigeon I shot with Billy Ray? It was hemorrhaging. And the pigs...remember last fall when we killed Zula's hogs?"

"Hemorrhaging—I get the picture. Dang, Jimmy, I was so worried about that sight, that it might traumatize you or something. But you know, I think you're taking it better than that ol' boy back there," Homer marveled. He was staring again in his side mirror.

"No, Homer, I don't think it was the sight of blood that did that to the guy. Didn't you see all those flies coming out when the guy open the door on that Volvo? Didn't you get a whiff when we passed? I sure did. It was bad. Worse than the time I had to help Dad clean out the septic tank. Those folks were ripe!"

"Well, you answered my next question: 'Do you think we should go back to help them?' Obviously they're past any help we can offer; God rest their souls."

"Homer, the guy in the front, the driver? He looked out when the sports-car guy opened his door. He's still alive, I think!"

Homer again studied the cars and the people now receding in his rearview mirror. *Oh, boy, decision time, Lord.* The sports-car man had gotten out of the road, and cars were again moving on, catching up behind his truck. *It'd be very difficult for me to turn and go back right now,* he reasoned, *assuming that someone would even let me in. And I've got the boy to think about. And Zula!*

But he continued to look for escape routes. "I think the traffic seems to have lightened some. Most cars are trying to turn north, toward I-40, and are mixing it up with the cars coming from Pigeon Forge, also trying to go to I-40. See ahead there? No, Jimmy. I don't think I'd dare try to turn around to go back and help those folks. Maybe on the way back, if the Lord wills it."

"And that guy's still got that gun," Jimmy helpfully reminded.

They crept on in silence for the next mile.

At the intersection, a county sheriff's deputy was trying to maintain order—and failing. His patrol car, its red lights flashing, was more or less an island, and cars were inching around both sides. Wild-eyed drivers were mostly ignoring his frantic hand waves and intermittent whistle bleats; everyone was doing what they thought best for themselves—and that included Homer. "Boy, there's no way in the world I'm gonna go on up there and get in that mess. Now hold on to something," he said. With that instruction, Homer shifted to his lowest gear, the one he used to cross deep mud holes, and drove over the low curb and onto the adjacent, freshly plowed field, away from the frantic whistles of the frustrated deputy.

"They're going to build a shopping center here, Jimmy. There'll be a new Winn-Dixie over there and a Co-Op over there." Homer conversationally narrated the tour as he drove. "And we're going over there." He was pointing at a brick building that fronted 441, the road to Pigeon Forge and Gatlinburg. "That's the drugstore. We've just cut off the corner, you might say."

He pulled around to the front of the store and parked close to the door. Their travel across the parking lot's fresh black asphalt was clearly marked in red from the clay that had come with them from the field. Homer looked back as they climbed out. "I reckon that'll wash off with the first rain. Let's go see the druggist." He pushed Jimmy ahead.

At the door the boy gave a mighty tug. *Locked.* "Homer, I don't think they're open." He cupped his hands around his eyes and searched through the glass door. "Hey, there's Mr. Cline. See?" He stepped aside to give Homer room to peer in the door. Mr. Cline, a short, exceedingly thin man, was bobbing up and down behind the pharmacy counter at the back of the store.

"What the heck?" Homer said. "Cline!" he yelled, rapping on the glass with his key ring. "Cline, you got customers out here! I see you back there! Stop ducking down! You look like a woodchuck!"

After considering his alternatives and deciding he had no alternatives, the tight-lipped Mr. Cline came from behind his counter to dart from gondola to gondola, making his way through the store to then halt for another minute or two for additional surveillance from behind the Hallmark card stand. Finally he broke for the front door and frantically opened the thumb lock for Homer and Jimmy then immediately closed and relocked the door behind them.

"What can I do for you boys?" he asked, when he was again behind the card stand and doing his best to appear nonchalant while he smoothed a tuft of unruly white hair.

Homer gave him an appraising look. "You can start by telling me what the dickens you're doing, Cline."

Mr. Cline gave him the appraising look right back. "You not been listening to the news, Homer? You don't know all what's going on out there?"

"Probably not what all you know and probably secondhand at that. Zula just sent me down here for some Wampole's Creo-Terpin— she's caught a cold—and me and ol' Jimmy here weren't listening to the radio or anything. Why? What's happened today?"

"The world has gone crazy, Homer! Since the CDC announced the…Do you talk in front of the boy, Homer?"

"Yeah, go ahead, Cline. He needs to start finding out, and I think he knows more than he's letting on anyway. Besides, I'm finding out Jimmy here has the soul of a maggot." Homer patted the boy on his back and pulled him to his side.

Mr. Cline looked to Jimmy then back to Homer and cleared his throat. "Let me start again then. Yesterday the CDC announced that this here disease was spreading across the United States—said it was much like the bubonic plague of the Dark Ages, like around the fourteenth century or so in Europe. They think it started in the North, maybe along the coast, but it could have come in from around California too. Or maybe Canada." The pitch of Cline's voice steadily rose. "Anyway it seems to be getting to the older folks like us and…and they ain't got nothing to stop it! They say it's killing all us old people, Homer!" For the moment Mr. Cline had lost his battle for nonchalance.

"Here, Cline. Sit down here and…We're OK. We're all OK," Homer said evenly. "There's certainly more to this than we know, but for now we're all OK. Understand?" He was guiding the druggist to the waiting-area chairs near his pharmacy counter. "We might have heard something like that ourselves, Cline…on the news. And Zula talked to the motel people down here last night. But nobody's saying nothing about this stuff killing all the old people…that I've heard." *Maybe.* "Not around here anyway. Besides, you're too contrary to die from something you can hardly spell. Now sit down, and tell me what's going on around here. They said something about the gas station across the road having to close." *Was that only last night?*

Cline sat down, took a deep breath, and continued. "Homer, folks here *are* dying too. See? I heard it on the news, and the next thing I know, I've got people in my store wanting penicillin and antibiotics and all—that was yesterday. And all without prescriptions! Well, I couldn't give them that, Homer—you know that. So then someone pulls a gun. They didn't want my money; they wanted medicine and drugs. Pain-killers! Maybe not because they were sick; maybe they wanted them just in case. And you know, these weren't local folks, Homer. These were people who were going home—up North… and South. I saw one ol' boy with Florida tags on his car. Miami. Everybody was panicking. Scared to death. And they didn't care if the sheriff caught 'em! Guns, Homer! Reports of folks shooting into houses and stores!"

"Did you call the police then?" Jimmy asked.

"Oh, my, yes. First thing. Yesterday evening. They were directing traffic over there…" He jabbed a finger toward US 441. "…and a cop just walked over here, just walked over here. See? And then the damnedest thing, Homer: Here's this cop in here asking about the robbery, and another guy walks in carrying a gun. Just walks in! From Connecticut. He was going to rob me too, but the policeman shot him dead. Dead, Homer! Right there! See what's left of the stain that I couldn't clean up? That's when I closed up. And got this out." Cline held up an old .28 caliber revolver that he pulled from the front pocket of his baggy pants. "Five-shot," he proudly proclaimed.

"Dang, Cline!" Homer said, clearly impressed. "That gun's barrel is as long as your forearm."

"And loud too. I saw my mama shoot a stray dog in her chickens from a hundred yards away using this here pistol."

"Well, I don't know how you're gonna manage to keep it in your britches, something that long—and that ain't a compliment. Anyway, suppose you just wait 'til me and the boy are out of here before you go putting any of those old cartridges in that gun? Where's your Creo-Terpin, Cline?"

"Just a minute," Mr. Cline said. He got up and wandered around the end of the shelves to rummage in the dark among the bottles and boxes there. "Here 'tis—next to last bottle," he announced. "Not many people want this stuff anymore, Homer."

"Well, tastes a lot better than straight turpentine."

"Not a lot of folks doing their doctoring with turpentine these days either. Maybe you ought to think about taking Zula up to the clinic. Your cousin, Nick Clark, came in here early yesterday and decided he'd go over there to be checked out."

"Nick did?"

"Well, his daughter did. Ol' Nick was looking for that other bottle of Creo-Terpin when he coughed and sprinkled blood all over my counter. You know, now that I think on it, maybe he…" Cline's voice trailed off, and he looked toward his pharmacy counter. His eyes wide with new fears, he turned back to stare at Homer.

"Naw," Homer consoled. "I'm sure he's just got that sinus condition again. Always had that problem, he did. Even as a kid. Tell you what: I'll run by the clinic to check on ol' Nick—he's about ninety now, so the least thing can be serious for him—and I'll give you a call back when I've heard what his daughter says. OK?"

"Homer, I'd appreciate that. I surely would." Mr. Cline's gratitude was evident on his face. "Here. Take this bottle—you don't owe me nothing. Besides, I'll never sell that stuff to anyone else anyway. And here…take these too." He was holding out a white-capped container of pills—prescription-type pills. "For Zula, if she gets to really hurting. And maybe for…Never mind."

"Why, Cline, I appreciate that too. I'll let Zula know." Homer patted Jimmy's shoulder. "Jimmy-boy, we've got to get going. The ol' woman will be wondering where we are, and it's getting late. She'll have a dozen things for you and me to do before milking, I'll bet."

Mr. Cline led them to the door. He stood there for a moment, carefully surveying the parking lot again before he clicked open the lock, then almost pushing Homer and Jimmy through the tiny opening. "Take care," he called after them, through the glass.

Jimmy turned to wave, but Mr. Cline already was disappearing into his back room. "Wow! He's already gone to the back of the store. I bet he's sleeping somewhere back there, guarding his stuff and all."

"Bet he is too," Homer replied.

At the truck's door Jimmy snapped his fingers. "Oh, wait, Homer. We forgot the hair spray and stuff for Thelma. And the candy bars."

"Tell you what, Jimmy ol' boy. Let's go ahead and get in the truck, and I'll stop at the convenience store when we're leaving the clinic. I didn't want to ask for candy bars in there because ol' Cline wouldn't have let us pay for them anyway—and I didn't want to impose, you know. He gave us enough already. Understand?" Homer was holding up the bottle of cough syrup.

"Sure, I understand," Jimmy answered, and he did. That was one of those old-timey country rules—*Like when you never stay for dinner unless you're asked a second time. The first asking is just being polite.* Certain courtesies were unwritten but well understood by all.

***

Making their way to the clinic, as he had promised Mr. Cline, Homer steered through residential neighborhoods, staying mostly away from the main roads, sometimes even cutting across plowed fields if the crops appeared to be mostly done for the season. Along the way they met up with few cars on the road, though they saw a lot of cars still parked in driveways. "Folks must be staying in today," Homer observed to Jimmy. "That's maybe what we should have done, huh?"

Arriving at the one-story clinic, they found the parking lot almost empty and a rent-a-cop standing at the little bridge over the ditch. "Help you, buddy?" the guard asked when they had pulled in from the road and halted and Homer had rolled down his window.

"Yeah," Homer said. "We're here to see my cousin. He came in yesterday with the flu."

"The plague, you mean." The cop smiled a nasty smile. "You local?"

Homer smiled back. "Yeah, local."

"Then park over there, close by the front. Watch the grassy area too, though your truck looks like you wouldn't mind if you mired it up or not."

Homer nodded and pulled forward, over to the spaces the guard had indicated. Soon they were tugging open the clinic's double doors; the automatic door openers obviously weren't operating. Through the glass they saw another uniformed guard—an armed guard—waiting inside. "Any guns, knives, or drugs?" he loudly inquired as soon as they entered the lobby. He looked ready for action—any action—with his thumbs hooked in his pistol belt, one hand resting on the butt of his holstered pistol, his shoulders drawn back, his face set hard.

"Noooo," they replied in unison.

"Yeah? Really?" he challenged, as if he had doubts, sneering his question and obviously not expecting another answer. "Really?" With the palm of his right hand still resting on his gun, he casually circled Homer, inspecting him up and down, poking his side pockets. "What you got there, old man?" he snarled.

"Keys and change." *Danged glad I forgot my Barlow at the house. Hope to heck Jimmy forgot his pocketknife too.*

The guard took another step. "How 'bout there?" He tapped Homer's bulging back pocket with his fingers.

"Just my pocketbook."

"Your wallet, you mean."

Homer nodded meekly in agreement.

The guard made another circuit then abruptly dismissed them. "OK, now go on over there, to the reception desk over there," he ordered. "And hurry!" He turned to resume his position of authority, standing just inside the glass entrance doors and facing the parking lot.

Following Homer, Jimmy looked back to see if more people were coming through the door. *Nobody. What's that guard's rush?*

The blond receptionist watched them approach, having already looked up from her reading to observe the guard's examination, her finger still marking her magazine page. "Why are you here?" she brusquely demanded.

Manners apparently are being put aside today, Homer thought. "We're here to see Nick Clark," he replied. *These people obviously aren't in any mood to be wasting time with visitors. Must be feeling pretty powerful...but then I don't know what they've had to go through today.* He held his peace.

"Isolation room one," she directed, and went back to her reading.

Homer's eyebrows rose. *That don't sound good.* He put his hand on Jimmy's head and turned him around. "You wait out front in the chairs over there, please. Stay away from the front window. Don't be talking to the guard, and don't go back out to the truck. OK?" Jimmy nodded and sauntered over to the chairs in the waiting area.

Homer strode around the blonde and her reception desk and through the propped-open double doors beyond. In the hallway he found that only about half the overhead lights had been turned on and that all the doors to the rooms along the way were shut tight. *Must have had a power failure.* He walked on, reading aloud the numbers over the doors.

"Room one," he announced, finally stopping before a closed door after having walked the entirety of the long hall, almost to the far end of the building. He slowly pushed against the door and peered in through the space. *Room's very dark, curtains drawn awfully early in the day. Three beds in here, very close to each other—look to be all occupied.*

"Nick," he whispered.

"Here. That you, Homer?" the dim shape in the first bed responded.

"Yeah," Homer replied, now pushing the door wide-open. Then the scent hit him: blood, vomit, diarrhea—all together. He leaned back out the door, determining if either a CNA or a nurse was nearby and to catch his breath. *Nobody's around. Nobody to ask. Where is everybody? Oh, well.* He went in, making sure the door stayed latched to the wall and open.

"Quite a mess, aren't we, Homer?" Old Nick had pushed himself up against the headboard; he was holding a plastic trash container in his lap. It was obvious from the smell and the flecks on his beard that he'd been in the process of using it.

"Not so bad, Nick. Here, let's see what we can do." Homer crossed the room to the sink against the wall, intending to wet a towel for Nick's face and hands. He had learned how to breathe through just his mouth years ago when his father was dying with cancer; he could abide the smell, and his actions had been automatic. But now he couldn't find a towel or washcloth in either the tiny closet or the space under the sink. *Wet paper towels will have to suffice, and there aren't many of those—pretty sad shape around here.* He separated three paper towels from the half dozen or so and wet them all.

"So what are you in for, old man?" Homer talked as he wiped Nick's face and beard, moving the trash can to his far side. "Trying to get out of hauling in your hay?"

Nick smiled but seemed not quite able to laugh. "Thanks, Homer. I wish I was just...trying to get out of work. But this stuff... is pretty bad, I think." Nick was talking in hushed, breathy bursts. "I heard some of the news reports...so I believe I know what I have... and I'm sure...you do too. First I cough up blood and...then I shit all over myself. Or maybe it was...the other way around. Anyway, coughing...throwing up blood...diarrhea, lumps, fever...who knows what's first? Don't matter no how. Those ol' lumps, though...hurt like the dickens."

"What? Down here?" Homer lowered the stained sheet from Nick's shoulders and lightly touched his chest and sides. *Dang ol' man is skin and bones.* Nick winced when Homer's fingers ran over the buboes in the pits of his arms. "Oh, those lumps. Yeah, you've got a couple. I'll see if I can do anything about them." He carefully pulled up the sheet again.

Nick looked up at Homer, his eyes bloodshot and fever red. "Listen, I know I'm going...to die, Homer. I can stand the dying, but...I just don't want it to get...real bad in getting there. Understand that?"

Homer wiped and dabbed at the corners of Nick's mouth. "I understand," he said. "I do understand." He had known Nick for a long, long time now. He thought back to that day when Nick had returned home from World War I, his breathing then labored from the gas he had encountered, his soul depressed from the sights he'd seen. He and Nick had spent a lot of time together back then, talking, just helping each other along.

Guessing Homer's thoughts, Nick continued, "Got through that damned ol' war...and the Spanish flu, I did, but Homer...I'm not going to get through this. But you know...I don't mind. I'm an old man. Those are old men." He nodded to the beds to his side. "We've all lived our lives...so I hope this will be it for this stuff...just old folks. But you know, Homer...I don't think this *will* be it...and I need to tell you this...I need to tell everybody this...I had this dream, you see...That's the way the Lord's talking to me...in dreams." Nick was straining now to complete his sentences, willing his thoughts to remain unbroken and his voice strong. He had gripped Homer's hand and was squeezing it, drawing strength from him. "Homer, the ol' Devil's gonna have his day and...I don't think this is gonna stop... with just old men and old women. I think ol' Satan's...gonna winnow the world before he's done. I...don't know why he can do it...but I guess that's not for me...to say neither." He had to stop to gasp for breath before continuing in his spectral tone. "But I do know that... God is in control...and all will be made right...for his purpose. Ain't that what you once told me, Homer?" Now he smiled and patted Homer's hand.

"Gosh, Nick, that was a long time ago when we talked. I guess that was something that stuck with you."

"A seed planted, Homer…at the right time…the right words. Led me to the Lord. You never know."

"I guess that's the way it works, Nick. Say, old man Cline told me your daughter was bringing you here. She still here?"

"No, Homer, no. She…brought me here…turned around… went home. She heard on the radio…She's worried about…her family now. What we got…" He waved to the other two beds. "…might be catching. I don't blame her. Yesterday…this ol' clinic had full staff, today just old people…taking care of old people. Patients that could walk…got themselves out. Only older nurses showed up today. Doctors? I don't think I've seen…a doctor in here today. They're the ones…could 'ppreciate this stuff. They're showing it. A healthy respect…I'd say."

Homer bit his lip and said nothing, but his cheeks and forehead had noticeably reddened. He reached for the Dixie cup on the bedside table and after smelling it, making sure it contained only water, held the cup to Nick's mouth. "Drink?" he asked.

The old man took several gulping sips, straining sips. "Yeah, Homer, you know…I don't mind. Those ol' fellows don't mind." He again indicated the patients in the other beds. "They're past caring. I been getting them…some water and stuff, but…you know…I'm to the point…I don't believe…can do 'nother trip. Had one nurse… earlier…think she got…frightened with what she was seeing. It wore on her. She ended up getting…right mean…with those ol' boys. I told her to go on out. I'd do what I could…for 'em." Nick took several deep breaths and dropped his chin to his chest. "But that weren't for long…was it?" He patted the garbage can he was holding.

Homer finished wiping Nick's face and hands and turned to the others. "I'll see what I can do for them too. Maybe even see somebody in the hall—at least about the boils."

He walked around to the next bed and lowered the sheet from the man's face; the old fellow was looking back. Rather the man was looking, but Homer could see that his eyes were unfocused. If the man was seeing anything, the sight was not of this world. Then the old fellow moaned and rolled to his back, his sheet slipping from his necrosis-darkened fingers down to his pale, bare chest. A foul smell rose from the bed like a cloud, and Homer drew back. Mouth breathing or not, there was no way he could continue to stand at the bedside. The dying man was lying in his own filth and vomit, and it was obvious he had been that way for the better part of the day.

"Whew!" Homer took a large detour and went to the next bed; it was no better, maybe worse. This man's nose and upper lip were black with decay. And he began also to groan—a truly pitiful sound. Homer returned to Nick's bedside. "I...I don't..."

"Homer, I don't expect...there's anything to do," Nick offered, "but it was...a lot quieter in here...before you started." He wearily smiled at Homer. "Why don't you go ahead? Go home. Take care of Zula...and yourself. You look tired yourself...in your eyes."

Homer knew he really wasn't feeling too good, and there *was* this cough he seemed to be getting. *Maybe I'll just sit down for a while—to rest.* He saw the chair beside Nick's bed.

But Nick placed his red-speckled trash can on the chair and leaned back again in his bed, still watching Homer; he was throwing his cousin out of his room.

"Yeah, OK, but I'll be back," Homer promised.

"Well, I don't expect...I'll be waiting...if the Lord is willing and takes me. I don't know...how much leeway...he's given the ol' Devil."

"Ah, Nick, you don't really believe that, do you? God's good, and he'd never want something like this to happen." Homer was shaking his head. He couldn't stay silent.

"'Want' and 'let'...different things, Homer. 'Use' is another. God'll use this...as he wants. We don't know...what he wants. His ways are mysterious. Right?" Nick was now looking out the window, staring into eternity. "And you and me...pondering on it...ain't gonna change a thing...even if we agree on the vote. So...see you later, my good friend. Tell Zula...I'll see her later too."

Nick fell silent, breathing his deep gulps, his eyes closed and pinched.

Oh, the pain. Homer looked about to do something—*anything.* Seeing Nick's metal water pitcher, he lifted it then took it over for refilling at the tiny sink, returning it to Nick's table and to its companion Dixie cup. "Nick?" he whispered. He wanted to tell him that more water was in his pitcher, but the old fellow looked to be asleep; the other two men continued to moan, perhaps even louder. "Nick?" Homer straightened and backed toward the open door.

This is hard, and it's going to get worse. "But I can't do anything more for you...none of you!" Homer explained in a harsh, choking whisper to the room, his extended hands held open and empty. "I can't!" He had wanted to shout out the last words and run from the room. *But that would just be for me, Lord. Just for me.*

Then he heard the familiar voice, the soothing inner voice he knew but never could quite describe: *They understand. It's all right.*

Comforting assurance washed over him. *Yes, Lord, they do. Thanks.*

Homer turned and walked to the door and out. *Yeah, and now I need to be home.* He was thinking of Zula, back at the house, *and the boy I need to be looking out for.* He increased his stride.

Arriving at the hall's end, Homer noticed that the frosted-glass doors were now closed, the exit sign now extinguished. *Why'd they unprop the doors? They could use the light down here. Maybe something fell down.* He cautiously pressed his hand against the metal rail and pushed, feeling something blocking the door's swing. *I think that's one of the chairs they were using to hold the doors open.* He allowed the door to swing back and caught its edge with his fingertips, opening it back into the hallway. *Swings both ways.* Silently slipping through the opening, he saw shards of glass and plastic littering the floor just inside the lobby. *From the exit sign, I suppose. What's going on here?* He carefully stepped around the chair and over the pieces, scanning the big lobby as he entered. *That Jimmy there? Too dark to see his face. Why don't they turn on the lights around here?* He thought that was

Jimmy there across the room, sitting toward the middle of the row of chairs lined against the far wall, his head and shoulders silhouetted in the floor-to-ceiling windows. *Is it just Jimmy in here?* Then he saw the guard walk from behind a pillar, his hands on his hips, and cross in front of Jimmy, then stop and stand in front of the boy. The receptionist was gone from behind her desk, and no one else had come in.

Wrong! Something's changed. Something's wrong here! Alarm bells rang in his head. *The way that man is standing.*

With the sound of Homer's footsteps on the tile floor, the guard whirled around, his hand reaching for the revolver strapped at his side. "Jeez, man!" he yelled. "You scared me, sneaking up on me like that! I coulda shot your old, withered ass, you know...old man!"

Homer stopped where he was, holding his hands in the air. "Oh, gosh! Sorry! Sorry! I didn't mean to startle you!"

"You friggin' asshole," the man swore.

Now anger replaced Homer's alarm. *No need for that.* The guard's tone was, well, bullying and was much more threatening than necessary for the circumstances. Something more was in his voice than just his irritation at being startled. *That ol' boy's mad about being interrupted.*

"Sorry," Homer apologized again, raising his hands higher in surrender and looking past the guard to Jimmy. "I'll be more careful because I know you're on high alert and have a lot of responsibility right now. I should be more careful. I'm very sorry."

"Damned straight!" the man growled.

Behind the guard's turned back, Jimmy was gesturing, warning Homer by waving his arms to show alarm and caution, clenching his teeth to show the presence of great danger. But he couldn't tell if Homer was seeing him. *Gotta do something.* He noisily cleared his throat and slowly raised himself from the squeaking chair. "Well, Homer," he said, clapping his hands as if dusting them off, "we should be going, I guess. The guys in the truck will be wondering why you're taking so long, and we need to be getting back to the hunting camp before dark." The guard turned to look back at the boy.

Homer understood. He resumed walking, detouring toward the door as if he were looking through the big windows for his vehicle in the parking lot, maybe parked just around the corner and out of the guard's line of sight. "Yeah, yeah, you're right, Jimmy. Both Fred and Billy Ray are coming this way now. See? They're looking for us already." The guard turned back and sidled along the windows, trying to see what Homer was seeing, his hand still on the handle of his gun.

Homer was now at the entrance doors and pushing one side open. The other rent-a-cop was no longer at the door, guarding the building's exterior entrances.

"Hey old man!" the guard called, still moving along the windows, looking for Fred and Billy Ray. "Hey! Hey! Hold it right there!"

Streaking along in his noiseless sneakers, Jimmy skirted behind the guard and, quick as that, was out the door held open by Homer. They both made for the truck without exchanging a word.

"Hey, old man! Kid! Stop! Stop right there!" the guard yelled from behind the window. He was pulling out his pistol and running for the closing door.

This time Homer's aging knees were ignored. He was jerking open his door on the old truck as Jimmy was just closing his; he almost had outrun the kid. "First time I've run in thirty years," he later told Jimmy. Keys in ignition, hard turn to the right, and the motor caught. "Get down!" Homer yelled. He popped the clutch, and the truck leaped forward, roaring across the lawn, aiming toward the corner of the building and, perhaps, cover. Then the back window exploded as the sound of the guard's gun reached them.

Homer stomped on the brakes, and the truck slid to a sideways stop.

Jimmy at first thought the old man had been hit, but then saw Homer reach back to the rack behind his bench seat and pull his twelve-gauge pump from its mounts.

"Stay down!" Homer ordered, as he snapped the gun's fore-end mechanism in and out, jacking a shell into the chamber, then slid from his seat to the ground, pushing open the truck's door with his foot as he dropped, all in one fluid motion. He crouched, leveled the gun at his waist, and let loose—just like that—with no hesitation.

The explosion was terrific, and his aim was true; as the guard cleared the rear of the truck, he was spun around by the impact, his revolver thrown into the air and landing about three yards behind where he fell. Then all was quiet again.

Homer didn't try to shout a warning or anything! He just twisted out the door and fired! Boom! Jimmy, having dropped to the floorboards along with the glass from the rear window, was now staring at Homer through the open door, his mouth gaped wide. *So fast!* Jimmy hadn't had time to even think about seeing what was happening with the guard. "Homer? Homer? You OK? You get him?"

"Hard to miss with buckshot," Homer said with a shrug. Then he calmly got back into the idling truck, put it in gear, and proceeded to make a wide turn on the grass, steering far around the trees and the guard's prone body to again cross the little bridge over the ditch to the road. "I didn't think the ol' boy was gonna give us the time to circle back," he explained, "and there's a big ditch back there that I didn't think we could jump."

"Did you really shoot the guy? That him back there? Did you kill him? How'd you know what he was doing? When did you know what was happening? When did you know?" Jimmy peppered Homer with his questions as he soon as he had crawled from the floor. He was kneeling in the seat and looking backward, having brushed aside the glass crumbs from the upholstery and gripping the sides of the empty rear window.

"Well, when I saw it right ahead of us."

"No, no, not about the ditch. When did you know the guard was ready to do something to us? Probably rob us!" The boy's voice had risen an octave or two.

"When I saw your big ol' eyes. Looked like raisins in a couple bowls of milk. When did *you* know?"

Jimmy slid around to again face the front. "Well, you know, you were barely out of the room when the receptionist up and said she'd had enough of this you-know-what and was getting the heck out of Dodge. Well, she didn't say 'Dodge' either—she was pretty foul— but she'd had enough of old people, and she was gonna take care of herself. So she and the guy outside took off in his car like they were boyfriend and girlfriend and—say, Homer, I've got a new word I need you to explain."

"You're already a teenager; I doubt there's few words you don't already know the meaning of." *That kid can recover faster than...* "Go on with your story first."

"Well, they left, and the guard came over to talk. See? He wanted to know where we were from and where we lived and such. And he wanted to know if there were other people back at the house. I guess he'd already assumed that we'd come there alone. By the way, the story about Fred and Billy Ray—that was really good. You're pretty quick sometimes. You know—"

"Jimmy, the story?"

"Yeah, I guessed about then he was a little *too* interested in us, so I said I needed to go back to see you in the patient room. He blocked me in and said he 'didn't think so'—something about kids going back on the floor. And then he unsnapped the strap on his pistol and let me see how loose it was in his holster. Then he asked if you kept a lot of cash at the house and if I'd like to go with him out West somewhere. He said he could show me a lot of things he had learned. Hey, did you know that guy was in prison once? He showed me his tattoo on his arm. It looked rather ragged, but I didn't tell him that. You know, I did a better one on ol' Donnie Lincoln back in the fourth grade with a number two pencil. Anyway, about that time you came tromping in. So what do you think he could have shown me that he'd learned in prison?" Jimmy looked over at Homer, innocently blinking his eyes.

"I think kids grow up entirely too fast these days. That's what I think." Making his little tsking sounds with his tongue, Homer turned his attention back to the road.

They rode on in silence for a few minutes, and then Jimmy asked, "Homer, what about the guy you came to see at the clinic?"

"Nick?"

"Yeah."

"It wasn't too good, Jimmy. Ol' Nick caught the tail end of a war and another epidemic that occurred long ago. He's had a hard life, and he's filled it with a lot of living—a very interesting guy. And he's actually ending it pretty well. I know you know Christ, and so does Nick. So he can see the big picture and isn't afraid of dying, you see. In fact I think he's been spending a lot of his time in the other realm already, the true and eternal one. He's ready. But I really hate to see him hurting so."

Jimmy saw that Homer's eyes were shiny; he turned back to watch the road ahead. "How about that guard fellow? Think he was ready to meet his maker?"

Homer shook his head sadly. "No, I don't think that ol' boy was ready. But you know, I'm not so sure he's gone already either; he was wiggling when we passed him by, but I didn't feel an obligation to get out and check on him just then. I'm going right now to the sheriff's office to tell them what I've done. The high sheriff will do what he wants with that ol' boy…and with me for that matter. Fact is, I gotta tell him, but I don't think this situation, drastic as it is, will be the sheriff's highest priority right now. I fear there's a lot more evil afoot right now." He then paused and looked over to confirm that Jimmy still had the shotgun propped up against his leg. "And we're gonna need to keep that piece somewhere we can both find it in a hurry. More shells are under your seat. Hey, did Billy Ray teach you how to cock and shoot that thing?"

"Yeah, remember the time we shot the guinea hens for supper? I used your gun then. Like to have broken my shoulder with that thing." Jimmy had raised the gun and was looking at it in the fading sunlight.

"Should have held it tighter," Homer advised. "And as I recall, you boys used quail shot on those birds. I remember I almost broke a tooth on a pellet—that's kind of hard to forget."

Jimmy laughed. "Yeah, that'd be the time. So what were you saying about evil being afoot right now?"

"Oh, it's just something Nick was saying. He said God talks to him in his dreams and all. And I'm sometimes feeling we're in for some kind of testing and all too. Frankly I don't think we're anywhere near the end of this plague thing—and we may be in for a time when a lot of evil people will be doing evil things in this world. See, in the generations that have gone on, we've seemed to have gotten away from God in our relations to him—like the ol' Israelites. I bet you can see that in your school, what with the ACLU fighting prayer and… What's that up ahead?"

They were nearing the intersection on 441 that led to I-40; it appeared to be total gridlock, and the deputy sheriff they'd previously seen trying to direct the traffic was standing atop his car, waving his arms frantically in all directions. Everyone seemed to be ignoring him, and his emergency lights no longer flashed.

Homer studied the situation. *Deputy's car is either out of gas or its battery ran down. Better not bother him.* "You know, Jimmy, I can see the lane to Knoxville is open with all the traffic blocked here. We might just want to go back the way we came and skip visiting Sheriff Noland right now. It's totally blocked back that way anyway. Besides, I suppose we can call him from the house or a pay phone; he can come on out our way when he's ready to talk." With that said, he made a left then a series of other turns on secondary streets to eventually bounce into another plowed plot running alongside Chapman Highway. As he drove through the field, parallel to the road, he studied the line of traffic ahead. "See any openings, Jimmy? We need to cross that line of cars there to get to the other lane to go west to our turnoff."

Jimmy was again sitting on the edge of his seat, his nose inches from the windshield. "No, Homer, I don't. It looks like a lot of those cars don't even have people in them anymore. See those people walking over there?"

Then they heard a gunshot that echoed around the knobs and hills…and another…and another.

"Lord help! Jimmy, them folks are getting into a gun battle! Hang on." He pulled hard on the steering wheel, making a wide turn in the field and heading back the way they had come.

Jimmy held up the shotgun. "Homer, we got this."

Homer nodded. "Yeah, and I got *you*…and I'm going to keep it that way."

They bounced back onto the paved street. "We'll go the back way and come up around Panther Creek. That'll get us home. There're a lot of old roads around these hills that only old folks and moonshiners know about." Homer winked at Jimmy.

***

Hours later they pulled out onto White School Road, stopping briefly to let Jimmy hop out to open and close the gate to the cow pasture they had just crossed.

"Hey, Homer. What do you think this is?" Jimmy had climbed back into the cab and was holding out a sheet of paper, maybe a handbill.

"Where'd you get it?"

"Stapled to the telephone pole back there."

Homer took the handbill and, holding it up to the fading light, read aloud, "Faith healing service this week. Held nightly. Pastor Dilbert Davis, preaching and officiating. Pastor Daniel Davis, healings. Come one and all. Faith offering accepted. Youth membership encouraged. Come join the cleansing crusade tonight at seven. Come before it is too late."

Homer lowered the paper. "Well, what do you think of that, Jimmy?"

"I didn't know Daniel was a reverend now."

"I didn't either—a healing one at that."

Jimmy looked over. Homer sounded as if he were about to do some cogitating right now—staring at the fading sunset, stroking his short scraggly beard, and just thinking. *He is,* Jimmy confirmed.

He waited for a few minutes, listening to the truck idle, before asking, "Say, Homer, are you thinking about going to the service?" *Sometimes Homer needs some reminding where he is.*

"Well, Jimmy, I'm thinking the good preacher is taking advantage of a very bad situation and seeing how he can make some money off this. And that ain't nice what I'm thinking, but I…" Homer's head lifted with the arrival of another thought. "Jimmy, you might want to be staying close to home tonight and the rest of the week. If Daniel's enlisting a youth membership—you know how those younger boys follow after him—he just might take it upon himself to…"

Homer's voice trailed off. He didn't know how he could let Jimmy know of this thought, his fear, without also telling him about his suspicions regarding the fate of Lassie—and Daniel Davis's involvement with it. The dog had taken off on his own, chasing after a bunch of boys they had surprised in the lower pasture late one evening, just a few days after Jimmy had gone home last spring. Homer had heard them laughing and seen them shooting at ol' Red with their air rifles—*shooting at his eyes and privates*—and he was certain the gang was Daniel Davis's motley gathering of ne'er-do-wells—*and Daniel was right there with them*. But he wasn't quite as sure whether Lassie really had nipped Daniel. Regardless, the incident got the preacher's attention; Reverend Davis came knocking at his front door early the next morning, demanding the immediate execution of Lassie. Homer smiled at that memory: Zula had walked in about that time, and he had related the previous evening's events to her there in front of the preacher. Without even asking Homer's thoughts on the matter, she had invited Reverend Davis to "get off our property" then proceeded to escort the sputtering man down the steps and to his car without so much as another word. Actually, Homer remembered, the preacher had even seemed to be exceptionally cooperative, given that Zula had just come from the kitchen where she had been cutting up a chicken and had brought her old butcher knife with her. *Zula must've liked that ol' dog after all.*

But now Homer wondered if it wouldn't have been kinder to ol' Lassie to have gone ahead and dispatched the dog himself. He knew the animal had suffered mightily under the hand of someone that following week. Lassie had been blinded, disemboweled, burned, and left hanging in a tree beside the creek in his pasture. *A real mean someone.* And Homer felt deep inside that "someone" was Daniel, seeking revenge on the dog and him.

And yesterday he had again given Daniel cause in his sick, twisted mind to seek vengeance, this time on Jimmy.

"Yeah?" Jimmy prompted.

"Oh, sorry." Homer looked around, getting his bearings. "We'll just go right here and on up White School Road to the house. Zula and Thelma will be wondering where we are. Getting hungry, my lad?"

"Heck, yeah!" Then it was Jimmy's time to do some cogitating. "Say, we didn't eat anything all day long. You know that, Homer?"

"Well, now that you mention it, I guess we didn't. I didn't learn to boil eggs, and you didn't get that Milky Way bar or that milk shake. You ought to be starved!"

"I guess it's been…an eventful day." Then Jimmy remembered. "Hey, Homer, I didn't tell you all about Gus this morning, and we still got to do something about that fence ol' Red pulled down. Remember?"

"Yeah, let's do some planning. I'll let you off at the gate—the cows should all be waiting for us—and while you're bringing 'em up, take 'em up the hollow way. I'll tack up a strand or two between fence posts to maybe keep Red in. You'll have the cows, so he'll be less likely to wander. But you'll have to be watching for ol' Red as you take them up. OK?"

"OK. But you know, I kind of wish ol' Lassie hadn't started sucking eggs and all. He was always good to watch out for Red for me. Say!" Jimmy was pointing at the white clapboard house set back from the road. "Isn't that Mr. Shanks coming out?" A Ford truck was crunching down the gravel driveway, coming toward them.

"Yeah, it sure is. He's all loaded up like he's moving. Let me pull over here a minute." Homer steered his Chevy to the shoulder, giving Mr. Shanks room to turn onto the road and to pull up beside his truck. "Maybe he'll have time to talk a minute."

He did. Mr. Shanks pulled his truck alongside Homer's; he was leaving opposite the way they were coming.

"Bill," Homer greeted the other man, while eyeing the heavily loaded bed of the Ford truck. "Mrs. Shanks." Bill's wife was seated at his side, holding their baby; suitcases filled the remainder of the space in the cab. "Looks like you're going on vacation or something."

Shanks snorted a bitter laugh. "You been listening to the news, Homer?" Bill was a ham radio buff and kept in touch with other amateur radio operators all over the United States. Jimmy could just make out the man's tall radio tower against the failing blue of the evening sky, back behind the little white house.

"There's an epidemic happening, and a lot of folks are dying. I heard people are going in grocery stores and grabbing up everything. And there's shootings and stuff going on back toward Knoxville, and the governor's declared martial law. The national guard has been called up." Jimmy also knew Mr. Shanks was a guardsman. "But I can't go," he said, as if he were reading Jimmy's thoughts. "I've got my wife and baby to worry about."

Mrs. Shanks leaned forward to wave, and Jimmy, also leaning forward, was reminded anew what a beautiful woman Mrs. Shanks ("Call me Judy") was. In fact he was pretty certain that his feelings for her qualified as love and that he had been desperately in love with her for as long as he could remember. On Sunday mornings he'd hurry Homer and Zula along so as to get the pew seats right behind Bill and Judy, causing Zula to once remark that Jimmy was "sure fervent" in his seeking of the Lord's word. On weekdays he listened for opportunities to visit the Shanks's house, even inviting himself along on Zula's visits if Homer wasn't to be going that way. But he also knew he wasn't alone in his love; he had noticed that the eyes of the other boys—and most of the men—lifted when she walked past. And then there was that time she had kissed cheeks under the mistletoe.

Jimmy felt a minor rush of guilt. *Here Mr. Shanks is talking about the terrible state of affairs, and I'm thinking about his wife.* He again tried to concentrate on what Bill was saying.

"Homer, we're packing up and getting into Maryville, where Judy's parents live. They're gonna need us, and you know, things might get rough way out here in the country. The preacher's kid, Dan, has been here twice today with his gang of thugs...offering their assistance to Judy, you know," Bill sniffed, adding a skeptical tone to his voice. Jimmy suspected now that Bill also had noticed the other men's admiring glances. "I don't trust that kid. He's almost bigger than me, and with those—you know, we should be going to another church, Homer. I should be out looking for another church. At any rate who knows how things are going to get out here, and the law sure won't be around."

"You still working over in Oak Ridge, Bill?" Homer asked.

"Yeah, and that's another thing. I had to come home by Knob Creek and then by Sugar Loaf. Chapman Highway was barely moving. It took me an extra two hours to get home this evening. You know, we might oughta go on down to Florida and just get out of these hills. I hear they have a lot more hospitals if…you know." He quickly glanced over to Judy.

"Bill, things are gonna be all right," she said, patting his shoulder. "Shoot, we might even want to bring Mommy and Daddy back up here with us to minimize, you know, contact with germs." She now leaned past Bill, to smile and wave. "Hey, Jimmy," she brightly called to him. "You doing OK? You coming down to visit when we get back?"

Jimmy smiled and waved back. He was in love all over again; he would defend this fair maiden with his life against all who would dare threaten her well-being! And he sure hoped neither Homer nor Bill noticed the crimson hue he felt warming his face. *Come on, darkness.*

"Well, Bill, we've got to get on down the road," Homer said. "You know we'll be thinking of you and keeping you in our prayers. Let me know how it's going down there. We'll keep an eye on your place if you want."

"Gosh, Homer. Thanks. We got to be going too but we gotta stop by the church first; the preacher sent word he wanted to talk with Judy before we left. And we'll be thinking of you and Zula and Jimmy too."

Not Thelma? Jimmy knew that she and Judy had once had words. *I guess Bill's gotta be courteous to Judy's feelings right now too.* He had no idea that Thelma had propositioned Bill, cornering him in the church kitchen when Judy had missed choir practice and Billy Ray was in New York—and Bill had shared the specifics of that encounter with his wife. Jimmy knew only that Thelma and Judy didn't speak to each other anymore.

Bill and Judy waved again as they rolled on past and away down the road. Bill turned on his headlights and was soon gone from sight. Jimmy watched from the glassless back window until they had rounded the corner and were out of sight. "I think Mr. Shanks is in a hurry," Jimmy said as he turned back.

"Yeah, and we should be too."

Three minutes later, Homer slowed for the pasture gate, and Jimmy dropped from the running board to the gravel. The cows mooed at him as they shifted restlessly on the other side of the wire. Jimmy was late, and they wanted to be milked!

"Back, back," he ordered as he opened the gate, bottom loop first then the top. "Now come on out." He swung the wire back and leaned the post against the fence. *Might as well leave it open again.* The cows filed through and made the right turn, heading home without his direction. They were comfortable with their world.

***

"Honey? Thelma?" Homer softly called when he had closed the porch door behind himself, pressing against the frame to quiet the latch. "Honey? Thelma?" he called again as he climbed the steep, narrow staircase. He tapped on Zula's bedroom door. The short hall-way was dark, but he had no trouble moving in the familiar space. He cracked the door and eased it open. "Honey? I'm sorry we took so long. Gosh!" The smell hit him like a wall. And it was very famil-iar. *Like that smell in the clinic, in Nick's room. Crap and vomit!* Homer backed up and gagged—or rather dry heaved. He hadn't eaten that day, so he had nothing in his stomach to vomit.

"Oh, Zula," he anguished.

6

DAY TWO

J immy woke well before dawn, feeling as if he'd hardly slept during the night. It wasn't as if he hadn't been tired when he had gone to bed. He *was* tired—bodily tired, tired to the bone—but his mind just would not slow down and permit him to drift along in untroubled sleep. *I must have tossed and turned all night long, worrying about things and listening to those dang crickets.* At least the phone had been silent—tourist inquiries abruptly had ceased—and his sad bouts of homesickness had abated. But now he was a kid with a burden, a big burden, and it was keeping him from sleeping. He kneaded flat the lump of his pillow and lay back into it, to think more about things.

When he'd left Homer yesterday, he had driven the cows on up through the shadowy hollow, along the tiny stream and up the steep hillside to the barn, all without incident. Knowing that Big Red was roaming free somewhere in the area—in the knobby, wooded acres surrounding the barn—he had been especially watchful along the way, half expecting the big bull to come crashing out of any one of the many thickets that lined the trail or to come charging up the path from behind at just such a time as when his escape options were especially restricted by the steep hillsides. But all had been quiet...almost too quiet. When he had reached the top of the ridge, he had found the barnyard abandoned and silent—neither of the mules awaiting him there, ready to race him to the fence again. And unlike being merely wary for the bull along the way, he actually had anticipated an ambush by either Whitey or Blackie and had been careful to position himself behind a cow or two when they had first filed into the barnyard. But no, there had been no greeting thunder of big hooves, no accompanying snorts from starting mules. *Just a big ol' empty barn. Not that I minded, but it was strange. I wonder where they were. Maybe Red and the mules mixed it up some and did themselves in.* But just in case, he remembered, he had made sure to securely fasten the barnyard's wire gate when the last cow had passed through.

He guessed that he and Homer had been lagging behind maybe two hours or so in their routine, from the time they usually milked in the evenings. The cows had most definitely reminded him of his tardiness even as they'd made their way in from the pasture, stopping every so often to cuss-moo back at him then picking up a double-time pace to cause him to run just to stay up with them. Then, inside the barn, they had lined up at their respective stables, pushing at the latches and bawling at him to get a move on; they all had wanted to be milked—right then! *Too bad Homer wasn't there yet; he'd have thought all that was pretty funny right then.*

Jimmy had waited in the barn for Homer for a while more, completing the preliminary tasks of preparing the disinfecting water and filling the feed pails before deciding to go ahead *(it was getting really dark and the cows were really mooing)* and start the milking on his own—his executive decision, as Homer had called it. As it was, when he finally had heard the creaky opening of the big wooden gate out front, he already had milked the Jersey, the Guernsey, *and* the Ayrshire.

"About time, Homer!" he remembered yelling from the stall, expecting some irreverent reply from the old man. But he had heard no reply, not even a reverent one. Curious, Jimmy had picked up his bucket and followed the cow through the stable door into the main bay, all the while grousing loudly about the old man's punctuality. "Well, you stayed away long enough that I risked my life and milked your danged ol' wild Ayrshire and..." And there, at the front, he had then seen the *old* man—Homer—just entering the outer reaches of the overhead floodlight, not even slapping at the dive-bombing bugs drawn to the glare, just walking slowly, hatless, his chin to his chest.

Despair. That was the word that had come unbidden to his mind when he had emerged from the stall with his stool and pail and had seen Homer standing there at the barn's entrance. *Just standing there with his head down.* He remembered he had been uncertain as to what to do next; he had been readying himself to joke and replay the events of the day with ol' Homer, to discuss their amazing adventures and escapes, and had come out to find...an old man...a really old man...all broken and bowed with despair in a lonely pool of light.

So he had done nothing...except watch. He had watched as the slight breeze lightly fluffed the soft white hair that ringed Homer's balding head and had tried to recall any time in the past when he had seen him outside the house without his brimmed hat. *Never.* He had watched the shaded jowls and tried to remember any time previous when he actually had noticed that the old man's shirts hung open and loose at the neck or that his overalls were about a size too big. *Never.* In fact, he remembered, he had found himself wondering whether it had really only been an hour or two since he had last seen Homer down at the road, waving back at him from the cab of the truck...or if years had passed since then—such had been the change in the old man's appearance.

After several minutes of their standing like that, Homer had seemed to rouse himself on his own and had looked up, appearing almost surprised to find Jimmy ahead and just watching. "Hey boy," he had softly greeted and then had plodded forward—his slow, slow walk—to cover the remaining ten yards of ground space between them, and had tentatively placed his calloused old hands on the boy's shoulders, saying simply, "Jimmy, we need to do some talking."

"Homer? Zula's gotten worse?" he had asked, alarmed with the possibilities. He recalled also how blue—fevered blue—Homer's eyes had appeared to him there in the barnyard, in the glare of those harsh floodlights. *And how utterly sad.*

Homer had just nodded, affirming nothing—and everything.

"Well, shouldn't we be taking her to the hospital, the clinic? Homer? The emergency room?"

Homer had first deeply sighed, in a tired, resigned way, causing his body to appear to shrink even more. "Jimmy," he'd said,
"I've tried calling the clinic in Sevierville, the hospital in Maryville,
Blount Memorial—where your mother works—and two hospitals in
Knoxville. The phone lines are bad...and when I did get through,
they told me not to bother coming in. They have more on their plate
than they can handle already. They said they wouldn't even attempt
to admit her if I *was* to bring her. Blount Memorial said they had
people outside, in their cars, waiting to get in. And they told me a lot
of the doctors and nurses weren't even able to come in themselves—
you know, like we saw at the clinic here—so they're working with
only a fraction of their staff."

"So there's nothing we can do? But we can't just give up! Maybe..."

He had paused there, with Homer looking at him with those
crackling blue eyes—he remembered how strange, how nervous
that had made him feel—and how it had stopped him midprotest.
"Jimmy," Homer had softly said, "I've cleaned Zula up as best I can
but...she's in the Lord's hands now. She'll mostly need our prayers
now. You need to understand that and accept that the Lord is in control. OK?" He must have dipped his head then, nodding once and
looking like he'd either accepted or at least understood, and Homer
had continued on. "And there's more you'll need to know about...
about what I've heard on the radio." The old man had appeared to
be carefully choosing his words. "You heard ol' Cline say this here
disease is something that might have happened before, maybe cen-
turies before now, maybe all the way back to during the Dark Ages?"
Jimmy had quickly nodded again. "You did? Then have you ever
heard or read about this thing that they're now calling the plague
or bubonic disease, Jimmy? About how back in the Dark Ages it had
affected the world...the whole known world?"

I think I must have shook my head then or sniffled or something, Jimmy
thought now. *Maybe I was about to cry. But Homer kept talking.*

"I didn't think so. I knew about it but not about the particulars
of it, and I've been around a lot longer'n you. And bear in mind,
the CDC—that's the Communicable Disease Center in, I think,

Atlanta—and the state board of health folks in Nashville are just guessing at what it is...so everything might not be as bad as what they're saying on the radio...and what everybody's making it out to be. Anyway, I've laid out some books at the house I want you to read when we get back there. OK? You need to know what they're saying in case...We've just got some planning to do. For you and me and Thelma and, yes, for Zula. Now see, these books that I laid out—"

"Well, OK, thanks, Homer. I'll read 'em later, but what about the cows?" Jimmy had interrupted, trying to change the subject right then. "I can try to milk the other cows, but you know, the Holsteins and their big ol' tits...And ol' Red and his fence—we gotta do something about that." He must have been feeling very impatient with the old man about then and thinking Homer was going on and on—*and forgetting...those cows and milking...important stuff. Stuff we always do that we need to think about.*

But Homer had just smiled again, in his own understanding way, and said, "Son, what say let's let the cows go dry now? I don't know what's going to happen. I think it's a good time to let them rest for a spell. So unless you just want to go on milking the Jersey, like for fresh milk in the house, let's just let them alone tonight. Feed 'em and just let them alone to graze."

"Stop milking them? Like just stop milking them and open the gates?" he had asked, incredulous at the thought. *He was telling me that he's giving up. And you know, somebody besides me might still want fresh milk in the house. Unless...*He couldn't finish the thought.

"Yeah, open the gates. You can let them graze around these hills around the barn and back behind the tobacco patch. There's plenty of grass there. And you won't have to take them down to the pasture across the road anymore." Homer had then ruffled his hair like he always did. "Wouldn't you like that?"

"OK, but it's apt to be a bit noisy for a while." He had pointed over his shoulder with his thumb at the Holsteins still standing just inside their stall doors.

"Well, yeah, but I believe we can put up with that for a while, can't we?" Homer had managed another sad grin. "And if you would,

would you take care of Zula's chickens for her too? I think it'll be a while before…Those birds might just come in real handy soon."

That was another strange thing for Homer to say. "Well, I expect they're handy right now," Jimmy had replied, wanting to state, and thereby stabilize, the obvious.

"Yeah, you're right," Homer had agreed.

Then Homer had gotten real serious again, he remembered. "Son, we can talk about…the other things later. But I need to tell you one other thing now so you can do some thinking. I…I just might have caught something myself. Now I don't know if it's like that plague stuff," he had hurriedly qualified, "but I've got chills and…other stuff…and I just might be laid up for a while. I've taken some more of that ol' cough syrup and maybe a pill or two, but…you know…just got to work through it. So anyway, I'm appointing you to be in charge—to take care of things around here if I can't, you know. And, ah…" Homer had been rummaging around in the front pockets of his overalls with one hand. "…I want to give you this here to help you keep tabs on everything." He had then held out his gold pocket watch for Jimmy to take.

"I can't take that! You love that watch, and I bet it's the most precious thing you've ever owned. No, I can't take that, Homer! You're not gonna get sick, and I can't take that!" He'd stepped back then, away from the hand that had remained on his shoulder.

But the old man had persisted, still holding out the watch and reaching again for his shoulder. "No, no, you'll need it to keep time for your tasks, and…I tell you what: Maybe I'll ask for it back when I start feeling better!"

"Well, OK then," he remembered agreeing. *Under those conditions,* he'd thought.

"Under those conditions. So ol' Jimbo, you'd better be getting up and getting out to it," Jimmy commanded himself, sitting up in bed and reaching over to locate the straight chair where he had draped his clothes last night, to feel around for the watch with his fingertips on the chair's seat then lift it up in the blackness of the bedroom against the faint light from the window so he could see the watch's roundness. *Wow!* He noticed the watch still seemed warm—*Maybe from Homer's pocket!*—and held it against his cheek for a little while. It felt comfortable when so much suddenly had become uncertain.

"That's enough of that," he said, still talking aloud. He swung his legs to the floor, stood, and tap-touched the chair again to find his shirt and jeans, then quickly slipped them on. *Feels right, tag to the back side.* "Now to see what's got to be done first," he declared, his voice loud and singular in the dimness but somehow encouraging. Slipping the watch into the tiny pouch at the top of his front jeans pocket, its tiny gold chain left to hang to the outside for easy retrieval, Jimmy straightened and felt his way to the door, resolving anew to make Homer proud of him. *I'll take good care of things.*

He touched his way down the familiar, squeaky stairs to the closed-in room at the base of the staircase. This room, once an exterior porch, and the downstairs bathroom and kitchen had all been added on well before the time he had been born, squaring the corner of the house and adding amenities—and the beginnings of indoor plumbing—to the lives of the young Clark family. At the staircase bottom, he turned to his left to bypass the kitchen route and located the ancient chest freezer against the wall there, sliding his hand along the length of its cool metal side as he padded across the long room, making his way toward the outside door. As he went he also felt ahead with his bare toes, feeling for the crack in the flooring that outlined the cellar door, confirming that it was indeed closed, that someone hadn't forgotten to lower the heavy portal cover where, in the dirt-smelly gloom below, lurked the monsters of his childhood. *Heck,* he thought, *I still hate going down there for jelly and canned green beans and stuff, and I'm almost grown!*

He tapped his way along to the outside wall then to the door— the solid door. *Homer must have closed up the house last night. Sure makes it dark in here.* Usually, in the warmer weather, only the screen door was closed for the night, its flimsy eye-and-hook latch securing the entryway. Very quietly he turned the knob, pulling inward on the wooden door then pushing wide the screen door, slipping through the space to stand for a moment on the top step of the stairs there, in the cool dimness of the new day. He loved this time, so early in the morning—this time of quiet and peace and beauty and possibilities. But as he stood there now, more thoughts came to him, unfortunate memories, about last night.

After he and Homer had talked earlier in the barn's center bay, they had returned to the house for supper, splitting the remaining corn bread from the previous morning between their tall glasses of buttermilk and quartering two apples Zula had left in a bowl atop the refrigerator. Neither of them had been especially hungry, and the fare was satisfactory to both. Then Homer had wished him a good night and ponderously climbed the stairs to spend the night in Zula's bedroom, tending to her, while Jimmy had gone into the TV room, where Homer had placed the *World Book Encyclopedia* on the little table he used for bill paying. The red-covered book, volume D, had been left open at the section labeled "Disease."

After turning on the green-shaded lamp, he had slid onto Homer's cushioned chair, where he pulled the book close and read the book-marked section. He had voiced aloud certain words or phrases he had deemed especially memory worthy: "'Bubonic plague, zoonotic disease, rats, and fleas—generally believed, Black Death, killer of twenty-five million people, sixty percent of the European popula-tion.'" He had to stop for a minute to consider the extent of the ruin. While twenty-five million people was hard for him to visualize, 60 percent of the world's population was easy to imagine. *That's more than half the people in the world! Imagine how empty the cities must have seemed. Imagine how whole families were wiped out.*

He had read on: "'Buboes or inflamed lymph nodes, gangrene, two to five days after exposure, fever, chills, seizures, bleeding, vomiting, diarrhea...death in two to five days after exposure!" *No!* There he had stopped...and had put the book away, back in the bookcase.

Even now, standing and beholding the makings of another warm, beautiful day, he shivered, not with the morning cool but with a fleeting mental image of what possibly was happening to Zula. *No!* he again told himself. *She's got a cold, and I need to tend to the cows and chickens.* He pushed the image from his mind and let the screen door close easy behind.

After slipping on his still tied tennis shoes—still tied because he hadn't wanted to touch the manure-soaked laces last night—he rumbled on down the few back stairs and trotted across the lawn, first to the chicken lot beyond the smokehouse, where he watered and fed the waking, murmuring hens, then on to the barn, where he milked only the little Jersey. The rest of the cows were again waiting at their stall gates, but this morning only the Ayrshire and Guernsey bawled their demands at him. The Holsteins apparently were over much of their discomfort and only turned with minor interest in him as he passed with his partially filled milk bucket, heading back to the house. He would give them each only about half their feed ration, as Homer had instructed, and then would let them graze freely around the barn and the surrounding hills.

Whoa! Surrounding hills! he thought with sudden alarm. *Ol' Red and the mules are out there!* He had left open the wire gate in the encircling fence last night and hadn't thought to resecure it this morning when he had walked over from the chicken house. And now, without first thinking about the animals and safety—*his* safety—he was about halfway across the wide-open barnyard and toting a heavy bucket of milk.

And there's ol' Whitey right there!

The big mule apparently had walked into the fog-wisped, dew-quieted barnyard and taken up a position at the front wooden gate—between the boy and the house. She now heard his steps and turned her head slowly, deliberately to watch him, to nod to him and study him. He imagined he also could see her to smile—*grinning with those big ol' yellow teeth.*

Jimmy carefully lowered his bucket to the ground. *Easy, easy.* Thinking he would retreat into the barn, run lightly through it then circle around on the outside of the fenced perimeter, he straightened and began to shuffle backward toward the security of ladders and stalls and doors. *Easy, easy, easy.* Whitey snorted once and violently shook her head, slinging her slobber to the sides.

Snort! An answering one—just behind him!

Whoa! Dang! Blackie's right behind me! Jimmy whirled to find that the other mule had come silently through the barn and now stood maybe five yards behind him, dead center, in the main bay.

Oh, damn! Jimmy knew his day had now come. The mules had waited years for this moment, to catch him between the two of them, with no fence to duck under and no ladder to scramble up. "Oh, dang!" he breathed, frozen in place, waiting for the stomping, biting beasts to charge him and convert him into a limp, bloody mess right there amid the cow piles and corn shucks.

But it didn't happen that way. In fact nothing happened…immediately. With big-hoofed, scuffing steps, Whitey shifted on around so as to face the boy fully from her front, putting him directly ahead of her. She then took a step—two steps—toward him. Hearing the sound and sensing her movement, Jimmy spun partially back, trying to keep both mules in sight at the same time. His head jerked back and forth, from one side to the other, while the mules…studied him, eyeing him up and down and sniffing. Then, after a long minute of consideration, Whitey apparently decided she knew enough, and the kid was no longer of interest to her; she blew once again, wheeled, and trotted heavily across the yard and through the open gate. Blackie followed, trotting in the way that mules do, his head held high and proud, passing by the boy a scant three feet away.

"Amazing!" Jimmy watched them go, through the gate and out of sight down the hillside. "Darn, don't that beat all!" Suddenly he felt wilted and in need of a place to sit for a while, at least until his heart returned to a normal rhythm. *Whew!* But more than that, he now realized he needed to find a place to pee—and quickly!

"Yeah, a really close call, that was. More ways than one." Standing in the yard's corner, behind the woodpile, the boy continued to shake his head with wonder. *And don't that beat all; those ol' mules had me and let me go…just let me go! And they let me know they weren't afraid of me neither. But maybe because I didn't—couldn't—run away. Maybe to them, their constant chasing after me was just…for fun?*

Minutes later, recuperated and lurching along, milk bucket in hand, on his way back to the house for breakfast, Jimmy continued to mull over his close call, refining the recitation he planned for the old man: "See, Homer, those ol' mules were circling, gnashing the air and closing in for the kill—whoa!" He almost walked into the side of a car that had been parked across the walkway.

What the heck? Thelma's Corvette! It wasn't in its usual place, secure in the garage at the front of the house. He hadn't noticed it on the way to the barn because he had first gone to the chicken house. Then another unfortunate memory came to him: Thelma had returned home late last night after he already had gone to bed; he remembered having heard a car crunching up the driveway. He had heard her then, coming in through the TV room and dining room…where Homer apparently was waiting for her. Jimmy seldom had heard the old man raise his voice, except to holler for the cows or pigs, but he remembered he'd heard Homer holler last night. He and Thelma really had a few words to say to one another. And then it had gotten quiet in the house, and Jimmy had heard Homer slowly mount the stairs back to Zula's room and her door clicking carefully, respectfully closed. Later, about an hour or so, he had heard Thelma making her own way to bed, stomping heavily up the stairs and slamming her bedroom door. Apparently she had still been pretty mad. *I wonder if all that woke Zula up?*

He stepped back to walk around the front of the car. *What's that?* In the better light, with the sun now clearing the eastern horizon, he saw that the Corvette carried a long scratch down its side, the passenger side, and a dinged-up front-quarter panel—definite signs of an accident. *Whoa! No wonder Thelma was in a foul mood last night. That car's her baby.* And he supposed that, with the way Zula was sick and all, Homer was out of sorts himself too. *Maybe that's what it was last night.* He walked on.

At the back door, he found the old man waiting for him and holding a large manila envelope. *He's not smiling; he looks sick—the chills!* Homer's words returned to him from yesterday. "Ah…morning, Homer. You look like you're a bit…You're OK now, aren't you?"

"Here, Jimmy, let me take your bucket," he replied, brusque but not unkind. "I need you to run this down to the mailbox and wait for Gus. I need you to give this to him when he comes by. It's some records and our letter telling him—and Mayfield—that we won't be having him pick up our milk...for a while." He added the last words when Jimmy glanced sharply up. "Anyway, if you'd wait for him and give that to him, I'd appreciate it."

"OK, Homer. I'll wait there. By the way, I just passed Thelma's car, and man, there's fiberglass showing around the right wheel well. Did she get in an accident or something?"

Homer looked past him, out to where the car was parked. His eyes narrowed, and his complexion seemed to darken a shade or two. "Ah, no, well...I don't know." He cleared his throat. "She hasn't said anything to me, Jimmy. She, ah, got home pretty late last night and didn't say anything at all about it." But Homer knew she probably *wouldn't* have said anything about it in the first place—because then he could have asked her where she had been...and that would have been that. As it was, they had argued anyway when she'd arrived *(talking like a drunk and looking like a...streetwalker)*, griping and whining her usual complaints—her lack of this or that, her distant husband *(who she made distant)*, and life's generally unfair treatment of her—the usual complaints. *And after she dumped all that, she didn't ask me even that first question about her mother's health or about her at all! And I couldn't just let that pass...like usual.* He was tired, he was sick...and last night he was angered, angered to his very core over his daughter's absolutely uncaring, selfish attitude.

When did it all happen? She could be that way to me, to others...but to her mother? He knew his daughter to be self-centered (*She's an only child*), and he thought she was often too demanding and demeaning in her treatment of her husband (*They'll work it out—not my business*), but he always had believed she would come through when those rough times arrived, if they were ever to come. *Well, the rough times are here, and Thelma doesn't give a damn about her mother...or me.* He could no longer pretend and hope. *Thelma's heart's dark, unrepentant, evil.* She would be of no help when he was beyond his ability to care for his wife—and he knew that time was coming. He had coughed up blood this morning and had felt the painful lumps growing in his thighs and armpits. Soon, he knew, he would no longer be able to abide even his shirts and pants touching him, rubbing against him there. *And soon I'll be shitting and puking all over myself.*

I don't even know if I'll be able to talk to Jimmy for much longer…or with Billy Ray when he calls again. The face of his son-in-law came to him, and Homer remembered his daughter's passion-perfumed smell last night; she had been too drunk or perhaps too uncaring to wash up, freshen up, before she had driven home to her own bed. And Homer wasn't dumb; he knew the world. More doleful feelings roiled his guts, rising to tighten his throat, feelings for Billy Ray. *But Zula's dying. Please, Lord.*

"Homer? You OK?" Jimmy asked. Homer had zoned out on him, still holding out that envelope and looking as if he had more instructions to impart.

"Oh, yeah, sorry," he croaked. He coughed and refocused on the boy. "Now take this to Gus, please, and come on back. Meantime I'll see if I can find something for breakfast, and we can eat and talk some more. OK?"

Jimmy smiled and quipped, "Yeah, sure, and you're the guy who has yet to boil an egg. Hah!"

Homer absently nodded his reply and opened the screen door to go back inside the house.

***

Down at the mailbox, Jimmy waited for Gus and threw rocks at fence posts. A full hour dragged by before he finally heard the roar of the Mayfield truck as it climbed the hill beyond Fred's place. Gus would first pick up Fred's milk cans, Jimmy knew, and then he'd drive on to their cans. But this time the truck didn't halt at Fred's; it slowed, but it didn't stop. *Fred must be late getting his milk out.* The boy made a mental note that he would tell Homer, and maybe the two of them would walk over to the Rogers's house after breakfast.

Now the big yellow truck was slowing for him, its brakes screeching like always, and Gus was looking down at him from his high seat.
Wait! That's not Gus! The driver was a younger fellow, sporting a mus-
tache and wearing a long tie and a white shirt, a dress shirt. *He's not
even wearing a uniform.*

"Where's the milk can, sonny?" the stranger yelled from across
the truck, through the open door. The truck's front doors had been
slid back inside their paneled sides.

Jimmy stepped up into the passenger-side doorway, pulling himself up with the chain stretched across the opening. He held out the
big envelope for the driver to take. "Don't have any," he answered.
"We're letting the cows go dry now. We'll let Mayfield know when
we're ready to start milking again."

"Start milking again?" the driver sneered more than asked. "Let
me guess. You got old farts here, and they're dying on you. That
what's happening, kid?" The driver had turned away from Jimmy
and was looking up the hill toward the house.

Jimmy felt the warning bells go off—and he noticed stuff, all
kinds of stuff, that the driver had wedged back in the walkway that
led to the refrigerated part of the truck: a couple of chain saws, a
webbed lawn chair, a shotgun stock, and the back end of a bicycle,
all obviously intended to be hidden from sight with a ratty old army
blanket thrown over it. "No, no sir," the boy replied. "That's not it
at all. We're doing fine. And Billy Ray's home again, and my folks…
We're all doing fine. Thanks for asking. So where's Gus today?"

"Well, ol' Gus ain't doin' fine. He's in the hospital in Knoxville—
Fort Sanders—and might be dead already by now. He's got this stuff
that's goin' around, see, and drove his truck right into the emergency room yesterday. Caused a whole shit-pot load of trouble for
the company and all. Are you sure that, ah, Mr. Clark's OK, kid?"

The driver looked like he might be somebody important, like
maybe a manager at the milk company, but still Jimmy felt the man
was showing entirely too much interest in their circumstances. "Yeah,
he's fine. They're all fine." He pointed past the driver. "See? Here

comes Thelma now, probably going to work." The Corvette scattered rocks as it came on, speeding dangerously down the long driveway.

"Hey, Thelma!" Jimmy yelled, and waved as the car reached the intersection and almost slid sideways onto the paved road, bouncing rocks their way, some actually dinging off the truck's tires and rims.

"Hey! Watch it lady!" the driver yelled, pulling his feet back into the truck. He had turned in his seat, preparing to drop to the road and probably intending on walking up to the house—until Thelma came rocketing down. She gave him a middle-finger salute over the top of her car and proceeded to speed away, disappearing in seconds around the bend in the road ahead.

"Crazy bitch!" the driver spat, returning her gesture to the empty air.

Jimmy was still hanging on the door chain, leaning back so he could watch her go. "I bet she and Billy Ray are having a fight or something," he explained, speaking loud to make sure he had the man's attention. "See, Billy Ray sometimes gets all mean and nasty, and he's actually pretty dangerous to be around. And see, he's got all these guns and rifles, and well, I just might have to go on over to the Rogers's myself…for now." *That sounded pretty good.*

"That those folks next door?" the man asked, his eyes squinty with sudden interest.

"Ah, no. It's the other Rogers. They live farther down the road toward White School." *Dang! I forgot he's probably got a route book or something with names in it.* "You know him, I bet. Deputy Rogers? You know him?"

The driver scratched at his dark-stubbled chin. It was evident he hadn't shaved today, tie or no tie. "Really? No, I ain't ever heard of him. I was just going to say that the folks next door look like they've left—gone away—in a hurry. Their front door's standing wide open, and their garage doors are open. No car inside. They didn't put out no milk cans for me neither." The driver was again studying Jimmy. "Reckon they're letting their cows go dry too, kid?"

Jimmy shrugged. That was all he could think to do.

"Yeah?" the driver drawled, his suspicions evident in his tone. "I was thinking maybe I'd go see about them when I saw you standing up here. What do you think?"

"Oh?" Jimmy marveled. "Gosh, Homer was just saying that me and him and Billy Ray and my dad should go over there later on to see them about some stuff but that we should go in full daylight. So I'd be careful about just going in over there, if I were you. See, Fred's got guns, and he hunts and stuff." He figured that since he was lying, he might as well get creative about it. "And you know, he shot an egg-sucking dog the other day...from all the way across the pasture! Ol' Fred's some shot."

"Well, I'm not too bad myself." The man leaned forward and pulled a large revolver from a recess in the dash. "See, kid, it's getting kinda dangerous all over these days, especially out here in the sticks." He glanced back to Jimmy and saw that the boy's eyes had grown to the size of silver dollars; he liked that. "Say, haven't you been out and around in a while? Haven't y'all been watching TV or listening to the radio?"

Jimmy shook his head.

"Shit, kid! All you've got to do is go out there to Chapman Highway, and you'll see what's happening out there. All these old suckers are dying all over the place. Us younger guys are having to take over, having to do their jobs, and bury their asses. Shit, boy, the national guard's been activated, and they're out there with tanks and bulldozers pushing stopped cars off the road right and left! Just getting to the turnoff today was a real pain for me. And some of those cars are filled with dead old farts and..."

The driver's voice trailed off. He was now staring intently into his long rearview mirror. "Say," he asked Jimmy without looking at him, "do you know that car a'coming here?"

The boy leaned back, looked, and allowed that maybe he *did* recognize the big ol' Cadillac now creeping up the road. "I think it's the preacher's car from White Road Church—White Road Independent Church. You know him? Preacher Dilbert Davis?"

"He the one putting out all those handbills on power poles and in mailboxes—about a healing service or something?"

"Probably so. I think so. See, yesterday, Homer and I—"

The driver interrupted. "Kid, there are a lot of guys in that car for it just to be a preacher out sticking his handbills in mailboxes." He ground the truck into first gear. "Gotta go!"

Jumping down from the vehicle, Jimmy barely kept himself from falling forward on his face in the gravel as the man revved his engine and jerked forward. As it was, his momentum still carried him on across the ditch and into the tall Johnson grass, almost clear to the barbed-wire fence. And there he lay, splayed out and listening for the approaching Cadillac. He figured that if the vengeance-seeking Daniel Davis were driving the car, he'd be safer where he was. *Maybe Daniel didn't see me fall out of the truck.*

His wait wasn't long. When the truck sped forward, the Cadillac also roared and accelerated, slowing only momentarily at the mailbox before continuing down the paved road after the now vanished milk truck. Jimmy peeked through the grass, trying to see whether the car's driver was indeed Daniel *(Make that "Reverend Daniel" now)* and whether it was filled with those young thugs Davis called his youth fellowship. *Can't tell—least they ain't slowing for me. I gotta go tell Homer. They got rifles sticking out the windows!*

Jimmy counted to one hundred and one, adding the additional "Mississippi" as he pushed himself up from his hiding place to a kneeling position, to first retie his tennis shoe. *Manure's dried,* he noted. Then: *Bang! Bang! Bang! Bang!* He heard gunshots, the reports echoing back and forth through the knobs and knolls. *Dang! Sounds like World War III.* He stood, impulsively thinking of running to the road and around the curve to see what was going on, but there was no cover there. Then he thought maybe he would crawl through the fence and run across the field, but again he saw that there was little cover remaining in the open field—the grass had been mown short for hay. *Heck! Maybe I'd better go back to the house for now—or maybe go down the hill out beyond the tobacco patch.* He bent again, to tie his other shoe and to count off a few more seconds before dashing back across the road.

What's that? Another car's coming! He heard the low crunch of tires on gravel and the distant ding of pebbles hitting the vehicle's under-carriage. He dropped back to his hiding place just as the Cadillac rounded the curve. *Daniel!*

The engine then quieted, the driver allowing the car to coast—silently, slowly—up to Homer and Zula's driveway…and on past. Parting the tall grass, Jimmy peeked out again. The car's occupants all appeared to be scrutinizing the house and not looking his way. He raised himself above the grass and clearly saw Daniel at the wheel. And he counted three other boys in the car, recognizing them from church and noting they all were carrying rifles—hunting rifles with telescopes and ammunition clips.

The Cadillac coasted on and soon reached Fred's house; it turned up the drive and disappeared from Jimmy's sight. *Probably saw the open door and thought they'd look in to see what they could steal.* Knowing the boys, he doubted any of them was above theft if given the opportunity. "I just hope the milk guy's wrong," he muttered. "Or maybe it's better if Fred and Juanita *are* gone. And I bet maybe it was that milkman and Daniel's guys doing all that shooting back over there. I wonder what's going on?" He really needed to talk to Homer.

Jimmy crept down the low bank, searching both ways up and down the paved road and listening for more engine noises. *Nothing.* He slunk through the weeds to the road then across, running up the driveway to the concrete steps and following the broken-marble walkway up the front lawn and on around the house.

"Jimmy!" Homer called. The boy had run past the boxwood hedge where the old man was waiting for him. Two days before, Jimmy had waited near the same place—to ambush him. But Homer hadn't wanted to frighten the boy; he could see Jimmy was wild eyed already and clearly alarmed about something. But the boy jumped anyway, almost a foot in the air.

"Homer, you like to have given me a heart attack! As it is, I think I've messed myself!" He stopped himself then; he saw only pain in

Homer's face—no humor, no teasing. Everything *had* changed in two days.

"Jimmy, I'm sorry. I thought I'd heard…Let's go find something to eat and then talk."

"OK. Zula? How's Zula doing?"

"Not good. Not good at all. I'll let you talk with her after while. She's asking about you."

***

Homer was seated in one of the yellow plastic-covered chairs at the kitchen table, resting his head on his folded arms. He mumbled to the tabletop, "Jimmy, Jimmy, Jimmy, I don't know where to start."

The boy was standing at the sink, filling a pot with water to boil their eggs and waiting for the old man's words. Hearing Homer begin to talk, he turned off the faucet, leaving his pot in the sink, and pulled out a chair for himself. And again he waited. But sitting there, waiting, he also studied his friend and cousin. In the full morning light, the old man had aged another ten years; his skin was pale and thin. This seemed especially remarkable to Jimmy because Homer was *always* tanned and thick skinned, even in the winter. Working outdoors every day, he'd say, in the sun, rain, wind, whatever—that did that to a man; it darkened and thickened a man's skin. *Fred's like that too. But now Homer looks old and pink! And wrinkled—like he's shrunk in his skin!*

More minutes passed. Jimmy sighed and quietly stood again, returning to the sink for his pan. He moved it to the stove and dropped in the eggs. *Two for me, two for Homer, two for Thelma, and one for Zula.* He still had hope.

"Well, Homer," he broke the silence, turning and leaning against the stove. "I guess I could be telling you all about what I've seen this morning. See, first, the cows are fine, and the chickens are good."

Homer looked up, his eyes red lined and weary. His mouth opened, and he appeared as if he were about to say something, but he shook his head and lowered his face again to his arms. "OK. Anything else?" he asked, his words muffled in his secure place.

"Yeah. Something's happened over at Fred and Juanita's place. Daniel Davis and his hoods are over there now, ripping off everything. Gus is in the hospital with the flu, and I don't trust the new guy who's in his place—I think he's checking us out to rob us—and Daniel's doing the same. There was a gun battle over toward Chapman Highway a little while ago, and Daniel and the milkman may have been at it. The milkman showed me his big ol' revolver and said that people were shooting at each other all over the place and that old folks were dying all over the place and that younger folks are taking over…all over the place. And the national guard's been called up…but you know that already." Jimmy turned back to the stove to check on the state of his boiling water.

Homer lifted his head and straightened in his chair, a slow smile coming to his eyes and mouth. He cocked his head, nodded, and chuckled. *That kid's grown ten years in two days. And he's not about to let me feel sorry for myself neither.* "Anything else?"

"Yeah, and this is important! You know those ol' mules? Well, I don't think they've been trying to kill me all these years after all. I think they've just been having a good time with me."

With that information Homer managed another smile. He rubbed the scar over his nose. "I don't believe I'd be thinking those critters are your good buddies now, Jimmy. Just don't get too close to them. Anything more?"

"Yeah. Homer, I read the encyclopedia you left out for me. I read all about the bubonic plague."

"Yeah?"

"Well, something *is* going around, and from what you said about Nick and the fellows that are with him, well, maybe they've got it, and maybe they don't."

"Jimmy, are you…are you thinking Zula's gonna make it? Be healed?"

"Well, Homer, I've prayed, and I can't believe God would allow—"

"Son, did you read the other book I left there, the Bible?" He was tired and heartsick, but he needed to do this. *God, please use me,* he prayed. "Maybe Romans nine, where I marked it? Or do you remember reading about Job, maybe about God's answer to Job in the last chapters of Job?"

"Well, yeah, Homer, but God is good and will protect us...when we call on his name." Jimmy was desperately trying to remember those verses, the good verses, the comforting verses: "'Now I lay me down to sleep...' No, no, that's not the one. Maybe, maybe..."

Homer softly chuckled at the boy's efforts. "Jimmy, read those sections again when you can. Remember that verse in Romans? 'Therefore God has mercy on whom he wants to have mercy, and he hardens whom he wants to harden.' See, God's the potter...and we're the clay that's being talked about. We may understand his purposes someday—when we're joined to him in heaven—or he may give us insight now; it's his choice. But we just have to trust him now, and that's called faith. And that's a good part of what's called love too, Jimmy. Read it again, OK?"

"OK, I will."

"But do you know what I really, really worry about, son?"

The boy shook his head, turning around to give Homer his full attention.

"That those eggs are going to be hardboiled and the toast stone cold. What say we eat now, and do some planning afterward?" *I am feeling better,* he thought.

***

Ten minutes later Homer slid his plate back; he'd been able to eat only one of his eggs, fearful that he would start to vomit again if he put too much in his stomach. And he *had* to be able to talk with the boy—now.

"So do you want to know what I really worry about?" he asked.

Jimmy nodded, wiping his mouth. He had finished up Zula's egg too; Homer had told him she wasn't the least bit hungry.

"Son," the old man began, "there's no use beating around the bush. I think you know what I'm about to tell you—no, no, no. Please. Just listen now. Please!"

No! Jimmy had gathered himself, ready to stand and perhaps run from the table. He *did* know what Homer was about to say and didn't want to hear it. *No!* But he didn't run; he stayed, allowing the old man's restraining hand to rest on his arm, keeping him there to know what he already knew. *And you really do, don't you, Jimbo? Homer's really sick, too, isn't he? But if I don't think about it, I won't have to worry.*

"You've got to think about it, Jimmy," Homer insisted, guessing the boy's thoughts. "See, I realize now that I soon won't be able to talk to either you or God. And I've…*we've* seen what this disease is doing, and I can feel it in me now. It's just a matter of time, hours maybe. And you've got to listen and harden *yourself,* boy. Understand?"

Jimmy dropped his eyes to the table as Homer continued. "First, soon I'm not going to be the least bit interested in talking with you and, I suspect, with God—that is, talking in any meaningful way. I'll be hurting, maybe hurting too much to move, talk, think. Remember those pills we got from Cline? Yeah? Well, they aren't working too good for me anymore, and not at all for Zula. And I've watched her and…she's about past the point of caring for anything; she just wants it all over. Understand?"

"But Homer…"

"No, no, let me finish. See? I'm not afraid—not afraid of dying. I'm just praying for God to give me that final moment of inspiration, of understanding, before he takes me over to the real side of eternity, to join with him there, as he's now here with me, in me, using me. Understand?" He waited until Jimmy nodded back. *He's listening.* "See, we've both accepted the Lord, and he sees us as acceptable—his sons forever—regardless. That brings me comfort and strength and will give you comfort and strength too in the days ahead." *But Lord, I pray this boy won't need such comfort in the days ahead.*

Homer saw that Jimmy was now staring back at him, watching him through teary eyes. He saw the boy was having to absorb and accept this reality in little bits and pieces—and there just wasn't enough time. *He's hearing but not perceiving. Lord. He'll need your guidance in any case. I'll need your guidance. Please.* He bowed his head, and for a long, long minute, the man and the boy sat together at the table—both silent—one's hand on the other's arm, both willing assurance, strength, comfort, and love for the other.

Then Homer broke the spell. "Amen. OK, boy, you've heard the worst. That's enough for now. Blow your nose, and let's do some planning and cogitating." He patted Jimmy's arm and pushed his chair back from the table.

"First thing: We need to get you home—to Maryville. I talked with Thelma about running you over, but well, she had to go to work to get her check and...well, you know Thelma...always busy." *And self-centered, arrogant, lazy—you know it all, Lord.* "So I tried calling your folks when you were down waiting for Gus. The phone lines are really bad, and we're on a party line, but by the grace of God, I got through for a few minutes and talked with your dad. And Albert said he'd been trying to come up to get you for a couple of days now"— that news tightened Jimmy's lips—"but he said your mother was having a tough time getting away from the hospital. He said Olivia was working almost all the time now. Anyway, he was saying that he was coming to get you, but well, we got cut off then. I didn't hear when he planned to come, but he's coming—or I'm taking you home." He leaned over and patted Jimmy's forearm again. "So what say we try to call him again later...like this afternoon when you're here with me?"

Jimmy nodded but didn't say anything. He couldn't trust himself to say anything right now. With the mention of his parents, those old homesick feelings had returned, rushing in, filling him up, mixing with those other feelings; he was afraid to even open his mouth. *Homer needs me to be strong.* But he still felt like he was going to drown; he couldn't breathe.

"Jimmy? You look like you're choking. Here, drink the rest of your water." *The boy's taking this all real hard—I guess I would too if I was fourteen.* Homer decided then that he would tell him at a later time the other parts of his conversation with Albert, the parts he'd heard before they were disconnected, about things in Maryville "going to hell in a handbag." The hospital was flooded with the dead and dying, mostly elderly folks, and violence was everywhere in the town, even there in the hospital. A doctor had been shot and killed because he had refused to admit someone. Young hoodlums had forced their way into the pharmacy and loaded up their sacks with drugs and narcotics. And all *that* had happened right across the street from the police headquarters! The cops were overwhelmed and virtually unable to answer all the calls for help—and that's assuming that all the phone calls were even getting through to them. Gangs of men were forming and were forcing their way into people's houses all over the town. That was one of the reasons Albert actually was encouraging Olivia to stay at the hospital; he was worried about her. In fact a couple guys had come to their door just this morning, wanting to come in, and Albert said he had to show them his shotgun to run them off. "Homer," Albert had said right before being disconnected, "what if I didn't have that gun? Would I still be alive?" *I need to make sure Jimmy and I talk about his protection too. And what he may be facing.*

Homer took a sip from his own water glass. "Jimmy, let me ask you again about what you've read."

"From the Bible?"

"No, about the disease. Did you read anything about how the plague affected the generations and about whether it affected the older people first before it got to the younger folks?"

Jimmy shook his head. "No, nothing from what I read. I guess it was pretty even: old, young, men, women. I think it said the bubonic plague just wiped out whole families, right there in their homes. Maybe they didn't even have hospitals back then."

Homer pulled out his handkerchief and coughed in it, glancing in and then folding it over. He cleared his throat. "I was just asking. The ol' flu that went around when I was young seemed to have actually affected the younger folks worse, hit them harder, harder than the older folks. I was just wondering if maybe this stuff was the opposite, seeing as how we haven't heard of a young person getting it. But then I've had the radio on, and some guy, maybe from the CDC, was saying younger people *were* getting it—not real young,

Jimmy, just relatively younger—and it makes sense, you know. I'm a little younger than Zula. You know how I kid her? Well, it's true. And she got sick first."

"Homer, Zula might just have the flu...and you too!"

"Jimmy, listen. Believe me, please. There'll be time...Just go along with me now. Please."

Jimmy nodded, looking down at his hands folded before him on the table. He had heard the frustration edging into Homer's voice. "OK, sorry."

"OK. For now just keep in mind that there might be an age-pro-gression aspect with this plague. Just keep that in mind, and God willing, it will mutate like the Spanish flu did and be less harmful as the succeeding generations are affected." He bent forward slightly to see whether the boy was still listening. He was.

"Now, Jimmy, I'm not saying this to make you think I'm comfort-ing you or anything. Maybe tomorrow the children will start catching this stuff, but I don't think so. I'm telling you this because I want you to know that there are other differences between generations—morality differences. From your age, looking forward, you can't see those differences, but from my view, I can see them. I can see the World War One generation as being more—well, not exactly more patriotic but more accepting of social situations, accepting of things bigger than themselves, or maybe just being less self-concerned. Maybe it has to do with our proximity to the Great Awakening reviv-als that spread across the nation in the prior century because they did have big effects in our history. You read history much, Jimmy?"

Jimmy shook his head.

"Pity," Homer said. "A pity but typical. History seems to be more interesting as we create our own, I guess. Anyway, getting to the point, I'm talking about our acceptance of death, of eternity. The older folks from the World War One generation seem to me to go down easier, more accepting of the eventual nature of death, than does, say, the World War II generation. And to them, they seem more accepting than the fifties generation...and so on. Maybe that's a result of parents wanting to make things better for their kids, or maybe that's a result of the development of mass communications and social control, or maybe it's a result of people moving away from God—kind of like the ol' Israelites or something. *Self* is a word that's used much more today than when I was a kid. Good? Bad? No difference? Jimmy, the only reason I'm telling you about my suppositions is that I think things are going to get worse around here before they get better. I'm saying that the philosophical 'Nick Clark' types of the world are apt to accept their fates, this fate, more easily than, say, the younger generations." He had wanted to say the "Thelma" types, but he didn't want to prejudice the boy. *But maybe he should be...warned?*

"So Jimmy, basically I'm saying that people are meaner now than you may believe...and they may be getting meaner in the future. Some people can accept bad circumstances in their own lives, but some may not want to suffer *alone*. You understand what I mean? You've known people like that already I bet, even as young as you are. It's a human trait, and as I'm seeing, as people become quicker to put themselves first, they're quicker to judge everything in relative measures, with themselves in the center of it all. It might come down to people feeling that it's not so much them being sick, but them wanting you to be as sick or sicker than they are. Know what I mean, boy?"

Jimmy shook his head. "Are you saying that...people might be getting meaner if more people get sick?"

Homer nodded. "Yeah, yeah...that's a start."

"Maybe like Daniel Davis and his being hateful toward others—others who may have something he doesn't have?"

"Yeah, I've noticed that too. That young Davis is quick to put himself first. I'd expect he'd be someone to watch out for, Jimmy." *Maybe someone special to look out for.* Earlier this morning, when Thelma had come down the steps for coffee, she had told him she was going to hire Daniel and his father, Dilbert Davis, to come to the house to try out their special healing service on Zula. "By the way, did you see Thelma leave when you were waiting for Gus?"

"Um, yes."

"Well, I might have been the cause of that. I, uh, told her I didn't want her bringing Daniel up here, and I might have called him and his father a pair of Pharisees or something like that. Now I'm not doubting their salvation or anything, but I swear, Jimmy, I see more of Jesus in you than in the both of them. They both have a way of finding the verses that suit themselves while ignoring the inconvenient ones and...I'm sorry. I've gotten off the subject." Homer puffed once and willed his blood pressure to drop. "Let's just let the Lord deal with Christians like that, and let's talk about Billy Ray... and Thelma."

"Billy Ray and Thelma? Homer, they aren't sick or anything, are they?" Jimmy stopped fiddling with his fingers and straightened in his chair, searching Homer's eyes.

"No, no. Fact is, I expect that Billy Ray's on his way home now and should be calling sometime today. And Thelma, well, I was going to tell you that Thelma can take care of herself. See, if...when I get so that I can't take care of myself, I don't want you to be around here. So that's why...Never mind. Just know that Thelma will take care of me, and you just look after your folks—no, no, they're not sick. Sit back down." Jimmy was half standing. "I'm just telling you about your priorities and that looking after yourself and your folks isn't the selfish thing I was talking about before. This is a time for self-responsibility—not like living a self-centered, selfish life all the time. Understand the difference?"

Jimmy nodded, saying "I think so" and sitting back down.

"Another thing..." Homer continued but abruptly halted mid-sentence, holding up his hand. He urgently dug for his handkerchief, pulling it from his back pocket and coughing loudly, painfully into it, then briefly glimpsing the sputum caught there before he refolded it and returned it to his pocket. He took another sip from his water glass and resumed. "Another thing, a second thing: See, I'm telling you people might get a little crazy before this is all over, and you need to be able to protect yourself. See? Sheriff Noland may or may not be able to keep the peace, but I'm betting he'll be looking for all the help he can get. And you know, the sheriff isn't much younger than me, so he might be fighting his own battles right now. Anyway, I know Billy Ray has let you shoot every gun we have here and…Do you know where ammunition is kept in the house, Jimmy?"

Jimmy was still thinking about the red he had seen in Homer's handkerchief. "What? Ammunition? You want to know if I know where the bullets are kept?"

"Yeah."

Homer was sounding a bit exasperated again to Jimmy, and he wondered whether that was because the old man was beginning to feel worse or was thinking there wasn't much time. He resolved to listen better. "Yes. You've got twelve-gauge shells under the truck's seat and part of a box on the back floorboard of the car, and there's twenty-two shells in that drawer over there." He pointed to the junk drawer next to the refrigerator. "And Billy Ray has shells for his guns in his gun safe in their bedroom. That right?"

"Yeah, that's right." Homer nodded. "Now you remember yesterday, when I…ah…shot back at that guard at the clinic?"

"Yeah, and you got him too!"

"Well, I guess I did. And I hope the young man was able to get help for himself because, well, hurting another human being is never good. There'll be times when people just got to protect themselves, you understand, and I believe the good Lord provides for that, but it would have been better if we'd been able to have avoided doing what I did. But that's past, and God has forgiven me of my sins, and if that was one, it was included—I sure felt sorry for it. Now Sheriff Noland may have other thoughts, so Jimmy, I've written out what I did and why. That letter is stamped and is out on the writing table. Would you put it in the mailbox when you go down that way again?" He unconsciously felt for his watch in the bib pocket of his overalls.

The boy noticed the familiar gesture. "Want to know the time," he asked, reaching for the little gold chain dangling from the watch pocket in his own pants, "for the postman to be getting here?"

Homer nodded. "Yeah. Did you wind it this morning?"

"Before daylight. See?" Jimmy held the pocket watch open so the old man could see its hands.

"Good. Thanks. Now, finally, let's talk about people in general. I told you to watch for changes in people if they catch this stuff. People are funny...even Fred and Juanita, and Bill and Judy Shanks. By the way, when you take the mail down, would you mind walking over to Fred's place and checking things over? About what the milkman said? And be real careful—go through the woods. Be real careful with all strangers from now on. OK? Your dad said something about people breaking and entering—well, you know about that already—enough said. Now I expect that Bill and Judy are on their way to Florida, so we should plan to, ah, drive over to check on their place too."

Jimmy didn't remember hearing anything about anybody "breaking and entering," but he did notice that Homer looked a bit pained when he said "drive." *Maybe just driving the old truck hurts him,* Jimmy considered. *Maybe Homer would be better off if he were to switch to the old Plymouth. It's ancient, but it's also an automatic. Shoot, even I can drive that car.* And there had been a few times in the past when Jimmy had done just that. For example, when he had visited earlier, back in the spring, Homer and Zula had gone away for the day to attend a funeral and had driven over to Ashville, leaving him and Wayne, an older cousin, in charge of the house. And they had left the keys to the Plymouth dangling on a coat hook in the hallway. So that early afternoon, Wayne, the holder of a learner's permit, had shown Jimmy how to operate the car, and they had spent the rest of the day visiting Wayne's girlfriends in the community—there were a lot of them—and giving them rides in the backseat with Jimmy driving, seated high on two catalogs. *Wayne's a great guy. I wonder how he's doing?*

"Are you listening, Jimmy?"

The boy realized then that Homer was still talking and was now staring at him. "Yeah, Homer, yeah. You were talking about food." Jimmy had caught Homer's last couple of words.

"OK, good. I'm just glad you already can cook some things. By the way, you fixed good eggs, but I could only eat one. Thanks."

"You're welcome. Those over there are for Thelma." He pointed at the two boiled eggs he had left on the counter in a small bowl. "I'll see if she wants your other egg too."

"Well, I'm sure she'll appreciate that." *Not likely.* "Wait…I think I hear Zula. We'll talk more later." Homer was standing, again pulling his handkerchief from his back pocket as he rose. He coughed repeatedly into the cloth—deep, violent coughs. "Whew! Almost lost a lung with that one, Jimmy."

"Homer, didn't you say Zula was asking about me? Can I go with you this time? May I go up with you this time? Mom's taught me about being around sick people, you know."

Homer had partially turned and was refolding his handkerchief away from the boy's view. "Ah, maybe." *Why not? You don't have much time left. You're about to vomit yourself, and those ol' pills aren't doing a thing with this ol' headache.* "Yeah, yeah, I guess. I guess you'll just be seeing what's happening out in the world now."

Dang! Jimmy wasn't so sure he wanted to see Zula now. But he fell in behind Homer, climbing slowly up the stairs to the landing then on up the second set of stairs to the bedroom at the top. There was a small nightlight burning there, just enough light to see the door's frame and its knob. Homer gripped it and slowly, quietly drew back the latch, then cracked the opening wide enough to peek in.

"I wanted to make sure she was decent," he explained. "Come on in." Homer swung the door wide.

Instantly Jimmy was engulfed with a smell he'd never known before. He had helped clean out septic tanks, had washed up after slaughtering hogs, and had mucked out stables, but this smell was more than those, or maybe a part of all those, all those fetid odors. He couldn't go any farther.

"Breathe through your mouth, Jimmy, your mouth. Don't breathe through your nose—just your mouth," Homer advised. "And Jimmy, this is still Zula so…" He didn't know what else he could say. He just didn't want the boy to reject her, and for her to know it.

Jimmy surprised himself and managed a thin smile, drawing from an inner resource he hadn't known himself to possess. "Yeah, I know, Homer. This is the way things are. Open the door wider so I can see. Got a light you can turn on?"

"Yeah, over here." Homer went forward and fumbled with a small lamp on the doily-covered round table in the corner. It looked like it was supposed to be an old-fashioned kerosene lamp except with pink flowers and green leaves painted on its chimney. "Zula seems to be bothered by the light, so I've just been using the flashlight and this here lamp. There. Can you see her OK now?"

Jimmy tiptoed around the foot of the bed and along the far side, between the bed and the wall. Zula was lying on that side of the bed with only the top of her head visible against the white of the pillow.

"Zula," he whispered. "Zula, it's me, Jimmy. Are you awake?"

"Jimmy?" she softly rasped from beneath the sheet. "Jimmy, are you here? Where's Homer?"

"Right here, darlin'," Homer answered from the other side of the bed. He was slowly pulling down the top sheet. "Baby, Jimmy wanted to say hello to you. Let me ease down the sheet a little bit more."

Jimmy noticed the wet, dark marks here and there on the sheet. He'd supposed the boils that he had read about, the buboes, had been suppurating, and the spots were from the water or pus that had seeped through. *Dang! I guess hope is really gone, left at the door, but Homer told me—he tried to tell me.* He now wondered whether he had ever really doubted that Zula—and Homer—had been infected with the disease, this plague. He must have shut down that part of his mind, telling himself over and over that everything was going to be OK, but deep down he knew different. *Lord, have I lost my faith?* He knew now that nothing was ever again going to be safe, quiet, the same as it had been.

Homer pulled down the sheet a little more, exposing Zula's face. He watched Jimmy, not Zula.

Whoa! Her nose is black! Jimmy took another deep breath, through his mouth. He hoped he was keeping the alarm he felt from showing in his face or, at least, was keeping his face in the shadows. "Zula, it's Jimmy." He lightly touched the sheet, feeling for her arm and her hand.

"Careful, Jimmy," Homer cautioned. "Her skin is really sensitive, and her joints ache terribly. Her fingers are also—well, be real tender with them. And watch your step over there. I might have forgotten to pick up her bucket from that side of the bed, and there might be some poop there. You know, we clean up every so often but…"

The boy looked up and smiled, "Homer, we still call it BM—bowel movement—at my house. You know—my mother? The nurse? And no, there's not a bucket over here. We're good."

Jimmy looked back to Zula and lifted the side of the cloth where he believed her hand to be. *Oh! Her fingers are black too—necrosis, Black Death. Like it said in the encyclopedia.* He slowly, carefully slipped his hand beneath her dark digits. "Does that hurt, Zula?"

She softly moaned but shook her head. "No," she whispered. "But Jimmy, I'm a mess. I'd like to fix you something to eat, but—"

"Zula, you've spent your lifetime waiting on others. It's your turn to be waited on."

The boy continued to hold the old woman's hand for many minutes, warming it with his own, until her eyes again closed. Then he carefully returned her hand to the bed and covered it with the sheet. "Good-bye, Zula, I love you," he whispered. Sniffing back his tears, he stepped sideways, back to the foot of the bed, where Homer stood, his old, white-haired head bowed as if in prayer. "Homer, is there anything I can do here? Maybe take a pail out? Maybe help you change the sheets?"

"No, no, she's resting now, and it's best if we leave her alone for a while. She hasn't had a…BM for a while and isn't throwing up now—probably nothing left to throw up—so just let me sit with her for a while. Maybe I can get some fluids down her. And maybe I should set myself down for a while anyway." Homer looked longingly at the recliner beside the round table. "Thelma should be back soon and…" He sighed heavily. "…I'll ask her again to run you over to

Maryville. OK? And Jimmy, thanks. I know this can't be pleasant for you."

"Naw, it's not hard on me at all. You know, mother, nurse…You probably wouldn't enjoy supper conversations at my house at all." Jimmy was smiling, but he was also lying. His mother never talked about her work at meals, and *he* was very close to throwing up. "Suppose I just go on downstairs and…Hey! I hear a car coming up the driveway. Sounds like Thelma." He crept to bedroom door and on out.

Homer followed, stopping at the landing as he descended the stairs. "I'll wait for her here," he said.

"OK, Homer. I'll tell her you're waiting, and then I'll go on out to the garden. Maybe I'll bring in a cabbage or two and see if there are any tomatoes left." He hopped from the bottom step and turned to the right to go out the back door through the TV room. Thelma was just coming in that way, throwing her purse onto the couch and her keys onto the writing table.

She lingered at the table and looked up when Jimmy came through the door. "What's all this shit?" she asked, pointing at the envelope and the bookmarked Bible.

"It's a Bible," Jimmy replied.

"Don't give me that crap. I know it's a Bible! What's it doing out here, and what's that letter for?" she harshly demanded.

"It's a letter to the sheriff about what we saw yesterday. Your dad asked me to put it in the mailbox when I have the chance." Jimmy absently drew Homer's watch from his pocket and checked the time. "I expect the mailman should be coming along any time now, and Homer said to tell you he's waiting up there to talk with you." Jimmy inclined his head in the direction of the stairs—and saw Thelma was looking hard at the watch in his hand. *Oh, gosh! Here it comes now!* He wished he had kept the watch in his pocket.

But she said nothing at all about the pocket watch, her eyes flicking up from his hand to his eyes, asking instead in a sweet lilting tone, "Oh, Dad's still up?" At his nod she dispatched him, saying, "Well hurry on, my boy. Hurry on. The mailman cometh. Oh, and

Jimmy darling, would you mind terribly sweeping off the front porch all the way around on your way down to the mailbox? I've noticed that lots of leaves and dust have accumulated out there. And please wait for the mail. I'm expecting something. OK? And thank you so very much."

Wow! Thelma must be... "Ah, sure, not a problem at all. I've left the broom there in the corner from the last time I swept the porch, so I'll go do it right now. And then I'll check the garden to see about any veggies for supper. OK?

"Sure, sweetie. Why, here comes Dad now. Hurry on."

The door was closing behind Jimmy when he heard Homer's heavy tread, stepping down to the bottom step. Thelma sat down at the table and pulled the Bible closer, as if she were reading it. Homer rounded the corner, and she looked up. "Hey, Dad, how's Mother doing now?" She took note of the pinkish hue of his skin and the obvious energy-draining effects of his minor exertion in just now descending the stairs and walking to the room; he was out of breath and looking for a place to sit down. And she noted that he had traces of blood around his mouth and nose.

Homer stopped just inside the room. *She sure sounds different from when she left earlier today.* "Hello, Thelma. Your mother's not doing well at all. I don't think that...that she's gonna get better for a while—a long while. She's very, very sick." Homer sank heavily onto the couch.

Thelma shook her head. "That's what I've wanted to talk with you about, Dad. I've been so *horrible* about Mother. It's just that, well, I've never hardly been around sickness before—you know that. The smell and the *stuff* is just terrible; I wasn't prepared to deal with it. It frightened me. Now I've talked to a few people and I think I have a better understanding about all that now. And it's just terrible! Why, it's affecting *all* the older people! They're dying all over the place! So many of my elderly bookings have called in to cancel. Imagine! And I was so afraid it was going to get to you too. Can you ever forgive me?" She lowered her face to her hands and covered her eyes with her fingers, softly sobbing in jerky breaths.

Homer reconsidered his earlier thoughts, as his distraught daughter, having gone already to the Bible for verses of comfort, was crying before him as if her heart were breaking—*a repentant heart.* He closed his eyes and took a big breath. "Honey, I'm sorry I was short with you. You're my daughter. I love you, and I'm sorry I doubted you. I, ah, knew you'd be here if the times got rough."

"Dad, I'm always here for you...and Mother," she sniffed. "Just show me what you need me to do...to keep things going around here. Cleaning and changing Mother, cooking supper, anything. They're closing the shop for half days now, so I'll be here to pitch in more. Just tell me what you need done."

"Well, I'd told Jimmy I'd get him back with his folks tomorrow in Maryville. Would you do that for me, run him over there? I know you said—"

"I'm sorry for what I said. Of course, Dad. I'll do it tomorrow afternoon. How's that? And I can run more errands you need then too. They've pretty well cleared the road to Knoxville, and I know the back roads to Sevierville. Need me to pick up anything, stop by the pharmacy or the bank or the post office? Maybe help you with the bills and everything?"

"Maybe so. The bank might not be passing my checks anymore since my hands are so shaky now. I can hardly manage to write my name."

But I can manage it just fine, Thelma thought. She had stilled her sobs and was now watching the old man from over her hands—hands that hid her slight, slight smile.

"And I need to tell you something else, so listen to what I say. See, yes, I've caught this stuff too, this plague stuff you've heard about, along with your mother. Now don't be alarmed again—I can see it in your eyes—just listen to me. We've got enough food and resources around here that you and Billy Ray can stay away—stay separate from all this sickness until things get better. Now I don't know if your mother and me...See, Thelma, I heard on the radio that the CDC is saying the plague is a resurgence of the bubonic plague, like from the Middle Ages. Now that went away, and I expect this will too.

But it killed a lot of people first. So you and Billy Ray can stay holed up, and most likely you'll come out fine. OK? But don't expect the same for your mother or me. Fact is, you mother might not last out the night. And me? I'm bleeding from my nose and have thrown up blood already. And I got these swollen glands here…" He pointed to the inside of his upper legs. "…and they're sore as heck. Fever, chills, you name it. Now I'm out of those pain pills from ol' Cline, and…I think I just might have to go lay down right now. Would you get me the bucket, honey? Right there on the stairs. And please hurry!"

Thelma was up in a flash, dry eyed and willing. She found the stainless-steel bucket on the third step and returned quickly to Homer, to hold it under his bowed head. *Just in time. I'd hate to have to mop that shit off the floor. I'd get Jimmy to do that for sure. Gaaa! I think it's all blood! It's splashing!* "Dad, are you OK? Want to sit a moment longer? Yes?"

Homer, still hugging the metal bucket, looked up with bleary eyes. "Yeah, yeah, I'll just sit here a minute more. I think that's all. I'm so sorry…"

"Dad, Dad, you don't need to be apologizing to me. I heard that's what a lot of the afflicted do—throw up and stuff. *And they have pink skin, blood coming out, boils, seizures.* You haven't been having seizures, have you?"

"Is that…is that something they say happens to people…who catch this plague?" Homer now wondered with whom she had talked.

"Um, just what I've heard on the radio. You know, the DCD or whoever you said, the disease people talking on the radio. And work—maybe some of the girls were talking about it. Why?" *You guessing I've been talking with some guy, old man? Well, you'd be right. Daniel Davis, as a matter of fact. And it's happening just like he said.*

Homer was slow to respond, appearing ready to use the bucket again. But the moment passed, ending with his sigh. "Oh, I was just wondering. I marked the encyclopedia for Jimmy to read about it… but you've never been much interested in those books." He nodded toward the bookcase. "If you want me to show you where more is written about it, the plague, hand me the D volume over there."

"Maybe later, Dad. But right now let's get you off your feet. Here, let me help you up. You maybe should stay in the bedroom on the ground floor on the other side of the stairs. You don't need to be climbing any more stairs today, and it's closer for me to watch you."

He started to protest. "But Zula..."

"No, no, no. I'll take care of Mother the rest of the day too. It's getting near late afternoon, and she should sleep for a while. Right? Now come with me." Thelma took Homer's hand and helped him to his feet. Then she led him around the corner to the tiny bedroom beyond the staircase.

She flipped on the room's overhead light, and Homer grimaced, closing his eyes and shading them with his hand. He was finding that bright lights were now beginning to bother him too.

"See, Dad, Mother already made up this bed for tourists, so this will be real nice for you. And it's so close to the bathroom through the kitchen; it should be real nice for you while you rest here. OK?"

Homer already had eased himself onto the bed, giving out with another sigh. "Yeah, this will be nice for a while. About Zula..." He didn't finish; he was already asleep.

Thelma watched him for a minute then removed his shoes and slid his legs around to fully rest on the bed. "Now I'll go check on Mother," she whispered. When Homer didn't answer, she pushed the bloody pail close to the bed where he could easily find it, turned on the bedside lamp as she turned off the overhead light at the wall switch, and left the bedroom, softly closing the door behind her. Then she strolled back to the TV room, pulling a candy bar from her uniform's apron pocket as she went. *I wonder if I can get channel six on the TV at this time of day.*

***

Jimmy trudged through the gap in the garden fence, carrying a couple of small cabbages, four fair-size butternut squash, and two overly soft tomatoes. The garden was almost through for the year for most of the vegetables and the greens were still too young to pick. So he had planned a menu in his head that centered around corn bread, boiled cabbage, baked squash, and sliced tomatoes. "Thelma probably will want those eggs too," he said aloud. "Otherwise maybe I can boil some more and devil 'em. Haven't done that in a while."

After he had left Thelma earlier to talk alone with her father, and before he had gone down to the mailbox, he had swept clean the long porch and sidewalk all the way to the concrete steps that led down to the driveway in the front. Then, balancing the broom upright in the palm of his hand, he had walked with starts and stops to the box at the road, to place Homer's letter inside and raise the metal flag that alerted the mail-truck driver to stop. Since he had the broom with him, he also had used the handle to squash the black widow that had taken up residence in the rear half of the mailbox. *Been wanting to do that for a while. The postman will like that. Those things are all over the place around here and can bite you—dangerous, like Daniel.* With that thought, he had looked around and decided he would sit in the tall grass on the far side of the ditch to await the postman. After another forty-five minutes had slowly passed—timed with Homer's pocket watch—he had concluded that the mail service was delayed for the day and that he would come down later, right before dark, to check again for any delivered letters and packages. *Besides, I'm going to pick up ticks, spread out here like this. Thieves may or may not be out cruising these back roads, but these ticks are certain.* Returning to the house, he had rehung the broom on the two nails in the corner of the covered porch and trotted on out to the garden in search of ready vegetables.

"Or maybe goulash? Maybe Zula's got some okra in the freezer, and there's canned tomatoes down in the cellar." He thought about having to lift the heavy cellar door then having to descend into the earthen catacombs below. "Well, maybe there's some canned stuff up in the cupboard." He'd check.

Coming in by the back entrance, he found Thelma stretched out on the sofa and watching a soap opera on TV. "Hey!" he cheerfully greeted her as he unloaded his bounty onto the rope-bottomed chair next to the door. "Hey, look what I got. How about some goulash for supper? I can make it."

"Gaaaa, no! I hate that shit. And shut up, will you? Can't you see I'm watching TV?"

Whoa! What's happened with her? Maybe she and Homer got into it again. "Ah, Thelma?" Jimmy softly asked. "Where's Homer? Back up with Zula?"

"No. He's lying down in there…" She pointed at the wall behind the sofa with her thumb. "…and you don't be bothering him. Got that? If he's got what Zula's got…probably going to die. Just leave him alone. Just go back outside. Do whatever you do 'til dark. Then come in, and you can fix…whatever." Thelma hadn't taken her eyes off the flickering TV screen. "Things around here gonna change," she absently mumbled.

Jimmy continued to stand there, just inside the door, holding a butternut squash and looking pole axed. Sure, he had reconciled himself deep down to the fact that Zula would die and that, most probably, Homer would follow her. But Thelma's distracted, careless attitude had astonished him. *Mean—that's mean! That's what Homer was talking about!*

Thelma noticed the gaping boy still standing there and abruptly sat upright, her face flushed and her hands held out, questioning, "What? *What?* Are you a deaf ass as well as a dumb ass? Drop that stuff and go! Go!" She fluttered the back of one hand at him.

So he fled to the barn, where Elsie was patiently waiting for him in her stable. And for several minutes more, she continued to wait for him, watching him there, as he gripped the rough planks of her stable's hay manger, on his knees, his face pressed to the wood, trying to make some sense of his feelings and—of everything.

"Whew!" he blew, when he had finally reached that place of emptiness, drained of the sad emotions that for the moment had claimed him. "Whew!" He blew again and turned with his back to the manger, his legs spread before him. The old cow took that as an invitation and stepped forward, rasping her long tongue across his face, chin to forehead. "Dang, Elsie! You're taking my skin off." She looked down at him with wise, brown eyes. "You think I'm crying, don't you?" he said. "You concerned about me? You understand all this, huh?" He dodged her next lick. "Enough, enough." *Well, maybe ol' Elsie really ain't so understanding, but at least I feel some better.* Jimmy hadn't actually cried, with streaming tears, big sobs and all, since that time his dog, Bullet, had been run over on the busy highway in front of his house. But this time there had been no holding back; it had all come out. He was lonely; he was mad; he was frightened about what was happening around him—all out of control now—and he was no longer liking very many people. He felt like he was six years old again, and Bullet had just died. *Ah, well.* He heaved a mighty sigh.

Snort! Elsie stepped up again and breathed her sweet, grassy breath in his face, her wet nose almost touching his. He laughed. "Want to be milked, ol' girl? Ready for milking? Get on with life, you say?" The cow was now nosing him to move away from her food. "OK, I'll get out of your way. And I'll talk with Homer later too; you don't pay enough attention."

Jimmy soon finished his milking and fed the other cows as they wandered in, inspecting each one as he poured out her grain, looking for any hurts or sores he'd report to Homer. Then he refilled the hay racks in the stables and headed back to the house, carrying his partially filled bucket.

It was fully dark as he rested his forehead against the screen door, leaning on it to push off one tennis shoe with the toe of the other. He then elbowed open the door, coming inside the house via the enclosed porch. He padded on to the kitchen, where he strained and refrigerated the milk and washed his pail, making everything ready for the next day. Then he walked on through the house, turning on the dining-room light, to the TV room, where Thelma still lay stretched on the sofa.

"Hey!" he greeted her, trying to move past their parting words. "For supper there's some boiled eggs in there…"

"Crap!" she blurted. "You made me miss what they were saying right then! Can't you learn to be quiet when I'm watching my programs?" Thelma wasn't so inclined to reconcile. "Besides, I don't want an old, cold egg or that other dirty shit you drug in—you eat it for *your* supper. I don't want it—makes me sick to think of it. Besides, I brought home my leftovers from lunch." She gestured to the table and a grease-spotted paper bag that Jimmy hadn't noticed before. "Now turn up the sound on the TV, and leave me alone," she ordered.

Since she hadn't offered to share, just continued to gaze fixedly at the TV screen and said nothing more, Jimmy turned up the volume and returned to the kitchen to fix his own supper, to eat the boiled eggs with this morning's milk. *At least we got milk. And eggs.* His vegetables had vanished from the chair and weren't to be found on the kitchen counters or in the refrigerator. *Wonder what she's done with them? Don't think I want to ask neither.*

After washing his glass and plate, Jimmy decided he would find out if Homer was awake, regardless of Thelma's orders. *That'd be OK with him if he's awake.* Turning out the lights, he tiptoed from the kitchen and through the house to the closed door of the small bedroom. With the cranky Thelma just in the next room, he hesitated at the door, fearing that the ancient latch would click loudly and alert the woman. So, for a minute or two, he stood at the door and simply listened. *Nothing, just breathing.* But it was labored, almost moaning breathing. *I gotta see him!* But he would ask Thelma if he could see Homer. *I'll tell her I'm going to bed.* Surely she'd let him see the old man and Zula to bid them good night as he headed to bed.

When he entered the TV room, Thelma swung her feet from the couch to the floor to sit upright. A commercial was on. "So did you eat something for supper?" she asked, her tone neutral.

Jimmy said he did and chanced his question. "Say, I'd like to tell Homer and Zula good night before I go to bed. OK?

"No," she replied, without a second of consideration. "I told you that the old man's sick and needs to sleep and that I'd take care of Zula. Understand? In fact Homer asked me to get you home tomorrow, and that's what I plan on doing. OK? So pack your stuff tonight, and I'll drive you home tomorrow. Understand?"

Standing there, looking down at Thelma, Jimmy was instantly awash in a flood of inconsistent feelings; he was elated to be going home but was suddenly concerned about the care Homer and Zula would receive from their daughter. He wanted desperately to see his mother and father, but since they hadn't called again, he felt a dark foreboding about what he would find there. And he was thinking about the care of the farm's animals; he was certain Thelma wouldn't bother to feed or water any of them. *I could just leave out several sacks of feed for the cows.* But while the mules wouldn't tend to overeat on the grain, he was uncertain what the cows might do. *Might founder—might kill 'em. They could just live on grass for a while, I guess, until I get back, or until Homer gets…*He had to stop then and shake his head. He knew Homer wasn't going to get better. The old man was going to die, and he needed to stop thinking that way—that there was a chance. *There isn't, and the cows can just live on grass until I get back.* Then he thought about the chickens and the fact that they didn't have a ready food source as did the cows. *I'll just have to let them out of their pen right before I leave.* He knew their chances with the area's predators were slight but were still better than if they had to depend on Thelma for feed and water. *Yeah, I'll let them out, but I can't tell Thelma. She might be pissed if the eggs…Wait, didn't she said she hated eggs just a little while ago?*

"Jimmy, you gonna just stand there with your mouth open? You look like a retard or something. If you're going to bed, go! My program's coming on again now. Just get packed." Thelma returned to the flickering screen.

Well, sir, that makes it easier about the chickens. "Ah, yeah, sure," Jimmy answered. "Sorry." Then he had another thought. "Ah, Thelma, reckon we can give my folks a call tonight? To make sure my dad's not coming here too?"

"Can't," she simply answered. "Billy Ray's supposed to call tonight, and I don't want to miss him. Besides, if they'd wanted you home, they'd have come to get you rather than make me to go all the way to Maryville to get rid—"

The telephone rang—two short rings, their ring on the party line. Zula had steadfastly refused to pay the extra two dollars per month just to get a private line so their circuitry was perhaps the last of the party lines in the entire country.

Thelma grabbed at it, almost knocking the handset off the end table and onto the floor.

"'Lo? Yes? Hold on a second. Let me get rid of Jimmy. No. Can't. Busy." Thelma lowered the phone, covering the mouthpiece with her hand and looking up at Jimmy. "Anything else, asshole? This is Billy Ray, and I want to talk with him…alone."

"Oh, *oh*, sorry. Yeah, I'll, ah, go ahead and go to bed. And pack. Tell him hi for me." Jimmy turned and walked from the room, slowing just past the doorway when he was out of sight, to listen.

"Hang on a second," he heard Thelma say, accompanied by the creaking of the sofa's springs. *Heck, she's getting up to check!* He double-timed it then, on tiptoes, past the stairs, through the dining room and kitchen and up the back stairs. *Not a sound,* he thought when he'd reached the top. It would have been embarrassing for him to be caught eavesdropping.

Well, maybe tomorrow she'll tell me about how Billy Ray is doing in New York. "But ol' Jimbo, you're going home tomorrow," he told himself. Despite his concerns, he whistled as he undressed in the dark of the bedroom.

***

Billy Ray returned the handset to its cradle with more force than necessary and swore aloud. "It never fails, damn it!" He was feeling hurt and angry, as he usually did after talking with Thelma on the phone. Never mind that the world was going crazy all around him and that he had things to say to the one person who, in this life, was supposed to be closest to him—his wife—but it always seemed to turn out this way. *I think all she really cares about is herself, and she doesn't give a damn about what happens to me.* He never had felt important to her—unless she was wanting something. "So then I guess I should feel important all the time, because she's all the time wanting something!" He grimly smiled to the mirror on the bureau at the foot of his bed. "Yeah, old man, face it! You got priority standing only when Thelma is wanting something. Otherwise you're toward the bottom of her list."

But having voiced that thought, he couldn't think now of anyone who would come ahead of him on that list. He knew it wasn't
her parents because, on most days, she was either fighting with her
mother, when she was with her, or bad-mouthing them both when
they were apart. She couldn't fight with Homer when she was with
him because the old man simply wouldn't fight with her; he'd listen
to her argue, complain, whatever, then turn and saunter off to the
barn. And usually, Billy Ray knew, ol' Homer would be praying for
her as he walked away, sending Thelma to new levels of rage and vit-
riol. "No, ol' Homer and Zula aren't any more important to her than
anyone else, I guess." He thought about the other people he knew
who moved in and through her life: her beautician pals at work, her
church friends, her relatives…those men she would tell him about
whom she had "just met" and who possessed talents, abilities, riches,
and aspirations he'd "do well to copy." Yes, he knew about the men,
and at one time, it had hurt him so very much. But now those feelings had dulled. Those men relations, like her friend relations, never
seemed to last, and soon she would be bad-mouthing them too.

So why do we stay together—married like this? he asked then answered
himself. *Just used to each other, I guess.* He again smiled his brittle smile
and nodded to his mirrored self. Divorce, he knew, was something
not regularly done by people of his generation and from his section
of the country. He had given his word back then, promised like he
did when he had enlisted in 1941, just a kid but knowing full well
what a promise was, and he had kept his word. And he supposed he
still loved her; heaven knows he worked at it. *Love.* To him that was
an action more than a feeling; he *loved* her. And he would, he knew,
until the good Lord took him home.

*Maybe I just never found the one I could say was more intended for
me than Thelma?* Billy Ray's thoughts usually circled around to this
and on to the thought that maybe he'd never taken occasion to
look around to find another. The life he had selected for himself,
he knew, hadn't been and wasn't conducive to the talked-about
searching periods any more than to the concluding married life. His
electrician jobs usually came through the union and usually were in

faraway cities, usually Northern cities. And at the bars he frequented with his buddies from the jobs he'd worked, he'd seldom attract the attentions of a lady. But it *had* happened a time or two, and like Thelma's menfolk relations, those attractions had faded with the daylight and the demands of a new workday.

Maybe it was me who done the changing? The war, he knew, had been hard on him. It had changed him inside and out; he had left Sevier County a boy and had come home a hard, cynical man, an aged man, from what he had done and seen. And to her credit, Thelma still had married him, becoming pregnant during the first month of their brief engagement. But the baby wasn't to be; she had lost their child shortly after the wedding ceremony. *Maybe the shared grief over the death of our baby is what keeps us together?* Regardless, Thelma seemed unable or unwilling to become pregnant after that, or maybe Billy Ray's extensive war injuries had limited his procreative possibilities to that one occasion. *The baby was a little girl too.* The child's development had reached the point that her sex had been discernable. *She would have been a sweet, sweet child.* He deeply regretted that he never would have kids.

But through the years that followed, Billy Ray had endured and found a measure of solace with the children he could share, those who came and stayed at Homer and Zula's to work and play on the farm. They all enjoyed the children, but Billy Ray did most of all. Big brother, father figure, friend—there he had found the type of love that wasn't a verb, an action to be performed. It just was.

Gosh, I'd liked to have talked with Jimmy tonight, but Thelma said he was busy. He sometimes wondered if his relationships with the kids rankled her—as if she weren't receiving the priority attention she sought. Like tonight she sounded almost if she had scorn for Jimmy...or hate. *That ain't right. He's a good kid. But maybe she's uptight about this disease that's spreading all around the world.*

Even to the Middle East. Earlier in the week, his landlady, Ms. Dorfman, an elderly Jewish woman who had leased him this efficiency at the rear of her house, had left a note on his door, inviting him to dinner the next evening. He had accepted and arrived home with plenty of time to wash up and even dress for the occasion, wearing his tie and his only sport jacket. *Not like today's trip home—damn fools. I almost didn't make it home at all tonight.*

Ms. Dorfman had appreciated his efforts and, even more, appreciated his company. Earlier she had received the news that her favorite nephew, Isaac Dorfman, a professor at City College, apparently had contacted a disease in his travels and had quickly passed away. "He visited with me just days ago!" she'd said. "He returned from Israel and had some very interesting news he was to discuss with me. He's an archeologist, you know, and that too is my avocation. In his correspondence Isaac often shared news with me of his finds from his dig sites across Israel. But this time he was most concerned with the epidemic that was ravaging the land, which started very soon after his last visit. Apparently a close colleague of his even contracted the disease. Maybe that was what he had wished also to discuss with me? Or maybe about the disease's proclivity toward older persons? Isaac was like that, a very caring person. He loved his old aunt, I believe. So very, very sad."

Ms. Dorfman had begun to fade after saying that, her retelling of the story having tired her more than she would have supposed. So Billy Ray had picked up and cleaned up after dinner as best he could—despite her protests—and had wished her a good night, leaving by her back stoop. *Yeah, she just needed to talk, like I needed to talk tonight with Thelma. And looking back now, that was the last time I saw the old lady, still standing on her own and in her doorway, waving to me as I crossed the backyard. She probably was beginning to feel sick even then.*

He did have much to tell Thelma tonight, but tonight she didn't have the time to listen. First he would have told her about Ms. Dorfman, who had indeed caught the disease and then about her house, now looted by those sworn to protect and serve. Returning home last night, he had noticed that her mail and newspapers were still in her box and had knocked repeatedly on her doors, both front and back. When she didn't answer, he had called the cops, who forced her door open and, finding her in the hallway, had summoned an ambulance. Billy Ray had offered to help, but the emergency attendants, dressed in their hazmat suits, had requested *(demanded)* that he and the other neighbors stay back from her door and well away from the dwelling, running their yellow crime-scene tape completely around the house and trees. Then, after all the authorities had departed, he had glanced out once more before going to bed and noticed they hadn't closed Ms. Dorfman's back door; it was swinging open with every wind gust. Slipping under the tape to close the door, he had then seen through the glass that the house had been ransacked and that the old woman's prized paintings and elegant furnishings were either gone or smashed. *So who could I call? Maybe both the police and ER workers had decided to help themselves to her belongings? Maybe that's the only reason they came to get her so quickly?*

He also would have told Thelma about his trip home tonight. He had gone in to work well before daylight this morning and had found, much like the day before, that only a few men on his crew had come in to work and that only a few of the others had even bothered to call in. "It's 'cause this disease panic that's come on the city," his site supervisor had supposed. "Only you and a few of the older, steadier guys weren't too…you know. 'Cause I saw on TV that people all over the city are running away, hitting the roads to get as far away from here as they can. But there's no place to run to—you and I know that already. This stuff is all over, so we might as well be here, huh? But then I don't know if they'll be keeping this job open without more men coming in," he had guessed. By noontime today the supervisor had known: They halted work on the construction site and handed out paychecks. With his check in hand, Billy Ray had thought to check for alternate construction work, phoning his union hall while still on site. But his repeated calls had gone unanswered; apparently the union officials also were out for the day. So he had headed home, back to his place and an empty afternoon.

His efficiency lay well west of Manhattan, a little off Route 1, and required a subway ride and a bus ride from the job site. He had driven up to New York from Tennessee but had left his old car parked in a rented spot behind a Sunoco filling station near his lodgings to avoid the aggravation and cost of driving into the city every day. This afternoon, as he had walked to his subway entrance, he had several times questioned the wisdom of that decision; it had just not *felt* good to be out walking—alone. He had immediately noticed an absence of *crowd*, of people and taxis, out there on the streets as he had strode along. He had been reminded of that *Twilight Zone* episode when all the people of New York City disappeared overnight, except for one old fellow. But the old boy had remained happy and unperturbed with the situation because he lived only to read great books—his sole joy. Then, on that first day of solitude, he accidently broke his thick eyeglasses, which he absolutely needed to read those great books. *Sad tale—creepy place, almost.* But it hadn't gotten that extreme, he reminded himself; there were still vehicles and people moving about, just fewer of them. And most of the people weren't much older than him. *Maybe it was because of what Ms. Dorfman told me that I noticed that. I especially was looking for older folks, I guess. Reckon they're all sick.*

He also had noticed that relatively more private cars had passed him as he had walked along the streets—private cars that carried usually three or four bodies, usually men, usually all slouched low in their seats. After one such vehicle had slowed, its occupants turning and scrutinizing him in passing, he had thought of his own safety. *The wolves of the city are out searching for the weak and the sick.* Opening the front of his coat wide, he had pulled his long Phillips screwdriver and his pry bar from his tool belt, choosing to carry these tools in his hands, exposed for the world to see—and to avoid. After that, no more cars seemed to slow near him, except for the two cops in their cruiser. And they only had slowed to look and to return his nod. *They knew what I was doing.*

In the subway tunnel, Billy Ray had found what he had been looking for: older people. He had met an elderly couple there on the platform...in the process of being robbed by a pair of young toughs like those he had seen upstairs. He had arrived about the same time as a transit cop, and together they had scared off the robbers. But the couple hadn't endured the ordeal any too well; the old guy's cheeks had been bruised black from the attack, and the old lady had been knocked unconscious, her nose broken and bleeding. *But the really sad part was that I couldn't comfort them.* Neither Billy Ray nor the cop had wanted to touch the old folks in any way. So the policeman had called for an ambulance, and they both had waited there, watching the old man as he cradled the woman's head in his lap and tenderly dabbed at the blood dribbling from her wounds. When his late-running train finally had arrived, Billy Ray had left the cop and the couple still there on the platform, waiting for the ambulance.

He would have told Thelma about all that, but she had been too busy to listen. *But I'm gonna go home tomorrow.* With no work for him to do in the city, it would be foolish for him to stay and keep incurring expenses. *'Course with Ms. Dorfman in the hospital, there'd be no one to ask for the rent.* But he knew the situation was only temporary; a relative or beneficiary eventually would arrive and demand all the rent money he owed the old lady. *Especially after those low-life creeps stole everything else she owned.* He knew also that in this temporary situation, even ordinary people soon would begin to do nonordinary things—things they wouldn't do with laws intact and enforced, things that hoods did every day. He had seen that happen in Germany when the law enforcers had disappeared. Soon, he expected, would come the burning and the killings, the wolves and the wounded. *Damn, I wish I had a gun!*

He hadn't brought any weapons from Tennessee because he wasn't sure how the New York authorities viewed private citizens' ownership of private guns. He had heard it was frowned upon in certain jurisdictions and didn't want to risk being arrested or fined or both. And his work friends had seemed to have no better or greater knowledge than he had on the subject. *'Course they might have their own guns and just ain't tellin'.*

So tonight he locked and bolted his door, packed his few belongings for an early start, and planned his route home, spreading his map on the bed. *Across the Pulaski to reach I–95 and then south.* He'd heard on the radio that the New Jersey Turnpike south of him was temporarily blocked with car wrecks and such, so he would avoid that route. Then he'd go on to Philadelphia, where he was more familiar with the roads, having worked there before for several years on various high-rise jobs. From there he'd work his way west to find I–81 and on south to Knoxville. *Tennessee, I'm coming home!*

7

DAY THREE

Several times during the night, Billy Ray awoke to noises coming from Ms. Dorfman's house: low voices, rumbling engines, boards breaking—all the sounds of the looting industry. *Like a pack of hyenas falling on a wounded antelope. Hyena? Wolf? Are we now back in the jungle?* He lay awake thinking about that, the thin veneer of civilization that seemed to have disappeared—*And in what...something less than a week?*—and wondering whether the jungle would reach his own doorstep tonight.

It did. Shortly after four, he heard the footsteps at his front door and the muffled voice just outside. "Hey, man. Did youse guys check out dis place already?"

Rising soundlessly from his bare mattress, Billy Ray groped for the fishing knife he had left unpacked and ready, there beside the lamp. Then, skirting the breakfast bar that divided the kitchenette from the rest of the efficiency, he crept to the door to stand just to the side, against the wall. *Just in case they decide to kick in the door.*

A second looter whispered his reply to the first, "No, man. Want da crowbar?"

I'm gonna need more space. Billy Ray inched farther back and away from the door, running his left hand along the wall as he went. He felt the wood of the cabinet doors...and the metal latch that fastened them. *Hey, wait! Maybe this thing will sound like...*He gave the latch two hard flips with his thumb and yelled, "OK, man, loaded—both barrels. Now open the damn door when I count to three! Ready? One!" From outside the door, he immediately heard grunts of alarm, low curses, and stumbling sounds, followed by the pounding of retreating feet. He moved to the door. "Two!"

He didn't call "Three," but he jerked the door open anyway and yelled at the backs of the dim figures running for the road, "Hey! Where'd dey go? Der! Der! Shoot! Shoot!" Then for good measure, he added, "Damn it! Der getting away! Get yer shoes on!" The fleeing shadows had reached the road and continued on, past the next house and out of sight.

Billy Ray stood in the doorway for a while, watching until he was satisfied that his visitors had all departed the yard. Then he closed and locked the door and returned to his bed to await the dawn.

***

Jimmy heard the keening of some animal way off in the dark of the night, perhaps in the thin woods alongside the garden patch, and it would *not* shut up. When he had first awoken to the eerie sound, he'd remembered his interrupted dream: something about a coyote ambushing a bunny and the latter, being an especially resilient rabbit, having continued to struggle against its fate, squealing in protest even while the coyote was chewing away at its flanks. He remembered wishing in his dream that the rabbit would just go ahead and quietly die—and now he was wishing that whatever was outside would just give it up too.

Ah, well. Sighing loudly he decided to go ahead and get up; he was past the point of returning to sleep anyway. He flipped aside the top sheet and sat up, sliding his legs around in the bed to dangle on its edge while stretching and rubbing his face. *It's so dark I can hardly make out the shape of the window over there.* Easing forward and tapping with his toes, he located his crumpled jeans on the floor and slipped them on, standing and pulling up his pants in one motion. Then he shuffled over to lean against the window frame, staring into the moonless void beyond the screen, trying to determine the direction of the haunting cry.

"Whoa!" he gasped, suddenly jerking back with his realization. *That sound ain't coming from outside! It's inside!* The weird wail was coming from behind him, from across his room…coming through the open door!

He turned and felt his way back along the bed, to the straight chair to snag his shirt then to the chest of drawers beside the door. Standing there now, listening and willing his pounding pulse to quiet, he definitely could tell the sound was coming from down the hallway. *Zula's room! Zula! Not some animal—Zula!* Her low, intermittent moans had morphed into a chilling, unwavering note that penetrated the wood of her door and the walls between the rooms.

Oh, golly! He was reminded of his impatient thoughts from the prior minute and instantly regretted them. "Lord," he whisperprayed. "Lord, I wasn't wishing just then that…that Zula should die right now…or even later." He paused to think about what more to say. "And just…be with her, please, God. OK? Amen." Now he *really* needed to talk with Homer. He resolved then that he'd sneak downstairs to see if the old man was maybe awake too—and listening. *That's what I'll do. Besides, Thelma's probably still sleeping, so it'll be OK. She won't even know I've been in to see him.*

Jimmy inched forward around the tall chest, running his fingernails along its smooth wooden side, and explored the floor ahead with an extended foot until he located the door's sill and then the short riser just outside the opening. Leaning in sideways and gripping the doorframe, he tentatively stepped down, feeling for the tread…as another ghastly, spectral cry washed over him from out of the inky well ahead. *Oh, gosh!* He hastily stepped back, breathing hard. "Ah…Lord," he prayed again, "one more thing: Please be with me too. Please…and protect me…please. OK?" *Oh, gosh!*

After a few more deep, fortifying breaths, Jimmy stepped out again, creeping down the back stairs and on through the dark house, touching along the walls and furniture until he stood just outside the closed door of Homer's temporary room, the small downstairs bedroom. With his hand on the knob, he placed his ear to the door, listening, expecting to hear either snores or the turning of pages.

Crying? He pressed harder against the panel. *Yeah, that's what it is.* Through the door he heard low sniffling and concluded that Homer must have already heard the moans he was coming to report—the awful, awful sounds of the old man's wife in her anguish. As he listened—and imagined Homer inside, prostrate and shaking in his grief—a soft sob bubbled up from his throat, escaping him along with the tears now rolling down his cheeks…and with most of his resolve. He turned away, blindly reaching behind for the table's edge, which would guide him toward the back door and away. *I can't see Homer now. I don't want to see him crying, don't want him to see me like this, blubbering like a baby. Embarrassing…but it's not about you!* He mentally heard the last words and stopped. Repeating them, he whispered, "It's not about you. Homer may need you now and only now. See him while you can." Jimmy turned back, blotting his eyes with his short sleeves while feeling the air for the door and its handle. Then, with teeth clenched in trepidation and another settling breath, he slowly turned the knob and eased open the door.

There were no lights burning inside the room to greet him and no illumination behind to fall through the open door to guide him. In the soft murk, he saw only vague shades of darkness and heard only the muted weeping ahead. He whispered in that general direction, "Homer? You awake? Can I help?"

The sobs ceased; Homer sniffed and coughed. "Hey, Jimmy. That you, boy? You can't sleep or something?"

Gosh, he sounds more concerned about me than about himself. "No, no, I'm fine, Homer. I just wondered if I should go up and see if I can do something…something for Zula. You know?" He scooted his bare feet along the floor toward where he judged Homer to be, patting the darkness with his outstretched hands, searching for the bed. "And you too. Can I do something for you? Like get you a drink of water or something?" *Dang, it's stinky in here.*

"Jimmy, that's real nice of you to ask," Homer answered, shifting his position in the bed, causing its springs to squeak under his weight, "but, no, no…I'm fine right now." He coughed and sniffed again, and thudded his steel pail into the nightstand as he moved it from the bed, slightly sloshing its contents as he set it down. *Gosh, I hope I didn't spill anything,* he thought, *and I hope Jimmy didn't hear that.*

"Maybe I can go dump your bucket, Homer?"

Despite his pain and discomfort, Homer smiled in the darkness. "No, Jimmy, I can't ask you to do that." *I don't want you to have to see and smell what's inside.* "Tell you what: I'm feeling a mite weak right now, and I want to straighten up myself a tad—alone—and then we'll talk. How 'bout that? Maybe after you've come back from the barn?"

"Oh...oh, yeah. That'd be fine. But before I go there, I didn't know if I shouldn't be doing something for, you know, Zula?" *Maybe ol' Homer ain't hearing her after all? It is a lot quieter down here.* Somehow he felt a flicker of happiness with that thought.

"Oh...Jimmy." Homer had to stop and clear his throat before he could go on. *The boy's just going to have to accept this.* "Jimmy, Zula's really beyond suffering. She's been unconscious for the most part... and Thelma's with her. So we just need to trust in the Lord that he's doing what's best...and in accordance with his plan. That's all we can hope for." *God, please give me the faith to truly know that myself.*

"But that still don't seem fair, Homer." Jimmy had reached the bed and found the old man's arm. He was now lightly rubbing it. "You know? 'Bout God and what's happening to Zula and all? Not fair at all." The old man's presence had brought him warmth and safety; he didn't want to leave it just yet. *Just another minute or so.*

Homer huffed a tired, one-breath laugh. "It is truly a conundrum, Jimmy, an earthly conundrum...isn't it? Know what that is?"

"Ah...a place with little bitty yards and old people living right up against each other?" Jimmy answered hopefully.

Homer huffed again. "Well, maybe, but what I'm talking about is a puzzling question that's been around as long as God put humans on this earth. Ahhhh!" In the darkness, the old man suddenly stiffened, holding his stomach as his guts clutched and released. He could abide the constant burning of the buboes in his groin and under his arms, but there was nothing he could do about his violent vomiting attacks and his loose, wet-bowel explosions. He rolled away, grabbing for the bucket again, pulling it close under his chin. "Huuuuhh! Huuuuhh!" he hollowly called into it. But this time nothing was to come as he retched—noisily, repeatedly, painfully—hidden in the room's deep gloom. Again and again the dry heaves rolled over him, giving him no relief. Finally his body stilled, and the feeling passed, leaving him weak and shaking. He lay back into his pillow. "Whew."

"Homer?"

Then he remembered Jimmy, still standing there in the darkness and now patting away again on the bed, searching for his arm.

"Son," Homer said, his voice hushed, his breathing quickening as if he'd been running. "My boy, Jimmy, I really do need some time for myself now. How 'bout seeing to the cows and coming back later?" He dabbed at the corners of his mouth with the sheet. "Please?"

"Sure, Homer, sure," Jimmy said, the disappointment evident in his voice. "I'll go to the barn and be back after while. And I'll feed the chickens while I'm at it. And then maybe…" His voice was fading slightly as he backed from the room, reaching behind and feeling for the doorframe. Then he stopped and turned back. "Homer? I… ah…" *Dang! I almost told him. Guys don't say that stuff to other guys!* "I'm going to the barn now, Homer," he said in a rush as he fled the room, glad for once for its darkness so the old man couldn't see the burning redness of his face.

"I love you too, Jimmy," Homer softly replied.

***

Morning came without further incident, and Billy Ray packed the ticking alarm clock that was still on the nightstand. *That should do it.* He unzipped the breast pocket of his fatigue jacket and slipped in the long, thin-bladed fishing knife. *Just in case.*

Then, hefting his stuffed suitcase from the bed, he trudged from the bedroom and across the tiny efficiency space to the front door, giving the cupboard latch another couple of flips in passing—*Sure does sound like the racking of a shotgun shell*—and stepped out to face the new day and the new world.

As he walked up the driveway, passing by the side of Ms. Dorfman's ruined house, he didn't slow to take another look inside. *No point in trying to return my key. I'll be back as soon as the work starts again anyway…*

after this panic dies down. He walked fast and purposeful; he believed people sometimes invited their own muggings with weak, indecisive strides. When he reached the avenue, he strode on, rounding the corner and heading toward Lincoln Highway and Rolando's Garage and Service Station.

When he had first leased his place from Ms. Dorfman, he had rented the parking spot behind the gas station, a place he thought his old '56 Mercedes-Benz would be mostly safe from theft and vandalism. The remainder of the car's security, Billy Ray believed, would come from the general unattractiveness of his ride: The tires were worn; the wipers were missing (removed and stowed in the trunk); the faux external radiator cap was gone (stolen before he'd bought the car); the upholstery was stained and splitting; and the car's paint was an ugly, faded taxicab yellow. And so far it had worked; no one had taken the time to further deface his vehicle or attempt to remove any attachment that possibly could be sold at the junkyard. Billy Ray also had taken pains to park the car with its fuel tank as empty as possible and its filler cap removed, the hole stuffed with plastic bags, so as to discourage gas thieves from drilling a hole in his fuel tank or cutting the line. He reasoned that if anyone wanted his diesel, they could siphon it out. *Don't think many people want diesel anyway.*

At the station Billy Ray noticed first that Rolando's garage doors were down and padlocked; he'd never before seen Rolando's doors closed and the bays dark. The garage was an informal meeting place for the neighborhood's large Puerto Rican population; Rolando rented bays out to anyone who needed self-repair space with a roof; someone was always there tinkering with a car, day or night. *But not today.* "Crap!" he voiced aloud. "Now I'll have to call Rolando to get my battery. And my diesel." He patted his jacket's side pocket. "At least I remembered my filler cap. Now damn it, Rolando, where the hell are you?"

Billy Ray had struck up a friendship with Rolando a few days after he had moved into the neighborhood. The old man had liked the character of the vintage Mercedes and had appreciated Billy Ray's shade-tree mechanic skills, which had kept it running, often asking him to assist in the repair of other locals' vehicles. Rolando was honest and reasonable, and Billy Ray was honest and reasonable; it was a good partnership.

He stashed his suitcase behind some nearby trash barrels and walked back to the sidewalk and the phone booth on the corner under the hanging Sunoco sign. He pulled out his rubber-banded wallet as he walked then fished out the tattered business card the old man had given him with his home phone number scrawled across the bottom.

In the booth and digging in his pocket for coins, Billy Ray looked up to find that the pay phone had been destroyed, pried open and emptied from a robbery that, unknown to him, had occurred yesterday at about the same time he was crawling under the yellow tape around Ms. Dorfman's house and immediately after Rolando had emptied his cash register for the stocking-headed man holding a forty-five. This latter occurrence was the reason the garage doors were locked today. Like many other New Yorkers, Rolando had decided to stay at home for a while; it simply wasn't worth the risk. Besides, as Rolando had told his wife that morning, he felt like he might be coming down with a cold or something.

"So now what are you going to do?" Billy Ray asked himself. He circled in place while scanning up and down, side to side, studying the surrounding houses and buildings in the early-morning light— something he hadn't consciously done before. "Nothing, nobody." Besides seldom being at the filling station during daylight hours, Billy Ray probably would have seen the area's numerous inhabitants rather than notice the structures they leaned against or the stoops they sat on. Today the buildings were conspicuous for their lack of people. No one was hanging out a window to talk with a passing neighbor. No one was waiting on the corner for the next bus. No one was begging him for money or trying to sell him something. *There's just nobody around!*

He backed into the street that fronted the station and looked up and down the blocks, both directions. "Nothing either way." *Damn!*

Only now did he really begin to grasp the pervasiveness of the fear that had gripped the city.

"Wait, wait, wait!" Billy Ray saw a car turning right a block down. It accelerated hard onto the street, squealing its tires, sliding, and coming his way. "Best get out of the street." He returned unhurried to the curb and the phone booth to lean against the Sunoco signpost, waiting for the car that had now slowed and was coasting. *They've seen me.* Billy Ray saw that the vehicle was an older Chevy, a heavy-bodied model that had been lowered on its springs and painted with the Day-Glo colors favored by the area's residents. *A lowrider. A gang car.* He straightened and tried to look bigger, chancing a furtive glance back to the station to confirm that his suitcase was still well hidden at this angle by the trash barrels beside the padlocked doors. It was.

The car eased to a stop in front of him. A heavily tattooed, muscular arm rested in the open window on the front passenger side; the riders were all sitting low, vague silhouetted heads barely visible through the glass. "Say, holmes," a voice called from the car. "That phone working?"

Billy Ray turned and looked toward the booth; he could feel the scrutiny of the car's occupants. *Looks like three in the front and three in the back.* "Naw, it's busted," he answered smoothly.

"Yeah?"

But the car didn't move on, and Billy Ray continued to stare into the shadowed interior, where he imagined the men's eyes to be. He brushed his front jacket pocket as if to scratch himself. *Knife is there at least.*

"Say, holmes, you Billy Ray?" A question from the dark of the backseat.

"Yeah, why?"

"Man, don't you recognize the ride, man? You fixed her in the spring. Remember?"

Ah, yes—a 327 with two four-barrels. With a leaking head gasket. Damn, I hope he was happy with the repair. "Oh, yeah. Maria. I recognize her now. You've had her painted, and I didn't recognize her."

"Hah!" A sharp laugh came from the backseat, and on the far side, the driver's door opened. A large, dark man in a plaid shirt unfolded himself to stand beside the car, still inside the door, leaning on the low roof. "*Si, si, si.* You remember now. Say, Billy Ray, what's you doing here this early…in front of Rolando's? Don't you know it's not good for you to be here?"

Billy Ray recognized the man and recalled his name. "Juan, I'm waiting here for Rolando," he lied. "He's on his way in with ol' Tony. Called me to do a repair job for him. Alternator." Tony—Antonio the Tool—was the quasi chief of the neighborhood's assembly of miscreants, a man whose name Billy Ray sincerely hoped was well known and respected by Juan and his associates. And he hoped his apparent familiarity with "ol' Tony" was likewise noted by the group.

"Oh, then you will be safe, my man. But you know the city is no longer safe here for the Anglo, Billy Ray. The sickness come, and the old ones die, you know. People leave. And the cops no longer come. And the Anglo…" Juan was shaking his head. "So I see you here, and I say to my *compañero*, 'There's Billy Ray.' And I know I need to see you are OK. Are you OK, Billy Ray?"

Juan must know Antonio the Tool…or of him anyway. "Yeah, I'm fine, Juan. Broke and needing this job, but fine." He patted his pockets. *That's for his next question—his real interest in me.* "But thanks for the concern, man. I'll tell Tony too. Say, he'll be here in a minute. You want to wait with me for him?" Billy Ray was betting on human nature, that the subordinates usually preferred to maintain space from their superiors—something to do with comfort level—until they needed them.

"No, no. Me…My *amigos* are to…We see Antonio later. Eh, Billy Ray?" Juan refolded himself and slid back into his seat, slamming the door as the car started forward.

If he waved in departure, Billy Ray couldn't see it through the heavily tinted glass. *'Course it could have been me feeling my pockets that he noticed. Mighta thought I had a gun or something in there. Ol' Juan seemed to be looking a mite nervous there at the last.*

He watched until the Chevy was out of sight, turning at the next light two blocks down. "Man, it hasn't been a week since this crap started, since they first announced the plague," he spoke aloud, again talking with himself. "You *are* in the jungle, Billy Ray. You're in with the wolves and hyenas and coyotes. And you best get out." He turned, heading back to the station. *I'll check on the Mercedes before I try to find a phone. Maybe ol' Rolando left me a note or something in the...* His eyes fell on the mailbox hung high on the wall beside the door to the first service bay. Since the station was seldom closed, he doubted the box was ever really used for mail; the mailmen would just walk inside. But there was that one time, he remembered, that Rolando had left car keys there. *Yeah, Rolando had to leave for some reason, but he told me he'd drop the keys inside the box for me. Yeah! Our hiding place.*

He slowed his pace and altered his course while continuing to survey the street and the surrounding buildings. *Still nothing.* At the building he leaned against the whitewashed wall, his shoulder directly under the mailbox, and reached with his opposite hand up into the box. *Aha! A note!* He pulled the folded paper from the box and scanned the parking lot once more before he opened and read Rolando's labored scratchings. *Damn guy's a genius with a motor but terrible with a pen.*

He read aloud, slowly. "I hope you ignor...idiot man find this letter because I go home. I come back just to put letter, you idiot man. I hope you are look for your battery. Put in box for old oil." *Aha!* Billy Ray knew that Rolando stored up used motor oil in metal cans until someone was around to help him pour and filter the stuff into the fifty-five-gallon drum at the back. The cans were stacked in boxes beside the drum. *Rolando must have put my battery in one of those boxes.*

He read on. "Damn thing heavy for me. Key is to padlock. Hand pump on wall. Gas in five gallons with handle. Should be enough." Billy Ray snorted. He remembered the first time he had siphoned out his diesel to store in the rear of the shop. Rolando didn't sell diesel, but he allowed Billy Ray to store his fuel there because it was much less volatile than regular gasoline, so there was little chance of accidental ignition. Plus Billy Ray allowed him to use the stuff to clean auto parts. Anyway, Rolando had watched Billy Ray siphon out gallon after gallon of diesel fuel, far more in volume than the capacity of any other car he'd ever seen. Whoever had first bought the old Mercedes-Benz, a 1956 180D sedan, apparently had ordered a greatly oversized fuel tank. Even now Billy Ray was uncertain as to the full capacity of the tank; his ready funds always ran out before the pump clicked off.

"No, Rolando, it probably won't be enough, but it should get me to the Tennessee state line." He folded down the last part of the note. "So my friend, maybe we see together soon or in heaven. But you probably not get there because you steal candy bars from under front counter on second shelf. So I pray for you. You are my friend. Rolando."

The last part brought a lump to Billy Ray's throat. "That tough ol' turd has probably never, ever called anyone his friend. Ah, well." He sighed and rubbed beneath his eye. "Now, Billy Ray, you've fooled around long enough." He stood and again scanned from side to side, searching down the road and the vacant windows across the way for a face or movement of any kind. "Nothing." He reached up into the mailbox and felt along the bottom for the key that Rolando mentioned. "Ah, there 'tis." He had to wet his fingers to lift the key from the flat bottom. *Now let's see if it works.* He knelt at the first padlock and fitted the key into the lock. *It works!* After another quick surveillance of the area, he rolled the garage door up and open enough for him and his suitcase to slip under and immediately pushed it closed. *Nothing moved out there.* He watched for a full minute through the narrow window set in the sheet metal before he went to the back.

Then, for the next fifteen minutes less the minute he used to scout behind Rolando's counters, Billy Ray moved his fuel cans along the back interior wall of the building, stacking them in front of the single, solid door that accessed the rear of the station. He knew that once he started to refuel his car, he would be less watchful and more open to intrusions—attacks. He would have to be careful…and fast.

He slipped the bolt on the rear door and peeked out. *Nothing.* He snaked through the narrow opening, leaving the door slightly ajar, and crept over to the pile of boxes beside the elevated oil drum. In the second layer, he found his battery—and the little Post-it note on one terminal: "Full charged." *Thanks, Rolando.*

For the next thirty minutes, Billy Ray wrenched, screwed, and pumped until he had his battery in place and tightly connected and his cans emptied. He was now fueled and ready to go. *Time to be the most careful.*

After pitching his suitcase onto the car's backseat, he skittered back inside the station, bolted the building's rear door, and ran to the pull-down doors at the front. Then, after a frenzy of opening and closing the big metal door, he clicked home the padlock. *I'll mail Rolando the key.* One minute more, and he was back around the station and sliding his own key into the Mercedes's ignition. *Burn, baby! Burn!* He was almost safe, almost there. He waited for the glow plug light on the dash to go out, proving that the cylinders were now heated and ready to burn the heavy fuel. *Light's out! Now catch, baby! Catch!* He turned the key a little farther to the right in the ignition, and the starter cranked...and cranked...and caught. The motor rumbled to life. *Whew!* Billy Ray breathed in his relief; he had passed his first hurdle and began to relax.

Then, ahead, at the far end of the alley, he glimpsed the Day-Glo orange of Juan's Chevy as it cruised slowly past on the side road, its riders looking for any signs of life in the buildings and streets, any easy prey in the jungle. *Oh, crap!*

The Chevy stopped and backed up, its motor revving, tires squealing. Billy Ray knew then that he had been spotted; the smoke from the newly started diesel engine couldn't be missed as it rose from the back of the Mercedes.

Now you're in for it! He looked from side to side then jerked his head to the rear, searching out and weighing alternatives. He could see ahead that the alley was wide enough for two cars to pass, but he doubted Juan would just pull over to allow him to pass. Behind him the alley went on for about two hundred yards and was walled with the backs of neighboring structures, unbroken except for the opening between buildings to Rolando's parking lot. *I can back up and swing into there.* But he knew Juan's car was much faster than his own. And his men surely had guns. *Just a matter of time.* He looked again to the front to see the Chevy speeding on, down the alley, almost to the… *Wait! Rolando's oil drum!* Rolando recycled used oil by selling it to his many customers whose failing piston rings burned almost as much oil as gasoline. He kept it in the big drum ahead, elevated on a welded metal frame for easy filling of the glass quart jars that were displayed out front between the pumps.

Ol' Rolando isn't going to like this. Billy Ray dropped the Mercedes in gear and rolled forward to the side of the frame. Then, slowing, he placed his bumper against one upright support and pushed on. *Damn perfect!* The framework tilted up, and the barrel rolled off and onto the asphalt alleyway, its lid cover popping off and its contents spilling out, rushing like a tidal wave toward the pretty orange car.

Juan braked hard, and the Chevy slid to a stop, but it was too late. The oil, funneled by the buildings, flowed around and under the car and past. He and his amigos were frozen in place; if they opened the doors now, they'd step into oil that would cover the tops of their shoes—their expensive shoes. If Juan accelerated forward, the dirty stuff would splash up and onto his new paint. Then he saw Billy Ray's Mercedes backing up in the alley and turning into the break between buildings—and saw red. With a curse that sounded more like a roar, he slammed down the accelerator as he grabbed for the thirty-eight tucked in his waistband. But the car didn't move *ahead;* rather, in the slippery roadway, the Chevy hopped and skipped to the side, its rear bumper grinding against the concrete of the building there. Then it caught some traction and leapfrogged forward to smash its front bumper into the back of Rolando's station, effectively wedging itself across the narrow alleyway.

All the car's doors now flew open, and six pairs of shoes, expensive or not, hit the oil-puddled ground. But they were too late; by the time they had slipped and slogged to the opening where Billy Ray had disappeared, they were just able to catch the last of the Mercedes's taxicab-yellow trunk as it bounced onto the avenue and away. But they shot anyway in their frustration, unloading their guns into the apartment building across the road.

Billy Ray heard the shots and now regretted a portion of his decision. *I shoulda fried their asses.* He felt around on the seat beside him and located the round-tubed road flare he had "borrowed" from Rolando's wall display, along with the four Milky Way bars from under the counter—precautions for the trip. *One pull on the igniter and one quick toss, and those guys wouldn't have troubled anybody again. Shoulda done it.* But that would have been taking lives, and heaven knows he had done enough of that back during the war. *And then there'd be more dreams.* "Naw, better what's happened the way it's happened." Still, he kept a close eye on his rearview mirror until he made the Lincoln Highway.

***

Jimmy scaled the planks, noticing that the sky had lightened somewhat and that he could now see well enough to survey the barnyard ahead to search for ol' Red and the mules before he chanced to drop into it from atop the wooden gate. *Looks clear.* He eased from his perch to the dirt below and hurried toward the barn.

"So where do you start, ol' Jimbo?" he asked himself. "You've definitely got a lot to do this morning." And if he'd been thinking about it, he probably would have added that he was also feeling much better now. Maybe he was feeling relief over being told Zula wasn't really feeling pain or anything, despite her strange cries. Or maybe it was just his feeding the chickens that made him feel better. While he enjoyed feeding all the animals, he especially liked tossing around the cracked corn to the milling, clucking flock. "They appreciate it so much," he once had told Homer. "And they sound like a roomful of old ladies at a social—just gossiping around to each other—kind of pleasant sounding."

On entering the barn's center bay, he located and flipped the big switch set high against the wall, sending power to the overhead lamps and causing the shadows to instantly disappear. Straight ahead, as he'd expected, he could see the little Jersey cow standing at the door of her stall, patiently chewing her cud while she waited. She blinked in the sudden flood of bright light.

"And good morning to you, Miss Elsie," Jimmy greeted. "Are you ready to be milked?" The cow turned and gave him a long stare. He laughed. "Yeah, you're telling me, 'Why else would I be standing here?' Dumb question, huh, Elsie, ol' girl?" He lifted the feed bucket from its nail on the wall and pulled himself up and through the tack room's high portal. Then, as an afterthought, he leaned back out the door. "You know, ol' girl, you really should work on your sense of humor." Elsie didn't disagree.

After milking the Jersey, he hung his bucket on a nail and followed her across the barnyard through the left-open wire gate to where the steep hillside sloped away. He hadn't seen any of the other cows this morning in the lot and was hoping to catch a glimpse of them; perhaps they were eating the tender grass down in the swale.

"Too early still and too foggy," he observed. The whitish haze was just lifting from the warmer ground below, rising off the little brook and covering the valley bottom. "Don't see them at all. Ooh…wait! There's a hole, and there's the ol' Ayrshire." The big red-and-white cow was standing with her front hooves in the creek and staring back up the hill at him. "Hey, down there!" he yelled. The cow tossed her head as if to acknowledge his hail then stepped backward, disappearing into the fog, probably to plod on in the opposite direction down the narrow path alongside the stream. He heard the other cows as they followed her, rattling rocks as they clambered from the creek bed.

Jimmy continued to watch, wondering whether they would reappear farther down the trail, where it rose and the haze had lifted. *There they are.* The herd passed on in a single file until they were again out of sight behind the hillside. *All there. Good.* Then he noticed a straggler hurrying to catch up—Big Red—meekly bringing up the rear. "Hah! Won't the ladies let you drive, ol' feller?" he yelled to the bull. Red slowed and looked back to seemingly give the boy a reproachful glare over his shoulder.

"Yeah, Big Red, I'd say you were pea whipped!" Jimmy loudly taunted, his hands cupping his mouth. He wasn't too sure what that meant other than it involved timid husbands, and Billy Ray's occasional use of the description usually drew an arm slap from Thelma, if she happened to be in range. *I'll have to remember to ask Billy Ray when he gets back here.* "Yeah, totally pea whipped, I'd say! Hah!"

He turned back to the barn. *All right, that's chickens—fed and watered, eggs gathered. Washed pails, cows...*Jimmy went through his to-do list, mentally crossing off his completed tasks. "Just pull down a couple bales of hay from the loft and put out some more feed, and you'll be finished. And then we'll see if the ol' man feels like talking some more." Jimmy clapped his hands together as he walked, ridding them of invisible dust...like Homer always did.

Passing along the barn's long side, striding toward the rear and the ladder nailed there, Jimmy looked ahead at the separately fenced tobacco patch. *Gettin' brown.* He saw that more ground leaves were drooping, and in some sections, whole stalks were beginning to wilt. *'Bout time to be cut and hung.* He made a mental note to bring that up with Homer. *'Course I don't know how I'd get it in the barn by myself—* another mental note to discuss.

Then, about a hundred yards away, the white mule stepped silently through the rising fog tendrils at the far end of the patch. She paused and casually turned to peruse the oncoming boy, who also faltered in his stride and warily returned her gaze. *Looks like a big ol' ghost. Wonder how long she's been standing out there keeping watching on me?* Then she dipped her head to nip at a blade of dew-covered grass and leisurely moved off, heading west toward the misty woods along the far ridge. Jimmy exhaled, realizing he'd been holding his breath, waiting to see what the big mule would decide to do next. *I guess maybe ol' Whitey really did tire of me and her ol' game.* But he'd keep an eye out anyway.

***

Back at the house, Jimmy made his second executive decision as he tried to find space in the refrigerator for the milk he had just brought in. *I believe it's time to let ol Elsie go dry too.* Neither Homer nor Zula were drinking milk now, and Thelma never drank the stuff. *No use milking the cow if it's just going to go bad.* There was no way he could drink that much milk by himself, and there was no more room in the refrigerator—and he knew he was going home very, very soon. *I can only eat so much more raisin bran.* With that thought, he realized he was actually enormously hungry and that a bowl of cereal sounded about right.

With his milk jug in hand and the latest issue of *The Progressive Farmer* tucked under his arm, he selected an appropriate bowl from the cupboard—*big, tall sides, white*—and a favored box of cereal from the pantry—*Not the Kellogg's Corn Flakes, 'cause they're about ninety years old*—and seated himself in the dining room to eat alone at the long table there. He figured he would be close enough sitting there, just outside Homer's door, to hear any noise should the old man awake and move about.

Jimmy was almost finished with his eating and reading when he realized that, besides not hearing any sounds coming from Homer's room, he also was no longer hearing Zula's strange wail. *Not since I got back from the barn. So maybe she's gone back asleep? Or maybe Zula has finally...*But he didn't want to think about that. *Anyway, I should check...maybe.* Because Thelma was staying with Zula in her room, he was reluctant to tromp up there for fear of disturbing them both. *Now that'd be some hell to pay.* Then he heard the upstairs toilet flush and Thelma's stumbling footsteps going back to bed. *To her own room! Thelma's not staying in Zula's room after all! So...well, I guess it should be OK looking in on her now,* he reasoned.

Standing and shuffling to the side, he pushed his chair back in under the table and picked up his bowl, intending to rinse it before he went upstairs. Then he heard the thin, thin call from Homer's room, summoning him. "Jimmy? Jimmy?" *All right!* He set the bowl back on the table.

After tiptoeing to the bedroom door, he twisted its knob and pushed, carefully nudging it open. *Homer's up all right!* Peeking through the crack, Jimmy saw that the old man had pushed himself up in bed and turned on the reading lamp clamped at the top of the headboard. *He looks pretty good too,* judged Jimmy. Then he saw the puke pail still within easy reach, still on the bedside table. *But maybe not that good.*

"'Morning again. Planning on staying in bed all day?" Jimmy teased, swinging wide the door and striding in, crossing the room to sit at the foot of the bed.

"Well, son," Homer replied, wearily smiling and tapping him through the bedcovers with his foot, "I just might, unless you keep bouncing me around like this. Besides, with you in charge, I don't expect I'm needed for much of anything around here anyway."

Jimmy smiled back—his biggest possible smile. *Everything's gonna be all right.* He patted the front of his jeans for his badge of authority: the watch and fob that were safely tucked in his pocket. *What's this?* In the tiny pocket, he also felt a card folded there, behind the watch. He edged it out with his thumb and lifted it to the light, reading the blurred, blue-ink printing on the outside. *Romans 9:14? Oh, yeah,* he remembered. It was the memory verse card Homer had given him after telling of Grandma Clark's daily scripture requirement. *Gosh, was that like a month ago when we saw the morning stars? Noo...* He realized that had only been a day ago, maybe two days ago. And then later Homer slipped him the card, telling him a little suppertime recitation might be good for him too. *Feels like so long.* He glanced up to see whether the old man was watching him. *No? Well, then, I'll just look those verses up later. Best not to get him started again...right now.* He palmed the card and pulled out another list, his memory list, for those questions to ask Homer that he had stored up from the morning's work.

Homer, in turn, listened and answered as each question was asked, sometimes requiring a moment to consider the question or else to gather his strength. "Yes, keep feeding with the laying mash. Yeah, it's OK to stop milking Elsie now. Yes, we need to call your mom and dad today. No, you don't need to stay. No, no, you don't. No, don't worry about the tobacco. That's not so important right now..." And so on he talked, until it seemed that every question required a pause, and the pauses were beginning to grow long.

Jimmy noticed. "Well, Homer," he said, "that's about it. That's all I got for now...except..."

"Yeah?"

"About Zula..."

The old man's eyes abruptly closed, and he lowered his chin to his chest.

Uh-oh, the boy thought, *wrong direction.* Long minutes came and went while he waited, growing increasingly uncomfortable in the silence. Finally, when he shifted on the bed as if to stand, the old man exhaled a deep breath and lifted his head. *Real tired eyes. Needed cogitating time,* Jimmy supposed.

"Son," Homer simply stated, "Zula's with the Lord now. She's dead."

Jimmy drew back with the news, returning Homer's gaze through tight, questioning eyes. When he realized the old man wasn't going to add anything more to his reply, he haltingly asked, "How? How do you know? Did you go up and see her? Did you...did you climb up those ol' stairs to see her?"

"No, Jimmy—and this is going to sound strange...I *felt* her soul leave her body this morning, just a little while after you and me started talking. I guess if you live together for as long as we have, well, you just feel such things about the...Are you OK?" At the foot of the bed, the boy had gone white and was looking somewhat wobbly. "Do you think you need my bucket?" Homer asked, swiveling around and reaching back for the stainless-steel pail.

"No, no, no, no. I'll be all right," Jimmy insisted. The thought of puking into someone else's puke, even Homer's, made him even more nauseous. "I'll be...I'll be OK." He swallowed and took several more deep breaths. "Homer, if Zula di—ah, passed away—shouldn't we be doing something now?"

Homer studied the boy and absently nodded. *Good, good. Some color's returning to his lips. And the blue in his eyes.* "Yeah, we will. We will...but that's not really so important...once a body's gone."

Jimmy didn't think the old man was getting it. "Homer, I mean don't you think we ought to be calling the doctor?" he blurted. "I mean, even if she's died, she's *dead!* Shouldn't we be calling some-body?" He never had encountered death so close before—not in his family, not in his friends' families, not with anyone he really knew—and suddenly death was very real. *Never to be alive here anymore!*

A new feeling—a confused mingling of seriousness, dread, lone-liness, and fear—settled on the boy, and he voiced his thoughts as they came: "You...you aren't able...Would you want me to...I been to funerals, but I ain't never touched...Aren't you worried about you too? I mean, if she died from the disease, you probably have it too! And you'll die? Homer, this is bullshit!" He jumped to his feet, vio-lently shaking the bed and causing the mattress to shift and thump against the footboard. *Oh, gosh!* He imagined that he'd knocked the bed off its frame—and the old man to the floor—and the thought momentarily froze him. But the bed held firm.

"Whoa, whoa, Jimmy! Whoa!" Homer ordered, taking advantage of the slight pause. He was waving his hands in the air, calming the air. *The boy's just now really understanding.* "Slow down, son. Slow...down. You've got me dead and buried, or will have with one more leap like that. And I don't think the bed slats can...Just calm yourself down and listen."

Jimmy shook his head; he couldn't believe Homer could be so unaffected at this time. *This is the big one—what could be more impor-tant?! And how am I supposed to think right now?* With his tone only slightly less agitated, he tried again. "Ah...ah...OK. OK. Sorry, Homer. I thought I'd almost...But I mean, Homer, aren't you afraid? I am! And what am I supposed to do now?"

"Sit down again. *Please.* Sit. Sit. Breathe. Rest. Listen. Just listen. OK?"

"OK, OK," Jimmy wearily agreed, resigned to the old man's con-foundedly placid attitude. He lowered himself onto the foot of the bed again. "So what's gonna happen now? What are we...What am I supposed to do?"

"Well, sir, right before you came in, I was just sitting here and thinking about how it's so amazing that God can talk to each of us in ways so different, but when we compare notes, there's a similarity, a sameness, under all his messages that he especially tailored for each of us."

"Ah...yeah, I understand. But Homer...maybe you should...I mean..." Jimmy's time of patient resignation had ended. *There he goes again.* The boy wanted to talk about real-life things—serious things—and not be talking about God and religious things. *That kind of talking is for another time. I can't be "relying on the Lord" right now.*

The old man sensed he was quickly losing the boy's attention; he would need to say what was on his mind, plant the seed of understanding in him that would carry him through. He leaned forward, wanting to physically touch Jimmy, but he was too far away—and the boy didn't move closer. "Son, let me talk...and then I'll rest. OK? Yeah, I need to rest, but I know this has been especially hard on you, and maybe you've been able to—*He's been detached, like in the movies, not real*—cope with the way things are—"

"Homer, I need to—"

"OK, to the point. Let me first ask a question: Remember when Jesus prayed in the garden the night before he was taken and crucified?"

"Ah...yeah," Jimmy replied. It was a basic Sunday school lesson that he had heard many times. That was easy for him to answer.

"Well, Jesus knew he was going to die, and he didn't want to. Remember that?"

"Yeah."

"Jesus concluded there in the garden that he was there to do God's will, 'the will of Him that sent me.' Jimmy, there was purpose in *his* dying. And I know there will be purpose in *my* dying. In the eternity that is to come, that I now feel coming, only then will I truly know. And my acceptance of Jesus's own purpose allows me the 'knowing' to accept all this as his will for my life. I'm not afraid, son. Besides," he sniffed, "I ain't crossing from the temporary to the eternal side alone; God's right there with me." Homer was nodding, smiling...knowing. "And you *really* should take the time to read Romans nine, verse fourteen and the next few—"

Click. The dining room lights were turned on, illuminating the tiny bedroom. Jimmy sprang to his feet, again thumping the mattress against the footboard. *Thelma!* She appeared in the doorway, noisily backing in with a tray held high in her hands. *Corn flakes?* He could see the big white box rocking on her tray.

She turned. "Dad, are you ready for break...What's going on here?" Her voice was harsh and loud in the small room. Neither Homer nor the boy answered; they both just returned her stare, their eyes wide. They hadn't heard her to come down the stairs.

She glared at Jimmy—then at Homer—then returned to Jimmy. "Boy," she addressed him, her words slowed, her voice now lowered and menacing, "Dad needs his rest...and I was looking for you. I couldn't find you in your bedroom or anywhere you *should* be."

That's why I didn't hear her. She came down the back steps. And dang, if her ears aren't red! "Well, ah, Thelma, I...I've been up for a while and, ah, been to the barn and all...and Homer called me when I, ah, was going to the kitchen...happened to be walking by here." *Yeah, he called me—good touch but not totally true.*

"Yes, yes, I called him," Homer seconded, without even glancing his way. He had seen the hate-filled glower his daughter had given the boy. "Jimmy isn't bothering me in the least."

"Just the same," Thelma complained, "he shouldn't be in here." She walked over to where the boy now stood and placed her tray there beside him, on the foot of the bed. "You need to conserve your energy, and you two don't need to...talk. We—you and I, Dad—we need to do the talking, the planning, the financial planning, for when...*if* Mother passes. And Jimmy, *you* don't need to be in here." She reached over and firmly grasped his wrist, pulling and guiding him to the door. "Out. Stay out." She pushed him from the room.

As Thelma was closing the door behind him, Jimmy heard Homer quietly tell her, "Your mother's dead. If you really had stayed with her, you'd know that she already died."

***

Still rubbing his wrist, Jimmy walked down the long sidewalk to the driveway, intending to take the hard road in the front over to Fred and Juanita's house. He had told Homer he'd go over and check on them at his first opportunity—and he couldn't think of a better opportunity than the present. With the closing of the bedroom door, he could tell Homer and Thelma were about to get into it, and along with the passing of Zula, Jimmy just needed some time to…He didn't know what. *Get back to hauling hay? Was that just two days ago? Go back home? Mom and Dad should have come by now. Maybe…? No. No, they're OK.* He realized now that he really didn't want to think at all…or remember what he'd seen in the last couple of days. *It's all a bad dream. When I get to Fred's, I'll see him rocking on his porch, and Juanita will have made banana pudding and…*Off to his left, he heard gravel hit metal. *Car coming!* He skittered back up the steps and dove behind the big white oak growing there beside the sidewalk and lay still, his face pressed in the grass, his body hidden by the tree. He stayed that way, counting seconds, until he felt reasonably sure that enough time had gone by for the vehicle to have passed. Then slowly he lifted his head and edged around to the side of the tree's base, to spy on the car Boy Scout style, exposing only his left ear and eye. *Dang! They're still there.*

The car—or cars; he now saw there were three—had slowed and were only coasting past the driveway. Crawling sideways to keep himself well concealed behind the tree's massive trunk, Jimmy watched until the last car had almost passed behind the low bluff to the west of the driveway. *Not just kids,* he observed. The cars appeared to be filled with ordinary-looking folks, out for a Sunday drive or something, and maybe just interested in the houses they were passing. Then an ordinary-looking passenger in the backseat shifted his position and momentarily extended the long barrel of a rifle through the rear window. *Maybe Sunday drives have changed too. But you know…* Jimmy went on to consider that perhaps the traffic on Chapman Highway had become even more congested, causing drivers to seek back-road alternatives, as he and Homer had done when they had returned from Sevierville. *Bet it has. But I bet those folks will run into*

Daniel Davis and his boys if they keep going on down that way. Or maybe there are a lot of "Daniels" out there these days…all toting rifles.

Jimmy counted to a hundred again, just to make sure the way was clear, and got to his feet. Since the road route was open to more sudden and perhaps unpleasant encounters with passing vehicles like these, he decided he'd go through the pasture and woods to Fred's place. *I'll go down the hill through Red's pen.* After one more check of the road, he trotted from behind the cover of the oak and across the front lawn, slipping between the barbed-wire strands that bordered the yard then skipping down the long incline to the rock ford at the base of the hill. He planned to cross the creek there and climb the knob on the other side. He knew of a trail that led right to Fred and Juanita's.

When he reached the lower corner of Big Red's pasture, he slowed to inspect a portion of the fence that Homer had temporarily repaired. *I'll say it's temporary.* Without a corner post, Homer had had to tack the wire to the remaining posts and had created a very long stretch between supports. As a result a determined cow could easily walk through the wire along this section of the fence and onto the road. *Well, maybe they won't come by here.* And with Red now being a part of the herd, there'd be little motivation for him to return to his enclosure. *But I'll ask Homer.*

A distant rifle shot cracked through the hills, holding him in place. *That's pretty far away from here,* he judged. *Safe.* But it reminded him that he needed to be on his way and keep his mind on what he was doing. He stepped through the wire and crossed the stream, hopping from rock to rock. Then, instead of paralleling the fence as Red had done a few days before, he followed an overgrown path to the woods that covered the side of the knob and climbed at a diagonal up the hill's steep side. It was a more strenuous route but he knew he would be well hidden from the road and the valley's bottom, and he would come out of the trees above and behind Fred and Juanita's house. He wanted to "scope out" the house before he went up and knocked on the door.

Thirty minutes later Jimmy reached the ridge top and the barbed-wire fence that separated their property from Homer's. Through the thinning trees, he saw the backs of Fred and Juanita's house and garage, and the side of their barn across the way on another small rise. Fred's tobacco patch stood in between; Jimmy would use that to hide his approach to the rear of the house. *Don't know who's going to be inside. Oh, wait! What's that?* At the front of the garage, he saw the three cars that had earlier coasted by the driveway. He would have to get closer if he wanted to see what was going on inside the house.

Zigging and zagging from tree to tree down the hillside, Jimmy reached the cover of the garage and, from there, the shelter of the rows of tobacco. Choosing a row, he low-trotted to the center of the plot where he could see through the tobacco stalks and into the back door of the house. Someone had propped open the screen door and had left the inside door pushed back. He saw movement inside as people moved from room to room, repeatedly crossing the center hallway. Then a man, white-haired and heavyset, maybe about Billy Ray's age, carried a box filled with canned goods out the back door, stacking it on top of other boxes on the porch. A woman followed with another cardboard box full of jars.

They're stealing Fred's food! Jimmy's anger flared, and he impulsively shouted, "Hey! What are you guys doing?" *Hey, yourself, dumb butt! They probably got their guns inside too.* "Hey!" he challenged again, slightly lowering his tone and now kneeling, staying well back in the tobacco plants and well concealed by their broad leaves. "What do you think you're doing stealing the Rogers's stuff? That ain't yours!"

"Where are you?" the man yelled back. The woman had moved behind him and was rocking from foot to foot, trying to see past to locate the source of the voice. Another man, a teenager maybe, came to the back door and remained in the shadows, a pistol butt poking in profile from the holster at his side. "Where are you?" the white-haired man shouted again.

"Never you mind!" Jimmy yelled. "I've got a rifle trained on you, and you're stealing Fred and Juanita's stuff. You get on outta here! Now!"

Another pair of men appeared from the far side of the house, creeping along as they moved apart. Jimmy saw that they carried long shotguns. *That's probably what I saw through their car window. Now they mean to outflank me.* He pushed backward through another row of stalks.

"Hey!" the white-haired man shouted. "Listen! We bought all this stuff! You hear? Bought it! They died. The Rogers died, and we bought all the foodstuffs in the house." He partially turned toward the doorway and said something to the teenager. A youngish woman, maybe in her twenties, emerged from the house, tentatively holding out a stiff, folded sheet of paper. Somehow it looked familiar to Jimmy, even from a distance. She handed it to the white-haired man, who waved it in the air toward the tobacco patch. "Hey! Here's my notice. We bought this stuff. Ain't stealin' it!"

"How'd you know the Rogers are dead?" Jimmy shouted in reply, moving along the row, trying to vary his position.

"'Cause they're laying in there in the back bedroom. Probably died of this flu stuff that's going around—they's old folks. Now they need burying." The man had lowered his arm and was motioning with his head, encouraging and directing the other men with his nods.

Seeing those men hasten their advance, the one at his left now shielded from his sight by the garage, Jimmy scrambled backward through another row of tobacco then ran down the row toward Fred's low barn. From there he believed he would be able to keep track of both men. He stopped once to yell, to warn them again. "OK, that's far enough! You walk up any more, and I'll shoot your asses off! Hear?"

"You sound like you're just a kid!" the shotgun holder closest to Jimmy challenged.

"And you sound like you're ready to die!" Jimmy screamed back. "Now y'all move to the center of the yard, or I swear to God I'll shoot your heads off! Now!"

The shotgun holder stopped momentarily, startled by the vehemence of Jimmy's threat—and its close proximity. But then he came on, increasing his pace and stalking forward, scanning the tobacco patch ahead and angling away from the others.

The white-haired man hollered again from the porch. "See? We're working with Reverend Davis! He got the sheriff to commission him to sell it all. He said he was commissioned to do that all around here, from the church all the way to the highway. That's what he said!"

Wow! "Reverend Dilbert Davis?" Jimmy questioned without thinking, way too loud and way too close to his intended destination, his next vantage point.

All eyes shifted toward the barn. "No," the white-haired man answered. "Reverend Daniel Davis. Dilbert—I hear he's holed up in a cabin up above Townsend. Wearing a surgery mask and trying to escape the disease—that, is if he's still living now. I heard he was pretty old anyway. You know Reverend Davis, do you?" The man was getting very conversational, and Jimmy knew he had slipped up.

Can't stay. He dropped to his hands and knees and crawled through the high grass around the side of the barn to the drainage ditch that he had watched Fred dig years before. As he reached the woods, having slithered through yards of blackberry briars in the gulch, he heard a twelve-gauge open up, spraying the tobacco and the side of the barn with shot. *Close.* But that was it; they didn't follow or attempt to pick up his trail. *Just a little target practice maybe, like shooting at a road sign on a pole.* Then he remembered where he had seen the guy's notice paper. *It's one of those poster papers, Daniel's poster papers like he'd nailed to the power poles about his healing services. Shoulda known it. But commissioned by the sheriff...?*

Now sheltered by the woods, Jimmy circled back around, skirting alone the border of Homer's property until he found another favorable spot for surveillance, where he could look down and see the full lay of Fred's property. As he watched from the heights, the people in the three cars finished loading their purchases, boarded, backed their vehicles out to the hard road, and drove away. Jimmy waited until the last car had disappeared around the farthest curve he could see and the road sounds had faded altogether. Then he willed himself to wait still longer—hidden and distant—just in case someone had been left behind in ambush, or another visitor was soon to arrive.

Commissioned by the sheriff? As he waited, he mulled over what had been said and supposed Daniel's bunch could have been the ones to have first found Fred and Juanita—since he'd seen them in their Cadillac turning up into Fred's driveway just the other day. They'd probably decided then to profit from their discovery. *Or maybe the milkman came back?* Regardless he knew Homer would appreciate it if he verified what he had heard—and perhaps attended to his friends' remains—before returning home.

He waited another thirty minutes, timed with the pocket watch, before pushing up from his hiding place at the base of a bushy hemlock tree and silently making his way down the forested incline.

"Patooey!" somebody spat.

Jimmy froze in his tracks and squatted on the hillside, straining to see movement through the sparse branches ahead. *The Henry boys!* He recognized them as they cleared the corner of Fred's house, spitting out their tobacco chaws and heading for the barn. *Didn't see or hear their old truck pull up.* He guessed the brothers had walked all the way from their small, poor farm down beyond the church, around the Pleasant Hill area. *And well armed!* He spotted the hunting rifles slung across their backs. *And...what's that?* Squinting and peering close, Jimmy believed he could see another of Daniel Davis's unique sales bills protruding stiffly from under the bib of the older Henry boy's overalls. *Yeah, ol' Daniel, both healer and vulture now, preying on the dead and dying. And who's in a position to stop 'em?* He'd seen how Daniel and his crew had chased after the Mayfield man and heard the gunshots when they'd dealt with him.

The Henry boys reached the barn and just walked in, glancing neither to the sides nor behind, as if they belonged there. *They're just attending to business, I guess.* Soon Jimmy heard Fred's Ford tractor rumble to life. *Gosh, maybe if I'd gotten over here earlier...dang!* "Was I just thinking that," he admonished himself, "while ol' Fred and Juanita might be lying dead in their bedroom just a few yards away?"

Suddenly, though he didn't like it, he could understand the motivation that caused these people to be out driving up and down the roads, searching out those opportunities that presented themselves now at every turn, all along the way…and probably beyond every dead body. *New opportunities for material wealth, fleeting opportunities for riches—a whole new world for the taking by those who've never had much of it, like the rich man building storehouses and losing his soul the next day.* He stood, blinking. "Now where did that last thought come from? Maybe, next day, that kind of stuff *will* be needed."

Jimmy glanced up; the sun was now almost straight overhead, and he needed to get back to the house. *Maybe I can go see the Shanks's place and swing back by here later this afternoon.* He left without waiting to watch the Henry boys drive off on Fred's tractor.

***

The going hadn't been smooth for Billy Ray. After he'd left the secondary roads, he'd found most of those missing New Yorkers traveling along the interstates—those people he had earlier noted as being absent from around Rolando's station. He had found miles of citizens in their vehicles creeping up Lincoln and Pulaski and apparently still lined up all the way to the Jersey Turnpike. He wondered now if he shouldn't have taken the lower turnpike loop, but the radio repeatedly had warned of crashes and roadblocks that effectively had shut down the southbound flow of traffic. And he thought of the warnings: Riots had broken out in parts of Manhattan and Brooklyn, so now, every five minutes or so, the radio announcers passed along messages from the city's officials, advising residents to remain in their homes and to avoid *any* travel if possible. *The problem is…most New Yorkers are already here with me, listening to these advisories in their cars while escaping the city and the plague.*

Billy Ray leaned forward and located the sun through the windshield, grousing aloud that *this* trip to *this* spot should have taken only about an hour at most and was now well into its fifth. And having eaten his candy bars in the first hour, he was feeling hunger pangs again. But he was reluctant to get out of his place in line. Several miles back a car in front of him had smoked to a stop with its radiator hose ruptured and spilling water all over the road. Making use of the flare—the one he hadn't used earlier on Juan—to caution those cars following, Billy Ray had slowed and stopped close to the stranded car, getting out and going forward to offer his assistance to the young driver and his family. But he quickly had found that giving aid along the roadway was more difficult than he would have imagined. Besides provoking a cacophony of horns and curses that immediately protested his attempt at assistance, the driver of the Ford station wagon had initially *resisted* his offer to help, refusing to even lower his window to talk. The young man was so frozen in fear that he'd been unwilling to loosen his death grip on the steering wheel to even roll down his window. *The dude probably didn't even realize he wasn't going anywhere.* After a long minute, with Billy Ray standing beside the Ford and cars inching by on both sides, the guy's wife finally had managed to get through to the driver that they were going nowhere and that he needed to talk. Only then had the car's door cracked open, with the man asking through the narrow space, "May I help you?"—like he was opening his front door to the Fuller Brush salesman.

"*May I help you?*" Billy Ray had erupted. Then he had caught sight of "the look" in the man's face, which he hadn't seen since his military days—a look of total panic held in check only by totally denying the situation. He'd seen it in the face of a navigator who had refused to crawl back with him to leap from their dying aircraft and later in the face of a young soldier/clerk who had gone numb amid falling mortar fire on the HQ; the boy had refused to leave the safety of his files. So Billy Ray had held his tongue and instead appealed to those capable of assisting: the guy's wife and some Mexican dude wearing a baseball cap and riding in the back of a pickup passing to the left.

"Help me push this car out of the way!" he'd ordered, jerking open the door and grabbing the young man's collar to pull him from his seat. "Now go to the back and push with the other fella, and lady, you steer to the right." The Mexican already had circled the Ford and was kicking at the door of an adjacent car, forcing it to make way for the station wagon to pass onto the shoulder.

"Wasn't worth it," Billy Ray commented aloud. "Coulda gotten myself shot." Since that time he'd passed two more stalled cars, and there they had stayed, blocking traffic in that lane until the desperate persons following behind, probably in much bigger vehicles, had nosed their way out and around, pushing traffic to the sides and allowing the following cars to continue to slowly flow like the waters of a creek around a rock in the middle. The odd-even traffic rule, common in big cities where commuters were forced to cooperate daily, seemed not to be in practice today. "I guess I could even have gotten shot when I pulled that fella out of his seat." But he also remembered the nod of gratitude the wife had given him when the Ford was safely parked off to the side in the emergency lane. "I hope those folks and their little kids are doing OK now." He'd heard on the radio that the national guard was out clearing the roads and directing traffic. *They'll probably help those folks. But I ain't seen none of those guards yet.*

The lines of cars moved slowly on.

***

The sun had moved noticeably westward by the time Jimmy had returned from Fred and Juanita's place. He had made his way back the same way he'd gone earlier in the day, except that when he reached the creek, he'd taken the cow trail north to the barn, walking up through the shady hollow. He felt that the other route, through Red's pen and parallel to the road, might be too exposed in the daylight to strangers passing on the narrow country pike. *Besides, the blackberry briars like to tore me up on the trip down the hill this morning.*

Now, passing by the parking area behind the house and Thelma's damaged Corvette, he spotted another car parked there—a long, black car. "Dang!" he blurted. *Reverend Davis's Cadillac! They're here!* He instantly halted and allowed only his eyes to move ahead, to probe the shadows of the thick trees, the interior of the Cadillac, the bushy hedge that spanned the space between the smokehouse and the broken-tile sidewalk, and the back side of the house, only partially visible through the overgrown bushes. *Nothing.* He lightly, quietly stepped backward to Thelma's car and dropped behind its cover to continue his scrutiny of the big car through the Corvette's windows. *Empty.* He saw neither people in the car nor movement at the house. *I'll have to get closer to the house to look inside there.* Stooping low, he warily edged around to the front of Thelma's car and, from there, dashed from tree to tree to the rear of the smokehouse. Then, after a minute or two for further surveillance from beneath the building's pier foundation, he scurried on across the yard to the corner of the house, still running in his hunched-over style, imaging he was lessening his exposure to the TV room's big windows along the back and eastern side. *They're maybe watching for me from over there at those window, waiting for me there.* With his back pressed tightly to the white boards of the house and willing his heart to slow, he considered his next move. *Maybe through the back? Yeah!* He would sneak in the back door and listen through the kitchen then maybe hide in the cellar. *No, no, not the cellar.* He'd climb the back steps instead and go through the upstairs rooms to the front staircase beside the dining room. There he felt certain he could hear any voices in either the dining room or the TV room. *Or Homer's room.*

He crept around the side of the house and tried the door to the covered back porch. *Not locked. Good.* Carefully depressing the handle, he slowly pulled open the door, just enough for him to slip sideways through the gap. From there he made his way through the house as planned and soon was sitting on the top step of the front staircase. In that position and with a little leaning, he chanced several tentative scans into the dining room and back toward the adjacent doorway to Homer's bedroom. *Closed. No voices.* He would have to tiptoe down the stairs, closer to the doorway and the TV room, to hear anything of the goings-on out there.

Carefully, carefully he moved; not a step creaked in his passing. When he finally reached the floor level, he slid himself along, his back to the wall, and peeked into the TV room. *Thelma's there, just sitting on the couch by herself...reading folded-over, stapled papers. Well, I guess I'll have to...*"Ahem!" He cleared his throat to announce himself—and avoid startling Thelma—and walked into the room. "Hey, Thelma," he casually greeted, as if he had not spent the last half hour sleuthing his way in and through the house.

But he apparently had startled her anyway. "Damn it, Jimmy!" she yelled. "Where's...What the hell are you doing skulking around here?"

She looked so surprised that Jimmy had to fight his initial impulse to laugh; Thelma wasn't good at recognizing humor, particularly at her expense. *No siree,* he thought. Instead he presented his innocent but repentant face: "Gee, I'm sorry. I was working out back of the barn and thought I'd break for a bite to eat. I didn't even know you were out here." He gave her his amiable smile, closed mouthed and friendly, while she continued to glare at him. He now wondered if she hadn't been so much startled at seeing him as disappointed in seeing him. *Maybe she was expecting...*"Ah...say, is the Reverend Dilbert here now? I thought maybe that was his car out there." Jimmy waved vaguely in the direction of the backyard.

"It is, smartass, but it's Daniel who's here—on business."

"For your mother?" he asked, his expression showing concern. He didn't know whether he should let on that he already had knowledge of Zula's death or that he had overheard Homer's remarks when he was leaving the bedroom earlier. He knew that Thelma always preferred being the one dispersing the information and that she might still be rather sensitive about the way she had received *this* information.

"No, dumb-a..." Her voice trailed off as she rethought her words. "Jimmy," she began again, now using her serious and talking-down tone, "Jimmy, Mother has passed. She died earlier today. That's it."

"Oh...I...I need...to sit down," he stammered, seeing and moving toward the straight-backed chair across from Thelma. He moved slowly, seemingly pondering her words. "She's died?" he repeated, his head lowered. "Dead?"

"Yes. Dead." Thelma intently studied the boy as he seated himself, a queer smile almost visible at the corners of her mouth.

After a suitable period of apparent thought and reflection, and a deep breath, Jimmy again raised his eyes and dared to ask his real question. "So Daniel's here for...Zula's funeral?"

Thelma's mouth now became the hard, taut line Jimmy easily recognized, having seen the look many times in the past while she sorted through her inventory of lashing, hurtful replies to inconvenient inquiries. "I'm paying him for services," she said, her tone surprisingly low, but her jaw muscles still bunched and moving. "Healing services for Dad, if it's any of your business. And I've already called all the funeral homes for Mother, but none are answering their telephone. So while maybe you think you can..." She stopped short of saying the words she really wanted to say but continued to glower at him while she worked over a new thought in her brain. "Maybe he *could* do something with Zula," she allowed.

"You mean Daniel?" Jimmy asked, incredulous at the thought of Daniel Davis performing any of the funeral duties he could imagine. "You mean his dad, Dilbert, don't you? I mean, Daniel's no real preacher let alone...Does Homer know anything about this?" He had uttered the magic words.

"Homer?" Thelma spat, cutting him off, her lips now contorted and ugly. She set her papers aside and got to her feet. "Boy, I don't recall ever asking your advice on the subject, but Daniel's old man's sitting somewhere in a cabin atop a mountain, eating his food out of cans and drinking bottled water. He ain't even here!" She now stood in front of Jimmy, glaring down at him, her feet spread wide, her fists on her hips. "So while you and Homer..." She spotted the watch chain hanging from Jimmy's fob pocket. "And another thing—about my old man giving you 'authority' around here?" She reached down and grabbed the gold chain, pulling free Homer's watch. "That's a laugh! The things you do around here ain't worth a tinker's damn—and you should know it. Don't you know you're just another one of those kids—pawned off by relatives—they have coming here all the time, just playing at farming?"

Thelma's insults hurt him, but her actions touched a real nerve. Jimmy's conciliatory smile faded, and his cheeks glowed red as he fumbled to his feet, forcing her to momentarily step back. "Thelma," he declared, "I know I'm in your way, and I regret that. But I'd be at home in Maryville right now if Mom and Dad had been able to get up here and get me…or if you could have found the time to run me home…like you told Homer."

"What did you say, smartass? I'd take you home right now if I wasn't tending to my father." She and Jimmy were about the same height, and she stood with her nose about six inches from Jimmy's. And since she was generally abrasive to everyone, she was quite used to altercations with others; she believed she would genuinely enjoy having it out with the boy here and now. After all, this kid had been especially irritating to her of late. "But you don't give a damn about him or us, do you, Jimmy?" she accused, almost screaming in his face. "My mother just died and my father is dying, and you just like to come here and play and take our money, don't you? Well, let me tell you something, boy!" But she was unable to finish because Daniel Davis came striding into the room, his tread heavy on the linoleum. They both turned their heads to look back at him.

"You need some help with him, Thelma?" Daniel asked, flicking an evil grin Jimmy's way with a tilt of his chin.

But she wasn't looking for help right now. She was feeling good—really good; she didn't want Daniel taking away any of this pleasure. She was remembering that, for some reason, she had been having dreams this past week—about Jimmy, specifically about hitting and hurting him, but she could never seem to be able to hit him hard enough. So yes, she wanted this…and she would really enjoy it. *It's something inside, something satisfying.*

*But in front of…*In the next instant, she realized that maybe she really didn't want Daniel to see her now—like this. She knew from experience that the vileness that could spill from her mouth would shock most men, and that man-boy, Daniel, wasn't really too bad looking after all; he had grown up a lot in the past year. Fact was, she was coming around to rather like his aggressive style and cockiness. *Yes, this might turn out to be something special.*

"Thelma?"

"Ah…no, Daniel," she declined, stepping away from Jimmy. "No, please. I apologize that you had to walk into this and see Mr. Juvenile Pisspot here showing off his ass. No, we probably should concentrate on getting Father back on his feet right now."

"Yeah, yeah, we could do that, Thelma. But you know, if you should change your mind…just call." Daniel's malevolent stare hadn't moved from Jimmy. "You know," he intoned, "I've long wondered about this boy's soul and his salvation. And I believe his demon might be right there to be seen—railing and reviling—fulminating against God himself. In fact the man Homer's sickness and the woman Zula's death may very well be in answer to what we're seeing here and now—in this *boy!*" Daniel's charges came smoothly to him; they were well practiced.

Jimmy swallowed and blinked. *My demon?* The awful anger in him that had flared out when Thelma had taken his watch had been blunted by her charges of unworthiness and selfishness—*Her mother has just died*—and his feeling of righteous indignation was now fading, almost as fast as his feeling of guilt was rising. *But me causing any of this—my demon?*

Thelma folded her arms and looked at him with new eyes. "You know, I hadn't thought about that before. We weren't having any of these problems before Jimmy came. And you know," she lied, "his mother told me sometimes this boy can really be wicked and that she really appreciates those times when she can leave him here and be shed of him for a while." She and Daniel were glaring at the boy and nodding in unison. "Real wicked, she said."

Jimmy looked back and forth between them, his mouth open, his eyes wide. He didn't really believe her. *But yet they haven't come for me—neither Mom nor Dad.*

"Thelma," Daniel said, partially turning to her, "if you're feeling, you know, somewhat threatened by this boy here, we have the Youth Brigade in operation at the church. Since the sheriff has been so tied up in dealing with this sickness stuff and all and is so shorthanded, we've kinda gotten together with some of the church leaders and started policing our own area, our own neighborhoods. You know, a protection service for the shut-ins and afflicted members? Property management, you might say." He now fully turned her way. "By the way did you get those papers signed by Homer—the ones I gave you?"

"Daniel," she replied, her emphasis hard on the first syllable, warning him away from the subject, "we'll talk about that when we've finished our discussion about Mr. Juvenile Pisspot here." She tilted her head, indicating Jimmy. "And about what you were just saying," she continued, changing the subject and again smiling warmly at Daniel, "I understand you've enlisted many youth *volunteers* to your little group. So maybe Jimmy could gain much from his association with your members? Hmm?"

"Yeah, yeah," he agreed, understanding where Thelma was going. "We do have quite a few younger boys working for—*with*—us. With so many people dead now, and parents running away from their homes and stuff, we've had to take responsibility for a lot of children, down at the church. We take the kids with us during the day to help out with carrying stuff and all, just letting them feel productive by helping us out and—"

"Wait, wait," Jimmy interrupted. "Are you trying to send me off, to enslave me to *him*?"

Thelma's eyes narrowed and gleamed with delight. "Oh, Jimmy, don't you think that's a bit dramatic? I'm not talking about selling you into *slavery*; you don't need to be wrinkling your nose in disgust with Mr. Davis like that."

Daniel's head jerked around; he hadn't been aware of Jimmy's disrespectful wrinkling. "You got something you want to say to me, punk?" he challenged.

"Boys, boys," Thelma intervened, resuming her adult role while still tittering. "Let's not be fighting here. I'm sure you two can work this out later." Her light patting of Daniel's arm had become a two-handed biceps rub. "Jimmy, I'm just suggesting that, with Dad down sick and there not being much to do around here, you'd rather enjoy helping out in the community during this especially trying time. But if you're so lazy that—"

"You told me you'd run me home today! You said—"

"Tsk, tsk, tsk." She stopped him, clicking her tongue and shaking her head. "I said I'd *try* to find the time, but the day is half over now. Can't you see that, or are you just *so* selfish? Tell you what…" She angled her head and folded her hands across her stomach—her condescending pose, according to Homer. "You plan on working with Mr. Davis, maybe this afternoon or evening—whenever he needs you—and I'll try to make a special effort to arrange my schedule so I'll have the time tomorrow to drive you to Maryville. Will that suit you, Mr. Juvenile Pisspot?"

"Umm…" Jimmy considered his options, rocking in place and vacantly rubbing his forearms—gestures that unconsciously revealed the extent of his fear and concern—and didn't immediately reply.

"Jimmy?"

"OK," he agreed, still grasping at straws. "For a while, but we go home tomorrow. Right?" *Hope?*

"I said I'd *try*."

No hope. He was trapped; he felt sick to his stomach.

She turned back to Daniel. "Now, Mr. Davis, I'll need your assistance in moving Mother downstairs. I believe I'll take your advice and temporarily place her in the chest freezer on the back porch while…" The TV room's screen door squeaked open; she turned in time to glimpse the back of Jimmy's shirt as he ran from the house.

Daniel made a quick move toward the short shotgun he'd leaned against the dining room doorframe, but Thelma stopped him, her hand again on his shoulder. "Not now, not now. He'll be back. There's nowhere else he can go around here. Besides, I believe you'll find Jimmy to be more, shall we say, cooperative when you come back tomorrow for the service—that is, if we are still in need of the healing service for Homer tomorrow." She smiled her secret meaning up to Daniel's eyes. "You may begin *using* the boy then. Now what say we get to the task at hand?"

"Yeah, what say," Daniel replied, caressing the side of her waist with his right hand while holding his left hand, palm side up, extended to her. "But what say we take care of the details first? I believe my assistance with Zula is worth, what say, an extra hundred?"

"Why, you greedy boy," she playfully admonished. "I had in mind another figure, perhaps a figure more appealing to your youth…and manhood." She fluttered her eyelashes up at him and pursed her lips. *Fat chance of him getting a hundred bucks out of me just for hauling Zula's ass down to the freezer. Why, if she didn't smell so bad, I'd leave her where she lays.*

Daniel smiled back, his thick lips twisted in lascivious comprehension. He needed no coaching to understand Thelma; he'd understood women ever since he was old enough to have hair. "Maybe it's just something in me that appeals to something in them," he'd once told his father when the old man caught him in the file room groping the church secretary. *But this old bag sure as hell ain't beating me out of my money. Hah! Not with somebody like Judy Shanks soon to be available.* "Whatever you think. But what about the boy coming back?"

"Didn't you see how frightened he is? I don't expect to see him before tomorrow morning."

***

Getting late. Billy Ray fumbled with the car radio. He had turned it off hours before because it was getting on his nerves with its series of unheeded admonitions: Stay off the roads; stay in your homes; do not call the hospitals; do not attempt to transport the ill to emergency rooms; do not, do not, do not—*Just die peacefully in your own house by yourself.* But now the sky was darkening, and he wanted to know the time of day. *Don't know what difference that'll make, but I do need to call Thelma again…and find something to eat.*

He then saw the sign indicating an off-ramp ahead; its roadway appeared to be clear. Like the broken-down Ford station wagon, more cars had now pulled off onto the emergency apron, sometimes clogging the exit ramps. And many more people were now walking alongside the slow-moving traffic. *But I do believe the cars have thinned some since I passed the Newark airport; it'll still be tough finding a break in the line of all that mess.*

Because traffic was moving so slowly, Billy Ray also had witnessed several attempts by pedestrians to create their own rides, forcing their way into backseats and onto truck beds, much like the hobos had done during the Depression era when they had hopped boxcars and ridden the rails. *But there ain't no bulls out here to keep order and to limit the hitchhikers.* In fact he had seen several vicious fights break out, the latest between a walker, trying to hang on to the top of a car, and its driver, an enormous black man armed with a baseball bat. The big guy had slammed on his brakes and leaped around his car to beat the interloper from his vehicle and back to the side of the road. *I think the ol' guy was too tired anyway from all his walking to have put up much of a fight.* The pedestrian was a bloody mass when Billy Ray had inched by the scene.

"But you know, ol' boy," Billy Ray told himself, "you really should be thinking about letting some other folks ride with you. Don't know why it didn't dawn on you before. Guess you was thinking the trip would be shorter, and passengers wouldn't likely want to go where you're going." He was planning to take the New Jersey Turnpike's fork over to I-276 and the Pennsylvania Turnpike then I-95 to Philadelphia. Since he knew the roads in that city well, he believed maybe he could stay over there, find himself something to eat and a place to sleep, and continue on in the morning. "I guess at this turnoff you just might find some folks who look halfway decent and won't try to rob you. What do you say, ol' boy?" He steered around a jeep, its rear end sticking partially out in the exit ramp, and moved cautiously through the broken line of walkers alongside the road, aiming for the McDonald's that was advertised on another sign as being down the road to the right, two-tenths of a mile.

The restaurant was exactly where it was advertised to be, but it wasn't really open for business. It was open, however, in the sense that the glass in the door had been shattered, and groups of people could be seen moving about and sitting inside at the tables. *They must have needed to use the bathroom.* But Billy Ray wasn't really surprised; he'd heard on the radio news that many fast-food places along the interstate had been broken into and vandalized. *This must be one of them.* Further he had heard that the national guard troops and local law-enforcement personnel were simply too sparse to adequately deal with the droves moving out of the cities and that peacekeeping efforts were to be concentrated around hospitals and other "high-value" areas. *Wealthy neighborhoods, I'd expect.*

Billy Ray circled the low building, accelerating through the drive-through lane to avoid unwanted passengers, and turned again onto the road, this time away from the interstate and toward, he hoped, a rural area and a town that was still relatively untouched by the panicked movement of people across the country.

And there was. Nine miles down the country road, Billy Ray first saw the flashing red lights and then the police cruiser parked under them, spanning the road's center line. A policeman with a shotgun waved for him to slow down and stop; another officer observed from the car.

Billy Ray rolled down his window. "Good evening, sir. Is there trouble ahead?" he calmly asked, as if he hadn't just exited from miles and miles of mayhem.

"Depends on you, boy. What do you want here?"

The cop, still sporting his mirrored sunglasses even though the sun had set, had loudly voiced his inquiry without moving forward to inspect either the car's contents or its occupant. *Now that's unusual,* thought Billy Ray. *The man is clearly here as a watchman rather than a law enforcer.* "Well, sir, I was just looking for a place to eat and rest up. Maybe a MacDonald's or a Burger King? And maybe get some fuel for my vehicle?"

The cop backed up some to consider the Mercedes. "Diesel?"

"Yeah."

"Good thing. Out of gasoline in the town, but the truck stop should be OK for diesel."

"Great!"

"But you can't stay overnight. Understand? Only locals here. Get your fuel and get out. Understand?" The cop raised his shotgun to emphasize his directive.

"But Officer, food?"

"Bologna sandwich and a can of pop—twenty-five dollars. I can tell them here on the radio if you want it, and they'll leave it out by the pump."

"Bit pricy, ain't it?" Billy Ray smiled; he thought maybe the policeman was having some fun with him. But the mirror-eyed man didn't smile back.

"Take it or leave it—your choice. But you tell me now. You'll also want to pay upfront for your fuel." He still didn't smile.

"But Officer…you're right. I'd better settle on just getting the diesel and going on my way. Thanks for your help, sir." *Bet he's mostly concerned about my germs anyway.*

The policeman turned and walked back to his companion in the car, who then lifted a hand mike from the dash; he kept watch past his partner as he talked. Then he nodded, and the shotgun-carrying cop turned back, waving Billy Ray on around the parked cruiser. Nothing more was said.

A mile and a half down the road, Billy Ray entered the city limits, passed several closed buildings, and spotted a second set of flashing lights in the intersection ahead. *Broadway and Main. This must be the business district.* The policeman in this cruiser didn't get out; he just pointed at the filling station across the intersection.

Billy Ray pulled into the brightly lit station, stopping beside the island with the green pump and the diesel sign painted on its front. He got out, stretched, and stooped to read the charge per gallon on the pump. *$9.99.9 per gallon!* He jerked upright and looked to the building. *You got to be kidding me! Damn price gougers!*

About that time a man in a baseball cap opened the door to the truck stop and stepped outside. He casually leaned so the big pistol strapped to his side was clearly visible in the high-intensity lighting.

Billy Ray swallowed and acknowledged the guy with a slight wave. *Don't think we're in New York anymore, Toto, with all these weapons showing.* His initial rush of anger and indignation dissolved at the sight of the gun. *I guess extortion comes with the jungle.* He sighed loudly, slipped out his wallet, and thumbed free the large bill he knew was on top. Then he strolled across the island to greet the man and, as he expected, to prepay for the fuel. *At least I'll get something for my money.*

"'Evening," Billy Ray called, forcing out a friendly tone. When the other man simply nodded, he continued, "I'd like a hundred dollars' worth, please."

The man pointed to the short, wide post that protected the front of the truck stop.

Billy Ray understood; he ambled over and put his bill on the post and backed up. "And I'll need to use the facilities."

The man advanced a step and palmed the money from atop the post. "No facilities. Piss on the side of the road."

"OK," Billy Ray amicably agreed and returned to the island to pump his $100 worth of fuel.

It dinged off rather quickly. *At $9.99.9 per gallon, you'd think the assholes wouldn't still short the pumps.* But he knew this was just another sign of the times; if they weren't limited by the pump's calculating power, they would've charged even more per gallon. Billy Ray rubbed the top of his head and looked up at the bugs that bobbed against the lights above. He'd be glad when he was in East Tennessee again. *Then maybe I'll at least know the name of the man robbing me.*

Soon, with darkness complete and flying insects rising in his headlights to splatter his windshield, he was cruising back down the country road, past the policemen sentries and their flashing red lights, and back to I-95. Another couple of hours, and he would be crossing the Delaware River then traveling south again.

***

The moon already had risen over the barn when Jimmy tossed his shovel from the hole and climbed out. "Whew! That was a lot of digging." He stood and turned to critique his work in the moonlight. "Pretty good, I'd say." He compared the length of this hole with the other one on the far side. "About the same."

He had started digging soon after he had run from the house, having heard Thelma's plans for Zula and the freezer. *Can't let that happen.* He had wanted what he believed Homer would want: a respectful burial, even if it wasn't to be done with proper funeral people and all. So he had taken a long-handled shovel from the tool rack in the barn and had set out to dig a grave, first walking the property to find the best plot on the land, a shaded spot at the end of the garden. "There's a great view of the mountains across the hayfield here, and Zula will get plenty of company when we come to work in the garden," he'd said. *Plus,* he'd thought, with a twinge of guilt, *it's not near as hard digging out here as back up behind the barn in that ol' red clay.*

When he had completed the first hole, he already had made up his mind to dig the second one. "It's gonna happen," he'd told himself. "And it's gonna be dark soon, but at least it's not real cold in the evenings yet. Maybe I'll get a bright moon too. I think the Lord will do that for Homer."

The moon was so bright that Jimmy could now see clear to the bottom of the second hole. "Pretty deep," he observed, leaning far over the edge, bracing himself with his shovel. "Now go get yourself cleaned up and something to eat." He drove the shovel's blade into the massive pile of dirt between the two graves and turned to go to the house through the garden.

As he walked he raked his arms along through the brown cornstalks, not caring that the rustling sound could be heard well beyond the garden's fence and probably by anyone sitting as far away as the front porch. But Jimmy didn't care; he had seen the black Cadillac rolling down the driveway toward the hard road at about the same time he had started on the second grave.

He reached the driveway and walked on, along the broken-marble sidewalk, past the TV room door, and on around to the other back door—actually a side door—to the closed-in porch. *Habit.* After he had scraped the bottoms of his tennis shoes and slipped them off, he realized he would have to pass the long chest freezer—*with maybe Zula already inside?*—if he went in the house this way. *No matter.* Two hours earlier he probably would have walked back to the screen door at the TV room but not tonight. He was just too tired. *Tired of everything.* He was ready to go home whether or not Thelma would take him. He wasn't afraid of her, and he was no longer afraid of Daniel. He just wanted to be away from the whole lot.

But you're forgetting Homer. He realized now that Thelma wouldn't take care of her father. *She didn't take care of Zula.* And he felt he owed it to Homer to be there for the old man up to the end. He was due that respect, like the kind of respect Homer had paid ol' Nick Clark by visiting him on his deathbed. *So long ago. Gosh, that feels like an eternity ago.* He pulled wide the screen door and walked in without turning on the overhead light. *Now that's a full moon,* he thought.

Stripping off his dirty jeans and sweat-sodden T-shirt as he walked, Jimmy tossed them on top the freezer as he passed, heading to the bathroom for that cooling shower. He had more jeans and shirts packed in his suitcase upstairs.

***

Yawn! "Man, I'm tired!" Billy Ray was yawning more often now, and his eyes burned. It had been almost four hours since he had retraced his ten-and-a-half-mile detour to the town, regained the turnpike, and journeyed on to the last exit ramp before entering Pennsylvania, right where he was to cross the river. Traffic had initially been as bad as when he had first left it; all lanes crawled, flowing around stalled vehicles as if they were islands, edging off onto the road's shoulders, where wrecks formed larger obstacles in the current, but still flowing onward. He also had noticed that, with the deepening night and waning moon, the numbers of walkers paralleling the traffic flow had significantly decreased. In fact he had passed maybe only two small groups of pedestrians in the last hour. *Maybe they've taken shelter for the night. Maybe with the increase in the speed we're moving...Ah, that's it—fewer stalled cars now.* He guessed that by now most automobiles and trucks were running out of gas, being unable to refuel at any of the stations he had seen alongside the road. *Probably few could pay the tariff anyway.* He took small comfort in his thoughts that, as soon as this plague was over, those gougers who were taking advantage of others would be called to account for their actions. *This is America! Land of the just!*

And then we'll bury our dead. Billy Ray had passed several sad bundles on the side of the road that could only be bodies—dead people. He, at first, had imagined the supine figures to be sleeping people, folks who were simply tuckered out from their walking and seeking momentary rest and warmth from the pavement. But then, more often than not, he saw skid marks before the bodies, where the walkers probably had chosen quick deaths under the wheels of oncoming cars, their spilled fluids forming dark pools surrounding piled tangles of cloth and luggage.

There's one now! He rotated his foot from the accelerator to the brake, his eyes automatically flicking to the rearview to check for closing headlights. *Nothing!* In fact the next vehicle's lights were only a speck on the inky horizon behind. *Traffic has really thinned. So maybe I can see if there's anything I can do to help this guy—girl; she's got long hair. Doesn't seem to be gushing blood or nothing either.*

He braked harder, slowing his car and stopping when he was about ten feet from the blanketed figure but still able to see her over his hood. He rolled down his window, allowing the Mercedes to idle while he looked around. *Be careful. Too dark to see much.* The road had narrowed, and the number of lanes had decreased since he'd left the last town and were now two and two, both directions. *Nobody coming either. Gosh, it's really late now. Nobody around.* That thought made him thoroughly nervous.

Billy Ray tried a couple of horn toots. "Ma'am!" he yelled, tilting his face to the open window. "Ma'am! Can I help you, ma'am?" *Nothing.* He shifted into neutral and twisted around in his seat again, searching the brush-covered median and the grassy roadway margin for any signs of movement or irregular shadows. *Too dark, too cloudy now for full moonlight. Flashlight?* He remembered that he once had owned a small, two-cell flashlight that might still be in the car, and leaned far over to open the glove compartment. *Damn!* The tiny light in the box flashed on, momentarily blinding him, startling him. He jerked straight and felt for the shift lever, ready to slam it back into gear should he hear the sounds of running feet on the pavement. *Stupid! Stupid!*

He waited, firmly gripping the steering wheel and shifter while the purple dots faded from his vision. *That wasn't too smart.* He waited until he could again see the outline of the trees and bushes in the median and was barely able to discern the gray of the fencing that ran alongside the road, on the other side of the low ditch. *Try again.* This time he averted his eyes as he leaned over and felt-searched the glove box. *Nothing…boy! That was a waste. Blind yourself and almost crap your britches…Now check under your seat.* He leaned forward and tucked his hand beneath the bench seat as far back as he could reach. *Ah!* He grabbed at one of the objects his fingernails brushed, a hard cylinder aligned toward the center of the seat. *More road flares? No, no, it's my bat.* He remembered now having watched Jimmy stow the miniature baseball bat under the front seat last spring. It had been a birthday gift from the boy. *He said I could use it to test the pressure in my tires, like the long-haul truckers do.* He smiled and rolled the bat forward until he could lift it from under the seat then tossed it onto the passenger side. *Maybe it'll come in handy to lower the pressure on me if somebody comes running up out of the dark.*

Reaching down again, Billy Ray searched and this time found the flashlight. He clicked it on and off to test the batteries, flashing it through the window and away from his face. *Looks good. Now to turn off the interior light switch.* He touch-felt the dome light, located its switch, and clicked it to the center. *Now.*

He slowly opened his car door and stepped out on one leg then quickly ducked back inside to retrieve his miniature bat from the seat. *Might need it sooner than later.* With his left arm propped on the door and his right on the roof, he methodically surveyed the darkness around him again, scanning both roadsides up and back. *Nothing. Try the horn now.* He reached inside, located the horn button, and held it down while keeping a close eye on the blanket and hair, watching for any movement, any sign of life. The blaring horn sounded ugly in the still of the night. *Damn! Nothing even twitched—don't look good.* "Ma'am?" Billy Ray called again. "I'm going to come over and look at you, ma'am. Hear me?" He exhaled a long breath through puffed cheeks—his sign of reluctance at leaving the safety of his vehicle—and stood up fully, ready to move from behind the door.

Then he heard it—the whoosh, whoosh of many legs running through long grass. *The ditch!* Over the car's roof he could see shadow men coming onto the road from its side, jumping up from their hiding places across the low swale. Billy Ray ducked to clear the door, to fling himself back into his seat. *Gravel!* He heard the crunch and the scattering of the roadside rocks behind as another man vaulted from the median. *No time! Window open!* He could feel the body behind him, reaching for him with murderous hands, coming fast. Billy Ray stood, lashing backward with the bat as he rose, a full swing with his weight behind it, as if he were aiming for the fence. *A homer!* He solidly connected with the head of his attacker, and the man dropped, thudding first into the sharp edge of the Mercedes's open door, his inertia being redirected by the force of Billy Ray's bat, then skidding to the pavement against the front tire.

Billy Ray was again in his seat, his hand pulling down hard on the gearshift, his foot pushing the accelerator to the floor. For a millisecond the car did nothing—the normal response for a diesel engine—then took hold. Billy Ray's heartbeat resumed with the engine's roar and with the rear wheels gaining traction, first sliding to the side then thrusting forward; Billy Ray barely had time to get his left leg in before the door slammed shut on its own. *Damn!* Then he felt the second slight skitter to the left as the spinning tires reached the downed assailant—he was too involved with steering his vehicle to even make the connection—and saw the prone body ahead—the reason for his having stopped in the first place. It flashed in and under his car with a bump that he felt and noticed. *Oh, heck!* He looked to his mirror, trying to catch some sight of the effects behind, maybe to see a human body tumbling along the asphalt—one that he'd forever wonder about...*Did I kill her, or was she already dead?*

***

"Forever" lasted almost until the time Billy Ray saw the exit-ramp sign for the state park. "You've almost made it to the river, to Pennsylvania, ol' boy," he told himself, the body in the road momentarily forgotten. With the passing miles, he had reasoned, probably correctly, that if the blanketed girl had been alive, she would have been a part of the ambush and most definitely would have moved when the commotion had started. Or the gang most definitely would have *not* used one of their own if there was any uncertainty the passing car would *not* stop. And he was quite certain *he* would not be doing any more stopping along the way to help anyone.

"Do you dare take a run through the recreation complex," he asked himself, "to see if they have a usable bathroom or maybe an operating water fountain?" He took his foot from the gas and allowed the car to coast. "Well, you'd better make up your mind quickly, ol' boy, 'cause the turnoff draws nigh." He again wished he had a gun. *Decisions would be so much easier.* "OK, ol' man, you can drive through...but keep your head down."

He turned the wheel and coasted on, rolling in under the tree canopy that began about a hundred yards or so into the park. Billy Ray reckoned that the entrance must be really gorgeous in daytime... and under less stressful times. *At least there's not a lot of broken-down cars coming into Pennsylvania this way.* He had noticed, however, that on the other side of the interstate, the side leading out of the state and away from the big city, there was an accumulation of stalled and parked vehicles lining the shoulders of the road, just like he had seen coming out of New York. *Maybe I won't be staying in Philadelphia tonight after all,* he thought.

He read the signs as he drove, a task made easier with the light of the coming dawn: RESTROOM, NO TRUCKS, CARS ONLY THIS WAY. He made a slow left and spotted the refreshment and bathroom building off to the right. "Should call it the relievement center. Hah!" The lights were on inside the building, and several flood lamps lit up the parking area. "Looks rather welcoming."

Then he saw them: a young woman carrying a baby and running for her life from a hobbling man, running from the refreshment area toward the interstate, moving in the same direction he was going. The woman seemed to have built up a sizable lead ahead of the limping guy, but she continued to scream anyway. Billy Ray sped up slightly and drew alongside. She seemed to stumble slightly, almost falling, while frantically gesturing to him, pointing to the baby and the pursuing man, imploring Billy Ray to stop. So he did.

He leaned over and unlocked the passenger-side door, tugging at its handle until it opened; the woman barely slowed to jump into the moving car. She wrenched shut the door, gasped, and pulled her baby close, burying her face in its blanket.

"Oh, sir, thank you so much for stopping. Thank you. Thank you. I don't know what—"

"That's good, ma'am. That's good, that's good. So how's the baby? Is he—she OK?" Billy Ray twisted in his seat for a better view of the child in the light of the passing floodlights.

"Oh, the baby's fine...but you gotta stop now," she answered, straightening to face him, her voice now calm yet somehow edgy, strained.

Billy Ray looked up sharply into her determined, frightened eyes. He saw the bore of a large handgun pointing up at him from the now loosened covering. *No baby.*

"Mister, suppose you pull over here, and let's sit for a while. We need your car. We need to talk some." She raised the pistol, holding it with both hands and pointing it at his eye.

Billy Ray saw the running man behind, no longer limping and drawing close.

"Ma'am, I don't think we have much to talk about," he said, and stomped hard on the accelerator. In that millisecond of diesel engine hesitation, he heard the gun explode. Then darkness came.

***

Billy Ray awoke. *Dang! What a headache!* He realized then that he was flat on his back and staring at the sky above through intertwining tree branches. *Early morning, I think.* Then he remembered what had happened to him. *State park. Running woman. Damn, boy, she shot you…you dumb ass.*

Another minute passed; he decided he should begin to see which parts of his body still functioned. Rolling his head from side to side on the ground, he tasted the coppery tang of blood in his mouth. *Lots of it.* He raised his hands to his face, covering his eyes with his fingers, his palms on his cheeks. *What's this? Damn, it stings!* He felt lumps: a flap-like scallop on one side that hung from his cheek and a ragged fringe on the other. *Flesh! My flesh! My skin's hanging from my face! She shot me in the face!* With light finger taps, he tried to determine the extent of his injury. *Right through my mouth, in and out. But my eyes work, thank God. And I'm breathing.* He pushed first to one side then to a sitting position. His fatigue jacket hung open, and his shirtfront felt clammy and cold against his chest. *It's wet. More blood?* He explored his chest and stomach with his hands, and his mouth with his tongue. *Shirt all wet—probably my blood—no big holes in my guts. Don't feel my tongue, though.* He opened his mouth and touched around inside with his forefinger. *Thought so—not much left of my tongue. The side of my jaw's mostly gone.* "Ouy mm uh ess." *I'm a mess.*

He pushed himself to a kneeling position then stood, uncertainly, extending his arms to maintain his balance. *Shaky.* Then more blood flowed warmly down his forehead and into his left eye. *Now what's that?* With more light finger taps, he felt a groove—a cut in his head—that extended from above his hairline to his crown. *That lady shot me in the head while I was on the ground! From the front—meaning to finish me off! Why?* Bile rose in his throat, causing him to bend, hands on knees, preparing to vomit if it came to that. *At least they left me my shoes.*

When the waves of nausea and dizziness had passed, and Billy Ray believed he could again walk, he turned in place, trying to sort out his surroundings. It was still early morning, but now there was enough light to see the trees and bushes all around—and the buildings beyond. *Rest-stop bathrooms!* He stumbled toward the closest building, the glass-fronted one with a sign over the doors: TRAVEL FACILITY. It looked well lit inside to Billy Ray…and safe. *But there's others!* He saw two men, standing and talking, beside the benches on the walkway.

Billy Ray halted for a time, watching the men, studying them while trying to stay hidden in the shadows. *Dressed OK, I guess. Uniforms…maybe state roads people. No guns. Now to try to walk that far… gonna wash up.* He stepped out onto the sidewalk and stumbled forward, his sanctuary just ahead. *Gonna be OK,* he assured himself.

The men called out to him when he tottered past, his hands extended, anticipating the doors' entrance handles. "Hey buddy! Where you think you're going? Gaaa!" They recoiled when Billy Ray stopped and turned to them. "Jeez, man! You got the plague? Get the hell outta here! Get away from here, ya friggin' zombie!"

Billy Ray tried to explain, his hands held out to them, pleading, "Ouy ot hot n ya hah." *I got shot in the face.* He could see that they were young guys, probably assigned to look after this rest stop, and guessed they'd probably never before seen people, despairing people, like they were now seeing pass this way. He was just as certain they hadn't come of age during any past wartimes to have encountered bloody torsos, blasted limbs, and gun-shot faces. He could understand their shock. But *they* couldn't understand him; they continued to stare at him, their faces twisted in revulsion.

One of the men, the bigger of the two, nudged his companion and leaned close to confer, whispering in his ear. The other man, the talker, nodded and held up the flat of his hand to Billy Ray. "Listen, old man, unless you got some coin—some dinero—you can't use this john. Unless you got some *money.* Understand? Money!" The big man moved to place himself directly between Billy Ray and the building, while the talker continued to edge along the sidewalk to block Billy Ray's escape or perhaps to distract him, slapping at his shoulder with the back of his hand. "Ya gotta have funds now, old man—money. Everything costs now. No more welfare, old man. You old guys are dying off now, and ya gotta pay. The funds, old man…Show us what you got, or get the hell outta here. Now!" He jabbed his fingers into Billy Ray's arm—hard—causing him to stagger backward.

Billy Ray couldn't understand this—this hostility. He was hurt and barely clothed; he obviously had no money. But he wasn't afraid of these guys. *This ain't panic, like those folks along the road. And these guys ain't gangbangers and killers, like Juan. They got no excuse to act like this. This is just plain meanness—evil—coming out. Maybe a week ago, they were nice guys, working guys, ordinary people. But now it's all physical. Blurred lines. The dirty guts of human nature coming out.*

He thought of Homer, of his summary of a situation involving some boys caught torturing and killing one of his neighbor's calves in the pasture: "Billy Ray, they've just got the ol' Satan in them, the ol' evil one. When they thought no one was around to see and punish them, they let ol' Satan out—had the opportunity and let ol' Satan out. And the little calf was defenseless and couldn't tell on 'em." *Homer understood this.* And maybe Billy Ray had seen the same old evil during the war, but the scale was much bigger, and he was younger then, not given to philosophical contemplations—just comprehension—and he had managed to forget a lot since then. But those old insights, those specters now rushed back. *Evil is poured out onto the earth.* He blinked and stepped back. *Where did that come from?*

The small man interpreted Billy Ray's hesitation and his backward step as cowardice and fear, and slapped at him again. "What's in that pocket, old man? You're dying anyway."

Billy Ray patted his jacket's breast pocket. *Yeah, I'm dying anyway.* He thumbed open the flap's snap and reached in with two fingers, touching the wooden handle of his fishing knife.

"Whatcha got there, old man?" The bigger one made the mistake of grabbing Billy Ray's arm, trying to turn him to see in his pocket while avoiding contact with the bloody shirtfront.

The blade flashed, severing the big man's thumb from the rest of his fingers. He pulled his hand back and dumbly looked at his member, the hanging digit. Then the pain came, and the guy screamed.

Billy Ray shuffled backward, keeping both assailants in sight. "Ev me own…na tral!" *Leave me alone. I wasn't looking for trouble!* He held aloft the knife, guarding his retreat as he crabbed up and through the flower bed beside the sidewalk, then on through the evergreen bushes on the far side.

But his caution wasn't necessary; the small man was staring bug-eyed at his wounded friend. "Damn, man!" he yelled. "I think that old shit cut your artery! You're squirting blood everywhere!"

Billy Ray crept away from the men, the building, and the parking-lot lights, fading into the patches of trees and bushes farther along the road that would lead back to the interstate. *Gotta keep going.*

DAY FOUR

Gotta keep going. Billy Ray had walked for almost two hours now. Looking back over his shoulder at the sun, he estimated it was near midmorning. The sun's rays felt good on his back, and he saw the rise of the bridge ahead. *Gonna be OK.* His bleeding had stopped, and he had bound his jaw with his handkerchief. *To keep it from jiggling.*

As he walked, he replayed the last forty-eight hours and all he had been through. It seemed to him that everywhere he had turned, everywhere he had looked, he'd had to defend himself—had to fight other folks just to keep what he had in his pockets, to just stay alive. Several times he had asked himself in his mangled whisper, "How can I make it through this? The world's gone crazy! I've gone crazy!" But he knew, just knew, that somewhere ahead there was real sanctuary—protection and the rule of law—and the national guard. *Just keep walking.* He thought of the two men at the rest stop and of his initially being mistaken for someone with the disease—a carrier—and the possibility of being turned away by those very same authorities he was seeking. "Oy en hot ey en. Hah!" *Or being shot by them. Hah! That'd be... What's the word... ironic?* He snorted again with the thought. *Talk about a wasted, useless way to die.*

Since leaving the park, he'd stayed well away from the paved surfaces, slogging along in the shorter grasses just to the inside of the bordering fence, and turning occasionally to watch for approaching cars. More vehicles were on the road now, going faster and heading into Pennsylvania. And in the full daylight, he was being ignored by their drivers…as he had ignored pedestrians yesterday.

Then he saw a semitrailer truck go by on the far side of the highway—the first big truck he'd seen on the road since New York. It was heading in the other direction, away from Philadelphia. *The world is starting up again! Commerce has returned.* He was feeling better; he liked it better when the world made sense to him.

He returned to his reflections, about all that had happened in the last few hours, the last two days. *Was that all real?* He touched his jaw and winced. *It's real.* But it was still dreamlike. He thought about his revelation at the rest stop. He'd never been what most folks would call religious; he couldn't remember having had an inspiration, let alone a revelation. However, for a moment there, he had perceived, grasped, understood a foundational truth of human nature: A flaw, a baseness, exists there, maybe held in check by laws and customs and social mores, yet the flaw remains—this tilt to the evil. Preachers had told him it was there all along, fixed in man after the fall from grace and personified as Satan, but he never had really believed it any more than he believed in the Garden of Eden. Yeah, he'd accepted Christ when he was a kid and believed in God and all, but he never really believed in an evil that existed in his deepest parts. *Maybe because it doesn't anymore, and maybe Christ's spirit is telling me that. So was that maybe God's gift to me?*

For a moment there, the curtain had slipped, and he understood and could see a measure of order in all the chaos now surrounding him and his existence. To him things needed to have reasons, and he hadn't been seeing that meaning, particularly since the inception of this plague. *An old plague, Black Death, from the Middle Ages. Can you beat that? Sure has put a knot in our world. I've seen a side of people I'd forgotten—a meanness I'd forgotten, the jungle that's waiting just outside our thin protection of law. But that's all past now.* He believed commerce and justice and consideration were here again. There would again be tangible order in existence. *And for me an intangible meaning in eternity: God's gift and the cleanliness of my soul. Intangible? No. As tangible as my thought and consciousness.*

There's the bridge. He climbed the steep embankment and crawled over the low steel fenders to stand in the roadway. He looked both ways, behind and to the front; he was alone. *I guess I'm gonna hafta be the only one right now on this big ol' bridge,* he concluded, feeling his anxiety ratchet up one more notch. While he'd avoided the few people he'd seen this morning as he walked the road, he disliked being alone now and away from any pedestrian cover. *Way too open, way too close to the pavement.* Though the bridge's railings were spaced far enough for him to stay clear and out of the paths of the intermittent vehicles, there wasn't the safety of a separate walkway alongside the expanse. *Maybe they want to discourage folks from fishing from the bridge. Hah! Ah well…at least it's daylight now.* He walked on.

He passed a few cars that had been abandoned along the bridge, and for the most part, they'd been pushed to the railing and weren't apt to impede traffic flow at all. But still they slowed his progress because he felt each one posed an ambush threat to him, requiring him to cautiously approach and survey each vehicle before proceeding.

He was skirting the last of these abandoned cars—a forlorn-looking Buick station wagon left standing with its doors open—when he heard tire noise coming fast from behind. *Oh, damn!* He'd almost made it all the way across the long bridge without encountering any traffic going his way; a few cars had passed him, but they all were on the other side of the bridge; none had passed on his side. Ducking low, he hurried back to the Buick to lean against its grill until the oncoming car, actually a van, rolled by, moving at close to the posted speed limits. *Yeah,* he thought with a chuckle when it had passed, *it's over. Sanity's come back.* A little boy was standing in the rear seat of the van and was smiling and waving to him. He smiled and waved back.

And I'm almost into Pennsylvania. He now saw the river's far bank and the two-lane road that ran alongside it, crossing under the bridge just ahead. He limped on, a little faster now.

He spotted a line of national guard vehicles convoying on the road below, coming toward him and the bridge, to cross directly under him. *Wow!* This was the first sign of the guards he had seen since he had heard they were providing order and protection along the roads. *Yeah, things are getting back to order. The jungle's been pushed back!* He waved and the soldiers returned his wave. *Yes.*

More tire noise! Another vehicle was coming across the bridge, slowing behind him now. Billy Ray glanced over his shoulder, noting that it was a pickup, with a couple of guys standing in the truck's bed, leaning over the roof of the cab. And one guy was holding something and smiling. *Yes.* Then he saw the muzzle flash from the rifle.

***

"So how'd you like that shot, Charley? Caught him just when he was looking back. *Kapow!* And he dropped. Knocked him right over the railing!"

"You're just so damn lucky to get those kinds of shots," Charles replied. "Hell, Richard, he even had a scarf or something tied round his head to aim at. You couldn't have missed!"

"Still a damn good shot," Richard groused.

"OK, so we're even now. OK? I get the rifle next time." Charles bent over and slapped the side of the truck, whistling for the driver's attention. "Jeffrey, after you turn at the crossover at the end of the bridge, me and Richard will swap with you and Ted for your turn! That's two up on you guys!" He straightened and smiled at Richard. "We're gonna win that case of beer," he declared, confidently nodding and winking. But then another thought came to him and his smile faded; his thick eyebrows knitted in concern. He leaned to again yell, "And cripples don't count—just kills!" He straightened, moving close to Richard. "You gotta watch ol' Jeffrey. He'll cheat you if you give him half a chance. Damned shame the way some folks are."

"Yeah, a damned shame," Richard agreed.

***

"Hello? Mom?" Jimmy whispered into the mouthpiece, cupping the phone with his hand.

He had risen well before daylight, his habitual wakening time, and quietly slipped out the back way, heading to the barn to complete his morning chores. *Such as they are.* Without having to milk any cows, he was done before the skies had begun to lighten. But he hadn't returned to the house, choosing instead to climb into the hay manger of one of the stalls to nap until daylight.

Now, with the sun high and his stomach rumbling, he had returned to the house, slipping in through the TV room after he had made sure Thelma was elsewhere in the house. He had planned on checking on Homer then exploring the refrigerator for any edibles he could take back to the barn. He'd spend the day there and maybe at the creek at the foot of the hill. *Until Thelma calls...If Thelma calls for me to take me home like she said she would.*

However, in passing through the room, he had spied the telephone and decided he'd chance a call home.

"Jimmy? Is that you, Jimmy?" His mother, Olivia, had picked up on the first ring; she sounded so far away.

"Yeah, Mom, it's me. It's me! Can you hear me OK?" he whispered louder.

"Oh, Jimmy, where have you been? Thelma said you and Homer had taken Zula to the hospital up there, and you'd call when you had a chance. Where have you been?" His mother was crying.

Thelma told her what? "Mom, when did you call? Thelma didn't tell me anything about your call."

"I called yesterday and the day before. Maybe it slipped her mind, what with her mother and all. I'd imagine she's really upset with her mother turning."

Yeah, like turning her into an icicle. "Yeah, it must've slipped her mind...like you said. So are you and Dad OK? Are you coming to get me?" *Please.* He wanted to plead with his mother, but he didn't want to alarm her, frighten her. *At least not yet.*

"Your dad's not doing well at all, Jimmy, not well at all. I should be at the hospital, but early this morning..."

"Yes, Mom?"

"...I called home from the hospital for Albert—we were going to come up and get you—and your dad didn't answer the phone."

"Yeah?" Jimmy could hardly breathe. He heard the strain in his mother's voice and heard her cover the phone while she sniffed and wiped her nose, but he didn't want her to stop talking.

"Well, they drove me home in one of their cars—one of the guards drove me home—and went with me inside. And there was your dad sprawled out on the living-room floor, like he was just fixing to come get me like we'd planned. But...Jimmy, did I tell you your father has caught the plague—the disease? I can't remember what I told you when I last talked with you." Her voice had risen steadily; she sounded very close to tears. "But anyway, he'd started to come down with the disease, and that was why we'd decided to drive up today to get you. We didn't know how much longer he'd be able to travel. Didn't Thelma tell you that? That shouldn't have slipped her mind because she told me not to bother because she was bringing you home."

"Well, Mom, she didn't say anything to me. But back to Dad—how is he now?"

She sniffed again, and Jimmy heard wiping noises. "The guard and I—he's a young fellow—we were able to drag Dad to the back bedroom and get him into bed. I've bathed him and given him what medications we have but..." Her voice faded as she searched for the right words. She knew her husband had little chance of surviving the plague—she had seen too many people dying at the hospital—but the beating he'd taken was so severe that he probably wouldn't even regain consciousness. *A blessing perhaps.*

When this had all started, when just the town's very elderly were trickling into the hospital's emergency room and were soon to pass away, Olivia hadn't been too upset, too alarmed. *After all, those persons lived long lives and were mostly accepting of their situations.* And the old folks were in anguish...death to them seemed more or less like a release from their suffering. However, there were a few, she remembered, who weren't so accepting and were lashing out, screaming to all who would listen of the inequities of the contagion, of their own innocence, and of the Lord's failure to rescue them in their hour of need. But they too eventually had died, leaving this world with their faces twisted in masks of bitterness and the hallways ringing with their accusations of betrayal. "I wonder what they're seeing?" she had asked herself and her coworkers.

As the hours had moved on, turning into days, and the inflow of people had increased, the mix of these aid seekers seemed to her to be tending to a younger generation—still relatively old but younger than those folks who first had come into her emergency room. And these people also were tending to be more demanding of her time, more insistent on immediate attention and instant healing, than the others. Some even had grabbed at her as she had passed, clamoring for her care as if they were the only ones in the room and threatening lawsuits and such if they weren't moved to the top of her triage list. *That was too much.* Dr. Dorfman, the ER physician, had seen what was happening and had relieved her, commanding her to find a place to rest for a while...and to check on her own family. Then he had ordered the few remaining nurses and aides to start issuing aspirin and placebo medications to the growing throng awaiting admission into the hospital—just to quiet them and allow the staff to do the work they could.

She had found a vacant office and the free phone line and had called home for her husband, perhaps to check on him but probably to tell him she had surrendered and to come rescue her from this repository of sadness and despair, where bodies were being stacked like cordwood in the back rooms and hallways. *But Albert didn't answer.*

"Mom?"

Gosh, I forgot Jimmy! What am I going tell him? That there's no hope for Albert...and me? Her nosebleed was heavier now. It had started at the hospital. *Maybe Dr. Dorfman noticed it after I returned from trying to call Albert? Maybe that was why he took me aside and leveled with me?* He had told her of a phone call he'd received four or five days before— from his cousin, a professor in New York and who was probably dead already—telling him of an international illness that had struck the city and soon would sweep the entire United States, and it had. His cousin also had told him of the disease's absolute mortality rate; no one had yet survived, other than an old fellow in Jerusalem named Abacus or Abbas or something like that; the old man had been the exception and was now the sole subject of ongoing pathogen tests and antibody studies.

Dr. Dorfman had then moved close to her, holding her by her shoulders and stooping to look her in the eye. "So, Ms. Burke, there's really very little hope," he had concluded, shaking his head. "Maybe no hope at all. You need now to tend to your own and go on home. You could have run like many of the others, but you chose to stay and help...without having known of the futility in running or, for that matter, any other response. That's a credit to you. Now it's time to tend to your husband and make your peace." He had then filled a small bag with pain-killers and walked Olivia down to the guards' station, instructing them to escort her through the milling crowd and drive her home.

"Mom?" Jimmy heard her breathing and sniffing. *She's going to start bawling any moment. Dad must really be in a bad way.*

"Son, I'm sorry. I was just thinking of...things. Listen, we're... we've got to do some planning here. And Thelma has *got* to drive you home. Hear? The roads aren't safe, and we don't have a car anymore."

"What?" He forgot to whisper.

"I think your dad was getting ready to come to the hospital when someone forced their way in." She passed over the part about finding the door ajar when the guard had brought her home and about the doorframe being partially chewed away by Albert's twelve-gauge. He obviously had put up a fight because of the blood pooled on the front porch tiles, but he must have only gotten off that one shot. The entrance door's broken glass and the pockmarked plaster indicated that whoever had come calling had brought automatic weapons. "They beat him unconscious and then went through the house. I think they took his wallet, his gun, his metal lockbox, and his car— that's all."

"That's *all*, Mom?" That sounded like a lot to him.

She misunderstood. "Yes, maybe they took more," she softly answered. "I guess, Jimmy, the time *is* short. And for him, for Albert, I wish I'd had those…"

Then the line went dead. Olivia hadn't the time to tell Jimmy that she thought the hospital guard may have helped himself to her purse and the relief-giving pills before he had left.

"Hello? Jimmy? Hello? Shoot! Well, I guess…should finish talking later anyway," she said, dropping the handset to its cradle. The shivers were now coming over her, and diarrhea was near. She might have just enough time to make it to the bathroom.

On his end, Jimmy was staring at a white-tinged thumb pressed hard on the phone's disconnect button. Following the thumb to the hand to the arm and so on, he now stared wide-eyed into the seething eyes of Thelma. She had entered the room without his having heard her and was standing beside him, huffing her foul breath in his face. *She's been drinking already.*

"What the hell do you think you're doing?"

"I was just passing through and saw that no one was using the phone and wanted to see if Mom was coming—"

"I *told* you I'd take you when I had time!" she screeched. "And I *told* you to stay off the phone unless I gave you permission!"

"Thelma, you never told me to stay off the phone," Jimmy objected.

"Jimmy, you, you…Never mind! Liar! That's what! I've told you and told you, and I'm telling you again: Stay off the phone unless I give you permission! Do you understand now, you…dummy? Is that plain enough? Billy Ray said he was going to call this morning, and if you caused me to miss—"

Right on cue the phone rang, then two rings—their phone number on the party line.

Thelma glowered at Jimmy. "If that's your mother again, and you cause me to miss Billy Ray's call…Now get out of here! Leave! Leave!"

Jimmy turned and fled but only as far as the doorway to the dining room, where he stopped to listen.

Thelma answered the phone, using her dripping-sweet phone voice. "Helloooo," she said, turning to face the windows. "Yes, this is Thelma Jones. Yes, Billy Ray Jones is my husband." Thelma was talking very loud, like she tended to do when she was on long-distance calls. "Yes, I know he's coming back to Tennessee. He was walking? He doesn't have a car? Well, let me tell you that he had a nice Mercedes when he left…Oh, OK. No car. He fell from a bridge? Onto the hood of a Pennsylvania national guard truck? What? Pennsylvania? *What?* Dead? Shot through the head? Oh, my god!" She lowered herself to the couch and her forehead to her hand; Jimmy saw her reflection in the window's glass.

And he felt his guts grow cold with the apparent news. He wanted—needed—a moment to sit, to think…to share. *Maybe I should go in to be with Thelma?*

Then she straightened and yelled into the phone, "No, screw you! We will *not* be responsible for damages to your truck's windshield!" She slammed the phone down and glared out the window; her eyes danced crazily to and fro, and her teeth were bared. "Damn it! Damn it!" she screamed. Then "Jimmy!"

He'd heard enough, and she was coming! Someone would pay for this, and he was readily available. He turned to run…and saw Homer's bedroom door…and made for it. *Safety!*

Slipping inside the unlit bedroom, he managed to quietly reclose the door behind himself; he followed the breathing sounds to the bed. Then, standing at the bedside, he patted the covers for Homer's body, frantically whispering into the fetid darkness, "Homer? Homer?"

The old man seemed to hear, pausing in his struggle for the next popping, labored breath; he gasped, his voice guttural and sticky with phlegm. "Whaaa…tizit? Whaat said? Zula?" But that was all; then his labored breathing resumed. Homer's condition obviously had worsened overnight.

Suddenly the knob clicked, and the door swung wide, loudly banging against its stop…and there stood Thelma in the portal.

Then she entered, step by step, flipping the wall switch, turning on the harsh overhead light as she came.

"I thought I'd find you here," she purred, her voice low and dangerous. "So just why are you in here, Jimmy?"

He retreated around by the far side of the bed, visually gauging the bed's clearance from the floor as he neared the wall. *Just in case.*

But there was no need; Thelma stopped short of the bed—to stand and stare at him. And for the moment, she had composed herself, knowing exactly what she wanted to say to the boy. "Take a look, Jimmy-boy. See the old man there?" She rapped the side of the mattress several times with the back of her hand. "Yeah, he's dying. Fact is, I don't know what's keeping him going." Jimmy glanced and saw that Homer was now pale as milk and that his eyes rolled wildly in their sockets as if in response to Thelma's raps; and then they closed again. He also noticed the large, uncapped bottle of prescription drugs lying on its side on the nightstand, along with a few capsules scattered about, spilled from its opening. Thelma had been either hasty or sloppy.

She was watching the boy's face, catching his study of the medication and the shadow of misgiving that had followed. "Yeah, spilled a few, didn't I? Well, I doubt the old man is going to make it through the night anyway. And you know, Jimmy, I want to get you home more than anything else I can think of. And I'll take you as soon as… Homer can be left alone for a while."

"Yes, Thelma, and I appreciate it. I really do. I hate that I'm being such a pain, and you know, I'll really appreciate it when—"

"Stow it! Just shut up!" she shouted, stopping him in midsentence. "I…I don't even want to hear your mealy mouthed words now; they grate on me so bad. I hate it too that you're such a pain in the ass. I've never cared for you kids they let stay here, and you know, I probably like you least of all. You know that, Jimmy? Least of all! There's something in you that just irritates me, and lately it's gotten worse. Something inside you and something inside me just don't get along…and I don't want you around here anymore. So now you've talked with your mother. Did she say she's coming for you? No? I bet she's telling you that your old man's sick. Oh, wait—maybe that was me she told. Gosh, that's right!" Thelma began to move again, to ease closer to the boy, swaying as she stepped and talked, her hands to her side and her fingers rubbing together, perhaps anticipating pinches and a firm grip on his ear. "Maybe that was me she told— that your ol' dad had taken sick. You know, Jimmy, I'm betting that he—achoo!" She violently sneezed once, twice, three, and more times through the fingers she now held to her mouth.

Jimmy had seen her edging closer to him; he took advantage of her closed eyes and heaving expulsions, springing forward and beyond, fast and low, as to dodge those grasping fingernails. Reaching the open doorway, he turned back, wanting to coolly confront her when her fit had passed—as if she had said nothing of importance to him or presented a physical threat to him. But nothing came to him; he didn't know exactly what he was going to say. *Maybe something about my intention of staying out of her way until she's ready to take me home. Or maybe something about my immediate wish to be on my way right now.* Then he thought about Billy Ray; he knew what he had heard and how much the man meant to him. And this was the wife of Billy Ray.

"Thelma, about Billy Ray, I heard you talking on the phone with the police..." he began.

She instantly whirled about to face him, the fingers of her one hand covering her mouth. Thin trails of blood ran from between her fingers and down the back of her hand.

Jimmy's eyes grew wide. *Thelma's caught the plague too!*

"Wasn't the cops, asshole," she said in a monotone. "That was the Pennsylvania National Guard...and it's none of your damned business...unless Billy Ray owes you money. Hah!" She laughed her mirthless laugh and extended her hand, seemingly to consider the bloody lines on its back, while she shifted closer to the boy. "Hah!" She made a sudden lunge at his head, but he was ready. He easily leaned to the side and skipped backward several steps into the dining room, placing the table between himself and Thelma.

"Thelma, what are you trying to do?" He couldn't now ignore her actions, her foulness. "You're trying to hurt me—to make me hurt for Billy Ray's death or something?" He was yelling too now. There was no longer any need for him to pretend there was friendliness or even courtesy between them. She hated him absolutely, and nothing he could do would change that. *But she's sick, and she's probably feeling sick—bad.* "Thelma, I hate this, and I'll…"

That's as far as he got. Thelma dug in her pockets to grab the weighty object she'd felt there: Homer's pocket watch. It was the only thing she had handy she could fling at the boy—and she did just that. In an instant she whipped out the watch and threw it at Jimmy with all her might, aiming for his face. But her aim was off, deflected by the intensity of her anger; she threw high, dinging the heavy gold case off the top of the boy's head and into the wall behind. It exploded into pieces.

Jimmy's hand went to his head, to feel for a wound as he glanced back at the wall. *I'm OK.* Scattered across the floor were the tiny springs and wheels and the bent metal pieces. *Homer's watch.* He straightened and looked again to Thelma, fully returning her gaze, staring long and hard into her demented eyes. Then he abruptly turned and walked unhurried through the dining room, through the kitchen, and on, leaving the house by the covered porch door.

Thelma heard the back door slam. She didn't follow after him, to chase after him. *I—and Daniel—will deal with him later. Damn, I hate that kid!* And she realized, for a second there, she had also felt fear. She returned to Homer's bed, to sit on its edge until she got her wind back, to think and plan.

✳✳✳

As her breathing slowed, her fevered thoughts congealed and her priorities hardened. Did she consider how her hatred of Jimmy had grown to such proportions, or why her anger was so overwhelming as to almost film over her vision with its red gauze? Or maybe think back to that date when she first had realized she loathed all the children— and Jimmy most of all? Or had she even realized the ramifications of her own affliction, its early stages perhaps indicated by the wavy red lines across the backs of her hands? No, her thoughts hadn't been allowed to proceed in those directions at all. She knew only that she needed to deal with those certain tasks at hand—those jobs she had started. That single-mindedness always had sustained her and carried her through; she would take care of herself—first. She needed now for Daniel to confirm that the papers Homer had signed were all that were necessary for the property—all the property—to transfer freely to her. *And to do that other thing he said he'd do.* Besides, if she was really infected, she wouldn't die without taking many more with her. *Better there to be no winners.* Somehow that thought calmed her, comforted her. *And there's Daniel too. With Billy Ray out of the picture, who's to know what comfort he can supply? He's young, but I could teach him a thing or two—and he's certainly got what's needed. Live for today, I always say.*

With that she rose from the bed and walked over to the nightstand, selecting one of the loose pills there. Then, with the glass of water in the other hand, she pressed the pill between Homer's gums and slightly lifted his head, placing the rim of the glass to his lips. "Here, Dad. Drink this, and swallow your medication." The old man obliged.

"Thank you...feels so good on my throat...so dry," he murmured, without once opening his eyes.

And a gun, she thought, as she was leaving the room, *I need to find either a knife or a gun or both. That pocket watch was worthless. Didn't even draw blood.*

Five feet directly below, Jimmy listened to her steps as she walked in Homer's bedroom. Minutes before, when he barely had exited the same room, he immediately had realized two things: that he would need shelter options for the coming night, since the evenings were growing cooler and the barn's hay wasn't all that warm and insulating, and that he must quickly accumulate supplies. In all probability he would soon, very soon, be hitting the road on his own. So, after loudly opening then slamming shut the back door, he had raised the dreaded cellar door and softly crept down the clammy stone steps, quietly lowering the heavy door behind as he had descended. *Thelma thinks I've gone outside.*

About a quarter of the way down the steps, Jimmy had slipped under the handrail and onto the bare dirt crawlspace off to the side. In earlier times of daring and tests of childhood courage, he and his cousins extinguished the hanging bulbs that illuminated the block-lined cellar below and for long, chilling minutes, gazed off into the dark recesses of the foundation piers and faraway walls in search of the poison-fanged snakes and hump-shouldered rodents they knew must dwell there. *Snakes, rats, and bogeymen.* However, today, he only wanted to be near Homer's room, to be able to hear the old man should he stir and be able to talk more. *It's possible Homer will pass on soon, and then there'll be no more talking face-to-face. Maybe Jesus allows for keeping in touch with people in heaven?* He would ask someday.

After pushing aside the sweet potatoes Zula had spread across the cool dirt there, close by the steps for easy reach, he had crawled away toward the metal grill set in the far foundation. His eyes had adjusted to the low light, and he had then been able to see the other grills and openings spaced evenly along in the foundation, allowing for good ventilation. Along the way he also had crawled past the odds and ends that had been placed there long years before—for temporary storage. *All kinds of valuable stuff's stored here and been forgotten: several coal oil lamps with high chimneys, probably used before they had electricity; thick, long boards, left over probably from maybe the 1800s when they were building the house; and iron traps with wicked, jagged teeth. Homer probably put them here because he don't hold with hunting animals.* Jimmy had wondered whether the stuff would be of future use to anyone.

Now Jimmy heard Thelma's quick, short steps as she strode above him. She stopped for a minute, and he heard her close the bedroom door. *Leaving Homer again.* Then she walked on, and he followed her in his mind's eye. *Going back to the TV room.* Thinking she might decide to use the phone again, he crawled across the packed red clay off to the right, over to where he estimated the desk to be on the floor above. *Yeah, she's dialing a number now.*

"Hello? Daniel?" she said. Jimmy clearly heard her talking. "Daniel, I've sneezed blood. I thought that healing I paid for was to fix that. Oh? Well, it had better. You know I can make it bad for you too. How bad? You naughty boy. You're never satisfied." Thelma's tone had turned coquettish. "You bad boy. I'll be waiting. Oh, a couple other things." She was back to business. "Homer is dragging on, and you know how I hate to see him suffer…He is *not* a heathen! Just because you and he believe differently—yes, I know. It's in your hands. And Jimmy too." Jimmy's ears perked up at the mention of his name. "He's ready for you to use him. *No*, he's not volunteering. But you know, first I need to make sure his mother doesn't show up today, and then he's yours tomorrow. Oh? So Bill Shanks is dead now? He was working for you too? Now that's a pity—I didn't know he was sick. Oh, I see. Well, you and your boys have to do what's necessary to enforce the law. Yeah, even with Jimmy; he's not above the law…and I agree with you about the Devil in him. I find I'm hating that kid more as each day passes. What time? Three? OK, see you then. What? I did—his third pill today. Yeah, out. He's aged like twenty years in the last two days. Better hurry, or I may not need you—no, no, I'll always need you, lover. Bye-bye, sweetie." Thelma hung up the phone and ambled away. Jimmy heard her humming as she mounted the stairs, going to her room.

Sprucing up for ol' Daniel, I would imagine. Jimmy realized then that he'd done his own aging over the past few days. *Maturing?* Maybe it was just concern about catching the disease and dying the horrible death that swirled closely by and around him. *Zula, the clinic, the people in the car, Homer, now Thelma.* Or maybe he was necessarily adapting to the hardness and cruelty he was seeing in others in these hard times. Maybe he was starting to truly see people for what they were—self-seeking and capable of anything as long as they got what they wanted. *Gosh, four days ago I was just worrying about Zula hearing me say a dirty word.* With such things to ponder, he crawled back over to the potatoes, for a snack. He rather liked them raw. Besides, he wanted to be back in position for when Daniel arrived here.

***

That wasn't a very long wait. Ol' Daniel's motivated, I guess. Through the grills set in the eastern part of the foundation, Jimmy heard rocks flying and dinging off the underside of a vehicle pulling up the driveway. He crawled over to the slits he believed to be alongside the TV room's doorway; he expected Daniel would come in the house from that direction. Soon he heard footsteps above as Thelma came downstairs and across the floor to stand directly above him. She apparently had expected Daniel to come in by the walkway too.

"Hey, handsome!" he heard her greet him. From the wet, smacking noises that followed, Jimmy guessed they were kissing. Then she coughed and murmured, "So lover, who are those guys out there at your car?" She must have been looking over his shoulder.

Daniel didn't answer right away, and when he did his voice was low and husky. "Them? Oh, they'll stay out there. I told them we were going to be...occupied for a while, sweet thing. Don't worry about them. I told them to check on the farm animals and crops in the meantime—you might be needing our property protection services. Might mean a bunch more money for you. You know folks are still going to be needing food and tobacco when this stuff blows over."

"Oh, OK, Daniel. But would you look over those papers first? Homer wasn't able to sign them all, but you know...he meant to. Can you still notarize them for me, big boy?" Jimmy imagined her fluttering her eyelashes at him.

"Oh, sure, darling. I don't even need to read them...seeing that they came from me. Oh, yeah, Thelma, I do believe you neglected to pay my invoice for, you know, services. Five hundred dollars, I believe, is due me."

She stepped back. "Daniel, I thought we'd worked it out, you know...that evening when you and I..." Then Thelma was off and flirting again, and Jimmy was beginning to understand what disgust felt like. *I mean, she just found out her husband was killed!*

Daniel seemed also to be understanding what disgust was like; it was evident now in his voice. "Thelma, knock it off. Quit doing that. That's not worth five dollars let alone five hundred. This is business now!"

"You asshole!" she squalled. Then Jimmy heard a slap and thump on the floor right above him.

"Thelma," Daniel said, his voice louder and harder now, "I want that five hundred dollars now, or I'm not going to finish with Homer. Do you want that? No, make it seven hundred dollars now. You want me to make it more?"

She must have nodded her head in resigned agreement.

"Well, all right then, lady. Now suppose you watch the door and I'll tend to Homer. By the way, where's that brat Jimmy?"

"You hurt me."

"Where's the kid?"

Thelma was getting to her knees. "When I caught him on the phone, he scooted on out the back door. But he'll get hungry. I'll grab him then or when he comes in to sleep tonight. But he's not around now. Maybe, we can...you know?"

"Yeah, maybe we can."

The house grew quiet, and for several minutes, Jimmy heard only scraping and rubbing noises on the floor above. Then he heard several deep grunts followed by a long moan. *Sounds like Thelma. Oh, gross!* Jimmy had spent much of his growing-up time on the farm and around the animals, so he had a fair idea of what was going on above him—and it affected him but not in a "reaching puberty" way. Rather, he was bothered in a revolting way—in a way that piqued him and that he was yet unable to verbalize, but he knew right from wrong. *And this is wrong. That's nasty...and Thelma's just barely found out her husband's dead! Yeah!* Maybe that was why he was so troubled, so incensed, by what was going on above...because of his loyalty to Billy Ray, to his friend. *I mean, it wasn't so cool when Mom found the torn-out* Playboy *centerfold under your mattress, was it? Yeah, but that's different. This is... Gross* was still the only word that would come to his mind. *Maybe it's just Thelma that's gross.* Jimmy crawled away from the sounds to the deeply shadowed part of the crawlspace, back to explore behind the stairs, where he believed he could stay hidden in the event that Daniel or his thugs came looking down there.

In the gloom he made another discovery: a hidden passage opening into the crawlspace. Behind the stone stairs, he crawled across another grate, this one set level with the dirt and covered over with the ends of long boards. When he pushed the boards from over the grate, he found that the metal bars were hinged to a surrounding iron frame and secured by a huge, old-fashioned padlock. "Bet this sucker was here before Daniel Boone's wagon. Ah, well." He let the lock fall back to its hasp and got to his feet, intending on duck-walking around to the stairs and, from there, back up through the cellar door to take his chances with sneaking outside. *Hopefully without running into either Daniel or his troops.*

As he pushed himself up to a squatting position, steadying himself using the rough-hewn joist above his head, he felt a squared nail protruding from the wood...and a key dangling from it. *The key to the lock?* He slid the key from the nail and examined it in the faint light. *Fancy at the end, either brass or copper, old, only one notch.* He returned to the padlock, pushed aside the tiny cover over the keyhole, and carefully inserted the key. *It fits perfectly!* In no time Jimmy had the lock open and the grate lifted, leaning it against the back of the stairs. *Now to see what's down there. Bet there's a big ol' snake waiting.* He looked around and, finding a sizable lump of red clay, dropped it into the hole. He immediately heard the thud; the shaft beneath the grate was only about four or five feet deep. *And no snake hissed back at me.* Scooting around on his rear end, he extended his legs down into the dark, searching for the bottom with his shoes. *There. Not even muddy.* He stood in the hole and tapped around its sides with his fingertips. *Another hole—a tunnel!* He knelt and felt around the inside of the opening. *Rock-sided and maybe mortared.* Someone had taken their time with the building of this tunnel, lining its sides with smooth river rocks and shoring up the roof with thick locust planks, like the ones often used for fence posts. Its bottom also sloped downward so Jimmy found he almost could stand erect just inside the tunnel's entrance. *Bet Zula's grandparents hid slaves here or something during the Civil War.* He had learned in seventh grade history that, during those years, most of the citizens in the eastern part of the state had sympathized with the Union cause and actively had resisted the Confederacy. *And I bet this ol' tunnel opens out somewhere in Big Red's pasture.* That thought gave him a moment's pause before he remembered that the big bull had forsaken that ground. "Should be OK," he assured himself and took a step into the tunnel.

Inching forward he ran his one hand along the rock wall while waving his other in the absolute darkness ahead—as if he were directing an orchestra—searching for probable spider webs. After nine or ten paces in and not having yet contacted a cobweb, he picked up his pace, sliding his sneakers along on the scraped tunnel bottom but still enthusiastically chopping the vacuity with his free arm.

When he had counted twenty steps in, he turned to look back to the tunnel's entrance. "Whoa! I can still see back there...a long, long way back. But the air's real good." The air *was* good; it felt cool and fresh as it moved through the tunnel and over his face. So he continued on.

Finally, after Jimmy had lost count of his steps and was to the point of turning back, he imagined he saw a slight glimmer of light far ahead. "No, no—yeah, yeah, that's really...That's gotta be the end." He shuffled faster.

Soon he was standing before the source of the glimmer: the daylight that filtered between the thick, wooden boards of a door that stretched from wall to wall, covering the tunnel's exit to the outside. And the door, he found, was secured by the mate of the padlock on the metal grate back in the crawlspace. *Crap!* He felt around in his pockets, wishing and hoping he had shoved the key into his jeans and hadn't returned it to the square nail. *Ah, I got it!* Maybe today was his lucky day after all. He slid the tiny hole-cover aside on the padlock and inserted the key...and the lock dropped open. *Thanks, Lord.*

Jimmy pushed against the door...but it hardly budged. Getting the door to open, he perceived, might be of greater difficulty than just removing the lock. In fact it would take him the rest of the afternoon to force the heavy planks outward far enough to get his hand—and pocketknife—through the opening to attack the limiting obstacles he felt there: the dirt that had built up on the far side and the roots and branches that had grown through and under the timbers. *Thank goodness for skinny arms and hands.* When he finally was able to push his head and shoulders through the widening gap, he was surprised to find that the sun already had dropped behind the high ridge to the west. "And this is definitely Big Red's pasture." Through the tall weeds and farther up the hill, he saw one end of the old clothesline pole...and a pair of jeans and some underwear he'd forgotten on the line. "I expect I'll be needing those clothes real soon." He pushed again, expanding the door's opening and stepping through.

Reluctant to leave the cover of the recessed tunnel entrance without first knowing the location of Daniel's men, he carefully searched the fence row above for any signs of movement before finally standing and dogtrotting out through the high weeds toward the clothesline. "Guess I'll find out where those guys—dang!" He felt his left sneaker squish in a semifresh cow pile. "Ambushed by ol' Red anyway."

At the lines he kept watch on the house as he unpinned his clothes. He barely could see over the curve of the hill, but he could see enough to ascertain that Daniel and his boys were there, still up at the house. They had grouped in the back, huddling on the walk, smoking and laughing, and passing a bottle from man to man. *Boy to boy?* And he heard Thelma before he saw her. *Having a gay, ol' time, they are. I wonder if she and them...gross!*

He rolled his well-laundered skivvies and jeans together and trotted through the weeds, back to his hiding place. To his relief he found that closing the door was much easier than opening it, and soon he was feeling his way back through the long tunnel toward the crawlspace. He hadn't relatched the heavy-timbered, outer door; he had wanted to preserve an entry alternative in returning to the house. *If those ol' boys find the door, they'd break it down or burn it down anyway.* But he was reasonably certain they'd never find that entrance. *I'd never notice it before.*

Back under the house, he also didn't relock the grate. *Maybe I'll need it for an emergency too. But right now...* He hung the old padlock and key on the square nail, slid a couple of the boards back over the opening, and crawled quickly across the clay to the foundation opening at the side of the TV room's door. Just outside, on the walkway, the party was breaking up and heading to the parking area. Thelma apparently had made friends with all of Daniel's men because she insisted on hugging and kissing each one before returning to the house. Then she slammed the screen door and noisily climbed the stairs to her bedroom. *Yeah, I'd say she has a toot on.* That was something his father would have said.

After she'd gone, Jimmy continued to watch the men through the vent. Daniel circulated among the group, handing each man a few bills. "Fifty dollars each, men," he said. "This job was for two hundred fifty, and we split evenly. Right? We share what comes our way. Right?" The boys mumbled their thanks, slapping him on the back as he passed. At the end of the walkway, they turned back, laughing at some joke Daniel made about a train, while another boy—Jimmy couldn't tell which one—hefted the now empty bottle, launching it clear over the pump house and onto the sidewalk at the side of the house. It smashed into a hundred pieces, and they moved on toward the parking area and Daniel's Cadillac. They were all very drunk.

Jimmy listened for the Cadillac to rattle back down the driveway to the road. "Jerk. I wonder how he'd like it if I went to his house and smashed a bottle on his steps? Ah well," he sniffed. At least he was reasonably certain with Thelma in her present condition he could spend the night upstairs, in his bed and undisturbed.

9

DAY FIVE

B am! Jimmy jerked awake and immediately identified the sudden, loud noise as being the bathroom doorknob hitting the wall. *Thelma's up—tripped or stumbled on her way to the toilet, probably put a hole in the plaster.* It was still early in the morning and still mostly dark. He watched his bedroom doorway and counted off the seconds, waiting for the sounds of her making her way back to bed. He was almost to three hundred when he heard the choking, violent heaves from down the hall; Thelma was vomiting—loud, long, and hard—like Homer had. *Homer!* Jimmy had forgotten to slip back downstairs during the night to check on him, when he was certain Thelma would remain in bed and fast asleep.

He swiveled sideways and slid from the bed. Since he had slept fully clothed and atop the covers, he moved quickly through the room, out the door, and down the back stairs. This time he wouldn't wait for Thelma to fall back asleep.

Through the kitchen and the dining room he crept, grateful for the wide windows there that lighted his path and, in a certain way, for the periodic retch that resounded down the staircase, allowing him to keep tabs on Thelma as he moved. Reaching the door of Homer's bedroom, he waited for her next round of vomiting then quickly twisted the doorknob, easing wide the door under the cover of her noise. *Dark, dark.* Since this room had no outside windows, he again had to touch his way along the wall, searching for the bed.

"Homer? Homer?" he whispered. *Nothing.* He patted the edge of the bed. *No sheets?* He felt only the slick cloth of a bare mattress. He passed his hands across the width of the bed. *No Homer!* Someone—*Thelma, most certainly…or maybe Daniel*—had moved the old man from this room. *Maybe they took him to the hospital? No, no, they didn't.* He remembered having watched the drunken group yesterday evening, and he had watched only Daniel and his cretins leaving in the car. *Then maybe another room in the house?* But he probably would have heard Homer's coughing and labored breathing during the night if he'd been moved to another bedroom—any bedroom—in the house. *I'll check anyway.*

Heading for the converted-for-tourists bedrooms arrayed along the front part of the house, Jimmy took the kitchen route again, tiptoeing down the short hallway from the kitchen, past the downstairs bathroom, to the covered back porch. There, in the dim light of the early morning, the boxy silhouette of the chest freezer against the wall caught his eye, and his throat tightened. *Did they put Homer in there too?* He knew Daniel had little regard for the old man, and he suspected Thelma's affections were also on the wane, sick and burdensome as her father had become. *But would they have killed him?* The mental picture of the spilled medications came then to the boy, and he recalled Thelma's words about money and services with Daniel. *Could they have killed him?* With this picture came his thoughts, his recognitions that people fundamentally *had* changed with the crisis—*for the worse*—and that seemingly the common constraints such as civility, laws, manners—the stuff his parents thought important and proper—existed no more. *Anyone—anyone!—is capable now of anything in the blackness of their guts, the stuff that's leaking out. But not Nick or Zula or Homer or…*He was having trouble remembering anyone else…Mr. Cline. *They weren't like that, hurting other people and being just mean. But maybe they were too old or were Christians or something? But Daniel and Thelma are…or maybe not. Enough!* "You need to do less thinking right now, Jimbo ol' boy," he whispered. "The 'why' isn't important anymore. Just watch out for yourself. Now go on!"

He detoured over to the long chest and gripped the rust-spotted latch that would flip open with a sideways pull and allow the lid to spring up. *And there would be Zula, all stiff and icy. Lord, I don't want to do this.* But he did. The top came up with a low, frosty crack; Jimmy held it so it wouldn't bang into the wall behind. He leaned forward to look inside, but with the rising vapor and the room's darkness, he could see nothing. *Oh, crap!* He'd have to reach in deep and feel around in the cold…and he did just that, holding his breath and closing his eyes. *Nothing.* He felt only the small, hard packages of wrapped meats and bags of frozen vegetables. *Zula's not in there!*

Suddenly he could see very well; someone had switched on the overhead lights. *Thelma!*

She hadn't returned to her bed but instead had come downstairs hunting for either booze or Homer's pain pills; she didn't care which. She had heard the latch click and the freezer's top lift open and had come to check on it. And there was the boy, half in and half out of the big freezer. *What the…* "Jimmy! What the hell do you think you're doing?"

He didn't answer. He'd dropped back to his feet and now took two or three tentative steps toward the far wall, toward the outside door.

"Now hold it right there, young man. I need you to…" But she didn't finish. As she leaned forward, readying herself to run at him and grab him with her clutching claws, Jimmy turned and dashed to the screen door, flipping up its little hook latch and slamming it open. In the next second, the door was banging shut again, and Jimmy was gone, swallowed up in the early-morning murk.

Thelma walked to the door, pushing it open and holding it as she looked through the screen up toward the barn. She heard the padding of his tennis shoes off in that direction. "Little asshole. No matter. Daniel and his boys can find him there come daylight." She was certain now that Olivia wasn't coming for him; she had called herself yesterday afternoon. "And his dumb bitch of an old lady is sick now," she murmured to herself, somehow getting satisfaction from the thought. "Dumb bitch," she repeated. "Sick herself now. Hah!" Thelma closed the screen door but didn't lock it, didn't return the hook to its eye. *Maybe the kid will decide to come in through it again.* She would much rather trap him inside one of the rooms in the house than try and run him down in the barn.

Turning off the overhead light, she wandered back through the house to the kitchen. After all that vomiting, she felt she should eat something, but nothing seemed to appeal to her. Then her bowels noisily twisted again. "Oh, gosh. Maybe I can make it…" She hurried back down the short hallway to the bathroom.

***

Up at the barnyard, Jimmy straddled the top boards of the gate and watched the lights go on and off in the house. *She's not coming after me. She'll leave that to Daniel.* He figured Daniel and his boys would be coming over in the late morning—*He won't be getting up early if he can help it*—to continue the search for him. And maybe to settle up with Thelma.

So what now? With Homer gone he desperately wanted to go home, and Thelma wouldn't be taking him. He would have to find his own way—walk if he had to. "Do you even know the way back to Maryville, boy? Maybe you don't." *Maybe there's a map in the truck?*

"And you need food and clothes—it'd be simpler if you had a pack or something." Jimmy was a Cub Scout when he was younger, and at about age eleven, he became a Boy Scout, but that had lasted only a year or so. He had enjoyed the camping outings and the swimming trips, but he'd hated the meetings and the endless documenting of those tasks that were required to be completed if he wanted to garner merit badges and continue to progress up the scouting ladder. It had begun to feel like competition to him, and competition wasn't something that appealed to him at that age. Besides, about that time, his father had allowed him and a friend or two to camp on their own in the nearby campgrounds, even pulling their old, tarp-covered utility trailer up to the Smokies for their shelter. Jimmy then had no further need of a formal structure to engage in those most enjoyable aspects of scouting.

"Maybe if I took the old Plymouth…" He was about to say that Homer wouldn't mind if he took the vehicle, but he suddenly remembered the shiny object he'd almost tripped over when he had run from the house. *Homer's bucket! Maybe…* "Thelma—or whoever moved Homer—just threw it in the yard rather than washing it out!" *Or maybe they dropped it when they took Homer outside?* That would explain why he hadn't heard the old man's gasps from inside the house. *Maybe they took him out to the smokehouse!* "I'll go look right now."

Then he felt a warm, wet tentacle encircle his ankle. "Gaaaaa!" he screamed, pulling away and falling from his perch, landing heavily on his face in the tall grass outside the barnyard. He struggled to get to his knees to face the monster that had attacked him, clutching his leg with its raspy finger.

Mooooo.

Elsie was looking down on him through the gate's lower planks. Jimmy saw her ears and horns outlined against the lightening skies. "Elsie! You liked to have scared the…crap outta me, sneaking up like that!"

Mooo.

Jimmy got to his feet, brushed himself off, and waited for his heart to slow. "You know, you could kill a fella slipping up on him like that…and licking him on his bare skin. Coulda given me a heart attack!"

Elsie didn't reply. She just stared back.

"OK, you just want some food, don't you, ol' gal? You've been missing your breakfast?" It seemed as if months had passed since he had last milked her, back when things were normal and Homer was…Hot tears came to his eyes and warm snot to his nose. He dug in his back pocket, hoping to find a handkerchief to wipe away both. *Got one…stiff. It'll hafta do.*

When he was through with his wiping and blowing, he climbed up and over the tall gate and walked on to the barn to get some food for ol' Elsie.

***

Keeping an eye on the house as he searched, Jimmy flipped through folded papers in the Plymouth's glove compartment looking for a local map that would show him how to get home. *Wait, wait, wait, wait. There's one.* He pulled the folded paper from the bottom of the box and held it up. "Florida," he read, disgusted with his find. "I guess I'll have to check the pickup." He supposed Homer must have parked the truck in the garage at the front of the house when Thelma had taken to parking her car around here, at the back. He eased from the seat and stepped out of the car, keeping his head low, in case she was watching from the windows. "Oh, wait." He reached in again and pulled the key from the ignition; keys were still commonly left in parked and unlocked vehicles in that part of the country. "Thelma or Daniel might grab the keys if they think I might take the car."

He quietly closed the car door and leaned against it to make sure it had latched. *Don't want to run down the battery.* Then he trotted low around the Plymouth to the front of the next parked car, the Corvette, and from there across the open area to the back of the smokehouse. When he saw no responding movements at the house, he slipped around the side of the smokehouse to the ground-floor door. There the stairs to the second story of the building partially concealed the lower doorway—and Jimmy—as he worked to unwind the wire that held tight the bolt in the bracket on the doorframe. That was something Homer had been meaning to fix—the broken lock and doorknob—for about the last fifty years now. *Don't think he'll be getting to that now.* Jimmy pulled the wire away, and the door swung inward; he could smell the cool air from within, unique with its mixture of cured meat, hickory smoke, and salt.

Slipping inside, he pushed the door closed, bracing it with a burlap sack of flower bulbs Zula had stored for the spring. After walking about, doing a cursory search of the dusty interior and looking behind the few boxes and crates that were there, he ascertained that neither Homer nor Zula had been redeposited in there. *Maybe upstairs then. But first…* Jimmy fished his knife from his pocket, unfolded it, and selected the smallest of the country hams dangling from the overhead hooks screwed into the bottom of the heavy plank shelf that spanned the length of the smokehouse. *Don't know when I'll be able to cook this, but just in case.* He set to work cutting a long slice from the moldy, ugly, delicious-looking lump of ham. He was licking his lips, anticipating a bite of the savory, hard-fried meat, when something dripped on his hand. *What is that? Reddish colored.* He held his hand to his nose and took a whiff. "Ewwww!" The odor was *terrible*, unlike anything he'd ever smelled. He shuffled around to better see what was dripping…and lost his slice of meat. *They put Zula up there! She's thawing out!*

He stumbled backward against the crates that lined the far wall and now saw the entire shelf. *And there's Homer there!* Beyond Zula he saw the bottoms of the old man's feet. He appeared to be lying on his side on the wide plank, facing outward. Jimmy glanced back to Zula. Mercifully she had been placed there with her face to the wall and her nightgown pulled down. *'Course she was froze that way!*

When Jimmy had calmed down and his heart had slowed to a more or less normal beat, he moved to the door and pushed it wide to get more light inside. Then, stepping sideways, he moved back even with the old man's head to better see his face, and to pay his last respects with silence and memories and prayer.

"Amen." Several minutes had passed, and Jimmy looked about again, selecting a suitable crate from the wall. He dragged it over and stood on it while he closed Homer's eyes and pushed his swollen tongue back inside his mouth. Then he coiled the rope that was hanging down—the rope that had been used to move Homer from the house and was still looped tightly about his neck—and wedged it under the old man's body on the shelf. *I wonder if he was dead already?*

"I'll be back soon," he promised them both as he pulled tight the smokehouse door.

After rewiring the bolt to the bracket, Jimmy next visited the garage at the front of the house, where the driveway forked, leading one way to the ancient, whitewashed garage and the other way around to the side and back of the house. To lessen his chances of being seen from either the road or the house, he had used the smokehouse to screen himself as he had circled around, back past the chicken house, through the barbed-wire fence behind, and then, reversing his direction, up through the lower part of Red's pasture, where he couldn't see even the highest peak of the house's metal rooftop. At the far side of the garage, he had waited, listening for road noise until he was certain no one was approaching, either on the road or down the driveway. Then he skittered around to the front and pulled apart the double doors, lifting the one side to keep it from scraping along on the rocks, then slipping sideways through the opening and quickly pulling the doors together again. He wouldn't need to keep them partially open to see around inside; the structure was so aged and weather-beaten that light streamed in from the dozen or so cracks in its sides and along its roof line.

Now, turning in the sun-dappled interior, the first thing Jimmy noticed was: *There's nothing here! No truck, no glove box, no maps, no nothing! Stolen? Yeah, of course.* That was probable since the building was never locked, and the truck key was usually left in the ignition. *Yeah, just another sign of the times.* "Shit!" It seemed to him that everywhere he looked, everywhere he turned, he found obstacles and problems...and more problems. *I'm never gonna get home! Everything's against me. How am I ever gonna...Somebody's coming!*

The sounds of vehicle tires on the rocks outside cut short his vent. He frantically looked about for a place to hide but saw only bare walls. *And rafters. Yeah!* He thought that maybe, just maybe, he could get to the crossbeams above by pulling himself up by the doorframe then grabbing a beam. *But first...*He ran to the doors and stared through the crack, trying to determine how much time he had before he was discovered. *Wait. The car—it's Daniel's car—isn't coming this way. It's turning to the right and going on up to the house.* "Whew!" he breathed his relief. *Now to get the heck outta here.* He would find a place—well away from here—where he could hide and wait until Daniel and his gang were done with their searching and were gone. *Today's when Thelma told him to come get me.* He had no idea what Daniel would do with him—how he would use him—but he had seen what he had done to Homer. "Betcha that's what he'd do to me."

Leaning against the door again, Jimmy peeked through the crack and waited. *Too soon is as bad as too late.* Then he heard a voice barking orders, back behind the house in the parking area. *Daniel's giving directions, telling them where to go. You gotta leave now, boy!* He lifted the door and moved it outward, far enough for him to fit through. He stepped back to take a final look around, just in case. *What's that?* He saw a magazine or pamphlets in a plastic bag left lying in the dirt beside the wall. *Maps!* He recognized the bag. *Homer's maps!* The bag must have fallen from the truck. He raced over to snatch up the bag and back, then slipped through the opening and scampered around beside the garage to the cover of the weeds and briars behind.

In minutes Jimmy was crossing the creek at the bottom of the pasture, stepping from stone to stone, heading for the safety of the woods that bordered Fred's place. The steep hillside and dense growth there, he figured, would hide him from Daniel and his boys while he waited. In the meantime he would lay out his route alternatives to Maryville, he believed, patting the front of his jeans where he had stashed the maps.

At the flat rock on top of the ridge, slightly above the thicket where he earlier had surveyed Fred and Juanita's place, Jimmy spread out the map of East Tennessee and western North Carolina, using several of the rocks scattered about the outcropping to hold down its edges against the slight breeze. "Let's see. Let's see. Let's see." He hunched over the map, tracing his finger along its red-and-black lines then retracing when he found the route not to his liking. Finally he straightened, nodding to himself. "White School Road on around to Sugar Loaf—or maybe overland north to Chapman Highway—then on those back roads: Cusick Road to…ah…South Rogers Road to Wye Drive if I have to stay off Chapman Highway. Let's see, that's US 441 to the mountains." He ran his finger along the double line to Sevierville. "Then on down Wye Drive…" His finger had slipped, and he had to find his spot again. "…and on down to Knob Creek Church area."

"Knob Creek Church," he said again, looking up, his eyes unfocused and distant with his memory of the church and Decoration

Day, the day that was to be renamed "Memorial Day." His father had taken him and his mother to that church, once a year, to put flowers on the graves of *his* mother and father, to reintroduce them to his kinfolks, and to have dinner on the grounds. *That's the only time I could ever get enough deviled eggs to eat.* The food would be potluck and plentiful and spread on the long, long tables off to the side of the building. It was usually too early in the year for his father to bring his specialty, fried okra, so his mother usually brought a pot roast or something else that could be cooked beforehand, while they were still in church, back home in Maryville. His stomach rumbled, reminding him that it was well past breakfast time.

Then, after everyone was filled with food—"tight as ticks," his dad would say—they'd walk through the cemetery across the road, his father showing him and his mother again the graves of Pap and Ma, his aunts and uncles, and so on; it seemed to him that an awful lot of Burkes had been planted there. And Jimmy would look at the dates and marvel at his father's recitation of the historical events that had occurred during his ancestors' lifetimes. *Didn't Dad's oldest brother also die of the flu? Like Homer's cousin? The flu epidemic of 1918— like today? Will it be like that now?*

"Let's see, where was I? Oh, yeah. The road becomes Jeffries Hollow Road and then on to Ellejoy Road and the Ellejoy area, and to Tuckaleechee Pike and to 321 and to Maryville. That'll do it." *Now if I can just remember all that.*

The wind blew harder, parting the limbs of the trees toward Fred's house. Jimmy caught a glimpse of the lightning rod he and Homer had helped Fred fasten to his chimney the previous year. *Maybe I should go check on Fred and Juanita?* He didn't really want to. The man he had seen taking the Rogers's foodstuffs *had* said the couple had died and were still in their bed in the back bedroom. *Gosh, they'll really be stinking by now.* And he didn't really want to have to bury them; his blisters were still fresh from digging in the garden. *Besides, I need to pay attention now for Daniel and his gang. I can't be digging and watching for them. But Homer would have wanted me to at least look in on them—and they've got a telephone too.* "OK, Jimbo, just go look then."

He refolded his map, fitted it back into the plastic bag he then slipped down the front of his jeans, under his T-shirt. *Hmm.* He decided he'd take the trail that slanted down the hillside, almost parallel to the Rogers's driveway. *That path will be quieter,* he reasoned. He wouldn't be scrambling from tree to tree, grabbing on to each one to slow his descent, and he could watch the road and the front yard as he walked.

***

"OK, Jimbo, all clear." At the bottom of the hill, he stepped from behind the juniper bushes that grew alongside Fred's driveway and ambled up to the house, trying to look as normal and supposed-to-be-there as possible. Skipping up the front porch steps, two at a time, he tromped across the porch and banged loudly on the doorframe. *Front door's open.* He tried the screen door—it was open too.

"Fred! Juanita!" he yelled through the screen. He had watched the windows at the side and front as he had descended the trail and had seen no movements inside, nothing to make him think someone was hiding, waiting there. And now, just in case someone *was* inside, he didn't want to surprise them and get himself accidentally shot. "Fred! Juanita!" he tried again. *Nothing.* He pulled open the screen door, its return spring screeching in protest. *I guess they don't have much company come in this way.*

"It's Jimmy!" He poked his head around the doorframe then walked on into the front room. It was empty of furnishings. Even the old-fashioned, round rug had been rolled up and pushed against the wall, as if awaiting pickup. He tried a whistle; it sounded shrill and hollow in the empty room. "Anybody here!" he yelled. *Nothing.* He'd look around.

"Well, there's nothing left in the sitting room; they even took the pictures." Jimmy turned in place, studying the brighter rectangles of wallpaper here and there where once there were tranquil scenes of the Jordan River and scowling visages of ancestors, ivory hued with age. "Yeah, even the pictures." *Now what would anyone want with those old pictures?*

He strolled on, slowing making his way through the house, heading for the bedroom in the rear corner. Dining room, hallway, past the bathroom—it didn't take long. The house was small and the rooms tiny. *I guess Fred and Juanita weren't all that well-to-do, but all they had is surely gone now.* The door to the bedroom was partially open; Jimmy could see from the hallway that there was no longer even a bed in the room. *No Fred. No Juanita.* He'd seen what he had needed to see; he didn't need to go in. He would leave now the way he had come, to wait in the woods above the barn for Daniel and his boys to depart.

Bang! The back door slammed shut. He whirled in that direction, back toward the kitchen. A man was coming toward him, silhouetted in the hallway and the sunny yard behind! *A big, fat guy!*

"Jimmy?" the figure inquired.

"Bernard?" Jimmy gasped in answer. He'd recognized the voice: Bernard Goodman. He and Faith were members down at the church. They were friends of Billy Ray and Thelma, often coming home with them for Sunday dinners.

"Jimmy? I was looking…wondering about how you've been doing. What are you doing over *here*, boy?" Bernard sounded like he was smiling, friendly—his face was still shadowed—and he didn't seem to be wanting anything from the boy, other than news from him.

"Well, ah…Homer sent me over to check on Fred and Juanita. I heard they'd caught that ol' disease…and it had done them in."

"Where'd you hear that, Jimmy?"

"Well, ah…I'd come over here earlier, and a fellow was here loading up stuff with a lot of other people. They said that they thought Fred and Juanita were sick and that they were coming in here to buy the food they'd put up." Jimmy was still feeling his way with Bernard, keeping open his escape option—the unlocked front door to his rear.

"Other people? Did you hear them say anything about Juanita's medication, Jimmy? I know she used to have rheumatism and took a lot of prescription drugs. Did they say anything about them?" Bernard's voice had taken on an urgent edge.

Uh-oh! Jimmy scratched his ear, as if were was trying to remember. "No, I don't remember hearing about that. Why?"

"Oh…well, Faith—you remember Faith? Of course you do. Well, Faith, she come down with that stuff too, and she's in a lot of discomfort, and I thought maybe…Juanita could spare some drugs for her." Bernard breathed a deep breath. Faith's condition was obviously weighing him down.

Seems on the verge of crying or something, with his heavy breathing. "Bernard, I'm sorry," Jimmy commiserated, biting his lip and shaking his head, "about Faith…and for you. I know when Zula took sick, well, Homer…it's been real hard on him too. I'm so sorry." Then he appeared to brighten a degree with his fresh thought. "Tell you what. There's been a whole lot of people stopping by the house, like Sheriff Noland and his deputies," he lied. "I'll ask him about the drugstore and about old man Cline. I bet they'll know how he's doing with the drugstore in Sevierville. Maybe me and ol' Homer can run over there for you while you watch Faith. Your phone still working?" As he talked, Jimmy had noticed the wall telephone's wires hanging from its bracket, next to where Bernard stood, twisting his cap in his hands. *Dang!*

"Ah, yeah, our phone's working good. Do you need to use a phone? Maybe to call home?" He straightened, studying the boy again.

Bernard wasn't as slow as Jimmy had hoped; he obviously had noted the dangling wires there too. "No, no. I meant that I was going to call you when I heard something about the pharmacy…from the sheriff. But you know, I guess you could just call old man Cline yourself, couldn't you?"

"Yeah, I could. That's still a good idea…a real good idea. You know, Jimmy, if you want to ride along, to come back by the house with me, I'm sure Faith would love to see you again." Bernard was putting his cap back on his head, preparing to leave and beckoning for him to come along, to come closer.

Pow! A gunshot sounded, echoing through the knobs, seemingly coming from behind the house—and close. The big man's head jerked up, cocked to one side and listening for the next shot to gauge its direction. "Jimmy, that sounded like it come from backa Homer's place," he guessed. "Think somebody's out hunting back there? A little early for hunting season, ain't it? Maybe we should go out and check?" Bernard turned sidewise in the narrow hallway, as if he were creating space for the boy to squeeze by his big gut.

"Maybe ol' Homer's shooting some squirrels or something," Jimmy allowed. "He really likes 'em, you know. And I don't think they have a season." He was becoming very uncomfortable in the big man's presence. "Anyway, I should be going."

"Well, if you want to ride out to the house with me…"

"Yeah, maybe I could walk on down later in the day. We were coming that way later on…to visit with Bill and Judy Shanks…Bill is going to help us cut and stack our tobacco soon—it's getting that time." Jimmy was on a roll, creating events and people—lots of people—all around. "But it's getting up in the afternoon, and ol' Homer has got a lot of stuff for me to do. I guess you've got a lot of stuff you want to do too, huh, Bernard?" He backed away faster as he talked and was now easing open the screen door with his butt.

"Yeah, I guess I do," Bernard replied. He hadn't moved any farther into the tiny living room, and his features were still shadowed by the light coming in through the kitchen door. "Yeah, I guess I do," he repeated, turning now and striding heavily toward the back door. "See you around, Jimmy!" he yelled over his shoulder.

"See you later too. Tell Faith 'hey' for me," he yelled back, letting the screen door slam shut behind him. Then he stomped halfway down the front steps…and right back up, flinging himself down behind the low, solid-board wall that bordered the porch deck. *He won't see me here when he leaves.* Jimmy wasn't through with the house; he knew Fred had a second telephone extension, down in the basement, high on the wall to the side of his worktable. He wanted—needed—to call home, to check on his father and to plead with his mother. *I gotta get outta here!*

***

"Blade, you and Wing go on down to the road and go east, all the way to Chapman Highway. See if the road is clear all the way down there. Then come on back, like you're coming to the house, and come up the little hollow down there…" Daniel was pointing to the garden patch. "…and come up the hill alongside the barn. Ol' Jimmy-boy might be off down there and hiding. Right, Thelma?"

She was nodding and looking off in that direction. "Yeah, I saw him with a shovel and heading down that way the other day, like he was going to do some digging or something. He's all the time digging hideouts and caves and such to play in…when he shoulda been working." She had come out to greet Daniel and his men when she had heard them driving in. "When I last saw him early this morning, he was heading out yonder, toward the barn." Since she was carrying a tray, she pointed with her uplifted chin. "Say, you boys want anything to drink before you go lookin'?"

"Whatcha got there, Thelma?" asked Blade. That wasn't his real name; Daniel had renamed him when he had joined the Lord's Army, which used to be called something else too, when it was the youth ministry at the church. Daniel had said King David had given his Israelite soldiers new names when they had chosen to follow him and to fight with ol' King Saul. *Daniel said we'd be getting uniforms too,* Blade recalled. *Black ones. With those button things on the shoulders and our Lord's Army names embroidered on our pockets.* He liked the name "Blade"; he was getting quite used to it.

"I got some milk, and I got some water. That's all I could find in the fridge, Cedric."

"Blade," corrected Blade.

"Oh, OK…Blade. That's all I got in the refrigerator. If I'd known you guys were gonna be so late in coming today, I mighta made some coffee…but I didn't. If you had just called…"

"Thelma," Daniel admonished, "we got here just as soon as we could. You know we got a lot of responsibility now, keeping the peace and watching for troublemakers and all. It's a big job for big men, and it takes up a lot of our time." He rested his palms on the butts of the holstered revolvers slung low on his hips; they were brand-new. Daniel apparently had managed to find time to visit the Western store in town. He also sported a brand-new, scroll-pocket shirt, its fold marks still evident in the front. "Yeah, a big job," he added.

Wing stepped in. "Ah, Daniel, Chapman Highway—that's the big ol' woad down that a way?" He waved toward the barn.

"Yeah, Wing, the big ol' woad way down yondo. That big ol' woad I've taken you down a bunch of times, where all the caws were wecked and people were wotting? Wemember, Wing?"

Wing hated that name. He had a hard time pronouncing the letter "r," and he felt Daniel and the others were making fun of him in giving him that name. "Oh, OK. Ah...Daniel, can we take the Cadillac—dwive down in the caws?"

"No, not my Cadillac. Take B Team's truck. Ah...wait." He remembered then that he already had dispatched Bernard in the truck to guard the Rogers's place, just in case Jimmy was to try and hide over there. "OK, never mind. You guys just walk down to White Road and turn east—like you were going to Chapman Highway—and then walk up the hollow up behind the garden and the barn. Got that?"

"Yeah," they answered together.

"And me and Miss Thelma will take a look around the chicken house and the smokehouse there." He winked at Thelma standing beside him. "And look through the house from top to...ah...bottom." He patted hers.

"Reverend Davis!" she exclaimed in mock protest, looking up at him with what she imagined to be her demure expression.

Daniel caught the coy glance, and it made him laugh inside. *Damn, lady, you're old enough to be my mother. I oughta charge you another hundred or two just to tug at my zipper. 'Specially since I got somethin' better back in the church basement right now.* "And boys, if you catch anybody around there, bring 'em on back up here. Unless it's Jimmy—you can just shoot his ass and lay him here in front of the pump house. Hah!" Laughing at his own joke, he turned and pulled wide the door, shooing Thelma and her tray along with his hat. "After you, my dear, after you. Let's me and you go do some huntin'."

Ten minutes later he heard the gunshot. He and Thelma hardly had gotten undressed. "Damn!" Daniel swore. "They've shot that little asshole already!" He pushed Thelma aside and swung his feet around to the floor, standing then and pulling up his jeans from around his ankles. "They've shot him, and I bet they've killed him! I bet I ain't gonna be able to watch him die," he whined, tucking in his shirttail and carefully smoothing its front before cinching his belt tight.

"Slam, bam, thank you, ma'am," Thelma voiced from the bed, clutching the wrinkled sheet to her bare breasts. "That all you gonna do?" she asked, her voice hateful, accusing.

"Well, I believe that's all I have to do. Thank you, ma'am. But if that's the kid they shot, then I believe you owe me another two hundred dollars too, ma'am."

"What! I paid you the seven hundred for Homer *and* the boy. *And* for the healing—that freakin' healing, Reverend…That ain't work-ing! Do you know that?" She threw aside the covers and her pretense of modesty, swiveling around to her side of the bed and reaching for the bra and bathrobe draped across the chair there.

In a flash Daniel was around the bed and on her, pushing her back to the bed and straddling her. He held her by the neck with one hand and repeatedly, viciously slapped her with the other. *Slap! Slap! Slap!* "You damn whore of Babylon," he yelled. "How dare you stand to me, you spawn of Beelzebub! Dare thee to accuse me, thee hea-then? Ye of little faith, ye shall indeed perish! What the hell! Thelma, you pissed all over me! And that's blood right there that you got on my new shirt! Damn you!" He was pulling the material from off his stomach, examining the tiny spot on his shirt while he still straddled her torso. "Well, little lady, you're gonna be paying for this here new shirt too!" He backhanded her across the face once more before disentangling himself and standing, now studying the spot closely.

"Damn it!" He looked at the naked woman, lying on her side and holding her bleeding nose in the bunched sheets. "And it smells like hell in here, Thelma. Like shit and vomit...and piss!" He was holding his pants away from his legs. "Hell, woman!" He furiously pushed over the chair and stalked to the door, snatching up his twin holsters from the bureau in passing. "I'll be back for that two hundred dollars," he promised.

At the top of the stairs, Daniel paused and then turned back, coming to stand just outside the doorway, his hands fumbling with the buckle on his gun belt. "Thelma, why do you do that to me—accusing me of cheating you, causing me to lose my temper? You know that's not like me, is it? Why do you do that?"

She sat up in the bed, her eyes blazing as she wiped her nose with the bloody sheet. "I don't know, Daniel," she murmured. "I guess the ol' Devil has just got me." *And broke my goddamn nose!*

"Well, sister," he said with a smile, "I'll be praying for you." He turned and tromped down the stairs and out the back door. He saw Wing walking to the house from the parking area, just now reaching the end of the long sidewalk. He would wait for him beside the pump house.

"Boss, you'll be weal pwoud of us," called Wing. "You'll never guess who we found coming from back behind the bawn."

"Jimmy, I hope."

"No, it was that ol' Tom Pawton. You know, the ol' boy what beat you up."

"He didn't beat me up!" Daniel heatedly corrected. "He hit me when my head was turned when I had a bale of hay in my hands. He didn't beat me up! Who told you that?"

Wing dropped his head to look at his feet.

"Who?" Daniel persisted.

"I dunno...sowwy. I got it wong, I guess."

Shaking his head with disgust, Daniel looked past Wing to where Blade still stood beside the lump out in the barnyard. They *had* gotten Parton. Now he couldn't be too mad...unless. "You didn't kill him already, did you? He's still alive and conscious, isn't he?"

"Well, yeah. He'd alweady been shot a couple times. Blade just got him in the legs." Wing didn't want Daniel to think *he* had critically wounded the boy, but he did want Daniel to know there was some effort, some danger involved—not that Tom Parton had just come wandering through the trees, lightheaded from his loss of blood and looking for his mother. *Skinny shit looks mostly starved anyway.*

"Good, good. You done good, Wing. Now suppose you go in there in the house and visit with Miss Thelma until I get back. Keep her downstairs and away from any guns. OK?"

Wing nodded and went inside while Daniel marched to the barnyard.

"Say, Blade, whatja got there? Wing tells me we're honored by a visit from that famous…Philistine, Tom Parton." Daniel couldn't think of what to call him. "Judas" didn't quite fit the situation, so "Philistine" was about the worst name that had come to mind.

Blade looked up; he was kneeling at Tom's side. "I didn't even know he was Jewish."

"You're not a Jew if you're a Philistine. You've just got to hate our Lord. Besides, you knew what I meant."

Daniel moved to the other side of Tom, waiting to see if he would open his eyes. He didn't, so Daniel kicked him hard, square in the ribs.

"Ugh!" Tom cried, his eyelids fluttering open.

Daniel stooped close to his face. "Parton, do you see me? Do you remember what you did to me?"

"Heard he beat the shit outta you," Blade volunteered.

"No, he didn't!" Daniel angrily replied. "He hit me in the back of the head with…a hay hook when my back was turned. He coulda killed me if I hadn't fought back." He rubbed his head as if the lumps were still there. "So what do *you* think I should do with him?"

"Kill him?"

"Yes, I shall kill him," Daniel replied, somewhat pompously. "I shall grievously smite him, hip and thigh, and he shalt die."

"Well, I think you'd better hurry because the Philistine's about to do it on his own."

On cue Tom began to shiver, rolling onto his stomach and burying his face in the barnyard dirt.

"Crap! Cedric, you grab that rope hanging from the pulley on that side of the barn door. I'll get the other one. Leave the hook on it." The rope and pulley setup was used to lift hay bales from the wagon and into the loft. It would work well for what Daniel had in mind.

"Blade," corrected Blade.

"Blade, OK. Blade then goddamn it! Just do it!"

Using the hooks, one for each of Tom's armpits, Daniel and Blade soon had the boy standing, held erect by their tension on the ropes.

"Daniel, I think he's passed on," Blade observed.

"Yank him on up. We'll see if there's any life left—any pain to feel."

They heaved, and Tom came off the ground...and screamed once, twice, and then he was gone.

They left Tom there, hanging high in the barn's doorway, his arms outstretched, his head lolling to one side. His blood would continue to drain for a little while but not long, as he'd lost most of it from the wounds he had received earlier in the day. A gang of scavengers had ambushed him while he was coming from his garden. They had followed the narrow dirt road through the knobs and found his remote homeplace, his family, and their scant possessions. And they had taken everything, including lives; only Tom had escaped, for a little while.

At the walkway, Blade turned and looked back at the barn. "Say, who does ol' Tom remind you of, hanging up there that way?"

Daniel glanced back once then stopped and turned fully around. "Damn! He shouldn't look like that! Blade, you go back up there and untie him before—"

"Daniel, Daniel!" yelled Wing, running from the house. "Daniel, Thelma says Jimmy is over at the Wojoses' house. She just how'd him tawking on the pawty-line extension!"

"Damn it! That's why Bernard's over there! He's supposed to be watching for him over there!" Daniel dug in his pockets for his keys.

"Come on!" he yelled, pushing Wing ahead of him. "Run and get in the car! We'll go over there and get him!"

Wing looked back at the house; he'd left Thelma alone in there. "But Daniel," he began, just in time to see the muzzle flash through the screen door. Then he felt the stinging pressure on his forehead; he never heard the shot.

But Daniel did. He saw the dot appear on Wing's face; he saw the blood spray when Wing's head recoiled. Then he dove for the ground. "Blade, get the hell down! Thelma's got a gun in there! She just shot Wing!"

But Blade had heard the shot himself and guessed that it was coming from the house; he leaped behind the pump house while Daniel dove in the opposite direction. Two more shots rang out, kicking dirt and grass up from behind Daniel as he rolled madly across the ground toward the quasi cover of the birdbath pedestal, before Blade remembered he still carried the pump shotgun. He racked a shell into the chamber and blasted out the top of the screen door. He fired again and blew away the door's center. He pumped in another round—and then he listened.

Aaarrrrggghhh! The scream came from the dark interior of the house. He'd hit something, but it didn't sound human. *Aaaaaaaiiiiiiii!* The thing was coming! It stumbled on the bottom part of the screen door—the only portion that remained intact. It was Thelma! She had taken pellets in the face and was coming out the door, cocking and recocking the bolt-action rifle she was carrying but not firing a shot.

Boom! Blade let Thelma have the next load full in the face and briefly wondered whether he had any shells left. No matter, Thelma ran the bolt-action open and closed once more—and crashed to the sidewalk, the remains of her face making a wet splash on the broken marble.

***

Long minutes passed, and then Bernard's truck crunched by the side of the Rogers's house on the gravel driveway there. Jimmy peeked through the little gap between the porch floor and the railing wall, hoping to see which way Bernard was looking. But the man's head was hidden by the truck's roof; from his position, Jimmy saw only stomach through the truck's window, and no higher up. *Ah, well.* He waited for the truck to turn onto the hard road below and for its sounds to die away. *Ol' Bernard must be doing good for himself. That looks like a new pickup.*

Jimmy pushed up from his position and reentered the house, heading straight for the narrow hallway door that opened to the steep steps that led down to the basement. *It'd take a skinny little guy like Fred to regularly make it up and down these stairs.* At the bottom step he stood on his tiptoes to search the outside again, through the dusty little window over the coal bin.

There was another tiny window in the foundation on the far side, at the western side of the house. Since it didn't open like the one over the coal bin, Jimmy supposed its sole function was for light. *Good thing.* The other two windows set in the foundation were at the front of the house and opened beneath the high porch; there the encircling latticework limited any additional lighting that could come in from that direction. *But they work; they open out.* Fred had pushed him through one of those windows just last spring to retrieve a possum that had chosen to crawl in and under the porch to die. The decomposing animal had grown quite fragrant, and Fred, not wanting the additional work of tearing down and replacing the wooden slats of the lattice, had bribed Jimmy to crawl out through the window and to haul back the remains using the coal scoop. As it was, they had had to wait until Wednesday night, after Juanita had gone to her prayer meeting, to carry the evil-smelling load up the stairs and through the house.

Still OK, he assured himself. He could see the driveway there, to the side of the house.

He jumped from the step and circled around under the stairs to Fred's ancient worktable. *Great!* He saw the phone secured high on the center supporting beam, hidden in shadow. *Wonder if it's still working.* Using a stool to climb onto the table, Jimmy lifted the handset from its cradle…and listened. *Whew!* He heard a dial tone. Carefully he mashed the buttons, leaning close to the numbers in the dim light. *Ring…ring…ring.*

"Hello? Jimmy?" His mother had picked up and spoken his name without really knowing it was him calling.

"Hello, Mom. How are you? How's Dad? Where *are* you?"

There was a long, long pause. "Jimmy, we're here. Dad's…not doing well at all. And Jimmy, I've…I've contracted the disease too. Neither of us is doing too well today."

"Yesterday!" Jimmy almost shouted into the phone. "Yesterday you were better. Why didn't you come then?"

"Jimmy…" His mother had started to reply but then began to weep—to softly weep.

Oh, gosh! Here I am, thinking just about myself. "Mom, Mom, I'm sorry, Mom. That was so selfish of me. I'm so sorry. Please, please forgive me." He was blubbering now.

"Son, we—I would have found someone to take me…but Thelma said not to. She said she was on her way down and would be bringing you."

"Oh, yeah?" Jimmy's tears receded. "She told you that? She said not to come?"

"Jimmy?" His mother's tone was now uncertain. "Has something happened up there? Has…something happened to Thelma? Is she acting…strange? Maybe hostile?" She remembered the way people were becoming at the hospital: aggressive, selfish, demanding, maybe mean. "Has Thelma done anything to you?"

"No, Mom. No!" His mother didn't need more problems, more things to worry about. "I just didn't know you'd called. That's all. I didn't know Thelma had told you that and—"

"Jimmy!" Another voice came on the phone: *Thelma's voice!* She'd picked up on the party line next door.

Gosh, I hope she didn't hear what Mom said.

"Olivia! I told you—I told you and Jimmy—that I would get his snotty little ass home! You don't trust me anymore? Well, let me tell you that as far as I'm concerned—"

She heard! "Mom, I'm hanging up now!" Jimmy shouted, trying to drown out Thelma. "I'll get home. Don't you worry! I'll get home. Now please hang up the phone! Don't listen to this stuff!"

Thelma was now hollering to someone close to her, telling him to run and fetch Daniel. Jimmy knew then that he would have to leave quickly; she would guess that he was next door, over at Fred and Juanita's. He slammed the phone back in its wall bracket and jumped from the table to run around to the stairs.

"Jimmy, is that you down there?"

Bernard! That was him at the top of the stairs; he had come back. Jimmy stopped on the first step and leaned back, looking out the tiny window. *Yup, that's his red truck. Came back when I was calling.* Now what was he to do?

"Jimmy, that sounds like you down there."

The boy then realized that Bernard couldn't see him, standing as he was on the bottom step in the darkened basement. But he definitely could see Bernard at the top, blocking the doorway with his big body…and with his shotgun in hand. The man's eyes apparently hadn't yet adjusted from the bright sunshine outside. *That'll give me some time.*

Jimmy eased back down to the concrete floor, his footsteps silent in his sneakers. He crept back past the side of the workbench and on around behind the stoker and the furnace, looking for the place of deepest shadow where he could hide. *Dang!* The bare bulbs hanging from the floor supports above flashed on; Bernard had found the light switch on the wall at the top of the stairs. He had only seconds before the man would make his way down the stairs, to him.

Windows! He didn't think he'd have time to make it over to the coal bin, to climb out through the window there. *Besides, the coal level is too low for me to reach the window.* He looked to the front of the basement. *The windows under the porch!* He saw that Fred hadn't yet put away the stepladder he had used earlier in the year to retrieve the possum carcass. *Bless Fred's procrastinatin' heart, as Zula would say.*

"Jimmy, stay right there. I'm comin' on down."

"I'll be right up, Bernard. I just need to finish with this right here…" He didn't know what else to say; he needed time to get to the window, to get it open—*Please, Lord*—and get his rear end up and out that tiny window, then break through the vine-covered lattice outside. That would take time, and he needed to delay the big man. "By the way, Bernard, I thought you'd gone. Did you forget something?"

"Yeah, Jimmy, I forgot to get that rug out in the front room. You know, I bought that rug off the Reverend Daniel Davis. He's been handling the law around here since ol' Sheriff Noland passed on…about two days ago, Jimmy. You know how I know that? 'Cause Daniel's handling the law here now."

"Oh?" That was all Jimmy could think to say. *Bernard's not as dumb as he looks.*

"Yeah, you know what else?" The stairs creaked under Bernard's weight; he was managing to squeeze his bulk down the narrow staircase. "I also was supposed to check on the state of the tobacco back behind the house because…ol' Bill Shanks and me were supposed to cut it and stack it."

"Oh?" Jimmy was on the top of the ladder, pulling at the window's handle; it wasn't working! *I think this was the window?* "Well, Bernard, I guess we'll have to have to compare our schedules so ol' Bill can help us both."

"Hah!"

The boy heard Bernard's laugh. It sounded a tad cynical to him; he'd have to hurry. He jumped from the ladder and moved it beneath the other window.

"Yeah, we'll have to do that. 'Cept I got ol' Bill out in the truck out there. Deader'n a doornail. He ain't gonna be helping either one of us out."

"Dead?" Jimmy paused for a second before climbing the ladder again. "When—how'd he die?"

"Well, it was the strangest thing." Bernard was enjoying himself. "That ol' boy just walked in front of this here ol' shotgun, and you know, it bit him. Nigh on took his head off, it did. Just this morning. Or maybe it was yesterday that it…"

The stairs creaked again. *Dang! Bernard's almost to the bottom. And there's no handle here! It has to be the other window.* Jimmy dropped from the ladder, grabbed it, and moved it back to where it had been. He dashed up its rungs to the top step and jerked at the window's handle; then he noticed the slide locks on each side of the window. When he slid the bars from their holes, the window opened easily. He lifted it and slipped the little hook on the bottom into the eye screwed into the rafters above, to hold the pane up and open.

"Yeah," Bernard continued, "ol' Reverend Daniel told me to take care of him right before he told me to come over here...to wait for you. Guess he thought you'd come visiting all right, Jimmy. And I guess he's taken a shine to that Judy girl. Figured she'd hang around, seeing as he has her baby."

"Was it true then, Bernard, about Faith and her illness?"

The man stopped on the bottom step to consider the question as well as to scan the basement. "Well, yeah, that's true, boy. And me too. But we've got the Lord taking care of us. Reverend Davis has prayed over us and laid his healing hands on us. We'll be OK, Jimmy-boy. But now about you and your wicked kind..." Bernard jumped from the bottom step, swinging around to bring his shotgun to bear on the worktable and beyond, where he figured the boy to be standing. "Hold it right there!" he yelled, aiming at the window to the front.

Boooom! Jimmy barely had gotten his legs from in front of the window and was now scrambling to the lattice work at the side of the porch. *Bernard won't be able to shoot straight at me through the window over there.* He turned on his back and raised his legs, pounding with his feet on the wooden strips. Fred hadn't taken the time to secure the frame at the bottom, so Jimmy heard the satisfying crack of the wood right away.

"Hey! Boy!"

As Jimmy pushed his head and shoulders under the frame and rolled beneath the lattice, it split and disappeared above and to the side of him. *Boom!* Bernard had found his way to the window and had shoved his shotgun through it, firing sideways.

"Damn! Damn! Damn!" the man cursed. The gun's recoil had painfully twisted his fingers and almost broken his elbow against the windowsill. "Ow! Ow! Kid, you're going to pay for this!" he roared.

Outside Jimmy was on his feet and running. When he passed the shiny new pickup, he glanced in the window and saw the keys dangling from the ignition. *Thank God for small towns.* He yanked open the door and grabbed them, then raced around to the back of the house. He figured the big man would be slow in climbing the stairs and would first go to the front of the house. He didn't know that Bernard's shotgun was now back under the porch, too far away for the man to reach through the tiny window. *I'll go out through the barn and out the back to the woods there. Maybe grab a pitchfork. Daniel will be coming up the road, I bet.* For a second there, he thought of the new truck. *I coulda taken that, but I'd probably have met Daniel and his boys coming up the driveway or the road.* He had made the correct choice. *Wonder if I could have seen Bill's body in the bed of the truck? If that was true.* He then decided it had to be true because Bernard wasn't apt to have made up such a story—like he would have.

At the barn's door, Jimmy paused and flung the key ring far into the woods, off to the side. *He'll never find them, but I could if I ever need to.* He ran on through the barn, searching the walls as he ran, looking for a weapon: *pitchfork or swing blade would do.* "Whoa!" He'd tripped over a tarp-covered mound in the center of the bay. *Soft.* He scrambled back to the edge of the tarp and flipped it over, and a cloud of flies rose up in his face. "Shit!" It was Fred and Juanita, laid out side by side, covered by the tarp. "Dang!" Someone had chopped at them with a briar scythe; the handleless blade had been left in Fred's almost severed neck. "There's no call for that…meanness. No reason at all." Jimmy knelt and lifted the blade straight up. Maybe he'd take it with him; he might have a need for it. And if he was able to return it to Fred and Juanita's killer, well, that'd be all the better.

"Jimmy!"

The boy jumped to his feet and dashed on through and out the back of the barn.

In seconds Bernard followed, limping heavily. It hurt him to run, but he knew Daniel would be furious with him. He'd been told, "If you see the kid, just blow him away. Don't talk to him. Don't do nothing except shoot him." Then he had forgotten that his shotgun was in his truck's tool chest, remembering it only after he had started over to Homer's place, looking for help from either Blade or Wing in running down the boy. He hadn't had it with him when he had first come in from the barn and had found Jimmy coming in the front door. And then he had fooled around talking with the kid when he *did* have the gun and the boy was already down in the cellar. Daniel would have his skin; he'd said the boy might hide in woods and may flush across the Rogers's property—but he hadn't believed him. He had been out back in the barn messing around with those bodies. *There was sure a shitpot load of maggots and blowflies eating at them already!*

Wait! Bernard saw the kid just ahead, going into the tobacco and heading to the woods beyond. He believed he just might be able to catch him. "Damn, I wish I had my ol' shotgun right now!"

When the big man reached the fence behind the tobacco patch, he realized he had vastly underestimated the boy's speed. There, at the edge of the woods, before slipping away into the shadows, Jimmy was waving to him. *The little shit ass.*

Boom! Boom! There was silence for a moment. *Boom!* The shots were coming from over the ridge to his right. Both Bernard and Jimmy looked in that direction, and then Jimmy disappeared into the woods. Turning back, Bernard wasn't even certain where the boy had been standing when he had looked away. "Couldn't run after your ass anyway. Don't even see leaves moving. Well, it don't matter, Jimmy-boy," he said. "We won't be telling Reverend Daniel about what went on over here anyway—'cept that you shimmied out through the window, and I chased you back into the woods. He won't know no different. And I'll tell him I think you'll be coming back tonight and I'll be waiting for you, little man. With my shotgun." *Mighty fine. So you might as well get yourself over there now.*

Bernard actually disliked spending much time around Daniel. *I'm a middle-aged man, and the boy's included me with those other numb nuts in his youth group, even giving me a friggin' name.* "B Team?" *What's that? What kind of name is that? Sounds like the second string. Sure wish Reverend Dilbert was back.* "Aw, well." He turned and retraced his steps through the tobacco, back to his truck.

Swinging into his seat, he glanced in the mirror, checking out the wrapped body of Bill Shanks in the bed. "Sure glad Faith is ugly as…ah, shit!" He was grabbing thin air at the truck's ignition switch. "That little shit stole my keys! Stole my truck keys! What's the world coming to?" Then he realized he would have to hike over to the Clarks' place to get the spare key from Daniel. "Shit!" He hated that. But he'd hated it more when Daniel wouldn't give him both sets of keys in the first place. "Just in case, B Team," ol' Daniel had said. *Like I was a little kid or somethin'.*

"Aw, well." He dropped from his seat to the ground and slammed the truck's door. "And I'm feeling like crap right now—headache." *Like Faith!* For a second there, he wondered whether they really had…or maybe still had the plague. *I gotta be strong and believe, or I'm doomed.* He headed down the long driveway toward the hard road.

10

DAY SIX

When Jimmy heard the shotgun blasts, he knew he should be putting more distance between himself and his pursuers. He had waited for Bernard, willing him to follow him into the woods so he could then circle around, back to the telephone in Fred's basement. *To call Mom again.* But the close shots alarmed him, panicked him; he supposed that Daniel was on his way over. He waved once to Bernard and trotted away, up into the heavily wooded hillside and on along the crest of the ridge to the rock cliffs at the back of Fred's property. There he followed the trail along the rocky outcrops to the western end of the Ogles' farm.

It had been more than a year since he had last gone there exploring, but he remembered the way very well. The ridge continued north toward the highway, tapering down to where the big road cut through. Homer once had talked about the steep grade of the old road there, back before they had built Chapman Highway, and how they sometimes had to hook up two teams of mules to pull their loaded wagons up and over the ridge on their way to the market in Knoxville. Jimmy wished he could have seen it as it was back then.

The big chunk of property between the ridge and White School Road and adjacent to that section of the highway had been owned by the Ogle family as far back as anyone could remember. And even though most of the land was straight up and down, they had farmed it until the midforties, when Grandpappy Ogle had gone off to Detroit to build cars. When Jimmy had walked there before, probably in the guise of Daniel Boone or in search for arrowheads, he'd noticed that

261

the knobs had once been plowed but reckoned that must have been long before. The rows that circled the hills like an elevation map had been worn and brush covered, no longer being seen but rather being felt through the soles of the intrepid explorer's worn sneakers. Even the bottomland on the property hadn't been turned in years; the creek meandering there had left the land covered with the stones and debris of its numerous floods. But the Ogles' ancestors had chosen to build their barns and big stone house there, close by the flat fields and the country road. And that was where Jimmy now aimed himself, toward the Ogles' house and their telephone. *Their hopefully working telephone.*

That was not to be.

***

Ah, heck! In the fading light, Jimmy saw that the stone house had burned, its roof fallen in and its windows gone. At first he wanted to walk down to the house, to search for treasures and feel the heat of the ashes. He believed the burning had only recently happened since he and Homer had waved at the house when they'd driven by just a few days before. But it was getting late, and he realized now he had no choice other than to return to Homer and Zula's house. *Or maybe spend the night in the barn. At least I can chew on some of the mule's oats there.* He hadn't eaten anything since he had gnawed that potato while hiding in the crawlspace. *Yeah! I can go get some potatoes too!* He hurried his pace, trotting along in the deep shadows off to the side of the hard road.

Earlier, when he had crossed the knoll that overlooked the Ogles' home and could see across the fields to the highway, he had stood watching there for a long while, studying the road to see whether the situation had improved since he and Homer had last driven to Sevierville. He'd noticed that only a few vehicles were inching by, silent with the distance and careful in picking their way around the abandoned cars that remained from the jam five or six days ago. *Volume ain't hardly nothing, less than even on a Sunday.* And he had noted that no cars seemed to be turning onto White School Road. *Should be somebody coming home from work.* He knew there were many people living throughout these hills who, like the Ogles, no longer farmed but worked in nearby towns and cities: Knoxville, Sevierville, Maryville, Oak Ridge, Alcoa—*A lot of folks work at the aluminum company*—choosing better-paying factory jobs over tedious farm lives. When evening time came, Jimmy often sat on one of the hillocks on either side of the driveway and watched the line of cars coming up White School Road, returning to their homes back in the hollows and coves. *But today nobody's turned in. Why?* Jimmy had made a mental note that he would have to drive back down in the old Plymouth when the coast was clear—and when Thelma was away from the house. *And Daniel.*

And Bernard too! He remembered the man, and his neck hairs stood up. *That ol' boy's probably hiding and waiting for me somewhere.* Jimmy knew that, given a choice, Bernard would have been home right then, maybe watching the evening news, but since he apparently was working for Daniel now, he probably would be detailed to spend the night somewhere close, waiting for him to return. *'Course he could be over at Fred's. No, he couldn't—no beds.* Jimmy was virtually certain that Bernard, and maybe one of the others, would be waiting for him ahead, either in the house or in the barn.

Then maybe I should check out the barn first. "Ow!" Planning his approach as he jogged along, Jimmy suddenly felt the pain stitch his side. *Gotta stop for a minute. Rest.* He would need to walk, maybe turn in well before this side of the house and climb up the hill to the back side of the garden, to rest there. He'd been running for a long time and the sky was growing dark; he was leery of staying on the paved road for much longer. *Just asking for trouble.* If he were going to be ambushed, he supposed, this would be the time and place for that to happen.

He crossed the wooden bridge over the creek and stepped through the barbed-wire fence at the side of the road, taking a short-cut by following one of the cow trails around the hills to the garden. *Where I dug the graves for Homer and Zula.*

The pathway was steep and its sides were overgrown, but soon he was lying on his stomach on the soft mound of grave dirt, surveying the darkened house at the far side of the garden. *Looks quiet. Nobody moving about. I suppose they may have left, but it's too black to see behind.* Suddenly the floodlights along the roof of the house flashed on—and Jimmy thought he'd been discovered!

"Damn it, Blade!" someone at the house yelled, and the lights faded. Apparently someone named "Blade" had been fooling with the light switches and had turned on the outside lights by mistake. *Well, I guess I don't have to suppose anymore.*

Jimmy continued to watch the house. Soon another light, the tiny bulb over the back door, came on—and stayed on. *Ah, that's what that was about.* He guessed the light was intended to be inviting to him in the gathering darkness, beckoning him to come in the house by the TV room door.

But how many people are in there? The voice he had heard sounded like Daniel Davis, but he didn't know anyone named Blade. He would have expected Bernard and either Cedric or the Yokum kid to be in there with Daniel, since they'd been with him earlier in the day, but now he was concerned that even more members of the Lord's Army had arrived. Yet, in the brief flood of light, he had seen only four vehicles parked out back among the trees: the Corvette, the Plymouth, the black Cadillac, and the red truck, Bernard's red truck. *But others could've walked up.* "Or ol' Daniel or Bernard coulda gone and got more of 'em." Jimmy settled down to wait and watch some more, now nervously casting backward glances down the overgrown cattle trail.

At about midnight he reckoned, he saw the desk lamp in the TV room come on. It blinked as the people inside walked around and in front of it. *They look to be packing up to go. Bet ol' Thelma has...No, that's nasty.* He now heard the murmur of distant voices as they came to the door. *I'll need to get closer before I can understand anything.* He stood...and immediately froze in place. *Someone's coming out!*

Two men emerged from the door—one walking backward, pushing the screen door open with his shoulder. They obviously were carrying something between them. *Whump!* At the end of the walk-way, they unceremoniously dumped their load and returned to the house. *Still can't tell who they are.* The light over the door was so very dim.

A few more minutes passed, and the men again left the house, extinguishing the outside bulb as they pulled the door to, locking it and jiggling the handle to make sure it latched. "Ja get t'other uns?" one man asked.

"Did you get the other ones?"—that's what it sounded like to Jimmy. He couldn't hear what the other man said in reply, but his voice was like Bernard's. *Maybe that's Bernard's nickname: Blade. Bernard the Blade? Makes sense.* "But what other ones? And why are they locking the doors?" he whispered. "Bet ol' Thelma's gone off to bed, and they're thinking I'm not coming back tonight." He smiled in the dark; he'd go in through the tunnel to the crawlspace. "So just what are you going to do inside," he asked himself, "with her upstairs with Billy Ray's guns?" He'd never before considered that Thelma could shoot him. "Naw, she wouldn't. I'll just carry out some food and stuff...to hide." He approved of his plan, nodding to himself.

Bernard the Blade was now past the dumped load, crunching along on the gravel driveway. He walked on to his truck, hopped in and started it, and drove it over to the end of the walkway, where the other man waited. "That's far enough," he yelled.

That's Daniel there, waiting for Bernard.

Within the minute the two men had heaved their loads—"loads" because Jimmy heard a second thump hit the bed of the pickup—and Bernard the Blade crawled back inside his shiny new truck while Daniel, slapping the truck's side as he passed, walked on to his Cadillac.

Soon Jimmy watched their lights disappear down the driveway, heard them brake before the paved road, and then turn to the right, accelerating west toward the church. All was quiet again. *They've gone. Whew!* He stood there in the garden for maybe five minutes more—he slowly counted to three hundred—before he dared take his next step toward the house. Then he crept along, searching the shadows and feeling very exposed in the dried-out garden. *Glad the moon's clouded over.* At the driveway he walked slower still, fearing the noise of the loose gravel, and paused at the head of the broken marble walkway. He looked around his feet for any indication of the contents of the packages that had been tossed into the truck's bed. "Something here." He knelt and dabbed at the dark spot on the ground then smelled his fingers. He recognized the coppery odor. *Blood!* "They've taken away ol' Homer and Zula, damn it! Threw them around like garbage!" If he hadn't been so mad, he might have cried. "Well, damn it, I got a good mind to go on up there and get Thelma's dumb ass outta bed! That's what I'm gonna do!" He strode to the door and reached for the screen door's knob. *But there's no screen door!* He felt around and found that only the outer frame of the door was intact; the rest of the door was gone, ripped out, screen and all. *What the heck?* He felt for the inside door. *It's still there—locked.* He ran his fingers around the glass panes set in the top of the door then pressed his face to one, trying to see inside. *Too dark.* He couldn't even see the TV's power light across the room, where he imagined the set to be. *It's OK. I'll go around.*

When Jimmy turned to go, he felt the stickiness under his shoes. *Molasses?* Then the smell reached him. *More blood?* He couldn't imagine what had gone on here. He'd definitely ask Thelma.

The circuit around to the crawlspace under the house took him about thirty minutes—through the side-yard fence, down the hill in the pasture, into the tunnel's dark maw, and on to the house—before he was pushing up the cellar door, fastening its little hook to the eye on the wall to keep it open, and studying the room's shadows, trying to see everything at once. His eyes seemed not wide enough to identify everything that could be waiting for him up there in the dark of the covered porch. He lingered on the cellar's top step, listening and waiting. *All OK.*

He stepped up and skulked across the room, past the bathroom to the hallway to the kitchen. He looked back in the dimness and saw the black rectangle of the rear stairs he and Homer had tiptoed down just days before, on their way to the barn to milk the cows.

Only days ago? Now a sickness has changed the world. He moved on, not wanting to spend any more time right now considering the "why" of his new world. *It just is…and it's real.*

Through the kitchen he walked, only now and again reaching out to touch familiar places in the dark, dark rooms. *Dining room, the table, Homer's room off that way, the stairs—the stairs!* He would climb them and go up there and listen at Thelma's door. He would wake her and get some answers. Then he would come back through and fill his pockets in the kitchen. *That's what I'll do.*

As Jimmy slowly, quietly mounted the stairs, he strained his eyes, trying to see anything above at the top of the flight then in the short hallway that ended with the door to Thelma's bedroom. *Not Billy Ray's anymore.*

He listened at the closed door but heard nothing. *No breathing, no snoring—nothing. She's not in there,* he concluded, slowly turning the doorknob. He stepped back to allow the door to fully open then eased his head into the room, confirming his conclusion. "Unmade and empty," he whispered. But he definitely *hadn't* seen Thelma leave with the men, and he hadn't heard her—or anyone else for that matter—move or breathe when he had made his way through the rooms below. *That doesn't mean she wasn't in the car already. Or out front in the other bedrooms.* "Jimmy, Jimmy, be calm. Be calm." He searched around, grateful for the wide windows in Thelma's room. He could see better here than in any other part of the house. He saw the chair piled high with Thelma's clothes, her nightstands, the dial on her clock, the guns in the rack…*guns!* He would need a gun, and he had better get it right now.

After taking another precautionary survey through the door and down the hallway, he tiptoed back in, going to the gun rack above the bed. "The Mauser's gone. Dang! Wait, there—it's at the top." He had wanted that rifle because…*It's Billy Ray's favorite. But you probably should take the twenty-two because you've shot it the most. And there's lots of ammo.* He reached for the boxes stacked on the shelf under the rifles. *But there's lots of other ammunition too.* So he lifted the larger-caliber rifle from its rest and tossed it onto the bed. *Now go!* He pulled down two boxes of the heavy bullets and held them close to his eyes to see the caliber markings. *Too dark.* He had no choice; he'd have to turn on a light to check the writing on the box. He gripped the neck of a lamp on one of the nightstands and quickly turned it on and off. *Yeah, it's the right box.* He pushed a box into each of his front pockets and tightened his belt; the extra weight was pulling down the front of his pants. *And the purple spots aren't helping.* The brief flash of light had temporarily destroyed his night vision. He would have to feel his way back through the house before it improved.

Then he heard the running footsteps outside. *They were waiting for me to turn on a light!* He grabbed for and found the rifle where he had laid it on the bed. Then he ran for the door, feeling his way along. *The doorframe, the hallway, the bathroom doorway, the corner of the staircase. But they're coming in the door!* He heard the keys clanging against the deadbolt; someone was trying to fit a key in the lock. He knew then that he couldn't go back down those front stairs. *The back stairs!* He felt his way to Zula's bedroom then through and out her other door to the back hallway and staircase. He danced down those stairs to the covered porch to the cellar door. He grasped the edge of the heavy frame, flipped back the retaining latch, and lowered the door above his head as he descended the stairs. *Bam!*

Seconds later the cellar door was ripped upward again and flashlight beams stabbed the darkness below. "He's down there!" Daniel yelled. "I heard him! Down there! We got him!

"Where's the friggin' light switch for down there?" yelled another man.

Gosh, that sounds like Cedric. Jimmy was in the crawlspace, around on the back side of the stone stairs, pushing the planks from across the grating. But that was only a fleeting observation, for he had no time for another. He *had* to get in the tunnel and away before he was trapped. He raised the grating, slipped through the opening, and lowered the grating again—all in one continuous flow of motion. Then he reached back through the bars and pulled the planks forward to cover the hole as much as possible. *There.*

But he needn't have rushed; Daniel was satisfied with where he thought Jimmy to be. "Blade," he said to the other man, "I think you have to pull down on the string on the bulb there. See my flashlight beam? But there's no need to go running him down tonight 'cause I don't want to go shooting up all those canned foods down there in the dark trying to get him. Those jars are gonna be worth more than any shit-ass kid. Let's just push that freezer on top of the door—that'll keep him in 'til morning." But Jimmy couldn't hear any of that; he was crouched, running through absolute darkness, one hand holding his rifle and the other extended, brushing along the side of the tunnel and reaching for the heavy wooden door at the end.

When he reached the far end and cleared the covering gate, he quickly closed it again, falling heavily against it and listening for the sounds of Daniel and his guys following him in the tunnel. Many minutes ticked by, and Jimmy began to replace the brush against the door. *Safe for now. Must not have found the grate.* But he'd still sit for a while, he decided. He needed some time to think about what he should be doing before daylight came. It was clear to him that the house was no longer an option. *The gun!* He'd forgotten about the rifle he now carried. *That'll make a difference, expand my options. Maybe even run Daniel off.* But he'd never fired a shot at a person before— for real. Sure, he'd been in a BB gunfight or two, but a BB just left a welt. *A bullet's forever.*

Jimmy thought for a while and concluded he could think better if he weren't shivering; he'd move over to the barn and its warm hay. *Until daybreak.* Then he'd try the highway again. *It's the fastest way home, and there weren't many cars on it anymore. And I got the gun.* He also was confident Daniel wouldn't pursue him in that direction. *Ol' Daniel's got his own realm now to run.*

He stood and scanned across the weeds and briar clumps of the field, taking extra time to examine the ground up toward the house. The clouds seemed to have thinned from over the moon, and Jimmy believed he could see better now than before, when he was hiding across the driveway. *Yeah, I can see the house pretty good now. And the yard all the way over to the smokehouse.* That reminded him: *Maybe I should sneak up and look in there again…just to make sure.* But the thought alone caused a certain sadness to begin to well up. *No, no, not now, Jimmy-boy. Not now. You're tired, and you should rest. Go on now.* He nodded in agreement and started down the scuffed-out cow trail that led to the north, toward the lower end of Red's pasture.

Soon he saw the barn roof as he again climbed the hill farther up the hollow. He took his time, even though he was certain Daniel and his gang members were now all sprawled throughout the house and sleeping away the early-morning hours. *Wait a minute.* He realized now that he thought he'd seen only Bernard and Daniel hauling the bloody bodies to the truck and that there had been no one inside the house trying to trap him or grab him when he was making his escape. *Thelma could have stayed in the car down at the road, but I only heard a few people running to the house—maybe only two. Hmm, maybe ol' Daniel's losing his soldiers in the Lord's Army? I'll have to wait 'til daylight to see.* He wished he had grabbed the telescopic sight for the rifle. *Ah, well.*

He was at the left-open gate to the side of the barn. He paused to listen for any sounds, including—out of long habit—any mule noises. *Nothing.* He trotted over and leaned against the side of the barn, peeking around the corner into the first bay. *Looks OK.* Then he shuffled on around and stood just inside, waiting for his eyes to adjust to the deeper darkness. "Nothing," he finally pronounced. He could see only the familiar shapes of the old wagon and the other farm implements Homer had kept stored in this bay.

He raised his rifle midchest and moved deeper into the barn, intending to take the central pass-through between the stalls to the center bay. *Did I cock this thing?* He had remembered how to load the gun, sliding the brass stripper clip in through the top chamber. *But did I pull out the clip? Did I have to?* He felt the slide mechanism; it was closed. *OK. Did I take the safety off?* "Damn it, Jimmy, you did!" he whispered. "Stop being so nervous!" With his sneakers silently testing the ground ahead, he moved on, past the corncrib, past the plows, crossing over to the black rectangle that led to the center bay.

At the end of the pass-through, he peered between the slats of the adjacent stalls, looking for any movements or unusual shapes. *Nothing.* He was beginning to breathe again. "Whew!" He crept out into the main bay, moving toward the front of the barn where the wooden ladder was nailed against one wall. "That hay will feel so good," he muttered. "I just wish I had more time to sleep in it."

"I can take care of that, boy!" A big arm shot out of the stable door he was passing and grabbed the barrel of his rifle.

Jimmy yanked back on the gun and pulled the big man from his hiding place, where he sat just inside the door. *It's Bernard!* He recognized the fat, balding man and instinctively struck out, pulling and swinging the butt of the rifle at him. "Let go!" he screamed. "Let go!"

"Hey!" Bernard yelled, coming fully to his feet and striking back at the boy, jabbing with the barrel of the shotgun he held in his other hand. "You don't hit me, boy!"

Jimmy acknowledged the man's greater strength and abruptly let go of his rifle, hoping Bernard would hit himself in the face with it from the force of his own tugging. That would give him enough time to race away, through the barn and out the other side.

It almost worked; Jimmy managed several pumping strides before he heard Bernard ratchet a shell into the shotgun's chamber. Instantly he dove through the door of the next stable and crawled madly through the layers of old straw and manure, searching for any openings or any cover. There was nothing; he reached the solid back wall. *Oh, crap!* He turned and looked back at the doorway behind, where Bernard now stood, blindly scanning the darkness inside the stall for any movement, any sound.

Jimmy knew he had only seconds before the man would pick out his shape in the dimness and blast him away; he would talk to him… ask for his mercy. "How's Faith, Bernard?"

The man snorted then coughed and spat. "So ol' Jimmy-boy is concerned about ol' Bernard and Faith now. Well, you weren't so concerned yesterday when you were giving me the finger at the far end of the garden."

"Bernard, I just waved at—"

"Shut up! I know you ain't really thinking 'bout me and Faith. Ol' Faith is probably laying on her deathbed right now, shittin' and pukin' her life away. And you know why I ain't with her right now?"

"No, I—"

"Shut up, I said!" Bernard was waving the shotgun's barrel toward where he believed the voice was coming from. "You don't… You know why I'm here? It's because ol' Jimmy-boy ran away and wouldn't come with me back to Daniel. Ol' Daniel was just wanting you to join up with him and his boys. But *nooo*, you had to run away, and I got told to sit out here, waiting for when you chose to show your sorry ass again."

"Bernard, I thought—"

"Shut up! Or the next sound you'll hear is this here gun talking." He was shaking the shotgun around and inching forward into the stall. "Yeah, Faith is dying, and ol' Bernard is waiting up here in the cold and probably dying too. See?" He was holding out his hand as if Jimmy could see it in the murk. "See? See the blood there? I'm coughing up blood now, and I should be in bed resting. This is all your fault!" He paused, as if waiting for Jimmy's response. But the boy said nothing.

"Well, Mr. Smartass Jimmy. Your whore cousin got her due yester-day—remember those shots yesterday? That was when your Jezebel was catching it full in the face. Hah!" Bernard thought he'd said something mighty funny. "Get it, kid? She got it full in the face."

Jimmy said nothing.

"Yeah, ol' Blade like to took her head off after she shot Wing."

"Who's Wing?" Jimmy chanced a question.

"That dimwit Yokum kid. You know, the one that can't talk worth a damn? Ol' Daniel gave us names when we enlisted in his army. Cedric's called 'Blade' now. He thinks he's hot shit."

Oh? "Well, that does sound pretty good. So what's your name then, Bernard?" Jimmy was beginning to see some hope. *You don't kill somebody you like.*

The big man didn't answer right away. Instead he lowered the muzzle of his shotgun to where he thought Jimmy was sprawled. "He gave me some dumb-ass name, some juvenile name that pisses me off every time he talks to me. Like this is some kind of game or something, and he's more than some murdering teenager. You know, yesterday I had to come over here, *walk* over here when I was feeling as bad as I am, and tell the boy king you took my truck keys. You're just another dumb-ass juvenile who has no respect for your elders."

Jimmy saw his hope fade.

Bernard pulled his handkerchief from his back pocket and blew his nose with one hand, wiping and seemingly studying the cloth afterward. "Blood—my blood, Mr. Juvenile Jimmy. You know, I'm thinking I'm not going to live much longer, but I'm taking as many of you snot-nosed kids with me as I can. Ain't one of you sick at all while us older folks are dying right and left—the ones who made this nation great. How's that for fairness?"

Jimmy took another chance. "But do you think that's the way God would have you to do? You're a Christian and—"

"I told you to shut the hell up!" Bernard took a full step inside the stable, still appearing unable to see the boy in the shadows. "Fact is, I'm thinking the Lord and me just never got together anyway. It was never personal with me—like it is with God and...I was gonna say, 'God and Daniel'...but now I don't know. Anyway, I guess it didn't take with me. And you know, I've looked around, and I don't think it took in many of those phonies down there at the church house. All ritual. All just sayin' the right things to each other but deep down not really believing any of it. Can you, boy, right now, look inside yourself and say you really believe in Jesus—God? Deep down?"

Jimmy thought for a second or two. "Yes, Bernard, I believe I can. You know, some doubt is natural, and like Homer says, you gotta expect it, but our part is just to let him live in us. We believe in the man Jesus."

Bernard snorted again. "Well, Jimmy, then you're going to enjoy meeting him after while. You know, I think I'll just wing you a bit then string you up like they did the Parton boy. Hah! That son of a bitch looked like Christ on the cross when they had me to cut him down yesterday. Christ on the cross. That's what I'm gonna do with

you—put those ol' hay hooks in your wrists and pull you up high
and find the pitchfork. Maybe I'll pierce your side too, while you're
hanging there. And then I'll call ol' Daniel over to look. That'd piss
him off real good because he fancies himself some kinda disciple of
God or something. Maybe like a prophet of old, calling down some
damnation on his enemies? Yeah! Then turning around and rapin'
and whorin' like he does. Yeah, some Moses he is."

"Bernard, did they kill Tom Parton too?"

"Yeah. Wing and Blade did. They caught him back yonder…" He
tilted his head to indicate the direction. "…and blasted him in the
legs. And then they strung him up to bleed out. But Jimmy, know
what? He wasn't completely bled out; he was still a little alive. And
you know what I did? I took the mower blade and removed his arms.
That's the way I took him down—chopped off his arms. Lots easier
that way. But he didn't split apart like Fred and Juanita did; they were
just probably riper."

Then a dark shape shifted behind Bernard…and Jimmy noticed.
The day seemed to have lightened a tad more—or his eyes had
adjusted more—and he thought he'd seen a shadow move behind
Bernard's big form…and then it was gone. *Won't be much longer before
Bernard will be able to see me too.*

"You know, Jimmy, I don't think I'll shoot you at all before I string
you up. I think I want to poke those ol' hooks through your skinny
wrists just like you are." He raised his shotgun and leaned slightly
forward, reaching downward with his free hand.

Sniff. Clump, clump. They both heard the sounds. Bernard
straightened and twisted to the door. *Whap!* He caught a big hoof
square in the mouth, knocking him off his feet and to the ground—
on top of Jimmy.

The boy caught the full weight of the big man on his stomach. With
his breath knocked from him, he could do little more than squirm
beneath Bernard and gasp out in pain. But minutes passed, and his
breath returned to him before consciousness returned to the other.
Jimmy continued to push and finally rolled the heavy body off him
and scrambled to his feet. His shirtfront felt warm and damp from the

man; the familiar smell told him Bernard was now bleeding—bleeding badly, judging from the thorough wetness of his shirt and pants. Dropping again to his knees, Jimmy patted his way through the straw toward the doorway, hoping to find the shotgun quickly. *Aha!* He felt the cold metal at the foot of the feedbox alongside the manger. Clutching the gun to himself, he stood, his finger on its trigger, and leaned forward against the wall alongside the door. He chanced a furtive look into the main bay. *Whitey!* The big mule was now standing just outside the doorway, her long head lowered and her black eyes peering under the lintel, seemingly checking the results of her work. When the boy appeared to the side, just inches from her nose, the massive animal started back, wheeled, and thundered from the barn and away, through the wire gate to the open hillside.

Jimmy was as startled as the mule. Whitey went one way; he went the other, tripping backward, his rear end landing solidly on Bernard's head with a loud crunch. But nothing more happened; the man only grunted. Gripping the shotgun with one hand, Jimmy felt around behind with the other as he tried to rise. His fingers slid into the pulpy mess that was Bernard's jaw. "Ewww! Dang!" He sprang up, stamping his feet and wiping his hand on the leg of his jeans. "Dang, man!" he yelled at the unconscious form. There was a time not so long ago when Jimmy would have joined the man on the floor, fainting away when confronted with blood and gore—but no more. The boy had changed.

"Dang, man! That's terrible! Gonna be a long time before you're eating anything." He shivered with revulsion, feeling no need to further inspect the wound or give aid. "At least you're still alive, Bernard."

Backing through the door, Jimmy turned and scurried first to the place where he thought he had lost his rifle. Finding it easily in the improving light, he hurried to the front of the barn and, after a cursory survey for any activity down toward the house, trotted across the barnyard and out, leaving the big wooden gate pushed back and open. *Don't think there's a need to keep any of the animals penned up any longer.* He was heading home to Maryville.

He trotted on, across the parking area to the side of the smoke-house where he waited, studying the house. When he was sure no one was yet moving about inside, he scampered back to the chicken yard, to open its gate wide, and then to the fence beyond the hen-house. *I'll retreat this way.* He leaned the shotgun against the opposite side of a fence post there—*Just in case,* he thought—and pulled the two boxes of rifle shells from his pocket, hiding them under some leaves farther along, under the barbed-wire fence. *Danged things are almost pulling my britches off.* Then he returned with his rifle to his observation spot behind the smokehouse. He glanced around at the sky. "'Bout six thirty, I'd judge. Shouldn't be much longer. Maybe lay down here for a second." Jimmy stretched out alongside the smoke-house. From there he could still see the back door of the house through the foundation pillars. Soon he was fast asleep.

***

Bang! The smokehouse door slammed shut, and Jimmy almost cried out. Pressing himself into the low space between two pillars, he saw the big backs of Daniel and Cedric now leaving the smokehouse, each man staggering under the weight of bulging croker sacks. *Whew!* He wondered how he had managed not to be seen when they had entered the smokehouse. *Thank you, Lord.*

"Blade," yelled Daniel, "you don't think the smell got into these hams, do you?"

"Naw," Cedric answered over his shoulder. "They been smoked and salted, so they ain't apt to pick up any more smells. 'Sides, you ain't eating 'em anyway. Just don't tell anybody where they come from."

"Yeah, you're right. But maybe we should pull Homer and Zula out of there and drag them on over to the hillside. Their smell's gotten so bad it might start stinkin' up the stuff stored upstairs, up top the smokehouse."

Cedric stopped walking and turned around to face Daniel. "Yeah, we should do that. People will be looking upstairs and buying

the stuff that's up there. And there's lots stored there—unless you'd
rather we carry it all down here."

"Naw, let's just move them two. Less work." The boys proceeded
on their way to the house. "Reckon, ol' Zula will fall apart when we
try to move her?" Daniel asked.

Cedric laughed. "Yeah, good point. We can just tell folks to hold
their noses and carry their own shit downstairs. Say, they'll be coming this afternoon. Do you have those handbills to stick around?"

"Yeah. I'll go get ol' B Team to do that. I didn't tell him we'd
trapped Jimmy in the root cellar; he's still up there guarding the
barn. Hah! Funny, huh? Anyway, I think he can cover the road
from here down past Sugar Loaf in about an hour. That should be
enough time." Daniel stopped and looked toward the barn; he now
was about halfway across the backyard. "Say, it's daylight now. Ol'
Bernard should be up and moving about by now—that is, if he ain't
totally sick and up there fouling himself. Hey! Somebody's left the
barnyard gate open. The cows might've already gotten out. Damn it!
I told Bernard…Here, you take these hams on into the house, and
I'll go see what he's doing. Can you do that?" Daniel dropped his
sacks without waiting for an answer. He pulled the pistol from his
gunbelt and jogged to the barn.

Best you get yourself outta here now, boy! Jimmy scooted from
between the foundation piers and lightly loped toward his hen-
house escape route, keeping the smokehouse between him and
Blade and watching Daniel as he raced to the barn off to his right.
Jimmy was stepping through the barbed-wire fence when he heard
the crack of a handgun, the sound coming from up around the
barn. *I reckon ol' Daniel isn't one to save the wounded. Bet Bernard didn't
have much to say about seeing me neither. Probably Daniel just shot him
laid out there with his mouth all smashed in.* Jimmy then wondered if
he would be able to kill a man when the time came. He'd planned
on maybe shooting Daniel at the door of the house this morning,
but he had fallen asleep. So now he was again wondering if he
would be able to shoot a man. *Yeah, I think I can…but you didn't shoot
Bernard this morning when he was just lying there.* He retrieved the

shotgun, uncovered the boxes of bullets, and ran to the tunnel's entrance at the side of the hill.

***

It was midnight in Israel, and Maymum Abbas passed away. He died in the isolation ward of the Jerusalem hospital without the attendance of either a hazard-suited physician or nurse. He died alone. Since Dr. Eliphaz had last seen him, maybe four or five days ago, before the doctor himself collapsed and died, few people had ventured into the ward. And those persons were there only to draw blood from Abbas then quickly retreat through the heavy plastic curtains. He had received neither food nor water from them.

In the first few days of his admittance, Abbas's blood had been distributed to laboratories around the world, maybe just ahead of the spread of the bubonic plague. The younger clinicians had worked at a frenzied pace around the clock, growing cultures then trying to kill the bacteria with antibiotics, while the older clinicians simply had died. After a day or two, the younger scientists had begun to abandon their labs, choosing to spend their remaining hours in the company of their loved ones. They were the first to fully understand the situation.

The efficient Israeli army also had ceased their interdiction activities around the hospital, and around all the hospitals throughout the state. At first, when the existence of the plague had been made known to the populace, citizen soldiers were mobilized and manned barriers guarding all health facilities, their goal being more to restrict the discharge of the infected than to limit admissions to treatable levels. But that had done little good as people continued to sicken and die, in the order of generations—a pernicious phenomenon without explanation.

When it had become obvious the disease was not endemic, and the Palestinians in the West Bank and Gaza also had experienced its spread, the question of the continued maintenance of border security also had become moot; panicked people seeking food and medicine would not be denied access with mere guns and razor wire. Throughout Israel, as in the bordering countries, security considerations had for the most part degenerated into the formation of local militias of families and friends rather than sovereign organizations. Political concerns had been set aside in favor of simple victual accumulation—the stuff needed just to make it through another day.

While, in the Middle East, these evolving militia units were generally better armed than in other parts of the world, the national concerns once dominant in the area and throughout the world also had dissipated and disappeared within days; no one thought much about nuclear oblivion any longer. Point in fact, those persons who could have ordered the use of such weapons probably had died within the first week of the plague.

Religious conflicts and terroristic acts also had waned in this new environment. Personal relations with God, where such beliefs endured, had become of greater importance to the individual than any desire to proselytize beyond the militia unit. Goals, desires, and ambitions had been reduced to daily strivings for continued existence—that most basic of human drives.

***

It was about five in the afternoon now, and Jimmy was concealed behind a log on the high knob above the broad pastureland south of the hard road. He felt safer over here, with the vast woods and mountains to his back. If he were to be chased, he'd have farther to run on this side.

He watched cars and trucks come up the road from the direction of White Church and turn into Homer and Zula's driveway. *Daniel's selling everything, like he did over at Fred's.* The thought made him furious. *It's not his to sell!*

When Jimmy had gone back into the cellar earlier, following the tunnel to the crawlspace, he had carried potatoes and canned goods back to the grate and then into the tunnel. He had expected Daniel and his gang to soon descend on the foodstuffs stored in the cellar and wanted to hide as much as he could for himself and his trip. But his time had been cut short; he had soon heard heavy footsteps coming to the cellar door and the sound of it being wrenched open. Rough men had spilled through, with guns and flashlights, looking for him. He'd barely had enough time to pull the planks back over the bars of the grate when he had heard Daniel screaming for him, demanding that he give himself up...then cursing because Jimmy had smashed all the light bulbs in the basement on his last foray through the shelves. *That actually felt good.* Now, from far across the valley, he watched as people arrived at Daniel's invitation from their neighboring farms—to steal and plunder Homer and Zula's belongings. *And livestock!*

As he watched, a man came down the driveway leading ol' Elsie toward a truck parked on the clear rise to the right of the driveway. *Dang! The cows didn't make it out of the fence. And isn't that guy...?* He thought he recognized the man holding the rope as one of those people he had seen over at Fred's place, carrying away their food and furniture, trying to shoot him. Now he was seriously mad, furious in fact.

He flipped the safety on the Mauser. *Off.* Lining up the distant figure in his sights, he held his breath...and squeezed the trigger. The man halted midstride, having been violently jerked to the gravel with the bullet's impact, all well before the sound of the shot had reached the driveway. *Wow!* Jimmy had not been certain that he could shoot at another human being when the time came—but he had just done it...and it wasn't that hard. His immediate feelings were not what he had expected, and his thoughts were frantic and random. *Wow! Lucky shot! Must be the gun.* He *had* noticed a long line of notches carved under the stock of the rifle.

Then Jimmy was up and slithering to another tree. His instinct for self-preservation kicked in as any compulsion toward justification receded; this was something else—this was battle! His fear was gone. Even his anger had been set aside. He functioned; he responded. He was capable.

Those guys probably have scopes, and I don't. But all he heard in reply was a single shotgun blast...and a cow's anguished bawl. *Those assholes shot Elsie!* He steadied his rifle on the tree's trunk and sighted on the man running to the downed cow, his knife flashing in the sunlight and held ready. *Maybe to cut Elsie's throat.* Jimmy watched. *Yeah.* When the deed was done, and Elsie was squirting her lifeblood away, Jimmy squeezed off another round toward that man—but aimed only close by him. He somehow reasoned that the guy had at least put the cow out of her misery. *But was he the one who shot her?* Jimmy looked again; the knife-wielding man *was* carrying a shotgun, so Jimmy fired a third time, aiming at the man's head. He missed, he believed, but made the man stumble backward, falling over Elsie's legs and behind her heaving bulk.

Suddenly several muzzles flashed at him, winking from the shelter of porch columns and truck doors. Bark and leaves rained down on him from the surrounding trees, and he heard the rat-tat of many rifles. *Sure didn't take them long to find me.* He turned and retreated up the hill and over the crest, beyond the sighting ability of any telescope. Hidden by this elevation, he sprinted to another vantage point, a pile of rocks toward the top of the hill. There he found a space under a large, flat stone that he believed would minimize his own muzzle's flash while giving him a commanding view of the house and the surrounding buildings. He sighted and blew out the truck's windshield as a test; no one returned his fire. *It works.* He decided he would fire on any vehicle that turned in the drive and would shoot any adult person he saw with a gun. *Maybe they'll all go away then. Supplies. That's all I want.*

All was quiet for about an hour. Then, in the fading light, Jimmy spotted several men running from the back of the house toward the garden and the hillside beyond. *Trying to outflank me, I'd say.* The guy in the lead was big and, to Jimmy, looked like Cedric. He concentrated on the man, watching him dart from tree to tree and then break across the garden's dusty rows, dashing on to the honeysuckle-covered fence. Jimmy sighted in and felled him with a single shot. *Dang! I think ol' Cedric ran into that one.* He held the rifle at arm's length, regarding it with newfound respect. *Maybe those hours I spent plunking pigeons off the barn roof are paying off.* When he again looked through his observation hole, he saw that the other men were retreating to the cover of the house, dragging the wounded one with them.

More quiet time passed, and then someone emerged from the truck at the front. It was a woman; she was waving a white cloth. *That's her all right.* Jimmy recognized her as the older woman he had seen at Fred's. They apparently were the owners of that truck, and she was requesting Jimmy's permission to move. He held his fire. More minutes passed, and the woman, still waving her white garment, backed slowly to the prostrate man in the driveway, knelt, and rummaged through his pockets. Then she stood, holding something at arm's length, maybe for Jimmy's perusal—*Probably the truck's keys*—and walked to Elsie's body to assist the man there to his feet. Together they hobbled to the truck, started it, and backed up to the driveway to their fallen comrade. After much difficulty they lifted the body to the tailgate then slowly drove away in the direction of the church.

No one seemed to have moved from the time the woman had begun waving her white flag; all onlookers were engrossed in the play that had unfolded on the hillock to the right of the driveway's entrance. And Jimmy was now experiencing complex and conflicting emotions...but mostly a feeling he interpreted as a great regret over his actions. The adrenaline charge from the gun battle and his morning's escape from Daniel's gang had passed from his body; now he was just feeling very sad that he had forever killed someone who'd only been trying to cope with this new world. *Just trying to feed his family. But what was the alternative? What have I become?*

And Thelma's dead. He blinked with the thought. He'd actually felt nothing when Bernard had imparted the news. Maybe it was the way the man had delivered the information? And maybe the sorrow would come later? *It's not that I never liked her—hated her. It's just that recently she'd turned.* He almost had ceased to think of her as Thelma, his cousin. *She changed. The meanness.*

He looked again through his rock-framed hole and saw that another truck was slowly moving down the driveway, coming from the back of the house, its occupants vigorously waving their own white flags through their side windows. Their tailgate was down, apparently to show that they were hauling no wrongly purchased goods. One by one they departed—in cars and trucks—all showing white shirts or handkerchiefs at their windows, requesting Jimmy's permission to leave.

Daniel was the last to depart, displaying little of the solemnity of the other trespassers. If the others had perhaps been shocked back into a place and perspective where they could again see their own actions as craven and reprehensible, such a revelation obviously hadn't reached Daniel. In the twilight of the evening, he roared down the driveway in his black Cadillac and fired his pistol, shot after shot, in the general direction where Jimmy stood watching.

But Jimmy hadn't responded, even though he knew the big, black car would be an easy target. He was leaving here tomorrow, and he was sick of what he had seen of this new world. Once again he had felt a kinship with his fellow man but suspected it was only transient, fleeting. With the dawn he and the others would forget this tragedy and the memories that had been evoked. Once there had been faith, justice, responsibility, and respect in the world. Now there was only survival.

Jimmy softly cried as the darkness settled about.

11

DAY SEVEN

It was the dawn of the seventh day since the bubonic plague had come to White School Road.

After thoroughly scouting the way ahead, studying the front of the big house on the hill, and listening for the cars that could appear on the road at any time from either direction, Jimmy jumped to his feet and sprinted across the asphalt and up the graveled driveway. He looked back, remembering having hid in the same patch of tall weeds just days before when he had seen Daniel's gang racing by, chasing after the Mayfield truck. *Was that before or after Homer died?* He couldn't remember. *But I'm sure the grass wasn't all wet with dew then.*

After he passed behind the cover of the red-clay bluff to the right, he slowed his stride, now taking his time in walking up the driveway while keeping an attentive eye on the tall windows of the house. He watched for any sudden movement of draperies and listened for any unusual sounds. *It all seems so…so very normal.* In fact, with the warmth of the rising sun on his face and the morning chirps of the birds happily greeting the new day, he felt as if he should be hauling an empty milk can up from the road—like he usually did—instead of toting a rifle and a heavy shotgun. *Except you just passed a dead cow that used to give you that milk, boy. Anyway, that's all gone now, and you're gonna be leaving in a little while.*

By the time Jimmy reached the backyard and the beginning of the broken marble sidewalk, he had just about decided he should try the door first this time, to see if maybe it had been left unlocked. *Sure would save me the time and trouble of going in through the tunnel.* After all, he'd seen no movement of any kind while walking up the drive—no flutter of a drape in the window or parting of a blind—no movement that would indicate that someone was waiting for him inside. "And I sure could use the john about now." His stomach rumbled in reply, and he rubbed it. "Been kinda rough on you, hasn't it, Myrtle?" With Homer now gone and the name presently unused, he had renamed his own tummy. He reckoned he'd always liked "Myrtle" much better anyway—much better than "Ralph," which he'd originally picked for his stomach. "Well, I guess a steady diet of raw potatoes would be a bit hard on anybody's system, huh? We'll get some better food for you when we get back to Maryville. OK?" He turned at the top of the sidewalk.

"Whoa!" The walkway at the front of the pump house was speckled here and there with little pools of oil—or blood. *It's blood—and it can't be from Thelma; that'd have to be up more toward the door. Must be Cedric's.* He looked around, half expecting to see a tarp-covered mound somewhere in the yard, since he hadn't seen anyone leaving with Daniel when he'd roared off in his Cadillac. *Yesterday evening—but I was a long ways off too.* "That reminds me…" He turned and walked back the way he'd come, back up the sidewalk to the driveway, then trotted on toward the barn. "Might not have been a pile of rags I saw yesterday neither."

It wasn't. When Jimmy pushed wide the big wooden gate to the barnyard, hooking it back so it would stay open, he startled several dark forms grouped about the small mass there alongside the barn—forms that scurried away, thumping and crowding one another before rising from the bare dirt then madly pumping wide wings to soar over the fence and away. "Danged buzzards!" he swore. He walked on and knelt beside the pile, pulling back cloth fabric from the top. "So ol' Mr. Tom Parton, I guess that's what's left of *you*." He recognized the torn material as the work shirt Tom had worn the day he'd helped him with the hay bales in the loft—and had rescued him from Daniel. The actual remains were beyond identification having been visited overnight by the assorted scavengers of East Tennessee. "Doesn't seem fair, does it, Tom? I mean, to be born with so little and to work so hard all your life and to be finished off by a sadistic…Wait here, Tom. I gotta go check something."

Jimmy stood and walked inside the deep shadows of the barn to the back stable, where Bernard had trapped him. The man's body still lay where he last had seen it.

"Dead and supine," he observed, kicking at the man's foot. "But I'm not going to check you for a bullet hole—I suspect I don't care anyway—and I'm not going to bury you neither…you asshole." He pulled shut the stable door and returned to the front of the barn and Tom's side, after first detouring to the tack room to select a pitchfork and the horse blanket he then used to drag his friend's remains to one of the graves he had dug earlier, out beyond the far side of the garden.

He next visited the smokehouse, removing first Homer's body and then Zula's, using a garden hoe to roll them from their high shelf and onto the tarpaulin he'd spread on the floor. It was a grisly task, one likely not ever to be forgotten by the boy. But Jimmy persevered, driven by his love and respect for his cousins, numbed by a sense of unavoidable circumstances, and empowered by his special mouth breathing technique. *I really don't have a choice…but at least I didn't have to hear Tom go splat on the floor…like them.* He was also thankful that he was pulling the bodies on the tarp; that way he was out ahead of most the smells and the hovering masses of blowflies.

He was soon ready for the burying, having moved both Homer and Zula, relocating them to the second grave there in the garden. Tom had been placed in one grave while the couple shared the second. *They won't mind.*

After covering both plots, Jimmy stood over the heaped soil and prayed, trying to remember the words he had heard at the few funerals he'd been obliged to attend. *Seems like the right thing to do, to pray.* But those funeral services had been long ago and the relatives distant; nothing particularly profound or religious would come to him today. So his parting words were brief, including his apology for the rough handling in dragging the dearly departed to their graves— "Couldn't hardly shovel y'all up in the wheelbarrow and push you over," and ended with a thin amen. Regardless, he knew he would remember them for as long as he was to live. *Which might not be long if I don't get a move on.* He estimated it was now almost noon; he had wanted to be on the road much earlier.

***

Dana Bishop lived within the city limits in Sevierville, a few blocks from where, days before, Jimmy and Homer had come upon the wide intersection clogged with the cars of the tourists seeking US Route 40 and their Northern homes and families. She lifted the side of a gauzy curtain in the upstairs bathroom and squinted to the west. *Damn road's not any better.* She turned to the open doorway and yelled, "Are you planning on going back in to work this afternoon, Mother?" She worked at a pawnshop in Gatlinburg.

They had moved from Nashville to the area about a year ago, escaping from a developing situation: Dana's stepfather had begun to develop an abusive streak toward his wife when he drank a bit too much and an unusual interest in his stepdaughter whether or not he drank too much. So they had moved east and her mother's divorce was finalized last month.

Ms. Bishop—she was using her maiden name again—strolled from her bedroom, still brushing at the back of her hair. "Of course I'm going in, dear. You'd be amazed at how much business we have right now."

She had applied at the pawn brokerage when they'd first come to town, and Saul, the store's owner, had hired her after only a twenty-minute conversation. He had liked her quickness, saying, "No amount of education will keep you going in the pawn business—you either got it or you don't." And over the next few months, Ms. Bishop had come to agree with him; in her prior employment life, she had worked for several attorneys and CPAs and believed that none of those professional men possessed capabilities that came anywhere close to Saul's general business acumen. His ability to read people, value their wares, and understand the market still amazed her every day.

"Mother, I worry about you. Look at it out there—it's still a mess. And I heard on TV that the schools aren't expected to start on Monday because of all what's going on."

"Dana, sweet Dana," comforted Ms. Bishop. She stopped brushing her hair and placed her hands on the girl's shoulders, gazing with her through the window. "Saul told me the national guard will be clearing the intersection this weekend, and then things will begin to move again. I guess we should be happy the out-of-state traffic has slowed, and we can still get around town on the back roads. And we didn't catch that...disease. We have *so* much to be thankful for."

"I know, I know. But school—"

"And Dana, I'm *so* happy you've decided to complete your last year rather than take the GED."

"Me too, Mother, but you're changing the subject."

"Listen, I know you're worried about what's been going on around here, but things *are* getting better. Floyd told Saul—"

"Floyd? Is that the cop who picked you up this morning? And brought you home for lunch?" Dana gave her mother a sideways look. Ms. Bishop *was* an attractive woman.

"Oh, honey!" She playfully slapped at her daughter's shoulder. "Yes, that's Floyd. Saul hired him to help out at the store and help keep order around there."

"Good thing. You saw what those people did at the Pig. Those people just came in and grabbed groceries and stuff off the shelves then ran out! It was crazy! And some of those rednecks had guns!"

"I know, Dana. I know, dear. But hopefully that's all behind us. I'm just so glad you weren't hurt and were close enough to immediately come home. They *should* have closed the Piggly Wiggly hours earlier when they first began to notice how people were acting up."

"They did, Mother! That's what I told you! Those people just kept coming in—broke in with crowbars or something. Right then Mr. Jones went ahead and opened the doors and called the cops; there was no choice. And then he told us all to go home." The girl's eyes narrowed. "You know, I still have a paycheck coming too. Did you happen to look yesterday when you were going to work? Did you see if they've done anything at the store?"

"I looked, dear, but nothing appears to have changed. The broken windows haven't even been boarded up, and the doors are still standing wide open. And it's dark inside, so they've probably cut off the power there."

"Oh? What about where you work? Did a mob of scared people try to break into your place too? I mean, you have a ton of guns there."

"We have an arsenal—and that's what kept those thieves away. I mean, yeah, some of those people were frightened and just wanted to make sure they had food in their houses, but lots of those men were simply stealing and were—*are*—planning on selling that stuff if the stores don't open again soon."

"Any chance of that happening?"

"Well, you know Saul, and he's usually far ahead of anyone else in knowing what's going on. He said food stores, pharmacies, and medical-supply stores naturally would be the first places to be mobbed in a national emergency—and that's what this is. Of course, he said, our politicians probably will be of no help—even if people listened to them; they'll be looking after their own behinds. But I'd imagine most of those people would have died early on anyway—being old and all. That's what Saul's saying; the old and the weak are gonna be the ones to be killed by this bubonic plague. He said he saw it like this when he was a kid and living in the Middle East. Did you know this disease has occurred before in the Middle East and—get this— even the United States?"

"Mother, they said on TV that it's much like the Black Death that killed lots and lots of people in Europe and Asia in the thirteen hundreds and fourteen hundreds. Just how old is Saul anyway?"

"Hah! I'll tell him you said that. He's about my age…maybe a little older. Thirty-something…OK, maybe forty-something."

"Well, so what's keeping the military running, Mother? And the cops? Why are they still working? And the TV people? Why are they still broadcasting instead of running away?"

"I asked Saul the same thing. He said America *could* somewhat revert back to what it was like during the medieval period: barter, militias, guilds—that sort of thing. But today so many Americans have moved far from their hometowns and families that only in a minor way does he expect family units will become the controlling thing. He said people now tend to identify as much with their coworkers than with brothers and sisters half a continent away. That's why some places you see open are still open. Those people are the groups where people are finding security."

"Is that why you're still going to work?"

"Maybe so, sweetheart. Maybe so. I'm not afraid there, and I know the police—another group of employees still coming to work—are looking out for you here as well as looking out for their own families."

"Think so?"

"I know so. Floyd as much as told me that."

Dana partially turned and smiled back at her mother. "Think that maybe ol' Floyd has taken a special interest in you?

"Maybe so, maybe so. It's a good time to be appreciated, ain't it? Hah!" She continued to gaze past her daughter out the window, now with a smile on her lips. "Anyway, back to what Saul was telling us—notice that the lights are still on? That the power is still on? That's because of automation and a younger workforce. The worker bees are younger and know how to generate electricity and so on, keeping routine things running. And the military: younger with a stronger chain of command at the lower levels—coworker loyalties. Soldiers fight more for one another, Saul said, than out of any sense of patriotism. I don't know about churches, but I'd expect, around here, a lot of militia groups are forming out of religious relationships—local denominational relationships. I doubt we'd see an army following the pope around, though—if he's still alive, that is. He's pretty old." Ms. Bishop patted Dana's shoulder; they were Catholic but since their move they had not attended any local services.

"And you asked about TV people? Much of that's automatic too, I guess, and the places are probably well protected with security people. But if the TV does go out, please don't...don't be afraid. OK, dear? Especially if I'm at work. Just expect that to happen sooner or later. OK?"

"Oh, I've been expecting that," Dana assured her. "When Mr. Dilfer left when this first started happening, he said we should barricade ourselves in with food and water and guns and—"

"Mr. Dilfer is a *banker*," Ms. Bishop interrupted, her lips tight, "a banker who's never known or felt workplace loyalties. See, they hire young and fire young in that business, certainly well before they're due to vest in their pension plans. And he'd probably just spun the dial on his big ol' safe and was running himself. I bet he's holed up in the mountains somewhere and—"

"Uh-oh, looks like I touched a nerve."

Ms. Bishop's smile returned. "Well...maybe. But Mr. Dilfer's just not a good one to talk to when times are tough, Dana. When we first got here...but I don't need to talk about that right now."

"What about the next family down? They've gone too, I think. And he works at Alcoa."

"Maybe they've gone to their folks' or something. So many older people are sick, you know. Oh, that's another thing Saul was talking about—about workplace loyalties. See, he has this theory about why the governmental bodies will be ineffectual—like that word?— in these kinds of times, especially this kind of time. First, age and seniority are big parts of advancement in the government. And if the old folks are the first to die off, well, you can imagine the turmoil and confusion with the vacuum in leadership. Anyway, Saul was saying that with big labor unions and stuff like that in place, like so much in the government, you'll find a lot more older people in managerial positions than in smaller, private businesses. Second, he said he's known a lot of people who've retired from governmental jobs and big industry jobs, and none ever seemed to have had a lot of memories of great achievements or workplace relations or...a sense of purpose—that they'd want to talk about; they don't seem to have those kinds of relationships. So, he said, we shouldn't expect much from our government and big corporations. But I told him there are exceptions. Remember your grandfather? Remember how he'd talk about his time at Cape Canaveral? I told Saul about him."

Dana glanced backward. "Yeah, but they were working to send a rocket to the moon when he passed away. They probably had an extraordinary sense of purpose that *would* have kept them together." She moved past her mother and started downstairs, angling toward the kitchen at the bottom. "So maybe that's what you guys got? A sense of purpose?"

"Oh? Maybe so...maybe so," she mused, as she followed her daughter down the short flight of stairs to the kitchen. "Maybe that's kind of the way things are going to be for a while—the only order we're going to see for a while. Say, did you get enough lunch, Dana? You didn't eat all of your sandwich."

"Yes, Mother, I'm filled up. God knows you fixed enough for two meals."

"Well, I just hate to think of you going hungry."

"You've squirreled away enough canned goods and pasta to last us until next fall. Hah! But, you know, we *are* about out of milk. Do you think...Never mind. Water is good for now. I hope those kinds of people have a workplace loyalty that keeps them coming to work. Or are the water utilities and sewage systems mostly automatic and being run by real young, real smart people now?"

"Hah! That's funny. It's good you've still got a sense of humor, baby girl. That's important now." Ms. Bishop stood at the kitchen window, looking up and down the lane outside. She turned back, holding up an index finger. "And another important thing: Do you have the pistol handy that I gave you?" she asked.

"Yes, Mother. It's there beside the door, and the shotgun's there next to it. Say, do you really expect me to ever use that thing?" She grimaced. "It'd knock my shoulder off if I shot it."

"Better your shoulder than..." She walked over and took Dana's hands in hers. "Darling, you just don't know what can happen now. That banker and other men...well, you just can't trust anyone now, especially men. Floyd says they're working to control the situation, but there are just too few cops and too many yahoos out there with guns. And many of these self-styled militias have newer and bigger guns than the cops! I just wish…Never mind. Say, did you just hear a horn toot? Floyd's here to take me back to work, I guess." She grabbed her purse and leaned to kiss her daughter on the cheek. "Lock the door behind me, sweets, and I'll see about picking up some milk somewhere on my way home tonight. I'll ask Saul—he'll know. There are people from the country coming around now, selling their home-canned stuff, green beans and tomatoes and stuff, and fresh milk and meat. It's expensive, but what are you gonna do? Love ya, darling. Ta-ta." Then she was gone, her footsteps echoing off the pavement as she hastened to the waiting police car.

Dana stood at the kitchen window now, watching the cruiser pull away. Theirs was the end unit in the complex, and their kitchen faced to the front, to the road. She leaned in to look back toward the end of the cul-de-sac.

Especially men, huh, Mom? She hadn't told her mother that the banker already had knocked on their door and asked her to go with him—and it *had* been to go to the mountains. Since Mr. Dilfer had moved in several months back, he seemed often to be working in his tiny yard when she'd arrive home from school, calling out to her to come see one or the other of the new flowers he'd planted. At first he'd merely been friendly, but soon he was telling Dana how lonely he was, now that he had divorced, and that maybe she "would like to come over for a little while—maybe have a beer or two—and talk about the day and all." Then, one afternoon, he offered her money, and she stopped turning aside to see his latest planted posies. *Yeah, Mother, I think I know about men already.* She padded over to the door, slid together the chain lock, then walked down the short hallway to recheck the deadbolt on the other door which opened into the garage. *Now to go watch the soaps.*

About thirty minutes later, the TV screen went to fuzz, and Dana spent the rest of the afternoon vacuuming and dusting.

***

Jimmy jogged lightly across the gravel to the old Plymouth, trying to look both ways at once—toward the house on one side and the barn on the other. *Safe!* He ducked low, leaning back against the car's grille, waiting for his breathing to slow. He hadn't heard or seen any vehicles enter or even pass by the property while he was doing his burying. *But you can't be too safe. They could've walked up the drive or the front walkway.*

Then, when the time felt right, he eased around to the passenger side, slowly opening the door and slipping inside, and wriggled his way across the bench seat to the driver's side, leaving his two long guns there on the floor. As he levered himself up in the seat to retrieve the key from his tight jeans pocket, he remembered to check the backseat. *In case somebody's hiding back there.* Jimmy had seen more than a few reruns of *The Naked City* and *Dragnet*; his heroes often had been ambushed from the backseat. *It's OK*, he determined. Then he slipped his key into the ignition and turned. *Nothing!* There was no grinding or clicking in answer to his key twisting. *Oh, dang!* He checked the gas gauge. *Nothing—no power. I'll have to go look at the engine and see if I can see anything.* He wasn't much of a mechanic, but he had learned a few things from working with his father—before one or the other of them had gotten angry and stalked off. He wished now he had been more attentive and respectful around his dad. He found the hood latch easily enough and was soon standing on the front bumper and leaning far into the motor compartment. *Battery's gone! When they couldn't find the keys, they took the battery, I guess.* He raised up and looked over to the Corvette; its hood wasn't completely closed. Jimmy jumped down, raced to the other car, and lifted its hood. As he had feared, its battery also had been removed. *Those boys are intent on keeping these cars here. Or selling batteries.* He knew then that he would have to walk home. *Maybe.*

Yesterday, when Jimmy had crossed the bottom en route to the knob across the way, he had spotted Fred's old plow horse wading along in the creek, nibbling at the watercress that had accumulated in the eddies behind rocks and along the banks. Ol' Hammerhead obviously had learned long ago that the surest way to avoid reminding his owners of his availability was to maintain as low a profile as possible; his galumphing along in the shallow waters that flowed through the deep gulch definitely had kept him invisible to the road and the farmhouses beyond. *If you don't see 'em, you don't use 'em. And that probably has kept the ol' horse from getting shot by Daniel and his troops too. What if…?* He thought to ride the horse out of here and back to Maryville. *Yeah!*

He lowered the cars' hoods and closed the doors on the Plymouth, leaving the heavy shotgun hidden under the front seat. Soon he was hopping down the hillside, running toward the lower gate at the end of the hollow. After furtively crossing over the hard road there, he stayed close to the vine-draped fence and the drainage ditch that bisected the pasture. It was still early in the afternoon, and there were few shadows in the open field he could use for cover should he hear a car or truck speeding along the road. At the creek he quickly located the ancient horse very near the same place where he'd seen him the preceding day.

"Hey, ol' boy. Hey, Hammerhead, baby. Wanna go for a ride?" Jimmy crooned. As he approached, wading along up to his knees in the creek, the horse raised his head and sniffed the air. He was suspicious of the boy coming his way and the hands holding out big clumps of freshly torn grass. That *could* mean work for him—something he detested. He could have wheeled just then and splashed away, thundering up the path and through the knobs to the back pastures, but he also knew that the grass—the boy-delivered grass— always tasted like something special. So he waited for Jimmy and his fistful of fescue.

Jimmy fed the horse his offering and then, using both the animal's mane and the adjacent creek bank, hoisted himself onto its broad back. Now came the test: On a good day, ol' Hammerhead didn't mind being ridden at all; on a bad day, the horse was quick to find the nearest low-hanging tree branch to brush off the nuisance rider. Today turned out to be a good day, and the big animal splashed on, responding well to the boy's knee pressures and prodding heels.

At the drainage ditch, Jimmy steered the horse out of the creek bed to lumber back the way he had come, crossing the pasture, mostly hidden from the road by the weeds and low channel. Then, with more luck and the compliant mood of his mount, Jimmy got them both over the road, through the gates to the long hollow, and eventually up to the barn. Once there, and with Hammerhead ensconced in a stall with a door, he treated the old horse to a gallon can of oats and a good curry combing. *Dang horse has got more bugs than a dog. I'm eaten up with 'em.*

Leaving the horse, now secure in the barn, to rest, Jimmy raced back to the tunnel's hillside entrance and to his food stores hidden beneath the grate in the crawlspace. He quickly filled his burlap sack to capacity, ready to return to the hillside via the tunnel. *But it might be a lot quicker to go through the inside of the house.* And he always could use more of the now convenient ammunition up in Thelma's room. He returned to the grate, pushed aside its covering boards, and climbed from the hole. After circling around to the front of the stone steps, he paused there for a minute, looking down on the shelves below. Even in the cellar's gloom, he could see there were significantly fewer jars of canned foods there than a day or so before. *Ol' Daniel already has made off with some stuff, I bet. I wonder what he's taken from upstairs.*

Jimmy climbed to the top of the stairs and pushed against the big cellar door. *Locked.* He was unable to raise the door; the outside metal hasp just clanged with each mighty push with his back. *Bet ol' Daniel's put a padlock on the door to keep people from stealing stuff*—an ironic thought for sure. *And I'm not going to be able to replenish my supply of bullets right now. Dang! Well, I guess it's a good thing I got the food.* He crawled back around to the tunnel, lowered the heavy grate again, and pulled the boards in place. *Just in case.* This time he reached back through the bars and fitted the antique padlock in its bracket, locking it with the brass key. *That'll be there in case they find the opening.* At the hillside gate, he also took extra care in concealing the tunnel's mouth with cuttings from the nearby thornbushes and briars. *Ain't nobody gonna find that now.*

Back at the barn, Jimmy soon had the horse bridled and his stores divided in two tied-together sacks thrown over the horse's shoulders.

He decided that, with much light still left in the day, he'd take the back route through the woods and out to the highway. Then he'd canter the horse along on the road's grassy shoulders to Route 411 and then on into Maryville. He tapped his shirtfront making sure he still had Homer's maps tucked safely in his jeans. *Maybe four or five hours, I expect.* After fashioning a strap for his rifle with some bailing twine, he slung the Mauser across his back, mounted his stead, and was on his way. *Probably none too soon.* As heavy-footed Hammerhead shuffled his way past the gateposts, heading to the dense woods north of the barn, Jimmy heard the distant whine of an approaching truck, coming from the direction of Fred and Juanita's place. *They're probably coming back to get the rest of the stuff here.*

***

When they reached the fence at the back of Homer's property, Jimmy dropped to the ground to open the taut barbed-wire gate to the Ogles' woods. The opening was so hidden in brush and its post so difficult to unhook that the boy guessed he was probably the first person ever to attempt to open it. Indeed it took him a good ten minutes of grunting and pulling to free the bottom of the post from its looped wire restraint. *Dang! I'll have to ask...Never mind.* It wasn't going to be easy for him to remember that Homer was dead now. *No reason to close the gate either, I guess.* He remounted and rode down the hill toward the flat pastureland.

Emerging from the woods and skirting around the Ogles' burnt-out house, Jimmy urged ol' Hammerhead forward, trying to get the horse to trot the short distance along the paved White School Road to the divided highway. He began to suspect his idea of a brisk canter to Route 411 wasn't likely to happen. *This is gonna be ol' Hammerhead's top speed, I reckon. Well, a ponderous plod will get us to Maryville sooner or later—but probably a lot later.*

Minutes passed, and as they drew near Chapman Highway at the end of the country lane, Jimmy heard the sharp crack of a rifle shot, echoing from beyond the curve ahead. Then he heard another shot and another. "Dang, Hammerhead. That's too close! Let's don't go—whoa!" The horse already had decided he wasn't about to go that way and made a hard left off the road and over the steep bank, sliding through the clay and dense brush to the once plowed field below. As they skidded to a stop, Hammerhead popped lightly to his feet—as if this were something he did on a regular basis—shook himself, and looked around his hooves for any promising patches of grass. On Hammerhead's back, still entangled in mane hair, Jimmy opened his eyes. "My gosh!"

They stood there for a while, the horse pulling at the puny grass within reach and the boy rearranging his bags and picking leaves from his hair, both listening for any indication up ahead that they'd been discovered. *Nothing. Thank you, Jesus. And I suppose we're only slightly worse for the wear.*

"Ready to go again, horse?" Jimmy quietly asked. He'd retrieved the dropped reins, and they sauntered on, staying very close to the line of brush that masked them from the roadway above.

Slowly, slowly. Lying flat out on Hammerhead's back and looking up, Jimmy saw something that looked like a car bumper extending far over the bank. They crossed almost under its shadow. *Don't sneeze, horse. Don't sneeze.* For once he was glad they didn't have a saddle, which probably would have squeaked and creaked with every step.

"Whew!" Now that they were clear and the highway intersection was just ahead, Jimmy looked back and saw that the bumper thing was the rear end of a burned school bus left sideways and blocking the road above. *That's why no one's been turning in White School Road. They've got a barricade up there!* Another shot sounded then, as if to punctuate the thought. "Oh, man!"

They ambled on, following the deepening ditch. Jimmy leaned far over to the side of the horse's neck, patting and rubbing him there. "Well, ol' boy," he whispered, "you done good by going over that ditch when you did. You probably saved my life, because we were fixin' to turn the corner and run smack into them." He twisted sideways to again scan the top, trying to see more of the wreck. "I can't tell who's up there, but I expect ol' Daniel's replenished his Lord's

Army by now." Then he straightened and studied the land ahead. "And what are you gonna do if there's another something-something army up there claiming the other side of the highway?" he asked himself, still whispering. "You can't even tell who they're shooting at up there. Gosh, now I could use some stirrups to stand in."

Soon they reached a ninety-degree turn in the ditch, where it emptied into the brush-hidden creek that flowed from under the roadways, and Jimmy slipped off Hammerhead's tall back. "I'll be walking you through the creek here, ol' boy. I don't think they'll be able to see us from back there, but we need to stay low. Besides, there could be holes and such in the streambed, and I don't need you dumping me then falling on top of me." He flipped the reins to the front of the horse and walked ahead, probing the shallow water. "Besides, we maybe should just go through that big ol' culvert over there and walk *up* the creek and through to the other side. It's flatter over there on the other side of the highway." They waded upstream for several steps before Hammerhead suddenly shied back from the dark hole ahead, pulling his head high and jerking at his reins.

"Dang, horse! Come on, boy. It's just a little ways to the other end! There's two big ol' tunnels here, see? And this one only goes over to the median under the two lanes on this side—ain't too far." Leaning in to estimate the distance, Jimmy looked through the culvert. Then he saw the multiple pairs of yellow eyes looking back at him, watching from some middle island, their large bodies silhouetted by the light at the far end.

"What the heck! Dogs?" The animals looked like maybe coyotes to him. *But they're way too big! Wolves? Not around here.* Then the low growls reached him, and a set of eyes elevated as one of the animals stood.

Jimmy turned and ran, splashing to the far side of the creek and dragging the now cooperative horse with him. They ran on into the field alongside the highway until they were hundreds of yards from the culvert. "Dang, Hammerhead! Did you see that? Do you reckon they've let animals loose from the zoo or something?" Still scrambling, he glanced backward several times, past Hammerhead and the open field, confirming that nothing had pursued them from out of the void. "They look like they're hyenas or something—big ol' yellow eyes! Way too big to be just dogs or coyotes! Maybe panthers?" They hurried on.

As they climbed the incline up to where the next road, Pleasant Hill Road, connected with Chapman Highway, the boy was still recalling the names of the predators he'd seen the last time he had visited the big zoo in Knoxville. "Panther. Cheetah. Maybe they *were* wolves, Hammerhead. Lions! Yeah, maybe lions! Dang!"

Nearing the top, he slowed, unslinging his rifle and flipping off the Mauser's safety, preparing to find another fortified barrier there like he'd seen back on the other road. He carefully, carefully peeked over the curve of the hill. *Nothing. No roadblocks here. Great!* Since this narrow lane connected with White School Road after a mile or so through the knobs, Jimmy was somewhat surprised—and relieved—that he encountered no barriers there at all guarding Daniel's domain. "Maybe they're farther down the pike. Or maybe the ol' boy don't have enough soldiers to watch all the entrances at once. Besides, without seeing a street sign there"—he'd noticed the broken-off road marker—"you'd just have to know this was a turnoff here." The country road crested over a slight rise before intersecting with Chapman Highway, causing the paved area to appear simply as a wide place in the road.

As if on cue, a station wagon emerged into sight from around the distant curve, driving slowly up the long hill toward them, toward Sevierville. When the vehicle drew near and its driver spotted the rifle-toting boy and his mount standing at the roadside, it abruptly lurched to the far inside lane, its occupants lining the side windows to exchange wide-eyed stares with the pedestrians—from behind the safety of their tinted glass.

"Just like that, ol' boy, just like that," Jimmy murmured, concluding his thought. They both watched the car until it was out of sight. "Well, we'd better be on our way, ol' horse." He looked around once more then led the horse to the crash barrier that began at the top of the incline and continued down along the highway. "I'll just have to use this thing to get back on top of you."

As he climbed up the metal fender, he noticed movement at the top of the hill in the other direction, back toward town. "Uh-oh. Another car's coming, Hammerhead. Let's wait 'til it passes." The car came on—a big Lincoln with its windows down. *Black.* Then Jimmy saw the flash at the driver's window and heard the bullet zigging past, right above his head, and then he heard the gunshot. The horse bolted, jerking its reins free and galloping along the crash barrier back toward White School Road...toward the oncoming car!

"No, Hammerhead! No!" wailed Jimmy.

More shots rang out, and Hammerhead screamed, crashing sideways into the steel guardrail and skidding to the rough asphalt. For several seconds more, his long legs flailed the air, spastically pumping and trying to regain his feet...before quieting.

Jimmy was still standing atop the steel barrier when the roaring engine brought him back to reality. *The car's crossing over the median!* He jumped backward, dropping behind the post as bullets dinged and ricocheted off the guardrail. The car roared on—on toward the boy. Jimmy again checked the Mauser's safety then stood and fired, aiming his first shot at the car's windshield, the driver's side. In the next microsecond, the Lincoln hit the concrete drain in the median and leaped into the air, airborne for ten to fifteen feet before crashing back to earth, digging up huge clumps of dirt and grass with its front bumper. Yet it came on! Its engine continued to roar, and the car continued to climb from the median toward him. Jimmy worked the bolt and squeezed off another shot, aiming this time for the open side window. Then, not waiting for the results, he turned and sprinted down the hill, running for the pasture fence at the bottom. *Too far! Too bare! I'm toast!*

Rat-tat-tat-tat! The boy heard a machine gun open up off to one side—a very heavy-caliber machine gun. He glanced over his shoulder, trying to keep his feet under him and locate the source of the sound at the same time. *A truck!* He sighted the top of another vehicle coming from the opposite direction, cresting the hill. It looked like one of those big military trucks. *The national guard!* He often had pedaled his bicycle through the armory's parking lot on Parham Hill when he had delivered newspapers; he knew what those trucks looked like. *They've got the canvas off and a machine gun's mounted on top!*

Rat-tat-tat-tat! The machine gun again ripped the air, and Jimmy heard bullets thunk into metal in reply. *Gotta be a fifty caliber.* He had stopped now, to listen and watch. A soldier stood high in the truck's bed, gripping the back of the big gun, his arms and shoulders twitching with the recoil of his short blasts. Belted shells, each the length of a man's hand, jerked up the side of his gun. *But I can't see the car!* He ran back up the hill toward the guardrail. *Rat-tat-tat-tat!*

Jimmy reached the top of the hill and threw himself down in the grass, pushing flat the weeds under the fender. He saw the Lincoln now, halted and partially in the road; it was burning. *Rat-tat-tat-tat!* The big gun coughed again and metal ripped from the car's right fender; the tire exploded. Fire licked from under the hood, and smoke rolled from the windows.

The military truck slowed and coasted onto Pleasant Hill Road then turned back toward the burning car and stopped. Its high, passenger-side door opened, and a combat-garbed man carrying a machine gun dropped to the ground. Jimmy stood where he was and raised the Mauser over his head.

"Over here, son," the man ordered.

Jimmy immediately obeyed, walking along the fender toward the truck. He saw the gunner high above glance over once, twice, while keeping his big gun directed at the Lincoln. "Nobody's moving, Sarge!" he yelled.

"Just keep an eye on it then," the sergeant yelled in reply, still watching Jimmy as he walked.

"Whatcha doin' here, son?" he asked when the boy was close. "And put your arms down. I ain't worried 'bout you."

Jimmy slowly lowered his rifle to his side, its muzzle pointing to the ground. "I'm going home, sir."

"You know them?" The sergeant partially turned and casually pointed with his gun at the burning Lincoln.

"No, sir. We'd just come from back that way down yonder," the boy replied, raising his thumb over his shoulder, "and just when we got on the road, that black car came driving up from that direction and shot at us."

"And then they got your horse, huh?"

"Yessir." Seemingly close to tears, he looked at his feet.

"Damn shame. A good horse is worth more than a human these days." Sarge was watching the burning car. "Damned shame. Say, you say you come from over that way?"

"Yessir."

"What's going on over there?"

"Well, a lot of people have died—"

"No, I don't mean from the plague. Are people shootin' each other up? What's it like? Any large gangs of men out killing and robbing? Raping? How much disorder's going on down that way?"

"Well…" Jimmy desperately wanted to tell the sergeant that Daniel Davis and his gang were out killing everyone in sight and that he should take his men and go blast the hell out of him and his Lord's Army. But in truth he really didn't know much about what was going on beyond his own backyard and, aside from crazy Bernard and what he'd said, he didn't know if a lot of raping and other stuff *was* going on. It was all very confusing. Violence seemed as bad or perhaps worse right here on the highway and in town, in Sevierville. "Well, there's one ol' boy named Daniel Davis," he began, "and he's blocked off the roads and gathered up a bunch of guys from around the church, and they say they're enforcing the law, since the sheriff's not around, but they've shot the Mayfield man, and I don't know if there's raping going on but they've got one woman named Judy Shanks, who's got a little baby and might be kidnapped, and well, I guess—"

"The Reverend Daniel Davis?" Sarge interrupted. "He the one who's blocking the next road?"

He knows Daniel? "Ah…yessir. Across White School Road. And Homer and Zula Clark have died, but they'd gotten the disease, and

Fred and Juanita Rogers have died, but that was probably from the disease too, and a guy named Tom—"

"Just farms down that way?" Sarge interrupted again. "I mean, are there any stores down that way? Like banks or pharmacies or grocery stores? You know, like a little town or something worth something?"

Jimmy was staring at the sergeant now, uncertain of what the man was asking. "You mean like a lot of money or maybe some important people living around here?"

The sergeant intently stared back. "Yeah, I mean if we go down that way and get our asses shot off in the process, what's in it for us? What's it gonna accomplish? We can only do so much, and we've gotta be heading back to Knoxville real soon."

Jimmy felt as if he'd been punched in the stomach. That almost sounded like unless there was something for them personally—to carry away—the military man wasn't interested in him or in protecting any of the folks down White School Road. "Well, some people have their egg money buried in their backyards, I've heard, and—wait! Food! We've got a lot of food in the house that might be worth a lot."

"Son, we got all the rations we want back at the armory. How 'bout gasoline? Any gas stations or big tanks of fuel on those farms back there?"

Jimmy shook his head. "No, no, not really. Most people drive out here for gas…but we've got a few cars and trucks that people might not be using." He was thinking of Thelma's Corvette. *That's worth a lot. Maybe that'd be enough to get them to…* He then remembered he was leaving; he was on his way home. If he got the national guard to shoot up Daniel and his boys, it still wouldn't bring back Homer or Zula or Fred or anyone else. It just wouldn't matter. It probably would be better if the sergeant and his men turned around and went back to keeping order in Knoxville. "No. Other than livestock and trucks and cars and stuff, there's not a lot of wealth back there."

"Didn't think so. And if you look around, there's cars for the taking all along this road. But there ain't no gas to run 'em." The sergeant was looking at the sky again. "Well, boys, the major told us to only go out as far as 411 then come back. We're well past that, but I don't care. I'm not too sure if that old man's gonna be around much longer anyway."

"You said '411'?" Jimmy was interested again. "What's it like between here and 411?"

"Hah!" The soldier laughed. "You planning on hiking down to 411 tonight, boy?"

"Well, you can see they've shot my horse."

"Yeah, and I'm sorry about that. I don't think those ol' boys there will be shootin' anybody else's animals, if that makes you feel any better. Anyway, from here to 411 is a long haul. You can't make it in the dark. And there's more men in big ol' black cars like that back toward Knoxville too. You were just lucky we came along when we did, or I don't know what they'd be doing with you now. But you wouldn't be enjoying it, that's for sure. Hah!" Sarge laughed again then gave Jimmy a salacious grin. "Unless, of course, you *do*."

The soldier manning the fifty caliber laughed now, and Jimmy's eyes burned. He knew what they were talking about, but he also knew they were just having fun with him. He shuffled the gravel with the toe of his sneaker.

"Say, boys!" Sarge yelled to the truck. "What say we give the young lad a lift to 411 on our way back?"

"Aw, Sarge!" the driver and the gunner chorused. "You said we'd be stopping at a jewelry store and that pawnshop in Gatlinburg today...and it's gonna be getting dark soon," the driver yelled through the window.

"Yeah," the gunner added, "and dropping the kid off on 411 won't be doing him any favors either. That's where they had all those wrecks and the big backup last week with all those people trying to leave town. You from Maryville, boy?"

"Yessir. That's where I was going."

"Well, there's been a lot of shooting up and down Sevierville Pike, boy. Lots of local militias with guns running around, I've heard. Lots of residences up and down that narrow road. You might be better off around here—out in the country. It don't get any better back that way."

Jimmy was nodding. *I'm still going to Maryville.* "You're probably right, but if you *could* drop me off at 411—"

"Naw, I'm sorry, boy," Sarge spoke up. "I shouldn't have made the offer without talking with the corporals here. We gotta look out for each other too, you see."

"No, no, I understand. That's OK, sir. I'll try to sneak past that roadblock and back to the house for the night and see what I can do for tomorrow later. But you know, I really appreciate your saving my life—'cause that's what you did." He shook hands with the sergeant and waved at the other soldiers as he turned to walk back the way he'd come.

When Sarge reached the truck, he called back to Jimmy, "Say, boy, don't walk too fast back that way. If we can see the roadblock from the highway, we might have to soften it up a bit in passing. Hah!" He waved again and climbed aboard as the truck stuttered forward.

Jimmy shuffled along the road's shoulder, back toward his supply sacks and Hammerhead's sprawled carcass. As he walked, he watched the national guardsmen in the distance as they dipped into the entrance of the country lane. No sooner had their truck slowed than the Lord's Army men opened up with rifles and pistols, the sounds of their shots echoing throughout the valley. While the bus barricade was beyond Jimmy's line of sight, hidden by the hills and trees, he saw—and heard—the guardsman gunner reply with his fifty cal—*rat-tat-tat-tat*. And then it was over; when the corporal ceased firing, all was quiet…and the truck continued on. *Just like nothing had happened.*

His supply sacks now draped over his own shoulders, Jimmy took his time retracing his way. Having no desire to again cross in front of the culvert, he paralleled his route staying up on the highway's surface. *And it's beginning to get dark.* He walked faster, soon reaching White School Road and then the silent school bus.

Jimmy noticed first that the vehicle had rolled backward, its undercarriage lying on the ground and its rear wheels hanging free over the steep bank. *Wouldn't have taken much for that thing to have rolled on over the edge.* There was ample space now, between the front of the bus and the graded hillside, for a car or a truck to pass.

Jimmy stepped sideways through this gap using the big yellow frame for cover. He held his rifle to his shoulder and kept his finger on the trigger as he moved around. Two boys about his age lay across each other there in the road—very bloody, very dead. The large-caliber military bullets had torn fist-size exit holes through the metal sides of the bus and had skipped unblocked underneath. The boys had almost been cut in two.

"About instantaneous, I'd say." Jimmy cautiously advanced and stooped down, trying to see whether he recognized the boys. He did. Had he enrolled in White School, the pair would have been in his class. "And if ol' Daniel had found me and taken me into his Lord's Army, I'd probably been out here guarding this road right now. That would be me laying there. Thank you, Lord."

It was getting darker. He needed to go.

***

Dana was worried. *Mom should be home by now.* She'd tried calling her mother, but either the phone wasn't working or no one was still at the pawnshop. *The phone must be broken.* She knew Saul was spending his nights in the store. *He's there for sure.*

She went to the front door and slid open the chain lock. Having made sure all the lights were out on the ground floor behind her, she eased open the solid door. *Looks like a full moon tonight.* She could see all the way to the end of the cul-du-sac in one direction and to the main road in the other. *Nobody's moving around.*

Dana slowly walked out and around their little curve of a sidewalk, and on down the driveway to the road in front. Then she turned and studied the other apartment fronts, down their side and up the other side. *Looks about half occupied now.* The power was still on, and lights glowed warmly at the neighbors' windows. Suddenly she had an urge to race to one of the other doors and pound on it, asking to be let in, to stay until her mother returned home. *But it'd be my luck to find Dilfer's twin.* No, she would go back inside, find her book again, and read herself to sleep. "Mother will soon be home." Saying that aloud made her feel better. "Yes, Floyd will soon be driving up, and Mother will hop out and say good night and come inside, and we'll have hot dogs and iced tea for supper. That's what we'll do." She sauntered back up the drive and up the sidewalk to her door. "What's that?" She heard a truck shifting gears, coming down the main road at the corner. "Damn, that's probably Mother, and here you're standing!" She pushed open the door and stepped inside to watch from the shadows.

The truck rattled past the entrance of their road. It was a big military vehicle and hadn't even slowed when passing their street. *I bet they're here trying to clear out that mess at the intersection. None too soon, I guess.* She firmly closed the door and slipped the chain lock in place again. "Mother will be here in…soon. I bet she's trying to buy milk or something. God, I hope things get better soon."

✳✳✳

"What do you think, Sarge?" the corporal asked from his high position behind the big gun. They were parked at the far edge of the asphalt, about forty yards from the building, between two pools of light cast by the pawn brokerage's huge metal halide lamps. There were no other vehicles in the parking lot between them and the shop's thick plate-glass windows.

The sergeant was standing at the truck's open door, closely watching the entrance to the low, flat structure. "Well, I dunno," he replied over his shoulder without looking back. "I told them we'd appreciate any contribution to our retirement fund they thought fair and reasonable—reasonable to us of course. And I repeated it so I don't believe there'll be any unfortunate misunderstandings. We just need to give some time to ol'…ah…Saul, I think. Yeah—Saul. It's there on the sign. Saul's Pawn and Brokerage."

The other guardsman, the driver, snorted and slapped his steering wheel. "Yeah! A contribution to our pension plan. Hah!"

Sarge glanced over and smiled at his corporal. "You know, it's good when someone's around who's smart enough to appreciate humor. Yeah, I told them we represented the military might sent to protect this hamlet, and we were invoking our powers to tax. And seeing as how this area was so inconsiderate as to have their jewelry stores so thoughtlessly depleted and abandoned, they must feel an especially great urge to contribute on behalf of their God and country...and town—can't forget the town bit." The driver rewarded him with another guffaw.

"Well, I hope they hurry up," the gunner replied. "The major's gonna have our hides if we're not back soon."

Sarge smiled again and looked back over his shoulder. "You boys leave the ol' major to me. When he gets his share of the stuff you've got piled up around your feet, he'll be all right. I just wish we coulda gotten the pain-killers and drugs he was asking for. But that was not to be." He nodded, again focused on the barred doors. "We tried the two pharmacies here and the one back on Chapman Highway. Those are the only ones I know about. Plus we tried the clinic here—all empty and looted."

"What was it like in there? In the clinic?" the gunner asked. He'd stayed outside to watch the gun and hadn't gone in.

"It was weird—all those rotting bodies in all those beds. The smell there liked to have knocked me down when Snyder yanked open the doors."

"Yeah," the driver, Snyder, agreed.

"Now that was a stink!" Sarge raised his arm and smelled his sleeve. "Shit! My clothes reek of that stink!"

"Gonna have to burn 'em, Sarge," the gunner opined. "I can smell you from up here. Sure glad I'm up here, and you and Snyder are riding together in the cab."

"Well, I oughta make you...Wait!" Sarge stood erect in the doorframe of the truck and stared at the storefront. "Didja see a shadow move over there? I think they're about to tell us what they can spare for us—for us protecting their valuable asses."

As they watched, a long bar slowly slid across the double doors from the side, and the inside lights blinked off.

"Well, I'll be damned!" the sergeant swore. "I think they mean to give us a fight." He reached inside the cab and retrieved his machine gun. Stepping down and clear of the truck, he sighted in on the overhead glare and let loose several bursts, blasting apart the expensive parking lot lamps. "Snyder, forward! Sanders, light 'em up!" He screamed out his orders as he climbed back to his seat. Sanders complied and swept a spray of fifty caliber bullets across the windows and doors.

At first the projectiles just chinked at the glass, ricocheting into the night. Then, as Snyder moved the truck forward, and Sanders continued to fire, the big plate window exploded into fragments, leaving a gaping hole of interior darkness. The gunner continued to fire, waving his stream of bullets and tracers back and forth and into the hole, and the driver continued to move slowly forward. *Rat-tat-tat-tat!*

"Cease fire!" the sergeant commanded, and the firing stopped. He again opened his door, standing up through the opening and surveying the broken scene ahead. All was quiet, and the truck braked, its headlights illuminating the counters and racks inside. "Looks like we got 'em."

Pow! A shot flashed from inside the store, and the sergeant lurched from his perch, felled by a single shot through his left eye socket. Sanders opened up again, not expecting an order. He raked his gunfire from side to side, exploding the thick glass in the doors and the other front window. His tracers covered the store's interior; his bullets penetrated shelves, counters, and walls. *Click.* He reached the end of his belted ammunition. Again all was quiet except for the softly idling truck engine.

Snyder tenderly mashed the accelerator, coaxing forward the big truck and stopping only after its front tires climbed to the smoothness of the broad sidewalk, its headlights exposing the store's total interior, wall to wall. He saw four—*No, there's three*—people scattered around the store: a uniformed man sprawled facedown at the door, a balding guy holding a pair of pistols spread over the counter, and a long-haired woman shoved back against the long gun displays at the rear of the store. "She's got the rifle, Sanders! I bet she's the one who shot Sarge!"

Sanders aligned another belt of ammo, cocked his weapon, and sent the next long volley her way. She violently twitched with the sustained impacts and was driven from sight, thrown behind the counter. "I don't think she'll be shooting anybody else!" he yelled from above the cab, as if the woman had been the cause of the fracas. He ripped another short burst at the counter, blowing away big chunks of plywood. "That should do it!"

After another long moment of silence, broken only by the ticking of his cooling gun, Sanders leaned down to the side window. "Snyder, best you get in there and hurry. I'll keep watch, and you grab anything of value. We don't want any visitors interrupting us— not now."

Soon the guardsmen were hurrying back to Knoxville, returning the way they had come. Sanders had joined Snyder inside the truck, and the sergeant was stowed in the truck's bed. They drove in silence down the highway, occasionally slowing for abandoned vehicles blocking a lane but meeting no one traveling in the night.

***

When the sun had dipped below the knobs off to the southwest, the big wolf atop the soft sandpile rose to her feet and stretched mightily then ambled over to the cool waters that flowed around the mound and on through the culvert. The creek water tasted good to her after so many years of drinking chlorinated city water. And it felt good to eat the meat that seemed freely available and all about, softening in the sun and ripening to a tenderness she hadn't experienced in the years since she had been trapped as a pup and sold to the zoo industry. Fragrant, tender meat—that's what she remembered most about those days—plus the absence of fences…and the absence of noisy, smelly people moving along the far sides of those fences.

But it was these more recent experiences—with humans and their noise—that had kept her and the pack from fleeing the sanctuary of the big culvert when all the gunshots and explosions had erupted on the roads above. And it was that same experience that had kept her inside when the young human had passed, walking alone up the narrow country road and carrying the oiled metal she associated with the noise. She would lead her pack along that country lane after first consuming the best parts of those other humans she smelled, left for them up on the road. She would allow her members to eat the available food for now, but she also would train them for the life ahead—when times would be even better, and they would hunt to fill their bellies. But she also was feeling something different now—an urgency, an inner command, a growing presence strengthening and hardening her, and giving her strange new desires. Something was expanding inside her—with needs and demands far greater than those of her pack. She would obey.

***

"It's gotta be almost midnight." Jimmy had walked all the way from the highway back to the house. "I'm darn glad the moon's out. Otherwise I'd probably still be laying and waiting in a ditch somewhere back there." Only one vehicle, a small Ford pickup, had passed him on his way up the hard road, and that was only a short time ago; he'd heard it coming in plenty of time to hide in the ditch. He'd expected Daniel's guys to be coming down to relieve the boys at the bus, but the truck had carried only the driver. And it hadn't returned. *Maybe he was the midnight relief for those guys?* In that moment he felt a slight stab of sorrow and whispered his hope that the boys' parents were real old and maybe dead or dying already. *I bet it's real hard on a mother or father to find out you've outlived your kid.*

He turned up the driveway, walking briskly and unafraid for the moment. "Elsie's gone! Dang! Somebody's come and hauled ol' Elsie away. Well, maybe she didn't go to waste then and is being made into hamburger or something. Too old and tough to be used for much else anyway, like Homer's always...said." *This remembering's going to take a while.*

Jimmy slowed his pace, creeping along the rest of the way, bypassing the house and going through the open barnyard gate directly to the deep shadows of the center bay. By touch he found the handle for the door set high in the wall then climbing up and mounting the stairs that led to the loft. He soon found the safe place he was seeking, crawling between bales of stacked hay to the special hidey-hole he'd constructed back in the spring. It felt so good, and soon he drifted off, listening to those faraway dogs howling at the full moon.

***

Having finished their eating, the pack members sprawled beside their leader, each wolf licking its muzzle while clearly savoring the last of the heat that emanated from the asphalt surface. The sun had set long ago, and they were unhurried; they sensed no cars passing along the road to disturb them and no humans about to take up the oiled metals scattered on the road. On an earlier evening, this would have been a time to rest and enjoy their new life.

But tonight the big female was unable to relax; the inner urging was strong—demanding; it was time to hunt. The pack, two males and a female, felt her unease and watched her, awaiting her signal. When she stood and sniffed the air, they also stood and sniffed, readying themselves to follow.

Her quarry's scent was still strong in the air, having passed this way only hours before. A young male, she determined, judging from the fragrance that lingered on the bus fender he had rubbed along in skirting the blockade. And he had walked away from the big road and toward the south, she noted, his smell hanging in the still air off in that direction. *Yes!* Setting off at a brisk trot with her head lifted high, she followed the invisible trail to the boy.

With their ground-gobbling stride, the first mile sped by quickly—then mile two, then three. She heard a vehicle coming and led her followers to the creek bed alongside the road, waiting there until the little pickup rumbled by. Then back to the road and mile four. Once more the big she-wolf paused as she followed the scent, this time to examine the ditch at the side of the road. She allowed her followers to group around her, sniffing the dirt and vegetation that had lain beneath the boy, before resuming their stalk. The wind had begun to move the air, so she more often now dipped her nose to the road to confirm her quarry's route.

Around a curve and up a rise, she detected her human's divergence from the hard road and turned north and up a broad, rock-covered pathway. She abruptly slowed and the next wolf, one of the young males, almost collided with her. He had been closely following his leader and was distracted by the odor of an injured cow. He knew this smell well because chunks of raw, bloody beef often had been fed to them back at the fences. It was a comfortable smell to him and a flavor he much preferred over the human flesh that was now most available to them. And even though they had just eaten their fill, he experienced a fresh rush of hunger when they entered the invisible cloud of fragrance.

The she-wolf snarled and wheeled on the youngster, driving her shoulder into him and forcing him to the ground, pressing her bared fangs against his exposed throat. She wanted to kill him—she needed to kill—now! *The boy, my darling. Go to the human.* The big female pulled back, shaking her head, reluctantly turning aside and continuing up the driveway, allowing her pack only seconds to scour the ground where Elsie had lain.

She felt danger now—being close to the den of the humans and their oiled metal—and slowed her pace. But the smell of the boy was very strong, and the youngsters behind began to exude their own odors—of tension and excitement. The kill would be swift. But the trail seemed to lead on, past the humans' den and the vivid smells of their spilled blood, passing on to that tall structure that smelled of more meat—strange meat. She raced on to the barn, her keen eyes searching the shadows ahead for the prey.

Inside the scent lifted, replaced by the animal smells, so thick and cloying in her nostrils, rising from the ground all around her, confusing her. It was as if the boy, like the fowl quarry she occasionally chased, had risen into the air, to be smelled but roosting far above and out of reach. His smell was still almost…warm…and sour, pungently sour. She howled in frustration, setting off a chorus with her pack members. So close. So very close.

Her inner voice soothed her: *Wait, my darling, wait. There is still time. Grow and be strong.*

12

DAY EIGHT

Dana awoke to the sound of a garage door opening. *Mother's home!*

She looked about the room. *Wow! It's morning! Sun's up, and I've spent the night in the chair.* She groaned and stretched. "Whoa, girl, you've seriously strained something there. Ooh…so stiff. Really pooped out or something last night." She stretched again, arms in the air and toes pointing hard at the TV, and slowly pushed herself to her feet, feeling years older than any teenager should. "Old recliner's great for reading but terrible for the neck." She rocked her head from side to side. "Better go let your mama in now. Wonder what's kept her?" This was a first for her mother—staying out all night. She sometimes had arrived home well after dark, but she'd never been this late before.

Padding barefoot through the apartment to the hallway door that opened into the garage, Dana glimpsed the covered pan still on the stove in the kitchen. "Forgot about the hot dogs. I hope they're still good after being in water all night." Her stomach rumpled in reply. "Maybe they'll be good fried…with breakfast. Mother had better be hungry too." *If she's spent the night with Floyd, I'm really going to be ripped. The least she could've done was to call—maybe.* She wondered whether the phone service might have been down during the night. "Better wait and listen to her story first. Times are weird, and who knows what's happened at the shop?" Dana often talked aloud to herself when she was alone—and even more often when she was alone and alarmed.

She unlocked the deadbolt on the door and pulled at the knob. *Whoa!* Her mother's little Ford Mustang was there, but the garage door was down, and the light was off. *Oh, that's right.* Dana remembered now that her mother had ridden in with Floyd yesterday; she hadn't taken her car to work. "Damn!" Dana pushed tight the door and ran back down the hallway to the kitchen, to its window. Dividing the curtains, she saw the neighbors across the lane backing out of their drive; the garage door sounds had been theirs. "Damn!"

She continued to watch at the window. The driver seemed to be having a difficult time backing his car down the short driveway; he was about to run over his mailbox. *Crack!* He did run over his mailbox.

"Don't see something like that very often," Dana muttered. "Maybe, girl, you should go see what's happening?" She knew the neighbors, but she didn't know them that well. They were a younger couple with a small child, and she had babysat for them twice when they'd both had to work. "Maybe you should go see if they need some help." Dana hurried to the front door, slipped the locks, and walked out. Across the street the neighbor was trying to drive forward from off the broken post. "Oh, gosh, that don't look good. Now what's his name? Or rather, what's *her* name?" She saw that the guy's wife was the one behind the wheel; the husband was sitting on the passenger side, his head propped against the window.

"Hello!" Dana called. She had walked down her drive to the street on the passenger side of the car. The man rolled down his window as if he were about to return her greeting. Then he leaned farther out and violently vomited down the side of the car and onto the pavement.

Gross! So now what are you gonna do? "Ah, ma'am? Ma'am?" Dana squatted and yelled from the road, trying to see around the guy's head and into the car. "Do you need some help, lady?"

The woman must have caught sight of her; she seemed to have flashed a wave in Dana's direction right before she grabbed the gearshift. Then she began to rock the car to and fro on the broken stub of the mailbox post, sawing the shift lever back and forth, as if she thought something were wrong with the transmission.

Damn! I hope she doesn't suddenly hit the gas pedal right now. The lady looks panic-stricken or something. Maybe epileptic. She was rolling her head wildly from side to side, her motions growing almost frenetic. *Definitely past being able to drive a vehicle. I need to go around to the other side.* Dana cautiously circled wide around the back of the bucking car and approached the driver's door. "Ma'am? Ma'am?" she again called out. *She's not even looking.* "Damn it, Lynn!" Dana screamed. The woman jerked erect and searched ahead, looking for the source of the call.

Lynn! Yeah! That's her name. Lynn. "Lynn!" Dana yelled as loud as she was able. "Stop it! Damn it, Lynn!"

Lynn stopped…then slowly turned to regard Dana, her eyes wide and frightened. Recognition seemed to come, and she lowered her head to her hands to sob, her neck and back shaking with her hysterical gasps. "Oh, God. My God! What am I going to do? What am I going to do?"

Dana edged closer and extended her hand, cupping the door handle. "Lynn, where's the baby? Where's little Jeffy?" she demanded in her most authoritative voice. "Where's Jeffy?"

"Jeffy?" Lynn answered, straightening as if she were coming out of a deep sleep. She again stared to the front, out the windshield.

"Jeffy, your son," Dana tried again. "And your husband—is there something wrong with your husband?" Dana couldn't remember the man's name. She just knew he was several years older than Lynn and was the meat-market manager at the grocery store in Townsend. Lynn had been a cashier there when she and her husband had first met, she'd once told Dana.

"Lyle?"

Crap! How could I forget that? Lynn and Lyle. "Yeah, Lyle. What's the matter with Lyle?"

"Lyle's sick," Lynn answered, using that same dreamy voice. "Lyle's sick, and he's going to die."

"Well, maybe and maybe not. Lynn, think hard. Where's Jeffy now?"

"Jeffy?"

Dana lost patience. She wrenched open the car door and flung herself across the woman, pushing at the shifter to get it into park. Struggling to her feet, she grasped Lynn's arm, forcing her fingers into the woman's armpit and lifting her, exactly like her mother had done to her when she was younger and slow to heed a command. Lynn followed her up from her seat exactly as Dana had been obliged those many years before. "Ow! Ow! Ow!"

Dana then pushed her back against the side of the car, leaning against her, steadying her. "Lynn, where is Jeffy?" she demanded, her face inches from the woman's. "Where is your baby?" Dana caught a faraway spark of recognition, flitting through the blackness of the woman's dilated pupils. And then it blazed!

Lynn pushed back, suddenly throwing Dana to the grass with superhuman strength. She spun around, frantically searching the streets and the yards. "Those damn dogs got Jeffy!" she yelled. "Those damn wolves got my baby. At the clinic. I took Lyle to the clinic! Jeffy! Right out of the carrier! Took my Jeffy! Gotta go back to the hospital! Animals coming! Mountains!" She continued to scour the area, searching all around, her eyes wild and anguished. Then she stopped and stared down at Dana, questioning, "Where?"

Dana didn't know what to say. "Lynn," she started, "let me try to call—" That was as far as she got.

"*Nooooo!*" Lynn screamed to the world. In the next instant, she was diving back inside the car, plunging it into gear, and stomping the accelerator. This time the car shot forward from off the post, its tires squealing onto the lane's pavement, barely missing the swale that bordered the main street. At the intersection Lynn wheeled the car, tires still screeching, hard to the left, heading south. Then they were out of sight. In the front seat, the guy, Lyle, had done nothing the whole time except rock from side to side with the motion of the car—and maybe throw up again.

Dana stood in the tiny yard, bewildered, listening to squalls of the fading tires and the roaring engine. "Whoa! What *is* going *on?* What did Lynn just say? Her eyes…That lady's *got* to be crazy." Soon there was only silence. "Crazy," she repeated, looking around now at the fronts of the other units. No one had come out to help…not even to gawk. Not even a curtain fluttered at a window. *Just by myself. Crazy.*

She turned back to face Lynn and Lyle's apartment. *Left the garage door wide open. I'd better shut it.* Her first instinct was to protect her neighbors' property, even though, after what she'd just seen, she had no idea when—or if—her neighbors would return. She once more circled in place, scanning door fronts while replaying the words and the scene in her mind, still searching for meaning—witnesses, assistance. *Still no one's around. And that whole thing took what? A minute? Less than a minute?* She walked up the driveway and into the garage's shadow, tapping the overhead door's "down" button as she passed to the side of the rear entry door. As the garage door rattled down, she partially opened the unlatched entry door and called out to the interior, "Anybody there? Jeffy, are you in there?" *As if the kid could answer me.* She pushed wide the door and strode in. Lynn and Lyle's floor plan was exactly like theirs—except in reverse—so Dana took a right then another right, with the intention of exiting through the front door, simply pulling the door and locking it behind as she left. *But you know you'll go ahead and take another quick look around the house,* she told herself. *Mother's little ADHD child that you are.*

Outside the master bedroom, Dana knocked once and tentatively opened the door. *Whew!* She wrinkled her nose as a fetid odor greeted her from the dark gap, washing over and about her. *Damn, that's bad!* She fanned the door a couple of times to disperse the smell before opening it wider, pushing against some obstacle low on the other side. Then, holding her breath and reaching inside, she patted the wall and located the light switch there. In the resultant brilliance cast from the unshaded overhead bulb, the extent of the room's dishevelment was unfiltered and shocking to her. The bureau drawers all stood open, and the mirror above the dressing table had been shattered, its broken pieces leaning dangerously from its frame. The big double bed had been pushed hard against the far wall, and its splotched mattress was bare, its sheets wadded and thrown here and there all around on the room. She kicked at the discarded sheet that partially blocked the door and saw the dark, seeping stains of either blood or feces. "Gross!" she gasped. "And it smells like the toilet's backed up in here or something! What's that?" The plastered wall beside the closet was dotted and marked, like someone lying in bed had tried to write words there with maybe a reddish-brown marker. Stepping inside for a better look, she was almost to the closet when she realized the deep-pile carpet was squishing beneath her feet. "Gross! I should've put on some shoes!" She backed quickly out of the room, scrubbing her feet through the drier-feeling carpet toward the edge as she retreated. At the doorway she turned and looked back once more. *Dresser drawers all open and stuff hanging out—apparently a lot of searching and packing has gone on here. Activity of some sort. Lynn and Lyle's life.* Dana was appalled but still curious about the room, seeing it as a summation of sorts—a sad memorial of a family's life now ending. *But somebody else sure the heck is going to have to read what's written over there.* She turned off the light and pulled tight the door.

In the next room, the nursery, Dana tripped and almost fell as she crossed the dim space, going to the window to open the blinds. She looked back, now seeing she had stumbled on the baby carrier on the floor in front of the crib. A certain weariness then came over her; a sadness seemed to weigh on her chest, momentarily making breathing difficult for her. She could only imagine what Lynn was feeling. "Is that what she said? 'Right out of the carrier'? Is that what she said?" She nudged the baby blanket with her foot then lifted it from the carrier, seeing the wide stains in its folds. *Bloodstains maybe?* The fabric *was* stiff, and the carrier bottom was tinged a rusty hue, as if it had been clumsily wiped.

But could Lynn have done something to the kid herself? With all that's going on and her husband sick and maybe dying? Those wild, crazy eyes... Dana was having a hard time believing a dog could—would—rush up and grab an unattended baby, a human child, and an equally hard time believing a woman, crazed or not, could harm her own, sweet child. *Beautiful little Jeffy. But there's no wolves around here,* she reasoned. *Some of the kids say maybe a bear or two might wander down to town every so often, but we don't have wolves or even dog packs around here.* "Poor, poor suffering woman," she concluded. "Her husband's stricken with…the illness—I really didn't think he was that old—and she's totally lost. I hope, I hope, I hope the police or the people at the clinic have just taken little Jeffy away from her." It had been a long time since Dana had prayed, but she made the attempt now, standing in the shambles of the nursery with a profound heaviness in her guts. "Please…about the baby. Please, Lord. Amen."

In the bathroom she found pills scattered across the top of the vanity, some having fallen to the floor. She looked around for the container. *Here it is. Hydro…codone…something, something. Wonder what that is?* The big-city drug culture had yet to invade Dana's world, and her stepfather had preferred booze. She scraped the capsules back into the container and picked up the pills from the floor. *I'll take them with me just in case. They're medicine.*

She opened the wall cabinet, scanned its contents, and took the bottle of aspirin from the upper shelf, putting it in her shirt pocket. Then she noticed an unopened tube of toothpaste on the lower shelf and picked it up but immediately set it back down. *That's getting like stealing rather than safekeeping. But Mother did say the pharmacies were the first stores to get mobbed, along with the grocery stores.* She reached back into the cabinet for the toothpaste and the floss. "I wonder if she has any hair spray. Mother's about out. Whoa, Mother!" In all the excitement, she'd forgotten about her mother—she needed to be looking for her mother.

In the closet at the front door, Dana quickly located the house key on the top shelf she'd remembered as being kept there. *In case me and Jeffy went for a stroller ride. Darn! I really hope nothing has happened to that sweet kid.* She felt the hot tears well up again, and for a moment there, everything was bleary. *Hey! You've gotta go find your mother, girl.*

She left the apartment, locking the door behind, and crossed back to their place. *Darn!* In the excitement she also had forgotten to lock their own door. *Now watch—somebody's probably slipped in on me.* But no one had, and soon Dana was watching their own garage door raise in the Mustang's rearview mirror.

OK, ready? Dana was old enough to get her driver's license but hadn't yet taken the time to actually go and get it. Her mother usually had the car all the time anyway and wanted her to take a drivers' education course first—for the lower insurance premiums. But they also lived close in town so her bicycle was really most adequate for the places—work, movie theater, work—that she frequented. *Maybe when I have a few friends I want to visit,* she'd told herself.

She turned the ignition key and the engine caught immediately. *OK, next?* She was well familiar with this next part—backing up. Ever since she'd grown tall enough to reach the pedals and see over the steering wheel, her mother had allowed her to back the car out and return it to the garage after washing it in the driveway. It was just the driving-down-the-road part she hadn't yet practiced to any great extent. *Well, it's gotta be easier than straddling the seats and trying to steer while being shoved over against Mother.* So after backing into the lane, she turned to the right for a few practice runs around the little cul-de-sac.

Wasn't hard at all. Ten minutes later Dana had accomplished all the basics of driving: stopping, starting, changing gears, turning the headlights on and off, and—most important for a teenager—finding the only radio station that still seemed to be on the air. It was playing big band music from the forties, but it would have to do for now. *Maybe some news or some rock music will come on after a while.* But that wouldn't happen. The station's engineer hadn't shown up for work that morning, and the DJ, feeling somewhat sick himself, had put the looped recording on to play for as long as the electricity flowed, locking the door behind as he had left.

"OK, girl. Now go that way and over to the highway." She figured the national guard had cleared some of the main roads by now. "And then all the way to Gatlinburg." But that also wasn't to be. She soon found that the line of abandoned cars still stretched from the big intersection, the one to Interstate 40, to the secondary road she was on. "But there's no traffic at least. Let's go across and down."

In the next block, she realized she also wasn't seeing any people moving about. "Like a *Twilight Zone* episode I saw," she remarked. "Like I'm the only one left." Then, coincidentally, as she slowed for the next small intersection, she saw a form crumpled in the cross-walk—a nonmoving person. *An old lady maybe. But I've never seen a dead person who wasn't in a coffin!* She slowed further as she skirted the body.

The clothing was that of an older woman, but the head was that of a scarecrow: black button eyes, coal nose, and stitched mouth. Dana steered closer and stopped. *No, those are holes and teeth.* The woman was well into turning into a skeleton, and her face was almost cleaned of flesh. *Just probably rotted away, I guess. I wonder if her pet—no!* Dana shook her head, willing away the thought; she didn't want to imagine that cats and dogs could chew on people who may have been their masters. It had made her think of Jeffy again too. Then, as she still watched, she saw the bottom of the old woman's dress begin to move, ripple, and a large rat popped out and scurried for the storm drain at the curb. "Gross!" she cried, accelerating and steering the car forward, around the two abandoned cars crunched together and partially blocking the intersection.

"Now how in the heck can someone just die on the street and just stay there to rot?" Dana asked her dashboard. "Why can't the cops or somebody at least take the body somewhere and bury her?" But *she* didn't want to do it, couldn't do it, didn't feel obligated to do it... nor apparently did anyone else who'd happened to pass by. So Mrs. Goldner stayed right where she'd had her last conscious thought about six days before.

At the next intersection, Dana slowed again and looked down the intersecting street toward the river—just in time to see something big lope across the pavement that way. "Damn! That's the most gigantic otter I've ever seen!" The big animal had crossed the road in two bowed-back leaps and disappeared in the bushes. *Or was it a panther? Well, at least I don't think it's a wolf like Lynn was talking about.* She clicked her door locks again, just in case, and felt for the pistol. She had remembered to bring the guns her mother had left for her. The revolver was on the seat beside her, and the shotgun was propped over it, leaning against the door. She wanted the big gun to be visible to anyone who got close enough to look into the car.

Still don't see anybody walking along. She was traveling north, she believed, slowing now as she drove through a residential neighborhood of very old homes. She examined every front porch and each door as she coasted down the street. There were no vehicles parked along the road so she wasn't too concerned about running into one as she surveyed her new world. She was taking her time.

Movement! Something sparked ahead, like a flash of sunlight. As she drew nearer, she saw that someone had parked a car, a silver car, in the middle of the street, and its door was open. *The flash happened when the door opened.* Dana slowed even more, trying to see what was ahead before she drove farther along the street and past the intersection just ahead.

"That's a big moving truck backed in and some people out front. Do you want to go on by them, girl? There's not much space." She stopped in the intersection to watch the activity ahead. Several men were carrying furniture from the house and into the moving van. They were like a string of ants, running in a line, truck to house and back, carrying boxes, clothes, and furniture from the house to the truck.

Then Dana realized she wasn't alone. A woman, maybe in her early twenties, had emerged from the corner house and also was watching the scene from her front stoop. She and Dana exchanged stares...and cautious nods. After another minute of watching the men down the block, the young woman walked from her porch, down her steps, and toward Dana's idling car. She was carrying a butcher knife in her hand. Dana checked her doors again. *OK.*

The woman stopped at the curb, keeping both Dana and the working men in front of her. She called out to Dana: "You with them?"

Dana partially rolled down her window and shifted her left foot to the brake and her right foot to the accelerator. *Just in case.* "Ma'am?" she called back.

"I said, 'Are you with them?'" yelled the woman, much louder this time.

Dana blinked, thinking the woman's tone was too loud—harsh and unduly confrontational—so she replied in kind, "No! Are you?"

The woman's lips pursed with Dana's reply. She must have then realized how she could have sounded to the young girl in the little car. "Listen, I'm sorry," she apologized. "I've just been…stressed, I guess. Don't know how to talk to people anymore…bad times. And maybe bad people—like over there. I've seen men at different houses…and I don't know any of them! That's Mrs. Hill's house they're carrying furniture out of, and Mrs. Hill went to the hospital a few days ago. She's not even at home or anything."

Dana nodded, acknowledging the apology. *She's probably by herself too. Watching her world being invaded.* "Do you think maybe those are Mrs. Hill's children or relatives?"

"No, I'm sure they're not. I've called the police, but they don't answer." The woman stepped from the curb so she wouldn't have to talk so loudly to Dana. She was hugging herself, as if she were cold. "No, Mrs. Hill had no living relatives that I know of. Mr. Hill died about two years ago, and Mrs. Hill rode with me to church. No, I'm thinking those are just men who are going around, knocking on doors, and breaking into houses when no one answers. That's what they were saying on TV was going on in Knoxville—before the TV went dead." The woman continued to look over the top of Dana's car, keeping track of what was happening at the Hill house. "Yes, I'd heard young men were banding up and attacking older folks. Even those who weren't sick with…you know."

"Have you been out and around?" Dana hopefully asked. "Have you been up toward Gatlinburg? Have you seen anybody else around?"

The lady took another step forward, still hugging herself, her shiny knife blade held off to one side of her face. "No, not for a day or two—or maybe three or four. The main road over there was all gummed up and all. I've had to go all the way down that way"—she nodded toward Mrs. Hill's place—"to get out on the road to go to Pigeon Forge to the grocery store there. And there were parts of the road going there that were still gummed up, so I had to drive around stopped cars to get there. And when I got there, the store was all broken into and just about empty, from what I could see—unless I wanted cleaning products. And those were at the front, probably for the taking if I'd wanted to get out of my car. No, I don't think... uh-oh. I think they're coming over here now!" Still watching over the car's roof, the woman took several steps back to the curb, toward the safety of her house.

Dana glanced over and saw that, indeed, several of the men were coming their way. She turned back to confirm the woman's observation, but she was gone, racing for her yard and for her door. One of the men shouted to Dana, "Hey, stop! We wanna talk." or something like that, and they all ran toward the car. *They've got guns too!*

With that Dana stepped hard on her accelerator—and on her brake. The engine roared, and she was astounded she wasn't moving. "Oh! Oh!" Then it occurred to her to lift her foot from the brake and the car instantly moved, dancing sideways for a millisecond before the screaming tires gained traction. For the next few seconds, Dana spun her steering wheel back and forth, trying to aim the front of the car down the street and away from the running men. And then she was gone, miraculously avoiding the big maple trees that lined the roadway.

Pook! Pook! Bam! Bam! She heard first the bullets hit her car and then the explosions from the men's rifles. She yanked the steering wheel hard to the right, aiming the car in that direction at the next intersection; it looked to be the most open. Far ahead she saw the cars still blocking the main road.

What if they chase after me? She remembered the parked silver car with the open door, there in front of Mrs. Hill's house. *I bet they'll come after me.* So just in case, she took the next right to the north, rounding the block and recrossing the road where she had seen the moving van. Searching farther down the road, she spotted the rear of the silver car as it disappeared toward the south, the direction she'd initially taken. "Damn, they *are* chasing after me! Thinking I'd go on down and get stuck at the blocked intersection, I bet!" Dana pushed down a bit harder on the accelerator, braking only when she approached the hump of another intersection.

About four or five blocks down—she lost count—she turned again to the right and then to the left after four or five more blocks. *There, that should be far enough.* She slowed, trying to figure out where exactly she had ventured. "I bet if I go down this road, I'll cross the big road up to Pigeon Forge and Gatlinburg." So she drove on, mulling over the closeness of her own escape and wondering about the fate of the young woman who used to drive Mrs. Hill to church. "Yeah, I bet women are almost a commodity now too. Like groceries and gas. Without police and laws—and being chased by men—I bet that could happen. It *is* happening! I hate to think what's happening to that lady back there now." On she drove, thinking and talking, not noticing the houses had thinned and intersections were fewer.

A pickup pulled up from a dusty side road ahead, as if it had been waiting there for her, and turned in her direction. *Oh, my gosh! I'm out in the country!* She didn't recognize anything around. *Maybe I should...* She accelerated now, but the truck ahead seemed to slow. *And it's turning! It's going to try to block the road! Maybe if I...* She floored it and flashed by, her right wheels almost in the ditch, mere inches from the front of the truck. "Wow!" She somehow had lucked out, having found one of the few county roads in all of East Tennessee that had wide shoulders—and she had needed every inch of that dirt alongside the pavement to avoid crashing into the pickup. In the rearview Dana saw the truck still straddling the lanes, and the men now standing in the truck's bed, watching her recede in the distance. *That was too, too close, girl.*

But what was she supposed to do? She suspected there would be more pickup trucks ahead, trying to block her, and she didn't want to return the same way she had come. *I'm just by myself, and God, you know the rest.* She would have to get to Gatlinburg to find her mother and her mother's friends. *That's the world now. That's safety.*

She turned at the next dirt road, heading to the south, she supposed. *Maybe I can follow back roads around cow pastures back to Sevierville and the main road.* She drove on, watching for any road signs and pickup trucks.

***

When Jimmy's eyes fluttered open, at first he couldn't decide where he was. All he could see was hay—bales of hay—on all sides, stacked clear up to the sheet-metal ceiling. *Oh, yeah—the hayloft. Makes sense.* Sitting up he remembered his return to the barn late last night and his prodding around in the dark, looking for the entrance to his hidey-hole. *There's the entry hole right there.* He was looking at the narrow gap between the two bales at his feet. *Gosh, it's getting hard now to keep things in order—to think of just when everything has happened. Yesterday...the highway...Got ol' Hammerhead killed yesterday, I did, on that highway,* he remembered. And he remembered the dogs howling at the moon. *Real close by. Musta been a full moon or something.*

After spying out the area beyond the gap, he crawled through, into the open loft. There, standing and stretching and looking about, he eyed the bare rafters high above his head. *I guess we would've had tobacco hanging from up there right now...if that ol' plague hadn't come along when it did.* "Ah, well." He brushed the straw from his shirt and pants and walked around, searching for the supplies he'd carried all the way from the highway last night. "There they are." He had dropped the burlap sacks at the top of the stairs.

Fishing his Barlow from his jeans pocket, Jimmy carefully cut the bailing twine from the tops of the sacks and folded the cloth down around the canned goods he had selected from the cellar. "Dang!" he murmured. A jar of beets had cracked during the trip, maybe when he had climbed the stairs, and the sweetened red vinegar coated the contents in one bag. "Well, those ol' beets will be good for breakfast and these beans will do OK for now too." He set another jar aside and lifted the remaining unbroken jars from the one sack, wiping them with the damp rags that were in the sack for cushioning then adding them to the contents of the other sack. "That'll have to do. I'm surprised more jars didn't break with all the banging around they've been through." He hefted the single sack, testing the strength of the burlap. "That'll do too," he judged. "Now for the rest of it." He twisted open both of the set-aside jars and filled their lids, one with green beans and one with pickled beets. "Breakfast of champions," he grimly announced, settling himself on a bale that gave him a good view of the barnyard out front.

He held up one exceptionally large, unbroken bean. "Too bad ol' Zula never liked to pickle eggs or do anything like that." He remembered the eggs Homer often bought for him when he'd go with the old man up to the filling station. "And pickled sausages and dried jerky and pickled pigs' feet...No, maybe not pickled pigs' feet." He had yet to sample those ghostly pale appendages that floated in the yellowish liquid there in the glass jars alongside the cash register. "Yeah, maybe *even* a fat hog's fat foot right now," he declared, changing his mind. The boy was truly famished. "And I'd be getting back that quarter I bet Billy Ray way back then too." That had been the standing wager they'd had between them since Jimmy was six years old. "One big ol' bite of pickled fat!" Billy Ray finally had done it— once—ate the whole foot, and Jimmy knew that one day he'd do it too. But then he thought of Thelma...and the long-distance phone call...and remembered he'd never see Billy Ray alive again. "Ah, well," he said with a sigh.

Jimmy poured a few more beans and beets from the jars into their respective lids and ate in silence, seated on the hay bale and staring out through the top of the barn door at the empty barnyard and the big house below. *Empty too.*

After eating his fill, he left the opened jars on the loft floor, hoisted the sack of unopened jars, and tromped down the stairs to push wide the door at the bottom, pausing to look around for the mules before he dropped from the safety of the high stairwell to the dusty barnyard. *Them ol' mules are probably miles from here anyway. Wish*

I could ride a mule. You know, maybe I could—that made him think of the skinny-wheeled wagon parked out back in the other bay of the barn—*use 'em to get home to Maryville*. At times in the past, Homer had hitched the white mule to that wagon and given them all rides down to the highway, back and forth. But when the county had paved White School Road, Homer had pronounced the surface as being too hard for the unshod mules, and that had been the end of the rides. *Too bad. But there's no way in the world I'd ever be able to hitch either of those mules to a wagon...and live.*

"Well, there's always the wheelbarrow," he reminded himself. The deep-bucketed, rubber-tired wheelbarrow was stored on the other side, next to the corncrib. "That'll probably work to haul what I'm taking down to Maryville." He let the roped weight draw the door closed, holding on so it wouldn't slam, and then, rehoisting his burlap bag to his back, he walked on around to the front of the barn and into the next bay to look for the wheelbarrow; it was right where he'd remembered. In the next minute, he was wheeling past the front gate, heading for the old Plymouth and the stowed shotgun.

"You know..." Jimmy was having another of his brainstorms—he'd noticed the unlatched hood on the Plymouth. "I can maybe get the battery out of the tractor and tie it in and start the car...maybe. But I'm not sure whether the tractor battery is six volts or twelve volts." He set the wheelbarrow down on its legs and trotted across the dirt parking area, detouring to the empty chicken house and the adjoining shelter where Homer kept his ancient yellow tractor—when it wasn't broken down at the end of some distant row of corn. It was there; the tractor was parked facing into the tiny shed. *No matter.* He was skinny enough to slide sideways between the shed's rough wall and the tractor's big-treaded tire to get to the front. Within the minute he reemerged, again sliding between the wall and the tire. "Dang!" he swore to the open air. He'd found a vacant space where the battery should have been in the tractor's engine compartment. "And I got a butt-full of splinters from those planks for nothing," he grumbled, walking back to the wheelbarrow. *I'd sure rather have ridden down the road back to Maryville instead of pushing a wheelbarrow.*

At the Plymouth he retrieved the shotgun from under the front seat and the partial box of shells from the rear floor. He loaded them into the bucket alongside his Mauser and ammunition, his burlap sack of provisions, and the big water jug he'd taken from its nail in the tack room. He was now ready to go, figuring he'd make the twenty or so miles by nightfall. "'Course you don't know what you're gonna meet along the road that's gonna take up your time."

Then Jimmy realized he actually was feeling unusually calm this morning. *Maybe stupidly so.* He hadn't scouted around the barn first when he'd awakened. And he hadn't been watching the house for any movements or listening for any warning sounds. *Shoot, I've been running around here and mouthing off as if nothing has happened at all. But it's as if I'm somehow sure nobody is waiting for me to walk past the house or hiding in one of the outbuildings.* He wasn't sure why he felt that way. He just…*knew.* He lifted the wheelbarrow's handles and started down the driveway at a brisk pace. He was going home!

***

"OK, girl, you're on Chapman Highway now so you should be seeing a sign soon about Pigeon Forge or Gatlinburg. Or the national park—there are always all kinds of signs around about how to get to the Smokies from here. Then I'll know where I should go." Dana checked her gas gauge again. "You've got almost a full tank. Things are going to be OK," she assured herself.

Even though she hadn't encountered any more pickups or farmers trying to block her on some narrow county road, she was still pleased to again be on the wide, divided highway. *It's just more familiar. Besides, that tangle of cars should be right up ahead, and then I'll only be a few blocks from my house.* "Maybe Mother will be home now. I should go by there again before going on to Gatlinburg. I bet she'll be pissed when she finds out I took her car. Maybe I shouldn't be so happy about getting home right now," she said with a laugh. "Kidding, Mother, just kidding. She'll be—we'll be so happy to see each other that it won't matter anyway. Now if I can just find another radio station." She drove on.

At the top of the next hill, the road curved to the left then straightened. Dana saw a bridge ahead, over a small creek at the base of the next rise. *I don't think I've ever noticed that creek before. Gists Creek.* She read the bullet-riddled sign as she coasted past. "Now I know I don't remember that tiny creek on the way into town. I'm lost! Must have turned the wrong way back there and have been driving to—I don't know—maybe Knoxville. Turn around, girl. Turn around. Damn it!"

There wasn't another turnaround after the bridge. She'd have to go on up to the top of the rise to see if there was another paved section crossing over to the other lanes. The grassy median looked too overgrown to her. *There could be any number of rocks and stuff hiding in there.* "You've already driven way out of your way. Going to the top of the hill ain't gonna kill you, girl."

"Yes!" There *was* a crossover at the top of the rise. In fact there were two; the closest one was for the traffic turning into the unmarked hollow off to her right, and past a black, burned-out car was the second, to be used by that traffic turning into…She couldn't tell. There didn't seem to be a road in the other direction. "But there's a big paved shoulder over there. I can get out and pee there too." She hadn't been to the bathroom since she'd left home this morning, and the paved area also seemed to offer a good view in both directions, up and down the road. Now that she thought about it, she had seen very few cars passing in the opposite lanes since she'd first gotten onto the divided highway, but she was still watching the road ahead, looking for places she could be boxed in and stopped by cars filled with men. She had slowed those few times when she had spotted a car coming in the other direction, locating all the open spaces and escape routes. *Should the need arise. But you've been lucky.* So far all Dana had seen in the passing vehicles were wide-eyed, apprehensive faces, probably much like her own, staring back at her. *Maybe families…going somewhere but certainly not girls like me out driving by themselves.* A chill ran up her spine. *All alone.*

She signaled her left turn, even though there wasn't another car in sight. It was just something her mother had drilled into her on those training drives around the neighborhood when Ms. Bishop had Dana scoot over close to her and take over the wheel. Her mother handled the pedals, but everything from their laps up was Dana's responsibility, including the turn signals.

Pulling across the double lanes, Dana saw now that the paved area actually was a road that continued over the hump and down into a very pretty valley. And she could saw a road sign that had been pushed over and made invisible to drivers on Chapman Highway. "But it'll still work," she decided, parking the Mustang in the center of the country road so she faced back the way she had come. She turned off the engine, and suddenly the world was quiet, except for the insects singing in the tall grass alongside the road, soaking up the sun's declining rays. Dana now saw she had turned to the west rather than the east when she'd gotten on the main road. "No matter. I'll soon be back in Sevierville, and I'll know my way then." She gazed for a moment back over her shoulder and listened for automobile noises. "OK, now!" She skittered from around the front of the car to the corner of the guide rail. That would give her something to lean against.

A minute later, the deed done and her jeans rebuttoned, she slowly strolled back to the car, enjoying the warm sun and the stretching of her muscles as she walked; she hadn't realized before how long she'd been driving around the countryside. She leaned against the car's hood and surveyed the sky and the hills around her. The raised position at the top of the rise gave her an excellent vantage point to consider the land and a place to contemplate the altered vista of her life. Nothing was the same, and nothing was ever going to be the same again. The plague had come and changed all that. The missing baby, the old woman in the street, the shooting men—that was all today. Just today. She couldn't begin to speculate what tomorrow would bring. Then the light breeze shifted.

"Whew! Damn, something's died around here." She looked up and spotted vultures wheeling and circling overhead. "Man, they're everywhere." Studying the skies to the east, she saw dozens of the black birds sailing low over the woods and fields. "As far as the eye can see. I never knew there were so many of those things about. And there's probably lots of food out and around now. Ew, gross! It's probably not roadkill either, what with the fewer cars and people running around. I wonder what's died around here?"

Dana butt-pushed herself off the hood and sauntered out to the middle of the eastbound lanes, scanning both directions and still listening for approaching cars. "What's that over there?" She walked over to the burned car on the shoulder that was facing the wrong direction. "Damn! That ol' car's been shot to pieces." She noted that the multiple holes in the metal were much bigger than the holes she was used to seeing in the road signs. "Really pissed someone off with a really big gun. Ewww!" She had just then noticed the blackened human skull hanging over the seat on the driver's side. "Damn! No wonder the buzzards are circling." She scurried back across the road.

"Whew, smells as bad over here!" She spotted the back leg of a horse sticking out from under the guide rail. From the blood trail and the plowed gravel, she easily could see that the horse had been pulled from the road's shoulder and under the metal braces. "Something's dragged that dead horse back there, trying to eat it. And it wasn't one of those vultures." She looked up again, to restudy the birds drifting overhead in the steady breeze. "Coyotes, I guess." The mental image of the laughing baby Jeffy came to her for an instant then was gone. She shivered despite the afternoon heat. "Time for me to be getting out of here and head to Gatlinburg."

Dana returned to the car, started it, and fiddled some more with the radio. "Nothing. Just that old music. But it's better than nothing." *Movement!* She looked again, far down the road ahead. From this hill she could see one or two miles of road, to where it turned and disappeared, rising over another hill far in the distance. "Looks like some cars and trucks coming this way. Two cars and three trucks—a convoy." With a trembling hand, she rubbed her mouth and chin. "Don't know that I want to be going back down that way, past that bunch. Gotta bad feeling." *I wonder if they've already seen me?*

She pulled hard to the right, steering the Ford in the direction of the country road. *Hope I'm not too late.* She read the pushed-over road sign. *Pleasant Hill. I wonder if it really is pleasant down this way.* She sped on, hoping to turn the corner far ahead before the men in the convoy caught sight of her from across the fields. "That's what they are. Just a pack of wolves out hunting for anything they can find. Taking anything they want now that the law's not around." She pushed a little harder on the accelerator.

Watching her rearview mirror, she was alarmed to see that she was leaving behind a sizable dust trail to rise and spread in the light breeze. *They're going to see that for sure! Oh, man. Oh, man!* She raced for the cover of the next corner. "If I can make that, I'll be OK. Oh, crap!" She glanced up again at her mirror and saw that the line of vehicles had sped up too. They now seemed to be close to the first crossover. "Oh, damn!" She pushed harder…and almost ran off the road at the curve. The rock-covered road made a tight bend at the top, turning hard back to the right. And it dropped right there, so the turn was doubly hard to make; Dana barely was able to keep her wheels from falling over the shoulder and rolling down the embankment. She sent rocks flying off the road and over the edge.

"Oh, man! Oh, man!" breathed the girl. She'd made it. "Whew! Man, I almost went sailing into that field way down there." But she knew she still couldn't slow. *Not now.* Those guys could be chasing after her. She would have to make it to the next sweeping curve to the left, about a quarter of a mile ahead, before she could see whether she had company. She could look back then and see the road behind. "Oh, man. Oh, man."

At the middle of the wide curve, Dana also could see farther ahead and saw the stop sign off to the side. "Well, I guess Pleasant Hill Road or Drive or whatever ends there. Right or left? Right or left? Which way, girl?" *Left.* "OK, left it is. More woods that way."

Dana slowed at the stop sign. *Road's paved—great!* She made a hard left and looked for pursuers on the dusty, rocky road behind. "There they are!" She didn't see cars and trucks, but she saw new dust clouds waft over the plowed field. "Oh, damn! They'll be coming around the corner any minute!" And they were. The lead car suddenly appeared and sailed off the road and over the wire fence, crashing nose first into the field twenty feet or so below the road's surface. *Bam!* Red dirt and dust flew everywhere, effectively hiding the car as it thumped heavily back on all four wheels. *Wham!* The following truck was skidding sideways on the rocks and gravel, trying to stay away from the drop-off, raising its own huge dust cloud.

Better git, girl, before the smoke clears. Dana floored it, and in the next second, she was hidden behind a thick curtain of oaks and maples. "Now this road may go all the way back to the highway…or it may just curl around and dead-end somewhere back in these hills, probably in some hillbilly's front yard. Probably some hillbilly with twenty-something horny young sons. Maybe you'd better look for a place to hide for right now, girl, and see if you can find a map." Dana watched the roadsides ahead for breaks that would indicate driveways. "Maybe you can pull up behind some vacant house or barn for a while and see if those guys keep chasing you."

In the next series of curves, she saw what she was looking for—an overgrown, two-track trail through an open fence gate and across an almost dry brook to a dilapidated barn set deep in thick bushes and briars. *The lanes are stony and overgrown. Yes! They won't see my tracks.* She slowly turned in, mentally willing soft, unnoticeable tire prints. Driving up to and through the cantilever barn, she steered in behind the board-covered end so the Mustang was hidden from the road. "Whew!" she blew out. "I bet no one's come back here in years. I should be safe here for a while. Now to find the map." She leaned over to rifle through the papers in the glove box.

"Hot dog!" Dana found the detailed map her mother had bought when they'd first moved from Nashville. She quickly located herself. "That must be White School Road. I wonder if there really is a school on the road? Yeah, there it is. Back that way." She traced the line representing the road the way she had come. "Yeah. I'll wait here for a while and rest and see if those guys go away." Suddenly she was exhausted.

***

Hoo-hoo-hoo.

Dana opened her eyes. It was getting dark. "Oh, man! I don't know if…anything! Those guys might or might not be gone. And I'll have to drive back to Sevierville in the dark. Crap!" She sat upright in her seat and felt around to the side, pushing the tiny lever that allowed the seat's back to spring to the driving position. *Zing!*

"And is that an owl hooting?"

"Yeah," Jimmy answered. He was sitting in his wheelbarrow alongside the driver's-side door.

"Shit!" Dana started, flinging her map over her steering wheel. She jerked around and glared at the boy. "Who the hell are you? How long you been there?" *Damn, I think I peed myself.*

"Me? Oh, 'bout three, four hours, I guess. It's getting dark now, so I'd say it's been at least that."

Dana continued to stare hard at the boy. She didn't know what to say, and the kid seemed to be content, sitting there and eating. "What the hell are you doing?" she brusquely asked.

"Eating supper. Want some?" He held out the jar lid to Dana.

She eyed the lid. "Green beans?"

"Yeah. I got some pickles too, but I broke the only jar of beets I had. They were probably my favorite too."

Dana didn't take a bean. She continued to eye the boy, wondering whether perhaps he was one of those imbeciles the kids talked about at school—as being half retarded because of inbreeding and poisonous white lightning, content to spend their days back in these hollows picking at banjos. "What…is…your…name?" she slowly asked. She wasn't taking any chances.

"Jim-my," he replied. "What…is…your…name?" *Poor girl must be a little slow.*

338

"Dana." She examined him through hooded eyes. "Are you fart-ing around with me?"

"Girl, until now, I didn't even know your name. But I do know you missed your friends earlier. They roared by here in both direc-tions until they got run off by—*She wouldn't know Daniel*—another bunch of guys down here. But if you hurry—"

"No, no, that's all right. I don't know anyone around here and…" She stopped to breathe. "I don't know them—they were chasing me."

"I figured. From the way they were driving up and down this road here, I expect they wanted to find you a lot." It was Jimmy's turn to scrutinize. "You got something they want?"

"I'm a girl, asshole. They probably saw me and…I'm a girl. So what do you think they want me for?"

Jimmy nodded. "Must be your charming vocabulary then. No, I was asking, like maybe, if you'd stolen something from them." He was again speaking slowly to her, carefully enunciating his words.

Dana twisted in her seat to squarely face him. "Steal? No, I didn't steal anything from them, idiot! You don't have to steal anything from anybody these days. Don't you know that? They saw me and chased me. People are nastier now—more malicious and stuff—because they can be, I guess. Maybe because there's fewer cops around to keep laws and protect folks. I don't know. They probably wanted to…My mother says men want…Oh, never mind. You prob-ably wouldn't understand anyway."

"Oh…Want a bean?" Blushing furiously, Jimmy again held out the lid.

"No, I just want to get the hell out of here! I want to go home. I want to go to Gatlinburg and find my mother. I want things to be normal. I want…" Dana closed her eyes and sniffed. "I want to go home to Sevierville."

"Might not be too good an idea tonight. It's supposed to be a bright moon, and like you said, there are a lot of mean people out there now. Heck, there are a lot of mean people right here now." He ate another bean from his lid, holding it up first in the fading light to see if any strings were still attached. He had eaten a badly broken bean a few minutes ago, and the string got stuck in his teeth.

"And?" Dana encouraged him to finish his thought.

"And Daniel's put more men to guard Pleasant Hill, the way you came, and White School Road, that hard road out there. I was up there"—Jimmy indicated the knob behind him with a tilt of his head—"in the woods, scoping out the situation, when I saw you come tearing down that turnpike and…Heckuva of turn back there, wasn't it? I was surprised you made the curve. See, these ol' roads were made for wagons, so you'd expect they'd follow the lay of the land around hills and such." He noticed Dana was giving him her "idiot" look again. "So anyway, I come back over here, where I'd stashed my 'barrow, and lo and behold, you'd taken up residence here behind the Burchfields' old barn. I circled around to close the gate at the barbed wire—so those ol' boys wouldn't know you'd come back here—and when I come back, you'd already sacked out." He ate another bean after holding it up and examining it against the sky. "So anyway, those ol' boys chasing you came looking for you and probably would have found you but for Daniel's gang finding them first. It's pretty amazing that you'd sleep through all those gunshots but wake up with an ol' hootie-owl calling. Bet you *were* tired." Jimmy paused, examining another bean.

"And?" Dana tried again.

"Oh, yeah." Jimmy grinned. "Since Daniel's boys had to deal with invaders, you might say, he put more guards on both roads. I saw them drive by earlier. I expect they're out there right now, guarding the entrances off Chapman Highway." He ate the bean. "So I don't expect you'd make it through their blockades tonight. Better to wait until tomorrow. I don't think ol' Daniel has that many men right now to guard the roads for long."

"And do what? Sleep here tonight? With you?" Dana again gave Jimmy the once-over. "Not that I should worry about you. I think you're a mere child anyway."

"Not if you saw me in the shower," Jimmy replied. His response was automatic, coming from his junior-high phys ed days. Being one of

the late bloomers—not having yet attained puberty—and wishing to
endure the open locker rooms, he'd accumulated an impressive store
of retorts for the taunts of those earlier-maturing boys. And due to the
boys' code of silence outside the locker rooms, this was the first time
Jimmy had used the deflection on a girl. It seemed to have worked;
Dana appeared to be looking at him with newfound respect.

"Yeah, sure. You wish," she said.

Well, maybe not. "No, I don't expect you to sleep with me…in that
way. I just think we need to hide for the night, and tomorrow I'll show
you how to get out of here and back to Sevierville. Homer and I once
went through the back pastures—*How many days ago was that?*—to get
to Sevierville and to miss all the congestion at that big intersection."

"That's where I live." Dana was sounding hopeful.

"You live in an intersection?"

"No, silly. I live a couple of blocks from there, and I need to get
to Gatlinburg to join my mother."

Jimmy studied Dana for several seconds. "Just how old is your
mother anyway?" Jimmy asked, his tone hushed.

"Oh, no, she's not like one of those old people catching the
plague. She's kinda not that old at all. I think she's even got a boyfriend." She smiled at the boy's obvious concern.

"OK then," he agreed. "You and me, we'll stay here until it gets a
bit darker, and then we'll walk back to the house over that way and
maybe sleep hidden in the barn. There'll be fewer bugs there; it'll
be off the ground. And I need to see if I can find some more ammunition. I might need it for the trip. And you can tell me about your
family while we wait."

Dana thought about it for a minute. "OK, but come around and
sit in the front seat. Bring the pickles."

***

It was fully dark now; the moon was just beginning to rise over the
hill ahead. "Yup, gonna be a bright night," Jimmy observed. "Ready
to go, Dana?"

They had talked, waiting there and eating pickles. Jimmy now knew more than just Dana's name and how she had come to White School Road—from the time her mother had first married her step-father back in Nashville. And Dana now knew Jimmy was anxious to get to Maryville. The time had passed quickly.

"Yeah. Should I bring the gun?" she asked, her hand on the door handle.

"Just the handgun. But before you open that door," Jimmy hurriedly added, "can you cut off that dome light first?" He was covering his eyes in case he was too late in asking.

"Dome light? Oh, the overhead light. Yeah, I can flip this little thing up here—see?—and it won't come on when we open the doors. That's a good idea," she noted. "Say, it sounds like you've been sneaking around here for quite a while. So when did your Uncle Gomer pass away?"

"Homer," he corrected. "And he wasn't my uncle. He and Zula were cousins."

"Cousins? They were both cousins to you? But weren't they married to each other?"

Jimmy laughed. "It's complicated. See, their moms and dads were cousins—in fact they were probably double second cousins… No, they weren't related at all…You're giving me that funny look again."

Dana smiled. "Sorry. So when did Homer pass away?"

Gosh, she sounds like she's really interested. "Well…" Jimmy was counting on his fingers, "…about three or four days ago. It's kinda hard keeping my days straight now."

"Nice guy?"

"Yeah. Kinda old and all. I guess that's why he got sick and died so quickly—him and Zula."

Dana looked thoughtful. Her features were now visible in browns and yellows—like an old sepia photograph—in the first beams from the rising moon just peeking over the ridge. Jimmy was studying her profile and thinking this was the longest conversation he'd ever had with a girl. *Kinda nice.*

"Do you think the plague is about over now—now that the older people have died, Jimmy?" She turned to study him now.

He quickly averted his eyes to the windshield, staring out as if the moon needed his full attention. "Um…I don't really know. Homer was telling me he didn't know if this stuff was God's will but that God was in control; he would use it for his purposes. So I don't know how far it's gonna go. I think Thelma caught the plague, and she wasn't really all that old. She was Homer and Zula's daughter."

"*Was?*"

"Yeah. I don't think she's still around either. I was told Daniel and his boys mighta done her in too. Say, see how high the ol' moon is there?" he asked, changing the subject. "We'd better get going, or soon it's gonna be like daytime. Besides, we got enough light to see the road now and won't have to walk through the woods. It's maybe a mile or two farther that way, but it'll still be faster. Probably kill ourselves walking through the woods anyway."

"Jimmy, are there wolves out in the woods?" She leaned forward so he'd turn his face to her.

He did…and paused a minute before he spoke. *Gosh, she's pretty.* He also saw see the anxiety she felt asking the question; he needed to be careful now. "Well, some zoo people, knowing they themselves were dying…I suppose some of them would let the animals out, being merciful and all. But I don't think they'd let out dangerous animals unless they didn't really care about other people. But now that I think about it, I suppose some of the meaner people out there could have let out dangerous animals." He didn't want to tell her about the pack of animals under the culvert.

"What about all the mountains all around here?" Dana waved her hand as if she were introducing the trees.

"Bears, then, I guess. Coyotes, hogs, elk…maybe red wolves. But they're smaller and not really all that aggressive compared to the things you see in the movies." Jimmy was nodding his head, willing confidence into his voice. "Heck, they're gonna come down if fewer people and less traffic's around. But remember that anything you see around here is gonna be more afraid of you than you are of it."

"Did your mother tell you that?"

"Do you want to open your door and pick up your gun?"

Dana laughed and pulled at her door handle. "I take it you're through talking."

Jimmy didn't reply. He quietly opened his door and got out, soundlessly circling behind the car, back to his wheelbarrow. He was lifting his Mauser from the bin just as Dana gripped her door, intending to slam and lock it. "No, no, no—you don't need to do that. Just push on it 'til it clicks. And don't worry about locking it. Nobody much stops just because a door is locked these days."

"Yeah, I guess you're right. Leave everything else as is?" She leaned against the door with her hip, listening for the click.

"Yeah, we'll be back in the morning." He pointed at the shotgun, its barrel glinting in the moonlight from between the seats. "We'll get you some more shells for your twelve-gauge there too. Or do you have more shells for it in the back?"

"Um…" Dana looked vacant.

"That would be no then. You know, you might even want to throw away the shell that's in there already if it's real old and stuff." He nodded and walked past Dana without waiting for an answer. "We'd better be going."

Dana followed and quickly caught up to walk even with Jimmy, striding along beside him in her own overgrown track back out to the road. *The kid's just now getting into high school, I bet.*

At the hard road Jimmy turned around and looked back at the barn from various angles. "Looks good. I'll leave the gate open like it was. I don't see any reflections or anything that will give the car away back behind that part of the barn. It should be OK for the night." *I sure as heck hope so. That car would make getting back to Maryville so much easier. But there's her mother first.* "You normally go through Pigeon Forge to get to Gatlinburg?" he asked.

"Hmm. Never thought about it. I didn't know there are other ways to go. I suppose so."

"Well, there's Wears Valley then back through the mountains on old 73, I guess. But that's a real long way of going. I hiked it once with the Scouts. You *are* still wanting to go to Gatlinburg, aren't you?" He looked hopefully to her, and she glared back. "'Nuff said." He put his rifle on his shoulder and crunched on down the road, Dana to the inside.

They walked quietly for a while, neither saying anything. The roosting birds had ceased their late-evening tweets, and the lightning bugs had come out.

"Wow, look over there!" Dana was pointing at the field off to their right. "Look at all those fireflies."

"That's one of Fred's fields. He mowed it a week or so ago and, I guess, never got around to baling it before he…It sure makes it nice for the lightning bugs. Without the moon being out, you'd see them even better. Sometimes, before it gets too late in the night, those things seem to flash together, to coordinate their flashing. I think it has something to do with mating. Probably the male with the biggest flash attracts more females or something like that."

"Nothing to do with the size of his hands?"

"Pardon?"

"Nothing."

They walked on in silence for a while.

Oh…oh…oooooooooh!

"What the hell? Jimmy?"

"Just somebody's ol' dog howling. Or maybe a coyote."

"That's not a bunch of wolves?"

"Of course not," he scoffed. *Please Lord, please, please.*

"Well, it kind of worries me."

Jimmy made a tsk-tsk sound with his tongue, trying to sound older, wiser. "Nothing to worry about. Besides, that's another reason to sleep up high in the loft—besides the bugs, of course."

"Of course. How much farther?" she asked, puffing with each step. She *was* getting rather tired.

"See that?" Jimmy was pointing at the knobs off to his right, far across the pastureland. "That dark line along the foot of those hills is a creek I sometimes fish in, and those fields are Homer's. It's just a little ways from here."

"I was happy just to get over that last hill. That was a *long* one."

"Yeah. That's the hill before Fred's place…where we just passed. You can hear the milk truck for a long ways when it's trying to climb…" He caught the sound of a truck or car coming from behind, now climbing the long rise.

So did Dana. She looked at Jimmy, her eyes wide with alarm. "What's that?"

"That's our call to get off the road. Ahead—over there's a gate, a gap in the fence. Leads up a little valley. That's where we need to get to." Jimmy had first thought about sliding over the bluff to the right, but the grass wasn't very long in the pasture below. And Fred hadn't taken away all his old barbed wire when he had put up new wire last year. He could visualize Dana getting tangled in the mess and being lit up in the headlights of the approaching vehicle. "We just have to keep on running past this bank here on the left." He was hopping sideways, encouraging Dana.

"Don't…don't think I can make it," gasped Dana.

"Sure, sure, it's right here!"

When the automobile crested the hill, its lights caught the white of Dana's tennis shoes as she followed Jimmy along the road's shoulder. Its engine roared.

"This way! This way!" Jimmy pulled the girl's arm, urging her down the cow path and through the break in the fence. "I didn't put the gate up, so it's open. Come on!"

"I'm trying," sobbed Dana.

They were inside the fence, running beside the little brook and almost to the trees along the path when the spotlight caught them. "There they are!" a man yelped. "Get 'em!" Car doors slammed, and fresh feet pounded the path behind.

Kapeww. A bullet sang by Jimmy's head. *Dang! Too close. We aren't going to make the woods. Gonna hafta fight.* He couldn't tell how many men were chasing him; he just knew there was more than one…and his rifle was a bolt-action single-shot. And he knew the kinds of guns Daniel's troops carried.

Jimmy slid to a stop and dropped to one knee, sighting at the blinding light as he flipped off the safety. He started to squeeze off his shot when the big light abruptly jerked upward, lighting the overhanging limbs as it streaked off through the underbrush to the right and up the hillside.

Mwaaaaaaa! The sound caused the leaves to vibrate around him. *Damn! Big Red's bellow!* He'd recognize it anywhere. Jimmy stood and watched.

A second and a third light diverted now, focusing on the underbrush off the trail. These puny beams were nothing compared to the spotlight, which now seemed to be stopped and pointing back through the weeds from the hillside, lighting the trail where two men stood, holding the flashlights and their rifles. "Jed!" one of the men shouted. "Jed, you OK? God almighty!" Their twin beams had joined, illuminating Red's broad face and disfigured horns. *Mwaaaaa!* He was coming again, crashing from the underbrush and charging downhill, slinging snot as he ran straight at the men.

Pow, pow, pow, pow. The men had full magazines and semiautomatic weapons. Their rifles barked as fast as they could pull their triggers.

Oh, God! Red doesn't have a chance! Jimmy turned, caught sight of Dana's disappearing tennis shoes, and scampered after her. He found her again up at the end of the fence line, where the trail crossed the creek and ascended the hill. She was holding her side with one hand and bracing herself with her other hand on her knee. The shots and sounds had motivated her to go this far.

"Dana, wait a minute, wait a minute. It's OK for a minute," Jimmy assured her, searching back along the trail, looking for waving lights and listening for the sounds of battle. But all was quiet. "I've got to go back."

"Jimmy, no!"

"I've got to. We won't know what to be looking for the rest of the night. That was Big Red who took them on back there. He's a big ol' bull that's as cantankerous as they come. But I expect they shot him down and now are regrouping for us. I've got to see what happened back there. Understand? There won't be a better chance. Understand?"

She didn't. She dropped her head, still trying to catch her breath.

"Wait here. OK? Won't be a minute." He trotted away.

Jimmy knew the trail well, and his eyes had quickly recovered from the blinding spotlight; he soon reached the battleground. Off to his right, high up on the hillside, the spotlight still burned, lighting the scene below as if in a theater play. On the pathway, he saw Big Red, his legs splayed, his massive head resting on the ground. Drawing closer, Jimmy saw the black blood that still flowed from the bull's nostrils—the huge nostrils that expanded once, twice with big huffs as he inhaled. Then nothing more; Big Red died, his eyes still open and still red with fury. *Just like that. And the danged bull looks... satisfied, I guess. Well, maybe he is. Done something he always wanted to do.*

Jimmy walked up into the underbrush and retrieved the spotlight. He shone it around in the tall weeds until he found the first man, his face still carrying his surprise and amazement, even without having much of a chest below to support his head. *Dang bull gored him and liked to have cut him in two.* "The guy's gone," he mumbled, stating the obvious and turning the beam back along the trail. He wanted now to see where the other two fellows had ended up.

Stumbling back down to the clearing, he spotted a shirt off in the briars. It was ripped, bloodied, and torn—and was still being worn by its owner. Jimmy didn't even have to walk over to know the man was dead.

Back on the trail, he quickly located the third guy, on his back and on the far side of Big Red. *He's still alive!* The man's legs were pinned under the bull's massive bulk, but other than that, he seemed to have emerged relatively unscathed. Jimmy walked around the bull, keeping the spotlight trained on the fellow. "You OK?" he asked. *Stupid question.*

"Don't think so...all broken-up inside," the man feebly replied. He lolled his head to the side, looking up at Jimmy.

"Miser?" the boy asked. "Are you related to old man Miser? You look kinda like him."

"My uncle. Damn, that hurts!" The man coughed, and blood splashed out, speckling his mouth and chin. "I think that ol' bull done kilt me."

"Mr. Miser, do you work for Daniel? Were you out looking for me? Do you know who I am?"

The man looked back to the skies, as if considering the moon and stars—and his options. "Yeah. Daniel said...Daniel said you'd be in the house or barn...Sent me and other two...Gonna burn 'em down." The man coughed again and blood dripped from the sides of his mouth. "God help me...and you're in trouble too."

"I don't have Daniel's healing, so I'm gonna get the bubonic plague?" Jimmy guessed.

"Yeah, I suppose," Miser whispered. "And Daniel..." The man again coughed his wet cough and tilted his head to stare at Jimmy above the light. "He's gonna get you...He hates you."

"Jesus's representative hates me? Doesn't that seem a little weird?" No answer.

"Mr. Miser?" Jimmy turned the spotlight back at the man. His eyes were glazed over. *Dead.* "Well, I guess there will be no more debate tonight—'absent from the body, present with the Lord'... Second Corinthians, chapter five, verse eight. I'm just glad I didn't have to shoot you to put you out of your misery. Actually, I don't know if I *could* have shot you with you just lying there like that. But I can move your vehicle from off the road." He stepped closer and felt the man's front pocket then reached two fingers inside for the car keys. "At any rate, Mr. Miser," Jimmy continued, standing and again focusing the beam on the dead man's face, "you're probably now knowing the answers to a lot of the questions that I still have."

Ten minutes later the boy had stashed the old Chevrolet in the pasture amid the briars and brush, and well below the rise of the red bank so it couldn't be seen from the road. After another ten minutes, he had rejoined Dana at the foot of the hill that led up to the barn.

13

DAY NINE

Jimmy knew the end was near; Daniel Davis had caught him, had pinned him to the ground, and was about to pound a spike through his nose. He felt the great weight on his chest, and the spike tickled his nostrils. *Achoo!* He sneezed several times. *Dang! Daniel's got beautiful eyes!* Then he realized his own eyes were open…and he was no longer dreaming.

"You sneezed on me," Dana said, staring down on him from a height of about six inches.

"You—you scared the heck out of me!" Jimmy exclaimed, staring cross-eyed at the straw she was holding, guessing she had been using it to tickle his nose. "I thought something was…Never mind. Dang!"

"'Dang'? That's it? That's the most unemotional scare I've ever witnessed." She pushed herself to a seated position, using Jimmy's chest for support. "I was expecting at least a pitiful scream or something from you. You should work on that," she advised, her mouth set in a mock-serious line.

"Well, that must be something new. I used to be much better with fright—much more expressive. Maybe since…" He finally shrugged, unable to come up with the right words.

"Yeah," Dana agreed. "I hear you. See so much scary stuff, you just get tired of it all. Didn't I tell you about yesterday at home?" She looked around and continued, not really expecting Jimmy to answer. "Say, how'd you find this place? Did you stack up the hay bales this way to give yourself a hiding place?"

Jimmy sat up, scooting backward in the straw to lean up against the broad planks that formed one of the walls. Light from the rising sun streamed in through the cracks between the boards. *Kinda liked it better when she was lying on top of me.* "Well, yeah, I guess so. When we were hauling hay, I was stacking it, see, and ever since I was a little kid, I've played up here. I wasn't really thinking about a plague coming or really needing a hiding place. I did it, I guess, because I was playing when I was stacking the bales. Ol' Homer probably wouldn't have liked it none if…Naw, he wouldn't have minded if it took up extra space and all." Jimmy looked around, as if he also were studying the high walls for the first time. "See, when you live on a farm, you've got to kinda create a lot of your own fun. So when I'd come visit and stay here—"

"You don't live here all the time?" Dana interrupted.

"No," Jimmy replied. "I guess maybe I didn't say anything yet, but I actually live in Maryville and go to school there. High school," he added, watching her.

"Maryville? I just thought you had somebody there, maybe one of your parents, who you were worrying about. I didn't realize you lived there. We play Maryville in football and basketball—sports." She continued to gaze at him. "Are you really in high school? You just seem rather…ah…small."

"You haven't seen me…" He stopped, remembering he'd already used that line. "Well, I've been sick."

"Have you really?" she asked, now sounding genuinely concerned.

"No, dang, girl, you don't leave a fella…Yes, I'll be in high school this fall. Yes, and through the magic of heredity, I've always been a bit shorter than most of the guys in my class."

"Girls, too," Dana helpfully noted.

Jimmy sent a scowl her way, his eyes hooded, his lower lip drawn up. "Yes, Dana. Thank you for the correction. Yes, most girls are taller than me too. But someday I'll become a man." He lowered his voice on the last sentence, imitating a cartoon character he'd once seen on TV.

She laughed. "You know I'm just having fun with you, don't you? I mean, you *are* the first boy—man—that I've spent the night with." She laughed again, harder this time, at the sight of the blush rising in Jimmy's cheeks. "Jeez, you're *so* easy."

"Well, you know…" He smiled with her, smiling at himself, smiling at her laugh. *Dang good-looking girl!* "So how do you feel about some breakfast now?" He changed the subject.

"More pickles?"

He laughed this time. "Probably. No, there may still be some stuff in the cupboards in the house. Since I'll be going inside for a couple more boxes of ammunition, I'll see if there's anything left on the shelves. Ol' Daniel and his gang's stealing stuff—hoarding it, I guess."

"They're selling it in the cities, Mother says." That thought brought Dana back closer to reality. For a little while there, she'd forgotten about missing her mom. "My mother says people in the country are bringing food into Sevierville and selling it—or trading it. Probably trading more now. I can't imagine paper money is worth as much now."

"Yeah," Jimmy agreed. He went on and told her of his trip to Sevierville, ending with, "And that was just…ah…twelve days ago." *Dang, has it been so long? Golly, we were just sitting around the table eating breakfast with the tourists.*

Dana saw the boy's face cloud over. "Missing Homer and Zula now?" she guessed. "The world *has* changed, and we're having to cope with it…and with what's happening to the people we've always known—and loved." She paused, waiting for him to raise his eyes. "And I suppose I'll have to wait until you've become a man." She lowered her voice on this last part, imitating Jimmy. "So let's go look for some food."

They crawled to the gap between bales at the base of the hay wall and wiggled through. Now standing in the open loft and brushing themselves off, Dana turned back toward the stacked bales. "You know, if I hadn't just crawled through that hole, I wouldn't have even noticed it was there. How'd you manage to find it last night without turning on a light?"

"Luck. Plus I've done it before." Jimmy pointed to the barn's far wall, to the left of the open front entrance. "We'll go down over there. OK? There's some stairs there that almost go to the ground. That'd be easier than climbing back down the other side, down that ol' ladder nailed on that side. You know, I've always worried about pitching backward off one of those ladders and falling on a pitchfork someone left upright, sticking up below in the hay."

"Damn, Jimmy, you're one strange kid," Dana observed, walking past him toward the stairs. "Your folks ever talk to you about needing some counseling?"

"Well," he reflected, following along, "after I killed and ate my baby sister—the second one, you understand—they did say—"

"Jeez! Jimmy!" Dana cut in. "Just forget I said anything! Right over there, huh?"

At the base of the stairs, she pushed open the door and looked down. "Now I suppose there's a good reason for having the stairs end so high off the ground."

Jimmy looked past her. "Yeah, I guess there is too, but I've never thought of it. Maybe it's to make small boys climb those straight-up-and-down ladders, like over there."

"Yeah...and to fall on those conveniently placed pitchforks—better than birth control."

"Pardon?"

"Never mind. It's a girl thing."

"Like that time in seventh grade when they ran all the boys out of class to just talk to the girls?"

"Yes. Exactly. Now do I have to jump from here?" Dana asked, leaning far out from the doorframe.

"Yeah, if you'd like. Or do like this." He eased past her, gripped the side of the door and swung himself to the side where there was a foot hole in the boards, about halfway to the ground. Jimmy then easily stepped down to the dusty ground. Dana followed.

"See over there." Jimmy pointed around the barn. "That's the room where we keep the harnesses and stuff and the cow feed. And over there in the other bay is the corncrib and—"

"What are those right there?" Dana urgently whispered, grabbing his shoulders and spinning him, then pointing back through the barn. Her finger quivered.

Jimmy understood the tone and quickly sighted the objects. *It's the mules!* He saw their large bodies silhouetted in the open barn door at the far end of the bay. *Whitey and Blackie.* The animals calmly stared back, their heads held high and alert.

"Those would be the mules that have spent their lives making my life difficult," he answered in a low monotone. "We need to back slowly out of here, and now wasn't a good time for me to have left the front gate open. Serious…stay close and back out slowly…slowly."

As Dana and Jimmy stumbled backward, out from the barn and through the lumpy yard, the mules followed, plodding along while maintaining their constant distance.

"Aw, look. They're hurt," Dana said quietly, as the mules emerged from the shadows into the full sunlight.

Jimmy looked closely, noting that both mules appeared to have been in a scrape or two; Blackie had several open, red gashes across his broad chest, and Whitey sported four or five deep wounds along her sides and flanks. "Dang, you're right! I think they've maybe bumped into something less domesticated than themselves. And I wonder why they're staying around here now."

"Dang!" Dana shook her head. "Damn it! You've got me saying that now. I was going to say that those mules are probably staying around here because it's home. It's where they've been safe all their lives. Aww, see how they're following us? They expect you to protect *them* now." Dana was looking at the mules with dewy, loving eyes.

Jimmy glanced over at her then glanced back again. *Women!* "Well, those ol' mules shoulda started wanting to be friends some ten years ago. I'm still feeling like they're really only wanting to come run us down and pound our heads into puddles even now. It's not a good time for me to be changing attitudes." *'Course they did do me a good turn with Bernard and all. And Big Red did kinda save our butts last night.* "I'll go back and throw down all the oats and shelled corn we still have there in the tack room. Will you wait here for me?" Dana said she would, and the mules obligingly shuffled to the side, giving him enough space to cautiously pass. A few minutes later, he rejoined her at the barnyard gate.

"Aw, that was so nice," she said, watching the mules munch on the grain spilling from the open sacks. "You must be quite a nice little kid sometimes."

"Haven't seen me in the showers lately, have you?" He walked on by, aiming for the henhouse off to the right.

At the shed they checked the nests for eggs but found nothing. "I don't even see a bird hereabouts now," Jimmy said. "Either they've moved to the woods, or some animals have gotten to them already."

"I bet they're living happily in the woods now. What's that tall building there?"

"That would be the smokehouse," Jimmy answered without turning. "Let's not go in there. Homer and Zula were put there…and we probably shouldn't eat any hams we might find there. Besides, the house itself looks clear now. And we might be getting company real soon."

"So let's do it," Dana urged.

They found the screenless doorway open but the inside door was closed. Jimmy tried the handle. "Not locked," he noted. "That's a relief. And at least we won't find a bunch of skunks and possums in here." He slowly pushed the door inward, listening for any noises in the house. "Suppose you stay here at the back door, and if you see somebody drive up, just yell at me. I won't be a minute. And if you hear me shoot, run for the back of the barn…and I'll catch up later." He held out the Mauser. "OK?"

"OK," she reluctantly agreed. It was clear she'd rather stay with Jimmy. "Just hurry. OK?"

Stepping inside the house, Jimmy first noticed that several pieces of furniture were missing from the TV room. "Dang! They were fast.

But I guess TVs aren't all that much in demand anymore—ours is still here."

"Just hurry," Dana said from beyond the door.

Jimmy took the stairs two at a time. He wasn't really hopeful that Daniel had left any guns in the bedroom; he was just hoping the boxes of shells had been overlooked. But they hadn't. *Even took the dang twenty-two shells. Didn't even leave any shotgun shells. Ah, well.* He shut the door to Billy Ray and Thelma's room, and felt a wave of sadness with the finality of the action. *Even Thelma was mostly OK before she started taking sick. I guess that's the way it works.*

After dropping back down the stairs, three steps at a time, Jimmy made a left turn at the bottom, toward the kitchen. There he found the cabinet and cupboard doors all standing open; nothing remained on any of the shelves. "Man, they even took the stuff in the back that Zula had since nineteen fifty-six. I wonder how the petrified hominy tasted? Probably like those old cornflakes."

At the cellar he found the same thing—the lock was no longer in the hasp; the trap door in the floor was open and leaned against the wall. Below the floor, with the partial daylight filtering down through the opening, Jimmy saw that the shelves below were totally bare, emptied of those hundreds of jars he had washed with his skinny hands and Zula had filled with the bounty from her garden. "Worth the look, I guess." He retraced his steps through the house to the back door, detouring only briefly to Homer's room for some private business.

At his reappearance Dana stood from the seat she had taken on the single step of the pump house, brushing off her backside. "Nothing?" she asked. "You didn't find any food to take from inside? No bullets?"

"No. Ol' Daniel's boys did a good job cleaning out everything. I didn't open the refrigerator or the freezer—didn't know what I'd find. Besides, the power's out now. Nothing in there could still be any good."

Dana looked around. "Yeah, I bet the power's out just about everywhere now. I wonder if the radio station is still on."

Jimmy looked interested. "You know, I once read a book about a time when everyone had to run for the countryside—maybe a bomb or a maybe even a plague too—and a radio station kept broadcasting where the remaining, nonlunatic survivors were regrouping, getting together again. Maybe we should be listening to the radio for instructions."

"Forties radio?" Dana asked dryly. "That's the only station that's on."

"Top forties? You must have been doing a little boogying this week."

"Nineteen forties, Jimmy. Swing and big band music." She rolled her eyes.

"Well, to tell you the truth, I kinda like that music," Jimmy admitted.

I do too, she thought.

"So no radio rendezvous for now?" he concluded. "Too bad—the book was great. Then let's head over that way." Jimmy waved vaguely toward the barn. "It's too light now to walk along the road—too few places to hide if someone comes along. We'll walk through the woods back there and up and down a few ridges to get back to the Burchfields' place, where you left your car. OK?"

Dana nodded; she was looking forward to those pickles back at the car.

As they passed back through the barnyard to follow along the trails beyond, Dana saw the two mules still eating at the sacks of oats and corn Jimmy had brought them. "Won't they eat too much and get sick?" she asked. "I've heard they can eat too much and get sick."

"Founder," Jimmy replied.

"No, get sick. At the stables they had us measure out our horses' food to keep them from overeating." Dana was still watching the mules eat, her brow furrowed in concern.

"Well, those ol' mules," he said, pointing at them as they neared the corner of the barnyard, "and all mules, I guess, are a lot smarter than horses. They can plot and scheme and don't overeat like horses do when they get in somewhere with a lot of grain and stuff. I think horses founder or get colic or something like that maybe—I'm not a farmer, you know. Ol' Homer told me about a horse he once had that foundered on grain, but I can't remember whether the horse got sore feet or just shit all over the place."

"Ooh, I don't think I've heard you cuss before, Jimmy," Dana teased, covering her mouth with the back of her hand in mock horror.

"Um, I think 'shit' is OK to say around a farm. There's sure enough of it around here anyway." He nodded at her feet. "You just walked through a big pile of it."

"Shit!" Dana cursed, pulling up the legs of her jeans.

"Yes," Jimmy replied, trying not to smile. "Exactly."

They were now walking alongside the fenced tobacco plot. The boy was studying the tall plants and shaking his head.

"That's tobacco, isn't it?" Dana asked.

"Yeah. That was Homer's cash crop for the year. But I don't guess anyone is bringing in tobacco now. Do you suppose people are still smoking and chewing?"

"Hmm," Dana said, looking thoughtful. "Good question. I haven't really noticed anyone doing either—oh, wait a second. Mother smokes, and she was smoking…day before yesterday, I think. Dang—damn, I see what you mean…about losing track of time. But I haven't seen anybody else smoking."

"Well, I don't think this crop will be brought in…"

Whump! There was a muffled explosion behind them—a punched pillow sound—and Dana whirled about.

"Just keep walking, please," Jimmy softly requested, pulling at her arm.

"But I see flames coming from the window at the house! It's on fire!"

"I know," the boy calmly replied. "I set it when I left. Everybody's gone…and it just seemed the respectful thing to do. I didn't want Daniel Davis doing it neither."

They walked on in silence, with Dana turning back every few steps to watch the leaping flames. "It's coming through the roof now, Jimmy," she reported.

"The timbers are old and dry. It won't take long. We won't be coming back this way again, Dana." He refused to allow himself even a glance. *That's all gone now.*

✳✳✳

The Mustang was where Jimmy and Dana had left it, hidden behind the Burchfields' ancient barn. They surveyed it from afar for a while, furtively peeking around the bulk of a massive oak even though Dana had wanted to immediately rush down and "get started." The insect bites from their having waded through wet brush and woods seemed more bothersome to her than to Jimmy. "I just need to have some cool wind blow over me," she whined.

"I know, I know," Jimmy empathized, sounding more like a tired, put-upon parent than a fourteen-going-on-fifteen-year-old boy. "We just have to reconnoiter around before maybe blundering into an ambush. See, if I were Daniel, that's the way I'd think—hide back in the woods and take out the first guy from perhaps those rocks over there. Then, in our case, the fair damsel would be there for the taking."

"Ah...do you really think I'm pretty, Jimmy?" Dana asked, fluttering her eyelashes at him as she clawed at the chigger bite on her butt.

He knew she was just having fun with him, but he still felt the heat rise in his cheeks. "Well...ah...ah."

Dana laughed. "Jimmy, you're gonna knock 'em dead in high school with that Southern charm and all. Gosh, I love watching you blush. Didn't your mama tell you to stay away from girls like me?"

"I think I'd like girls like you." *Whoa! That came out way too quick.* Jimmy felt the color rise faster in his face.

"Why, thank you, Mr. Burke. I may have misjudged you. You might do very well for yourself in high school." She was smiling furiously at him now. "You know," she continued, "in a way you remind me of a guy…a guy I used to date back in Nashville."

That brought up the question Jimmy really had wanted to ask. "Did you date a lot…ah…do you guys date a lot in high school?" *Too close. Gotta keep it generic.*

Dana saw the strange new expression on his face. "Why do you ask, Jimmy? What are you thinking about?" Suddenly she felt…protective. Here was a boy who suddenly looked very young again. *Fragile even.* "Are you wondering if you'll ever make it back—to attend high school?"

"Yeah…yeah," Jimmy enthusiastically acknowledged, grateful for her conclusion. *She might think I like her or something. This is better.* "Actually," he continued, mulling over the new subject, "I guess we really don't know if there *will* be a school again this fall. The old folks are now probably all dead…and the next generation—Thelma's—is maybe sick and dying too. You know, I don't know about the next group, but we'll fit in there somewhere too. Isn't that inevitable? Do you ever have thoughts like that, Dana?" *And don't you think that's a little overkill, boy?*

She didn't think; she just reached out and pulled him close, pressing his forehead against her cheek. *Taller than I thought.* "Jimmy, Jimmy, Jimmy. Just when I feel I—I've…experienced so much more in life than you, you surprise me and…in many ways, I feel you're… so much more mature than me. I can only imagine what's going through your mind right now." She was rocking with him, back and forth, back and forth.

Dang! Dana's got boobs!

She felt his heart pounding now, felt the warmth of his breath on her neck, felt his…"Jimmy! You stinker! Let go of me!" She pushed him back against the tree. "Damn! Typical boy! And no, I don't want to see you in the shower."

Jimmy was breathing hard…and blushing…and smiling. "Dana, I'm sorry—couldn't help it—but that was…actually…wonderful! You know, I think I'm going to enjoy…puberty."

"Yeah, if you live through it. Another stunt like that, and you won't. I think you're a lot more mature than…Never mind. Now how about getting done with your 'reconnoiter'? We need to get on the road. These damn bugs are eating me alive!"

After a few more minutes, Jimmy's breathing slowed, and he was able to stop himself from smiling. When he eventually felt he could talk again in complete sentences—he was going for an even, non-committal tone—he asked, "Dana, you know it's gonna be danger-ous going up to Gatlinburg, don't you?"

"Jimmy, you promised!"

"Dana, we're going to go. But you know, we might have to dodge a few more things on the way than some ol' farmers in pickups."

"Like what?"

"Like, for example, have you thought about how you want to get out of here, to get back on Chapman Highway?"

"Well, I figured…" She paused, her eyes squinted in thought. "…we'd just go back the way we came in. Couldn't we just go back that way?" She knew he was getting to something with his question.

"If I were Daniel, I believe I'd have more of a barricade up that way now. I mean, you and those guys who were after you came in that way. So ol' Daniel Davis probably will have done more to fortify his position there, so it'd be a real gamble for us to go out that way. And they might have pulled that bus on across the road at the White School entrance to Chapman Highway, to totally block off the road."

"So?"

"So maybe we should go the way I told you about—through cow pastures and up the ol' logging roads to come into the back side of Sevierville and 321. We won't need to get on Chapman Highway at all that way. But I wish we had the ol' pickup—it rides higher off the ground, and it rained some last night. By the way, have you been keeping your eye on your little car down there?"

Dana leaned around the tree to scan the surrounding woods. "Looks good to me."

"Did you see the kid on the bike in the barn?"

"A kid? On a bicycle? Did he find my car? Maybe he damaged it already so we can't drive it." Dana's eyes grew wide. She was close to panic, jumping ahead to think that her way to her mother was perhaps blocked now.

"I think he *just* found it, and he's going to be pedaling back to report it. So here's what we can do." Jimmy was ready with his stratagem. "An intricate scheme, I have to say: While you walk down the hill and distract him, I'll scoot through the woods this way to the road and head him off." He cocked his head to one side, hoping his toothy grin was at least calming to her. "I can't see if the kid has a gun or not, but he looks pretty young. I'm betting he doesn't, so I'll come in off the road while you make some noise coming down the hill through the trees. Got it?" She nodded, and he turned away then turned back. "Do you sing?" he asked.

Dana stared suspiciously into his eyes—wide, innocent, blue eyes. "I can. Why?"

"I think it'll keep the guy's attention. Do you know any Beatles music?"

"Jimmy!"

"OK, OK. Pick out your own song then. Thought maybe you'd take requests…" He walked away, mumbling to himself with pretend irritation. *It's hard to stop feeling good.*

Dana watched Jimmy as he bounced away, down the ridge, heading to the road. When he had disappeared from sight, she counted to ninety-nine and set off down the hill, singing at the top of her lungs. She chose to sing Eddy Arnold's "Cattle Call."

Far below, on the hard road where the tire ruts through the grass began, Jimmy smiled. *That figures—she's from Nashville.* He stepped into the nearer track, slinking silently toward the barn, the car, and the boy.

He'd figured right; the kid was about nine years old and was straddling his bicycle, ready to pedal off at the first sign of danger. *The young lad's still listening so I guess "Cattle Call" doesn't sound all that bad to him,* Jimmy thought. *I'll have to compliment Dana.* Still smiling, he crept forward until he was in front of the boy—at about the same time the kid turned away from the hill, ready to race back to the road and away, to alert Daniel.

"Gosh!" the boy blurted, almost falling from his seat.

"Going somewhere, stud?" Jimmy calmly asked, standing astride the bike's front tire and patting his rifle meaningfully.

"Ah...ah...no, sir!" the boy answered bravely, while the moisture stain spread rapidly down the front of his worn jeans.

***

"Weren't you a bit hard on that child?" Dana asked, steering her car from the ruts and onto the paved road.

"Naw, see, I'm throwing his britches out right here." Jimmy flung the garment through his window and onto the bushes beside the road. "They'll need to dry out anyway. He can pick them up when he pushes his bike up this way." He was enjoying himself. This was the first kid he'd talked to in many days who was younger—and smaller—than him. "He can't ride back with those flat tires anyway."

"But he didn't have any underwear on, Jimmy. You really embarrassed him."

"Oh, that *was* a little unexpected," he agreed. "But that's probably not going to be anything compared to what Daniel's going to do to him. Yeah, now I feel bad for the kid too. I bet Daniel's got the boy's mother or sister locked up down at that school building too, to keep him from running away. Or maybe at the church." Jimmy was leaning forward in his seat, staring backward in the passenger-side mirror. "Probably at the church. That's probably the base of his operations. Dana, go on down that way for a few miles, and watch for the first little bridge," he instructed. "Then turn right into the cow pasture after that; I can't remember if I left the gate open, but I think I did. Then follow the tire marks through the grass. There's rock there, so you won't bog down in the soft stuff. Then go straight on around the knobs and up the little hollows. Then go south on 441 when we get there. You'll know your way then."

"Are you seeing anything back there, Jimmy?" Dana asked.

"No, but it's a bit of a walk up to that barn. And the kid wasn't wearing shoes either. We'll have plenty of time behind us, I think. I worry more about what we might find ahead of us around one of these curves." He rolled his window the rest of the way down, extended the Mauser's muzzle through the open window, and casually rested his arm on the emergency brake—beside Dana's arm.

They rode in silence, Jimmy praying for bumps in the road ahead and Dana steering with only one arm, her other arm brushing lightly against Jimmy's on every bump.

***

"Isn't...wasn't your house—Homer and Zula's house—just over this hill and around the curve?" Dana asked, allowing the Mustang to slow on the long grade.

"Yeah, and be careful rounding the curve. I can still see a lot of smoke up that way."

"Crap! You're right! It's blowing down and...Do you think the woods are on fire too?" Dana leaned forward in her seat with both hands now on the wheel. She was anxious about driving through the smoke.

"No, everything is pretty green all around. It rained a tad last night too. And other than trees, there's not much near the house that's apt to burn. Actually I wasn't even thinking about...Ah, yeah, that was the plan all along—setting the fire to distract Daniel and his boys from the Burchfields' barn in the event they'd found the car. Yessiree." Jimmy was smiling smugly and nodding.

Dana shot him a sideways glance. "Sounds like what I stepped in earlier today."

Jimmy's smile grew broader. "Say, there's the mailbox, where I'd set out the milk cans. Just keep going, and I'll do the looking up toward the house."

They rolled on through the smoke and past the driveway, now cresting the hill. Jimmy suddenly leaned back in his seat and blew air through his puffed cheeks, "Woo-ee!" His eyes were big.

"What'd you see, Jimmy? What'd you see up there?" Dana took her foot off the accelerator.

"Just drive. Please just drive. We need speed now."

"What? What?" She sped up again.

"Just up the driveway and past the smoke, there's cars and trucks parked and guys watching the fire. Lots of guys, Dana. I had no idea Daniel had so many men still following him. Wow! There must've been a hundred!"

"Do you think they came just to watch the place burn down, Jimmy?"

"No, I think they had other plans…and we need to put some distance between ourselves and them right now. I think a couple of those ol' boys spotted us as we passed the driveway. If they can turn their cars around, they'll be right behind us. Just past the bridge up there," he instructed.

A minute passed, and she saw the bridge. "There's the gate. Thank God it's open. What are you doing?"

The boy had cracked his door. "I need you to stop now. I need to close the gate."

Dana slid to a stop, and Jimmy bailed out, racing back to the gap in the fence. In seconds he returned, diving through the open door, his feet muddy from the wet ground. "Dang! That's about the fastest I've ever closed a barbed-wire fence!" He was puffing from the exertion.

Dana started again, following the faint tire marks through the grass. "Why did you want to do that?"

"Buying us time, I guess. Maybe they'll go on down to the ol' bus and pass right by the gate." Jimmy was fully turned in his seat, watching behind them. He saw a truck and a jeep streak by on the hard road, heading to the blockade before the highway. *Too close.* He straightened to watch the trail ahead. Soon they skirted the first knob and were hidden from the paved road. "Whew!" he breathed.

"I saw them too," Dana simply stated. "Determined lot, ain't they?"

The boy knew what she meant. "Yeah, I think ol' Daniel's got a special place in his heart for me. But maybe he'll stop chasing me now. He's gotta know all I want to do is leave here and get back home. But he might have seen you…" He let the observation hang in the air.

"Now how would he have seen me?" she demanded.

"From those ol' boys chasing after you—I expect he didn't kill them all. Or maybe he'll hear about you from the kid. I think that kid on the bike had the hots for you." Jimmy was feeling safer now; his broad grin had returned.

"Why do you think all those men are joining up with Daniel?"

"Well, he gives them a lot of stuff in addition to some security. I guess that's why they were at the house too. We musta left just ahead of them. But there's no getting around the fact that the ol' boy is a gifted talker." Jimmy was rubbing his chin as if he were cogitating on the subject, as Homer would have done. "Yeah, he and his dad can sure talk…and quote Bible verses. But not around ol' Homer, because he'd correct them when they started. And I don't think Reverend Dilbert Davis cared much for Homer because of that. But there are a lot of scared people now—like Thelma—who'd grab at any chance to avoid the plague and the dying. I think they see Daniel now as having answers, and if they act like him—do what he says and act like him—then they'll piggyback on his beliefs. Are you a Christian, Dana?" he casually asked.

"That's a little personal, Jimmy," she curtly answered. "That's between me and God."

"Oh, sorry. I didn't mean to sound judgmental or prying. It just seems there's not a lot to be private about anymore. Homer used to say that a lot of folks tend to view their religious beliefs as something like a menu: 'I'll have what he's ordered.' And a lot of religious leaders are like waiters, just agreeing with and confirming the order. That makes for a nice, pleasant dinner."

"That's what Homer used to say? He talked to you about that kind of stuff?" Dana slowed for the slight dip where a wet-weather creek crossed the path.

Jimmy braced for the bounce. "Yeah. Personal or private—it was all the same to him. What you really believe wasn't a secret for long around Homer. Too important, he'd say. But he wouldn't let me copy what *he* believed. He'd say I had to go to the kitchen and fix supper before I really knew what I'd ordered. Every plate was special, he'd say, for each customer."

"Then I guess I should have spent more time in the kitchen."

Jimmy laughed. "Sometimes I feel like I'm still working on my appetizer."

They talked like that the rest of the way to Sevierville, back and forth, each voicing their own thoughts and questions, each answering as best they could, either through experience or inspiration, neither feeling obligated about having to appear a certain way to the other.

"Jimmy, you're right," Dana said at one point. "At this time there's nothing too private to talk about. I'm glad you asked about me."

"I feel better having met you...Dang! What's that?"

From behind the dark mound up ahead, the big cat stood, its huge yellow eyes unafraid, now calmly appraising the approaching car. The animal was on a rocky snag that extended over the creek running alongside the tire ruts. Jimmy had been watching the mound as they drew closer, wondering what it was and if it was alive.

"I think it's a damn cougar!" Dana opined.

Jimmy was now sitting erect in his seat, one hand braced on the dash and the other on his rifle. "Ah...yeah. That's what it is...and eating a dead pig—a big ol' cougar. 'Cept around here they'd call it a mountain lion. Or panther. I had an uncle who once raised peafowl. Some of the old men told me the peacocks' cries reminded them of panthers. Or maybe they said 'painters.' Anyway, I didn't think there were any more alive around—"

"Jimmy! Is it going to attack us?" Dana's interest in mountain lions was more immediate.

"Oh, gosh, no. As long as we don't try to take his pig away from him. Isn't he beautiful?"

"*Beautiful?* What the heck do you think he's doing here?"

"Well, I expect with the mountains here and fewer cars around…
Aw, look. He's leaving." Jimmy's disappointment was evident. The
big cat leaped from its perch, bounded across the tiny brook and
the tire ruts, and disappeared in the bushes on the far side. "Dang!"

"You know," Dana said, "I think I saw one of those things run
across the road down toward the river—within Sevierville's city limits! I thought it was a big otter or something."

Jimmy was rubbing his chin again. "Bet we'll start locking the
doors now." He laughed. "But I guess we'd better go on now. It's the
afternoon, and we've still got to find a place to stay tonight."

Dana mashed down on the gas, and they moved on, bouncing
on the rocks and holes in the twin ruts. Ten minutes later the ruts
broadened to become a scraped dirt road and then, a few miles later,
a rock-covered turnpike. Houses and yards now appeared and disappeared to the sides of the road.

"So far, so good, Dana," Jimmy observed.

"Yeah, but we haven't seen anybody yet. There's nobody at those
houses we're passing, and we're seeing cars again looking abandoned and all off to the sides. I'm kinda worried what we're gonna
run into up there." The Mustang's tires thudded at the start of the
asphalt surface. "The road to Gatlinburg is right up ahead." They
saw a car and then a truck drive past on US 441.

Dana braked to a complete halt at the stop sign and looked both
ways. "Do you drive, Jimmy?" she asked.

"That's a little personal, Dana," Jimmy replied.

She gave him her hooded-eye look. "Listen, smartass. I was going
to let you drive for a while, but—"

"Dana, please accept my heartfelt apology for my rude comment.
Now, please, please, please, let me drive, please."

"Jeez. I think I prefer smartass to fawning. OK, after we find a
place to eat—say, do you have anything other than pickles and beans
in those jars?"

"Now that you mention it, I do believe we have a jar of peaches.
How's that sound?"

"Great!"

"Now if you want to turn here and go down a few blocks, I think the drugstore is down this way. Maybe Mr. Cline is still around," he added hopefully.

"I know him, but I kinda doubt the old guy is still alive. He's about a zillion years old." Dana turned, and soon they were crossing the driveway into the pharmacy's big parking lot.

"Park down there," Jimmy pointed. "I know we can get out that way if someone wants to trap us in here. Besides, after we eat, I want to look around inside the store." They were passing the storefront; its windows were smashed, and the shelving inside was broken and splintered. "Dang! It looks like the store's been shot up with a really big gun." He now remembered the bullet holes in the bus on White School Road and the torn-apart bodies behind it. "If we see cops or even military people along the road, we need to be real careful before we drive up to them. OK?"

"'The best way to find out if you can trust somebody is to trust them,'" Dana quoted. "Mr. Hemingway, I believe."

"We don't get second chances around here anymore, girl," Jimmy replied. "That would be from Mr. James O. Burke. Besides, didn't ol' Ernie end up shooting himself? And not in the foot?"

"Point made, sir. I shall be careful. Now about those peaches…"

***

After they had eaten, they pulled around to the rear of the drugstore and rested for a while, studying the traffic on the highway beyond the plowed fields while they took turns napping. The moving traffic was sporadic, and for the most part, vehicles now all seemed to be traveling in caravans along the road.

"That must be for protection," Jimmy observed aloud, once they were on US 441 and heading south. Dana was allowing Jimmy to drive the car to Gatlinburg. "Notice how we aren't seeing any single cars passing us now even? I guess most people in the cities are staying in and hiding or are forming alliances with neighbors and family. Back where we were, neighbors are far apart, and churches are religious and social and family relationships all rolled into one. But in the cities, the folks might be closer to their neighbors...and maybe that's why gangs are there and not here, even when the threats and fears about a plague aren't around. 'Course they might have threats there that I don't know anything about that'd cause people to join gangs."

"I'd rather be a Jet," Dana said. She was slouched in the front passenger seat, watching the road roll slowly by.

Jimmy glanced over. "What? A jet?"

"You know, the Jets and the Sharks. I think the Jets were the Puerto Ricans, and the Sharks were the...Irish?"

They rolled on in silence. Jimmy glanced over again. "Are you talking about the gangs in *West Side Story*?"

"Yeah." Dana clicked her fingers and moved her hands from side to side, dancing in her seat in time to the tune she was humming.

"Man, I don't...Woman, I don't believe you," he declared. "Here we are, almost nabbed by a mob of men, dodging strangers, worrying about a plague, and losing loved relatives to whatever...and you're singing a Broadway musical? That's incredible!" Jimmy *was* falling in love.

"Oh, I thought it was a movie. Besides, you got me singing back there at that barn—and it felt good! I'm so tired of being afraid, Jimmy." She leaned his way, laying her head against his shoulder. "No fun at all."

"Well, I don't know the 'be an American' song you were singing, but I can help with 'Tonight,'" he volunteered.

Dana smiled up at him and started to say something.

Berruwwww! Jimmy heard the bullet pass by, just outside the window, then heard the gunshot. He punched the accelerator and looked to the rear in his mirror. A pickup truck had slipped up behind them while he was flirting around with Dana. He cursed under his breath and concentrated on the road ahead. The little Ford had lots of pep and surged forward, but he had his hands full dodging the stalled cars parked here and there alongside the double lanes. *Dang! There's nowhere to turn off. I've got to outrun 'em!* He chanced another quick glance in the mirror and saw he was just maintaining his distance from the truck. *Barely.* And he saw two men standing in the truck's bed, trying to align their rifles on him as the pickup swerved and dodged those same stalled cars.

They were now approaching—now entering—the long bridge back over the river, and Jimmy had no idea what it would be like on the other side of the hump. He steered to the middle of the two lanes and yelled to Dana, "Wrecked cars, blockades. Dana, would you…" *Kaboom!* Suddenly he was deaf in his left ear as he struggled to keep the car straight between the bridge wall and a parked station wagon.

"Ha-ha, got their asses!" whooped Dana from the backseat. When she'd heard the shot from behind, she had pushed herself into the backseat through the gap between the seats and grabbed the shotgun, letting fly a return shot through the open rear window. Her good luck—and the rabbit-shot load—had taken out the pickup's windshield on the driver's side. She and Jimmy—in his mirror—watched as the truck braked hard, skidded, and rammed the station wagon. *Kaboom! Crash!*

Jimmy slowed to avoid a couple of other wrecked cars ahead. "Dang, girl, you almost deafened me!" he complained. With his ear still ringing, he doubted he could have heard her if she had answered him. Steering the Mustang around the two-car pileup, he continued to coast, allowing for obstacles yet to come and yelled again to Dana, "Are you OK back there?"

"Your shotgun almost broke my arm!" she answered in his ear. She'd leaned forward between the seats and was rubbing her shoulder. "My whole arm's gonna be bruised. I don't think I'll ever again be able to use it again. My arm, not your gun…but maybe both. Say, did you see that shot? Why didn't the truck explode when it hit that other car?"

"Dunno. Maybe that just happens in the movies. But that *was* a good shot—my compliments. I think there were about four or five other cars following the truck, and they all got stuck behind him when he hit the car. I saw that just before we rounded the curve. Tell you what: We've got time. We could go back for a look-see."

"No! No! No! Just keep driving, boy. Or...hey, I don't know how to reload this thing."

"Just pull the slide back and forth...OK, you've got it. Now put the safety back on and point it out the window—not at me!" Dana had jacked in another shell and had lowered the gun in the process so that it was pointed at the back of Jimmy's head. His eyes were huge as he watched in the rearview.

Dana giggled and laid the gun back on the seat then wedged her way through to the front. "A little touchy there, bro. Not getting enough rest or something? And I notice your hearing doesn't seem to be bothering you as much either."

"Yeah, you have the power of healing all right. Try whispering in my other ear now."

"You wish. Say, we're not going close to my place, are we?" She was sitting forward in her seat, swiveling her head around to take in all the sights.

"Not going up that way—can't. Too much stuff blocking the roads that way. We turned south on the highway, and that was the bridge back there that's south of town. I'd thought you'd be recognizing where you were by now."

Dana continued to search around. "Gosh, everything's changed. The lights are all off, and there's so many wrecks and abandoned cars off to the sides. And nothing's open! See all the restaurants and hotels that are around here? None of them are open. I don't see anybody walking around or anything!"

Jimmy took his foot from the gas, allowing the car to coast again; he wanted to look around too. "Say, there's some people over there at that red truck—at the Holiday Inn. Let's get a little closer." He steered into the outside lane.

Dana reached back for the shotgun and placed it between her knees with the long barrel leaned against her shoulder; she wanted it to be easily seen. "Uh-oh, I don't like the looks they're giving us. Are those dead people in that cart?" The small group—three men and two women—were standing at the open tailgate of the pickup. Two of the men carried rifles. The others appeared to have paused from their labor: moving corpses from the large luggage carrier to the bed of the truck. They were scrutinizing the approaching Mustang just as carefully as Jimmy and Dana were studying them. "At least they aren't pointing their guns at us," she noted. "I think it's gonna be OK to talk to them."

Still coasting, the boy veered the car around the spilled garbage bags and trash in the right lane and onto the apron to roll almost to a stop directly across the grassy plot from the hotel's covered entrance. He figured they and the people would be able to exchange shouted inquiries from that distance. The group remained bunched at the back of their pickup—and watchful.

"Hey!" Dana yelled, waving and greeting them. The gesture seemed to Jimmy to be rather inane for the moment and the times. Yet, by far and until two weeks ago, that was exactly the most common of greetings to be exchanged between strangers. People just weren't being nice to each other anymore.

"Hey!" the ladies responded as a duet, a gesture equally astounding to Jimmy.

Gosh, I've missed that. Now what are we going to say? he wondered. "Ask them if they come from around here," he suggested to Dana.

"Jimmy, shush! That sounds stupid." She slapped at his finger tapping her unbruised shoulder.

"Are y'all from around here?" one of the ladies shouted.

"Tell her she's stupid, Dana. Tell her she's stupid," Jimmy whispered, still tapping her shoulder.

Dana slapped at him again while hollering back to the group, "Yeah. We're from Sevierville. We're on our way to Gatlinburg where my mother and her friends are waiting for us. Are those folks dead from the disease?"

The woman looked at the prone figures on the cart and in the back of the truck as if she were only now seeing them. Jimmy was almost expecting her to question back: "What folks?" But she didn't.

He whispered to Dana's back, "'Bring out your dead. Bring out your dead.' Hey, that's from a movie I—"

"Jimmy! Shush!"

"Yeah. They were in some of the rooms up there," the woman replied, pointing at the drive-through cover and the towering edifice above. "They're not so decayed that they can't be moved...and we're needing a place to stay for a while. We were camping on the North Carolina side of the park, and we're trying to get home. We're from Sweetwater...Say, you don't have any extra gasoline, do you? Nothing's open and..." The woman was standing there, looking as if she were searching for the right words.

Jimmy moved his right foot to the accelerator. *Just in case.* The fuel inquiry set him on edge.

"And?" Dana encouraged.

"And we tried to get some yesterday in Gatlinburg...but there's some unfriendly people up that way. We got through town OK, but we got some bullet holes in our truck now. They were shooting at us from some of those buildings up close to the road."

Damn! Dana grimaced. "Ma'am?" she yelled. "Did you come down 321? By the East Parkway? That's where my mother's business is located."

The woman was slow to respond. Jimmy was hoping that few of the new holes in the truck had been created in that locale.

"Girl," the lady yelled back, "there's a lot of destruction thereabouts—a few burned-out stores before there and a lot of fellows trying to stop us past there. I hope you find your mother OK up there. But we need to get back to what we're doing here. We wish you God's help and protection in your search, and maybe if you come back by, we'll have things a little more livable then."

Jimmy was watching Dana. She was studying the dashboard and rubbing her hands together, seemingly engrossed in thought and obviously not intending to reply to the group's well-wishes.

"Thank you, ma'am," Jimmy yelled through Dana's window. "Yeah, we'll see how you guys are faring when we come back by. Is there anything we should be looking out for?" The last question was just on impulse.

The man without a rifle responded, "Yeah. Past Pigeon Forge—do you know the tunnel there? Well, stay out of there. Drive the southbound lanes going and coming. There's some ol' boys blocking it off and trapping people inside. They're robbing and killing 'em. Must be twenty or thirty of 'em, what we saw."

"Thank you, sir!" Jimmy pressed softly on the gas and the car moved forward, gathering speed. "Well, Dana, that was some valuable information, I'd say." He glanced over at her when she didn't respond. She was still staring at the dash. *She's processing the fact that her mother might not be waiting for her. Best to let her think now, I guess.* He moved over to the inside lane and maintained his speed at a comfortable twenty miles an hour.

They were passing more restaurants and hotels now. *There's the cutoff over to Wears Valley,* he noted to himself. Jimmy's father usually brought them up that way in the wintertime, to see Pigeon Forge and the Christmas decorations and lights adorning the shopping centers and recreational attractions in that area. *"Tourist traps,"* he'd call them. Over the years, the area had expanded extensively and now catered to the dollars brought in by vacationing families and bargain-seeking shoppers drawn by the miniature golf courses, go-kart tracks, and discount outlets spread throughout the valley. *Then Dad would say, "When I was a kid, there wasn't anything here 'cept the people who made pottery—and that was reason enough to visit."* Likewise, Jimmy had seldom visited the town's attractions. *The Smokies are reason enough to visit.* So as they drove along the widely divided highway, Jimmy observed buildings and structures he was only now really seeing, as if for the first time. *Dang! Is that a brand-new pancake restaurant? One, two, three—I can see three pizza places from right here.* But as he passed some buildings, he was unable to determine what they'd been selling. The windows were blasted open, and the interiors were burned and ruined beyond identification. *Now that's a grocery store.* The expansive parking lot and the tall sign at the entrance gave it away, even though the windows were completely gone and its contents were completely torched. *Or stolen. Didn't Dana say people were now trading for stuff, trading for food?*

"Dana?" Jimmy almost whispered. "Are you doing OK? Say, does this look like the right way?" He was watching her, hoping for a flash of the beautiful smile that warmed him from inside.

She looked up and gazed around. "Yeah," she breathed. "This is actually the only way up here, so you can't get too lost." She reached over and patted the boy's arm. He smiled back—an almost grateful smile. She chuckled. "Got you worried there, big boy? Do you think ol' Dana's gone over the edge? And if something's happened to her mama, that's she's really gonna fall apart? That what you're thinking about?"

Well, I wasn't thinking about it just now. "Ah, maybe," he replied. He *had* been thinking exactly that, but when she voiced his thoughts, they sounded so hard and self-centered.

"See, I was thinking exactly the same thing about you. Yeah, I know you've already seen stuff that I don't ever want to see—people shot, bleeding, and broken—and people puking and crapping all over themselves with the plague. But suppose when you get back to Maryville, suppose nobody's there waiting for *you*? How are you gonna take that? Rough, huh?" She watched his profile, watched his face compress and close inward. *Oh, shit!*

"Jimmy, I…I don't really expect that to have happened, but see, that thought helped me. See? It made me think of how sad I'd be for you and that my problems aren't the end of everything." She glimpsed the shiny tear trail down his left cheek when he looked over. *Damn! He's really never thought his mother and father would—could— be dead. That's what's been keeping him going!* "You know, you told me God makes use of situations, and his purposes are ultimately for our benefit—and that made me feel better." She was hurrying now. "And don't you think Homer and Zula—and I know this sounds trite—are in a better place now?"

Jimmy sighed and nodded in answer.

"Well, I do too," Dana said. "I think they're in a better place too." *He looks better.* "So, see, those thoughts about *you* helped *me* feel better about…if anything has happened…to my mother." She now had to avert her own eyes.

"Do you really?" he softly asked. "Do you think she'd be in a better place?"

It was Dana's turn to nod and sigh. "Yeah, I do. My idea of an afterlife might be different from yours, but what you said about the unseen and the eternal, about consciousness and the indwelling spirit, and about God calling himself simply, 'I AM' kind of turned on a light for me. Even about eternity and his purpose for us—I thought about that, and for a second there, I understood." She looked over to him and was amazed. *A second ago he was about to bawl, and now he looks like I've given him some big present or something.* She imagined that his face actually glowed.

"Oh, Dana, I understand exactly what you're saying and—maybe that's inspiration too—that thought of your connection makes me... happy." Jimmy was watching the road again and shaking his head. "Now why do you suppose that would happen when I should be sorrowful and all, thinking about what could have happened to my parents? See, it was different with Homer. He wasn't the least bit sorry or bitter or fearful. So he died, and I felt sorry for *me*—not for him. He was OK with it all."

"Maybe that's just Jesus in you...being happy?"

"Yeah," Jimmy agreed.

They drove on in happy silence for miles.

***

He saw the fires far ahead. Long tongues of flame licked from the tunnel on the northbound side of the divided highway. Men were emerging from its darkness; a few were running down the road with their clothes ablaze. *Dang!* Jimmy slowed to watch but kept a careful eye ahead. A deep, swift-running creek divided the lanes, so he wasn't too concerned with the thought that men could be spilling over onto his side, but other cars could be stopping ahead, goggling at the sight. Then he heard the sudden rapid series of gunshots. *Brraap! Brraap!* "Ambush!" he gasped, stomping hard on the accelerator and shrinking low in his seat. They rounded the corner—"on two wheels," as Dana later would claim—but no salvos of bullets erupted after them, crossing over to stitch through the few trees and rip at their car. *And the road's clear ahead! Nothing waiting for us. Yes!* As the din died with distance, Jimmy allowed the car to slow again. "Whew!"

"Whew!" Dana seconded him, giving him a hard stare from her side. She had been dozing but was now hanging on the support handle above the door. "Take one more curve like that, boy, and we won't be having to worry about anything! You scared the holy crap out of me!" she scolded.

Like a turtle seeking cover, Jimmy lowered his head and hunched his shoulders. "Ah…sorry," he offered. "The shots—they surprised me—I thought they were coming from behind. Hah!" He was having a tough time finishing his apology while trying to stifle the snorts he felt rising in his chest. "It's just that when I'd scare Dad like that—with my driving—he'd say something like that and that we'd need to go get a crowbar…to pry him loose from the seat covers. Hah! Get it? He'd be so frightened that—"

Dana maintained her icy glower. She was not sharing his gush of relief.

"Well, I guess you'd had to have been there. Sorry." *No, I don't believe ol' Dana enjoys surprises when she's napping.* He looked away and changed the subject: "You know, this here car's got some accelera-tion, huh? It's really got some horsepower." He glanced over. *She still looks a mite peckish.* "Yup, really got some power this ol' car has…"

Seconds ticked by, and he kept watch across the creek.

"Say, we're getting close to the other end of the tunnel over there, Dana, so you just might want to…" he warned, tapping her elbow with his fingertips, touching her as he would an animal that was prone to bite.

"Got it," she acknowledged, slightly lifting the shotgun she now held.

Smoke was pouring from the tunnel on this side too. Several cars and trucks were halted in a line before the gaping hole. Jimmy pointed through his window. "See? That looks like a long caravan of vehicles was moving down the road, driving to Pigeon Forge, and didn't know about the ol' boys stopping and robbing cars in the long tunnel. So I expect they had a fight on their hands that neither gang expected."

"That's OK. Maybe they'll kill each other out of existence."

"Oh?" *A tad vehement, I'd say. Apparently still cooling.* He focused on the road ahead.

"They're just out hurting others as it is," she explained. "I can't pretend to understand their motivations or feel any compassion for them even when they're dead. It's like people stopped being human anymore."

"It's OK. I understand." *Like wanting to take potshots at folks.*

"Sorry," she added. She didn't like Jimmy seeing her like this. "Just being honest."

They drove on, and soon they no longer heard the gunfire.

"Getting darker," Jimmy observed.

"Yeah, and now I'm thinking maybe we shouldn't come back this way again. Know what I mean? Try to find another way?"

He nodded. "Yeah, we'll try to find a way," he affirmed. "Gotta be a better way."

***

As they approached the city limits of Gatlinburg, Dana pointed ahead. "Say, there's a detour up ahead—a small road that winds up the mountains and around, above Gatlinburg. It comes back in on the far side of town on the Little River Road. Know that way?"

"Yeah, my dad told me his dad and some ol' boys dragged their car up that way when it was only a trail. Or maybe it was railroad tracks. Anyway, he said Gatlinburg was more like a Wild West town back in those days. Gambling. Whisky. Dancing girls." Jimmy managed a leer for Dana's benefit, but she seemed not to notice. "So yeah, I know that way," he added.

"OK, great," she continued. "Up toward the top, there's some places we can pull the car over and get off the road." Another minute passed. "Fancy spending the night with me again?" she asked.

"Well, if it can't be helped. But I get the backseat, and you can't drape your feet over the seat right above my face."

This time she laughed.

That was a good sound to him. "By the way, Dana, how is it you have knowledge of such remote parking spots?"

"You don't want to know, darlin'. You don't want to know."

Awwww. He knew she was kidding. *But still.*

They found the detour without further incident. They met no one coming down from the mountains, and they saw no one going up. At the top they parked at an overlook and spied over the town far below, seeing only an occasional car move along the main street.

"I do believe, fair maiden, that we may even chance a tiny fire if your hidden spot is far enough off the road."

"Then we shall have a bonfire," Dana replied, smiling her own knowing smile.

That night, after a supper of pickles and green beans, they retired to the Mustang thoroughly warmed by the adequate fire. About midnight it rained and the weather cooled, and Dana lowered the backs of both front seats, slipping over to warm herself against an elated Jimmy.

14

DAY TEN

"Jimmy?"

"Mmmmm?"

"Jimmy, are you awake?"

Ooohhhhh. His dream, one of the usual ones where he walks through many dark rooms in a vast house, stopped midframe. He was just reaching for the knob on the closed door, and light was brilliantly shining from under the crack at the bottom...and all faded away.

"Jimmy, I'm hungry. My stomach's rumbling, but your pickles and green beans don't even sound good to me."

The boy tentatively cracked one eyelid then the other. *It's dawn—still dark. I'm sleeping in the car.* He stretched wide his eyes, blinking repeatedly, forcefully, then squinting, trying to focus on...*Dana?* He twisted in the seat and raised himself sideways to an elbow position to face her. "Dana..." he croaked, stopping then to cover his mouth, to cough and clear his throat. *Morning breath.* He began again, this time talking to the back of his hand. "Dana, it's barely light out, and I...I don't think we have anything else to eat right now. What time is it anyway?"

She was lying beside him, half on the backseat, half on the lowered front seats, her feet propped against the door. She answered in a rather languid way with her eyes still closed and her hands cradling her head. "Dunno. I woke up when I heard the truck climbing the hill. Do you know you snore?"

Suddenly Jimmy was very awake and very interested. He could see her profile in the early-morning light; he concentrated on her mouth. "Rea—really?" he managed, his voice going high at the end.

"Yeah, but not all that bad, really. My stepfather used to snore so loud that—"

"No, no, I mean about the truck. When did you hear the truck? And which way was it going? It didn't stop, did it?"

Dana turned her head to him and opened her eyes. For a long minute, they considered each other in the dim, colorless light. Several strands of her fine hair, still tousled from the night, had lightly fallen across her face; she moved them aside, blowing upward from the corner of her mouth. Then she smiled at him—an easy, lazy smile.

Dang! She's pretty even when she's just waking up! Jimmy had totally forgotten his series of questions. He hadn't even thought to return her smile while he struggled with this sudden and confusing desire, this impulse...to kiss her. *Right on the mouth!* Other than a few cheek kisses with his mother—and that time in the dark theater with Anna Sue Alexander, an eighth-grade classmate who'd been twice held back in elementary school—he'd never before purposely kissed another human being. His family and relatives weren't of the huggy, touchy sort, so he'd had few occasions in the past to attempt the maneuver. He just wasn't sure what to do next—and his panicked state showed.

Dana giggled and leaned up, brushing aside his hand to briefly touch her lips to his. Giggling again, she lay back. "Military truck, I guess. Coming up maybe from Pigeon Forge."

"Wha—what?" he blurted. Now he couldn't even savor the kiss.

"The truck. It sounded like it was coming from back down the road, from Pigeon Forge. In fact it sounded like the big truck I saw a couple of nights ago—a national guard truck, I think." She was now watching him, watching the morphing of his face from enthralled to concerned—and that concerned her. "Why?" she asked. "What are you thinking? The truck was driving real slow because, you know, the road's all eroded and washed out, I guess. But they *did* go on by,

Jimmy. And they didn't shine any lights back this way, so I don't think anyone knows we're here, if that's what you're thinking."

Jimmy still looked distressed. "Well, these days it seems we can't even expect the military to..." His eyes met hers, and he paused—and then he nodded. "But you know that already, don't you? We've talked about trust and changes and all that already. I was just... thinking about something else." *School bus.* He pushed up from his elbow position, his hand on the seat. "And I thought about some other stuff we really need to do while we can, before we go on to... Gatlinburg. So..." He froze in this halfway-up position and smiled down on her—a slowly developing, devilish grin.

Dana squinted back. "What?" she asked rather sharply.

"Guess what I just found," he said, passing something from his one hand to the other, "from under the edge of the seat back." He held the object over her head so she—and he—could see it in the window's light. "A candy bar! A...ah...Forever Yours?"

"Damn!" *Whew!* Dana was instantly up, grabbing the tiny chocolate bar from his hand. "My favorite! Let's split it. OK?"

Jimmy struggled to swing his legs around to sit upright. "No, no, no," he said with a laugh. "You go ahead. It's all yours. I'm not all that hungry. Besides, I didn't even think they still made those things. It's gotta be almost petrified from being under the seat."

"You sure you don't want half?" she persisted, scooching up in the seat to give him room to turn. "I know it's probably from Halloween—a year or two ago—but it won't make you sick or anything, I'm sure."

That thing does look good. "No, no, you go ahead. I'll finish off that one open jar of beans." *I'm getting a tad tired of canned green beans myself.* "Breakfast of champions," he added, hoping she hadn't caught his involuntary grimace as he turned away to open the car door.

Crawling out and stepping onto the pine needles, he stood there for a moment and stretched, twisting from side to side to loosen his spine. He had enjoyed Dana's warmth during the night but had worried over her comfort, wondering whether she had room enough to sleep comfortably. So he had tried making himself small, sleeping sideways and pressing himself hard against the seat back.

"It's gonna be a beautiful day," he predicted, grunting from his stretches as Dana extracted herself from the car, wiping at the corners of her mouth and tossing the candy wrapper toward the gray circle of wood ash remaining in the center of the clearing.

"Think so?" she said. She joined him in stretching. "Jimmy, *you...* uh...are the *eternal* optimist. You know that? Do you know what... uh...that is?" She continued without waiting for his reply. "With you there's always something good...uh...to be found in everything. Uh! In everybody—no matter what. Uh! People—girls on pedestals. Uh! 'All is for the best in the best of all possible worlds.' Uh!" She stopped stretching. "Say, have you ever read *Candide* by Voltaire? You should. You'd recognize the central character. His name should have been 'Jimmy.'"

He *had* read it, and he wasn't too sure he understood the comparison. He'd have to think about that. His smile faded in thought.

Dana, seeing and misinterpreting his expression, quickly added, "But I'm not criticizing, see? I really did like Candide...and I wouldn't have you any other way, Jimmy. Truth is, I don't know what I would've done if I hadn't found you—or you found me."

"Then you must be my Cunégonde," he replied, meeting her eyes.

Dana looked shocked. "Damn! You *have* read the book! I didn't even know it existed until this year and only because it's required reading. I thought that...Why would you read such a crappy book unless they made you read it?"

"It rains a lot around here in the wintertime. There's not much to do other than spend the weekend at the library. And that one, that book, was actually a very good story—the English translation of course. I don't read French."

"It was written in French?"

"Yeah. Originally." He fluttered his eyelashes at her.

"Damn it, Jimmy!" She popped him on the arm with her fist. "Smartass!"

That was good. He liked her reaction. Smiling broadly in return, he leaned backward with a final grunt and stretch. *Now's the time to ask.* "Dana?" he ventured. "I been thinking about things—like during the night—planning things, you know. Would you, by chance, consider staying up here with the car while I go down and scout around the town? See, that way, I can—"

"No way, José," she interrupted. "My mama, my job. Now if you want to wait up here while *I* go look around down there, I'd agree to that."

Jimmy shook his head, feigning irritation and clucking his tongue. "Then we shall together go down unto Gatlinburg to slay the Philistines—or at least to confound the foe. Kind of biblical sounding, eh? But there *are* a couple of things I really, *really* need for you to do. The first thing being…" He held up a finger and strode past the girl and on around to the back of the Mustang. He unlatched the trunk and lifted the lid, leaned in, and pulled a pair of faded green coveralls from the compartment. After vigorously shaking them, he held them out to Dana and continued, "The first thing being putting these on to go down there with me. I saw them when I was putting stuff in the trunk."

Dana looked at the patched garment and recognized it as her mother's gardening coveralls. She kept them in the trunk should she ever have cause to change a flat tire far away from home; she was careful like that.

"OK," Dana agreed, without protest. *Nobody will see me anyway. And they look clean enough.* "Next?"

"Next"—*this is gonna be hard*—"you gotta let me cut your hair… short." This time Jimmy watched *her* face transform. While he had innately realized—and appreciated—Dana's regard for her own appearance, he recognized in thinking about it now that she took actual pride in her hair. *Maybe all women are like that.* He recalled the earlier moments when he'd noticed the way her fine, reddish-blond curls tumbled lightly over her forehead and eyes as she had awakened. *Dang, she looked sweet!*

But "sweet" had vanished from Dana's visage, and her hands rose automatically, protectively, to cover her hair. "You want to do *what?* Cut my hair? Why? Why in the world would you want that, Jimmy?" In truth she knew the reason, and she actually, probably concurred; she just needed a moment…and for him to ask her.

"Because you can't look good to go down there," he stammered. "Because you can't look like a girl—a beautiful girl—to go down there around those men." The compliment was honest and easy for him to pay, despite his pained expression. "I don't know what all's going on in this town but, back around Homer and Zula's place, I think the men are beginning to be lusting after the women and fighting over them."

Wow! That was more than she'd expected. "Lusting after?" she innocently asked, teasing him because she could.

"Well, with the plague and all that's gone on, I know I'm being… I'm just afraid that a lot of the courtesies, I guess, and respect paid to women have been put aside in favor of…ah…those baser instincts in men." He was searching for the polite words. *Too bad she hadn't grown up on a farm.* "Like ol' Daniel back there wanting to…lusting after Bill Shanks's wife, Judy. But I mean, that wasn't really something new; he's been eyeballing her since way before the plague came, wanting to…So now that I think about it, I bet him and his men did that to ol' Bill—killed him—because he loved her so and all. Had to, I bet. And I bet that baby of hers is what's keeping her down at the church and compliant with…ah, you know, their requests." Dana's eyes had grown distant while he circled back to the subject. She appeared to be just nodding politely while she thought about something else.

But she was actually still listening. *I knew I'd have to do something with my hair. But cutting it short?* Having no pins or clips handy, her options were in fact limited.

Jimmy didn't know what more he could say. *Wait! Those guys chasing her—what did she say then?* "Um…those guys chasing you from off the highway—remember what you said about why they were doing that?"

"Yeah, maybe," Dana allowed.

"So it's the same down there—just a lot more of them to worry about. See, I didn't notice any women at all walking along the street last night when we were watching the town. I'm betting women are in short supply there too or are being kept hidden somewhere down there. That's what I'm thinking." Jimmy paused, looking at her. "Understand?" He half expected for her to say she didn't understand, and he was running low on explanation words—and breath. And if Dana didn't want to cut her hair, he knew he couldn't make her do it.

"Ah…yeah, OK, not a problem," she simply agreed. "I understand. And you're not being…whatever. Heck, I'm not too sure where I'd find my hairdresser these days anyway." She smiled mischievously. "You know, I expect even *he* would be a commodity these days…to certain segments of our society." She'd expected a laugh from Jimmy, but he said nothing. Instead he was looking thoughtful again.

"Well, how old is he?" the boy asked.

"Damn, Jimmy! See? The guy who does my hair is gay, and you know, these days with the decreased number of—just forget it," she concluded, frowning in disgust. "Make a great joke and…Are you thinking the plague is still going around? I mean, you and me, we're doing all right, aren't we? And it's been around for a while now."

Jimmy sighed. "Yeah, I think it's still around, but it may be going away. I read that it did just go away like that back in the Middle Ages. But those guys yesterday—those with Daniel, and at the hotel, and at the tunnel—did you happen to notice many older fellers yesterday? I didn't. I didn't see a single older person—what I'd call a middle-aged person—all day yesterday. Everybody who's out and around seems to be, well, younger—they look college-age or younger. Twenties or so. Even those women at the hotel. So how 'bout you looking around some too? Maybe *that's* just my imagination, you know—my paranoid imagination."

"Yeah, OK. I'll pay attention to people's ages too from now on. So age, hair, and coveralls—anything else?"

"So glad you asked," he replied. "May I carry your thirty-eight down there too? I didn't see very many people carrying guns down there, so I'm expecting we'll draw attention if we carry our long guns with us. I suspect they're limiting the guns in town, and they might just take ours away if they have the chance. It's probably easier to control a population in town if only the leaders get to carry guns."

Dana was nodding again. "Yeah, sure. The pistol's pretty heavy when it's loaded anyway. You can carry it...but I get to drive the car."

"Ah...Dana, that's another thing. Would you mind if we just left the car here and walked down the trail to town? That's another thing they might want to take from us—especially since it has gas in it." *Maybe now's the time to ask about that other idea too?* "You know, to go into Gatlinburg, I'm asking a lot from you, but, say, if we were to go to Maryville first then we could—"

"Jimmy, we'll walk down the trail to town. OK? Anything else?" She was beginning to sound stressed again.

"No, no, that's about it, and that's OK," he agreed, hastily withdrawing his Maryville idea. *I got concerns about Mom and Dad, but she's got her concerns too.* He could wait.

He softly closed the trunk lid and looked about the clearing once more. "If anything happens, and we get split up, we'll just meet back here. OK?" He held up the keys and jingled them. "And we'll leave the keys right here under this rock in front of the tire. Crows will take shiny things sometimes, but they should be safe under here. No need to be carrying the extra weight, huh?" He was doing his best to sound reassuring. "Dana? Did you get that?" She was still staring at a fixed place on the ground, her brow furrowed, her eyes unfocused.

"Yeah," she answered after a long pause. Looking up, she smiled weakly. "Yeah...if we get split up. So let's do it."

Their plans now complete, Dana changed out of her clothes and into her mother's coveralls on the far side of the car while Jimmy sharpened his Barlow, leaning with his back against the vehicle as so ordered, but frequently holding aloft the knife's shiny, wide blade to gauge the sharpness of its edge—maybe.

***

Dana led the way down the mountainside, feeling more relaxed but still grumbling as she walked. "You know, you cut way too much of my hair off the top; I could've put it up under my cap anyway. And why couldn't we just have walked down the road, Jimmy? I mean, this way is so steep that my toes are cramping in my shoes."

"Too long. It's way too long to walk all the way down to—I think it's called Newfound Gap Road right there—to the road down below. This way's a heck of a lot shorter and not too much steeper. And your hair looks real nice." Jimmy was studying the closely shorn back of Dana's neck and the slight stubble that disappeared under the band of her baseball cap. He had found the Atlanta Braves cap stuffed in the trunk with the coveralls; it completed her ensemble. Now Dana looked to be just another boy. *A skinny-necked boy at that—with a really crappy haircut. I sure hope I'm not around when she finds a mirror.* He choked trying to stifle a laugh, causing Dana to glance back over her shoulder.

"You OK?" she asked.

"Yeah, yeah," Jimmy snorted. "Just swallowed a...gnat." He coughed again and sniffed in validation.

After a few more minutes of silence, broken only by the sounds of their tromping and deep breathing, he spoke again, his voice low and serious. "Ah, Dana?"

"Yeah?" she replied, straightening and cocking her head to the side to better hear.

"Dana, would you mind spitting a few times before we get into town? Like just off to the side of the trail? Just a practice spew or two—nothing that could blow back around this way. I really think you should work on your spitting and nose blowing before we get to town."

"I'm *not* going to blow snot out of my nostril."

"It'd add to the boy appearance," Jimmy insisted.

"I will neither do a one-handed snot blow nor perform an enthu-siastic ball scratch," she declared without looking back.

"Dana!" Jimmy exclaimed from behind, his hands raised to his ears in affected horror. "So vulgar! Besides we usually call it 'scrotum scratching.'"

"Just the same," she evenly replied.

They walked on, with Jimmy still behind, smiling and chuckling, obviously pleased with himself.

Another long stretch of silent minutes passed. "Say, Dana, know how Gatlinburg got the name?" Jimmy was puffing now, timing his words with his steps and trying to catch up to her. She ignored him. "Seems it was once called White Oaks but was renamed after a guy who might have been a relative to the guy who invented the Gatling gun. But this particular Gatlin was a shopkeeper and postmaster for the town, so the office got named after him. Later, when he was run out of town during the Civil War—he was a Confederate sympathizer—by the Union support-ers, the name stuck even though there wasn't a Gatlin around anymore."

"Jimmy," Dana puffed back, "are you teasing again? And if that's true, how is it you know all this stuff? Surely it didn't rain *that* much around Maryville."

"Forty days and forty nights, Dana—but that's another story for another time. See the buildings up there ahead?" They were nearing the city limits, and the trees were thinning. "Just follow me between those two there, and stay close to the road in case we pass people walking the other way. OK?" Dana nodded, pulling the bill of her cap lower over her nose.

They stepped through the weeds between the two low buildings and emerged on the sidewalk. Then, turning to their left and away from the national park's roadside marker, they strolled on, side by side, along the mostly deserted walkway toward the far end of town and Saul's pawnshop.

Dana chanced a glance over her shoulder, back toward the park's entrance, then glanced a second time. She motioned to Jimmy, for him also to take a look. He did and saw what she had noticed: a pickup truck parked across the road just past the Great Smoky

Mountains National Park sign. The shadows were deep there, this late in the morning, but Jimmy could see well enough to count the men standing guard: five armed men grouped behind the truck. "See," he whispered. "They'd have stopped us coming in that way this morning." *But at least there aren't too many guys there, and there's space around the truck. We might have made it.*

They began to pass odd pairings of men, all walking along the sidewalk in the opposite direction; no one seemed inclined to exchange greetings in passing. Dana was keeping her face low anyway, walking far to the outside of the sidewalk to minimize facial exposures. *So far, so good,* she thought. *Just about a half mile or so to the 321 split.* About that time and a block down, several open jeeps turned their way and idled slowly up the road toward them. Each carried four men, all armed with high-powered hunting rifles. Dana held her breath, concentrating on taking that next normal step until the last vehicle in the convoy had passed them.

"Jimmy," she whispered, "those guys all had black armbands on!"

"Yeah, I saw that," he whispered back, his hand making a patting, calming motion above his thigh. "But don't worry. Not everyone's wearing them. Maybe you get an armband if you're carrying a gun... or maybe it's vice versa. Must be a militia thing." They walked on, their eyes darting from side to side.

"Jimmy, look! There's a restaurant over there, on the other side of the road. The door's open. Do you suppose they're selling food now? I'm really, really hungry."

"Yeah, me too. Let's cross." He fought the impulse to touch Dana's shoulder, to help her, to turn her to cross the lanes to the restaurant. *Guys just don't do that to each other.* So he rapped her arm smartly with the back of his hand, pointing across her to the restaurant.

"Ow! Damn it, Jimmy! You do that again, and I'm gonna slap the holy you-know-what outta you!"

"Dana, it's a guy thing to do," he urgently whispered back, still staring straight ahead, his lips drawn tight to stifle a grin. He knew he should quit fooling around, but he just felt too good, walking along beside Dana and all.

They crossed the street without seeing a car coming from either direction then trotted on across the opposite sidewalk, up the two steps at the front of the building, and through the open door. Jimmy stopped to read the sign thumb-tacked to the placard that stood just inside. *Looking casual here, just looking normal, just letting my eyes dilate.* Just the same, he clasped his hands over his belt buckle as he read, leaning forward to feel the reassuring weight of the thirty-eight hidden in his waistband. "Looks like eggs, grits, and corn bread's the fare today," he called to his partner's back.

Dana didn't reply, choosing instead to stride to the table in the near corner. *I can see both ways this way, while Jimmy can watch out front through the windows.* She pulled back the chair to the wall and dropped heavily into it, tugging at the crotch of her coveralls and adjusting her imaginary genitals.

Jimmy followed her to the table, seating himself across from her and leaning in. "Now, Dana," he softly cautioned, barely moving his lips as he talked to the back side of the menu she held, "guys don't normally spit on the floor *inside* a building. And if you keep scratching at your privates, you're gonna have to go wash your hands before you eat." Dana glared back at him from over the top of her menu.

He chuckled to himself, having actually enjoyed the theatric touch to her boy role. *But now to business. Let's see what we're dealing with here.* Turning slowly to both sides and scanning the room, he counted an even dozen men sitting at six separate tables. *All scattered around, normal-like.* The faces of the men seated at the backmost tables were barely visible in the flicker of the candles placed on those tables. *No electric power. They must be using propane for the stove for cooking.* The men returned Jimmy's gaze, having watched him and Dana enter and cross to the corner of the long room, breaking their stares only when Jimmy met their eyes and nodded to them. *Nothing to see here, folks. Just a couple of good ol' boys coming for breakfast.* Soon the comfortable buzz of conversations returned to the room.

As Jimmy listened in on the discussion at the nearest table, trying to make sense of the stray words, the place suddenly quieted again. A waitress emerged from the kitchen, swinging wide the double-hinged door as she entered. Jimmy glanced over—and then looked back again. "A woman, Dana," he whispered. He slid his gaze past the waitress to the men around the restaurant, catching their reactions. "Anybody do a double take?" None did. "They must all be regulars in here." But they all had rotated in their seats as she passed—studying her—in the same manner that a pack of wolves would study a deer. *Or a menu.* "But nobody's doing nothing about her. Just looking on subdued-like." He felt certain now that some sort of local order had been established and was being maintained in the town. "Wonder who's heading up this pecking order here and what she is to them?"

The waitress ignored her audience and scooped up her pad from beside the cash register as she passed, veering toward the new arrivals in the front to take their order. But then a large group of the men—most of them seated against the back wall—stood, screeching the legs of their chairs on the tile as they rose in concert. The waitress stopped and turned back to them, standing as if she were awaiting for something. *Perhaps some instruction, some signal about us!* Jimmy dropped his hand to the pistol at his belt. *Here it comes.*

But the moment passed, with the bearded man at the center table merely tipping his Shell Oil cap to her and the other men only gesturing with their bobbing heads. They then sauntered on between the tables and out the front door, picking at their teeth with the restaurant-furnished toothpicks, their thumbs hooked in their front belt loops. Now half turned in his seat, Jimmy watched over his shoulder, while Dana lowered the menu she pretended to read. He turned back to her, noting, "They all got those black bands but no rifles, and they don't seem inclined to remit payment for their meals neither. Not even a tip. Wonder what's the deal?" When the men had exited through the open doorway, the waitress returned to the register desk, where she retrieved a chained clipboard from beneath the counter. As she counted on her fingers, she made marks on the clip-held sheet of paper. "Looks to be a member-only proposition, Dana. Hope not. That'd be bad for us. Maybe barter? No money changed hands," he whispered. "Just a check-off." Jimmy now directed his attention to the two remaining men at the nearby table.

They weren't sporting black armbands, and *they* were eating. He'd have to watch to see how they paid their bill.

Grabbing her order pad again and this time snagging the water jug from the far side of the register, the waitress detoured over by the two men on her way to Dana and Jimmy's table. Stopping to refill their water glasses, she chatted with the men, nodding and answering their murmured questions, "Yeah, of course I'm going to the meeting. What choice do I have? Noon. No, no, we'll open again while Mr. Husky and Reverend Davis talk...coming over here for dinner in the reception room...no alternative either." The men looked to be in their early twenties, about the same age as the waitress. They were now standing, and one of them, the taller man, reached for the waitress's hand to press something into her palm.

"No, this is for you," he said, in a louder voice. "And *this* is to pay for the meal." He held paper currency in his hand; it looked like a twenty to Jimmy.

"Whew!" Jimmy whispered, straightening in his chair. "It's good to see they still use money—paper money—around here. I was getting worried how we were gonna pay for breakfast. You *are* catching the tab, aren't you?"

Dana didn't answer; she was still watching the men and the waitress across the room. "He's given her a bracelet too. Looks like a diamond bracelet!" she whispered.

"No, no, it's for you," the tall man was now saying. "Keep it. Just don't tell your pa. He don't have to know everything."

"Yeah," the other man added, his voice high with irritation. "The Whaley and Husky families don't run *everything* in this town."

"Careful," the first man warned. He had turned in their direction when he said that, Jimmy noticed. *Leadership must be a sore subject around here too*, he thought. *Some things don't change, I guess.*

"And I don't care who they are neither!" the other hissed through clenched teeth. He snatched his hat from the table and stalked through the restaurant and out the front door, not even glancing in Dana and Jimmy's direction. The tall man followed, after muttering apologies to the waitress.

"At least they seem polite and respectful in here," Dana observed, her voice low, her eyes watchful. "But did you hear what they said a little while ago? About Reverend—"

"Davis?" Jimmy finished her sentence. "Yeah, I heard what she said. I told you the ol' boy was expanding. I wonder if that's the meeting today, the meeting with Mr. Husky like she said?"

"Damn it!" Dana whispered.

"Yeah, I know. That would be bad, but we can—"

"No, damn it!" Dana was looking past him again. "I know the waitress—Vera Whaley. We're in the same grade at school. Gosh, I bet she'll recognize me. Let's leave. Oh, damn! Too late. Here she comes." Dana lowered her head.

"What are you guys having?" Vera Whaley asked, her pen and pad raised high from long habit.

Jimmy flourished the menu he had taken from the napkin holder. "Well, I would say we're having…eggs and grits and corn bread. Are there alternatives, my lovely lass?" Jimmy was heaping on the theatrics, trying to keep the waitress's attention away from his companion.

"Not unless you brought 'em, bub." Vera turned to Dana; she was obviously hardened to flirting, especially the flirting of an-almost-fifteen-year-old kid.

"But darlin'," Jimmy persisted, scraping his chair legs on the tile as he pushed back, "we'll also need to negotiate the price of your wares—the value of the victuals."

"Victuals? What?" Vera was scowling at him, her upper lip curled with scornful impatience. "Anyway, it's all on the sign. Or can't you read?"

Great customer skills, lady. "Not that well, my dear. Suppose you just tell me the prices, and then we'll try to get along better." Jimmy was standing up, *his* eyes now flicking to the closed kitchen door. *We might be needing to leave real soon.*

"Hah!" Vera laughed. "You're just a kid. What do you…The price is thirty dollars for breakfast for the two of you. Coffee is ten dollars." She had seen a glint of danger deep in the boy's eyes. *The kid's not that big, but he looks crazy—off or something. And the way he talks is nuts.*

"Better. Now do y'all barter? Gasoline? Ammunition? Drugs—legend and others?"

"What's legend?" Vera asked, her order pad now held low as she reappraised the kid, her scornful lip curl gone.

"Prescription drugs—legend drugs," Jimmy replied, making his own tsking sound of impatience. He was running out of bravado, and the girl still seemed not all that impressed.

"Well, sometimes...but I don't know the bartering rates. We've only been open again for three days. I'd have to get my father... Dana?" She had just recognized the seated girl.

Dana automatically had glanced up, hearing a noise at the kitchen door. She again raised her head to the waitress. "Hey, Vera," she greeted.

"Dana, are you with *him*? I mean, what have you been doing? Where have you been? I thought all girls..." Vera was now whispering and taking her own glimpses over to the swinging door.

Dana leaned forward and whispered back, "Same as you. Just trying to stay on my own."

"But my daddy said...I thought your mama was...I'd heard..." Vera saw Dana's eyes widen. "Nothing. You're coming here to find your mother, ain't you?" The waitress was now standing straight and no longer whispering.

Something's changed! Jimmy stepped forward, ready to grab the woman's hands with his farm-toughened mitts if necessary. *Better find a story quick.* "We're with Reverend Davis," he hissed, "and you need to quiet down. You do understand what's happening here, don't you?" Jimmy was doing his best to appear menacing while playing for time.

Now Vera's eyes grew wide. "I thought we were going to have an alliance with the Lord's Army. I thought that's why y'all were coming here today—to negotiate. That's what my daddy said." Again her eyes flicked to the closed kitchen door.

"Then you need to keep quiet about our presence here," Jimmy warned, trying to think of all the ways he could keep Vera quiet while he and Dana made it back to the car. He didn't want to shoot her, but his options appeared limited. "Where's ol' Whaley anyway—your father?" *Sounds good—"ol' Whaley"—just like we know each other.* "I'm here to talk with him. Just with him—and your mama. This conversation—and our presence here—is to remain quiet until after the Reverend Daniel Davis gets here. Do you understand?" Jimmy was having to process a lot of information quickly. It was making sense to him now: The importance of the waitress's father was the reason she was allowed public exposure like this, and this same importance was why the old man wasn't now coming through the kitchen door; he was with the other town leaders, mapping out their strategy for the upcoming meeting. *Noon, she said.*

Vera had started to take tiny shuffling steps backward while staring down at Jimmy's hands, holding her own hands close to her stomach, as if he were already gripping her wrists. "Um...um," she stammered. "He's back in the kitchen, with the cook. I'll go get him." She turned toward the swinging door.

But Jimmy was faster; he stepped between her and the door. "No need to bother," he advised. "Better I see him back there anyway." He slipped his hand in under his shirt, gripping the handle of his thirty-eight as he turned from her sight. "You and Dana just do some visiting right there."

"No! Wait!" she blurted, trying to keep up with him.

Jimmy kicked wide the door, storming in with his hand still under the front of his shirt. But there was no one in the room. *The place is empty!* The boy looked from side to side, seeing only the simmering pot of grits on the Sterno-fueled camp stove on the center island and the can-filled shelves along the far wall. *The stove and griddle's not even lit. Nobody's around at all.* Vera ploughed into him from the rear, unable to stop herself when she burst through the door following its next swing.

Jimmy whirled, his revolver in hand. The girl froze, her frightened eyes moving up and down, bouncing between his gun and his face. For a long minute, they stood like that, across from each other, neither speaking and both mouth-breathing as their excitement ebbed.

"Damn it, kid!" Vera recovered first, feigning the wrath that had worked so well for her in the past. "If you broke that door, you're gonna pay for it!" But Jimmy just continued to stare until she dropped her eyes from his, shifting her feet with her growing uncertainty.

"Where's Whaley?" he asked, hearing no emotion in his voice and feeling that same cold calmness he'd felt on the ridge that day, shooting at the scrambling figures far across the valley. He knew if he had encountered anyone in the kitchen—anyone who might have threatened their escape from this town—he certainly would have shot them dead right there. *And that's the way it is.* He wasn't afraid, and he wasn't curious as to why he wasn't fearful. It was just the way it was now: no fear, no guilt.

"Gone—I don't know—to the meeting with Mr. Husky," Vera answered, wisely deciding not to even attempt to lie. *This little shit will shoot me!*

"Do you have a cook in here?" Jimmy saw that the back door was open. If someone had been in here, they'd already fled the building.

"Yes."

Whew! Jimmy huffed, puff cheeked in thought. *Now what the heck to do with her?* He knew the cook would soon bring backup, and a freed, screaming Vera would fetch that backup sooner.

"I won't say nothing," Vera volunteered.

"And why is that?"

"'Cause Dana's always been good to me in school. She's my friend, and I don't want anything to happen to her. And my mama's died, and my father is sick and probably will die and...I just want to stay out of all this stuff. I just want to work in our restaurant and let all this other stuff go by!" Her face sagged like warming wax, and the tears came; she turned away.

Jimmy studied the sobbing Vera. *Gosh, I want to believe her, but I don't know if I can.*

Dana slowly, carefully pushed open the door behind Vera. She'd been listening on the other side, and she didn't want to alarm anyone, thinking maybe Jimmy already had drawn his gun and was holding it on Vera. She had seen his face, his intensity, when he had leaned close out there, talking with Vera. *He went dark, very dark, all of a sudden.* Coughing lightly as she entered, she waited until she could see the boy, see his hands, and know that he saw her. Then she said, advised, "Jimmy? Jimmy, I think we should believe her. She sounds to me like she means it. I think we'll be OK to leave her here." She looked to Vera. "Besides, these days, us ladies gotta stick together," she added, smiling and trying to ease the tension in the room.

Vera looked over and smiled weakly at Dana, nodding her thanks; then they hugged.

Jimmy watched them and considered the situation for another minute. "OK," he concluded. "We'll leave now, Vera, but you've got to stay put for a while. I may wait outside for a while too, just in case." He was still trying to sound menacing. "And if someone gets hurt, well, you know the rest. It'd be your fault. Deal?"

"Yeah, deal," she immediately answered, drying her eyes with a dinner napkin pulled from her apron pocket.

"No second chance," he again warned.

"A deal," she affirmed.

Just the same, Jimmy made Vera sit in a chair in the middle of the room while he slipped out the front door, following Dana. He didn't wait to see if Vera was good for her word.

So far, so good. This time, as he and Dana had agreed, he would stay several steps behind her as they made their way down the main road to the 321–East Parkway split, to where the pawnshop stood. As they walked, Jimmy gawked at the building fronts, at the garish signs and the promised fun and entertainment just inside those doors. Many of his annual elementary school field trips had been to Gatlinburg and Pigeon Forge. He had watched more fudge being made and taffy being pulled than an average human being could eat in a lifetime. He'd bought stuffed bears and fake vomit; he'd invested in pinball and foosball games; he'd journeyed up and down the mountainside in elevated chairs; he'd done it all in Gatlinburg. And he realized just now that he was actually having some fun just walking along its broad boulevard. *But there are hardly any cars around now.* Normally trucks and cars moved slowly along the street, filled with tourists watching tourists, at all hours of the day and night. That was the difference. That and the fact that all the people strolling today looked like boys and men, like the disguised Dana walking purposefully about five strides ahead of him.

As Jimmy walked he thought it prudent to glance back every so often, to reconnoiter behind. He now turned abruptly, as if to study the tall cardboard advertisement in Ripley's front window: a picture of a man driving a long nail up his nose—*Believe It or Not.* He immediately felt and heard the hurried movement yards behind; it obviously related to his own action. A boy of ten or so had stopped and suddenly ducked into the narrow alcove between the knife shop and the candied apple shop. But Jimmy had noticed in passing that both establishments were closed and dark; there was nothing to see in the windows of either business. Two other men then passed the alcove and briefly glanced aside, perhaps at the curious sight of the boy pressed tightly against the locked doors. *And avoiding me—I'm being tailed!*

Jimmy turned back and continued on his way, allowing Dana to pull far ahead of him. Then, at the next crosswalk, he decided to change street sides and strode out across the pedestrian crosswalk, moving to the sun-washed side of the street. As he continued down the sidewalk, he watched the boy cross over too, choosing to follow him. *That's good. Only a block left to go, and then Dana will probably be with her mother.* He felt a slight pang of loneliness.

At the next intersection, 321 branched off to the right and became East Parkway. Saul had situated his pawnshop there because of customer visibility on three of four sides. And the site was clearly visible now, both to Dana, emerging from a line of buildings along the same side of the street, and to Jimmy, strolling along on the far side of the street and stopping at the spit of a corner that formed the bottom angle of the reverse K-shaped intersection.

Jimmy saw the store, or rather the remains of the ruined, burned-out building, and he saw Dana throw her arms in the air in the typical display of alarm—for females. *Oh, dang! Dana, hold on,* he prayed. He looked around for other onlookers who may have noticed the gesture, and there seemed to be none. The other pedestrians seemed engrossed in their own affairs and hadn't noticed Dana's surprise... and her moment of anguish. He turned his attention past the girl to the destroyed edifice. *No doubt about it. Those holes in the walls are from something as big as the gun that shot up the bus.* He remembered the fifty caliber, long-barreled machine gun mounted atop the big national guard truck. *That would do it. I wonder if...*He decided he'd save those thoughts for later. He needed to get to Dana and get her off the street.

Looking to his left and readying himself to sprint across the wide intersection, Jimmy was astounded to see a string of vehicles coming from that direction, up the slight rise into town. He was shocked because the caravan was led by the same truck he'd just been thinking of—the national guard truck. *It just looks like it,* he told himself. And as the truck passed, he noticed the insignia was the same and the mounted machine gun was the same. But he couldn't say if the few bullet holes in the trucks doors were the same. *That wasn't something I'd thought to remember. Besides, those would change anyway with every battle.* The big diesel roared past, blowing black smoke from its tall stack. Then the following car passed...and suddenly screeched to a sliding stop just beyond the intersection. *Dang! The black Cadillac! Daniel!*

Daniel Davis had spotted Jimmy standing alongside the road, waiting to cross over. He recognized him instantly, even through deeply tinted windows. Screaming at his driver, he had halted his car and his armed men spilled out, his bodyguards from the front seat joining the one riding beside him in the backseat. But then, standing at the side of the car, they didn't know whom to shoot; men on both sides of the street were milling about and staring at the stopped Cadillac, uncertain what was going on. As the bodyguards stooped, leaning back inside the car to ask for instructions from Daniel, all the pedestrians came to their senses and scattered in every direction, running for alleys and open doorways.

Jimmy chose the opened door behind him, which led into the multistoried, multistored exhibition building. From past visits he knew each floor had an open concourse from one end of the building to the other, and each shop along the side had an entrance doorway to the central corridor. He'd find someplace to hide inside. He just needed to get far away from Daniel—and Dana.

He raced by the elevators to the stairs, bounding up them three at a time. He was on the top floor, the fourth landing, when he heard the shouts far below. *Ol' Daniel's got lots of men in those other cars and trucks.* He knew heavily armed men would soon reach his floor, to pull at every door to search through every open room. *And it won't do to break into any of these shops.* He also knew it would take too long to rip through the chainmail stretched across the storefronts, and even if he were able to rip through the barrier, the sight of a damaged entrance would just lead the Lord's Army to his hiding place.

"Bathrooms!" He remembered his last elementary school field trip, when he and another boy had attempted to scale the bathroom wall in this building and crawl across the hanging ceiling to the adjacent bathroom—the girls' bathroom. They had been successful and spied on several unsuspecting girls before the heat and boredom overcame them. Then they took to whispering and whistling at their quarry, and before long, cops and janitors were swarming the floor. That evening, traveling home on the crowded school bus, Jimmy heard the first tales of the haunted stores of Gatlinburg, having been built on the violated graves of the town's former inhabitants, the Cherokee Indians. *Imagine that.*

Jimmy quickly found the men's restroom, located down a short hallway, and scrambled into the last stall, up the partition to the ceiling tiles then into the crawlspace above. The space was smaller—and hotter—than he'd remembered, but it would have to do. He also hadn't remembered the long battens of fiberglass insulation blanketing the space. *Oh, yeah. Now I remember—itched for three days after that. Definitely not worth the sight of the tops of a few heads. Juvenile.* He now felt somewhat embarrassed. *Won't tell Dana that story.*

Ten minutes passed, and the heat and boredom again reached Jimmy. Looking around for alternatives, he noticed that the roof actually extended out over the far wall. If he could quietly make it over to the edge, he believed he could look down onto the sidewalk in front of the building and keep tabs on what was going on outside.

The trip across the insulation—he tested each hanging frame before he put his weight on it—took another ten minutes. At one point he heard men enter and search the bathroom below then use the facilities before they left. *Dang guys didn't even flush or wash their hands. And it's so dark in there they probably didn't even hit the toilet.*

At the wall Jimmy pried the long vent from its frame using the small blade in his Barlow, allowing him to see the sidewalk through the gap and most of the street out front. But he couldn't see across the road and wouldn't know whether Dana was still waiting there, maybe staring at the ruined pawnshop.

***

An hour passed and the shadows lengthened, crossing over to the opposite side of the street. Jimmy waited until the men returned to the jeep parked at the curb. He watched them start up and move on down the road, joining a line of about twenty cars now passing in front. *They must be getting on with their meeting,* he guessed. Then he spotted the red bill of Dana's baseball cap as she crossed over from the other side. She was walking fast and clutching herself as if she were cold. *Like a girl!* thought Jimmy. *Dang, I gotta get down there!*

He left the vent where it was and pulled up the edge of the insulation batten where he was sprawled; he didn't want to take the time to return all the way to the ceiling over the men's restroom. *Now for the tile.* The square panel under the batten also lifted easily, and soon he was swinging down into the janitor's closet. As he dropped into the small, dark space, he suddenly thought of the door. *What if it's locked?* He sincerely hoped it wasn't, because he kicked nothing as he dangled—nothing below that would help him if he had to return to the ceiling. He let go, landing lightly on his feet. *Whew!* He hadn't fallen on his butt...and the door wasn't locked. He eased it open, peering through the crack at its hinges as it swung outward. *Nothing.* He listened for footsteps. *Nothing.* He looked back around in the janitor's closet; light spilled past him from the tall windows at the end of the hallway.

And there's the mop sink! The fiberglass insulation had penetrated through his T-shirt and pant legs; his stomach and thighs were on fire. He'd splash himself with the cooling waters there before racing back downstairs. He turned on the spigot and the drops fell—about ten in all—into his trembling hand. *I didn't even think about that!* Without electricity the town's pumps wouldn't work, and apparently the huge water tank above the city was depleted. He would have to press on; there were no other choices. He brushed himself off as best he could in the light of the windows, taking off his shirt and flapping it up and down to remove any remaining fiberglass fibers. *Whoa! Better not do that—apt to attract someone's attention outside.*

Looking down, Jimmy spotted Dana now standing, waiting beside a trash can and staring off to the west as if someone were coming. "The kid!" The boy who had followed him down the sidewalk from the restaurant was walking up to Dana and talking to her. He gestured, and she gestured back, dropping her body-clutching arms. He pointed, and she pointed—and nodded. The boy took her by the elbow and started back down the street toward the restaurant. *Dana's almost leading him! Must have said something about her mother.* He needed to get out there.

He ran down the short hallway to the shadowy concourse then slowed to look and listen. Then he crept forward, going on through the building and staying close to shop fronts along the sides. Not having the lighting on would hide him, but it also would hide anyone left to guard the property. But Jimmy's luck held; he encountered no one along his block-long scurry, and he found a brimmed hat and a jacket on a chair at the base of the stairs. *Bet there's usually a guard here.* He slipped on the jacket and hat and stepped through the exit door into a side street. "Hey!" He felt something in the jacket's pocket and pulled it out. "Dang! Just a plug of tobacco." He was hoping for another candy bar. *I'll keep it just in case,* he thought, returning the plug to his pocket. He had once tried to chew but had just gotten sick. He set off at a trot, following along the way he and Dana had come earlier.

Jimmy sighted her and the boy ahead, crossing over the road in the next block. *The kid's taking her back to the restaurant.* He slowed and reconnoitered the street; traffic, both foot and vehicular, had increased since he and Dana had walked down the road, and appeared to be turning to the south, up a road a block or so before the restaurant. He joined the flow, intending to skirt behind the buildings along the narrow alley he had seen from the restaurant's rear door. He felt safer now, mixing in with the hard-faced men, all seemingly concentrating on their own thoughts and oblivious to him. *They're all younger guys—not a one even in his thirties, I bet.* He kept looking about as he trooped on with the men, turning the corner with them. "Airport road," he murmured, reading the signpost. He would walk up a half block then cross over.

Probably the plague's over and only us young, healthy people are left. But he had Dana on his mind; he couldn't be thinking about that now.

As he stepped into the street, another fellow brushed past him, almost running him over. Jimmy stepped back to the curb and watched the big man march on, running headfirst into a telephone pole that bordered the pavement. *Whop!* The man staggered back and collapsed, falling heavily to the sidewalk. Jimmy hesitated before going over to help, fearing the drawing of attention to himself. He was seeing more of the town's black-armband men moving along this road with him—and a smattering of Daniel's camo-clad men. *Smart of ol' Daniel to choose camouflage. There must be tons of that clothing in stores around here.* He snorted to himself. *Or at one time there used to be.*

As Jimmy continued to observe the fallen man, he noted that no one at all seemed inclined to turn aside to help the guy. The moving groups of men simply parted when they came to him and flowed around him, rejoining on the other side. *Oh boy, don't attract attention now,* he warned himself. But he had to do something. So he shoved his hands deeper in his pockets and strolled nonchalantly over to the prostrate figure, tapping the man's pockets with his feet. He figured that selfish self-interest wouldn't draw attention in this world. He was right; no one even glanced in his direction as he searched away.

"Uuuhhhh." The big fellow groaned as Jimmy rolled him onto his back. Standing over him, he saw that the guy was bleeding freely from his nose and his mouth, and attributed the injury to the vicious smack from the pole. Then he noticed the vomit caked at the front of the man's shirt and smelled the familiar odor of fresh diarrhea seeping down the guy's pant legs, darkening the fabric as it went. "So much for the end of the plague," he whispered. "This guy looks relatively young too."

Jimmy turned and walked on across the street and into the alley. *Couldn't help him anyway. But that armband maybe would have come in handy.* The man had sported the identification of the firearm carriers, but he had been unable to force himself closer to the smell and blood to take it from the guy's sleeve.

"Jeez, this place stinks too!" As Jimmy strode farther into the shadowed alleyway, he became acutely aware of the cloying, decayed smell that seemed to hang over the town. He'd noticed it when they'd first walked between the buildings, but the slight breeze from the mountains had spread the odor, making it less offensive. Here, in this narrow alley space, the stench was overpowering. "Dang garbage is rotting everywhere!" He would have expected some trash buildup with the interruption of municipal collection services in the cities but hadn't thought beforehand about the additional refuse created with the interruption of electrical power and, in turn, refrigeration. "It's amazing!" He eyed the heaped mounds that lined both sides of the asphalt, piled high against the backs of the buildings. Swarms of flies rose from the masses as he passed.

"Ah, *that's* gotta be the back of the restaurant—and none too soon. Shoo!" Crates of rotting meat filled the garbage cans and Dumpster outside an unmarked door. "This is what I saw from the inside." Jimmy circled in place, studying the walls of the adjacent buildings, searching for any movement in the blank windows set high in the walls. *Nothing.* Turning back to the closed door, he noticed a cow carcass wedged behind one of the heavy steel cans.

As he squatted to get a better view, he saw that beneath the mat of maggots wriggling feverishly on the surface of the beef, the body had been torn and shredded. "Chewed on by a bunch of big critters," he observed, whistling softly to himself. "Man! Some of those are big bite marks! Bet they've got lots of bears and coyotes coming down at night now from the hills and higher elevations." He'd want to be out of here by dark. "Can't risk running into one of those guys."

Standing again, he pressed his ear to the door. He heard a soft murmur, like people talking far away. He tried the door; the knob moved easily in his hand. Taking the gun from his waistband, he held it out, ready for use if necessary, and flung wide the door. The surprised boy seated at the small telephone table just inside the doorway froze, his eyes wide and frightened above the massive square of corn bread he was holding to his mouth. It was the same boy who had led Dana away, down on the sidewalk in front of the mall. He was wearing Dana's Braves baseball cap.

Jimmy's finger tightened on the trigger. "Don't move. Don't say a word," he whispered, "or you shall surely die right here and now." Maybe it was the whitening of his trigger finger or the fury darkening Jimmy's face, but the boy stayed still and silent, his hands holding the corn bread to his mouth. "Now slowly, quietly, stand up and back up to that wall there." With a wave of the thirty-eight, Jimmy indicated the wall beside the walk-in freezer door. The boy stood as he was ordered, still holding the corn bread, and shuffled the few steps to the freezer door. He pressed himself at attention against the drywall.

Jimmy followed, never allowing his eyes to break from the boy's fearful gaze. He reached over and pulled forward the metal latch, easing open the heavy freezer door. It moved easily on its hinges. *Empty.* Jimmy had guessed that the pile of offal out back had once been the freezer's contents. "Now step inside," he ordered, and the boy immediately complied, sliding sideways into foul-smelling space.

Jimmy continued to hold the door open, allowing light to fall across the kid's face. "What's your name, boy?" he whispered.

The kid moved his corn bread aside. "Gary...Gary," he whispered back.

"Well, Mr. Gary, you led a boy here a little while ago. I'm betting that pone there is your reward for bringing him here. Now you want to tell me where he is?" Jimmy lowered the barrel of his pistol; Gary's eyes followed its movement.

"Didn't bring a boy back here," he muttered, a petulant child now, with his fear of sudden death having apparently ebbed. He stared back at Jimmy, his eyes narrowed, his mouth pouting with hate.

"Gary, I'm exactly thirty seconds from putting a hole through that Braves hat—and I know where that hat came from. And Gary, this little ol' gun, it don't hardly make any noise at all."

Gary's belligerent eyes dropped. "Wasn't no boy. It was a girl."

Jimmy stared at the boy, watching him, waiting for what else he had to say. He cocked the hammer on the pistol. "And?"

The words spilled out: "She's in with the waitress here. She'll go to the house up there to be with the other comfort girls. They got a gun on her—the waitress and that other guy. They're waiting on Mr. Whaley to come back...from the meeting with the reverend feller. That's all I know. I swear to God. Please don't shoot me, sir." Gary had dropped the corn bread and was clutching his hands to his chest.

"Gary, what's a comfort girl?"

The boy looked from side to side. "That's a girl that's for you-know-what...screwin'...you know." He started making a back-and-forth motion between his hands, the index finger of one hand enclosed in the fist of his other. "That's what they call them—comfort girls—for screwin'." Gary managed a twisted leer, a conspiratorial grin. "You know...for the men." And he tried to wink.

Damn! How old is this kid? Jimmy slowly raised his cocked pistol and sighted in on the boy's forehead. Squinting, he tightened his trigger finger. "Gary, you have no idea how mad I am at you. I really, really want to put a hole in the middle of your friggin' forehead. But you've given me a reason to pass over you—like the death angel in Egypt. Do you really know God to be able to swear to him, Gary? 'Cause, you know, I'm going in there, in the restaurant, and I'll probably have to kill Vera and anyone who's with her. If the girl you led here is still OK, we'll probably just leave out the front door—unless you make some noise to remind me you're here. But if something has happened to that girl, I'll have all the time in the world to come back in here and...You understand me, Gary?"

The boy farted with fright—his face rigid. "Yessir!" he asserted. "Yessir, I understand. I won't move or make any noise. I promise to God. I promise!" A sob escaped his throat.

Jimmy couldn't do this anymore. He pushed the big door shut and snapped the latch. After taking a deep breath, he fitted the padlock hanging from a slender chain at the side of the door through the double holes in the latch. *There. That'll keep him until I decide what to do next. There's enough air for a long time...unless he's shit himself.*

He tiptoed around the center island and its simmering pot of grits over to the swinging door that led to the dining room. Slowly he pushed it outward. In the widening gap, he saw them, Vera and a man, profiled in the glare from the front windows. They were seated at a round table to the side of the cash register stand—about fifteen feet from him—and were watching out toward the front. *Probably waiting for ol' Whaley.* Then Vera leaned to one side, and he saw Dana seated on the far side of the table, facing him. *Lucky, lucky.*

Jimmy pushed some more, and the gap widened, enough for him to slip through. Then, holding the thirty-eight close to his side, he crept silently on toward the table...and Dana apparently spotted him; she made a pointing sign with her finger—a warning sign— her hand barely raised from the table's surface. He couldn't see her face—her head was silhouetted against the windows—but he followed her pointing finger to the hunting rifle propped against the table, between Vera and the man. Jimmy nodded his understanding and crept on. Then, when he was close, so close as to make his presence felt without being seen, the man jerked his head around and lunged for the rifle.

"Halt!" Jimmy shouted. *Where the heck did I get that?* The man froze but the waitress twisted in her seat, gasping in surprise. He extended his pistol hand, making sure both clearly saw the gun. "I mean, you don't want to move, or I'll shoot you dead where you stand. You neither, Vera. But I think I'd like to shoot you anyway, you traitor."

"I…I didn't…We…we didn't hurt her at all!" Vera stammered. "Don't shoot us! Please don't—"

The man suddenly pushed up, aiming himself to ram his shoulder into Jimmy while he grabbed for the rifle. *Pow!* The thirty-eight barked once, and the man tumbled forward, missing the boy and his gun and falling heavily behind Vera's chair. *Whump!*

That was it—hardly any sound at all from the gun, and Jimmy was staring down at the crumpled human bulk at his feet. *I didn't even think before pulling the trigger. Dang! Popped him right through his temple.* He watched the man's blood pulsate from the tiny hole above his ear…and then it stopped.

"You killed Harold." Vera breathed her accusation. "He's dead, and you killed him!"

"And it's your fault, Vera," Dana flatly stated, rising from her chair. "If you'd left me alone like you said you would, and hadn't gotten that kid to bring me back here, to prostitute me, then your boyfriend would still be alive."

Boyfriend? Jimmy moved around to the side to get a closer look at the guy. He now saw that the man was the same fellow who'd earlier tipped Dana as he and his friend were leaving the restaurant.

"Why didn't you just leave me alone, Vera?" Dana was holding out her hands toward the seated girl.

"Because that's the way things are now," Vera snapped. "You showed up, and…I didn't know what you were up to! That's the way things are now! My daddy would ask. He'd want to know what you're doing here. And what *he's* doing here!" She pointed at Jimmy. "And you son of a bitch, you killed Harold…and Gary! Did you kill Gary too? Did you kill him too?" She swung her fiery glaze from Jimmy and back to Dana. "Your mama's dead, you whore! Your mama's dead and blown to shit! You didn't know that, but I do—and I'm glad! They come in that big ol' truck and shot that pawnshop apart with their machine gun and stole almost everything worth stealing, my daddy said. And your mama's in pieces, you bitch! And you're gonna—ow!"

Jimmy had popped her hard on the top of her head with the barrel of Harold's rifle. "Shut up, or I'll give you something to really cry about," he warned, repeating the line his mother had so often used on him in his childhood, which worked no better now.

"Goddamn it! Goddamn it! You busted my friggin' head, you asshole!" Vera screamed at him as she vigorously rubbed the knot rising on the top of her head. "You probably gave me a friggin' concussion!"

Dana came around the table to stand beside Jimmy, taking the rifle from him. "Then you'd better shut up and do what he says," she advised, "because I don't doubt he'll kill you if he has to. And I sincerely hope he has to." She stooped and pulled the black armband off the fallen man's arm and handed it to Jimmy. "Your choice."

Nothing like an efficient woman. "Well, I guess she can join the boy in the back. Or I *can* just shoot her right now and she can join her boyfriend right here on the floor."

Vera immediately voiced her desire, opting for the former alternative. Still rubbing her damaged scalp, she walked meekly ahead of Jimmy, following his pistol's direction to the kitchen and its freezer. Jimmy, in turn, acquiesced to her request to latch the door using only the hasp at the top of the door so that it would stay slightly cracked, allowing in both air and light.

"Now, just to be sure you understand," he growled through the crack, "we're staying out in the restaurant until it gets dark. And I'm locking this here door with the padlock and taking the key with me. Understand? So if either of you decides you want to call for help before it gets right dark, I *will* walk back in here and shoot you both—right in your faces. *Your* choice." From the freezer's darkness, Vera and Gary readily indicated their understanding.

Jimmy waited there for several minutes more before he tiptoed from the room to rejoin Dana, leaving the padlock key on the center island as he passed. Back in the empty dining area, he found Dana seated at another table, well away from the dead man.

"What did they tell you about what's going on around here?" Jimmy asked, taking glasses from the center of the table and filling them with water from the metal pitcher. "Did Vera say anything more about Daniel Davis being here?"

Dana drank almost her entire glass of water before she answered; she was amazed at how thirsty she was. "Well," she began, blotting her mouth with a paper napkin, "you can probably guess she lied to me about my mother, telling me I'd be going up to be with her at the big Marriott at the top of the hill…where most of the women are gathered for safety—that's what she said—until their 'guard' guys got control of things around here. That's those guys who have the black armbands."

"And they prostitute the women?"

"No, no. Vera didn't exactly say that. Remember the short dude who was here earlier with the man you just shot?" Jimmy nodded. "Well, before he left—he was here with the big guy when that little turd, Gary, brought me here—he eyeballed me and winked and said he'd see me later, like probably up at the Marriott. So I just guessed the rest, including what happened to my mother." Dana dropped her chin and closed her eyes when she said this.

"Whew!" Jimmy puffed. He wondered now if she'd be incapacitated somehow and more vulnerable. *Maybe so grief stricken that she's flipped out, unable to continue with me.* So he said nothing, leaning forward on the table and attentive.

"Yup," Dana said, again sitting erect. "That's when I figured that out…and Vera just confirmed it."

"So you gonna be OK?" Jimmy softly asked, turning toward her, shifting in his seat.

"Yeah." Dana was nodding her head; her lips were firm lines. "Yeah, I'll be OK. I know what you've been going through too, and well, there's not much else we can do anymore, is there? We just carry on…or we don't. I don't see the Lord in control like you said you did. But he'll let me know in his time, I guess. So let's just carry on." She again dipped her chin to her chest and closed her eyes.

"Ah, Dana, about Daniel..." Jimmy encouraged.

"Oh, yeah, you asked about him." She lifted her face to look at him; her eyes were clear and sharp. "They said Reverend Davis is here to meet with the men of Gatlinburg. Apparently he's managed to gather a small army—still called the Lord's Army—from around here and all around the mountains: White, Townsend, Walland, Sevierville, the smaller communities, you know. And he's coming here to enlist Gatlinburg's guard to join him and march on to Knoxville. He's saying he's got God behind him...and he's saying he has protection against the plague. Do you think he really does, Jimmy?" Dana placed her hand on his arm with the question.

He looked long into her round, blue eyes before answering. "No," he replied. "I don't think the Lord's with him." He was tempted to allow her hope, even if it was false hope, but decided against it; he wouldn't lie to her. "I've known him a long time, and I haven't felt the Lord's spirit in him in my spirit. I know we aren't supposed to judge, but I've read about 'knowing' in my spirit. And I know." Jimmy lowered his eyes, now confiding, "Actually I've sometimes wondered where Daniel really is getting his direction. Have you ever had a sense, when something bad passes by, that you can feel the badness and danger inside? Kinda makes your hair stand on end? No? Well, that's the way Daniel affects me—like something mean and evil is in him. So if he has power..." He abruptly pushed back in his chair, its legs making that screeching noise of wood on tile; he'd noticed the subtle change in Dana's expression. "But that's just me—obviously."

"But there's more," she asserted. "He's supposed to have some *vaccine* against the plague! They said everybody's supposed to assemble in the convention center's parking lot when the sun drops behind the mountain. And then Reverend Davis is supposed to speak and afterward pass around the serum...Maybe we should be there at least for *that*." Dana was hanging on to Jimmy's forearm, squeezing it.

"Well, it's getting late, and the sun will soon be gone," Jimmy said. "I haven't seen anybody moving along the street outside, so if there's more coming, they'd still be coming in from the northeast side of town. I guess we can fall in with them—or maybe just go out the back way again and see if we can get to the parking lot around and behind buildings." He raised up from his seat and looked toward the open door. "There's some hats and coats on that rack beside the door. We can find new outfits."

"Jimmy Burke!" Dana admonished. "Those are probably clothes left by dead people."

"Then they shouldn't mind."

"What about germs and viruses?"

"The way the plague's spread, I'm not so sure it can't just move through the air. Besides, like you said, it's been around for well over a week. If we're gonna get it, I think we'd already have gotten it." He paused for a moment, weighing his thoughts. "Um…about that vaccine, when I came over here looking for you, I saw a guy that'd caught the stuff—dropped on his face in the street right out there. And Dana, he wasn't all that old—maybe in his twenties. He had on one of these bands"—Jimmy was tapping the black band now on his arm—"but he also wore camouflage clothing, like one of Daniel's men. So…never mind."

"*What?*"

"I was gonna say if that guy was one of Daniel's men, you probably shouldn't even try the stuff he's calling a vaccine—because it don't work; it ain't working. And it may be something that'll hurt you. I know I'm not going to try it."

Obviously disappointed, Dana dropped her eyes, thinking and now chewing on her lower lip. She suspected Jimmy was right, but still…"Well then, Mr. Smarty, I guess we'll just wait and see what they're doing. OK? You ready to go?"

Jimmy nodded. "I'll go lock up." He pushed his chair in and moved toward the front, sidling along the wall just in case someone chose then to show up at the door, looking for supper.

When the door was shut and securely bolted, he selected their hats and jackets from the coatrack against the wall. He chose a tractor-advertising cap for himself and a plain blue hat for Dana. "Eat Mor Possum" was stitched across its front.

"Very funny," she said when he handed it to her. She put it on anyway and adjusted it to her head. "Say, did you know Gary is a relative of Vera's? I think Mr. Whaley's his uncle or something. And from what he said walking over here—I think the guy's a little slow or something—ol' Whaley's about dead already. Gary said the man was puking blood when he left this afternoon to meet with Husky and the others."

"Then I guess I'm glad I didn't shoot ol' Gary. I almost did, you know, when I saw him in here wearing your cap." They were now passing through the kitchen, leaving through the back door, and Jimmy was whispering. He pointed at the slightly cracked freezer door; they heard the low murmurings of either Gary or Vera. *No need to say good night.* He eased the back door shut and continued with his thought. "I suppose maybe that's why nobody else was coming in. If ol' Whaley was fixing the food and sneezing and bleeding, that'd slow down your appetite no matter what. Hah!"

***

Seeing several men walk by the alley's far end, Jimmy steered Dana to the right. "We'll go between buildings up here and come in the back way to the convention center's parking lot. There's some woods bordering the back of the lot. We can watch from there."

By the time he'd guided her between the buildings and through the woods and underbrush, the last of the sun's rays illuminated only the tallest trees on the knolls east of the parking lot. From the west the pair spied down on the scene from atop the bluff that began where the asphalt ended. "This'll be fine," he judged, parting the weeds and grass with the hunting rifle's barrel. "See, they've positioned their trucks and cars around the perimeter of the parking lot so Daniel's men can keep an elevated view of the proceedings. And they've spread those traffic barriers in between to keep the crowd together. Dang! There's a lot more fellers here than I would've expected." Jimmy raised himself above the weeds. "Lots more."

Dana patted his back. "You'd better get down. Somebody might see you."

"Yeah, yeah, you're right," Jimmy agreed, pointing. "There's a lot of activity right here in front of us. I bet that's where they'll distribute their vaccine. See the dippers and those pots—looks like some kind of soup, different from what I'd expected. And over there to the right, they've got a stage set up, and it's backed up against the wall. I bet that's where Daniel will be. They've got the cyclone fencing down the sides that's keeping people out in front too. Good thing it's cooling off now. Earlier in the day, those men couldn't stand being out there in the—"

"Attention, attention. May I have your attention, men of Gatlinburg?" The announcement came from the little man on the stage, effectively silencing the crowd. His voice was amplified through the sound system's two large speakers positioned on both sides of the stage, seven or eight feet above the men's uplifted faces.

With the crowd now stilled, Jimmy heard the putt-putt of the generator providing electrical power to the stage. *Ol' Daniel's really got his show together now.* And somehow that thought was shocking to him; he suddenly felt shaky, as if dreading what was happening but unable to put his finger on anything specific that frightened him— that had awakened him.

The little man continued. "Y'all know me, but I'm Commissioner Dwight Husky, the grandson of our departed mayor. Y'all probably know this already, but the Reverend Daniel Davis requested yesterday to meet today with our city council about joining up with his Lord's Army—he's the general or whatever of that army—to improve our security against armed groups from Nashville and Knoxville and Virginia that he thinks are eventually coming this way." Dwight cleared his throat and thumped the microphone against the palm of his hand. "Can you hear me? Y'all so quiet."

"We're just listening, Dwight!" a black-banded man yelled from the front row. He raised his shotgun to show where he was, and a light laugh rose from the crowd.

Jimmy leaned to Dana and whispered, "They don't look too intimidated by either their leaders or Daniel's men. I bet ol' Daniel didn't know Gatlinburg had so many men neither."

"All right, just checkin'," Dwight continued. "Anyway, the reverend has addressed our city commission, and for the most part, the meeting was civil, and both sides could see benefits. Some of the members couldn't be here tonight, but three or four are here and will be available to answer questions, if need be. That's my dad, Mr. Alton Husky, there in the middle seat. He's had a lot of sun today, so he asked me to stand up here for him." Dwight nodded toward his father, who looked as if he were sleeping sitting upright in his chair. He had a blanket spread across his knees.

"That dude's dying if he ain't already done it," observed Jimmy.

"I'll get to the point—and the reverend has asked to speak a few words himself at the close of this assembly. In short we've already bought his vaccine with the money from our treasury, so gettin' or not gettin' the vaccine won't enter into the decision to be made here tonight. You're gettin' the vaccine anyway." The little man pointed at the twin tables set up under the bluff. Jimmy ducked his face to the dirt, suddenly feeling very exposed with so many faces turning their way, looking for the distribution tables. "In short, exclusive of the plague drug, Reverend Davis is offering us protection if we give him ourselves, our women, our land…everything else. He's sayin' the Lord has brought this plague on the land to rid it of evildoers so that his disciples, principally him, will rise to rule our country. Now if Mr. Blalock or Mr. Whaley could have stayed for this assembly, or if my dad hadn't worn himself out in the sun—see, the old man still keeps his hoes and he gardens every day—they'd be telling you what I'm sayin'." He paused for a minute, allowing the polite chuckle from the crowd to pass. He had no idea that those men doing the chortling had heard "whores" and not "hoes."

"In short we don't think the reverend's deal is all that hot—and we've turned it down. Now we've tried to stay a democracy and made sure each family is represented in our defense group. And we haven't tried to take your guns away—that was one of the reverend's conditions—and we didn't take wives away from husbands. And we made the young, single womens available to all, so nobody had that to fight about. And our childrens are kept with the womens and are protected with our womens by our defense mens. In short I'm gonna allow the good reverend to now say his peace, and afterward we'll have our voice vote like we usually do. Everybody understand?"

After a general murmur of assent swept through the crowd, Dwight exited the tall stage to the right, handing off the microphone to a dapper Daniel Davis, now passing him from the stairs to the left of the stage. Two men in camouflage helped Dwight down the stairs and accompanied him to the vacant chair beside his father.

"Good evening, men of Gatlinburg," roared Daniel in greeting. When no one responded, he tried again, this time holding his microphone out to the crowd. "Good evening, young men of Gatlinburg." This time a polite "Good evening" came back to him in reciprocal greeting, like it might at church. Daniel tightened the knot in his tie and checked the button of his suit coat; he appeared quite at ease before the group. "Yes, men, as Dwight Husky said, the vaccine for your *salvation* has been freely provided and is available *now* for your inoculations." He gestured at the tables and at his men who manned the dippers and held out long tubes of paper cups. "Because I *care* about your time—and my time—we will *proceed* to inoculate while I address you, men of Gatlinburg. See, fellows, it's getting late, and you know how wild and wooly it can be down toward Sevierville after dark." This aside line got a few more laughs than Dwight's garden joke.

"Now as you line up—and there's plenty for everyone—I want to tell you about two things. First, don't take more than one cup. Those darn paper cups are more dear today than you'd think." He paused again for the titter that came. "Second, I want to tell you about the vaccine. I believe God is a ho-lis-tic healer. Holistic. He provides his medicines through this here world he made. Now if you were to look up the word in the dictionary, you'd see that *holistic* means *analyzing* a whole system of beliefs, characterized by the view that a whole system of *beliefs* must be *analyzed* rather than judged simply on its *individual* components. Did you get *that*? Do you believe *that*?

"Well, I don't!" Daniel shook his head and glared at the crowd. "There's just one way, and that's *God's* way. And God speaks to *me*, men of Gatlinburg. He speaks to *me* and tells *me* what I'm to tell *you*. And I point to the Bible in proof, men. I can show you where it says what I say and what that means!" Unlike in his church, Daniel didn't get an amen at this point.

"And God spoke to *me* and spoke this vaccine into existence just like *he* spoke this world into existence—that's what the Bible says. Genesis. God *spoke*! Do you believe that, men?" Daniel received more positive crowd noises this time; the statement sounded vaguely familiar to them.

"He told *me*—God told *me*—to gather the herbs of the field and the produce of the land and to make a soup, like the red soup Cain made for Abel to take away his birthright," boomed Daniel. He was constantly mixing those two Biblical figures up with Esau and Jacob in his sermons, but few people ever bothered to correct him; they knew what he meant. "But I don't want your birthright. I just want your *friendship*, my friends. So the good Lord told *me* what to pick, the good fruits of the land, and how to prepare it—and you see us standing here, dear lambs. Whole and happy and healthy."

Jimmy searched around. "Do you see any of Daniel's men who look a day over thirty—or even twenty-five?" he whispered to Dana. "To me they don't look like their population is faring any better than these folks here in Gatlinburg."

"Strong and healthy, my friends. That's what my offering will do for you. It'll protect *you* and your loved ones. And all I'm asking is your allegiance." Daniel was watching the crowd. He would be careful of his demands and accusations until more of the crowd had taken of the brew. *Damned stuff is getting harder and harder to come by*, he thought. His men and the children down at White School had needed several days to accumulate the mushrooms used in this concoction. They had turned over about every cow pile in western Sevier County to get at the fungus for the soup in those two kettles. *But it should be enough to make every one of their pinheads spin.* He knew what the mushrooms could do. He and his buddies would gather their crops a couple of times every year; you couldn't do it too often, as a curious neighbor would report you to the sheriff. Once, he had tried to explain why he was traipsing around in the dead of night in an old feedlot with a bucket and flashlight in hand; the deputy had asked him why he couldn't just smoke pot like the rest of the kids.

Daniel droned on with his words; the rhythm was more important than the actual words. When he estimated that more than half of the eyes gazing up at him were unfocused and perceiving the sights as he was describing them, he switched to the meat of his sermon—and then they'd take that vote again.

"Men of Gatlinburg, if you search further in that *dictionary,* you'll find that holistic healing considers *all* factors when treating illness, taking into account all our physical, mental, and social conditions in the treatment of illness. And that's where the *Lord* has led *me.* Men of Gatlinburg, the Lord has sent *me* to make you whole…and holy unto him, dear brethren. I *am* the way, the truth, and the life. No man comes to the father 'cept through me." Daniel wasn't sure where he'd heard that; it was probably something his old man was fond of saying. "I and the father are one!" he declared.

He looked down at the sea of glazed eyes and knew the men below probably were seeing lightning bolts shooting out of his ass about now. "So you know that *I* am the great *redeemer* who was sent to lead *you* to the Lord's house, to live under *God's* protection, to bring *you* healing. You now know that now, don't you?" He got a flowing wave of nodding agreement now, much better than before. *Almost there.* He looked over and saw Dwight trying to help his father to his feet. Neither of them had yet partaken of the vaccine, and the old man was trying to get onstage to speak to his citizens. *Can't have that.* Daniel made eye contact with the camo-clothed men standing behind Dwight and Alton Husky's chairs and slightly shook his head.

"Are you hearing me out there?" he roared to the crowd, drowning out all other sounds. They answered and applauded, trying to match his volume.

Daniel raised his hands high when he figured they'd clapped and hollered enough. He glimpsed the men to his right and noted with satisfaction that the Husky men had sat back down, almost lolling in their folding chairs against the smiling men standing to their sides. *Now's the time.* He made patting gestures in the air to quiet the crowd. Several of the men had started singing "Rocky Top" but their efforts petered out when they caught sight of Daniel's shushing motions.

"Men of Gatlinburg!" he bellowed. "A week—two weeks—ago, God sent judgment on the earth in the form of this great plague. And our angry God made forth to send *me* to bring redemption to your town—and like Jonah being summoned to witness to Nineveh, *I* have been summoned to bring witness to *you.*" He found this story particularly easy to remember because he sympathized with Jonah, who was pissed off when the inhabitants of Nineveh actually repented, and God didn't destroy the town as Jonah secretly had hoped. In fact Daniel found many of the Old Testament stories easily remembered because he enjoyed reading about God and his selected people wreaking wrath on his nonselected persons. He often felt he had been born out of time; he should have been walking the earth when God was directing the sons of Israel to lay waste to those cities and civilizations that objected to their territories being reparceled to the wanderers from below the Dead Sea. *Damn, that would have been fun!*

He now watched the national guard truck quietly chug into place, there at the back of the mass where its big gun had a good angle on the entire parking lot. *Best thing since satin sheets and birth control, that truck.* His men had found the vehicle parked along Chapman Highway, its driver loosening his bloody bowels over the guardrail alongside the road. *Damned nice acquisition.*

"I brought to *you* this healing medicine today," Daniel continued, "not for the sums of monies your deceitful city leaders slung at *me*, seeking to allay the judgment of the Lord. No! Brethren, I bring medicine, that vaccine, out of *my* love—*God's* love—for *you!*" He noticed there was no longer a line to the kettles; everyone had been served who was going to be served. "Yes, dear brethren, me and God have desired that *you* join with *me* and my Lord's Army to go forth and conquer the surrounding lands *before* they come to conquer you. And they will come, my people. Don't think they won't. They will come to steal your food and goods from your storehouses. They will come to steal your womenfolk, to rape and pillage and have their evil ways with them. They will come to kill your children, because they will be jealous of their youth like the old people were of us. Yes, brethren, my own father did seek to end my life, much like Saul tried to do with David. Remember?"

At their bluff position, Jimmy rolled to his side and whispered to Dana, "I heard old Preacher Davis took to the hills to stay in his cabin when the plague hit. This is news to me. You know, I never thought ol' Daniel would make a good disciple."

"So, men of Gatlinburg," Daniel thundered, now spreading wide his arms like he remembered Charlton Heston doing when he had a sea to part, "you've got a decision now to make. *You* can join *me*... or send me on my way—I will love you either way. You can continue to follow to follow the Ogles and Huskys and Whaleys, who have run this town as long as I can remember—not allowing you to prosper and share in the glories—or *you* can choose to follow *me*, to submit to the Lord's will and follow *me*. Just as you are. Just as you are, dear brethren. Now listen to me while I pray for God's guidance for you. I want every eye closed. Listen to me." Daniel had returned to the singsong rhythm familiar to most of the audience, his voice low but clear and modulated, his lips pressed tightly to the microphone. The soft hiss at the rear indicated that the national guard truck was in position; the slight metallic tinkles on the perimeter meant his men were locked and loaded. "Every eye closed. No looking around now." *Unless you're wearing a camouflage shirt.*

"Listen to me. Listen to *me*. Now is the time for decision. I will ask you first if you will obey the Lord—every eye closed, every head bowed—and you will raise high your arms, both arms, high to the sky. Then I will in turn ask if it is your decision to turn aside to the broad highway and follow the world. That means not to choose to follow me." Daniel wanted to be perfectly clear. He and his men were scanning the crowd, locating those rifles held by the guard members. He noted with satisfaction that most of the men with the black armbands unconsciously had allowed their weapons to slip from their grasps; he saw men standing on their guns all along the front. *Those mushrooms have a way of doing that to a man.*

"Every eye closed, every head bowed. No looking around. This is one of the most important decisions you'll ever make for your soul." Daniel scanned about the down-turned heads, searching for his men, making sure they were attentive with their rifles ready. *They know the sign.* "Now," he yelled, "if you will join with *me,* join the Lord's Army, and silently raise your arms, raise your hands high above your heads. No talking, please. Every eye closed. Every mouth closed. Listening to me." One fellow in the front row pitched forward to the ground face-first. *Too much medicine,* Daniel judged. That could happen. "Have you made your choice? Have you raised your hands? Keep them up, please, while I count. Every eye to stay closed."

Above the lowered tiers of heads, Daniel saw that maybe 20 to 25 percent of the assembly had voted to join with him. He was visibly disappointed—and mad. *I wasted a damn bushel of mushrooms on these turds.* Without waiting to ask for a show of hands of the men selecting to remain with their current leadership, Daniel turned and strode quickly to his right, down the stairs and past the slumped Huskys. "Every eye closed while we count." He'd laid the microphone on top of the big speaker, which was now being covered by an enormous metal plate, a sign stolen from a nearby roadside. The Lord's Army had learned from their first time—when they had blasted away a perfectly good set of speakers.

Rat-tat-tat-tat! The big fifty-cal opened up with its measured voice, its barrel spitting flame against the dark profile of the western mountain ridge. Daniel's men also opened up with their rifles and shotguns—the explosions joining in volume, resounding from the hills. The Gatlinburg men had nowhere to run. They couldn't find their rifles, and the trucks and cars hemming in the lot seemed all to have a shooting man on the opposite side. The stage was solid in front and was backed by the cinder-block walls of the buildings. There was no escape.

Gradually the movement on the asphalt lot became individuals—running, crawling, or just aimlessly circling in place—and then nothing. There was no one standing any longer, and the rosy flashes along the back half of the lot ceased. There was no one left to shoot.

"All right, let's finish up here. Before it gets too dark and we can't tell if they're dead or not." Daniel had returned to the stage and reclaimed his microphone. The steel signs protecting the speakers were being carried to the pickup truck that had brought them. "And don't waste your ammunition if they don't need finishing off. Hear? Damn bullets are getting too damned hard to find." He paused for effect. "And you'll be happy to know we got some men on their way to the Marriott up this road. That's where we'll spend the night." A cheer rose from the men coming around from behind their barricade of vehicles. "Yeah," Daniel said with a laugh, "we all know what that means. But I got first dibs on that blond-headed girl down at the restaurant."

Dana reached over and squeezed Jimmy's arm. He looked back and rolled close. "That means we gotta get out of town right now," he whispered. "They'll know from Gary and Vera that we might still be conveniently close. And I think Daniel's got as much of a thing about finding me as he does you. Like I told you, we go back a ways. Follow me."

Jimmy scooted back into the weeds to the point where he could stand without being seen over the top of the bluff. "We'll work our way over to those woods there, in the national park, and then we'll move through the woods parallel to the road and cut across behind that roadblock you spotted when we first got to town."

"Didn't you say that's a longer way?"

"Yeah, but it'd probably be safer. They can't hardly track us in the dark, and since Daniel's shot up all Gatlinburg's guards, we won't know if they're still watching the park's entrance at the roadblock.

We can't see them either. So if we make a wide loop, I expect we'll come in behind them."

"Jimmy, with the Marriott and the new girls, do you really think they'll be looking in that direction?"

Jimmy smiled. "Good point. Follow me." He turned and retreated through the long grass and weeds, along the path they had come. Twenty minutes later they were climbing the shortcut back to the bypass and the scenic overlook where they had stowed the Mustang. When it got darker, and if the road traffic stopped, they'd drive down to the main road back through the mountains—the Little River Road—and follow it down to the Y then go on to Maryville. He knew the route well.

***

It was fully dark now, and they'd reached the clearing where they'd parked Dana's car.

"You know, Jimmy, my mother's got a flashlight under the seat." The sight of the vehicle reminded her of it. "I know it's a little late, but we got that."

"I noticed your mom left a roll of duct tape in the rear too. I'll use that to shade the headlights, make them less noticeable from the sides. I'll tape the side lights too. Smart woman, your mother."

"Yeah."

Jimmy heard the tears in Dana's voice.

15

DAY ELEVEN

"So what do they call you, son?" asked the Reverend Daniel Davis, his eyes pinched and focused on the bowl of his pipe, which he was attempting to relight. The match flame flared and disappeared, flared and disappeared, in reverse time to the hollowing of his cheeks, briefly illuminating the upper part of his face between each long drag. *Damned stuff is damned hard to keep burning!* His men had found Commissioner Husky's weed stash in the town's safe when they'd taken the clerk back to her office to withdraw the remainder of the city's treasury funds. *Ol' Dwight's got some good shit here, even if it don't burn any too good.*

"Gary," the boy replied. "Gary Husky, sir." He was standing to the far side of the table that held the flickering coal-oil lamp. The diesel generators on the back side of the Marriott Hotel had run out of fuel days before, and kerosene lamps, formerly scattered throughout Gatlinburg's many antique shops, had been confiscated and carried up to the big hotel on the hill. Since most of the town's free-walking citizens were now spending portions of their evenings up at the big building—where the female citizens happened to be sequestered "for their own protection"—that was where light was most needed during the evening hours.

Daniel raised his eyes. "You a relative to ol' Dwight?"

"I heared third cousin twice removed, sir." Gary continued to stare straight ahead. He barely had known his cousin and couldn't remember ever having talked with him. He looked down at the puffing Daniel. "That's what I remember. I'd have to ask my mama to be

426

sure, but she's daid...that ol' sickness, you know. Kilt lots of the old folks."

"Who's been taking care of you, son?" Daniel had surmised that the boy had some mental challenges.

"Well, sir, I been working and cleaning up around at the restaurant—ol' man Whaley's restaurant—and they been feedin' me and puttin' me up. They's my cousins too."

Daniel flipped away his match and leaned forward on his elbows. "Incest is best. Keep it in the family, huh, Gary?"

"Pardon, sir?"

"Nothing, Gary." Daniel silently read from some of the pages scattered on the table before him. He leaned back to ask his next question—and to study the boy and his response. "My men tell me you met a fellow by the name of Jimmy and a woman by the name of...Dana. Is that right, Gary?" He was gathering up the sheets of paper, tapping them into alignment.

"Yessir," Gary immediately answered. He had a feeling that his knowledge of the good-looking lady and the asshole who had locked him in the freezer was about to make him important...somehow.

"Well, Gary, what could I do for you so that you'd want to tell me all about your time with Mr. Jimmy and his cohort?" Daniel leaned back in his chair and motioned for Gary to take the other seat at the table. His pipe was going good now, and he was feeling very smart and very mellow.

"Well, sir, I don't know but..." Gary pulled at his ear, thinking of all the possibilities. This reverend wasn't like the reverends he'd known before; he sensed the Reverend Daniel would have more of an understanding of a man's real *needs*. But he wasn't quite sure how another man, this man, was going to handle that.

"Gary, would you like to see ol' Vera here naked?" Daniel asked, clear out of the blue, his thumb pointing back over his shoulder.

The reverend does have a talent in understanding those special needs of menfolk!

Daniel partially turned so the boy could see the sheet-covered figure in the bed behind him. "Do you understand what men and women sometimes do together, Gary?" He leered at the boy. "When it's dark and a man and a woman lie together in bed?"

The boy at first appeared confused—and suspicious. A lot of men had smiled like that at him. He tentatively tried out his finger-in-fist motion for the man now opposite him. There were several other men in the hotel room, seated on the sofa and standing just inside the open door; they all burst out laughing, like the men always did. Even the reverend grinned widely. So Gary added a bit more vigor to his hand motions and smiled all around. *These men understand the needs of men, not like that ol' Jimmy.* So for the next ten minutes, the boy freely told of returning Dana to the restaurant and of the words he'd heard while he ate his corn bread there in the kitchen.

When Gary paused, having fully disgorged his memory, Daniel heard the bedcovers rustle behind him. *So Vera's awake and listening.* He got to his feet. "Gary, why don't you just take off your clothes and crawl in back there—beside ol' Vera?" he suggested. "You know, she didn't tell me anything at all about meeting up with Jimmy earlier or losing his whore—what's her name? Dana?—there in the restaurant. She probably was going to tell me, though, but just hadn't gotten around to it since she's been so interested in pleasing me. And for good cause, I might add. I probably saved all y'all's lives by getting your butts outta that freezer down there and—"

"You know I would have, Daniel!" Vera loudly interrupted. "You know I would have," she affirmed, sitting upright in the bed and pulling the sheets up to cover her bare shoulders. "You know I'd have told you, but we've just been too busy here, Daniel. And you know, if you're ready, we could pick up again from where—"

"Where *what*, Vera?" His head jerked about. "Are you saying there should be more to come? That you weren't...satisfied or something?" The room grew quiet, and the men along the wall tried to make themselves small. They had heard this conversation before, and it usually didn't turn out any too well. "Horrible waste of womankind," they'd say to themselves when Daniel was no longer around, and they were maybe having to clean up the mess.

"Oh, Daniel! Of course I'm satisfied. You're such a man!" Vera was pretty quick herself. "I'm just waiting and longing for the next time when you touch me and...you know." She managed a wink and a knowing smile that ended with her tongue moving along her upper lip. Yes, she understood Daniel too. Then her moving tongue stopped, and her smile faded. *His pupils—like cats'!*

"Well, then, you'd better do your best to please ol' Gary here. I'll get a full report from him when I come back." Daniel turned and ambled toward the open door, hitching up his pants and buckling his belt as he walked. "Me and the boys gotta go explore these ol' hills around here now. It's past midnight—a whole new day—and I'm kinda feeling lucky. We might even be making a trip down toward Maryville today. Maybe do some shopping and enlisting tomorrow. What do you say to that, boys?"

"But Daniel," Vera protested from the bed, "Gary's just a kid... and my *cousin*."

"Then you should be right comfortable with him. Ready to go, boys?"

***

"So how'd you come to think of taping up our lights so they'd be less noticeable?" Dana asked, her face highlighted by the dashboard's glow.

Jimmy thought for a long minute, rubbing his cheek with the back of his hand. His window was rolled down and the wind flowed easily through the car. And Dana wasn't driving so fast as to make hearing difficult. "I guess I must've seen it in a war movie or something. I remember seeing pictures of the World War II bombings in London, and that was something they did over there to limit the enemy bombers' ability to spot their cars and trucks on the roads— over in England. Just taped up their headlights so the shine only came through the hole in the middle. Seems to work OK with you too, since you're driving and we're still alive."

Dana nodded. "Yeah, but I can't go fast at all 'cause I can't see *that* good. So it's probably going to take us all night to get to Maryville. It's good, I guess, that we got plenty of gas."

"Well, be careful. I'm betting the residents around here would like to have that gas."

"Jimmy, do people live back around here? Isn't this inside the park?"

They had left their concealed parking spot on the Gatlinburg bypass at about midnight, coasting down the long road to US 441, the Little River Road, that led to Newfound Gap and Clingman's Dome and eventually to the North Carolina side of the mountains—except they would take the turnoff at Sugarland and go back through the mountains, following the river down toward Townsend then Maryville. As they'd expected, after midnight Daniel's troops were no longer manning the roadblock they'd spotted earlier off in the shadows at the park's entrance. So tonight Dana and Jimmy had made their right turn unobserved and were soon speeding away, their taped-over taillights invisible to anyone who might have been walking the dark streets back toward the town.

"I'm not sure, Dana. I know there's people living just outside the park's boundaries, but other than the rangers, I'm not sure anyone does still live in the park itself. There were some people who lived in Cades Cove for a long time, but I don't think they do now. I don't remember seeing their house the last time I rode around the loop." Jimmy was squinting, trying to recollect. "No, I guess I don't know if anybody *is* still living in here. So maybe with us traveling in the night and all, we won't be seeing anybody the whole way." He sounded hopeful with that possibility.

"That'd be great," Dana agreed, "but there's sure as heck a lot of animals out tonight…all along the road. See there! See there!" She pointed at a pair of red eyes high in the vegetation along Jimmy's side of the road.

Resisting his initial impulse—to jerk his arm back inside the car while wildly rolling up the side window—Jimmy scoffed in reply. "Those animals are more afraid of you than you are of them, Dana."

In similar situations adults often had recited that very statement to him, but now, in saying it, he found the offering of that assurance required more effort from him than he'd imagined. The scoffing didn't take the effort; the effort was in keeping his voice from wavering while he scoffed. Besides, he wasn't sure whether he already had used the admonition on her.

Dana recognized the trite clause and glanced over to see whether he was serious. "Then I'd say those critters are crapping in the columbine right now," she lightly observed, deciding not to comment further on his yodeling ability, his quivery voice.

Jimmy turned toward her, studying her profile in the dash lights. "What the heck is a columbine?" he finally asked.

"A flower that's not in bloom right now. I just couldn't think of anything else to go with that fear comparison." She laughed. "Vulgar, isn't it? It's just that I've heard that saying about animals being more afraid of people all my life...and I don't believe it." *Especially from a kid no older than me.*

"Yeah, I see what you mean. And 'littering laurel' or 'ruining rhododendron' just doesn't convey the same...dang! Is that...is that a big ol' bear right there?" Jimmy was waving his hand toward the paved pull-off lane ahead.

"Yeah! And I'd get my arm back inside the car if I were you." Dana was slowing and steering far into the opposite lane. "He *is* a big 'un, ain't he?" The dark, shaggy giant was humped over, gnawing at something in the road and taking up nearly the entire right side of the lane while doing it.

Jimmy readily complied with Dana's advice, working the crank with both hands, as if that would make the window rise faster. *There!* He had the window glass up and now felt the security of its three millimeter thickness. They coasted on, slowly passing the huge animal; it hardly paused from tearing at its meal to acknowledge their passage. "Yeah, one of the dang biggest bears I've ever seen," he agreed. "Did you see the size of his head? It's as big as a basket! Imagine coming around the corner with just a flashlight in your hand and finding that ol' boy in your face." He whistled with this mental image—and waited for his heartbeat to slow. *Whew!* "I think I'd better go find that columbine myself now."

Dana snorted in reply.

There were no more bears feeding in the road, so on they drove into the night, carefully leaning through tight turns along the steep mountainsides yet continually checking to the rear for lights, making sure no one was catching up from behind. Soon they would be at the Y where the road forked, its left lane heading on into the mountains toward Cades Cove and the familiar campgrounds where Jimmy often had camped with his friends. But tonight they'd be taking the right lane through Townsend and Walland to Maryville. Soon he'd be seeing his mother…maybe.

As they entered the last curve, the long sweeping drop before the Y, Jimmy could see down along the river to the road there and the parking lot beside the road where tourists often launched their inner tubes to float down the now deeper, wider river. "Dana!" he warned, abruptly sitting erect and gesturing toward the windshield. He saw dark outlines of trucks and cars parked there—and men carrying lanterns and moving between tents spaced along between the vehicles. Dana braked hard, her headlights now angled toward the left shoulder of the road and away from the encampment. The men in the camp wouldn't be able to see their approach until Dana and Jimmy had rounded the curve going in that direction.

"Dana, we gotta stop. We can't keep going down this way. They'll see us. They're just setting up, but they'll see our headlights." Jimmy was lowering his window again. "See, there's a big ol' military-type truck over there across the road. I bet they've got a big ol' machine gun mounted on top like we saw back in Gatlinburg. Or maybe another mounted on a jeep they stole from the military. They're just setting up, preparing for daylight to see what's gonna come down this way."

"Then maybe I should cut off my lights"—and she did—"and while it's still dark go on straight that way toward Cades Cove after we get by that intersection." She allowed the car to continue forward, moving at a crawl. "But I don't know if I can see to avoid those big rocks down there along the median."

"Wait a second. Stop for a sec." Jimmy fiddled with the dome light, making sure it wouldn't come on when he opened the door. Then he slowly clicked open the door, holding his breath until he was sure he'd made the correct adjustment. "I'm coming around to walk alongside, holding your hand and walking beside the rocks on the shoulder of the road as you drive. It's so dark out that I can see hardly anything beyond the end of the hood…so I know they can't see us."

"Oh, Jimmy," Dana moaned.

But it worked. The shadowy men cursed and sweated in the darkness, setting up their blockade across the junction, oblivious to the boy walking alongside the idling automobile and tightly holding the hand of the girl at the steering wheel, passing just yards beyond the tall hood of their monster truck.

Soon Dana and Jimmy were around the next rock corner and the hairpin curve of the road. She turned her headlights on again while he ran around to reclaim his seat.

"Whew!" breathed Jimmy, dropping heavily into the car. "Talk about crapping in the columbine—I was afraid those guys would hear my heart pounding."

Dana gave his knee a couple of quick pats, comforting him and sharing, "I was afraid they'd heard us when I got into that gravel at the edge. Gosh! That was so loud!" She eased down on the accelerator, and the car picked up speed. "Who are they anyway? Are they part of Daniel's—the Lord's Army?" She was sitting straight up now, at attention in her seat and gripping the wheel hard, concentrating on the twin spots of light that occasionally disappeared over the road's shoulder and into the void that ended many yards below in the cold, cold waters of the creek that flowed alongside the road. "Do you suppose Daniel's men are all throughout these mountains?"

"Naw, I bet they're from out of Townsend and around there. Or maybe from Knoxville and Maryville if they've heard about the Reverend Davis and his army. That was a lot of men in one spot,

though…and looking like they were setting up camp for a long stay."
He was rubbing his chin again. "Maybe they're making ready to protect their homes like they had to do before."

"Daniel's been here before?"

Jimmy chuckled. "No, see, back during Civil War times—eighteen sixty-two or sixty-three—the rebels from North Carolina would
come over and steal produce and harass these folks—I mean, not
these folks but their ancestors. See, like in West Virginia, these folks
were Northern sympathizers, so they hid their guns and food as
best they could, awaiting the Yankee troops that were supposed to
be coming over from Knoxville. One time the rebs came over the
mountain pass, and somebody had stuck a flagpole in the ground up
there…and the American flag was flying on it, the Stars and Stripes.
The Confederate soldiers went to tear it down but their officer
stopped them, saying something about the flag once being the flag
for all of us and would someday be our united flag again. So they left
it unmolested…and the men from around the mountains here let
them pass unmolested. See, there were enough rifles trained on the
Confederates from behind about every tree in these hills that they'd
have been sliced to pieces in minutes. The officer maybe knew that,
too, and saved all his men's lives. And maybe he meant it; lots of those
men on both sides really didn't have a dog in that fight anyway."

Dana was nodding, still sitting leaned forward and concentrating
on the narrow lane ahead. "Another rainy weekend in Maryville, I
suppose."

"Fifth grade Tennessee history. Didn't you have that out around
Nashville?"

Dana sniffed. "I must have been sick on the day they taught that."

Jimmy swiveled in his seat, ready to tell her another amazing
tale about the origin of road they were now following when the roar
of gunfire rolled over them. "Slow down! Slow down! Dana, slow
down!" he yelled, leaning through his window. "Hey! I think they're
having a battle or something back there at the Y!"

She coasted to a stop then set the emergency brake and lowered
her own window, trying to hear all what Jimmy was hearing. "Damn!

Those *are* a lot of guns going off! What do you think's happening back there?"

He twisted back to the front. *Whew!* "I think we were only minutes ahead of the Lord's Army, and they ran into those fellows setting up shop back there. Gosh, I'd loved to have seen that!"

"Well, I think I can turn around up ahead," Dana volunteered.

"No! No, no, I don't think, ah, we'll have time to wait for the outcome of that."

"Gotcha!" she announced.

Jimmy heard her snigger. "Oh, for when we just met? When those guys…?" He nose-laughed. "Yeah, you got me all right. But seriously, you know, if Daniel blasts them outta there, he'll know we didn't go by that way. And then he'll know to come on up to the cove after us."

"That guy hates you that much? Hey!" Dana made her sound of sudden insight. "So how do we get back out of here? There's only this one road, and if Daniel knows—"

"There's more roads out. Don't worry. There's a primitive road out to the north, and then there's the road out by Parson Branch to the south. Since the first is a bit of an axle buster, I suggest we go out down around Cable Mill and out that way to Calderwood—you know, Chilhowee Lake—and then out by the Dragon to 411."

"Chilhowee Lake? I know all about Chilhowee Lake," Dana declared. The area was well known for its many roadside scenic overlooks—places of passion for hot-blooded teenagers. "You know, maybe we've seen each other out there before," she teased, pretty certain he'd had few past encounters with girls in any setting. "Maybe on occasion while we were watching the submarine races, huh, Jimmy? No heads above the seats and the car's windows all fogged up—that kind of thing? Or skinny-dipping in the moonlight maybe?" Her teasing worked but not for the reason she imagined.

"You've…you've been there a lot? You've been there before?" Jimmy's questions came unbidden and naked, the words slipping out before he could stifle the emotion clinging to them. He felt suddenly open, bared with his ears reddening. *Now this is silly. Why am I getting all jealous about a girl—who I've just met—going parking down at the lake?* He faced the front and waited, believing that an inspired response surely would come to him by the time they'd cleared the next curve. *I don't know why...but I am!*

Dana felt the silence...and enjoyed it. She heard what hadn't been said, and it meant he cared. *But I hurt his feelings.* There had been few people in her life who had cared about her without wanting something in return. *That's so cute. But mean. He's just a kid.* She'd explain. "Jimmy, I'm just teasing you." *Whoa, that's a tight curve in the road! Girl, you'd better keep your mind on where you're driving.* "I just heard about the lake from some people I know in high school. I've never been there. OK? I haven't been parking with a boy..."

Jimmy felt his ears reheating. *Dang! She knows!* For once in his life, he wouldn't know what next to say, no matter how many curves were ahead. He was very thankful for the dark.

"...maybe," she added. *This is too good.*

Now, mercifully, they crested the big hill that sloped down into Cades Cove. Normally and in daylight, the lane ahead would be packed with tourist cars crawling along, joining the queue and circling around Loop Road, stopping here and there to allow riders to dismount and explore around the few log cabins and frame houses left there by the National Park Service as representatives of the early settlers' abodes. *And bear jams!* Jimmy hated traveling the circuit when the tourists would spot a mooching bear alongside the drive; then the cars would back up for miles. But tonight there wasn't another vehicle in sight. *And no lights anywhere.* Jimmy had wondered several times whether some people would try to ride out the plague in the park, staying in camps, eating their rations, and using their bottled propane until the all-clear signal was sounded. Then he saw the padlocked drawbar ahead, crossing over the entire road, brightly reflecting its Day-Glo coloring and warning all approaching vehicles to go no farther.

"Road closed here. Park closed." Dana read aloud from the rectangular sign that hung from the bar. "Jimmy, I don't think I can get around that gate."

"Hold on. There's a trick to this. Open the trunk and wait here." Jimmy pushed open his door with his foot and hopped from his seat.

In the next minute, he returned carrying the jack handle he knew would be under the spare tire. "This'll just take a minute," he assured her. "Keep your lights on where they are."

Using the sharp end of the jack handle, some rope he'd found in the trunk, and a few handy rocks, Jimmy knelt at the far side of the asphalt and began to ratchet up the post there, raising up the steel barrier bar and its chain and padlock along with it. He pulled the post from its hole and carried it around in front of the car, pulling the crossbar parallel to the road. "Now drive up far enough so this thing clears," he yelled. "OK?"

In another minute he had replaced the post in its hole and was tumbling back into his seat. "Whew! All done," he breathed.

"Now how did you know about that?"

"One summer we needed a long pole to make a dam in the picnic area over there. So we traded out one of the parking-lot piers for that post—and it was a lot shorter. Didn't hurt anything, you know. This is the first time I've ever seen this gate closed anyway, so I doubt the rangers even knew about it."

"So now we know," Dana murmured.

"Now we know," Jimmy seconded her.

They followed Loop Road about halfway around its eleven-mile circuit before turning off the asphalt onto the rougher, rock-covered road that paralleled Parson Branch. The early-morning sky was beginning to lighten; the sun would soon make its appearance.

Jimmy yawned and stretched. "I heard the preacher who used to live around here died with his family from drinking the water," he said. "Typhoid, I think."

"Lovely," Dana replied. "Another wet weekend in Maryville?"

"Naw, my grandmother used to live around here. She never liked it here, so she left the first chance she got and moved to the south end of the county to live with relatives. But the parson and his family died way before her time; she was just telling me about it."

More minutes passed, and the road began to rise ahead; the sun now lit the very tops of the trees on the mountain's heights. "How could your grandmother stand to leave such a beautiful place?" Dana asked, thinking about the people who once lived in the cove.

"Well, if you had to work from dawn to dusk just to live—and you know, all the folks who lived around here weren't people you'd necessarily feel comfortable with today, especially around here in Chestnut Flats—you might not see the beauty of the place like you do now. And back then the fields were cleared, and there weren't all these trees around, so it looked quite a bit different, more like the hollows and knobs you see today throughout Sevierville and Wears Valley." Jimmy was pointing at the road ahead. "You'd better get some speed up now, or the car's not gonna be able to climb the hill. Watch out for the loose gravel."

Dana increase her speed, barely reaching the top of the hill before the rocks beneath her tires slipped and slowed the car's progress to a crawl. "Ah, made it!" she chortled, celebrating their small victory.

"You might want to hold that for now," he cautioned. "The next grade is a bit steeper and was eroded real bad when I was here last. I just hope the road's good enough for us to make it to 129 without busting a spring or snapping an axle." He glanced quickly in Dana's direction. "But I know we will...make it, I mean." He was sitting at attention and well forward in his seat now, just like Dana. "It just might be a mite touchy, that's all."

An hour later the sun was high in the east, and the scraped red clay of Parson Branch Road came to an end. The US 129 sign marked the amazingly wide and impossibly smooth pavement that ran in both directions before them. "Right?" Dana asked through clenched teeth.

"Yeah," Jimmy replied. "Go to the right."

The Mustang creaked forward through the turn. "A mite touchy, you said," Dana growled. "You know, I can't believe you let me drive up that cow path! My friggin' car's never going to be the same. And how many miles was that? Twenty? Twenty-five?"

"Eight."

"Eight? No way!" she shouted.

"Way," Jimmy muttered, looking out his side window.

"Damn! Then that's gotta be the worst road I've ever traveled on. I think I bruised my kidneys."

"Actually, if we'd gone out by the north way...Never mind." He caught the murderous look Dana sent his way. "Actually that was a real nice piece of driving there. Real nice. The car will sound better too...after a while." They drove the next twisted mile in mutual silence.

"If you really have to pee," Jimmy advised, continuing the conversation by voicing his latest thought, "you probably should stop well off the pavement here. People tend to treat this stretch of road like a racetrack—'Tail of the Dragon,' I think they call it. It's a big deal to the motorcyclists who ride it." He chanced a sideways examination of Dana; her face was a shade less pink now. "But we still lose a lot of riders here every year. It's a long way to the bottom over there toward the lake. And of course there ain't any shoulders to the road, and it's straight down."

"So this is Chilhowee Lake?" she asked.

Her kidneys might have healed. "Yeah...and we could go swimming if you'd like," he added, wiggling his eyebrows at her.

Dana smiled. "Yeah, you wish."

Jimmy smiled too—like he really was making a joke. *Dang!*

"So where now?"

"Well"—he shifted in his seat, pulling at the tightness in the straddle of his jeans—"just stay on this road and follow it around. We should run into 411 or see a sign showing the way."

***

Along the next series of deeply sloped and sculpted curves, the tall weeds thinned, and Jimmy searched the lake for boaters and the pull-offs for campers. He saw no one; they were alone on the lake. A big house would soon be coming into sight on the right;

he remembered it because it was built so tall and narrow to give its owners a consistently great view of the lake. They swept around the broad curve, but there was no mansion where he'd expected it to be. *What the heck?* There was only the burned pile of rubble, albeit a gigantic pile of rubble, to attest to the grandeur that once had been there. "Dana, the big ol' house that used to be there is burned to the ground."

She made no reply, and they drove on. By the time they saw the first road sign announcing their approach to 411, they had passed maybe twenty or more burned-down homes.

"Now what do you think it's been like around here?" Jimmy wondered aloud. "I feel like I've been away forever."

"Well," Dana offered, "judging from what we've passed, I'd say there's been a lot of fighting and stealing. There's probably gangs just like Daniel's all around now, except his gang is bigger than most. There's probably a lot of mean people we'd be uncomfortable with around here too. But I'm expecting there are some good people banded together too...somewhere. We've just got to find them."

"Wise lady. Then I expect we'd better go in on the back streets," he suggested. They were coming up to Old Niles Ferry Road now, and Jimmy was beginning to recognize landmarks. "Turn right. There's a restaurant up Niles Ferry that's a little less public than the ones on 411. My folks know the people who run it, so we'd better start looking for those good people."

"Good idea," Dana agreed, making a wide turn onto the well-paved two-lane road. "It might be a good idea if you drove now, just in case. You'll know the way better around here." She made a waving motion to her front. "We can change seats at the restaurant. Gosh, I'm starved!"

Twenty minutes later, Jimmy pointed her into a parking lot along the road. The large, white building at its center sported a racing motif, complete with finish-line flags arrayed along its roof and victory-circle banners hanging from the tall covering over the fuel pump islands to the side. "Was this once a gas station?" Dana asked.

"Yeah! How'd you know?"

"Just a guess." She pulled under the island covering where fuel pumps once stood. "Too bad they don't still have the tanks and pumps," she said, putting the car into park and cutting off the engine. "We're getting on the lean side for gas." She swung open the door then twisted to her side and pushed up from the seat. Then, standing beside the car and realizing Jimmy had yet to emerge, she bent down and looked back inside. He returned her stare, his head tilted at a rather strange angle. He was thinking.

"They do," he said.

"They do what?"

"They do still have the tanks underneath the ground. When they converted the gas station, it was going to cost too much to pull out the tanks, and with the EPA testing and hauling of dirt, it was really going to cost way too much. So they just left the tanks and decided to use them. They'd buy leftover gas from the gypsy truckers then let friends and family fill their cars with...an electric pump." Jimmy's voice fell with his disappointment. "An electric pump. Just when I was about to say things were looking better—with a place to get some more gas—I remembered we'll have to have an electric pump for the gas. Heck!"

"Well, couldn't we just siphon it up?" Dana suggested. "I heard guys in school talk about siphoning gas all the time—taking gas from cars. I could get a real long hose, and we could drop it down the hole that...What?" Jimmy had turned away, his hand covering his mouth. *I think he's giggling.*

His eyes glistened when he finally looked back. "Whew! Thanks, I needed that."

"Well, couldn't we?" Her face was rosy with approaching anger.

"You'd have to be able to suck a tennis ball through a garden hose to be able to pull gas up from fifteen or so feet underneath the ground."

"Oh." Dana sat back down in the car. "That *is* disappointing." She could understood the image that probably had flashed through his mind, and she giggled too.

"Yeah," Jimmy agreed, pushing his door fully open, "very disappointing. But maybe we'll find an old mechanical pump somewhere.

There's all kinds of antique stores around here. We might have to go back to the old ways to make do for a while, you know?"

Making do, using old ways, and banding together with the good people around here—that all sounded encouraging to Dana, and distracting. She hadn't thought about her mother for at least an hour or two. "Yeah—making do and planning for the future. Thanks, Jimmy. I needed that." She stood again. "Now let's go see about that food." She waited for Jimmy and took his hand as they walked around the side, toward the front of the building. With no cars at all in the lot, and no one moving about, neither of them really expected to find the doors open and the place in operation.

And they weren't and it wasn't. "Locked tight," Dana declared as she rattled the front doors. "I'm surprised no one has broken the window glass, you know, trying to get in."

Jimmy pointed at the rocks scattered about on the pavement. "I bet a lot of kids passing have tried but didn't have big enough rocks. That's Plexiglas, I think. And this road is a ways off the main road in from the south, 411, and maybe not many people have come by this way."

She nodded. "It's nice that it's not burned and everything, like all those houses along the way. Maybe things will be better the closer we get to town. Let's go around back and see if we can pry that door open."

Jimmy laughed and trotted after her. "Introduce you to a tire iron, and you go crazy. 'Give me a place to stand, and with a lever, I will move the whole world.' Who said that? Archimedes?"

"Like I'd know. But it doesn't matter anyway. Look." She pointed at the gaping back door, pried loose from its frame and hanging by its hinges. "Looks like another ol' Archimedes beat us here. Damn!"

But they cautiously entered anyway and searched around inside—and found nothing. The walk-in cooler was totally empty, its door left open. The freezers also had been left open and so clean that they looked swept. "They even took the smells," Jimmy groused.

"Ah, well," consoled Dana, "we still got our beans and pickles. Race you back to the car!"

With a sizable head start, she was well ahead of Jimmy when she rounded the corner of the building...but then she came to an abrupt halt, almost sliding to a stop. A half dozen kids were flitting around the Mustang, jumping from its opened trunk, rummaging in the backseat, all seemingly laden with purloined items clutched tight in grubby hands.

"Hey! Hey!" she screamed. "What the hell are you doing?"

All motion instantly ceased and six pairs of eyes fixed on Dana. Six children then slipped from inside and behind the car, studying her as they assembled, judging the strength and weaponry of this loud woman. And they obviously felt comfortable with what they saw as they casually arrayed themselves in a loose semicircle to await her approach.

"Whatcha gonna do about it, lady? You ain't even packin'," the tallest of the four boys challenged. He slid his knife from his pocket and expertly thumbed out its blade using only one hand. His other hand was occupied in securing the two large jars of canned beans against his side.

"Yeah, whatcha gonna do about it, lady?" chimed in a second child, a smallish girl standing beside the boy, her skinny arms filled with blankets and clothing...and the Mauser rifle.

Jimmy strode from the cover of the building, cocking the thirty-eight. "I'm gonna shoot your scrawny butts off. How 'bout that?" he yelled.

Instant commotion followed; kids went in all directions. The little girl dropped the rifle—that was Jimmy's prime concern—but managed to dash away with the blankets and clothes. The other children also skirted the car and escaped with their pilfered goods, streaking barefooted across the road and through the honeysuckles on the far side...and amazingly dropping only one pint jar of pickles to the pavement on their way. Dana and Jimmy watched them go.

"Man! Have you ever seen anything like that?" he marveled, walking to the rear of the car. "At least they left the car keys here hanging from the trunk." He slammed the lid and pulled the keys from the lock then stooped to retrieve his rifle.

Dana shook her head. "I...I don't think any one of those kids was over nine years old. Where do you suppose they live?"

"Well, I'd expect in those old houses over there," he replied, again scratching his chin. "This is still kinda out in the country, so they might belong to any one of these ol' farms here." He turned completely in place, looking around. "You know what seems funny? I believe they're about the only real kids I've seen in days now. On their own, I mean—not like the ones being held by Daniel at the schoolhouse. Did you see any kids in Gatlinburg?"

Dana thought for a moment. "No, I didn't see any. And I didn't think to ask Vera about any children thereabouts."

"With the plague taking the old ones first, I'd have guessed these kids' parents would've been young enough to last out the disease. But you know, like I said, I'm not seeing all that many people any-more who look much older than us—or you anyway."

Dana popped him on the arm. "Thanks, jerk. Make me feel like an old woman or something."

"Just sayin'." Jimmy grinned, rubbing his bruised biceps. "I can't imagine what's happening with the kids. Maybe these guys are on their own now, mother and father both sickened and dead, and they're the ones just making do. But they seem to be doing OK; they looked healthy. I'd rather they'd just asked, though, and we'd have shared our stuff, but—"

Bang! A bullet whistled by Jimmy's ear, coming from the honey-suckle across the road and ricocheting off the building. "Get in the car!" he yelled, firing a shot from his pistol in the general direction of the hedge but purposely aiming high. "Those little turds got guns!" He threw the Mauser into the back and dropped into the driver's seat, starting the car while Dana circled to the passenger side. Off they went, the car's doors slamming as he accelerated, through the pump islands and out the exit farthest from the honeysuckle hedge to skid sideways onto the road. Suddenly Jimmy felt much less con-cern for the children's continued welfare. "Those brats are gonna do OK, as long as they don't get too brave and shoot at the wrong people."

***

At the next large intersection, about two miles farther on, Jimmy took the bisecting road over to 411. "I've changed my mind, like you ladies sometimes do," he explained, talking loud to be heard over the rushing wind. Dana was positioning herself, searching the backseat to determine what the kids hadn't taken, and was blocking his rear-view mirror. "I think we'll do better if we have more road under us in case we have to do some, you know, dodging. Niles Ferry's only two lanes, and we're liable to meet more of those armed crumb crunchers. And the houses are real close to the road, and well, we'd be safer with four lanes." He paused for effect...and breath. Dana was about halfway through the gap between the seats, and her hip was against his shoulder, squishing him against his door. "Uhhh! Besides, there's a—are you ready for this? Dana? You're squeezing me! There's a brand-new Megamart right over the hill!"

She plopped back onto the front passenger seat and waited. He'd been talking, and there seemed to be more to be said. He glanced over once—twice—as if *he* were expecting a response from *her. Or he's making fun of me again.* "So?" she asked.

"You know, women, shopping, new Megamart...celebration time? Get it? Um...never mind."

They crested the hill. The unlit traffic light straight ahead marked Route 411, the broad avenue that ran along the top of the next ridge that was hidden now by the buildings ranged along its curbs. At the Megamart access road, off to the right before the intersection, Jimmy turned in, keeping to the center of the lane to slowly approach the store's parking lot, and stretching high in his seat to scan over the rise to his right. "Gotta be careful. You never know what we'll find anymore." The expansive store was there like he expected, its glass intact and its facade seemingly unburned.

But to the left of the lane, the filling station there was now completely gone, with nothing having taken its place—or better stated, less than nothing; there was only a gigantic crater remaining, its sides charred and blackened.

Jimmy whistled in amazement. "Hey, look over there. See that big ol' hole? This was actually once a little hill, and the gas station was on top. Now there's just this hole between here and 411—and scorched weeds." He whistled again. "I bet when the gas ran out, somebody tried to get at the remains that the pumps couldn't bring up. And I bet some idiot dropped a cigarette—no, I bet somebody tried to see down inside the tanks and dropped a match down one of those pipes where the tanker trucks unloaded. And...*kapow!* I bet the guy never even had the time to regret his decision. Those vapors are more explosive, you know, than the liquid fuel."

"Then I'd say it definitely was quick," Dana concluded, apparently much less impressed with the sight.

Jimmy shook his head and steered the car into the enormous parking lot toward the long, low building at the rear. "Dang." His standard exclamation was soft and halfhearted; he was clearly discouraged with this sight. "It's all dark inside."

"What?" Dana leaned forward in her seat and squinted as if to better examine the store's shadowed interior. "Sure it's dark, but we didn't really expect the electricity to be on—did we? But see, the cars are closer to the store here. Maybe some people are still inside in the dark."

"Well, I guess I'd hoped TVA power would stay on longer closer into town, but I suppose there's an end to hydroelectric power too. Too many little regulators and gizmos for anything to run on its own for too long, even if the water is still flowing by." He took a big breath. "I'd just hoped things would have stayed together better here in Maryville, better than where we came from."

"Maybe they are, and things will look better closer to your house."

"Yeah, maybe."

Jimmy slowly steered down the marked lane, still obeying the directional arrows painted on the pavement. "Jimmy," Dana said, "those cars all look to be empty, and some have their windows broken out...and most have their gas caps off. I'd say they were abandoned and their gas maybe taken later, if there was any to take in the first place." She pointed over her shoulder with her thumb. "At least they didn't use a match to see into the cars' tanks. Hah!"

Jimmy laughed too. "Give 'em time. Some fool eventually will do it. Hey, look at the bottom of that car. There. See that drip? There's a hole poked in the gas tank toward the bottom, I bet. That's probably the more professional way of getting at the gas than trying to siphon it."

"Yeah, you'll have to remember that…the next time you're about to strike a match."

He rounded the corner, still following the lines in the parking lot, and slowly braked to a squeaking halt. *Brakes don't sound too good. Dana's car might not be healing too well after all.* They had stopped in front of the wide bank of plate-glass entrance doors—intact but still closed tight.

"What now, Dana the Discoverer?" he asked, staring past her, trying to see through the glass doors.

"I'm not going in unless you go with me."

"We can do that, but I don't think we should leave the car unguarded out here. There might be some more crumb crunchers hiding out around the sides of the store. Or hiding out in those weeds in the field." Jimmy bumped his side mirror to and fro, watching for any movement in the open area beyond the garden shop. "I don't see anybody…but who knows?"

Dana still watched the storefront. It was getting late in the day, and the sun, now lower in the west, reflected its rays back at her from the doors' glass. "Crap! Even if they had the lights on in there, I still couldn't see inside. And we can't just sit here…"

One of the doors shook in its frame, clicked and slowly opened inward. A Megamart-uniformed boy about Jimmy's age edged through the opening to stand half in, half out of the doorway. He stared back at her, holding his shotgun high to make sure they were seeing it. "What do you want?" he shouted to the standing car.

Simple enough question. "What do you have?" Dana shouted back. "Maybe stuff to trade?"

The boy now stepped completely through the gap, and another shotgun followed, emerging from the darkness to reveal its holder as being a girl about Dana's age. She also sported a Megamart uniform. Then another couple of boys, maybe in their late teens, pushed out through the doorway. They all carried long guns.

Jimmy slipped his left foot onto the brake, holding his right foot slightly above the accelerator. He was clearly anxious now, his eyes flicking ahead and to his mirrors, waiting for the sudden appearances of more Megamart inhabitants.

The older boys took up positions on either side of the doorway while the girl centered herself; she obviously was going to do the talking. "We don't have any drugs," she announced, "except for some aspirin and stuff like that. No food that we can share; that all went in the first few days. We got paper products and toys and some clothes."

"How about camping gear?" Dana asked. "Do you have sleeping bags or camouflaged clothing? Maybe a Coleman stove?"

The girl shook her head. "No, no. When the plague came, people just come rushing in here, grabbing and taking. We got these guns and stayed in the back. After a while we got the people outside again and locked the doors, and the cops came. But by then almost everything was gone. Now, the cops don't even come by. Other than that…bedsheets!" she added, as in afterthought. "We got some fabrics we can trade you for. What do you guys got?"

Jimmy kept his feet on both the brake and the accelerator, still nervously surveying ahead and behind for any approaching people, while Dana swung her door fully open so as to better talk with the girl. She chose to ignore the girl's question by asking more of her own. "Was it just you guys who held off the looters? Weren't there any grown men here trying to take your stuff? How come they didn't just break out your doors?"

The girl backed up and held her shotgun higher. "Why do you need to know all that? There's more of us inside, for your information. Lots more. We can take care of ourselves. And we got lots of guns and lots of ammunition."

"You got ammunition?" Jimmy asked, leaning forward and yelling from behind Dana. That subject got his attention. He was concerned that his small store of bullets would be exhausted soon. "Do you have eight millimeter, like for a Mauser? Or seven point six five?"

The girl looked questioningly over to one of the boys to her side. She got a cocked-head response from him; he didn't know. "Yeah, yeah," she asserted anyway. "We got all kinds of pistol bullets inside."

Jimmy guessed then that they probably had only ammunition for the shotguns they were holding, the store having been cleaned out in the initial onslaught by panicked men. *That's what I'd have gotten if I'd been here. Ammunition. As much as I could have carried. Now that I know.* He went back to watching for ambushes from the store's sides.

"So what do you guys have to trade?" the girl asked again. She had stepped forward, coming to the center of the sidewalk so she could talk and hear better.

Dana rose from her seat to stand in the open doorway of the car, her arm on the doorframe. "We've got quite a bit of money to spend—"

"Can't use it," the girl cut her off. "What else do you got to trade? Do you want to sell the car?"

From behind, Dana heard Jimmy click off the shotgun's safety; he apparently had retrieved his twelve-gauge from the backseat, anticipating just such interest. "Absolutely not for sale—not the car, not my gas," she answered, keeping her face stony and her eyes fixed on the eyes of the other girl. Seconds rolled by with the two women staring at each other.

The Megamart girl broke the silence. "Doesn't hurt to ask, does it?" She gave a tight smile and raised the butt of her shotgun to her hip, its muzzle pointed to the sky. "So it looks like you guys really don't got anything to trade with us. That about the truth of it?"

Dana liked the girl's manner, deciding to return her straightforwardness. "If you don't have a need for paper money, then no, I don't suppose we've got anything you'd want."

The girl nodded, still smiling, and turned to the boys on both sides. They shrugged in reply and raised their guns skyward, still keeping the vast parking lot under surveillance. "So I guess we can only gossip then and watch the sun set."

Dana laughed. "I'd kind of guessed you guys are in about the same fix we are...except this is home for you."

"Megamart? Not hardly."

"Oh, I'd just thought with the uniform and all that you worked here."

The girl laughed this time. "Well, we do, but this ain't home. I live over there." She indicated with her shotgun barrel the direction of the development across 411, beyond the blackened hole of the former gas station. "I lived there with my father and mother until they took sick. Then, when I couldn't stand it anymore, and they were past caring for, I walked back over in the night and slipped back in. Mike and Tim were already here, and Jody came back later. I'm Sandra." The boys nodded as Sandra introduced them, pointing to them with a raise of her chin. "Tim found the keys, and we've started locking the doors."

"I'm not sure those glass doors will withstand a fifty-caliber," Jimmy opined from behind Dana. The girl and boys leaned down to look in at him, still seated at the steering wheel.

"I dunno," Sandra said. "That glass is real thick, definitely break resistant."

"Yeah, it looks it, but if you have a big ol' military truck back up against these pylons here at the front and just blast away, I don't think they'll stand up to that. 'Course the alternative is to just keep the doors open, and then even the halfway honest folks would be coming in and looking around. Maybe you're better off doing just what you're doing," Jimmy conceded.

"So tell me..." Dana persisted. "What's it been like around here, and how did you guys manage to hold out?"

"Well, it was like this," Sandra began, taking another step closer to the car. "When people got to hearing more about the plague, and the hospital filled up, and people were being found dead all over the place, a lot of folks got all panicky and decided the last days were here. So about every store was mobbed, and people stopped even trying to pay for the stuff they took. I was at my register when people started running out the door with their stuff. We didn't have guards, and the police outside just gave up and came inside to help themselves too. We really didn't have that many guns, but those were being snatched up when the manager called me and Jody to help her haul what was saved into the office with her. The pharmacy here already had given lots of their pain-type drugs—you know, like morphine and prescription stuff—to the cops for the hospital and doctors, so they were mostly closed already." Sandra lowered herself to sit on the sidewalk. "The manager then said there was nothing she could do, so she told all us to go on home. So I did."

"You just walked home?" This question came from behind Dana, from Jimmy. He now shifted the car to park and turned off the ignition. "I couldn't hear," he explained.

"So you guys aren't from around here?" asked Sandra.

"Well, he is." Dana indicated Jimmy with her thumb pointed over her shoulder. "I'm from Sevierville, but Jimmy lives here. He was visiting his relatives in Sevier County when the sickness came. Now he's trying to get home to check on his folks."

Sandra rocked to her side to better see Jimmy. "I think I've seen you before, but you don't go to Friendsville, do you?"

"No, I'll be going to Maryville High this year," he answered, adding, "That's if there's gonna be high school this year." Sandra and the standing boys all nodded in sad agreement, their thoughts momentarily turned inward, their despondency clearly evident in the hard, set lines of their lips and downcast eyes. These teenagers had become adults overnight, aging decades in mere days.

"So where do you go to school?" Jimmy asked, cutting short the depressive silence. His natural ebullience rarely allowed him to ponder long on humorless, existential topics. His mother said he had a positive outlook; his dad said he was silly. And right now Jimmy felt that silliness was the only thing that was going to get them through these times.

Sandra looked up from her cross-legged position on the sidewalk. "Friendsville," she said again. "That's why...never mind."

The boys added their "me toos" and Dana chuckled. *He's done it again.*

"Well, you just looked kind of familiar to me. So you were saying you just went home?" Jimmy was still very interested in what had transpired in his hometown during his absence. "What about you guys?" he asked the boys.

Jody, the first boy through the door, spoke up. "After Sandra and most of the others cleared out, Mrs. Thomas—she was the manager—and me grabbed up these guns and ammunition and went back to the stockroom and hid out atop the freezer. You'd just have to know the place was there because there ain't regular steps going up there. Anyway, when it got dark and the commotion died down and Mrs. Thomas cut off most of the lights at the back, we snuck down and gathered up most anything that was left—not broken and still left. People just broke a lot of things like plates and stuff, you know. And it was bad down here on the floor—shelves turned over, stuff thrown around in the grocery part—it was bad. Some of the gondolas, like the beer display, were completely pulled down. You know, I don't think there was a six pack left in the store by nightfall. Shows you what some people were thinking."

"Yeah, and when I came back in the morning"—this was Mike, one of the older teenage boys, breaking in with his story—"there were cars crashed into each other all over the parking lot. Seems some folks just got real mad and T-boned some other folks who got in their way. The cops were here—some cops were here—and they did what they could. One feller shot another feller because he got in front of him in the line over at the gas station. The cops couldn't do nothing, and somebody shot somebody else. It was getting real nasty. So I come on back over here to the store, and some people were still going in and out here, carrying stuff out, you know?"

"Well, how did you happen to come back over here, Mike?" asked Dana. "Didn't you have parents who wanted you to stay home?"

"Oh, he lives with his brother in some apartments over there," Sandra answered for him, pointing to the right down 411. "His brother works for TVA, and he come by here with some men to check on him and told him to stay put until he come back. But he hasn't come back yet. That's why we were watching out front and thought maybe you were them. But you weren't." She glanced over to Mike, where he stood, still keeping his intermittent surveillance off to the west. "But his brother kept the power going until just a day or so ago. Right, Mike?"

"Yeah, he did, so he should be coming by here soon."

"Has there been a lot of traffic by here?" Jimmy asked.

Sandra tapped the side of her nose as she thought. "No, not much anymore. About nine or ten days ago—it's hard to think now—there were a lot of cars around here. So many that 411 was blocked up over there. Then the police cleared most of them off to the sides, and cars began to move again. People were going everywhere, trying to find stuff before it was all gone. And then traffic died down with people trying to stay at home. My mom and dad began to get real bad then, and our phone didn't work, so I walked over here to the cop who was trying to direct traffic. He radioed in for me and said the hospital would send an ambulance...but they didn't." Sandra was talking to her lap now. "Then Dad died, and Mom was out of her head. She was seeing God and saying crazy stuff about heaven and all. And then she died; she died happy. Sicker than a dog she was—but happy."

"Sounds like Homer," Jimmy mumbled. "Just like my relative who died up in Sevier County," he said again but louder. "Homer was saying something about understanding or seeing everything, and then he died later—probably happy."

"Well," Dana added, "I'd imagine just not being sick anymore and pooping all over and hurting—that'd make most anybody happy, I guess."

"No, no, I think there's a lot more going on here," he declared, rubbing his chin again in thought. "There's a purpose to this, but I can't figure it out. Homer was trying to tell me, but sometimes words alone don't carry all the meaning. Maybe like a test or trial or something."

"Well, if God was just messing with us, I'd be mighty pissed with him," Dana concluded, turning to face him.

On the sidewalk Sandra shifted to a kneeling position. "Anyway, my mom and dad never got an ambulance, and when I went back to find the cop, he wasn't anywhere around. And there were carloads of creepy-looking guys going around then. I scooted back over here in the dark, and I've been here ever since."

"Same here," Tim spoke up. "I live with my father, and when he left to get some food and gas, he never came back. When somebody touched off the filling station over there"—he indicated the gas station with a dip of his head—"I walked over to see the sight. It was amazing! I guess you folks didn't see that, did you?

Dana and Jimmy replied in unison, "No."

"It was…amazing," Tim continued. "It was about dark, and like Mike said, there'd been a lot of men shooting each other over stuff like gas and food, so we'd just stayed inside. We have a house back down that way on Niles Ferry, so when the power went off, we could open our windows for air and stuff. And then my father left…" Tim's voice trailed off as he stared out toward 411.

"The gas station exploded?" Dana prompted.

"Oh, yeah. Oh, yeah," he said. "There wasn't hardly any gas left at the stations around here, and people were trying to lift gas with little electric pumps—you know what I mean? Those little pumps you can power with your cigarette lighter in your car?"

Jimmy didn't, but the thought put a smile on his face. *Maybe I could find one of those?*

"Anyway," Tim continued, "I'd come out onto our porch and was facing this way, and the most god-awful blast came from over the way. And then the sky lit up, and horns went off—it was amazing. I put on my shoes and locked the door and came on over here. I came around the back and around the side, so I didn't see all the wreckage until I cleared the building. When I was in front of the doors here, Jody came out and got me, and like Sandra, I've been here ever since. See over there?" Tim was pointing at the side of the parking lot closest to the crater. "There were cars over there, probably run out of gas already, but they were incinerated. And across the road, those buildings burned down."

"Yeah, and a lot fewer people came around after that," Sandra noted. "Jody had the keys, and we started locking the doors since then."

"See any gangs of men coming by?" Dana asked. "We saw a bunch of men up at the Y and thought maybe they were from Maryville."

Sandra got to her feet, standing and bending with her hands on her hips, loosening up. "They might have been from here. I worried about that, you know, about what might happen with the law breaking down and a lot of men running around with guns and liquor, but really, not much has happened in the last day or two around here. See those cars over there, the ones you passed coming in? There are dead people in there, decaying and smelling up the place. When the wind is right, you can't stand right here—way too stinky. And Mike and Tim and Jody dragged a lot of dead people off to the side there and just rolled them down the hill. So you can imagine that in daylight it looks pretty bad off in that direction too. I'm surprised you didn't see all the buzzards and bodies. It's real nasty looking. Until we started locking the doors, we had a couple dead persons in grocery carts just inside the door. It was hard on us too, but I guess it's been effective; people have about stopped coming around now, except for you guys."

"And all these people died from the plague?" Dana was leaning forward from her seat, looking both ways, up and down the sidewalk, as if she were looking for another rotting corpse or two just lying about.

"No, no. Most of the dead folks we've seen here died because somebody killed them—shot 'em or beat their heads in. When there was stuff here to fight over, people fought over it. But those folks out in the cars maybe all died from the disease; we didn't really look. They were probably real sick when they left their houses, and this was as far as they got—just died in their cars. We saw some people out here stealing their gas too. They didn't take the cars, so the people inside must have been quite ripe by then." Sandra studied the subject cars as she talked, staring over the Mustang's roof. "Now we've had some older Megamart people who worked here—like us—who...passed away. The boys here wheeled them over to the hillside…and left them there. Lavonne passed just yesterday."

"How old was Lavonne?" Jimmy asked.

"Twenty-something, I guess. Twenty-something, Jody?"

Jody nodded. "I'd say something like that."

"And there's nobody older than you guys now?" Jimmy continued.

The Megamart group looked from one to another. "Guess not," Jody surmised, a touch of sad realization in his voice.

"Well, you've got some younger kids over that direction"—Jimmy pointed back the way they had come—"who'll be glad to come over and make friends with you."

The boys chuckled. "That's why we're keeping watch," Mike said. "Those little assholes hide out around the sides and behind the cars and take potshots at us. I don't know where they're getting the ammo, but I'm just damn glad they can't aim worth crap."

Jimmy twiddled with the rearview mirror again, surveying the parking lot behind the car. "Well, Dana, it's starting to get dark," he said. "We'd probably better get on our way and find a place to spend the night."

"You can stay here with us," Sandra offered.

"Thanks, Sandra, I appreciate the offer. But I don't know if we'd have a car in the morning if we left it out here. And I don't want to spend the night watching for kids with high-powered rifles sneaking around in your parking lot."

"Then let us give you some stuff to last you for a day or so." She nodded at Jody, and he slipped back through the doors. "Do you have a can opener?"

"I got my Barlow," Jimmy answered. "I can open cans with that."

Jody came back out carrying several cans in a plastic bag. He handed the bag to Dana. "It's not much," he said, "but it'll keep you from starving for a day or two—sweet potatoes, corn, that kind of stuff."

"And you can always come back," Sandra added.

After more thanks, Dana swung her legs back into the car, and again they were off, heading to the north and Jimmy's home.

***

When the settlement that would become the city of Maryville had first been populated, the early pioneers had positioned the town proper and its main street atop a high ridge that ran in a southwest-to-northeast direction, its northeast edge ending in an elevation drop where Pistol Creek turned north then west, encircling the ridge and joining with Browns Creek to form the settlement's northern boundary. Route 411, the four-lane highway Dana and Jimmy now followed, split southwest of town with the right lane, still designated 411, becoming the main street, or West Broadway, and the left split, US 129, angling off to the west toward Knoxville.

"We'll stay to the right up ahead, Dana, and go down Broadway to my house. OK?"

She glanced over at Jimmy, wondering whether he was really asking for her concurrence. *Man, I don't know. Isn't this is your town?* "Ah, sure." *He's just really, really nervous now, getting close to home and not knowing what he'll find. What I found sure threw me for a loop.* "Broadway's fine." She studied the businesses and buildings they slowly passed, off to her right, narrating her impressions aloud to fill the nervous silence. "Filling station—looks new but closed and convenience-store door hanging open, glass broken out, pump hoses cut, one pump rammed by a truck, still balanced on the island. Small bank building—closed with doors busted in, burned police car in the parking lot. Another gas station, ditto to the other one but without the truck; Co-op store for the farmers—won't be selling any fertilizer or seed for a long time, glass out, looks burned inside, pallets of stacked birdseed pushed over and spilled, not many birds but a few rats running behind the pallets." On they drove, bearing to the right at the intersection where 129 forked off to the left, intending to follow Broadway through town.

"Hey, look here!" Dana ordered. She was pointing at a ruined grocery store on her side of the road. "There's a kid coming out. See? It looks like he's found something there. See the plastic bag he's carrying?"

"Yeah. Yeah. Look at him go! He's must have heard our car. Reckon we should turn in and check out the store?"

"Ooh, I don't know, Jimmy. We've passed the road to turn in, and the parking-lot entrance is blocked with those cars. Damn! They're really tangled together. Oh, gosh! Don't look! It's almost fresh, and there's kids and some young girls in the closest one!"

Too late—Jimmy was already looking. "Bloody mess," he observed. "Looks like the driver of the car they rammed is still in his seat. He's squashed. Look at the front of that Toyota there. It's just shot to pieces. And those girls and the kids are just tore up. Maybe there was a passenger in the Buick who managed to get out—with his Uzi. Dang! Can you imagine what it's been like around here?" He was now pointing across Dana at the store's parking lot. "There's cars smashed into each other all over the place. Looks like a demolition derby or something."

She followed his arm to where he was pointing. "Yeah. It's a small parking lot, and maybe they just descended on the store all at once."

"I would guess they did," Jimmy agreed. "There's several housing developments over on the other side of the road back there, and this grocery store is the closest for a lot of people. When the word got out about the plague going around, I bet this store was the first to be emptied. No…" He shook his head, having made his decision. "No, it's getting up in the evening, and with that kid coming out, we won't be able to take the time to carefully approach the store. Let's just… turn around here." He was already skirting the median where the lanes joined, becoming two lanes through town, and steering back in the direction they had just come. "We'll go back around that way toward Binfield and find a place to camp for the night."

"Why not just go on to your house? Was it something about seeing that kid back there?"

"Gosh, Dana, I don't know. Maybe. I just suddenly got a bad feeling about going down Broadway this late in the day. See, there's lots of shadows, and the road's kind of narrow—and there's just too many places to get bottled up and stopped. I want to be able to see far ahead, you know. Plus, there are a lot of houses and buildings on

Broadway that are up close to the road. If there are more of those kids out with guns, there'll be more potshots, and they just might get lucky."

"And…?

"And I don't want to get to the house in the dark. I—I don't know what I'll find."

"Then lay on, Macduff." Dana turned to face the front, sitting straight and attentive to the road ahead.

"Isn't that 'Lead on, Macduff'? Homer used to say, 'Lead on, Macduff.'"

"Jimmy? You're amazing. Your stomach's in turmoil over the road ahead; we've just seen some kids torn apart and blood all over the place, along with a squashed guy and ruined buildings; and you're correcting my quotation?" Dana was showing her amazed face to Jimmy, her head cocked in her questioning angle and her hands forward, palms up, as if awaiting the delivery of something of material substance.

Jimmy clenched his teeth and nodded. "Dana, that's true. I'm sorry. All this crap going on and I—"

"Gotcha again." Dana giggled. "Man, you're easy. I'm just picking at you."

He tried to frog her leg and missed, dinging his fist against the emergency brake. "Ow!" Then he laughed along with Dana while he rubbed his knuckle. "But you know, what you said is true. How many dead or dying people have we seen? I don't know about you, but I've gotten hardened by all this. Don't know what I feel anymore. Back up there, in Sevierville, I got to the point that I could shoot at living, breathing human beings—like I was in an arcade or playing a game or something."

"Maybe you felt you were protecting your home back there? Or yourself?"

Jimmy thought some more, making the turn onto Morganton Road, a two-lane country affair. He clicked on his headlights to better see the faded marker lines in the deepening shadows. "Yeah, Dana, you're right, I guess. Homer and Zula were dead—they got the disease and weren't killed by shooting—that I know of—and Thelma was getting weird. I guess I *was* in battle...and I don't think the Lord...I don't think I was being disobedient to God or sinning somehow then. 'Course now I probably can justify anything." He slowed the car to crunch over some fallen branches.

"You talk about God more than any boy I've ever known."

"Gosh, I hope you don't think I'm preaching at you or anything. I know some folks like for other folks to know how religious they are, but I hope I don't sound like that to you. It's just that God *is* a big part of my life. My inner place...of peace is close, and I go there several times a day; we talk. I mean, I went to church regularly and spent a lot of time there, and I'd hate to think I did it just to be doing something. Some people have a different relationship with Christ, I'm sure, but I've got what I've got, and it's easy for me." He laughed.

Dana laughed too. "Oh, Jimmy, I'd like to say I'm as close to God as you seem to be, but I'm not. Yeah, I'd go to church too sometimes but my going might have been more social with me. I mean, if my friends hadn't gone, I probably wouldn't have gone either. Yeah, I think God exists, but I'd be lying if I said I didn't have a lot of big doubts. I wish I could tell you I'm as good of a Christian as...because I don't want you not to like me. See...I'm still a good person, and I think God knows that."

Jimmy sighed. "You know, sometimes I think faith is a gift itself. But never something to show off about. He knows and you know."

"Thanks...I guess. And thanks for not telling me I'm going to hell because I was straight with you." *Jimmy, I'm sorry, but I just can't believe all that stuff.*

He nodded in acknowledgment. "I sometimes think I can recognize Christ in other people...but hell and that stuff? I don't know either. I've had friends who thought I should say stuff like they say or work harder at religious stuff, and then I'd feel like I was just trying to please another person, like you said. And some people can get mad real quick if you don't...ah..."

"Validate their beliefs? Be like them?" Dana had turned to him in her interest, ready to share more observations of Christian shortcomings.

"Yeah, maybe." Jimmy was distracted now, searching the sides of the road for something. "Hey, kinda watch over there for two dirt lanes going off into the brush. There's an old farm lane along here that leads to a long shed used to dry tobacco. I think we can hide the car in there, back off the road, and maybe get some rest before going into town in the morning."

"Sounds good. The canned sweet potatoes sound good too. There! Is that what you're talking about?" She gestured at a line of bushes that covered the ditch.

"Dang, girl, you've got good eyes." Now seeing the culvert mostly hidden by branches, Jimmy steered over it and into the brush, forcing the Mustang through the wall of foliage. The bushes parted, and he clearly saw the twin traces through the high weeds. "So in a minute or two…voilà! There 'tis. See that real nice shed over there?"

Dana snorted. "You make it sound like the Hilton."

They drew close, and he turned the car to back it through the double doors at the end and into the structure. Dana opened her door to step out, to run behind and slide the doors apart. "The roof does look like it'll keep out the rain," she allowed. Thunder then rumbled in the distance, underscoring her observation.

***

A blast of wind whooshed through the treetops, and the tin roof creaked with its passage. Rain pelted the metal in waves, its hammering being drowned out only by rolling drums of thunder. A lightning bolt lit up the spaces between the wide planks of the wall, instantly crackling with its close proximity.

"Whoa! That one sounded like it almost got us!" exclaimed Jimmy, the thunder peal still vibrating the rafters over their heads. Earlier they had opened a can of vegetables apiece, sharing the contents for supper, and were now reclined in the Mustang's seats, staring into the darkness above through their rolled-down side windows.

"Yeah," Dana agreed. "But like I told you, this ol' tin roof is as sturdy as they come. Did you remember to take out the trash?"

"Why? Do the garbage men come in the morning?"

"Funny man, funny man. I was just worried about rats and coyotes finding us, following the smell and giving us a visit."

"Yeah, I've heard rats and coyotes have a special liking for canned sweet potatoes and mixed carrots and peas." He sniggered at his own wit. "To tell you the truth, Dana, I don't think you left enough in that sweet potato can to draw a starving roach." He sniggered again.

"You're really enjoying yourself, aren't you, big boy?" she noted. Actually she enjoyed hearing Jimmy's quiet laughter; it gave her… hope for tomorrow. "By the way, Mr. Comedian, since we drove so far back this way, can we cross over to that main road tomorrow and go by the Megamart again? Maybe take a little detour?"

"Are you thinking of asking for more potatoes, please, sir…like Oliver Twist?"

"You know, I'm not too proud to beg. They were good, weren't they?" She laughed. "Oliver Twist—one of your playmates?" She laughed again. "I'd just like to check on Sandra and those guys again. After what we've seen, I don't think they'll be safe there if Daniel Davis and his thugs come here. Do you still think he'll come here?"

Jimmy exhaled a long breath. "I don't know. I think those were his guys back at the Y, so I think he expended quite a bit of effort already to come this way. You know, I don't know what he's got against me— why he hates me so. He surprised me back there in Gatlinburg with the way he sent his guys after me—little ol' me. We've known each other a long time, and we've never really liked each other, but that's kids' stuff. This is big stuff, and people are dying. And ol' Reverend's not comforting anybody, as far as I can see. He's just out doing evil like what he did up there to all those men. And I know he's always hated Homer because…" His voice trailed off, fading into the dimness of the rafters.

He's thinking and remembering, thought Dana. *Hey! The rain's stopped. The lightning's passed.* She smiled to herself then silently raised herself up on one elbow and leaned over the boy to lightly press her lips to his. "Good night, Sir James. Sleep tight." She was still smiling as she lay back in her seat.

Yeah, like that's gonna happen now. "Good night, Dana," he whispered. "And yes, it will be easy to detour over to 411 and the Megamart tomorrow morning. Get your list ready." He was smiling too, as he interlaced his fingers behind his head and listened to the rainwater from the tree limbs above drip-drop on the tin roof. *Maybe things will be better tomorrow.*

Suddenly many drops splashed noisily against the roof, as if something had shaken the tree. *Somebody's bumped the tree at the side of the shed! Or something big!* He slowly sat up, listening all around. *A sniff—something's smelling the wall outside! Crap! I should've thrown those cans outside!*

"Hear that?" Dana whispered. "What is it?"

Now Jimmy heard many sniffing creatures just on the other side of the thin planks. And digging—he heard them pawing at the side of the building, trying to dig under the structure. "Probably just coyotes. I'll yell at them to frighten them away." He pushed himself fully erect in his seat and aimed his yell at the wall, cupping his hands to the sides of his mouth. "Get out of here! Git! Git! Get away, dogs!"

Several fierce growls rose in answer to his commands—loud, unearthly growls—the kinds of sounds that had caused men to huddle closer to their fires since prehistoric times. A single chilling howl then rent the night, silencing even the insect calls that had begun with the storm's passing.

"My God!" Dana whispered, gripping Jimmy's arm.

But it was he who was already doing the real praying to God. He felt the presence of an ancient evil, a wickedness like he'd never known before. "Wolves," he breathed. But it was more than mere wolves, natural animals from a natural world…and he knew the walls couldn't withstand such beings. He had seen the silhouetted bulk and had run from the creature's eyes. *My God!*

"Damn, they stink!"

She was right. Jimmy smelled it too—the heavy odor of rot, a cloying stench that filled his nostrils. "They've been eating decayed, dead people," he guessed. The animals *had* been eating the dead, but the odor was preexistent to that.

And then suddenly they were gone, disappearing without the sound of running feet, without the breaking of a branch. "This wasn't their time." Jimmy whispered the words he understood in his spirit. "It was God's will."

16

DAY TWELVE

There you go again! Can't you just let me sleep for a minute? The voices had come again in the early morning, and Daniel could only listen to them. Sleep was impossible; the voices wouldn't allow it. They urged him on, accusing him of his worthlessness, his laziness, of his being one with the world. *Damn, they sound just like my old man!* He sat up on the edge of the bed, his feet still in his boots and his elbows on his knees.

He looked about the room. "So this is what a college boy sees every morning. Ain't much."

They had come down from Gatlinburg during the night. After they had caught the Townsend militia in the process of setting up their defenses at the Y, they'd met no other real resistance en route to Maryville. *I guess I should thank ol' Jimmy Burke for that—gave me a jump on those ol' boys.* When his convoy had rounded that last long curve, his lead scout had spotted the activity down where the rivers joined and had alerted his men. And they had made ready their rifles, knives, and their big mounted fifty cal. *They didn't know what hit 'em.* There'd been no one attending the militiamen's guns, and no guards had been posted along their perimeter. Daniel and his men had quite an enjoyable time and left no one alive to oppose them should he decide to return that way.

"Maybe I'd better go on to Knoxville, while I still got the manpower." He'd lost a significant part of his Lord's Army since leaving White School but not in conflict. One after another, his young men were catching the plague and were sickening and dying. He could go out this morning and lay hands on the sick ones and preach and swear…but he knew in his heart they would still be dead by tomorrow morn. His healing services, once a show for the troops, were now held only in private settings. *They're dying so fast now when they get it.* He imagined the thoughts behind those faces, those men who still followed him. *They're probably thinkin' God wasn't never using me to bestow the gift of healing on anybody, 'cause the afflicted have all died…or eventually will all die…Then, damn it, it's them that don't have the faith!* Just the same, Daniel would now only conduct his healings in private—with those healed souls being quietly escorted out afterward by the back door. "They'll need to recuperate some more," he'd tell any waiting family members or Lord's Army soldiers. "They'll be meeting up with you at home later."

Daniel and his men had entered Maryville from the east, coming down 321. And even though it was still dark, they had traveled up and down Broadway, searching for the address Daniel believed to be Jimmy's home. *That was a lot of fun too.* They had surprised several small bands of teenagers and kids sleeping in malls and stores. *Most of 'em couldn't find their pants when we spotlighted 'em, let alone their guns.* But there had been one sour spot; in a store down US Route 411, they had lucked out and flushed three guys and a gal. The boys had put up some resistance, but they and their shotguns, lightly loaded with bird shot, hadn't been much of a deterrent. *Just made the men mad, that's all.* Daniel laughed with the thought; he'd never before seen people skewered on long planks and used as torches, and he'd heartily complimented his men on their creativeness. "'Course it helped to have a lawn and garden shop in with the store; the materials were all right handy. Those ol' boys burned pretty good—lit up the whole parking lot. Now if they'd only gotten to that girl before she offed herself." That was the sour spot. Daniel had glimpsed the girl himself, in the distance, and had issued orders for her to be taken alive. She'd looked pretty good to him, and mature women were becoming somewhat scarce.

That thought reminded Daniel of Gary back in Gatlinburg, and he laughed again. "Dumb shit had better have used ol' Vera right quick. She sure as hell ain't long for this world, if I'm any judge." He'd heard her cough several times when he was with her. "Ain't long at all now."

"Say, that's maybe another of God gifts to me?" He'd noticed he could now seem to *feel* the presence of the plague in others—to sense it even before the diseased knew it themselves. He had felt it around Vera and some of his older men. *And they'd all had to be disposed of directly. Maybe that's my gift now?* "Must've come with the voices I'm hearing," he speculated aloud, his own voice sounding hollow in the bare room.

He reached over to the windowsill and picked up his pistol and the small notebook he'd placed there when he'd first stretched out on the bed—Zula's address book. He'd picked it out of her bureau drawer when he'd searched her house. He thumbed through the pages to the Bs. "Burke...Albert and Olivia. That's gotta be Jimmy's mama and old man. Hell, they's the only Burkes there!" The voices in his head confirmed it; the address was Jimmy's. "Murville," he said, reading further and pronouncing the name as did the natives, "Murville, Tennessee." Gary had told him he'd thought Jimmy and Dana would be heading for Maryville, having heard the girl mention the town a time or two in conversation with Vera. Regardless, Daniel knew somehow, even if he hadn't found the notebook and if Gary hadn't related the overheard conversation, he still would have come to Maryville. "The voices would've told me." In fact, after they'd passed the Y and he no longer felt the presence of Jimmy on the road ahead, he still knew absolutely they were soon to cross paths again. "And I'll be killin' him now," he whispered—a conclusion that came without breath. *Now that there's a revelation that's come surely under the guidance of God!* God never before had talked directly to him, but God often had talked to Daniel's father, and his father would then tell him what God had on his mind. "Yeah, this must have been what the ol' man was talking about—inspiration. Yeah! 'Cause God certainly does like his killin' and smitin'." And so did Daniel. It made him feel...justified!...and warm and quivery in his nether regions. *Vengeful! Powerful!*

He realized now that his breath was coming fast, with him simply seated there on the bed's edge and thinking. He pushed down on the front of his jeans and chuckled. "Well, looks like for sure I ain't gonna be getting any more sleep. Damn, I hope ol' Vera's hanging on for me to make it back." He stood. "I guess I might as well go down and see what the boys are cooking up." He heard the clicking of cutlery from downstairs and the murmur of voices through his open window.

Before daylight, Daniel and his caravan had returned to Maryville College, having earlier passed it on their way into town. The campus was large and open—easily patrolled—and its dormitories had many beds, all student free and immediately available for their occupation and respite. He'd selected one of the beds in a room over the cafeteria. The building was close to the center of the campus, making it easier for him to keep an eye on things going on all around. He returned Zula's address book to his shirt pocket and his forty-five to his holster, and tromped heavily from the room and down the stairs to the dining room below.

His men were arrayed around the room, sitting at small tables and eating rations from real plates. His newest lieutenant waved to him from across the room, pushing a chair from under the table with his foot and motioning for him to come join them—him and Daniel's other two in-charge men. *Damn, I can't even remember their names.* He'd been through quite a few lieutenants since Blade and Wing, always preferring the older men as leaders despite knowing they'd likely be the next ones to sicken and die. *Ah, well. Not likely to ever be in competition with me anyway. That's a plus.* He would just avoid calling them anything. " Morning, men. Are you ready for the day?"

"Yessir!" they responded in unison as he took the offered chair. While they feared him for his inconsistent temperament, they were in awe of his ability to seemingly go for days without sleep. They were each younger than him, but they knew they couldn't keep going for days on end the way he did. And even if he weren't apt to kill them should they attempt to separate ways with him, they stayed on because they were certain they'd exist longer *with* him than anywhere else. While Daniel's healing powers were sometimes questionable, his capacity for ruthlessness and treachery dwarfed all other leaders they'd known or heard about. And he was good about sharing his women with them.

A boy of about six or seven tottered through the kitchen's swinging door holding a heavy platter of fried meat and a jug of coffee. He slid the plate onto the table beside Daniel and held the jug ready to pour. Daniel turned upright the cup at his spot while offering refills all around. "Anybody want some more? OK, just for me then. And fried Spam? Anybody?" There were no takers. "Say, they got gas grills in this place?"

"They do," said the new lieutenant. "We had to cut the lock from the tanks. They got emergency stores here. And the canned meat was stashed under a counter in the back. We almost didn't see it 'cause of hidden drawers and stuff."

"Yessir," a second lieutenant spoke up. "This whole place is one big hidey-hole. One of the men flipped up that manhole cover out there aside the walkway and showed me a tunnel that led to other tunnels—one that opens up in that big ol' building over there on the west side."

"Do tell," Daniel replied, eating pieces of Spam from the serving tray. "I expect those tunnels were left over from Civil War days; I think this place was here then. Did y'all send anybody down them to scout around? Did you find anything hidden down there?"

"Yessir. We sent a couple of ol' boys down, but they didn't find nothing valuable there. You know, I 'spect most of the students going to school here never even knowed that those ol' holes were down there; there would've been more writin' on the walls if they had. The boys did find some old paper records and such over there in the basement of that big ol' building, but unless you're wantin' to build a big ol' fire, there ain't much use for that stuff that I can see."

For several minutes Daniel munched his fried meat, eating his way across the platter until there were no pieces left. "My stars!" he exclaimed, looking at the empty plate. "I believe I ate all the meat, and you fellers didn't take any. I got to thinking about having that big ol' bonfire and...had you eaten already?"

"Yes, yes," they assured him.

He smiled, knowing full well that they would have sworn they had no appetite even if they hadn't eaten for a week. *That's a sign of obedient minions.* "Well, boys, I believe we should be saddling up now. I expect there's a few places around town we should be visiting and places that'd stand watching."

***

"Oh, damn!" Dana was looking with wide eyes at the blasted-out doors of the Megamart. "What do you think's gone on here?"

Jimmy leaned forward to see past her through her window. "I'd believe either Daniel has arrived or others from Knoxville have come to town. Stay here and I'll go have a look." Leaving his door open and the engine running, he slipped warily from the car and around its front, pausing once to survey the wide parking lot from end to end. He turned to give Dana two thumbs-up and a tight smile, and trotted on past the barrier bars set in the sidewalk to flatten himself against the brick wall to the side of the gaping doors. After a couple exploratory head feints through the opening, he again gave Dana the positive thumbs-up signal, cocked the hammer on his thirty-eight, and twisted himself around the jagged doorframe and into the store's blackness.

Minutes rolled by, which seemed like hours to the waiting Dana. She heard the bugs loudly singing in the trees and weeds to the sides of the building, greeting the warmth of the morning sun...but nothing else. Nothing else. No wind. No vehicle noises. Nothing. *That smells like barbecue!* She leaned forward in her seat, searching for the source of the aroma. "That must be what I'm smelling." She studied the long planks leaning against the light poles in the parking lot. "I wonder what those smoking, blackened gobs are at the—" Then Jimmy slapped the Mustang's back quarter panel, using the side of the car to slow himself as he circled behind. He threw himself through the open door and into his seat, releasing the handbrake, ramming the shifter into gear, and finding the accelerator—all at the same time.

At the entrance to 411, Jimmy finally stopped the car and allowed himself to breathe—great heaving breaths. "Damn...damn...damn," he uttered, speaking to his lap with his forehead resting against the steering wheel.

Dana waited a minute—and then another—before asking, "What'd you see in there, Jimmy? You're beginning to sound like me! What'd you see in there? Did you see Sandra and the boys? Have they been hurt or something?" Her voice fell with the last question. Having seen the doors' destruction and the bullet-pitted brickwork on both sides, she had no real expectation of their salvation. "They're dead, aren't they?"

Jimmy nodded, turning his face to hers. "Yeah...I guess...Didn't see 'em all...found their guns...and fresh blood—lots of blood." He was still trying to catch his breath. "I found the guns there...behind some shelves they'd pushed to the front for cover. And you know... even if there'd been bodies stretched out there on the floor...I expect I might not have been able to recognize 'em. I didn't see them all that well yesterday and...and I'd told them—remember?—that they didn't know what they were up against, those fifty cals. They...they'd never even had a chance." He exhaled, blowing loudly and shaking his head in disgust—or maybe anger. "You know what they had those shotguns loaded with? Birdshot! How are you gonna fight with birdshot? And I bet it *was* Daniel who came here, and I bet it *was* those heavy-caliber machine guns he used on 'em too. Those shelves were shot to...heck."

"Sandra," Dana asked. "Did they...get her too?"

Jimmy knew what she was really asking. "I don't...Sandra had holed herself up in one of those little places at the front, the customer service desk, I think. To me it looks like she was trying...I think she shot herself in the head with her own shotgun. The back of her head was gone."

Dana crossed her arms and gazed off in the distance. "Well, if I'm about to be captured by Daniel and his thugs, I hope I'm brave enough to do that," she whispered. "I'd hope to be able to do that—to be messed up enough so they'd leave me alone."

Jimmy was about to say something about how drastic—and final—that act was, but he didn't. *I'm not a female, so maybe I'd have a different opinion if I was.* It just seemed to him that there were always alternatives. *And suicide?* He'd heard some preachers say that those who committed suicide were destined for hell. But he'd never had occasion to research it himself, and for some reason, he and Homer had never discussed it. *Just never thought about it, I guess. Homer would have known, though.* That would be a question, he decided, he would ask for himself. *One of these days.*

And Jimmy wasn't too sure Sandra really *had* managed to mess herself up enough to be left alone. He'd noticed that her clothes had been cut from her body and slung around on the floor. *Those guys are capable of anything.* But he said nothing further to Dana about that.

"Was that why you came running like that out of the store? Seeing Sandra like that?"

"Well, I guess that could be part of it," he replied. In truth he'd heard sounds off to the back of the building, like the clicking of long toenails on the tile floor. He'd heard the ticking sounds as they slowly moved across the back of the store then picked up speed as they came up the aisle toward the front—toward him! So he had run. After what happened last night, he'd dropped what he had in his hands—the ruined shirt he had intended to toss across Sandra's naked body—and run. He had run so hard he'd bounced off the jagged doorframe and jumped a grocery cart in the foyer. He wouldn't tell Dana about that either; his bleeding arm was on the other side anyway.

"Let's go, Jimmy," urged Dana. "Let's go to your house and see about your folks then just leave here—forever."

"You betcha!" Jimmy pushed down hard on the accelerator, and the little Ford leaped forward, its tires making chirping noises as they turned the corner hard onto 411.

***

"And see over there? That's where we'd go for ice cream. And right there—"

"Jimmy, is that a *tank* across the road ahead?"

He saw the black bulk of a large tracked vehicle farther down the road. It was almost in town, at the intersection where the first of other roads crossed over Broadway to slope down the ridge on both sides, where it then intersected with other streets that run northeast up the valleys and parallel to Broadway. He had planned on driving through town on this main road, but the mass of machinery may have made the route impassable. "I don't know, Dana. If it is, I don't think its cannon is pointed down this way, so maybe it'll be OK for us to keep on going." He took his foot from the gas, and they coasted on slowly, slowly. "It *is* a tank! Well, it's kinda more like an armored personnel carrier, but it's got a big gun. You know, I bet when people first learned of the disease and maybe began to run amuck...ah... get real disorderly around here...ah." He glanced over at Dana, who seemed to be grinning wickedly back at him. *Yeah—so that's another rainy Saturday library word. She enjoys pointing those out way too much.* He rushed on. "When people went crazy here and started stealing stuff and shooting each other, I bet they called in the national guard— that's a guard vehicle there. But people kept dying, and soon I bet there wasn't anyone around interested in sitting up there anymore." He squinted, examining the carrier as he steered around it and down the road that bordered the cemetery off to the right. "That machine gun on top doesn't have any bullets linked up to it; it's empty. The thing's just blocking the road."

He sped up slightly, making a left, intending to follow along the parallel road for a ways. "There used to be a lot of old rundown houses around here," Jimmy observed, pointing out more no-longer-existing residences, "and then something called 'urban renewal' came along and changed the looks of everything. See, this road ahead used to be dirt, and it circled back under the bridge." The short section of level road and uptown buildings now ended; the pavement ahead dipped precariously into a ridge-ending valley and continued far below over a low bridge that spanned the narrow creek at the bottom. "That's Pistol Creek down there," he said, keeping both hands on the wheel and nodding in the direction. "My father told me he'd delivered papers down there, and a lot of the folks were really poor around here and up that way. See that hill? That's called Parham Hill; the armory's there. A real fine house used to be up there too, but that was a long time ago. My dad said there wasn't nobody but poor people living up there when he was growing up."

"They paid for their newspapers?" *Damn!* She hadn't intended to ask any questions. *That just encourages him.* She wasn't interested in learning the history of Maryville right now, preferring that Jimmy concentrate on their present surroundings.

He laughed. "Yeah. Dad said they were his better customers." Glancing over, he noticed she appeared to be studying the long expanse of relatively new apartments or condos that covered the distant hilltop. "Ur-ban renewal," Jimmy continued, drawing out the syllables. "But you know, I wonder where the poor people went." He slowed now for the four-lane road that crossed at the top of the rise. "They had to go somewhere, didn't they?"

Dana made no reply; she was busy leaning back and forth, searching the road past the solid wall on her side.

She's probably wondering why I'm going this way. "I want to first go by the hospital," he explained. "My mother works there, and she might have gone there with my dad. And since we're already out this way…" He pulled into the near lane, turning to the right. There were more buildings on both sides, and it looked much like Broadway. "Doesn't look too bad over here, does it? And not a lot of traffic either, eh?"

"Well," Dana snorted, "it looks about like any other small Southern town I've ever seen. And there's absolutely no traffic at all—we haven't seen another car. Say, look over there. There, past the barbershop over there, up the railroad tracks. What's that place?" She was interested now and pointing at a gradually rising, grassy hill with several structures covering its crown. A newly resurfaced roadway bisected the lush lawn and wound up the hill toward an ornate sign that she was just now noticing.

"That's the beach," Jimmy chuckled. "If you go to school there, that's called 'the beach'...I think. See, that's a college. Maryville College, like the sign says. And as you might expect—"

"What's that?" Dana interrupted, waving at the distant forms moving between the buildings.

He could see what she was indicating. "I think it's a lot of vehicles, like those we saw Daniel and his guys riding in. I think they're forming up to leave!"

"They came here! Oh, my God!"

"Exactly. And we could use God's help to get past 'em before they spot us." Jimmy mashed harder on the accelerator. "Almost...a little more. OK!"

"Whew!" They both exhaled when they reached the cover of the building at the foot of the hill. Dana slumped back in her seat.

"Ol' Daniel and the Lord's Army must have spent the night up there," Jimmy surmised. "I bet they got here last night...before we did."

"With unbruised kidneys too, I bet."

He ignored her. "I bet Daniel got here then went searching around, searching for us. You know," he added hopefully, "since they didn't find us, maybe they're fixin' to go home."

"Is there someplace up ahead where we can hide and wait and maybe see them if they leave? I mean, this *is* 321, according to that sign, isn't it? Don't you think they'll go back to Sevierville this way?"

Jimmy was nodding. "Yeah. The hospital's up ahead—that's the way I'm taking us anyway. Maybe we can get in the parking lot and hide among the cars up there and watch for them to pass."

***

They reached the hospital's expansive parking lot with time to spare; Jimmy saw no vehicle movements behind them when he made the turn. Then, discovering there were actually few cars remaining in the lot to provide cover, he chose instead to park near the main building, taking additional time in backing the Mustang into the drop-off zone. *In the event we gotta make a speedy exit out the back way.* They settled down to wait.

Long minutes passed, and Dana rechecked the time on the dashboard clock; a half hour had crept by since they'd parked. "I think they must have gone another way," she opined, still sitting forward in her seat and keeping her attention focused on the wide avenue at the base of the hill.

"Yeah, I'd say," Jimmy agreed. He had less patience with the surveillance task and was now reloading the pistol he'd just cleaned and reassembled. With that completed, he turned in his seat to better survey the big building's lobby through the double banks of glass doors. Another minute passed. "You know, the hospital looks like it's empty in there," he said. "I been keeping a lookout that way and haven't seen any movement at all. Do you want to maybe stay here and keep watch while I go inside to look around?"

"It's my turn, kiddo. I need to get out anyway. Nature calls." She demurely batted her eyelashes at him and pushed wide the car's door. "You *are* going to wait for me, aren't you?"

"What?" Her question surprised him.

"Just kidding, dear boy. Just kidding. What's your mother's name anyway, in case I'm asked?"

"Mrs. Burke. See—Jimmy Burke, Mrs. Burke? And don't forget to wash your hands after communing with nature." Dana stuck her tongue out at him as she swung her legs around to the sidewalk.

He waited until she was at the outer set of double doors before he also eased out of the car. He figured he could do his business right there, standing beside the car, before she returned. "And I got a good view of the road too. Hoo-boy, hoo-boy, I thought my bladder was about to bust. Wow!" He glanced over at Dana's departing back; she was just inside the building between the double sets of doors. He watched as she tugged wide the inside glass door…and immediately covered her face with her hands and fled back outside, toward him and the car. *Oh, crap!* He almost snagged himself as he rezipped his fly. Then, falling back inside the car, he grabbed for the ignition switch. He was cranking the engine as Dana ripped open the door. "What is it?" he yelled. "Wolves? Wolves?"

She slid into the car seat, her cupped hands still covering her nose and mouth. "What? Wolves?" she asked in puzzled reply, now dropping her hands but retaining the quizzical arch to her brows. "Wolves?" Then she understood. "Oh, yeah…wolves, like last night. Those stinky animals we heard digging last night trying to get to our garbage; I thought you said they were coyotes."

Jimmy's eyes changed focus, moving from the hospital's almost-closed glass door to Dana's face. *No wolves. Not wolves.* He loudly exhaled and slumped back in his seat, visibly relieved. "Well, maybe they were coyotes. I just thought…that maybe something was waiting inside." He glanced downward. *I hope I didn't piss all over myself.*

"No, no, I came running back outside because that place inside there really stinks. See, it's hot and…and I didn't really go too far inside because, see, people are lying dead inside! I thought I saw one lady there in a lobby chair—about half decomposed and sitting in the chair next to the door; you know, all squishy and all slumped over like she'd melted! If there's anyone inside there, they shouldn't… they couldn't have stood that smell for long," she declared. "I wouldn't think there's been anyone alive in there for a while…and it was totally quiet inside—no noise whatsoever." Dana was watching Jimmy's face as she waited for her heart rate to slow. "But, you know, if you want…to go back inside and search around, I'll stay with the car and maybe drive around, checking out the windows. I realize it's your mother and father we're looking for."

"No, no, I think you're right." He lowered his head and again talked to his lap. "About wanting to come by the hospital…about finding my mother and father alive?" He took a deep breath then ran his tongue along his lips as he considered what he was about to say. "In sitting here waiting and thinking…ah, Dana, I—I really don't expect that to happen anymore. I'd like to pretend that my mother and father—well, the last time I talked with my mother, I think my dad was already gone. And my mom? You know, we haven't seen any older people around…since Gatlinburg. That older guy onstage? He was the oldest man I'd seen in a while, and he looked to be dying. And most everybody we saw there was less than half my mom's age, I bet…and a lot of them looked sick." He looked up to face Dana as he sadly shook his head. "No, I don't expect my mother has been spared. I can only hope that, like with your mother, it came quick. I don't want to think of her suffering. And if we weren't here watching for Daniel, we'd have just been wasting our time in even coming here."

Dana saw the pain in his eyes, and it affected her; she didn't like seeing Jimmy like this. "Jimmy," she began, her voice soft and consoling, "maybe don't you think God could have spared them? I mean you're pretty religious—you know about this stuff. Why don't you want to think that maybe God saved your mother? I mean, I didn't… until I saw where my mother…Don't you think that if God wanted to, he could save her?"

"Well, yeah, he can do whatever he wants. And he will. Like something Homer used to say: We can speculate on what God was doing when this plague came, but our ways are not God's ways. He'll use it, as they say, for his glory, but as far as instigating it—starting it and being behind it—we don't know about that." Jimmy was watching Dana's pursed lips. "You're getting ready to say something about 'if God is really a god of love'—aren't you? Well, as Homer used to say, 'God isn't one to be tested…or allow himself to be controlled by his love. Or control our love in general. His love…is free.'"

Dana puffed through her nose and turned away, to stare down the hill. "Just the same I don't understand that. If God is real, he should be expected…to do something about this!" Those words came out in a rush. "I mean, doesn't this just support the argument to be an atheist?" Her irritation had crept into her tone.

Jimmy smiled slightly. This thinking and talking had moved him away from the thoughts of his mother and father; he was feeling better. "You're not blaming God for taking your mother…and I'm not either—about my parents. Neither one of us is. We both know fixing blame and making ourselves feel mad sure wouldn't help things now. I can only say, with absolute assurance, is that we'll know—understand this all—someday. I feel that certainty down deep." He continued to smile at her. "And I'm certain God doesn't much worry about an atheist's unbelief. I mean, what does it matter to him? And if this all hadn't happened…Well, I'm very glad that *we* met."

Dana couldn't help smiling back at him. "Jimmy, I swear…don't you ever get pissed off about anything? I mean, here we sit, being chased after by a crazy priest—preacher—hungry, same underwear for days now, no toothpaste, no toothbrush, hungry. I mean"—she was now shaking her head—"what can you really, possibly say good about this situation here and now? And no flirting."

"Well, it's quiet."

"What do you mean?"

"The power's off and ordinarily that big ol' diesel generator over there would be roaring like crazy, and I wouldn't be hearing you talk now. When I didn't hear it when we pulled in, I kind of knew the air would be off inside and—"

"And you let me walk into that stinky place?" The irritation was back in her voice.

"Well, you had to pee, didn't you?"

"And I still do! And I'm hungry!"

"Here. Eat this—it'll tide you over." He was waving a granola bar back and forth in front of her nose. "And I'll stop at the first house that looks accessible. And safe."

"Where'd you get that?" she demanded.

"Never mind. Just eat it." He wasn't about to tell her he'd found it in Sandra's shirt pocket. *Not that she'd care about that right now anyway.* He watched as she downed the bar in three healthy chomps.

***

Approximately one hour later, Jimmy guided the Mustang slowly up East Broadway and past his house. He and Dana had left the hospital, taking the back exit to Sevierville Pike and from there across to the Everett Hill community. He'd stopped once, behind a tiny four-room house down a dead-end street, to allow Dana the time to "commune with nature." During the entire trip, they had passed no other cars and seen no other people.

"Jimmy, do you suppose there's really no one around now? I mean, we aren't seeing anybody, and we haven't seen anybody except those guys back at Maryville College. And there wasn't anybody in that house back there where we stopped so I could use the bathroom. We didn't see anybody along the road. Are we…do you think we're about the only ones left now in Maryville?" Dana was searching from side to side as they drove, scanning the windows of the closely spaced houses for any signs of movement and the shadowed garages for any dark forms.

"Oh, I don't know. I'm not exactly looking in places where I'd expect to find them right now. See, I actually knew the person who owned that little house; she was my junior high teacher. She was pretty ancient, so I'd thought that if she'd died, she would have gone with the first wave, so you weren't apt to be meeting her sitting on the john. But as far as not seeing anybody else along the way, I don't know what to think."

"Then maybe they've gathered in a public place, like maybe the churches. Or your high school, Jimmy?" Dana was now sounding as positive as he had.

"We passed my church when we crossed over Everett Hill. Remember that big brick building off to the left? That big, burned-out building you said was caving in? That was the sanctuary of my church. The other building's already had caved in."

"Wow! Maybe disgruntled members torched your church?" She was grinning, facing out the window.

"Maybe. Maybe even gruntled members." He grinned too, enjoying his own wit.

Dana ignored him, still staring at the houses as they passed to the right. "Say, smartass, when are we supposed to be getting to your abode?"

"We just passed it."

"What? Why didn't you stop?"

"I thought I saw a jeep parked back behind the house. I want to circle around and see if we can come in the back way, through the pear orchard. You know, scout out the area. Besides, since I'm not expecting either my mother or father—"

"You've got pear trees?"

"Are you still hungry?" Jimmy sniffed. "We got a few pear trees out back, but the peaches and cherries are all gone for the year. But if birds and possums haven't got to them, we should still have some pears—green pears. Sound good?"

Dana puffed her cheeks, blowing as if she'd just finished a task. "No, Jimmy, that granola bar was enough, I think. I don't feel so hot now. In fact..." Dana covered her mouth and puked granola bar mush down her shirtfront. She looked up at Jimmy with panic-filled eyes. "Jimmmyyyy! Oh, God! Jimmmyyyy!"

Oh, damn! Not her! Dear God, please! Not her! He patted her leg and searched for a place to pull over alongside the road. "Dana, you're... you're gonna be OK. That granola bar was old, and it just upset your stomach—that's all. You're OK." Jimmy was trying to keep his voice low and his tone settling, not like his screaming thoughts. "Look there ahead! We'll go up here and turn in past the ditch through those trees and follow that little road there. See? Doesn't it look just like the little two-rut path to the Burchfields' barn? Remember that place? In Sevierville? Where I first met you?"

"Oh, God! Jimmy, I've got a bad headache too. Didn't you say something about it happening like that?"

Yes, I did. "No, I didn't, Dana. A headache doesn't mean you're coming down with...Look! See, there's the little house my folks rent out." He was pulling the car in beside the frame house. He would run inside and see if there were beds—any place—where Dana could rest and recuperate.

"Oh, God, Jimmy! I think I'm gonna be sick again."

Dana leaned forward and heaved onto the floorboard. Then once more. The water she had drunk at the little white house came up last then nothing more. Her stomach was totally empty, so she could only dry heave and cough. *Damn, I feel so bad…and I think I pooped my pants. Oh, Jimmy!*

He recognized the odor that now circulated through the car. *Oh, no!* "Dana, I'm here, and I'm not leaving you," he assured her. "I think we can use this house for you to rest for a while. See? I'll run in for a second and make sure everything is OK, and then I'll come right back out and help you come in. OK? Will you just sit here for a minute? Please?"

Dana leaned back, her head lolling to the side on the headrest. She suddenly felt so very, very tired. Yet she managed a weak smile for Jimmy. "Go! Go! I'm not holding you up. But if they have a water bed, I call dibs on that."

Jimmy jumped from the car then returned to retrieve the handgun from the console, where he had stowed it. "Be just a minute," he promised again. At the door—the kicked-in front door—he cautiously peeked around the frame. Seeing nothing threatening inside, he quickly moved through the opening, dropping low and falling to his knees like he'd seen in the cop movies, his pistol held fully extended with both hands.

"Anybody in here?" he yelled. There was no reply. "Anybody in here?" he yelled again. "I've got a gun, and I'm not afraid to use it!" Still there was no reply.

Jimmy awkwardly rose to his feet, his hands still tightly grasping the gun. He flipped the light switch with his elbow, forgetting that electricity no longer flowed in the town. *Dang, it's dark back there.* He edged over to the roller shade covering the closest of the livingroom windows. After tugging hard on the bottom of the shade, he released it to flap noisily clear to the top of the windows. Light instantly spilled into the room, and tiny, quick feet scurried down the hallway toward the back bedroom. *Dang possum!* He'd almost squeezed off a shot at the fuzzy, gray backside of the escaping animal. "Get outta…Get outta here!" he loudly ordered, his voice breaking then deepening with hoped-for authority. "Get outta here, dang you!" The opossum scrambled from sight around the corner, and the claw noises faded.

Jimmy chose next to scout out the kitchen and the adjacent laundry room, scraping his back along the wall, past the ruined front door and through the kitchen door. The thick smell of decay greeted him. *Gosh!* He coughed and almost vomited. A cloud of flies instantly enveloped him, rising from the dark mound at his feet. He violently kicked at the vague shape, an instinctive response of panic and surprise, and his other foot, his planted foot, skidded in the fluids that covered the linoleum floor. He went down hard.

"Oh, shit!" Even though he quickly scrambled to his feet, his hand and backside had contacted with the mess; it dripped from him like cheap syrup and looked much like the glaze his mother smeared on the ham at Christmas time. But other than that, there were no further comparisons with anything he'd ever experienced. "It smells like...No, it's worse than that. Maybe a buzzard's breath. Damn, damn, damn," he softly cursed as he examined himself. With his clean hand, he slipped his pistol into the front of his pants and searched the room for a cloth or towel to wipe away the gunk. Spying a dish towel beside the sink, he crossed over and stood there, dabbing at his hand and clothing while reexamining the mass on the floor.

"It's the lady who rents the house." He recognized her bleached hair atop the gob he now determined to be her head. The flies had resettled, and their larvae, the maggots, continued at their task, causing the woman's hair to slightly move up and down in the breezeless room. Having made that determination, he anticipated what he would find next and moved to the doorway of the laundry room.

The woman's toddler son was there on the floor, laundry detergent still clinging to the corners of his tiny mouth and dusting his chin. To Jimmy, it was apparent that the boy had died much later than his mother and had been engaged in sating his hunger when he was felled. *I expect this wasn't his first meal of detergent. I bet he's been eating on that for a while.*

Still blotting at his clothes, Jimmy pushed aside the curtains at the pantry. "Nothing down low; nothing up high. If there were canned foods here, the kid probably couldn't have opened them anyway.

Somebody's been here and cleaned out any food the lady might have had there. I just hope they came after the little kid already had died. I bet ol' Dana will…" *Dang!* His thoughts jumped to the stricken girl in the car. Ceasing his wiping, he tossed the cloth back onto the counter, pulled his gun from his pants and rechecked the cylinder release, and returned to the living room.

Now pushing his one foot ahead, Jimmy eased down the short hallway that branched at the bathroom into the two bedrooms. He gingerly extended the toe of his shoe, hoping to rout any small mammals that might be waiting there in the dark. He first selected the bedroom to the right to search, rounding the walls of the room as he had done in the living room, making his way to the window to roll up the window shade. *If there's a possum in here, he's under the bed.* He circled wide around the bed, leaving plenty of fleeing space between him and the door.

With the window shade now high, he dropped to the floor, inspecting beneath the bed and under the chest of drawers. *All clear.* He would now go out and bring Dana to this room. The mattress was bare, but the bedspread was folded over the back of the straight chair beside the bed. *That would do for covers for now,* he decided. He trotted lightly back through the house and around to the side where he had parked the Mustang—well away from any prying eyes that may be lurking in the grove up toward his house. *This should do just fine for now, provided the wind is right, and Dana stays away from the kitchen.* He was also thinking of ways to remove the woman and her child from the house, relocating them someplace where he could later bury them. He hadn't know them well, but he still felt the dignity of a burial was due.

Dana was now fast asleep in the car, her seat pushed all the way back. From the door Jimmy watched her for several minutes, wondering if he should dare leave her there resting while he walked up to his house. Or maybe he'd wait with her until she woke, deciding then if she wished to accompany him or rest more, either in the car or in the house. *Her choice.* He watched her lips slightly open then close with each breath, and her eyes wander to and fro beneath her eyelids. *I wonder what she's dreaming about.*

He had now forgotten just how long he had known Dana. With all that had happened, he felt as if he had known her for much longer. *Like forever.* And he realized he had grown to love her—to really, really love her. He believed he had *liked* certain girls before the coming of this feeling, this perception, but this was so very different and special. Dana was perfection to him; Dana could do no wrong; her mere presence was desirable and pleasurable. *No one.* There existed no one else he would choose to be with, to watch sleep, or to just watch breathe. He would willingly die for her. *When had this all happened?* He didn't know; it just did.

He had supposed that love was something that would be age conditional—that he would have to be *mature* to really know. "But that isn't true," he whispered. "Not true at all." He watched her chest rise and fall, rise and fall. "Dana," he softly breathed to himself, "I love you."

She sweetly smiled in her sleep.

***

Where am I? Jimmy raised his head from his folded arms and looked up. Dana was watching him, still leaned back in her seat, her head turned toward him on the headrest. "'Morning," he offered.

"'Morning," she replied. "But it's not morning anymore."

He straightened and scanned around. He was sitting in the grass beside the car with his legs folded and his arms crossed on the driver's seat. "You're right. It's getting late. How long was I asleep anyway?"

"I don't know. I was sleeping too." She turned to the front to study the dashboard clock. "It's after six, but I don't remember going to sleep. I just remember…having to throw up. And something else—you might not want to have your nose in here, Jimmy."

"Whoa! It'll be dark soon. And I don't exactly smell like flowers myself either, so don't worry about it. Ow!" He was trying to get to his feet and staggering about. "Dang! My legs went to sleep. Ow! Ow!"

Dana chuckled. "Just a little pussycat, aren't you? Isn't that what you boys say to each other?"

"Yeah, I'm being just a little pussycat all right. So how are you doing? Hungry again? Stomach doing any better?"

She smiled her tired, tired smile again, with her head turned to the side and her eyes slowly opening and closing. *He wants to pretend... so let's pretend.* "Oh, I might be able to eat something soft and drink some water, but that'll wait until you check for your folks. Didn't you say your house is right around here?"

"Yeah." He bent low in the doorway, pointing up the hill off to his right. "Our house is over there on the other side of the orchard. See, these are peach trees here, and the pears and cherries are up yonder. I'll check the trees for pears; you'd probably like to just chew on the pulp for moisture then just spit it out. That's what I liked to do, when I was a kid."

Dana straightened to look closer. *He looks like he's gotten older or something.* "Jimmy, you're beginning to look pretty good to me. Right handsome, I should say." She softly laughed. "'Course I'm pretty sick right now."

He immediately lowered his head. His mouth was tight, and his smile strained when he again looked up. "But you're getting better," he declared.

"Yes, I'm getting better," she agreed. "Now how about getting yourself up there for some pears? Maybe they'll taste really good." *But I don't think I can swallow anything.* Her throat was sore, but the lumps in her armpits and groin made the pains elsewhere in her fevered body seem insignificant. *I don't think I knew what buboes were until Jimmy told me.* That thought seemed funny to her, and she chuckled. "Thanks, Jimmy."

"Aw, you'd better wait until I come back to thank me. I think there've been people through here, and they might have helped themselves to the pears. Just keep your fingers crossed." He crossed his fingers on one hand; he was holding the thirty-eight in the other.

"OK," Dana agreed, winking at him and holding aloft her intertwined fingers.

In her side mirror, she watched Jimmy walk behind the car. She had no inclination whatsoever to sit upright and turn around to follow his departure up the red clay trail through the trees. *Just don't have the strength. Just sleep some more. But first.* She reached up and tilted down the visor, adjusting its angle so she could see her reflection in the tiny mirror on the reverse side. "Dang, I look like crap...for Jimmy." This feeling was something new for her. While she'd always cared about her appearance, she'd never before wanted to especially appeal to another person. *Especially some boy!* Suddenly she felt his absence—a loneliness that welled inside her despite the waves of abdominal pains. *I need to just see him!*

She flipped the latch, and the door clicked partially open, drawn by the car's slight angle and gravity. Pushing herself up from the low seat, she leaned against the Mustang, inching down its side to the rear fender. *There he goes.* She could now see past the side of the house and up the hill where the tile roof of the tall house there rose above the expanse of treetops. She watched until the grove hid him from view. *Damn, that was stupid!* Yet she couldn't deny that she felt better in just catching the glimpse that she did. "Yeah, that was worth it," she decided. "Now where do you...ahhh!" Her bowels opened, and her gut twisted, wringing her to the ground at the back of the car. Her head bounced against the steel bumper as she fell, and she knew nothing more.

***

Jimmy pushed aside the boxwood branch as he peeked around the dense foliage, trying to see whether anyone was in the jeep. *Looks like one guy inside.* The windows were deeply tinted, but the vivid white of the garage on the far side of the vehicle profiled its occupant. *So now what? Supposing that the man is alone, I could just walk up there and open his door and stick my gun in his face.* He checked the release on the handgun again. *Off. Or I could circle around and go in the house by the front door.* He doubted the door would be locked. His parents had seldom if ever felt it necessary to do anything other than latch the door when they left the house. *But these are different times.*

He watched for another five minutes. *The guy's not moving. He's probably asleep or something. And he's by himself, I think.* Jimmy opted for the first alternative. *Here goes.* He crept from behind the bush, trying to keep the trunk of the big cherry tree between himself and the driver's side window. He held his breath as he lopped along, his footfalls silent on the thick grass. He covered the ground quickly.

"Get your hands up!" Jimmy snarled, wanting to scream out the words but fearing that his voice would break. "Get 'em up! Now!" He grabbed at the handle and jerked open the car door, keeping his pistol trained on the man. But the man didn't move to raise his hands. Rather, with the opening of the door, he slowly leaned from his position to crumple heavily to the driveway.

It's a trick—a decoy! Jimmy lurched to the side, expecting a bullet to erupt from some hidden place in the next instant. He hit the ground and rolled and rolled, toward the jeep and under its high chassis. From there he saw the crazy-white tennis shoes emerge from the front of the garage and heard their soles slap against the asphalt as their wearers sprinted into battle. *Pow! Pow! Pow!* They fired their guns into the car and into the trees beyond the jeep. *Pow! Pow! Pow!* The jeep's windows shattered, and the glass fell around Jimmy, bouncing onto his head and into his hair. He averted his face in time to see the prone body of the car's former occupant twitching with the impact of several shots. *Crazy shits are just shooting everything! Even each other!*

Then two more shots sounded, and the firing abruptly ceased. He saw a clip hit the ground in front of the car. *Out of bullets!* He rolled from behind the tire and onto his knees, pointing his pistol in a two-handed fashion at the three boys standing between the house and the garage, frantically trying to slide replacement clips into their weapons. Their heads lifted in concert, and their eyes widened, showing their whites in the evening light. Then one boy got his clip to fit and slammed home his pistol's slide. Jimmy shot him first, and then he shot the other boys as they too continued to reload.

For a long time, Jimmy remained in his crouched position, his gun moving from window to window in his house, from tree trunk to tree trunk off to the sides of the house. He waited, but no more shots sounded and no more brand-new tennis shoes slapped the ground.

That's it. He straightened and slowly approached the supine figures, kicking their automatics far from their reach. "Look to all be gone," he concluded, bending over the third boy and gripping his smooth face, moving his head from side to side in the deepening pool of blood. He had shot each boy in the head. *Never knew what hit 'em. And they're probably all of what? Ten years old?*

Jimmy turned back and walked around to where the driver lay on the ground. He wouldn't stoop to grip his chin or rock his head from side to side because he was quite sure the man was dead. However, unlike with the boys, Jimmy noted that the man was hardly bleeding from his newly acquired wounds.

He turned the big man onto his back and studied his face. "That ol' boy died of the disease. That's probably why they weren't sitting in there with him, in the jeep. I wonder how long they've been waiting?" He then noticed that the man and the boys were dressed in new shirts and britches—camouflage shirts and britches. *Lord's Army uniforms!* Jimmy felt a cold hand grip his heart, and he once again assumed his guarded stance. He searched all around again, even more carefully this time.

"Nobody else here." Jimmy finally breathed. "These must just be lookouts or something. Since they don't have radios—probably don't work these days anyways—I bet the good Reverend Davis will be sending somebody else back this way to check before much longer." He had no idea that Daniel was still on the Maryville College campus, dealing with the day's personnel issues. "I'd better hurry and check inside the house—*please, Lord.* And get back to Dana—*again, please, Lord*—before it gets to where I can't see anymore." His saying that gave him another thought. "Wait a minute." He walked toward the house, stepping carefully over the dead boys and their pools of blood, and around to the side where there was a narrow door set at ground level in the block foundation. He tried the knob and slowly pushed open the door. This was the small room his father had enclosed when he had built out the upper floor. *I was so little I could hardly reach this knob.* There was once a cistern down here, under the porch, that caught rainwater from off the steep tile roof.

He remembered that he played here as his father had worked and he had told Jimmy a story from his own youth about a neighbor's child having fallen into an unused cistern and drowning. So, even though his mother had really liked using the rainwater to wash her hair, his father had insisted they fill in the hole and concrete over it all.

Jimmy tiptoed across the solid expanse and listened for footsteps on the hardwood above. At the far end of the room, outside the open entrance to the basement, he paused again and listened at the short doorway before he finally slipped inside, guiding himself as he descended by patting the coal bin's planks to his left. When he reached the bottom of the cinder-block stairs and the basement floor, he again paused to listen to the wooden floors above. For once he was grateful for the age of his residence and the creakiness of its flooring. *No way in the world anybody can move up there without it squeaking.* He felt his way to the interior stairs and slowly mounted the steps.

The door at the top was locked. Jimmy turned the handle, but the door wouldn't budge. *We never lock this door!* His mother had sometimes locked it when he was small to keep him out of the basement, but she hadn't done that in years. "Nevertheless," he whispered, "it's locked." He felt his pocket and pushed his Barlow knife up and out. After thumbing open its big blade, he located the door's trim opposite the keyhole and slipped the metal in under the wood. Soon he had retracted the bolt from its receptacle far enough to ease the door inward. "It's been a while since I've had to do that." Putting away his knife, he again gripped his pistol and pushed the cellar door fully open. *Black, black, black.* Night had fallen, and it was very dark inside the house. Jimmy marveled anew at the deepness of the world's nights now—without distant street lamps and appliance lights, both of which could illumine a room, even without the flipping of a switch.

Moving from doorframe to wall, he circuited the house, inching from room to room, intensely alert for any alien sound, feeling his way along with his fingertips and the toes of his sneakers. Finally, upstairs now, having reached his parents' bedroom and standing just outside the doorway, he found only silence and fetid air—heavy with the smell of decay. He was unable to go farther; he couldn't go in. *Mom's dead here, and Dad's dead here. There couldn't be a chance. Still…*He whispered into the darkness, "Mom? Dad? Are you in here?" There was no whispered reply, no groans, no sniffles, nothing. The room sounded like what it was: a tomb.

"I gotta get a light." Jimmy remembered the tiny flashlight his mother always left dangling on its little chain at the foot of the stairs. "Yeah, that'd work!"

He felt his way back around to the steep staircase to the first floor. There he recalled the child gate his mother had strung across the gap to prevent him from falling down the steps should he wake up and wander during the night. "Hah!" He laughed a bitter laugh. "When I was a kid, I was so afraid of the dark that there was no way in the world I was getting out of bed." He proceeded down, carefully toe-touching his way from step to step. At the base of the staircase, he felt along the upper part of the doorframe until he found the nail. *No flashlight! Dang!* Then he heard a clicking coming from across the room—of long toenails on the hardwood flooring.

He couldn't breathe! Suddenly he couldn't breathe! Fear rushed from his paralyzed chest to his head, stopping up his ears and muffling all sounds. He challenged the darkness, "Who are you? What do you want?" But he only heard pounding in his ears, the pulsing of his blood. He saw movement—eyes! In the absolute darkness, he saw eyes! *Bloody, yellow eyes!* His mind flashed back to Sevierville and the long tunnel under the road. *Monstrous, bloody, yellow eyes! Deformed demon eyes!* Jimmy emptied his revolver into the eyes. Yet they came on. He smelled the foul breath—a stink beyond this world. *This isn't real!* He felt the hot wind on his face and the pressure on his head that made his cheeks squinch—and nothing more.

✳✳✳

"Damn it!" screamed Daniel. "Let's roll!" He slammed shut the big truck's door and slapped the dash. "We've wasted the whole day! It's gonna be dark soon, damn it! Let's go! Let's go!"

"Ah...sir?"

Daniel twisted in his seat to confront the source of this pitiful inquiry: his driver. It was his last lieutenant, the one who had waved him over to his table this morning at breakfast. He still couldn't remember his name. "Yeah," he snarled, momentarily enjoying the fear he saw in the boy's eyes. "What is it?" he screamed, even though they were scarcely three feet apart.

"Ah, sir?" he started again. He was hanging over the steering wheel, his cheek resting on his hands. "Sir, I don't feel so good. You might want to get somebody else to drive you."

Daniel jerked erect, his mouth drawing back on his teeth, his eyelids tightening to slits. He had transformed—now resembling a serpent preparing to strike. "What did you say?" he hissed.

"Reverend, when I climbed up here, I wasn't feeling any too good anyway, and see, I been waiting hours, you know, and—"

"And what, you mealy mouthed slug? And what? Are you saying I've kept you waiting, boy? Do you think I've been lollygagging around or something?" *Jeez! That's something my father would say.* "Have I inconvenienced you, son? You think I got nothing better to do than cause you inconvenience?" He drew out the syllables of the last word. "Well, you start this truck, and you listen here. You gonna do what I say, and you gonna back up this here truck, and we're gonna..." Daniel's voice trailed off. His lieutenant had fallen asleep on the steering wheel, his hands now dropping to his sides.

"Hey!" Daniel stabbed the kid in the ribs with his fingertips. "Wake up!"

The boy roused briefly, raising his head from the wheel and looking around as if all were now strange and different around him. He slowly turned his head to regard his assailant through unfocused eyes. And then he coughed—a soul-shaking, phlegm-filled gasp that started from the deepest lobes of his lungs.

Daniel drew back, looking at his own arms and his shirtfront. "You son of a bitch! You bastard! You unholy piece of shit!" The boy had sprayed him with his blood—gouts of filthy, diseased bodily fluids. He fumbled with the door handle, jerking it open and throwing himself from the truck's cab. When his feet hit the ground, he found his pistol and pulled it from his holster with such fury that he lost his grip and flung it against the side of the truck's fuel tank. "Goddamn! Goddamn!" He was on it in an instant, grabbing it up and aiming it at the open doorway and the boy slouched over the wheel.

"Goddamn you!" cursed Daniel. The guy's inattention to him— his disregard of him—angered him almost as much as his having spewed his disease all over him. "Look at me, soldier!" he roared. "You...will...show...me...respect!" The boy turned his face in the opposite direction and again lowered his head to the steering wheel. And Daniel pulled his trigger once.

That was enough. The slug caught the boy at the base of his head, splashing his blood and loosened teeth and skull fragments through the shattered side window.

Shit! thought Daniel. *It's gonna take the rest of the day to clean that up.* He stood erect now, circling in place and holding his pistol at head height and pointed to the skies. There were maybe four boys scattered across the campus, looking back at him. He leaned to see up into the high bed of the truck. *Shit! That kid's gone now too! Nobody's at the fifty cal.* "Damn it!"

That was the way his day had gone. Since breakfast this morning, he guessed he had lost maybe ninety percent of his men. They had stood on his order and filed from the cafeteria, carrying their guns and ammunition to the waiting jeeps and trucks. Then, as he had addressed them, speaking from the top of the cafeteria's steps, several of his troops had dropped to a single-knee position. Their coughs and gags had drawn his attention as they vomited on the campus ground. *Food poisoning!* That had been the first thought that had come to his mind, and he had pulled off his glove, ready to stick his finger down his throat. But then the other boys had shrunk back from the afflicted ones on their knees, shouting, "Black Death!" or "Disease!" to the others. *Hah!* Daniel thought grimly. *Everyone surely knows what that looks like by now.* But the strange part had come next. None of the boys had turned to him, to implore him to lay hands on them and to heal. In fact if anyone had looked up to him standing there on the top step, it had been only a glance—and a guilty one at that. *They know I've lost my gift of healing. That was plain.* So he had shot the boy closest to him.

In the ensuing confusion, Daniel had tried to quell any whole-sale desertions right then by loudly claiming that the boy had tried to shoot *him.* "That asshole pulled his weapon and aimed it right at me," he had screamed. "He might even have pulled the trigger." However, when he had returned from the bathroom—*Didn't want to chance it with the fried Spam*—he had found that he had maybe twenty soldiers still milling around the trucks, not counting the boys retching their guts out on the ground. So he had used the few men he still had, ordering them to a half dozen locations in town, making sure he covered those places where he most expected Jimmy and the girl to come to hide. He had even sent four guys to the Broadway address he knew to be the Burkes' home. *Even had to send Burl because the other troops didn't yet know how to drive. But they sure know how to pull the triggers on their guns. Hah! But they best not shoot Jimmy! He's mine!*

"Damn! Those guys have been there all day! I gotta go, gotta go." Daniel was feeling an urgency like he was going to miss something if he didn't hurry. He must go! He looked around for another driver. *And maybe someone to clean up the truck.* The four or so boys he had seen minutes ago were gone. He would have to drive himself if he expected to get to the Broadway address before it got really dark. *I guess I'll be by myself.* Daniel didn't like that thought; it had been a while since he'd done his own bidding. He remembered the guy he had fought in Homer's barn—the guy who had beaten *him* up. And even though he had avenged himself on him, he hadn't done it on his own. He was now unable to generate any traces of that satisfaction he must have surely felt when—*What's his name? Tom? Yeah!*—Tom Parton had been beaten to hell, stretched there across the barn door. "But there ain't all that many people left," he told himself. "So the Lord is saving you for the new world, Daniel." He then realized the voices had gone silent in his head. "First time in a week. Well, maybe I can get some sleep tonight." He would feel satisfaction again when he put his pistol into Jimmy's mouth. *Yeah!* "But you also ain't gonna find somebody to clean out that friggin' truck, idiot! Shoulda pushed him out of the truck before you shot his head off."

He ran to the closest jeep. *Key's in the ignition—great!* It started on the first crank, and Daniel was soon turning a tight radius and heading down the long hill onto the road at its base and then to Broadway. But he found the going slower than he'd expected; trash and wrecked cars littered the road. Sharp shards of metal and glass sparkled on the pavement in his headlights. "Sure wouldn't do to get marooned out here at night." He spotted a dark shape emerging from the brush when he crossed over a small bridge. "That's a damn bear!" He was amazed at how quickly the bigger animals seemed to be coming down from the mountains. *Littler ones too!* A fox sprinted across the road ahead.

"OK, almost there," he said. "Up this hill and to the left. There!" He saw the hulking outline of Jimmy's tall house against the lighter western sky. But there were no lights anywhere. He turned in and steered down the driveway toward the garage. "Where're my guys?" Their absence made him wary, but somehow he knew Jimmy was close—real close. And that made him feel good—real good, tingly-in-the-crotch good. "I been wanting to kill that bastard for so *long*. God's given him to me to *kill*!" With this sudden rush of feelings came a twinge of gratitude; he wondered whether he shouldn't take a moment and give thanks. In these past few weeks, he had enjoyed the world more than ever before in his life. He had watched while people died—people he hated—and hadn't regretted the death of any of them. *The Lord protected me that way. Yes, he did.* Daniel was powerful. He was chosen. He would lead the new world! "I will kill Jimmy Burke!" he screamed at the house.

"Damn, what was that?" He'd run over something in the driveway between the house and the garage. "There's our jeep and...that looks like one of my guys there under the open door." Daniel put his vehicle in park and pulled the emergency brake. He reached down and levered the heavy multicelled flashlight from its bracket under the dash. *I'll leave the headlights on, but I might just need this here torch. Especially if they've shot Jimmy.* He pivoted around in his seat and stepped to the ground. "What the hell!" His boots had skidded in something wet and sticky on the pavement. "Blood!" He turned the flashlight's beam downward, illuminating the pool and the boy's arm extending from under his car.

"Damn it!" he swore again, getting back in the jeep. He released its brake and put it into gear, backing up slowly over the boys' bodies sprawled in the driveway. For a long minute, he considered the broken, camouflage-clad lumps in his headlights. "Damn," he said again. "I'll probably have to get that shit off my shoes by myself. Ah, well." The day wasn't going well for Daniel at all.

Noticing the partially open doorway at the side of the house, Daniel again set his brake, grabbed the flashlight, and stepped from his vehicle. With his automatic held high in his right hand and the flashlight extended in his left, he circled behind the jeep and crept to the doorway. He listened at the crack for several seconds before he pushed the door fully open with his flashlight. Clicking it on, he played the beam around the small room, lighting the shelves and open rafters—and the open door at the far end. *That goes into the basement.* He moved quickly to the door, walking lightly and quietly, considering his large size; his head almost brushed the rafters. Stooping now, he directed his beam into the deep cellar, locating the steps: one set that led to the elevated wash area, and the other set, the wooden steps, that led up to the house's first floor.

He carefully descended the cinder-block steps to the basement floor and strode across to the base of the wooden stairs. He was now hearing sounds, noises that were low and wavelike, more like grumbles than words. *Like the growling purr of a big-ass cat. Hah!* He knew it wasn't his men because they were all lying outside. He flashed his light up the stairs to the closed door at the top. He saw the bottom side of another set of steps above these; they formed a sloping ceiling here. *Those go up to the second floor.* The purring sound seemed to be coming from the base of those stairs; he'd need to be extra careful now.

Creeping up the wooden stairs, he kept his feet to the outside of the tread to minimize squeaks. But near the top, there was nothing he could do to keep the stairs silent, so he climbed quickly and, finding the door unlocked, slipped through the opening and into the house. The purring stopped.

With his gun now held in his left hand, he extended the long flashlight to the right, around the doorframe and into the room. *That's the way to the upstairs side.* His beam fell on a mass at the far end of the room, another body. "Jimmy! Those shitheads done killed him anyway! Damn it to hell!" he swore. And then his light failed...and Jimmy's face became a purple splotch in the blackness of the house. "God gave him to me to kill!"

God? The voices in his head had come back.

Daniel shook himself. "Wh—what?"

You said God...that God had given him to you.

"What's going on?" Daniel asked the darkness. He asked...but really he knew. He knew with absolute certainty the source of the voices—voice now—the granter of his desires, his lord. He knew. But he couldn't call out the name of the expelled angel, the tempter of God, the unholy one! Fear rose in his chest, almost closing off his throat—almost. Feelings of betrayal and anger came too. "But you gave him to me! You promised! You promised!" *Huh? A promise from Satan?* The thought wasn't his own, Daniel knew. But the next thought *was* his very own: *You know, this might not be too bad.*

So he voiced the thought. "You killed him!" he accused. "You promised him to me, so you still owe me! You *owe* me!"

Daniel's flashlight flicked on; he focused the beam back on Jimmy's face and torso. But then something large and dark moved across and behind the body. The floor creaked beneath its weight. Enormous yellow eyes then opened, looking upward, returning his stare—foul yellow eyes over blood-dripping fangs. The flashlight's beam shook, and Daniel fought to steady his hand, dropping his pistol so he could use both hands. Somehow he knew the gun would be of no use anyway.

The thing's breath was rancid; its smell rolled over the room. It raised itself from over its dinner, its kill, until it was even with his height. *What do I owe you, Daniel?*

Daniel sensed that eternity was now; this would be the most important moment of his life, of anybody's life. "I want to rule and reign with you. I am yours forever, and we shall rule together! I shall be king of this world, and you will be my master. I shall worship you, and I shall be of this world!" He was quivering with emotion, his fist raised overhead in triumph.

The yellow eyes continued to gaze at him, revealing nothing except...humor, maybe? Affection? Mockery?

The eyes dropped, and the massive animal head returned to its disgusting, slurping task.

Then, Daniel, enter eternity.

Daniel first felt the warm dribble of blood flow from his nostrils and down his chin. Then he felt the bile rise in his throat and the anguish of his twisting intestines, their hot contents exploding forth and flooding down his pants legs. Yet what he saw now was worse—so much worse. He screamed and screamed, reaching for the door-frame, lunging and almost making it to the basement stairs before crumpling to the linoleum.

17

THE NEW DAY

*D**ang! I don't get this.* But then he did; he understood. *It's coming.* Jimmy understands.

There was pain for him, and then there is not. There was darkness all around, and then it is not. He rises, it seems. *But no, the world is spreading. Flattening.* Time passes as he rises, but then it ceases. Time is before him; eternity is before him: past, present, and future.

And Jimmy understands. He hears Homer; he *sees* Homer. The old man is reaching for the glass of water on his bedside table, there beside the unused lamp. "Jimmy, the Lord gave me some time before this stuff got so bad, and he's allowed me to think, even though I hurt so badly. And I've realized I'm probably more afraid of hurting than dying." He coughs into his hand, takes a sip from the glass, and continues. "Jimmy, I recognize now, in the midst of my suffering, a truer and deeper significance in God's word—in his instruction to 'follow,' to follow him, an eternal significance. See, no man knows the preface to his own story; he's never told that his soul is a warring place of good and evil, God and Satan. I now suffer, but it's not for my sake, or for the perfection of my faith and my reliance on God, or for my own purifying. No. That's all incidental. No. It's simply the will of God. See, I'm tempted to abandon God's right to my essence, to take back my right to myself and do his will according to my own understanding, still sanctified yet my own. But no, for as Jesus said, 'I came not to do my own will but the will of him that sent me.'" The old man looks up. "Do you understand that, Jimmy?"

Jimmy nods; he understands. These are Homer's thoughts, perhaps his unspoken thoughts, but his thoughts in a differing plane, the intangible and eternal plane. The plane where everything is now. The place of the great I AM.

Jimmy hears the prophets and sees Paul, there, scribbling a letter and murmuring, "What then shall we say? Is God unjust? Not at all! For he says to Moses, 'I will have mercy on whom I have mercy, and I will have compassion on whom I have compassion.' It does not, therefore, depend on man's desire or effort but on God's mercy. For the Scripture says to Pharaoh, 'I raised you up for this very purpose, that I might display my power in you and that my name might be proclaimed in all the earth.' Therefore God has mercy on whom he wants to have mercy, and he hardens whom he wants to harden. One of you will say to me, 'Then why does God still blame us? For who resists his will?' But who are you, O man, to talk back to God? Shall what is formed say to him who formed it, 'Why did you make me like this?'" *I understand. And all is now!*

And there's the Apostle John. Jimmy hears John struggling with his thoughts, his revelation he wishes to relate to others. But like Paul, he is unable to find words to translate, to re-create in his mind, his sojourn into the third heaven. *Trying to describe paradise. Imagine.* Jimmy understands.

He sees his mother and his father and he loves them. *This is love.* Love that encompasses trust, affection, companionship, satisfaction, pride, thanksgiving, gratitude—*it's all love! Freely given love.*

He sees himself, a kid in a pew, singing the sixth verse of "Just as I Am" and listening to the great I AM—trusting him, believing him. *Freely received love.*

✳✳✳

Satan returns to the presence of the Lord, saying, "It is done, God, and done. My thoughts were but foolishness; your creation cursed thee not while all the earth lies about, in waste and ruin—and the human seed is no more."

God replied, "Behold! My work is an eternity. My will doth reign and endureth forever and ever. My time is infinite; I and the seed are one and...I AM."

HathwaN lifted the window shade and looked to the north, up past the barn's roof line, to the early-morning skies above the gray hump of the distant mountain. *Gonna be a real nice day,* he judged. *Clear as a bell.* Solius Minor, the smaller of the two suns, had dropped below the horizon some two hours before, and he could now see a few distant stars, blinking clear and cold in the dim heavens. The few clouds above would soon show the first rays of Solius Major rising in the east, painting their fluffy bottoms golden and purple. *But not really many clouds to speak of.*

He bent across the bed and shook the mattress. "JastroM," he whispered.

The boy slowly came to consciousness, his first thoughts for the new day: *So I'm not in Flora Del in the middle of an earthquake. But it's still dark as...the second night? Where the heck am I?*

HathwaN whispered again. "Hey, sleepyhead. It's time we head to the barn."

www.ingramcontent.com/pod-product-compliance
Lightning Source LLC
Chambersburg PA
CBHW070826260626
47170CB00007B/2271